AUNTIE CLEM'S BAKERY

BOOKS # 10-12

P.D. WORKMAN

ISBN: 9781774680841 (KDP Paperback)

ISBN: 9781774680858 (Ingram Paperback)

ISBN: 9781774680865 (Ingram Hardcover)

ISBN: 9781774680285 (Kindle)

ISBN: 9781774680292 (ePub)

pdworkman

MUFFINS MASKS MURDER

AUNTIE CLEM'S BAKERY #10

To all those who are loyal, to a fault

CHAPTER 1

*A*h, finally." Vic took a long breath of air as they stepped off of the plane. "I can get warm again!"

Erin laughed and shook her head at her young, blond assistant. Vic had not been able to get properly warm since crossing the border into Canada. Even though she had bundled up on their Alaskan cruise, she just had not been able to get comfortable.

It hadn't been so bad for Erin. Her body was more acclimatized to Maine weather than to Tennessee, so she had fared better. But she had to admit that she still preferred being warm to cold. And while the cruise had been intended to be a nice diversion from her life in Bald Eagle Falls, things had not exactly gone as planned. A relaxed, carefree vacation it had not been.

"There's no place like home," Erin declared.

"There shorely isn't," Vic agreed, drawing out the words in her longest southern drawl.

"We'll need a vacation from our vacation," Officer Terry Piper said, as the men followed the women off the plane and through the corridor to the terminal.

"You're not kidding about that," Vic agreed.

Erin glanced back at Willie, who was characteristically quiet, to see how he felt about it. His skin, darkly stained from the mining and metal processing he did, was disconcerting to someone just meeting him for the first time, but Erin was so used to it that she hardly even noticed it anymore. A far cry from when she had first arrived in Bald Eagle Falls and had taken him for a dirty homeless man and had been afraid to let him help her carry supplies into Erin's new gluten-free and specialty bakery, Auntie Clem's. Now, Erin wouldn't have given it a second thought. Willie was one of the family. He might be nontraditional, picking up whatever odd jobs he felt like between working his mineral claims, but she knew he was a hard worker, not the layabout that many people seemed to think. He had been in Bald Eagle Falls much longer than she had and the townspeople should have known better. There was still prejudice against people who didn't conform, and Willie was about as nonconforming as they came.

Willie smiled and nodded at Erin, acknowledging her look, but didn't have anything to contribute to the conversation. He moved forward to put his arm around Vic, who also faced prejudice for her gender identity. He bumped against the cast on her arm.

"Just about time to get these off, Miss Victoria." He indicated the cast on his leg as well. "It will feel good to be able to get the darn thing out of the way."

"And to scratch," Vic said fervently. "If there's one thing I want more than to be warm right now, it's to be able to scratch this arm like a dog at a flea circus." She scratched around the end of the cast, sliding her fingers under the edge as far as they could reach.

Terry didn't take Erin's arm, but was trying to keep K9 under control. K9 wasn't usually on a leash, but was well-trained to heel and, other than when he had first met the stray orange kitten who had wandered into Auntie Clem's Bakery, Erin had rarely seen him out of Terry's control. But he clearly knew that they were going home. He was sniffing the air and dragging Terry along, eager to get out of the airport terminal and back to familiar settings.

"Heel," Terry commanded in a low, firm tone. "Come on, buddy. Let's show some professionalism here."

It took a few tries before K9 was finally at his side, behaving as was expected from a veteran police dog. But his nose still quivered and his ears pointed forward.

"Do you think he's looking forward to getting back to work?" Erin asked.

"Animals like routines. He's not used to being cooped up on a ship. Even though I walked him plenty, it's not the same as patrolling all day, and I'm sure he felt it worse than I did. I'm going to have to work off a few extra pounds here..." He patted his sleek belly. Erin couldn't tell that he'd put on any weight, but she knew it was bothering him.

"Who knew you could gain weight eating vegan food?" She laughed. "I was sure we'd all be thin as rails by the time we got back. Unfortunately... no such luck." She was so short, every pound she put on looked like two. Her frame was not nearly as forgiving as Vic's tall, slender physique. "But I can't tell you've gained anything, and after you've been hitting the streets of Bald Eagle Falls again, it will just melt away."

"I hope so. I have no intention of turning into one of those cops with a big beer gut hanging over his belt."

"I don't think you need to worry about that."

Erin couldn't help admiring her "Officer Handsome." He had boyish good looks, cut a very dashing figure in his police uniform and, when she made him smile, had the cutest dimple in his cheek. He was intelligent and kind, and it was a wonder he hadn't been scooped up by some other woman long before Erin had shown up on the scene. But he was married to his work, and maybe no other woman had wanted to compete with that devotion and the long hours of days and nights that he was gone. In a little town like Bald Eagle Falls, with its minuscule police force, he was frequently the go-to man, even when he wasn't supposed to be on call.

It was another hour before they finally got all of their baggage off of the carousel and were on their way. They retrieved Willie's truck from long-term parking and piled everything into the back before climbing up into the seats.

"Are you glad to be home?" Vic asked Erin, looking back over the seat of the cab to where Erin and Terry sat in the second row of seating.

"I'll be glad when I am home," Erin agreed. She might be back in Tennessee, but she wasn't in her house yet, and that was what she wanted. Just to be home and away from all of the drama and excitement that had surrounded their cruise, back in her familiar environment with her lists of things to do and her baker's schedule and something to keep her busy. The idea of a cruise had been nice, and Terry had thought that it would help Erin to be away from the stressful day-to-day business of running a bakery, but it had been more difficult not to have something to keep her hands and her mind busy, so she didn't have to think about finding the body of Mr. Inglethorpe, or the other traumatic events that had preceded the cruise. Erin had to admit that she wasn't a "fun" person. She wasn't interested in going out to a restaurant or dancing or watching a lounge act or going on a tour. She was happier following her set routine.

"You'll be happy to get back to your house, the bakery, and your animals," Terry agreed.

Erin reached down and scratched K9's ears. K9, being a specially trained service dog, had been allowed to go with Terry on the cruise without too much hassle. Erin bringing her cat and rabbit would have been another story, besides which, they wouldn't have enjoyed it at all. Like Erin, cats preferred familiar surroundings and routine. She didn't know what rabbits thought about changes. Marshmallow was pretty chill and took everything in stride, but Orange Blossom, who had grown from that straggly little orange stray to a sleek, luxurious adult cat, would have been miserable.

"I'll be thrilled to see them again," she agreed. "I didn't know how much I was going to miss them. Do you think everything is okay with them?"

"Adele would have told you if there were any issues. They don't take a lot of care, and they're not old, so I don't think a short vacation away from them will have been a big deal."

"She would have told me if one of them got hurt, or lost, or wasn't eating." Erin needed to hear the words to reassure herself. Of course Adele would have let her know. Except that they had not had much contact with Bald Eagle Falls while they'd been on the cruise, telecommunications being pretty spotty. And Adele had known the trouble they had run into there, and maybe wouldn't have wanted to put any more stress on Erin if something *had* been wrong with one of the animals. She might have just kept quiet about it, figuring it would keep until Erin got back.

"I'm sure she would have," Terry agreed. He rubbed Erin's back, digging down into the tense muscles and trying to massage the stress away. "You're going to see them in just a little while."

CHAPTER 2

*E*rin watched out the window, looking at the trees that surrounded Bald Eagle Falls. It was so lush compared to what they had seen in Alaska. She had gotten accustomed to the rocky cliffs and sparse trees that faced the ocean in Alaska, the gray water and clouds more reminiscent of what she had seen during Maine winters, and she had forgotten how full of life the Tennessee scenery was, even though it was fall and the weather was starting to get cooler. The trees were a brilliant canopy of oranges and reds, something tourists would be flocking from miles around to see.

When they pulled into Bald Eagle Falls, it looked just as Erin had remembered leaving it.

It wasn't like she'd been away for years. It had only been a couple of weeks. It just seemed like a lifetime ago. She finally felt like she had a home. A place where she belonged. She was no longer moving from job to job and from one sad, empty room or apartment to another. Instead, she had her own house, courtesy of Aunt Clementine who had left it to Erin in her will along with the bakery. She was the boss instead of someone who had to listen to everyone else and obey the whims of some old lady or frustrated high school dropout. It hadn't been easy, especially when she lost her first location to a fire, but things were running better than ever at Auntie Clem's Bakery 2.0, and Erin finally felt like she had some security.

Everything looked just right. A little more gold and yellow in the leaves.

9

The traffic was the same, the people whose faces she saw as they drove in on Main Street were the same familiar faces. It was all exactly as it should be.

And then they pulled onto Erin's street. She let go of a big breath of air she hadn't realized she'd been holding, the muscles in her body finally relaxing. There it was. Nothing had happened to it while she was gone. It hadn't been burned down or burgled or anything else.

She was the first one out of the truck and was at the door while everyone else was still climbing out and then pulling the luggage out of the back of the truck. Erin unlocked the door and disarmed the burglar alarm.

"Hello?" she called. "Where are my furry beasties?"

There was silence. Orange Blossom was a very loud and vocal cat, so Erin was disconcerted that he didn't answer and rush to the door, complaining loudly about her having abandoned him for so long. She looked around.

"Blossom? Marshmallow? Come on, guys…"

Marshmallow hopped around the corner and slowly approached her, then nuzzled her leg and nibbled at her pant cuffs. Erin smiled and bent down to scratch the white and brown rabbit's ears.

"Hello, Marshmallow. Did you miss me? Was I gone for a really long time? You knew I would come back, didn't you? I hope you didn't worry too much."

He didn't seem to be the least bit concerned about her absence, though her shoes clearly smelled very interesting. Erin moved farther into the living room and nudged him out of the way so that the others would be able to get in the door without stepping on a curious rabbit. She stroked his velvety ears and looked around.

"Where's Orange Blossom? Has he shut himself in the bathroom?"

It wouldn't be the first time. Reg suspected that he did it on purpose just to get attention. She walked down the hall to the bathroom to check, but the door was still open. His litter box was in there, looking as spotless as if Adele had just been there and refilled it. Erin checked the spare room and then her bedroom.

Orange Blossom was curled up in the center of Erin's bed, having made a little nest for himself in the blankets. His nose was tucked into his tail and he didn't move when she entered the room.

"Blossom! Oh, Blossom…!"

She poked and prodded, and eventually he deigned to lift his head and look at her. Then he stretched and tucked it back in again, shutting her out.

"Orange Blossom! What are you doing giving me the cold shoulder? Aren't you happy Mommy's home? We can cuddle up to read, and I'll give you nice treats…"

He ignored her, even though she knew he understood the word "treat." Even just the mention of a treat would usually have him trotting to the kitchen, meowing at Erin to follow and get him the promised goody.

She could hear the thumps of the others putting down the luggage and their voices as they talked to each other. There were footsteps in the hall and Erin turned her head to look as Terry looked in the doorway.

"Everything okay then?" he prompted.

"Sure, fine. I guess he's just mad at me for leaving him alone."

"He'll get over it. Then he'll be bossing you around and demanding that you feed him."

"I suppose. I don't like it, though."

"You're not supposed to like it; that's why he's doing it. To train you not to do it again."

Erin chuckled. "I thought I was the one who was supposed to be training him."

"Hate to tell you this, but…"

K9 made a huffing noise and Orange Blossom's head popped up. He glared at K9 and scrambled to his feet, fur puffing out as he hissed and made his opinion of dogs in the house known to them all. Erin shook her head.

"You're going to have to get used to K9 being around. Any other cat would have accepted him by now. I don't know why you have to be so stubborn."

The cat ignored her, staring at K9 and hissing at him to go away. Erin threw up her hands in exasperation. "Okay. We will leave you alone, how about that?"

She left the room, all of them going back to the living room. Vic was bending down to pet Marshmallow.

"Where's Blossom? Is he okay?"

"Oh, he's in fine form. I think I'm going to have to put up with the cold shoulder for a while. He isn't happy with me."

"His loss." Vic stepped into the kitchen, raising her voice slightly to make sure that the cat could hear her clearly. "I'm going to get Marshmallow something out of the fridge."

Erin heard Orange Blossom thump to the floor. She looked at the bedroom doorway and waited for him to come out. A little orange head peeked around the doorframe. When Blossom saw Erin watching him, he withdrew and did not leave the bedroom to investigate the possibility of treats. Erin suspected he was washing, pointedly ignoring her and pretending that he didn't want any treat anyway.

Vic gave Marshmallow a carrot. She looked at Erin and raised an eyebrow. "He isn't going to come?"

"Nope. He's pretty mad. I guess he's mad at both of us, not just me."

"Too bad for him. Shall we all have a quick bite to eat before we go our different directions?" Vic looked at her watch. "It's later than I expected, and I'm beat after the plane trip and waiting around. I'm going to either have a nap or go to bed early."

"You could get out some rolls and jam," Erin suggested. "That's really all we need. Well, it's all *I* need." She looked at Willie and Terry. "The menfolk may need something more substantial."

"A bit of bread and jam is good for now," Willie said. "I'm planning on hitting up Fatburger later on. I desperately need to top up my fat and cholesterol levels."

Erin laughed. "How about you?" she asked Terry. "I could see what else is in the freezer. Maybe you'd rather have a chicken sandwich? Something that will stick with you a little better?"

"Jam is fine. I need to start working this belly off."

It only took a few minutes to defrost some rolls from Auntie Clem's Bakery and to put out the various flavors of Jam Lady jams Erin had in stock. She wondered fleetingly whether Roger would ever be back with Mary Lou again to whip up some more batches of jam. If not, their Jam Lady supply was going to run out and they were going to have to go back to store brands or find another artisanal jam that was made locally. Other brands were sure to cost an arm and a leg. Jam Lady had always been very reasonably priced. Especially since Erin bought it wholesale to sell it out of the bakery.

Conversation lagged as they each spread butter and whatever jam they preferred on their rolls. Erin had given K9 a gluten-free doggie biscuit. He munched on it quietly while they ate. Orange Blossom still didn't show his face.

"Are you going to go back in to the bakery in the morning, or take a few days off to recover?" Terry asked Erin.

"I've just had a vacation. I don't need recovery time."

"Except that you didn't actually rest on your vacation. I'm worried you're going to try to do too much and your health will suffer."

"No, I need to get back to work. I need my job more than sleep."

"Okay... if you're sure."

Erin smiled. "You might make me feel guilty about jumping right back in if you weren't going directly onto shift tonight."

He looked sheepish. "Well... I do want to get back to normal police work. I know my town and what goes on here. I didn't like the uncertainty of living on a cruise ship. It will make me feel better to know what's going on in Bald Eagle Falls and to know that nothing has changed."

Erin took another bite of her sandwich. She understood exactly what Terry was talking about.

CHAPTER 3

They were finishing up when there was a knock on the front door and Erin heard a familiar young male voice calling out, "Where's that sister of mine? A little bird said you were back in town."

Vic hurried out of the kitchen. "Jeremy!"

"There she is!"

Erin looked through the doorway to see Vic and Jeremy hugging and slapping one another on the back.

"So, how was the trip?" Jeremy demanded. "Doesn't look like you wasted away to nothing or fell off the ship."

Vic threw an apologetic glance in Erin's direction. She drew back from Jeremy, smiling. "No, there was way too much food there to lose anything. In fact, I may have found a few."

Jeremy laughed. "Good. You put the rest of us to shame! It wouldn't hurt you to find a few pounds."

Vic rolled her eyes, smiling at being able to see her brother again. "And you survived while I was gone? Without your little sister to take care of you?"

"Well, it was tough, but I had—" Jeremy stopped abruptly and looked around for his girlfriend.

Beaver was standing just outside the door, looking back at the street.

Jeremy and Vic waited for her to come in. Erin stepped into the living room, wondering what was going on.

"Hey, Ro?" Jeremy called tentatively.

Beaver didn't turn toward the house or enter. She stood there, just in front of the door, looking intently over her shoulder. They all stood there for a moment, frozen, wondering what was going on. Eventually, Beaver turned around and saw everyone looking at her.

Her body relaxed into a loose, casual pose. She smiled widely, chewing on her ever-present gum. "Everyone waiting for me? You don't have to do that."

"What's going on?" Jeremy asked. "I thought you were right there behind me, and then you…"

Beaver looked back over her shoulder one more time and shrugged as if it was nothing. Her eyes sought out Terry, back in the kitchen behind Erin. She didn't say anything to him, but it was apparent from her expression that she wanted a word.

"What's up?" Terry asked.

She shrugged lazily, maintaining a casual and relaxed body language. "Nothing important, Officer Piper. How was your vacation?"

"You probably know more about it than anyone else around here… maybe even more than me, since no one wanted to talk to me in any official capacity. Things didn't go… exactly as planned."

Beaver chewed her gum, chuckling. "I would say that was an understatement. Can't you people even stay out of trouble on a holiday cruise?"

"We didn't really have any control over the circumstances." Terry looked over at Erin, gauging her reaction to the conversation. He smiled at her reassuringly and didn't bring her involvement into it. "Things just fell into our laps and I was the only police officer aboard, so…"

"They did have their own security forces. I assume you could have left it to them."

"You wouldn't say that if you had been there."

"No, I probably wouldn't," Beaver agreed with a sage nod. "Why don't you tell me all about it while you take K9 out for a walk?"

Terry's eyes went to K9, who was completely relaxed, stretched out on the floor in his favorite spot where everyone would trip over him as they cleaned up. "I don't think K9—" he started. Then he stopped. He snapped his fingers for K9, who looked up alertly. At Terry's signal, he got to his feet and went to his side.

Beaver nodded.

"Won't be long, Erin," Terry said. "I'll take K9 for a short walk and then I need to be getting into work. You'll be heading to bed pretty soon."

"Early to bed and early to rise," Erin agreed. She watched Terry and Beaver, wondering what it was that Beaver really wanted to talk to Terry about. It was clear that she didn't want to talk about it in front of everyone else. And Rohilda Beaven, with her three-initial federal employer, had every reason to contact the local law enforcement if something were going on.

She and Terry and K9 headed out the door. Erin looked at Jeremy.

"Is something going on?"

"Uh… nothing that I'm aware of. She didn't say that she needed to talk to Terry about anything, and was looking forward to a little something to eat." He looked at the food that was still out in the kitchen. "She shouldn't be too long, so could we leave this out a bit longer? If she's not back by the time you want to head to bed, I'll get everything cleaned up."

"Yes, of course. Let me just put the rolls in a bag, so they don't dry out. Rice flour makes them dry out faster than wheat rolls."

Jeremy nodded distractedly. He looked in the direction that Terry and Beaver were walking, their heads bowed as they talked.

"Everything was quiet while we were gone?" Vic prodded.

"Sure. Everything has been perfectly normal. Ro hasn't said that anything was bothering her. And I've just been working… everything has been quiet at the farm."

"No more ginseng poachers?"

"No, and it's getting late in the season for them now. They won't have much need for security in the winter months."

"Can't poachers harvest it any time of the year?" Erin asked, frowning.

"Sure. But they can't find much of a market for it. The government only allows legal harvesting until the end of December. They won't be able to sell it as legitimately harvested after that and the margins on black market ginseng are pretty brutal."

"Oh." Erin shrugged her shoulders and shook her head. "You learn something new every day."

"At least you got your harvest in good time."

Erin nodded. The surprise wild ginseng harvest had been a windfall for her. She was still getting used to the idea that she had money. Real money. She'd always been on the edge of poverty before, and had been struggling with running Auntie Clem's Bakery after the fire and rebuilding.

She wouldn't want her friends to know just how near she had come to closing down.

∽

Erin put the rolls into a bag and twisted it shut. She looked around the kitchen to see if anything else needed to be done.

"How about tea? Would anyone like a cup?"

Willie caught Vic's eye. "Maybe we could repair to the loft for some adult drinks."

"Oh." Vic looked uncertainly at Erin. "Well, I guess it would be nice to make sure everything is still where we left it. Uh, Jeremy, did you want to come up with us, or…?"

Jeremy rolled his eyes. "Oh, *please*. I don't need to be around while the two of you are making googly eyes at each other. I'll hang out here until Beaver gets back. I'll say goodnight to you now," he gave her a quick peck on the cheek, "and I'll stop by the bakery sometime tomorrow for my complimentary muffin."

"Complimentary? Sorry, you pay full price, just like everyone else."

"But I'm your brother," Jeremy pointed out, pouting.

"So I should charge you twice as much for all of the stuff you did to me when we were kids!"

"Twice?" Jeremy backtracked. "No, I'll pay full price. Full price is a good deal."

"Yeah, you'd better believe it," Vic agreed, giving him a little slap on the arm. "Now, goodnight. Come by tomorrow."

She and Willie said their goodnights and thank yous to Erin, and headed out the back door to Vic's loft over the garage. Vic paused to arm the back door burglar alarm, gave another little wave, and closed the door.

∽

Jeremy smiled at Erin. "If you want to get ready for bed, go ahead. Just ignore me, I can entertain myself. I'll just find a bit of string and play with... where's the cat?" He looked around, eyebrows raised.

"He's upset with me."

"What for?"

"For being away for two weeks. Cats don't like changes in routine. So he's rebuffing my advances... at least until he gets hungry."

"Silly cat. Where is he? I'll talk some sense into him."

"My room, last I saw." Erin checked the front door to make sure it was shut tightly and that Orange Blossom couldn't sneak out. He didn't usually try to get away, but while he was in a snit, he might decide to try it. She yawned. "I'm going to take you up on that and have a warm bath before bed."

"Let me just get that reprobate out of your way."

Jeremy went down the hall to Erin's room and looked in. He grinned, and in a minute he was back with Orange Blossom turned upside-down in his arms and looking awkward and embarrassed. "This little baby? He's the one who's been giving you trouble? Look at him; he's so cute!"

Erin reached over to scratch the cat's stomach, and he kicked at her with his hind legs. Erin narrowly avoided being raked by his sharp back claws. She shook her head. "You'd better have a good talk with him. Tell him scratching isn't very nice and Mommy won't give him anything but kibble in the morning."

Jeremy nodded and took Orange Blossom with him back to the living room. Erin got her nightgown and robe and retired to the bathroom.

~

When Erin got out, Beaver was back and Terry had already headed to work. Erin snuggled into her robe and nodded at Beaver.

"Everything sorted out, then?"

Beaver nodded. Her expression was still casual and relaxed, but her eyes were hooded and she wasn't about to tell Erin what the conversation with Terry had been about. Erin didn't know whether Beaver had told anything to Jeremy, but she suspected not. Beaver kept her own counsel.

"I had some nosh," Beaver said, nodding toward the plate with breadcrumbs and a few splotches of jam sitting on the coffee table. "Very good, as always."

Erin nodded and reached for the plate.

"Don't you dare," Jeremy warned, swooping in to take it from her. "I told you I would clean up. You can sit down and visit with Ro or go to bed. Your choice. But no cleaning up after us."

Erin watched him take the plate into the kitchen and then heard him clearing away the jam jars and whatever else was still out.

"He's well-trained," Beaver said. "Don't you worry about him."

"I'm not worried." Erin stood there for a minute, then decided that it would be rude not to at least visit with Beaver for a few minutes. She had just been away for a couple of weeks, after all, and it was only right that she should catch up on anything that had happened while she was gone.

She sat down on one of the easy chairs. Orange Blossom was watching her from the back of the couch and made no move to approach her. He was usually very cuddly, and Erin found it disconcerting for him to be giving her the cold shoulder for more than a minute or two. It must have really upset him that she'd been gone for so long. She hadn't thought it would make that much difference to him. Cats were more concerned with people meeting their needs than they were with specific people. Or so Erin had thought.

Marshmallow hopped over to Erin and lay down on her feet. Erin bent over and picked him up. She settled him on her lap and scratched his ears and stroked his short, silky fur.

"It's so nice to be home after being away. Vacations are nice, but nothing compares to being back in your own space where you belong."

Beaver nodded. "Always good to get home after I've been away. Not that you had much of a vacation, from what I hear."

"It was okay. We still saw all of the sights, and I enjoyed cooking with Chef Kirschoff while we were there. That part was fun."

"Well, that's good. A few days to recover from your vacation, and you should be right as rain."

Erin wasn't so sure that she was going to be right as rain. She had not been quite right before she had gone on vacation, and the vacation certainly hadn't fixed anything in that regard. She still had nightmares and anxiety. She had an oppressive sense of doom even when there wasn't anything to be worried about. She didn't like it and wished that things would just go back to normal.

She would sleep on her usual schedule, and get up, and make muffins, and everything would be okay again.

She hoped.

She really hoped.

CHAPTER 4

*E*rin tossed and turned after heading to bed. She had thought that she would hit the sheets and fall immediately asleep, but she should have known it wouldn't work out that way, despite how tired she was. It always took her time to get to sleep and, with the trouble she had been suffering the last few weeks, it was that much worse. Sometimes it seemed like she was trying to fall asleep for longer than she was actually sleeping. And when she did sleep, it was restless and disrupted and she felt like she was monitoring everything going on around her even while she slept.

She waited for Orange Blossom to come in, but was convinced that he wouldn't. He would leave her to toss and turn all night and still be pouting in the morning and withholding his affections. But after a couple of hours, she felt him jump up onto the bed and start nosing at her.

"Hey, you," Erin whispered. "Come and cuddle and help me get to sleep."

She stroked him and he settled in beside her and started purring. Erin listened to his breaths and the deep, loud purr, and waited for it to lull her to sleep.

~

Erin awoke with a start in the morning, just about jumping right out of bed with a gasp. She flipped Orange Blossom over by accident, luckily catching him before she rolled him right out of bed. He put his ears back, glaring at her, and squirmed away to jump off the bed and stalk off. She imagined he probably didn't like being startled awake any more than she did. So much for making up with him; he would probably be pouting the rest of the day about her scaring him awake even if he hadn't already been in a mood.

It was going to take a while before he was back to being her friend.

Erin picked up her phone to look at the time and decided she might as well get up, even though it wasn't quite time yet. She would continue to have nightmares if she stayed in bed, and she'd end up being even more tired than if she got up. She wouldn't get any more restful sleep in, so she might as well not even try.

She rubbed her eyes and climbed out of bed.

Orange Blossom was already in the bathroom using the cat box, so she detoured to the kitchen to put on the teakettle and putter around until he was out. No need to make things worse by intruding on a private moment.

By the time Vic's light came on in the loft across the yard, Erin had nearly finished drinking her tea, had written a list of tasks to be completed at the bakery that day, and had fed the critters, only one of whom showed any appreciation.

She didn't have any messages from Terry and wondered how his shift had gone. He had seemed just as eager to get back to the routine as she felt —two workaholics who didn't know how to handle a vacation. Of course, stumbling across s criminal conspiracy hadn't exactly been in the plans.

There was a tap at the door, and Vic let herself in and checked the burglar alarm.

"Already up?" she questioned through a big yawn.

"Been up for a while."

"Are you that excited to get back to work?" Vic put the kettle back on to warm up the water.

"No. Well... I am happy to get back to work and to make sure everything is okay and to get back into the swing of things. But I couldn't sleep any longer, so I got up."

"Are you okay?"

Vic had some inkling of Erin's disrupted sleep patterns of late, but didn't know all of the details. Erin tried to keep that to herself. And to Terry, who of course knew from the nights that he slept over.

"I'm fine," Erin dismissed. She studied Vic's face. "How late did the two of *you* stay up last night?"

"Well... maybe a bit too late," Vic admitted. "Wanted to get in a bit more vacation time before we got started again today. You see we..." She interrupted herself with another wide yawn. "*We* know how to enjoy ourselves."

"You keep telling yourself that when the afternoon slump hits. You're going to be asleep on your feet."

Vic shrugged. "I'll be fine once I get the motor running here."

They were both quiet while Erin looked over her lists and Vic petted Marshmallow and then washed her hands before preparing her tea. Orange Blossom was in the corner washing, still in a snit and ignoring both of them.

"How long is he going to keep acting like we've committed an unpardonable offense?" Vic asked, eyeing him with amusement.

"You'll have to ask him. I thought he'd get over it after a few minutes, but he's still nursing a grudge. And I startled him awake this morning, so he's started his day in a bad mood."

Vic shook her head. "Well, he's not going to get any treats while he's acting this way."

Everything was in order at Auntie Clem's Bakery, and Erin was happy to lose herself in the routine. She hadn't realized how much she had missed her regular customers. She smiled and greeted them all and enjoyed catching up on all of the little things that had happened in Bald Eagle Falls during her absence. The Fosters came by before school and Peter happily chattered to her about what had happened at school while she was gone. Mrs. Foster usually liked to do her shopping while the older kids were in school, so Erin appreciated that they stopped in before the start of the school day to give her a chance to see them. She had missed their happy faces and even cleaning the finger smudges from the glass of the display case once they were gone. She felt buoyed up by the visits and catching up on all of the local gossip. Everyone was full of questions about what the cruise had been like, and Erin and Vic were careful to tell them only the things they had enjoyed, staying far away from any mentions of murder or kidnapping.

Mary Lou arrived, her ash blond and gray hair carefully coiffed and her pantsuit neat and without a wrinkle. She gave Erin a warm smile, not quite as reserved as she used to be. A lot had happened during the time that Erin had known Mary Lou, and she was more open to their friendship since Roger's incarceration had turned many of the townspeople against her.

Erin couldn't understand how they could think that Roger's mental health issues were Mary Lou's fault and why they held his failures against Mary Lou any more than they did his getting lost before he had been put into care. How was she supposed to be responsible for everything he did? She had done her best to keep an eye on him, but it was more than one person could do.

"How is everything?" Erin asked warmly as Mary Lou considered the goods on display.

"Well, the new normal, I suppose. I haven't heard much from Campbell, but he is still around and I hear from him or Rohilda Beaven from time to time. So it's just Josh and I, and we're managing."

"Is he still having problems with school?"

"It isn't the academics... I thought at first that it was getting too difficult for him or he wasn't spending the time that he needed studying... but I think he's just too distracted by everything that has happened in our family. It's hard for a boy his age to understand what happened to his father or why Campbell left." Mary Lou paused. "It's hard for a woman my age! It's hard when we're just expected to go on as if nothing has happened. But what else is there to do?"

She pointed out the pretzels and rosemary pizza shells, deciding what she was going to need for suppers that week.

"Has he had any counseling?" Vic asked. "Maybe a professional could help him to work through it."

"We'd have to go into the city, and I can barely get him out of his room and to school most days. He doesn't want to do anything. I worry about the amount of time he spends in bed and on his tablet. I know he's not working on homework, but he won't talk about it. Just acts all... teenagerish about his privacy and me not interfering with his life."

"Isn't there anyone in town? There must be someone at the school that could talk to him."

"There is… but he needs someone who hasn't already heard about everything that happened from other sources. Someone who is more… impartial and unbiased. It's easy to say that a therapist has to be impartial and just listen, but they are human; they do form their own opinions about events without all of the facts."

Vic nodded slowly as she wrapped up Mary Lou's purchases. "I suppose so. One of the problems living in a small town. Everybody knows everybody else's business."

It was one of the reasons that she had left her own hometown. She hadn't been an adult yet herself when she had shown up in Auntie Clem's Bakery that first time. She knew what it was like to have everyone consider her a pariah because of something that was beyond her control.

CHAPTER 5

*A*s they finished ringing up Mary Lou's order, Melissa hurried in through the door, setting the little bells jingling wildly. Her wild brown curls bounced around her face and her expression was eager. She was not, Erin surmised, just excited about a chocolate muffin. She was definitely there to tell them something. Everyone had said that things had been quiet while they were gone, so Erin wasn't sure what kind of news Melissa had that was so exciting. She couldn't be in a hurry to tell them that everything had been normal while they were gone.

"Did you hear?" she asked breathlessly, approaching the counter.

Erin looked at Vic and Mary Lou, but neither of them had any idea what Melissa's news was any more than anyone else. Erin gave her a quick, discerning look, trying to see if there was anything out of place, but Melissa looked just the same as she always did, her full mouth set in an eager smile, ready to tell them all of the latest police department gossip. Even though she was only a part-time admin for the local police, she always seemed to know everything that was going on.

"Hear what?" Erin asked. "What's happened?"

"Terry—Officer Piper—just arrested Bo Biggles."

Erin looked again at Vic, who looked just as shocked by this news as Erin felt. With wide eyes, they both turned back to Melissa.

"Bo Biggles? What's he doing back in town? I thought he took off after the big drug bust, never to show his face here again."

"Well," Melissa leaned closer to them, oblivious to the treats in the display case, "I guess *never* is a lot shorter when you're a drug dealer trying to establish a business in a new town."

"What did Terry arrest him for?" Erin asked. "Is everything okay? Did he…" She trailed off, afraid to put her concerns into words. She knew that Bo Biggles carried a weapon in his car, if not on his person. "Is everyone okay?"

"Terry and K9 took him down. Just like an episode of Cops on TV," Melissa told them eagerly. "We're not used to such dramatic take-downs in Bald Eagle Falls."

"But Terry's okay?" Erin wondered how he felt about having to arrest someone like Bo Biggles on his first day back from vacation. Nothing like jumping right into the deep end.

"He's just fine. I'm sure he'll have some sore muscles, but he didn't sustain any injuries." Melissa gave a loud laugh. "Which is more than I can say for Biggles."

"He was hurt? What happened?" Erin wanted the whole story all at once without having to tease all of the details out of Melissa. Just get it all out, like ripping off a bandage.

"He didn't go quietly, let's just say that. Nothing serious, it isn't like Terry gave him a broken nose. But he was selling drugs near the school, and the PD does not look kindly on that kind of thing!"

"No," Erin agreed faintly.

"At the school?" Mary Lou repeated. She looked out the door of Auntie Clem's Bakery in the direction of the school, though it was impossible to see the school grounds from there. "Were there… any students involved? Do you know who he's been selling to?"

"I don't know anything about that yet," Melissa admitted. "I guess they'll investigate. But he's not going to be selling to anyone else in the near future, so you can stop worrying about that."

"A mother never stops worrying," Mary Lou said curtly. She clutched her shopping bag close to her, in danger of squashing all of the baked goods. She turned and walked out the door. Erin kept an eye on her as Vic and Melissa talked, watching her put her bag into the car and then immediately pull out her cell phone to call the school or her son to get more details.

~

It took a while to determine that they'd gotten all of the details out of Melissa that she knew, and then to get her to pick out the treat she wanted to use as her excuse for having come by the bakery and get on her way. Ramped up by all of the excitement, Melissa seemed inclined to stay there all afternoon, endlessly repeating the tidbits she knew.

When she was finally out the door, Erin looked at the time on her phone, wondering whether Terry would be off duty. If he'd had to bring in a felon, he probably had paperwork and interviews to do even though his shift was officially over. The sheriff could conduct the interviews, but Terry would want to do the follow up himself. Erin had a few hours left before she would be finished at the bakery. Hopefully, he would be off at the same time and could fill her in on some of the details that Melissa could not.

"I wonder if that's what Terry and Beaver were talking about yesterday," Vic said.

Erin turned to Vic, focusing on her words. "What's that? Oh, when they took K9 for a walk?" She considered. It was a possibility. If Beaver knew something of Bo Biggles's return to Bald Eagles Falls, then she would want to make sure the locals knew about it. She could have called the sheriff, of course, but she knew she was going to see Terry, so she had chosen just to tell him. "That makes sense, actually. I wondered what was going on at the time."

Vic nodded. "I think that must be it."

Erin looked back out to the street where Mary Lou had been parked, but she had since moved on.

"Mary Lou seemed pretty worried about it," Vic commented, noticing her glance.

"Of course. I would be too if I had a kid in that school. Especially since… Josh has been having problems since… you know."

"You don't think he's doing drugs?"

"I don't know. Mary Lou is worried, and she'd know better than me."

"Yeah. Guess so. Bella said Josh is a pretty nice guy. She went to school with him."

"Being nice doesn't have anything to do with not taking drugs," Erin pointed out. "I knew plenty of kids who were nice and still got messed up by drugs."

Vic nodded. "Yeah. I guess so."

They were both quiet, getting a few jobs done prior to the after-school rush. Erin started on some muffin mixes in the kitchen for the next day. Everything seemed to have been left in good order in the kitchen while they were gone. Erin had been worried about finding everything in a mess. Or worse yet, that there would be equipment missing. The last time she had lost her rolling pin…

She tried to focus on the job at hand and not on what had happened in the past. There was nothing to worry about.

Except Bo Biggles being back in town. What had possessed the drug dealer to show up again after he had run the first time? Why come back to a town that had just been through a huge drug bust? He had to know that people would notice him in such a small community. Especially after the public display he had previously made when Beaver had rear-ended him on Main Street.

Erin couldn't help grinning at the memory. She hadn't known who Beaver was at that point, but she had still admired the woman's pluck in standing up to the thuggish drug dealer. She had just stood there, chewing her gum and looking either bored or amused by his threats and imprecations. Beaver was always cool and unflappable, the kind of person Erin wished she herself was.

Erin glanced out the door to the front of the bakery to see that it was getting busy. She left the muffin batters to soak and went back out to assist Vic.

Terry hadn't stopped by the bakery during the day as he usually did, so Erin knew that he'd been busy and not able to keep to his regular foot patrol. The Bo Biggles case probably involved several other agencies and arrangements to be made. While closing up the bakery, Erin gave him a call to see what his expectations for the evening were.

"Erin," Terry greeted, sounding tired. "Sorry I haven't called or stopped by today. Things have been a little crazy today."

"I heard. Melissa was by to pick up a muffin."

He sighed in exasperation. "Some departments have leaks. This one has a fire hose. And I know the sheriff talked to her about it already. She's going to get herself fired if she keeps it up."

"I don't think she said anything confidential," Erin hurried to tell him. "It was all very general. Nothing more than someone who had seen it go down would know."

"She still shouldn't be sharing what she knows with anyone. She should be more careful than a witness."

"Please don't bring it up because of me. I didn't mean to get her in trouble."

"I won't say anything to the sheriff, but I should at least warn her she's going to get herself in trouble."

"Just… don't tell her that I said something to you. I really didn't mean to cause her any trouble. I don't want her to think that I'm causing her trouble."

Terry grunted. "I'll try to be tactful about it. But I think you could hit that one over the head with a hammer and she wouldn't notice. She's not exactly overly sensitive."

"Well… she is about some things. She may act like she doesn't care what other people think of her, but she does."

"Fine. I'm hoping to be out of here in a couple of hours. Do you want to do a late supper? Or will that make it too hard to get to bed in time?"

"I'd like to see you… if it's just a couple of hours, that should be okay."

"I'll do my best. You go ahead and do what you want to this evening, and I'll call you when I'm getting off. I don't want you to sit around waiting for me to get back to you."

"Okay. If I don't hear from you, I'll call you before bed."

"Good," he agreed, and she could hear the warmth in his voice. Tired and frustrated though he may be, she could still sense how he cared for her and wanted to be with her, even if it didn't always work out the way he hoped.

Erin hung up and realized that Vic was watching her, listening in on her half of the conversation. Vic raised her brows.

"He's not going to make it off?"

"Not yet. Maybe in a couple of hours."

"Willie and I are going out for supper. You want to join us?"

"No, you guys need some alone time. I have a few other things to do tonight, and if Terry gets off in a couple of hours, we'll eat then."

"We don't need to be alone all the time," Vic reminded, rolling her eyes a little. "In fact, I think we might need a little more time with other people."

Erin frowned. "What do you mean? Seeing other people?"

"No, I don't mean like that... just that... I don't know. Willie's been acting a little funny. Like... he doesn't know what to do with himself when we're alone together. Maybe it was too early in our relationship to go on a cruise together, but I thought it would be good."

Erin had wondered the same thing about her and Terry when they were on the ship, Erin feeling like she needed some space and separate rooms. They were used to living in different houses and only sleeping together on occasion. Being right on top of each other in the tiny staterooms had been a bit much for her. Vic and Willie had been together longer than Erin and Terry, but it was still a relatively new relationship, with lots of potential pitfalls.

"He'll be fine now that he's back to his mines and other work," she told Vic, hoping it was true. "He's not someone who likes to be tied down and have to operate on someone else's schedule. He just needs his space."

"I hope that's all it is. Okay, well, if you guys are going out for dinner later, then I guess it's just Willie and me. We're going to celebrate getting our casts off."

"That will make you happy. You guys have been so good about putting up with it, but I know Willie's about ready to take a saw to his himself."

"Well, you know him, he's used to being able to get around and do everything. Having a cast on his leg has put a cramp in his style. Climbing and caving and all of the other stuff he does are a little harder when you can't get around easily."

"I'm glad you both have healed quickly."

Erin studied Vic's face. It was hard to forget the horror she had felt when she realized that the mine had collapsed, blocking her friends' way out and possibly burying them. The hours of waiting for the rescue, not knowing even if they were dead or alive. She wasn't sure how she had gotten through it. But the scrapes and scratches had healed quickly, and now the bones had mended, and Willie and Vic and Jeremy could go on just as if nothing had happened. Erin found it hard to believe that anyone would want to go back into a mine or cave after something like that, but Willie seemed eager to get back to his work.

Erin, on the other hand, would never consider crawling into a cave again.

CHAPTER 6

*A*fter convincing Vic that Erin didn't need to join her and Willie for supper, Erin made her way home. She ate a small sandwich to hold her over until she knew whether Terry could get off or not, and sat down with one of Clementine's thick family history books to browse through it for new stories of interest. Marshmallow joined her, lying down on her feet, but Orange Blossom remained aloof. Erin eyed him for a moment, then decided to ignore him. If he didn't want to be sociable, she wasn't going to force him. Sooner or later, he'd come around.

She had been reading through the fading pages for an hour or more when there was a light knock on the door. Erin looked up but didn't see a vehicle parked in front of the house. Her heart pounding far harder than was warranted, she went to the door and looked out the peephole to see who it was. It was still light enough to make out the tall woman on the step, and she opened the door with a smile.

"Adele! Come on in! Would you like a cup of tea?"

Adele stepped in through the door and took a brief look around before answering. "Are you by yourself? I'm not interrupting anything?"

"No, just me. Come visit for a bit."

"Victoria isn't here?"

"She and Willie are out for supper. I imagine when they get back, they'll just head over to the loft. I don't expect to see them tonight."

Adele nodded and finally entered. "Okay."

"You don't need to avoid Vic, you know. She doesn't hold you responsible for what happened."

"Perhaps not... but it doesn't make for a very comfortable visit. I'd rather... not get in her way."

Erin shook her head. She didn't like to see fissures in her friends' relationships. She wanted them all to get along with each other and to be happy together. But that wasn't the way that life worked. She remembered what it had been like as a young girl in school to have friends that were always arguing with each other, breaking up, dissolving their friendships, and then making up a few days later. It had been hard for Erin. She was always the peacemaker, trying to get them back together again and keep everyone happy.

Adele looked toward the kitchen. "I'll put the kettle on. You just relax, I'm the one interrupting your night."

"I'm not doing anything, just reading. You shouldn't have to make your own tea when you come to visit."

"I'm happy to do it."

As soon as Adele was in the kitchen, Orange Blossom ran down the hall from the bedroom and skittered across the slick tiles of the kitchen, meowing excitedly. Adele laughed and spoke to him quietly as she moved around the kitchen, familiar with where everything was.

"Can I give him a treat?" Adele asked from the kitchen.

"Sure. Just one or two, though. He's been hard to get along with since I got home and I don't want to reward him for bad behavior."

Adele continued to talk to Orange Blossom in the kitchen. She didn't use a baby voice like Vic and some others did, and Erin couldn't make out her words, but it was a soothing, pleasant atmosphere.

In a few minutes, Adele returned from the kitchen, putting a cup of tea down for Erin and sitting down with one herself. Orange Blossom rubbed against Adele's legs and then jumped up beside her on the couch. Adele pushed him back, keeping him away from her cup.

"I don't want cat fur in my tea. Lie down and mind your manners."

In a few minutes, Orange Blossom was settled. He lay curled up against Adele's leg, one eye open to watch Erin.

Erin shook her head at him. "I can't believe he's being so lovey to you. He's been nothing but cold since I came home. Except for last night when I couldn't sleep, he did come in to cuddle after a couple of hours. But then this morning, he's right back to being aloof."

"He's just reacting to the change. He was pretty unhappy the first couple of days you were gone, so he's trying to decide whether you're going to stay or leave him alone again."

"But I made sure he was well taken care of. He didn't lack anything while I was gone. You were there to make sure he had everything he needed."

"Physically, yes, and I gave him all of the attention I could, but that's not the same thing as having his person disappear into thin air and not knowing if you were ever going to come back again."

"Well, I'm back now; it's time for him to start acting like it."

"He will. Give him time."

They both sipped their tea in silence for a few minutes. Orange Blossom closed his other eye and purred quietly.

"It's been very nice to have his companionship while you were gone," Adele commented. "I think I might have to get a cat of my own."

"Really? I thought you didn't believe in owning pets."

"Well... even though I don't quite cotton to the idea of owning another being... it is awfully nice having another creature around the house. There is Skye, of course, but he's a crow. He doesn't come into the house and doesn't always want to be around when I am outside. He does his own thing. Having a cat in the house... would be nice company."

"Well, if Orange Blossom doesn't shape up pretty soon, maybe I'll let you take him back to the summerhouse with you."

Hearing his name, Orange Blossom lifted his head and looked at Erin for a moment before deciding she wasn't addressing him and putting his head back down to sleep.

Adele was on her way out when Terry called to say he was finished work and could come over. Erin grabbed Orange Blossom before Adele opened the door. She didn't need him bolting for the open door and then having to chase him all over creation. With the way he had been behaving, he might decide he wasn't coming back again.

Blossom squirmed and yowled angrily, but Erin kept him under control until the door was closed, then let him go again. The cat jumped up onto the couch and watched out the window until Adele was out of sight. He gave Erin a kitty scowl and stalked back to the bedroom.

Erin was glad that he was no longer near the door. When Terry rolled up in his squad car, she didn't wait for him to come to the door, but immediately headed out to meet him, arming the burglar alarm before closing the door.

Terry opened the car door for her and was leaning his head back against the headrest when she got in, eyes closed.

"You look beat," Erin said. "You haven't slept in the past twenty-four hours, have you?"

"I got a couple of hours in partway through the day," Terry answered, opening his eyes again and giving her a worn smile. "It's not that bad. I've stayed up longer plenty other times. You take what you can get, and if you need to keep working to keep the town safe... well then, that's what you do."

"You need to get your sleep. I don't understand why they kept you for so long. You had the night shift. Couldn't someone else have taken care of Bo Biggles?"

"I wanted to be the one to arrest Biggles. Sure, Tom or the sheriff could have done it, but I was the one who got the lead on him being back in town and I wanted to be the one to bring him in. If I'd waited, he might have disappeared again. I just wanted to swoop in and arrest him before he knew what was happening."

"I still think it could have waited. If he's dealing drugs to the schoolkids, he's not going to do that today and go home tomorrow. He would have stuck around, once he'd established his business."

"Well, the entrepreneur in you has a point. But hoods like Biggles are unpredictable. Here today, gone tomorrow when someone looks at them the wrong way or spooks him somehow. I wanted to get him before he could do any more harm."

Erin got settled and pulled the car door shut. Terry sat up, blinked hard a few times, and put the car in gear.

"Are you sure you're okay to drive? You're looking pretty sleepy."

"No one else is allowed to drive the squad car."

"I could drive my car. You could leave the squad car here."

"I'm fine. Really. It won't be a problem to go that far. We'll just hit the Chinese buffet, if that's okay with you."

"Yes, of course. Whatever you feel like."

Erin kept a careful eye out for any possible hazards. Terry might say that he was just fine, but that didn't mean he was. People fell asleep at the wheel all the time. Or slipped on rain-slick highways. Or were just distracted when they needed to be focused on driving. She wound herself up so much that her heart was pounding when they got to the restaurant, but there hadn't been any problems. Everything was just fine.

"You can trust me," Terry said quietly, and Erin realized he could read her expression. "I'm not going to do anything that will put you in harm's way."

"I know. It's just... since Mr. Inglethorpe and the fire... things seem a lot more dangerous."

He leaned over and kissed her before getting out of the car. "I'll take care of you. Everything is going to be okay."

Erin tried to relax as they sat down together and ate. She had to keep telling herself that there was no reason to be anxious. She was at a restaurant with Terry; what was going to happen to her there? She was with a safe person, a person who would protect her if something bad happened.

K9 was stretched out under the table and kept bumping into their legs and feet. Erin saw him yawn a few times and knew it had been a long day for him too. Or maybe just a boring one, since he hadn't been able to go on the usual foot patrol with Terry, but had instead had to stay at the police department while paperwork and interviews were handled. That couldn't have been very interesting for him.

Erin looked up from her plate of food to smile at Terry, not wanting to be distracted during the couple of hours they would have together. Then she would be off to bed and he would hopefully hit the sheets as well and get the sleep that he needed to. He'd been awake for almost two days straight, and the fatigue lines around his eyes were clear. He needed to get a solid eight hours before he would be fully functional, and even that probably wasn't enough to make up for the sleep that he'd lost.

"I'm fine," Terry said, reading her worried expression. "It was a good day. It's always a good day when you can get a guy like Bo Biggles off the street."

"It's such a silly name for a drug dealer. You'd expect him to have some really serious street name. Mr. X or Ice."

"Biggles isn't a particularly scary name," Terry admitted, "but it is pretty unique, and one that people won't forget. You hear it once, and you remember who he is. That's a good quality for a street dealer."

"So…" Erin picked at her food. Even though she hadn't had anything big before their meal, she wasn't very hungry. Her body was probably still recovering from the menu on the cruise. They had all indulged a little too much on Chef Kirschoff's offerings. "Did you find anything out from him? When you talk to someone like that, you're trying to find out more about the drug network around him, right? Did he turn over anyone else in the business?"

"No, he was pretty closed-mouthed. But give it some time, we might still be able to get something out of him."

"He hasn't been sent to the jail yet?"

"No, PD is holding him for now, which means the sheriff is going to be sleeping in his office. Not exactly comfortable for either one of them. But we're hoping to get something out of him before he is transported, and we can't get him moved until tomorrow anyway."

"Not very often you can arrest someone like him," Erin observed.

"Bald Eagle Falls has its share of problems, but luckily, the drug trade has not been too bad within the town. Other than being used as a storage depot. The actual dealing that we've seen has been pretty low-key."

"There are always drugs."

"Always," Terry agreed, munching on some deep-fried shrimp. "But in Bald Eagle Falls, it has mostly been prescription drugs. Or pot grown in the backwoods. For the hard stuff, people have typically had to go into the city, which makes it a little easier to keep it out of the hands of young kids. Someone like Biggles comes into town, though, and starts handing out free samples and hanging around the school, and that's a big problem."

"I can't believe he would be so bold about it. He must have known that someone would see him and report him."

"He was keeping out of sight." Terry looked like he was going to say something else, but then he stopped.

Erin waited. "What?"

"Nothing." He rubbed his forehead and temples. "Just tired."

"We won't stay out too late. They don't have you starting too early tomorrow, do they?"

"Not first thing. I can sleep."

"Good. You need it."

He put his hand over hers. "And what about you? How did you sleep last night?"

"Restless. But I had Orange Blossom. It was okay."

His eyes lingered on hers and she knew he didn't believe she was being entirely truthful. He knew from sharing a room with her during the cruise that she wasn't just having nightmares every now and then. But he didn't jump in with the suggestion that she needed to get counseling. She appreciated that he didn't bring it up again. She knew he thought she should seek professional help. But Erin had dealt with enough therapists in the past and preferred to deal with it herself. The nightmares would pass eventually.

"So Orange Blossom has forgiven you?"

"No, not exactly. But he was happy to have a warm body to sleep with last night."

Terry let go of Erin's hand to pick up his phone. He looked at the picture on the screen and made a face.

"Sorry. I'll be quick."

He answered the call, turning his body away from her slightly as if that would give him some semblance of privacy.

"Piper."

Erin saw his face turn rapidly ashen.

"Terry, what is it?" She knew it was work and he couldn't tell her what was going on while he was in the middle of a call, but he looked like he might faint dead away at whatever news was being imparted to him.

"What happened?" Terry demanded, his voice flat.

He listened but didn't like what he was hearing. He turned farther away from Erin so that she could no longer see his expression. He held one hand up to shield the phone in case anyone could hear what was being said or read his lips.

"Who is coming?"

Erin tried to puzzle out what was going on with the few clues that she had. It was something to do with the police; it was obviously bad news. They needed someone else to come in to help. Was it something to do with

Bo Biggles? He'd made bail or escaped? It couldn't be bail if he hadn't even gone before a judge yet. He was being held until they could get him to the county jail, and then he could be arraigned and have a bail hearing. So it couldn't be that. Could he have escaped?

Terry ended his call and turned back to her. His face was gray, and Officer Terry Piper wasn't easily upset. He looked at her, not saying anything.

Erin didn't want to push him, but there was clearly something wrong and he would need to give her some explanation before he left. "Is it something to do with Bo Biggles?" Erin asked. "He didn't escape, did he? Or hurt someone?"

He shook his head. "Biggles... is dead."

CHAPTER 7

$\mathcal{E}$rin's mouth hung open. She tried to think of the appropriate thing to say, but it didn't come to her. Her first reaction was 'are you kidding?' but she had been in enough horrible situations to know that that was what people always said, for lack of a better response, and that it didn't make any sense. Of course Terry wasn't kidding that Biggles was dead. The police department wouldn't have called him as a prank, and he wouldn't be trying to tell her something that wasn't true. It wasn't a joke. As unbelievable as it was, Biggles was dead.

"I'm going to have to go back," Terry said.

"Yes… okay. Of course." He couldn't very well go home and sleep when someone had just died, someone he had just been talking to. He would have to find out what had happened and investigate the death. "Will you be okay? You haven't had any sleep."

"I'm not tired anymore. Adrenaline will keep me going for a while. I'll… I guess I won't call you tonight, but I'll talk to you tomorrow sometime, let you know I'm alright."

By the time he was done, she would either be in bed or be up preparing for another day at the bakery.

"What happened? Was it… suicide?"

"I don't know what happened yet." His expression was purposefully blank. He knew more than he was letting on. "I need to go in and find out."

"This is crazy. Maybe it was a drug overdose. He could have been… you know… carrying it internally. Or swallowed something when you arrested him."

"I doubt it. He's not a mule. But they'll have to do an autopsy to determine that."

"Okay… well… why don't you go ahead? I'll settle up here."

"You're not paying."

"I think that you're evolved enough to let me pay for meals now and then. I have the money. You need to take care of your job. Just go."

Terry considered her for a minute, then nodded. "Okay. Thanks."

He stood up and leaned over to kiss her before snapping his fingers for K9 and setting off at a brisk pace. K9 grunted as he got to his feet and hurried after his master.

Erin didn't linger at the restaurant after Terry was gone. She paid the bill, ignoring the waitress's questioning and sympathetic look, and headed back home. It wasn't until she got to the curb that she realized Terry had brought her in his car, and now he was gone again, back to the police department, without either of them recognizing that she didn't have a ride home.

Bald Eagle Falls was a pretty small place. It didn't take long to get from one place to the other. It was generally safe, despite Erin's propensity for stumbling across dead bodies. There weren't street gangs or muggers to worry about.

But despite all of that, she still didn't feel comfortable walking home after dark. Nothing would happen to her, of course. But it could.

Vic and Willie would probably already be settled in at the loft, ready for sleep. Erin didn't want to get them out again. She ran through the list of possibilities before settling on the one person she knew was a night owl and would not have any objection to picking her up. She called her half-sister and partner in the bakery.

"Hi, Charley?"

"Erin! Hey, I meant to get over to the bakery today, but I didn't quite make it. How was the first day back? Everything go okay? I made sure that everything was run according to your standards and put away and everything."

"Yes, it was all good," Erin agreed. "It was nice to come back to every-thing being where it should be."

"Good. I know it stresses you out when people don't follow your procedures."

Was it possible that Charley was actually maturing? She had, in the past, complained about Erin's lists and procedures and all of her rules about the way things should be run. It was Charley's bakery too, and she thought she should have more say in the rules. Even though she had said that she wanted to keep Auntie Clem's Bakery the same and to capitalize on the goodwill that Erin had already built up.

"So... I actually wasn't calling to ask where you were today. I figured you probably put in enough hours in the past couple of weeks that you needed a day off."

"Well, yeah. That's true. I didn't miss a shift, you know. Got there on time every day."

"Good for you." Erin couldn't help smiling a bit in amusement. For anyone else, that would have gone without saying, but for Charley Camp-bell, well, she liked to play things a little more fast and loose. "Charley... I need a quick ride. Are you in town, or did you decide to go away for your break?"

"I'm still in town. Where are you? Did that old beater break down? I told you it was going to."

"No, I didn't break down. I'm at the Chinese restaurant. I came with Terry, and he ended up having to leave in an emergency, and so he has his car and mine is at home. I could call someone else if you're busy."

"Not at all. I'll be right over."

"Thank you!" Erin didn't like to rely on anyone else for favors, but Charley didn't make her feel like Erin owed her anything for it. Erin had helped Charley out in the past when she had really needed it. But then, Charley had helped her out of some pretty deep holes too.

Erin put her phone back away and sat down on the bench outside the Chinese restaurant. It was well lit and there was still foot traffic down Main Street.

She rummaged around in her purse, looking for a notepad and pen. She really did need to clean out her purse and get rid of the junk that she didn't need. She flipped open her spiral notepad, and that was the first thing she put on her list.

Clean out purse.

Though, she hated cleaning it out. She always just ended up sorting everything, throwing out any used tissues, and putting everything else right back in again. She liked to have her possessions with her, to be able to physically see and hold them and know that she wasn't going to end up with nothing. Too many moves in the past. Too many times when she had lost precious items, no matter how inconsequential they might seem to other people. She wanted to be able to hold things in her hands. But that meant that she kept half the house in her purse and could never keep it all organized.

She added a few more things to the list, thinking about the way things had gone at the bakery, the upcoming Halloween season, and what kinds of treats she wanted to add to their repertoire. She liked to keep things fresh to keep people coming back. If they thought they were always going to get the same thing, they might get bored.

As much as she tried to focus on what she needed to do for the bakery, her mind wandered back to Bo Biggles.

How could he be dead?

Terry had been quick to dismiss the idea of drugs, but they couldn't be sure of that until an autopsy had been done. Biggles *was* a drug dealer, so Erin thought it wise to consider the possibility that it had something to do with drugs. Terry would have searched Biggles when he was arrested, but it was possible that he had missed something. Or that Biggles had swallowed something. Erin admitted that he probably wasn't muling drugs. Drug mules hid their drugs to transport them long distances and get them over borders; they didn't just do it to walk to the corner.

What else? Terry hadn't ruled out suicide. A lot of deaths in custody were suicide. But wouldn't he at least have waited to see whether he could get bail? He was an experienced organized crime member, not just a kid who panicked that his life was over because the police arrested him. Someone like Biggles, who worked with the Jackson clan, would know all of the ropes.

The Jackson clan. Vic's family. Vic didn't want anything to do with them. But her brothers and the rest of her family were still involved. Not Jeremy, happily. Vic at least had someone in her family that she could rely on.

It was possible that someone from the clan had killed Biggles to keep him quiet and keep him from implicating anyone else. Or maybe someone from the Dysons, the rival clan. That was who Willie had worked for when he had been younger, though he had gotten out of the business a long time ago after he had served his initial term for the family.

Charley's honk made Erin startle wildly. She'd shut out everything going on around her and had forgotten she was even on the street, let along waiting for Charley to pick her up. She put her hand over her rapidly beating heart. There was nothing at all to be worried about. Charley was there to take her home, and she could have a nice soothing bath and get ready for bed.

"Sorry," Charley apologized as Erin climbed into the car. "I didn't mean to scare you."

"I was off in my own little world. It wasn't your fault."

Charley waited until Erin was settled and had her seatbelt on, even though she wasn't wearing one herself, then pulled out onto Main Street with a squeal of tires that made everyone close by turn around and look at her.

"Charley!"

Charley giggled. "There's no need for everyone to be so stiff all the time. Why not have a little fun? What does it hurt them if I rev my engine or spin my tires a bit?"

"It doesn't… but you could be drunk or reckless, and you could end up hurting someone. They don't know. They just know that you're doing something that might be dangerous. Even though you were just showing off."

Charley smiled. She kept her eyes on the road and drove to Erin's house at a sedate speed. "So, what was the big emergency for Officer Piper? I can't believe that he just stranded you there."

"We were both pretty tired. Neither of us even thought about it. I got out to the curb before I realized that I didn't have a car. And he's been on duty since we got back to town, so he's a lot more tired than I am."

"If he hasn't had any sleep, then why don't they let someone else in the department take care of this emergency? They did manage to survive while you guys were on vacation."

"I think he wanted to deal with it himself. I'm sure he could have told them he was too tired and needed a break, but he wanted to go back in."

Charley raised her brows and glanced over at Erin. "And exactly what was so exciting that he would want to go back in again after working twenty-four hours?"

"I... really can't say."

"You can't say because you don't know, or because you don't want to?"

"I don't know what they want to share with the public. Best to wait and see..."

"If he told you, then he's not exactly keeping it confidential. Come on. Dish. What's happening?"

"I really can't. I just know because he was with me when he took the call. I was eavesdropping."

That wasn't exactly the truth, but Erin hoped that it would keep Charley off her back.

"If he's talking about it around you, then that's just the same as if he told you himself."

"No. Just wait and see. I'm sure it will be all around town tomorrow and you'll know more about it than I will."

"You are seriously no fun. What's the point in having a sister who is dating a police officer if I can't get the scoop before anyone else?"

Erin shook her head and didn't answer. "You'll find out soon enough," she repeated.

Charley pulled up in front of Erin's house.

"Do you want me to come in and keep you company?" Charley asked. "Are you going to stay up until Officer Handsome gets home?"

Erin's cheeks warmed in embarrassment. "No. Could be hours. I'm going to have a warm bath and head to bed."

"Okay. So you don't need any company?"

"No, that's okay. I didn't sleep very well last night, so I should try to get to sleep in good time."

Charley nodded her understanding. She was bright-eyed and ready to start her evening. She was a night owl. Erin looked out the window at her front door. Everything looked quiet. She knew she had set the burglar alarm, so if there had been any intruders, she would know it. But she was still reluctant to go in by herself.

"Watch me in?"

Charley raised an eyebrow. "What are you, twelve? Sure, I'll watch you in. If there's any trouble, I'm carrying."

Erin swallowed. That made her even more nervous. She didn't need

Charley rushing in and shooting things up. She should have thought things through before telling Charley to make sure she got to the door safely. But it would take all of ten seconds. Nothing was going to happen.

"Okay. See you tomorrow. You going to come by the bakery tomorrow?"

"I'm planning on it. Are we going to have a management meeting?"

"Tomorrow will be too busy, and I haven't figured out what our plans for the fall will be yet. Maybe Sunday morning while we get ready for the church ladies' tea?"

"Morning? How about after the tea?"

Erin rolled her eyes and shrugged. "Okay. After the tea."

"And don't make your plans yet. That's what we're supposed to be talking about. We're supposed to be deciding together."

"I mean... I haven't written down my ideas yet. I won't decide without you."

"Okay, good."

Erin opened her door. "Okay. See you tomorrow, then."

Her gait was awkward as she walked to the door. Like it always was when she knew people were watching her, and it suddenly seemed like she had forgotten how to walk properly. She looked around, watching for any shadows, listening for any movement. But there wasn't anything. It was just a clear, crisp night in Bald Eagle Falls, and nothing was going to happen.

She made it to the door and inserted her key. Nothing bad happened. She pushed the door open and bypassed the door open alarm, leaving the system itself armed. She shut the door and leaned against it, breathing hard, her heart pounding.

CHAPTER 8

*H*er night wasn't much more restful than the one before. She slept for a longer time, but kept waking up, worrying about Terry and about whether he was home yet. He had said that he wouldn't wake her up, he'd just let her know how everything was in the morning, but she wished she had told him to call her anyway. At least then, she would have been able to calm her mind and have a better rest, knowing that he was home safely and getting the sleep that he needed.

Instead, every time she turned over, she woke up, worrying that something awful was going to happen to Terry during the night. He would have an accident on his way home because he was too tired, or more of Bo Biggles's cohorts would be around and would jump him, or something equally tragic. Bad things could happen, even in a small town like Bald Eagle Falls.

Every time she closed her eyes, she was worried about the pictures she was going to see. Her dreams were filled with the images from Mr. Inglethorpe's murder, although the body in the scene was always different, one of her friends instead of the near-stranger. And all too often, the murder weapon was in Erin's hand.

She knew it was a dream, and she kept telling herself that, but that didn't reduce the terror she felt every time she found herself in the dream again.

Orange Blossom hopped up onto the bed and licked her face. Erin pushed him away. "Ugh, Blossom. Yuck. Don't lick me, just come cuddle. Purr for me. I always feel better when you're purring."

It was a soothing, steady sound. She felt safer knowing that he was there with her and that he was happy and calm. He wouldn't be purring if someone were breaking into the house or something else bad were to happen. He would know it, and he would warn her as he had in the past. He didn't like intruders, and he was loud and obnoxious when he was disturbed.

She rested her face on his body, absorbing his purrs. He was warm and soft, and everything felt right in the world. She could understand why people have therapy animals to help soothe anxiety. She always felt better when she was holding Orange Blossom.

And then her alarm was buzzing and it was time to get up.

Erin groaned and rolled over, looking at her phone in confusion to convince herself that it really was time to get up, and it wasn't just a phone call or some random birthday alert that wasn't supposed to be ringing. But it was, indeed, time to get up and tackle her day, so she forced her feet over the side of the bed, rubbed her eyes, and walked blindly to the bathroom.

A shower to wake herself up, and a strong cup of tea, and then Vic would be up and they would be able to keep each other awake until they were fully in the swing of things. She had several employees who worked shifts at the bakery now, but she liked it best when it was her and Vic. That was how they had started out, and Vic was the person she had the best relationship and sense of rhythm with.

The shower took too long to heat up, but the cold on her skin was probably a blessing because, by the time she got out, she was wide awake and ready to take on the day. She went to the kitchen to start the tea, looking around for Orange Blossom to make sure he wasn't going to trip her up. But he wasn't there. Unless he was already in the kitchen waiting for her, he was obviously still pouting.

Who knew a cat could hold a grudge for so long!

He was not in the kitchen. Erin didn't bother to call him. If he was going to pout, he wasn't going to get any special treats. She would top off his kibble and his water dish, but she wasn't even going to call him to tell him it was time to eat.

She put the kettle on and bent down to scratch Marshmallow behind the ears. At least he wasn't holding a grudge for having been away. He always had been much calmer than Orange Blossom.

Vic unlocked the back door and let herself in, disarming the burglar alarm. "Morning, sunshine," she greeted and covered a wide yawn.

"Morning."

"You sleep better last night?"

"Yes."

Vic poured herself a cup of tea and rubbed her eyes. She had pulled her long, blond hair into a ponytail, and would probably have it in a roll by the time she got to the bakery. Then topped off with her baker's hat, not a hair could fall into the muffin batter.

"Still no feline?" Vic observed.

"Nope. Perverse creature."

"Ah, well. In another day or two, he'll be getting underfoot and driving you wild, and you'll be wishing he was pouting again."

"Probably."

"So you and Terry made it out to supper last night?"

"Yes… for a short supper. Then he was called back in again."

"What? Why was he called back in?"

"Well, you know he arrested Bo Biggles…"

"Right. I was at the bakery when Melissa came by."

"And then he was dealing with that all day. And then…"

Vic raised her brows and nodded her head. "And?"

"He got a call back to say that Bo Biggles was dead!"

"No. Really?"

Erin laughed and shrugged. A predictable response. Like she would lie about Bo Biggles being dead. Like there was some big punch line. "Yes. Really."

Vic swore under her breath. "What happened?"

"Terry didn't know last night. I haven't heard anything yet today. No one will be up yet."

"Sheesh. The Bald Eagle Falls curse strikes again."

"There's no curse," Erin said, pressing her lips together.

~

Erin was happy to lose herself in the routine of the bakery. There were batters to bake so that they would have fresh, hot muffins and other bakery items ready as soon as the doors opened to accommodate the breakfast and pre-school rush. They would need to be arranged and labeled. There was a lot to be done, and even though they had the routine down pat, they couldn't afford to dawdle or forget anything. It all had to be run ship-shape.

Erin didn't want to think about ships, though. Enough about boats. She just wanted to think about her bakery and her customers. And Terry. Hopefully, everything had gone well the night before and he had gotten to bed in good time. No one was going to mourn the loss of Bo Biggles. There would be paperwork to file, and someone would have to investigate what had happened, but no one was going to miss a lowlife drug dealer.

"Are we going to do some pumpkin muffins this week?" Vic asked. "Now that it's October, I think pumpkins are in order."

"Yes, I think so too. We're supposed to have a management meeting Sunday, but I think we can sneak the pumpkins in before that without anyone being too upset about it."

"Has Charley got her panties in a twist over something?"

"No, I just promised her that I wouldn't be making all of the decisions without consulting her first. I have a partner and I need to make sure she's involved."

Vic nodded. "Even if she doesn't know anything about running a bakery."

"She knows more than she did a few months ago. And she ran things just fine while we were gone."

"That's true," Vic conceded. She and Charley did not get along very well. They seemed to feel that they were rivals for Erin's friendship. "But that's not just her; that's because you have everybody well-trained."

"I'm thrilled with the way it ran while we were gone. Maybe we can take other holidays."

"Somewhere warm."

"Yes, somewhere warm," Erin agreed. She had no desire to go to Alaska again. Victoria, British Columbia had been pretty, but Vic had been cold even there. "Somewhere tropical next time. And no murders."

"Exactly."

Erin looked at her phone to check the time, and moved to the front door. It was still a couple of minutes before she was officially open, but she would let people in to have a look and decide what they wanted to order.

Mary Lou wasn't usually there until later in the day, so Erin was surprised to see her with the small group waiting outside the door. She raised her brows and smiled, giving Mary Lou a friendly nod.

"Hey. Good to see you."

It was also unusual for her to be at the bakery two days in a row. Usually, she put in an appearance once and ordered what she would need for the week, only occasionally coming back a few days later to pick up something else for a quick lunch or dinner.

Everyone came in, smiling at the warm bakery smells. There was nothing like fresh bread and baking to put people into a good mood. And they were already carrying their travel cups of coffee, so they had their caffeine.

Erin went back behind the counter and finished putting the last few baked goods in the display case, while Vic stood by with the price tag signs ready.

"Good morning," Erin greeted the group in general. They all responded with various warm morning greetings. Mary Lou was hanging back, and she looked worried. Erin wondered what was wrong. She thought that Mary Lou would be happy to have heard about Bo Biggles's demise. But maybe words had not circulated yet. She would be relieved once she heard. There would be no more drug dealers hanging around the school her son attended.

The customers talked mostly among themselves. Some had heard of Bo Biggles's arrest, but it didn't sound like the word was out about his death.

Mary Lou allowed the other customers to go ahead of her, so it was quiet again when she reached the counter.

"Did you hear?" Erin asked in a low voice. "About Bo Biggles?"

"About him being arrested?"

"About him being dead."

Mary Lou looked back and forth like she might be overhead, then nodded. "I heard. The school sent out an email late last night, saying that there was nothing to worry about, it had all been taken care of and that Biggles wouldn't be coming back because he had died in custody."

Erin couldn't figure out why Mary Lou would be looking so worried if she knew that. Maybe she thought that someone else would come along to replace Biggles? Would the clan send someone else to take up the school sales again?

"You must be happy as two clams to hear that," Vic drawled. "I sure would be."

"I don't know."

"You don't know?" Vic repeated, frowning. "Why wouldn't you be happy about that?"

"Because it's going to cause a lot of trouble." Mary Lou looked at Erin. "You of all people should know the kind of trouble that comes from someone being killed, even if it was someone unpopular."

"Well…" Erin's heart sank. "Yes, I know that. But I'm not involved in this one, even peripherally, so… I wasn't worried about that."

"It's not going to be good," Mary Lou warned. "You mark my words. This is the beginning of our troubles, not the end."

Mary Lou didn't even pretend that she had come there to get a muffin. She didn't look at the display case once. She just looked impressively at Vic and Erin one more time, then turned and walked back out.

Erin swallowed. She turned to Vic. "Do you think…?"

"I don't know," Vic admitted. "I didn't think that anyone would care about Biggles being killed. Other than being happy about it, I mean. But she has a point. It isn't like the other deaths in Bald Eagle Falls have been uneventful. Even Charley's case in Moose River… the killing of a mob boss… that one came back to bite us too."

Erin nodded uncomfortably, not liking to think about it. Charley had been in jail, and even though everyone had told Erin to stay away from Charley because of her clan involvement, she hadn't listened. And some very nasty people had come after them.

Would the same thing happen with Bo Biggles? She didn't want assassins trying to track down the responsible parties. Even if Bo Biggles had overdosed or committed suicide, that didn't mean that the clan couldn't decide that someone in Bald Eagle Falls was at fault. Someone like Terry.

She had her phone out before she even formed the conscious thought to call him. If he had been up most of the night, he would be in bed and she shouldn't, but Erin's heart was pounding hard. She needed to be sure that Terry was okay. She hit the speed dial for his phone and waited, holding her breath and chewing on her lip. It was a few rings before Terry finally picked up. His voice sounded groggy and rough.

"Erin? Is everything okay?"

"I'm just… you didn't call me, and I wanted to make sure you were alright. I'm sorry I woke you up. I was worried… I thought that if the clan thought that you were responsible because you arrested Bo Biggles, that they could send someone after you… I just wanted to make sure you're okay."

"I'm fine," he assured her. He didn't rebuke her for having woken him up. "We'll talk later, and I'll fill you in on what I can. Things are… going to be tough for a little while. But it will all work out eventually."

"Tough? What things are going to be tough? What's going on?"

"I can't talk about it right now. I'm not awake enough to rub two thoughts together. We'll talk about it later, okay?"

"Okay." Erin just breathed for a moment, glad that she had called him even if it had meant waking him up. "You'll be careful? Don't put K9 in his crate, and keep your gun close by."

There was a long pause from Terry, and she wondered whether he had fallen back asleep mid-conversation. Then he finally spoke.

"I'll be careful, Erin. Don't you worry."

CHAPTER 9

*O*f course, telling Erin not to worry was no good at all. She was going to worry, and Terry couldn't stop her even with his most reassuring tones. It would have helped if he had told her that he'd had a burglar alarm installed, though when Alton Summers had come after her, he had managed to disarm her burglar alarm and just walk into her house. Orange Blossom had warned her then, and had even attacked the intruder. She hoped that K9 would be able to protect Terry if someone came after him.

And she should give Orange Blossom a treat. The memories of what he had done for her had somehow faded and she had forgotten his attack on Summers. Was she going to let Orange Blossom's pouting keep her from showing him how grateful she was to have him around? She should be showing him her appreciation for what he had done, rather than withholding treats and affection because he was a little upset about her having gone away. She would be upset if someone she loved disappeared from her life for weeks without knowing why too. She should be showing him that she had missed him too and still loved him.

"Erin?"

Erin turned to look at Vic. She lowered her phone from her face and put it away.

"Is everything okay?" Vic asked.

"Yes. He said he's fine. We'll talk about it later."

~

Erin was fully expecting Melissa to show up at some point during the day to give them an update on what had happened with Bo Biggles. She would have lots to talk about, even if she didn't know any facts. Melissa loved having gossip to share, and a little speculation had never stopped her. Everyone in town would be talking about the arrest of Biggles and his subsequent death.

But curiously, Melissa never showed up. Business was quiet. Maybe just because so many people had shown up the first day that Erin was back. They had all wanted to hear about how her cruise had gone and to tell her how happy they were that she was back again. So maybe they had all stopped by the first day and didn't need to come by the next day as well. That had to be why it was unusually quiet.

Even when people came in, they didn't talk about Bo Biggles. They studied the treats in the bakery case seriously and were subdued and didn't bring up the gossip that must have been circulating like wildfire.

When they locked the front door and were closing up, Erin shook her head at Vic. "That was one of the weirdest days we've had. Almost like when everybody was talking about boycotting the bakery because they thought I might be a witch."

"Has it really been a year since that happened?" Vic ran one of the big mixers, thinking about it. "I guess it was, but it sure doesn't seem that long. And it seems like Adele has lived here forever. We should remind her that it's her anniversary in Bald Eagle Falls."

"I'm sure she remembers."

"I guess so. But we should make her a cake or do something nice."

Erin nodded, her thoughts far away.

"Terry should be out of bed now," Vic offered. "The two of you can talk about Biggles and you can get the scoop."

"Yeah, I was hoping he'd be by here already." Erin glanced back toward the back door, expecting him to show up, but the door didn't open.

"He must have been exhausted. He was probably up half the night dealing with Bo Biggles kicking the bucket. There's probably all kinds of paperwork that has to be done when someone dies in police custody. You know how diligent Terry is. He wouldn't want to put it off until the next day. And there were probably investigators in from the city to help out with the case, because something like that is a little big for our little police department."

Erin barely heard a word of what Vic was saying. She continued to prepare the batters and doughs they would need the next day, her hands working from muscle memory while she pictured Terry in his house, unconscious or dead because no one knew he had been attacked. Anything could happen. They'd had enough experience with the clans to know that they didn't operate on logic. They were bold and brash, and why wouldn't they send someone after Terry if they thought he had somehow contributed to the death of one of their own?

She caught Vic looking at her questioningly, but then Vic turned away, leaving Erin to her contemplations.

∾

After they were finished at the bakery, Erin drove Vic home, but made no move to get out of the car herself. Vic turned back to the car and looked in the window.

"You going over to Terry's?"

"Yes. I have to make sure..." Erin choked up. She didn't want to give away how much she had been worrying about him and the possibility that he was in danger. Vic would laugh and say that she was overreacting and that there was nothing to worry about. Erin knew she was blowing the potential threat to Terry out of proportion, but she couldn't help it. As soon as she started to worry about something lately, her brain immediately swirled into thoughts of the worst possible scenario, and she couldn't get out of the rut. Vic didn't need to know how bad it had gotten.

"Of course," Vic agreed. "Go see how your policeman is. And give him my love." She gave Erin a little wave and headed toward the back of the house.

Erin let out her breath, relieved not to have to explain any further. She watched until Vic was out of sight, took one last glance around to make sure that there was no one lurking in the shadows or watching the house, and drove over to Terry's house.

~

His car was not parked in front of the house. Erin frowned. Had he gone out already, but she had missed him? Maybe he had shown up at the bakery right after they had left. Or perhaps he was back at the police department dealing with more bureaucracy. There had to be a lot of it surrounding a death in custody. Mary Lou was right. It was something that was going to cause them no end of trouble.

Parking in front of Terry's, Erin dug in her purse for her phone, then called Terry.

"Erin? Hi." He sounded much fresher, but there was a forced cheer in his voice. Erin put a smile on her face and tried to match his tone.

"Hi, Terry. I'm off work, and I thought I would stop by and see how you were doing. But it looks like you're not at home."

"I'm home. Come on in."

Erin stared at the empty parking space in front of the house where Terry's squad car usually resided. Maybe he had been too tired to drive himself home, so he'd had someone else drop him off. That had been a sensible thing to do. She was glad that he had decided not to drive, even that short distance, when he was too tired.

She slid out of her car, locked the doors, and went up to the house. Terry was at the door waiting for her by the time she got up the sidewalk. He kissed her and held her tightly for a minute, making her feel warm and safe and protected. They moved out of the doorway into the house, and Terry looked around, trying to decide where they should sit.

"Did you want to eat? I don't think there's a whole lot in the kitchen, but we could throw together some pasta."

"Sure, that sounds good."

Terry nodded, and they moved into the galley kitchen. K9 followed them in and nuzzled Erin's leg, looking for attention. She scratched his ears and petted him.

"You're feeling better now?" she asked. "It's amazing what a good sleep can do for a person."

"Yes. I was getting pretty frayed last night. And I didn't want to risk saying anything that might..."

He didn't finish the sentence. Erin looked at him, trying to figure out where he had been going with the line, but she couldn't match up an ending in her mind. Terry was quiet, pulling out his saucepan and filling it with water for the pasta.

"Was there any indication what Bo Biggles died from? I know you won't know the medical examiner's findings for quite a while, but could you tell by looking at him…?" Erin shifted uncomfortably, thinking of the other bodies that she had found or cases they had worked together. Too much history. Too many deaths. She wanted to know what had happened to Biggles immediately but, on the other hand, she didn't want anything to do with it. It wasn't just a matter to satisfy her curiosity about. It was a human life, even if it was someone who operated on the wrong side of the law.

"There are several theories," Terry said slowly.

Erin nodded, waiting for more. It didn't sound like it was obvious. Probably not a suicide, then. They would certainly not need to theorize if they'd had to cut him down after a hanging.

Terry didn't explain further. He continued to assemble their dinner, pulling a jar of bottled pasta sauce out of the cupboard to heat up, getting out their dishes, looking through the packets of vegetables in his fridge.

That was fine. Maybe he didn't want to talk until they could sit down and relax. Talk it all out at once and move on to nicer dinner conversations. Erin helped with what she could, but there really wasn't a lot to do. She found some rolls from the bakery in the freezer and set them to thaw slowly in the microwave.

They thoroughly discussed the weather forecast. Erin told Terry about Orange Blossom and her change of heart, deciding to pamper him instead of ignoring him. She talked about it being a year since Adele had shown up in the woods behind Erin's house, marveling that she had become such an old friend in such a short time.

"Some people are like that," Terry agreed, "even though they are newcomers, it feels like you've known them forever. They just click."

Erin nodded. She searched for other topics—Halloween, then Christmas. A lot had happened over the previous year. They hadn't even been together a year before, and now they were, as Vic said, thick as thieves.

They finally sat down at the little table, dishing up the spaghetti. Erin raised her eyes to Terry's. He didn't look tired anymore, but there was something else there. Discouragement? A weariness that didn't come from not being caught up on his sleep.

"What's wrong?"

Terry cleared his throat. He poked at his food but didn't eat. "I've been put on administrative leave."

"Leave? Why?"

"Because they need to investigate my involvement in Bo Biggles's death."

CHAPTER 10

*E*rin's jaw dropped. She looked at him. "Your involvement? What does that mean? They think you might have done something wrong?"

He nodded.

"But… that doesn't make any sense. They don't really think you did anything wrong. They just have to investigate, to show that you didn't. Right? It's just routine? That must be the policy when something like this happens."

"Pretty much," he agreed. "But… I'm afraid it's not all just academic. They really do… think that it could be my fault."

Erin shook her head in disbelief. "Who thinks that? The sheriff? He wouldn't be so stupid. He knows you. Without you, the Bald Eagle Falls police department would be nothing. There's no way they could operate without you."

"Biggles had bruises… there are concerns that there may have been excessive force used during the arrest or interrogation."

"That's ridiculous! They think you beat him?"

Terry nodded. "They're not using those words, but… yes."

Erin couldn't seem to catch her breath. She looked across the table at Officer Terry Piper, a man she knew to be kind and gentle. The idea that he would have used any more force than necessary was laughable. He had training in the use of force. He could take down a criminal when necessary. But he would never beat someone up.

"How long is this administrative leave going to last?"

"Until they have sorted out the cause and manner of death... and decided that I didn't do it."

"That could be a long time." Erin knew that such investigations could take months. Taking Terry off duty for that long would be disastrous. They would have to bring in someone from outside to cover his position while he was on leave. And his administrative leave would be paid, which meant that they would end up having to pay for an extra person, which would royally screw up the town's budget.

"It could be a very long time," Terry agreed. "I don't know what I'm going to do with myself. I don't think I can not work for three days, let alone weeks or months."

Erin knew the feeling. She had been so eager to get back to the bakery after a two-week vacation. If she had to stay away for months, she would go crazy.

"Maybe you can find something else to do while you're on leave. There's nothing to prevent you, is there? You're still allowed to work somewhere else even when you're on leave?"

"I'll have to check. They might say that I have quit if I do that."

"Yuck." Erin thought about Mary Lou's comment that Bo Biggles's death was going to cause problems for them. She had certainly called that one. Did she know that Terry would be accused of brutality?

"I'm sure the medical examiner will be able to prove that you didn't do anything wrong," she said hopefully. "The bruises he had were probably old, and he'll be able to tell that."

"Some of them probably *were* sustained during the arrest. Biggles didn't exactly go without a fight."

"But that's justified use of force, then. You can't be blamed for that."

"Just because it's legal, that doesn't mean people will take you at your word."

"But the sheriff and Tom—"

"It isn't just the sheriff and Tom. The sheriff answers to his constituents, and if the voters think that he's not performing his office, they can call for an election. The sheriff has to uphold the law, and if there is evidence that one of his officers has stepped over the line, he has to investigate it seriously. No matter what his opinion might be."

Erin was stunned. She sat there looking at Terry, then dropped her eyes to her plate of spaghetti. Neither of them was doing anything but poking at their food.

"They're actually going to investigate you for brutality? These people see you every day. They know what kind of a person you are."

"Not everyone is on good terms with the police."

Of course Erin knew that was true. There would always be people who took a stance against the police, even if they'd never been personally harmed or inconvenienced by them. Others had good reasons to be bitter about something that had happened in the past, and painted all officers with the same brush. But she'd thought that Bald Eagle Falls, with its tiny, friendly police department would have escaped that kind of judgment.

But it didn't matter that they saw Terry peacefully patrolling the streets every day. There would always be those who believed that all cops were monsters just waiting for the opportunity to hurt someone.

"Terry…" Erin cut a few strands of spaghetti with the side of her fork, worrying it. "This sucks."

Terry laughed. And it was a real, good-humored laugh with the dimple appearing in his cheek, not a bitter or forced laugh.

"You hit the nail on the head," he agreed. "It really does suck."

They scraped most of the pasta into the garbage and got out the ice cream. If there were any situation which required ice cream rather than complex carbs, it was Terry being put on leave and suspected of police brutality. They each heaped bowls with their favorite ice cream flavors and toppings, and sat down in the living room instead of at the kitchen table, trying to find some solace in sugar and cuddling.

It was a day when, even though it was still too warm to need one, Erin would have liked a fireplace to curl up beside. Staring into the flames and hearing the crackling of a really good fire was mesmerizing, and she could have used something else to pull her out of her growing anxiety.

Terry needed her. He needed her to be calm and collected and upbeat about the situation he was in. He didn't need her pulling him down with her moodiness.

"So he fought back against being arrested. He had bruises. They think that it was some internal injury that did him in?"

"Possibly. You never know when someone could have internal bleeding, or a concussion, or even just a weak heart. He never said that he was hurt and wanted to go to the hospital or to have a doctor check him out. He never said that a thing was wrong."

"Who found him? Was he on the floor, or still sitting in a chair, or what?"

Terry considered the question, likely evaluating how many of these details would be circulating town by the next day.

"We brought a camp cot into that interview room for him. I had gone to the restaurant to join you for supper. He had lain down on the cot to rest or go to sleep. Clara Jones checked in on him before she left. He was on the cot. She thought he was lying in an awkward position and wondered why. She pointed it out to the sheriff, and he opened the door and went in to check on Biggles. That's when he discovered that Biggles wasn't breathing."

"But there weren't any signs of violence. Like… a struggle. And he hadn't… done anything to himself."

"No. So the premise they are working with is that it was the result of something that happened in custody."

"But you hear about these kinds of things… about prisoners dying within hours of being arrested. It's not that rare."

"And what do you think whenever you hear about one of those cases? Do you think 'oh, I guess he just dropped dead'?"

Erin dragged her spoon through a pool of melting ice cream and chocolate sauce and took a bite. "No. I admit, I'm always a little suspicious of the police and how he was treated at the jail. They can say that there was no foul play, even that it was a natural death, but you always wonder."

"And now people are going to wonder that about me. It's always going to be a blot against my name, even if they can't prove anything. People will always remember that I had a detainee die in custody and got away with it."

Erin's heart ached for him. It was unthinkable that he had done anything wrong. He was always very careful about following protocol, and she knew him to be a decent and caring man. But now that he had this blot against his name, there would always be a cloud of suspicion over him.

Unless she could prove that Biggles's death had been caused by something else entirely.

CHAPTER 11

$\mathcal{E}$rin couldn't exactly jump right into investigating Bo Biggles's death. She had her work at Auntie Clem's, after all, and her employees who had covered all of the shifts for Erin and Vic while they were on their cruise now needed a break. But the bakery was a hot gossip spot and they always did their best business when something tragic had happened and people wanted to talk about it. Erin could find out a lot just by listening to what the townspeople had to say about the matter.

But it also meant that she had to grit her teeth and pretend not to hear what people were saying about Terry. If people were afraid to come in and talk about what had happened, she wouldn't find out anything.

She would have thought that with the number of years Terry had worked for the town and the number of people he had helped over those years, that he would have earned the respect of the residents of Bald Eagle Falls. But the townspeople seemed incredibly quick to jump onto the bandwagon and say that they didn't like to say anything unfair about Officer Piper, but it was awfully suspicious the way that Bo Biggles had died.

"They said he was covered with bruises," Erin heard Lottie Sturm say. She was always a troublemaker, and Erin tried to avoid crossing swords with her. So she focused on carefully packing the dozen cookies that Lottie had ordered into a box while she kept her ears pricked and listened for more. "You hear about police brutality in the big cities, but you never think that it could be an issue in a little place like Bald Eagle Falls. We've had such a good record up until now."

Bella Prost's mother was there to pick up some bread and to get Bella's schedule for the next week. "We've never had trouble like that before."

"But then, you remember when Kay Lourde's grandson was arrested?" Lottie mused. "There was a big to-do about brutality over that one."

Cindy Prost shook her head. "Didn't they decide that he'd been in a fight with some other boys a couple of hours before? His parents were threatening all kinds of lawsuits when they saw the condition he was in, and then the boy finally spoke up and admitted that it hadn't been the police at all."

"Still, you have to wonder. He might have been threatened into saying that. He did end up going to the state pen on those charges, and if the police decide you're a troublemaker and pass it up the line to the staties, they can make all kinds of trouble for him on the inside," Lottie said sagely. As if she knew all about the prison and how it worked. Erin was sure she'd probably never even driven past it. She was just repeating what she had seen on TV or read on the internet. There was always a conspiracy. The criminals accused the police of planting evidence or being dirty. The biggest problem in the prison wasn't the CO's; it was the other prisoners. They were the ones who were most likely to stab someone in the yard or the cafeteria.

"None of that had anything to do with Officer Piper."

"But it shows a culture of violence," Lottie insisted. "If one police officer is acting that way, you think the others are going to turn him in? They obviously didn't, and that means that they put up with it. They approve of it. It's a real problem in police departments all over the country. Once you get one bad apple in there, and the blue wall of silence... well, you may as well give up all of your rights there and then."

Erin shook her head, handing Lottie her box of cookies. "There you are, Mrs. Sturm." She told Lottie the total.

Lottie counted out her cash carefully, finding exact change so that Erin couldn't give her the wrong change back. She looked at Erin, her blue eyes glinting. "Are you still going out with Officer Piper?" she asked, as if she didn't know. Everybody knew that Erin and Terry were dating.

"Yes, ma'am, I am."

"Well, I'm just glad it's not you," Lottie said cryptically.

Erin raised her brows, but Lottie left the bakery, having stirred everything up like she wanted to.

"Land sakes," Vic declared, and let out a whistle. "It's a good thing she's not the one leading the lynch mob. I don't think Officer Piper would be making it to dinner tonight."

"It's not funny," Erin pointed out. "People like that... Terry will lose his job or end up in prison if people keep spreading things like that around."

"Everybody knows Lottie likes to cause trouble," Cindy said. Even though she and Lottie were fast friends, Bella practically worshiped the ground Erin walked on, and her mother had gradually changed from being antagonistic toward Erin to trusting Bella's opinion that Erin was a good, honest person, in spite of being an atheist. "No one is going to listen to anything she has to say, especially when she can't even keep her facts straight."

Erin nodded gratefully. She packed the bread and muffins that Cindy pointed out, giving her a couple of extra muffins for good measure.

"No one is going to railroad your sweetie," Cindy promised. "If he's innocent, that will come out."

If he was innocent. Cindy wasn't going to go all the way and say that she believed that Terry was innocent. She might be defending Terry's rights and showing kindness toward Erin, but that didn't mean she thought he was guiltless in Bo Biggles's death.

"Terry didn't do anything to cause Biggles's death," Erin said evenly.

"I believe that you believe that," Cindy said agreeably. She paid with a credit card rather than counting out her pennies as Lottie had. "But you weren't there and you can't know how hard Officer Piper hit that man, or what kind of damage he may have done. He believed he was arresting a dangerous criminal, so of course he did what he had to do to get him under control." Cindy shook her head. "You can just never tell."

"He might have been sick," Erin pointed out. "He might have had a heart condition or might have overdosed on drugs."

"Or it could have been an allergy," Cindy laughed. "If we're going to throw around alternate theories."

That one froze Erin to the spot. She couldn't say anything else until Cindy was gone.

"Ignore her," Vic advised. Her voice was low and soothing, the southern drawl pitched to calm Erin down. "She's just spouting off nonsense. She isn't accusing you of anything."

Erin cleared her throat. Her eyes were hot with tears and she had a hard time holding them back. She took a quick look at the customers who were waiting and decided that Vic could handle that many for a few minutes.

"Need to go check on those cookies," she blurted and went into the kitchen.

It was hot, and they tried not to bake too much in the heat of the day, but sometimes some special orders or events required more time than they could manage in the cool of the morning. Erin checked on the cookies Peter Foster's mother had ordered for his pre-Halloween costume-designing party, though she knew very well that they wouldn't be done. She slipped into the small office and turned on the desk fan while she sorted through the papers in her inbox.

When there was a lull, Vic left the front of the bakery and appeared in the doorway of the office.

"Are you okay?"

"I didn't give Angela Plaint anything that she was allergic to," Erin insisted, her voice cracking and tears spilling out of her eyes. She was so furious that Cindy would bring up allergic reactions like that, throwing it in her face as if it were a joke. "And I didn't give Trenton those muffins, either. That was Joelle. She planned it out. She wanted to get him out of the way. Neither of those things was my fault."

"No," Vic agreed. Her face was smooth and expressionless. "I know that. And everybody in town knows that. Cindy just doesn't like to be challenged. Everybody has their own opinions about what happened to Bo Biggles, but the fact is that no one knows what happened to him. Nobody is going to know until after the autopsy, and those things can take forever." Vic paused, looking away and pressing her lips together for a moment. "And chances are, they're going to come back and say that he died of unknown causes. Because this isn't TV. They can't always tell what killed somebody."

Erin wiped at the angry tears and set her face. She hated crying, and there was nothing worse than crying when she was angry, which people would take as a sign of weakness, as a sign that she was sad or hurt rather than that she was furious. "Do you think that someone might have killed him intentionally? It *was* just a freak thing, wasn't it?"

"Who could kill him when he was in police custody? No way it could have been murder," Vic dismissed.

CHAPTER 12

$\mathcal{E}$rin turned her thoughts to the possibility that Bo Biggles *hadn't* died by accident. What if it had been the result of a deliberate act? Or what if the cause was something that could be proven, thereby clearing Terry of any wrongdoing? He might always have that shadow on his reputation, but if she could prove what had happened, they could at least refute any accusations. That was something.

During their early lunch break, Erin called the police department, not sure whether she would get Melissa or Clara Jones, and not sure which one of them she wanted to talk to. It was Clara who answered the phone.

"Oh, hi, Clara. It's Erin Price."

There was an awkward pause. Clara knew that Erin had Terry's phone number and that even if Terry had been on duty, Erin could have just called him directly.

"Miss Price. What can I do for you?" she asked finally.

"I was just wondering… how you were doing?"

"How *I'm* doing?" Clara's tone was one of confusion. She and Erin were not friends. They knew each other, but that was it.

"I know you were the one who discovered Bo Biggles's body. That must have been horrible."

"Oh!" Clara's voice took on a bit of warmth. In all of the confusion and bureaucracy at the police department with such an unexpected death, no one had probably paid any attention at all to Clara and how she might be feeling or might have been affected by someone dying on the premises. "Well, yes," she drawled out the words, thinking it through. "It was pretty awful. I've never had such a thing happen here before. I'm sure you know we aren't accustomed to people dying in custody. This was a first for me, and it was shocking!"

"I'm sure it was," Erin agreed. "I've had… more experience than I would like in that department. I'm surprised that you're working today. I'm not sure I could."

"It's been difficult. But who else is going to keep things running around here? The sheriff may think that he's in charge and keeps everything running smoothly in the office, but without me… things would go downhill pretty quickly."

Erin laughed. "They always think they're in charge, don't they? But not even taking a single personal day… you're superwoman, Clara."

Clara made approving noises, happy to have the attention and accolades. "It wasn't easy to get up this morning and get in, I'll tell you. Knowing what I would be facing when I came in today… But you simply have to go on. There's a lot to be done. More than usual."

"Are there folks coming in from the city? The FBI or anything like that?"

"Some state boys. So far no FBI, and I hope it doesn't go that far. It's bad enough that the staties are coming in to have a look at things. It's really not their jurisdiction, but we have such a small department here…"

"I'll bet everyone is really happy about that."

"Oh, you know it. Tensions are running pretty high. And we still have the body here!"

"You do?" Erin was shocked. She had assumed that someone would have picked it up. An ambulance from the city, maybe. She didn't know who was responsible for picking up bodies in such a situation, but she would have thought that they would be there within an hour or two to get the body into cold storage and preserve any evidence from the scene.

"I know! Someone was supposed to be by this morning to pick it up. But no one actually wants to do that, so there are excuses about flat tires and a murder scene in the city they had to deal with and anything else that they can come up with. We're just the poor cousins; they don't want to have to pick up our garbage too."

"That's terrible. Does it… stink?"

"It's warm weather, dearie. It's going to be bloated and buzzing by the end of the day. If they don't get it into cold storage soon… I don't know what they're going to be able to tell from the state of the body."

"Ugh. I'm so sorry. I hope your desk isn't too close to the interview room."

"You know how small our office is. Everything is too close to the interview room."

Erin shook her head and let a few seconds of silence pass before inquiring further. "What was it like? I mean, when you realized something was wrong…? What exactly happened?"

Clara cleared her throat. She didn't answer immediately, and Erin pictured her taking off her glasses and letting them hang on the chain around her neck, looking around to make sure that there wasn't anyone nearby who was going to overhear her comments and get her in trouble for speaking out of school.

"I was getting ready to go home at the end of the day. It had been a really long day here, as I'm sure you know. We're not used to big arrests like this—a drug dealer, someone with outstanding warrants, known to be involved in organized crime. We're used to speeding tickets. Kids breaking curfew. Maybe some vandalism. When we make a drug bust, it's usually kids with a roach or two in their pockets. Nothing like that big drug bust the night your bakery burned down. We weren't even involved in that, just told to stay out of the way and let the feds do their thing."

"Right," Erin agreed. It had been chaotic that night, and she didn't know how many agencies had been involved in the cleanup, but it had been way too big for the Bald Eagle Falls police department.

"So we were busy getting all of the forms filled out and making arrangements to have Biggles transported in the morning. That meant someone had to stay here overnight to keep an eye on things, but that's not my job, luckily. In Tennessee, the sheriff is in charge of the jail. And even if we don't have a proper jail cell here, he's the jailer. That's his responsibility."

"And no one could come to transport him to another facility that night?"

"No… and to tell the truth, we didn't really want them to. Terry—Officer Piper—wanted to let him sit and stew, to give him a chance to think about what his options were and what was going to happen to him. Then Terry could talk to him again in the morning, and maybe he would have changed his mind and could provide some details about who else was involved with drug dealing around here. Terry wanted to do more than just arrest one person. He wanted to send the message not to mess with Bald Eagle Falls. We thought we scared the clans away with the big drug bust and that they would steer clear of here for a few years. Having Biggles show up again so soon… well, none of us were happy about it."

"Of course not," Erin agreed. She tried to move the story along more quickly. "So you were just getting ready to go home at the end of the day…"

"Right. The sheriff was going to have to stay and keep an eye on the prisoner, and I looked in on him to make sure that his dishes had been cleared away and that he was settled for the night."

"You went into the room?"

"No, I just looked in the window. I could have gone in; it only locks on the inside, you don't need a key to get in. But I wouldn't put myself in the room with a guy like that."

"He wasn't restrained?"

"No. You can't keep someone in handcuffs all night. There are guidelines, you know, to prevent…" Clara trailed off uncertainly. She didn't finish the thought.

"To prevent what?" Erin prompted. "I would think that if you don't have a proper jail cell, you would need to keep him in handcuffs, just for security. He could attack someone coming in the door. Or he could… I don't know… try to find a way out, or to harm himself."

"I know it seems like that. But there are rules because of… stuff like positional asphyxiation."

Erin blinked. She frowned at her phone, trying to figure out what Clara was talking about. Did she mean that someone could come in and smother Biggles while he was in handcuffs? Did he need his hands free to protect himself? That didn't make any sense. "What exactly is positional asphyxiation?"

"Normally, when you are sitting or lying down, you can breathe freely, right? But if someone does something to restrict your breathing, even just a little bit, it can eventually cause… well… asphyxiation. You can smother, just because you couldn't get your body in the right position to breathe freely. It's more common in men who are big and heavy, and Biggles wasn't any featherweight. If you lay someone face down, for example, then their weight can eventually restrict their breathing enough that they die. And the same thing with pulling their hands back behind their back, especially with someone who's pretty wide, because putting their shoulders back like that hinders their breathing."

"So you're not allowed to keep someone in handcuffs all night, because they could stop breathing."

"Yes. It's one of those things that we're supposed to do to help prevent… what happened."

Erin thought about that. "Huh. Things that you never know if you don't work for the police department."

"We have to be careful," Clara said sagely. "We're supposed to take good care of people who are in custody. You don't know how much trouble we could get into if someone starts making accusations… Because even if it never happened, people will believe it and be suspicious. It can throw a black cloud over the whole department, even if they never did anything. So we have to make sure that every-thing is documented, and you don't treat them… like the lowlifes they are."

Erin snorted. Vic looked over at her. She had been pretending not to be listening in on Erin's conversation, and she couldn't hear what Clara had to say, but it was apparent that she was paying attention.

"So what did you see when you looked in the window? Did… did he look dead?"

Clara hemmed and hawed. "Well, it's hard to explain. He didn't look dead, like he wasn't lying there with his eyes rolled back in his head and his tongue hanging out or anything like that. But he just… didn't look quite right. So I told the sheriff, and he went and had a look. Neither of us really thought that there was anything wrong, but he went in just to make sure."

"And that's when he found out Biggles was dead."

"Yes. After he checked him out to make sure that he was really dead, he had me call Terry. So that's when Terry came back in, and we have to inform all of the proper authorities…"

Clara had been the one to call Terry. Erin remembered how Terry had looked, his face drained of blood. He had been so tired and fatigued, and yet he'd had to go back in to deal with it.

"What did the sheriff think he died from? Did he have any ideas?"

Clara clicked her tongue. She didn't answer right away. But Erin wasn't ready to let her off the hook. Erin needed to find out what had happened if she were going to help Terry.

"Did he look like he'd smothered or choked on something?" she persisted. "Or maybe like he'd had an overdose?"

"How would we know? He looked... dead. That's all I can say. He was lying in sort of an awkward position, with his arm kind of thrown to the side and his face turned against the cot..." Clara cleared her throat and covered the phone receiver to speak to someone else in the office. Erin thought for a moment that Clara was going to hang up on her to cover up the fact that she'd been talking about the case. But there was silence for a few minutes, and then Clara was back, speaking in a lower, confidential voice.

"I know you want me to tell you that it wasn't Officer Piper. But I can't tell you that. He was the last one in there with Biggles. And Biggles had bruises. They weren't there earlier when he was brought in. I'm sorry, but... everything points toward Terry."

"No," Erin protested, the word escaping her lips before she had a chance to check it.

"What else could have happened? Somebody beat Biggles up. I don't know what he died of, but the medical examiner will determine whether he had internal bleeding or a head injury, or whether the swelling in his throat cut off his breathing. Officer Piper left here and thought he got away with it; he didn't know that Biggles would die and we would discover what had happened."

"Why would he do something like that?" Erin demanded. "It's not like he could think he was going to get away with it. There aren't that many people in the police department. It isn't like in a big city where they can all point their fingers at each other. If Terry did something like that, he would know that he would get caught. So why would he want to go to prison over someone like Biggles? He wanted him off the street, that's all. He didn't want him dead."

"Maybe he lost his temper. Terry wanted to get everyone who was working with Biggles. He wanted it bad. And what happened in that room… I don't know. But Terry was the one questioning him."

"Terry's the only one who talked to him?"

"Well… no. He wasn't the only one to talk to him. But he was the one who arrested Biggles, and he was the one who was in charge of the questioning. He took control of it. This was his case, not anyone else's. He was determined to keep dealers like Biggles out of Bald Eagle Falls."

CHAPTER 13

$\mathcal{E}$rin hung up the phone slowly and looked at her sandwich. She wasn't hungry. But ice cream for dinner the night before and tea for breakfast probably wasn't going to get her through her day. She didn't want to be fainting from low blood sugar during the afternoon rush.

"Are you okay?" Vic asked.

"I don't know. I guess so. I'm okay. It's Terry I'm worried about."

"You know he didn't kill that guy."

"I know he didn't... but I feel like you and I are the only ones who believe that. Clara works with him every day; how can she think that he would do something like that? She's acting like he's some vigilante and went after Biggles with... whatever you torture someone with... a rubber hose? She's acting like he's the villain, and he's not. He's just a cop that arrested a drug dealer."

"Clara's just overexcited."

"But she's doing real damage to his reputation."

"Depends on who she's repeating it to. Right now, it was just to you. You don't know that she's spreading it to other people. She knows she's supposed to keep the investigation confidential."

"If she talked to me about it, she'll talk to other people about it too."

Vic sighed. "Probably. But people know Terry. After they get over the initial shock, they'll remember that he's just the same cop who has been protecting them all along."

"Clara said Biggles had bruises. Bruises that weren't there when Terry brought him in. And she talked about his throat swelling. So... maybe some of the bruises were on his neck."

Vic considered this, carefully cleaning up the crumbs from her sandwich. "Well... that's not good news for Terry."

Erin felt like crying. They had to go back on duty soon. People would be waiting for her to flip the sign back to 'open,' and instead of finding something that would exonerate Terry, she had found the opposite.

"He could have been hurt before Terry arrested him," Vic said slowly. "Bruises don't always show up right away. Then they show up after a few hours... people think that means he sustained them while he was in custody, but that isn't necessarily what happened."

"Who would have beaten him up? He was selling drugs when Terry arrested him. If you were beaten up, wouldn't you go home? Take a hot bath or put some ice on your injuries, and worry about selling the next day?"

"Maybe he had to fight for the real estate. It was another drug dealer's corner, and he had to fight him to get it."

"There aren't that many drug dealers staking out claims around Bald Eagle Falls."

"No," Vic admitted. "It isn't like you see them staked out on street corners. But somebody else *could* have hit him or choked him before Terry arrested him."

"Right."

"Or... it could have been someone else in the police department."

"That's what I said to Clara. She said that it was mostly Terry's collar, but the others did have contact with him too. Something could have happened behind closed doors... that no one saw."

"Sure." Vic nodded. "But do you really want to accuse Tom or the sheriff? Do you see either of them doing anything like this?"

Erin liked Tom and Sheriff Wilmot. They had both been kind and respectful toward her and had helped her out in the past. Despite Erin previously falling under suspicion, neither of them had ever mistreated her. She had to admit that she couldn't see either one of them smacking Bo Biggles around.

Yet someone had.

~

Erin was exhausted after work. Not so much because of the early schedule and long hours that she kept as a baker; she was pretty used to those. But the emotional stress about Terry and worrying about what was going to happen to him was taking a toll. She called him as soon as she got home, not wanting to wait another minute.

"Hey, Erin," he greeted casually, as if it were just a typical day and not one of the most stressful in his life.

"Hi, I'm home. You want to come over?"

"Sure. About time I looked at that leaky washer in your bathroom."

Erin was startled by the offer. But she supposed he was probably looking for things to keep him busy and keep his mind off of the recent events. And events in the near future.

"Uh—okay. Sure."

"Great. Be there soon. You don't mind if K9 tags along?"

"When have you ever gone anywhere without K9?"

"I know… but that's because he's my partner, and since I'm not on active duty, I don't have to bring him, and I was just wondering…"

"Of course. I don't think I'd let you come without him. He could come without you, but not vice versa."

Terry chuckled. "Good. We'll be there in two shakes."

And he was. Erin had a sneaking suspicion that he had already been in his truck when she had called, just waiting for her to get finished at the bakery. He knew what time she closed up and often popped in to help her to tidy up and make sure everything was secure. When he was on duty, of course. Now that he wasn't, she wasn't sure what to expect.

Erin stood at the door to let them in, greeting Terry with a hug and quick kiss. "I was worrying about you all day."

"I'm fine," he brushed it off. "What's a few days of vacation?"

Erin was slightly hurt by his dismissal. She had expressed her feelings and he had simply ignored them. That wasn't something he usually did.

"Glad you called," Terry said as he looked around the living room, maybe sensing that he had responded too quickly. "I've been a little stir-crazy at home. After finishing most of the little jobs that I've been putting off for the last few months… I didn't know what to do. Do I like to read?

Watch movies? I'm told there's this thing about binge watching on Netflix. I could do that, I suppose."

Erin shuddered at the thought of him sitting in front of the TV or tablet in his underwear, a side table full of empty beer bottles beside him. She didn't want him to go to seed. He needed to stay sharp and feel like he was needed. There were only so many home repairs he could do around Erin's house too. A few days, and he would run out of things to fix.

"We can actually have an uninterrupted dinner tonight," she suggested. "I don't know when the last time was that we could do that without worry that you might get interrupted and called back on duty or to take care of some emergency call. Maybe never."

"Yeah, sure. Of course. Where would you like to go? We could go into the city if you like, that would kill a couple more hours…"

"I don't think I have enough time for that. It's still a 'school day' for me tomorrow."

"Oh, right. Of course."

K9 nosed at Erin, whining very quietly. "And I suppose you want a treat. Come on. Let's get you something. I guess he knows we're talking about food."

"Yeah, and he's wondering what I'm doing staying home all day. I don't know when the last time was that I didn't have to pop in to the police department for one thing or another, even if it was just to sign timesheets or some other report."

K9 followed Erin into the kitchen and waited politely while she got him a biscuit.

"And where's my kitty?" Erin called. "Orange Blossom! Come and get a treat!"

There was silence. After a few seconds, she heard Marshmallow's approach and got a stick of celery out for him. She scratched his head and told him how much she had missed him when she had been on the cruise, then called Orange Blossom again. This time, she heard him jump off of the bed, but when she poked her head out the kitchen door, he was not in the hallway.

Trying to decide just how much she needed to be punished by his cold shoulder, she supposed.

"Blossom…"

She walked down the hall to the bedroom, where he was sitting just inside the doorway. His ears flicked a few times when she saw him and he looked around like he'd heard a flying insect.

"I know you can hear me. Now come on. You want treats too, don't you?" She bent over and picked him up. This time, Blossom didn't kick at her or try to escape. He just looked into her eyes quizzically. Erin kissed the top of his head, scratched his ears, and took him into the kitchen.

He squirmed away when he saw K9, and stalked over to the corner, turning his back on the room while he washed. Erin went into the pantry to fetch his can of treats and started skidding them across the floor. Orange Blossom quickly forgot his aloofness and was running after them and jumping on top of them before tossing them in the air with both paws and then gobbling them up. Erin laughed.

"Yeah, that's more like it!"

She gave him a few more than she normally would to make up for the time she had been withholding them. And for the time that she had been on vacation, though she was sure that Adele had probably given him plenty of treats while she was gone. That wasn't the point.

Terry leaned his shoulder against the doorway and watched her. "So you two have made up?"

"I just had to make the first move. I decided there isn't any point in me holding back waiting for him to change his mind. Just who is the adult in this relationship?"

The dimple appeared in his cheek. "I'm not sure."

"Me!" Erin flicked him with the dishtowel she had just dried her hands on. "The adult is me!"

CHAPTER 14

They decided on dinner at the family restaurant, which Erin thought was a good choice as it wouldn't remind them of their dinner at the Chinese restaurant being interrupted by the call about Bo Biggles. But she didn't think about the fact that to get to the family restaurant, they would have to drive behind Town Hall, where the police department was located, right past the parking lot where Terry's squad car was parked while he was off the job. His truck was not as comfortable, but Erin hadn't said anything about that. She didn't want to do or say anything that would make Terry feel worse about his situation than he already did. He might be pretending that it wasn't bothering him, but Erin didn't believe it.

Terry slowed as they got closer to the parking lot, his eyes going to the van that was backed into the parking space the sheriff usually used. Erin looked at it.

"Who is it?"

"I don't recognize the van." Terry's eyes were sharp. The truck barely crawled forward.

"We probably shouldn't be interfering," Erin said anxiously.

"Interfering? What am I interfering with? I want to see whose van that is. I know all of the vehicles that are normally in this lot. I want to make sure that nothing is going on that shouldn't be."

"You're not on duty."

"That doesn't make me blind."

Erin chewed on a fingernail. She knew there would be no talking Terry out of it. And what was the problem with him looking to see what was going on at the police department while he was away? Were the state investigators going to come bursting out to demand to know why he was impeding their investigation?

While the truck was creeping forward, a man came out the back door of the Town Hall. Erin didn't recognize him at first. He had dark hair and a heavy build. It wasn't the sheriff or Tom or anyone she knew from the town council. But Terry sat up straighter.

"Do you know him?" Erin asked.

"Yes, and you do too. Or at least, you've met."

"We have? When?"

"When you were in Moose River."

Erin started to shake her head, and then she remembered. Jack Ward. Detective Jack Ward from the Moose River police department. She let out a breath.

"What does that mean? Is he here about Bo Biggles? What does he have to do with this?"

"I talked to him Monday. Someone from his department was supposed to be coming to transport Biggles."

"Does that mean that no one told him Biggles was dead? He thought he was coming today to transport him?"

"No... I don't think so. The sheriff would have let him know yesterday what had happened. Unless there was a miscommunication. More likely, he's here to transport the body now."

"Oh." Erin felt nauseated. She stared at Jack Ward, who turned around as if he felt her gaze and stared at the truck. Erin looked over at Terry. They looked suspicious just sitting there watching to see what was going on. But it would look even more suspicious if they peeled off. It would attract even more attention.

Terry pulled over to the curb and parked the truck. Erin put her hand on his leg. "Terry? What...?"

"Just wait here," he advised. He climbed down from the truck and walked partway across the parking lot. He didn't walk right up to Ward or attempt to get by him into the police department. He stood well back of the van and nodded to Ward. Ward approached him and they met in the middle of the parking lot. Erin rolled down the truck window, but couldn't hear what they were saying.

She waited, watching their faces and their body language, trying to tell what they were saying and thinking. Discussing what had happened to Biggles. Where Jack Ward was transporting the body to. Terry's administrative leave. Ward would be very interested in everything that had happened.

Eventually, Terry nodded, shook hands with Ward, and headed back toward the truck. Erin watched as he got back into the truck and put it back into gear. He did not comment on the window being open, though Erin was ready with a comment about how warm it was and that she needed the fresh air.

"Yeah, he'll transport the body to the medical examiner," Terry acknowledged. "Probably not the kind of thing we want to talk about before dinner."

"No... I guess not..." Erin took a deep breath and let it back out again. "You saw him after? When he was dead?"

Terry looked at her for a minute and then nodded. They drove the rest of the way to the family restaurant in silence.

"I heard he had bruises."

"Gossip isn't always accurate."

Erin wasn't sure it could be classified as gossip when she had talked to someone who was actually there. It wasn't just idle chatter that had been repeated from one person to the next. Clara was a witness. She knew. She might be exaggerating or trying to get more attention than she deserved, but she had been there.

"Yes, he had bruises," Terry admitted.

He climbed down out of the truck again and went around the vehicle to Erin's side to give her a hand down. She didn't need it, but it felt good to have Terry looking after her, taking her hand, steadying her as she hopped down from the cab. Terry stopped, looking down into her face, his eyes intense.

"Do you really want to know the details?" he asked. "I don't think this is something you want to hear about. You have enough nightmares without adding new elements."

He might have something there. That was all true. But it would be worse to lose Terry. Jack Ward was already taking his measure. Wondering, as he stood there talking to Terry, whether he would be transporting Terry

Piper to jail next. Erin had seen it in his eyes and the way he stood and held himself separate from Terry as they spoke.

If they put Terry in jail, they would have to put him in segregation so that he wouldn't be hurt. Criminals didn't like cops. It would be a lonely, miserable existence for him.

~

Sitting at the table, waiting for their 'meat plus three,' Erin answered Terry's question. "I want to know. About Biggles. I want to know what happened to him."

He looked across at her and took a sip of his drink. "Is that because you're planning on investigating it? Because I think we both know that's not a good idea."

"So it's true that he had bruises?"

Terry nodded. "He did."

"But he didn't have them when you arrested him?"

"Bruises can take a while to show up. It's conceivable that he had a fight before I arrested him."

"Will the medical examiner be able to tell that?"

"They might be able to tell how long it was before he died that he got them… but it won't be exact. And that's assuming that the body is still in good shape when they get it. It shouldn't have taken until now for it to be picked up. And I don't know whether Ward is going straight to the morgue. I assume so. You wouldn't want to be dragging a ripe corpse around for long. Kind of ruins the ambiance."

Erin wrinkled her nose. She did not need to be imagining the state of Biggles's body by the time it arrived at the medical examiner's office. "Why did it take so long for them to pick it up? Don't we have anywhere to store a body properly…?"

"Bald Eagle Falls is a small town. And bodies are not easy to move around. You don't just drag a man the size of Biggles from place to place without planning and at least a couple of men working together."

Erin nodded. "He couldn't have been easy for you to subdue, either. What do you do when you have someone that big who resists arrest?"

"I've got K9, a taser, pepper spray, a baton, and a gun. I'm well-prepared to take care of someone who resists."

"Did you have to use any of those things?"

"I used the taser," Terry admitted. "And the baton and considerable force. He wasn't going quietly."

"Wow. He must have really given you a fight."

Terry nodded grimly. "So there's no telling how many of those bruises might have been from the arrest. It took quite a bit of work to get him into handcuffs and the car."

"Were there bruises on his throat? I heard... that there were."

"I didn't choke him."

Erin nodded, accepting this. "But did he have bruises on his throat? If he did, then that means he did have a fight with someone other than you."

Terry considered his RC Cola. Erin suspected by the way Terry was looking at it that he wished he had ordered something a little stronger this time. He didn't usually have alcohol when they ate together. He felt that he needed to be prepared to be on duty at any time, and therefore, he did not drink regularly. But he wasn't going to get called in this time.

"Right. It would mean that he fought with someone other than me. Because I never put my hands or my arm around his neck. Chokeholds of any kind are expressly forbidden."

"So he did have bruising on his neck?"

"Yes."

Erin ran her finger around the rim of her glass, thinking about that. So Biggles had been in an altercation with someone else. Who? And had it been before he had been arrested, or while he had been in custody? "Could it have been someone else in the police department? You weren't the only one who questioned him?"

"I wasn't with him the whole time he was in custody. But I'm not going to accuse someone else in the department of having brutalized him."

"No... but at least you have some defense... an alternate explanation. And if we can find out who it was that hurt him, we might be able to prove that you weren't the cause of Bo Biggles's death."

Terry grunted. He took a sip of his drink. They were quiet for a while, holding hands across the table, just thinking about the situation. Sandy, a perky waitress who was always telling dumb jokes to the children who ate at the restaurant, bustled over with their orders.

"Here you go. Y'all enjoy your meals!"

They both thanked her. Erin took a couple of bites of fried chicken. "What about the taser? Could it have... caused heart problems?"

"So we're back to me causing his death?"

"No... if he's resisting arrest and is a threat, then you have the right to use your taser. They're supposed to be safe. I'm just... wondering if that might have had something to do with it."

"It's possible," Terry conceded. "There have been several cases where deaths in custody have occurred after a taser was used, particularly on someone who is very young, elderly, or has a preexisting condition. But Biggles wasn't any of those things. He was a big, strong guy. In the peak of health, by all appearances."

"Just because he looked strong, that doesn't mean he was. I mean... he did die. He might have been a drug user, not just a dealer. Right?"

"Could be. A lot of these guys use recreationally."

"So he could have damaged his heart with drug use, and then the taser, and the stress of being arrested... it could all just be 'natural causes' couldn't it?"

"It was natural causes. Because I didn't do anything to cause his death."

"Right. That's what I mean. It wasn't your fault. Either it was from these other injuries that he sustained, or it was natural causes resulting from his arrest. It wasn't because you beat him up."

"No."

Terry concentrated on his steak. Erin looked away from the bloody meat.

Erin heard familiar voices and was diverted by the Fosters traipsing into the restaurant. The Fosters, and young Peter, in particular, were Erin's favorite customers. She smiled at the busy little family. At first, they were only concerned with their seating arrangements but, in a few minutes, the children were bored and looking around, and spotted Erin sitting with Terry.

"Cookie! Cookie!" Traci insisted, pointing at Erin excitedly. She knew who gave them the delicious cookies when she was out shopping with her mother.

Erin laughed. "I'm going to have to start carrying emergency cookies with me. I feel bad about not having something to give to her!"

She excused herself from the table and went over to greet the family, being sure to say hello to each child. She left Peter for last, and he chattered excitedly when she reached him.

"Thank you for making cookies for my party! Well, it wasn't actually a party, it was an important meeting…"

Mrs. Foster gave a little eye roll at that.

"You guys were designing your Halloween costumes?" Erin asked.

Peter nodded vigorously. "We want to have really good costumes this year. Not just something bought from the store."

"Yeah? What did you decide on?"

"Before I was thinking a superhero costume. I've been a superhero almost every year since I was born. But Monday I saw this guy in an ape mask, and it was really cool. Like it looked real."

Erin nodded, smiling.

"No masks," Mrs. Foster said flatly.

"Mom! I need a mask. I need a really real mask like that ape mask I saw," he told her seriously.

"The school won't let you wear masks, only face paint. And you can't wear a mask when you're going trick or treating, because you won't be able to see properly. So no masks."

"It was so cool! It looked just like a real ape!"

"I'm sure it was very cool," Mrs. Foster agreed. "But you need a costume without a mask."

Peter sat back, rolling his eyes and looking just like a teenager dealing with an unreasonable parent. Erin wondered how many times she had given her foster parents such looks. She had tried to be 'good,' but not showing her exasperation was not high on her list of things to worry about. It was no wonder they had gotten so irritated with her.

"Well, I'm sure you'll work something out," Erin assured Peter, staying out of the argument between mother and son. She had observed negotiations between Peter and his mother, and Peter usually managed to get his own way. Maybe he'd be able to wear a monkey mask at his own party and face paint at school and for trick or treating.

She smiled and tousled his hair and gave a little wave to the children. "I have to go back to my dinner before it gets cold. You guys enjoy yours!"

Erin returned to Terry, still smiling.

"You've appeased your adoring public?"

"Yes, even without cookies."

CHAPTER 15

$\mathcal{A}$s they got into the truck, Erin caught sight of a familiar station wagon. Despite the weeks that had passed, Beaver hadn't repaired the damage to her front end. She had rear-ended Bo Biggles the last time he had been in town, resulting in a loud argument right in the middle of Main Street. Beaver had, Erin suspected, been trying to goad Bo Biggles into doing something he could be arrested for.

Terry started the engine. Erin put her hand on his arm to stop him. "Just wait for a minute."

He followed her gaze and saw Beaver's car. "You think something is going on?"

Erin shrugged. "Maybe. Let's wait and see."

Behind the seat, K9 let out a loud, exasperated sigh. Terry looked over the seat at him, the dimple appearing in his cheek. "Sorry, pardner. Stakeout for a few minutes."

K9 grumbled.

"You have to wonder how much they understand sometimes," Erin commented. She turned her attention back to Beaver's truck. "She's sitting waiting for someone, I think."

"Maybe. Maybe she's watching us, wondering why we're sitting here."

Erin pictured them both sitting watching each other and laughed. "Well, we'll see who breaks first."

But it didn't appear that Beaver had eyes on them after all. In a few minutes, another figure approached the dented vehicle: a slim figure, either a woman or a teenager.

"Who is it? Can you tell?"

Terry hesitated. He waited for a few seconds, then reached behind the seat, pushing things around until he came up with a pair of binoculars. Erin raised her brows. "You have surveillance equipment in your private vehicle?"

"What do you think I drive when I want to be unobtrusive? Besides, I didn't want to leave anything of mine in the squad car, in case…" He trailed off, not finishing the thought. He didn't need too. He didn't want to leave anything in his car in case he never got back to active duty again.

Terry raised the binoculars to his face and looked through them, focusing on the person Beaver was meeting with. He was still for a few minutes. Then he finally lowered them. He looked at Erin, frowning.

"Who is it?" Erin asked, reaching to take the binoculars from him and to have a look herself.

"Looks like one of the Cox boys. Campbell or Josh."

"Cam's been working with Beaver, so it must be him."

"Why would they be meeting here? I thought Campbell was out of town. Didn't he go into the city?"

"Yeah, but he could be here to see Beaver, or to visit Mary Lou. Who knows. There could be something going on at the school or something else that he wanted to be here for."

"Or there might be something else going on that he wanted to get the scoop on."

"Like what?" Erin took a couple of beats to connect it up. "You mean Bo Biggles's death? What would Cam have to do with that?"

"Nothing. At least, nothing that I can think of. But obviously there is something going on that we're not aware of."

He finally handed the binoculars to Erin and she took a look for herself. "Is that Campbell? Or is it Josh? They look so much alike, and I'm not sure I can tell them apart."

"I'm not sure either."

Erin watched him talking animatedly to Beaver. They were too far away for her to read their lips.

"Campbell is working with Beaver as some kind of informant. Maybe

Josh is too. He could tell her what was going on at the high school better than Campbell. Cam's dropped out, at least temporarily."

"At the school where Biggles was dealing drugs."

"Yeah."

"What would his involvement be? A customer? A middleman? Or just someone who was keeping his ear to the ground?"

"I don't know. Mary Lou said that he's been having a hard time in school. I don't know who or what he might be involved with."

"I don't imagine things are too easy for a kid when his father has been incarcerated."

"No, I think they're having a pretty hard time. Even Mary Lou has been having problems with people she thought were friends, judging Roger and judging Mary Lou for what Roger did."

Terry shook his head. "The man is ill. That's not his fault or Mary Lou's."

"And especially not Campbell's or Josh's, but kids are cruel. And having to deal with something like that can be pretty distracting from schoolwork."

"Yeah."

They watched Beaver in her car for a few minutes, then Terry shrugged. "Not really anything else for us to see."

"I suppose not. I was hoping it would be something significant. Beaver does know some things about Bo Biggles. I don't know how much she shares about what she knows."

"She can be pretty closed-mouthed."

Terry put the truck into gear, and they headed to Erin's house.

Erin tried to concentrate on Clementine's family history files, but her mind kept wandering and she couldn't keep focused on what she was doing. Terry was watching TV, something he normally did very little of. He looked over at her when she sighed and pushed the file away from her.

"Too tired?"

"Tired... and antsy... anxious and exhausted... I feel like a caged animal." Erin looked at their animal companions. "No offense."

"I would suggest getting some exercise or getting out to do something, but if you do that you won't be able to get to sleep tonight. A warm bath?

Or… maybe a massage…?" He raised his eyebrows, giving her a mischievous look.

Erin shrugged, trying to suppress a smile. "Maybe."

"Maybe?" He shifted closer to her. "What would I have to do to get you to a yes?"

"I don't know. Probably not too much."

"Good." Terry got to his feet. Erin stood up but, in a second, he had swept her off of her feet and was carrying her toward the bedroom.

"Hey!" Erin swatted at his arm. "I didn't say yes yet!"

"You will."

"I'm too heavy for you to carry!"

"You're as light as a feather." He took a deep breath, stopping to look her in the eye. "A very heavy feather."

"Hey!"

In a moment, he had carried her into the bedroom, and he pushed the door shut behind him to keep unwanted visitors out.

Terry dropped her to the mattress from a little higher than was strictly necessary, and Erin giggled as she bounced. One knee on the bed, Terry bent down and embraced her, brushing her cheek with a kiss.

"So, is it a yes?"

Erin nodded.

Terry's massage and the subsequent extracurricular activities relaxed Erin and cleared her mind so that she was able to fall asleep quickly. She awoke a couple of hours later and lay still, listening to Terry putting K9 into his crate and taking care of the other animals and the burglar alarm. He didn't usually go to sleep as early as she did, so it wasn't strange that he was still up. She lay there relaxed and drowsy, listening to his movements and, eventually, he returned to the bed and settled in for sleep. Erin cuddled up to him and, feeling warm and safe, dropped off to sleep again.

In the middle of the night, there was a loud yowl. Erin sat bolt upright in bed, heart pounding, trying to figure out what was going on. Terry moved beside her, not panicky like she was, but with stealthy, furtive movements.

"What was that?" Erin demanded, grabbing onto his arm. "Is it a burglar?"

"I armed the system. I don't think you need to be worried. Probably, Blossom just had a nightmare or saw a neighbor's cat in his yard. I'll go see."

Erin listened for any clues. "Be careful."

"I will."

She heard the soft clink of his belt buckle as he picked up his pants and pulled them on. He reached for something on the side table and then crept silently out of the room.

There was no noise of breaking glass or a car engine and tires as a vehicle made a quick departure. Everything remained quiet, the wind sighing outside, and the house creaking its usual old-house noises.

She heard Terry's low voice. "What are you making such a racket for, Blossom? You know you woke Erin up?"

And then she could hear Orange Blossom's loud, rumbling purrs. Erin relaxed, lying back down on her pillow and smoothing out her blanket. As long as Blossom was purring, she didn't need to worry that there was an intruder in the house. He did not take kindly to strangers being there in the night. He'd been her alarm more than once when something was not as it should be.

Terry returned to the bedroom. He was holding Orange Blossom and dumped him onto the bed on top of Erin.

"Maybe you can explain to him that yowling at things in the yard at two o'clock in the morning is not very polite. We need our beauty sleep."

Erin pulled the cat close and cuddled him. "It was probably just another cat, like you said. Or a possum. He doesn't like other critters in his territory."

"I didn't see or hear anyone nearby."

"Okay. Thanks for checking."

She heard him put his gun down on the bedside table and then the mattress sank down as he sat and removed his pants again. "Always happy to be at your service, Miss Price."

"Mmm. Then come cuddle up and help me go back to sleep."

He obeyed, putting his arms around her, and she let his warmth and Orange Blossom's purrs lull her back to sleep again.

CHAPTER 16

*S*he couldn't breathe.

There were hands around her throat, squeezing, cutting off her breath and the oxygenated blood to her brain.

Erin pried at the hands, trying to pull them away and get precious oxygen. She tried to protest, but couldn't make a sound, her vocal cords paralyzed by the pressure.

She reached out for Terry, feeling for him, trying to call for help.

The room was dark, but bright spots of light started to pop before her eyes like flashbulbs as consciousness began to fade.

"Erin."

She couldn't move. She thought she might be dead as he shook her and tried to get some response out of her. It was too late. The murderer had come and gone, and Erin was his latest victim.

Then she took a deep gasp of air, and full consciousness rushed back to her. Terry was shaking her, worriedly calling her name.

Released from her paralysis, Erin threw her arms around Terry and squeezed herself to him.

"Are you okay?" Terry demanded. "You scared me. Is everything okay?"

"I couldn't breathe."

"You're breathing now. Everything is going to be alright."

"I couldn't move. I couldn't call you. Everything was frozen."

He rubbed her back soothingly. "It's okay. Just another nightmare."

"It was just a dream?"

"Yes. Must have been a pretty bad one, huh?"

"Someone was choking me. Killing me."

"Oh, I'm sorry." He kissed her hair. "It's okay now."

Erin took a couple of shuddering breaths. "How did you know? I couldn't wake up and I couldn't move."

"I just woke up and couldn't hear you breathing. You were rigid. I thought you were having a seizure."

"Do you think that's what it was? I haven't had a dream like that before. Maybe something is wrong with my brain."

"I think it was just another nightmare. Are you worried? Do you want to see a doctor?"

Seeing a doctor would mean a drive into the city, then sitting in the emergency room waiting area for hours on end, only for the doctor to tell her that he wasn't sure what she had experienced, but there was nothing to indicate that she'd had a seizure or had anything wrong with her brain. And then she'd be stuck with a big medical bill for nothing at all. Better to stay home and go back to sleep. Or she could get up and start her day a few minutes early.

"No. It's okay. I don't need to see anyone. It was… just a dream."

"Maybe you have sleep apnea. You could get a sleep study done. Maybe there's a physical reason for all of the nightmares."

Erin already knew the reason for all of the nightmares. The dream of someone trying to strangle her was a new one, but they had predicted that.

"Someone choked Biggles," she said to Terry.

"Yes. I know."

"But it wasn't you."

"No."

"And he wasn't choked to death."

"Um… I don't know, Erin. We won't know until we hear back from the medical examiner."

"But if he was, that would mean it was someone who was at the police department. Someone you work with."

"Yes. But we can't rule that out just because we don't like it. Sometimes… people we know and trust can do terrible things. Things that we don't understand."

"If he was choked to death, he wouldn't already have a bruised throat when the sheriff found him, would he?"

"Hard to tell. I don't know how long it would have taken for them to develop. We took pictures. The medical examiner will have to tell us how old the bruises were and if that was the cause of death."

"What if it wasn't?"

"Well then... something else killed him."

"Maybe the taser."

"Maybe. But again... it wasn't until later. If it was the taser, wouldn't it have killed him right away?"

"I don't know."

"You should go back to sleep."

"I can't right now. Not when I can still feel those hands on my throat."

He rubbed her back and then stroked her hair back from her face, tucking it behind her ears. "You didn't think that it was me, did you?"

"That killed Biggles?"

"No. That was choking you. You didn't think I was choking you, did you?"

"Oh. No. I was trying to get to you... but I was paralyzed. I couldn't move."

"I've heard about sleep paralysis before. They don't know what causes it."

"Not a seizure?"

"No, I don't think so. We can ask someone tomorrow. Look it up on the internet."

"What if he was poisoned?"

Terry propped himself on one elbow to look down at her. "What?"

"Biggles. You had to feed him, right? Clara said something about picking up the dishes. So if you had to feed him, someone could have put something he was allergic to in the food. Or poison. Or he could have choked on something."

"Uh... I suppose. I couldn't see any sign that it was poisoning. And he didn't get welts like Angela did."

"But Trenton didn't either. Or the captain. Not everyone does. With some people, you can't tell."

"Go back to sleep. We can talk about it in the morning."

He wouldn't get up with her in the morning. He would still be sleeping when she had her tea and went to work.

"We won't be able to talk then. I won't be able to talk to you about it until after work, and then you won't want to."

"After work, we can make a list," he tempted, knowing how she liked to have everything written down in some kind of order. "If you go to sleep now, I'll help you to make a list tomorrow."

"Of everything?"

"Of everything. Whatever is on your mind. Anything that's bothering you."

"Okay." Erin yawned. "We should have made a list tonight."

"I think I enjoyed the way we spent the evening better than I would have writing a list." He chuckled into her neck, his breath giving her goose-bumps. Erin squirmed.

"You're naughty. You're going to try to distract me from making a list tonight too, aren't you?"

"Maybe."

She rested in his arms, her body molded against his. The dream was drifting away from her, the terror disappearing.

But for Biggles, it hadn't disappeared. For him, the choking feeling hadn't stopped until he was dead.

CHAPTER 17

*E*rin held Terry to his word the next evening, forcing him to sit down with pen and paper so that they could make lists and work through what they knew about Bo Biggles's death and what they needed to know to prove Terry innocent.

"I really just meant that if you wrote down everything that's been on your mind, it would help lighten the load," Terry said with chagrin, looking down at his pad of lined paper. "It's supposed to help to give you closure and get things off your mind."

"You said we could work on whatever was bothering me. I want to get this down. You said you would."

He grumbled, but he didn't go back on his word.

"Who was at the police department that day?" Erin demanded. "Working or coming in to file a complaint or anything. Everyone who was in and out of there."

"Well, me, of course. Sheriff Wilmot. Tom. Clara Jones. Melissa was in for a while, but not for a long time. I don't remember if Biggles was in custody when she was there or not... I think so."

"And who else? Anyone?"

"We had food brought over by Mr. Cooper, so that we didn't have to go out to get anything."

"Did he have access to Biggles?"

"No… I don't think so."

"Someone else took the food in to him? Who?"

"The sheriff. I'm pretty sure." Terry was still while he replayed the events of the day in his mind. "Yes, it must have been Sheriff Wilmot."

"Who made the food? Mr. Cooper?"

"I don't know. Maybe. Or maybe someone else at the store. They have a little catering department. I don't know who was working there that day."

"Write them all down," Erin insisted, noticing that he hadn't started making a list of the names. "Everyone who had access to the police department that day could be a suspect. And anyone who touched the food. We don't know if Biggles had an allergy or was poisoned. You don't know. Don't forget Roger Cox."

Terry nodded seriously. He started a list, putting down each of the names. "At least you hadn't sent over any cookies that day. And Melissa hadn't picked anything up from the bakery."

Erin nodded. "I don't need anyone adding me to the suspect list. I was far from the police department and have plenty of witnesses to prove it."

"Well, you and Vicky. But it isn't like you were far away. And you don't have customers there all the time. You could run an errand if you wanted to. Taking a tray over to The Book Nook or going out to the grocery or general store to pick up an ingredient that you needed while it was quiet."

"But I didn't. And Vic was there to confirm it."

He nodded, but didn't look convinced.

"I didn't have anything to do with this," Erin insisted, anger rising. She didn't know if he was serious or making a joke of it, but she didn't like to be accused of something she had nothing to do with. She had not been the one to take Biggles his food. And she hadn't provided any of the food that the man had eaten. She hadn't left the bakery, and she had someone to confirm that.

"I know you didn't," Terry agreed. "I'm just saying… when you're looking at alibis, you have to look at more than just what the person says. Of course they're going to say that they were never anywhere near the scene of the crime and that they have someone to provide them with an alibi for the entire time. But it isn't always the truth. People cover up or even forget. You might not remember from one day to the next when you had to take a tray over to The Book Nook or stop by the store to pick something up. People have faulty memories."

"Let's stick to who was at the police department. Because they are the only people who could have had anything to do with Biggles's death."

"Biggles's death was an accident. A freak thing. I know last night you had a nightmare about someone choking you, but that doesn't mean Bo Biggles was strangled. He appeared to be in perfectly good health when I arrested him. But a few hours later he was dead. But that doesn't mean that something I did when I arrested him killed him. And it doesn't mean that it was murder. Sometimes these things happen. People get panicked when they get arrested. They get stressed about it. They think that they don't have anything to look forward to in life."

"They can't talk themselves into dying."

"Well… I think they can. When people think that they have no reason left to live… they can die without any apparent cause."

Erin thought about that. She wasn't quite sure she agreed, but he had a good point. Sometimes people died of a broken heart, or stress, or died mysteriously after they told someone they were going to die. People were told that they had been cursed, and subsequently died just because they thought they were going to. Maybe Terry had a point.

But Biggles was part of an organization. He had experience. He would have known that a simple arrest wasn't a reason to give up. He knew that the clan would get him a good lawyer, that he could negotiate a sentence, that he would be protected on the inside by his gang affiliations and would be able to get out again and go right back to dealing and bringing in buckets of money. Or he could retire from crime and start something new. Second chances were a thing.

"Okay. Maybe he talked himself into it, but I don't think so. And I don't think he was hypnotized to kill himself or to stop breathing."

Terry smiled and shrugged. "No. It was probably something a lot more ordinary."

"He had bruises. Someone choked him either before or after you arrested him. Maybe it had something to do with his death and maybe not, but we have to find out who that was."

~

There was a tap at the door. Erin looked up from the table to see who it was and motioned for Jeremy to enter. He walked in, smiling and nodding at her, and Beaver entered behind him. She chewed on a thick wad of gum and looked them over.

"Hard at work, I see."

Terry shrugged and Erin caught an eye roll. He looked down at the pad of paper and slid his arm over the list, casually blocking it from view.

"We were just making some lists," Erin said, not sure why Terry would be concerned about keeping the information from Beaver, another law enforcement officer. She was afraid he was embarrassed to be seen making lists with Erin. Maybe he didn't think that it was a good use of their time.

"Have you solved Bo Biggles's murder yet?" Jeremy asked with a laugh.

"Biggles's death hasn't been determined to be a murder," Terry replied evenly. "It might have been accidental or suicide. We don't know yet. We have to wait and see what the medical examiner decides."

"If they decide anything," Beaver said. "It could just as easily end up undetermined. Deaths in custody can be tricky." Her eyes moved over Terry. "If he was killed, then the person who killed him may have been careful to leave no evidence."

"We don't know that anyone *did* kill him," Terry reiterated.

"That's what I said."

"Beaver, it wasn't me. I had nothing to do with his death."

"Well…" Beaver stretched the word out, "I don't know that you can say that you had *nothing* to do with it, when you were the one who arrested and interrogated him. You had at least peripheral involvement. That doesn't mean you were the cause of his death, but you were there. You are the person who had the most contact with him before he died."

"Which is why I am on administrative leave while they investigate it," Terry growled. "I'm well aware of that."

"I'm not accusing you of doing anything wrong."

He glared at her. "It certainly isn't coming off that way."

Jeremy hugged Beaver around the shoulders, pulling her toward him protectively. As if he needed to defend her. It was laughable. Beaver was both older than Jeremy and, as far as Erin could tell, had far more training and experience with physical threats than he did. She wasn't a defenseless little woman who needed his protection. Beaver leaned into Jeremy rather than pulling away. Her eyes were animated as she looked Terry over.

"I sometimes come across as provoking people when I mean nothing of the sort," she drawled. "Don't take me the wrong way."

"I don't think I am."

She just smiled and chewed her gum.

Erin's heart was pounding. She didn't like any conflict and especially didn't want to see it between her friends. She liked and admired Beaver, but the woman was an irritant, and intentionally so. Terry was Erin's partner, and she didn't want to see Beaver trying to get a rise out of him.

"Beaver doesn't mean anything," she told Terry, putting her hand on his arm. "It's just like you said; we won't know anything until the medical examiner comes back with a cause of death. It could be that his heart just failed."

Beaver chewed and nodded. "After he was choked."

"I didn't choke him," Terry said.

"And tased."

"I…" Terry's brows drew down. He looked at her. "How would you know that? That hasn't been released."

"It doesn't need to be released. It's part of your statement."

"And why would you have access to my statements? How are you involved in the investigation?"

Beaver just smiled and raised an eyebrow. Erin had never been able to decide which federal agency Beaver worked for. She was definitely involved in drug enforcement around Bald Eagle Falls so, even if she wasn't involved in the internal affairs investigation of Terry's actions, she might have still had access to his statement under her drug investigation.

"Everything I did was within the bounds of our policies," Terry said. "You know that."

"I did warn you that you might need assistance in bringing him in."

"I managed just fine without any help. K9 and I managed."

K9, stretched out at Terry's feet, raised his head to look at his master. Then he put his head back down again.

Erin looked at Beaver. "*You* told Terry about Biggles? Why didn't you arrest him yourself?"

"I didn't catch him dealing. I just saw him… in town."

There was a look exchanged between Beaver and Terry. Erin tried to interpret it. There was more that Beaver wasn't saying. She had told Terry that he might have trouble arresting Biggles. She knew he had used his taser. What else did she know that she wasn't saying?

"Did you see Biggles when he was in custody?" she asked thoughtfully.

"Did you question him too?" She looked over at Terry's list, which was still covered. He hadn't mentioned Beaver being there. But would he have? He'd kept her name out of it otherwise, even though she was apparently the one who had tipped him off to Biggles being in town.

"I might have looked in on him."

"So you could be a suspect in his death just as much as Terry."

"I didn't have any reason to kill Biggles. It was more beneficial to me if he was alive to testify against his co-conspirators."

"But he might not have been intentionally killed. You might have just..."

"Given him a little hug?" Beaver suggested dryly.

Erin had a momentary vision of Beaver choking Biggles. He was a big man and, although Beaver was tall and lanky, Erin wasn't sure she could have put him in a chokehold while he was standing. He would have had to be sitting, kneeling, or lying down. And Terry had said that chokeholds were forbidden. Beaver wouldn't have any excuse for choking him. No one did. No one professional, anyway. Someone with training would not have done that. Someone who was trying to defend themselves or attacking Biggles in a rage, however, that would be different. Where had he gotten the bruises on his throat?

"Nobody killed Biggles on purpose," Jeremy said dismissively. He gave Beaver another squeeze, then let her go. "It was just one of those crazy things. It wasn't anything anyone did wrong."

Erin sighed. She didn't want any of her friends to have had anything to do with his death. She'd had to deal with that before, and she didn't want to find out that someone else she knew had been pushed into killing someone. Even if there was good reason to permanently remove someone like Biggles from Bald Eagle Falls, she didn't want Terry or Beaver or the sheriff or anyone else at the police department to have caused his death. She wanted it to be an outsider. Someone she didn't know or care about.

"Maybe it was a clan thing," she suggested. "Could it have been someone from the Jackson or Dyson clan?"

They all looked at each other, weighing the possibilities. Eventually, everyone was looking at Jeremy for his opinion.

"He's Jackson clan," Jeremy said. "So it wouldn't be Jacksons. Could it be Dysons? Sure... but why would they kill him when he was in custody? And they'd have to know about the arrest pretty quickly for someone to get there and deal with him. And then… how would they get into the police department? That's a restricted area."

"But he might have had a fight with one of them before Terry arrested him," Erin pointed out. "He could have gotten the bruises earlier, not while he was in custody."

"And if he was in a fight with a Dyson, what happened?" Terry asked. "Why didn't anyone report it? Was he on his own or did he have Jacksons there to watch his back? And why a hand-to-hand fight instead of weapons?"

"I don't know. You're supposed to be helping me come up with explanations."

Terry gave a brief smile. "Yeah. Sorry about that. Forgot myself for a minute."

"If it was while he was in custody, it could have been the Jacksons." Erin pursed her lips and looked at Jeremy. "Maybe they were afraid he was going to talk? Turn in other gang members?"

Jeremy shook his head. "How are they going to get at him? He's locked in a room in the police department. You think they could stroll in there and no one would notice?"

Erin tried to visualize what she knew of the layout of the police department offices. She knew Clara Jones's desk and Terry's office. She'd been in Sheriff Wilmot's office. She wasn't sure of the room where Biggles would have been detained.

"Where exactly was he?" she asked Terry. "Near the back?"

He hesitated, looking at the question from several angles before deciding to answer. "Yes, the room he was in was near the back of the building. You can't walk back there without everybody else in the office seeing you."

"What if someone came in the back door? Like where Jack Ward was parked. Does that lead straight into your offices, or into the Town Hall?"

"There's a shared hallway with some maintenance rooms and a loading dock area. You'd have to go through a second door to get into the police department through the back."

"But you could do it. There is a way to get in through the back instead of walking past everybody else."

Terry shrugged uncomfortably. "Yes… but no one did. They still would have been seen. It's not that big of a place. And I was with Biggles most of the time. Someone coming in would have been face-to-face with me."

Beaver chomped on her gum, watching Erin's face with disconcerting intensity.

"But if they were watching, you weren't there the whole time. And you guys took a break to eat. Can you take me there? To see where the door is and how it's laid out?"

"No."

"Terry…"

"Erin, I can't even go back there myself. I'm on leave. I have no business going back there."

"Couldn't you find a reason? You need to pick up something personal that you left in your desk. And because you're just stopping in for a minute, and I happened to be along…"

"What are you going to see? Just my office. You've seen that before."

"I want to walk in through the back."

"You're not going to be able to see anything."

"But then I'll stop bugging you."

"Oh, will you?" he challenged.

Erin's face got hot. She shrugged and looked away from him, unable to suppress a smile of embarrassment at Beaver and Jeremy.

"You're not going to find anything," Jeremy chimed in. "It wasn't the Jacksons. You can be sure of that."

"How do you know that?"

He didn't come up with an answer. Erin fixed him with her stare, waiting for him to break. If he didn't have any more contact with the Jacksons, how could he state that they hadn't had any involvement? He couldn't know that.

Beaver tilted her head and looked at her young boyfriend. "Have you talked to someone?" she prodded. "Had any text or email exchanges?"

"No, of course not. I'm just telling you, I know how they work, and they wouldn't break into the police department to beat someone up and kill them while they were in police custody. That would be… like The Godfather or something. Things don't happen like that in real life. Or not with the clans, anyway. Maybe somewhere like New York or Chicago where they have big, powerful organizations. But in Tennessee? Come on."

CHAPTER 18

*E*rin? Earth to Erin!"

Erin blinked and looked up from her mixer to see Vic leaning toward her, trying to get her attention. Erin shook her head, feeling mesmerized by the noise and movement of the mixer. She obviously wasn't getting enough sleep if she could zone out that easily.

"Sorry, what was that?"

"I was asking you about treats for Halloween. Are we going to do some cutout cookies again this year?"

"They were a big hit last year, so probably," Erin agreed. "I'll make sure that everyone is onside Sunday."

"You'll make sure that Charley agrees with you, you mean."

"Well, she is my partner."

"I know, but she can't tell you what to make and not to make. And she doesn't have the experience that you do. You were here for Halloween last year, and you know how things sold."

Erin shook her head. "I can't believe it's been a year. For a few days there, it looked like everything was going to shut down completely. I didn't think the bakery was going to last."

"I know, I remember. It was scary. But this year, no controversy, no one is going to be boycotting us over rumors."

"Seems like there's always some kind of controversy. If it's not one thing, it's another."

"Terry, you mean?" Vic asked, looking sympathetic.

"Yeah. I don't know what he's going to do if he can't get back on active duty. Or if people decide that he's responsible for Biggles's death even though he didn't do anything. What are we going to do?"

"I don't know. I'd hate for you to even think about moving somewhere else. But if he can't work here… I don't know."

"I couldn't ask him to give up police work. It's what he does best. It's what he lives for."

Vic nodded her agreement. "I know."

"Tell Willie thank you for taking Terry with him today. I don't think he could stand another day just hanging around his house. Or mine. He needs to have a mission. Something to do."

"Willie will be around later; you can tell him yourself. He likes Terry. He's happy to help out."

"But there's only so much he can help Willie with too."

"Willie said Terry was going to help him with a security issue today," Vic contributed. "Which probably means stringing wire for a fence. And one day they're going to go fishing. I don't know if they have any plans other than that."

"Yeah. Then I'm going to have to think of ways to keep him busy… but it's going to be more than a couple of days. I'm worried it's going to be weeks… even months. I can't distract him for that long. I don't know what to do."

Vic shrugged, raising her hands up to shoulder height and shaking her head. "I don't know. Maybe he could get another job, temporarily. Security, like Jeremy is doing."

"I thought about that… I'm just worried it will drive him crazy. He's been such a good town cop, he's always got his eye on everything and knows what everyone is up to. It's not just walking a beat, it's actually caring about people and knowing what's going on in town. Just walking around a warehouse, even if he has K9 with him, is a huge step down from what he's been doing. Maybe if he could be a private investigator… but there's not a lot to investigate in Bald Eagle Falls. He'd probably be out of town all the time."

One of the ovens dinged, and Erin moved over to it to take the next couple of trays out to cool. She turned off the timer and looked at the hot, fragrant muffins in front of her.

"I'm going to take these over to the police department."

Vic's eyes widened. "What?"

"It's been a while since they had an order. We have to whet their appetites. Keep them coming back for more."

Vic stood there with her mouth open for a minute. "You're just going over there to snoop."

Erin couldn't help the guilty smile that crept across her face. "I'm just taking some muffins over. Have to keep the boys in blue happy."

"That made sense when Terry was there and you wanted to see him for a minute and do him a favor. Not so much now that he's off."

"And I have to show them that there are no hard feelings. We wouldn't want to lose their business just because Terry isn't there anymore, would we?"

"Well, no ma'am. We wouldn't want that."

"Then I'd better make up a box and take them over while they're still warm."

In a few minutes, Erin was walking down the street with her box of muffins. The days were getting cooler; it didn't feel like stepping out into an oven when she opened the door and went outside. It was pleasant, especially after the chilly days on the cruise ship. She hadn't been bothered by the cold as much as Vic, but it still had been a big change from the warm Tennessee fall to the cold Canadian and Alaskan autumn.

Erin saw Mary Lou through the window at The General Store and decided to stop in for a quick minute.

Mary Lou smiled and patted her hair when Erin entered, making sure that nothing was out of place. She smoothed her pantsuit. "What are you doing out and about today? I thought you were on at Auntie Clem's all week to make up for your vacation."

"I am. But it was quiet, and I decided to run some baking over to the police department."

"Oh." Mary Lou raised both brows, looking surprised at that. "Well, why not? You can take baking wherever you like; it isn't like anyone is going to turn you away." She smiled in good humor.

"I was thinking maybe I'd get one of those little jam and marmalade sets

I saw you selling the other day. They're so cute. And then if someone wants something sweet on one of their muffins…"

"Like they're not sweet enough already." Mary Lou shook her head at the idea of putting more sugar on top of the muffins. But she was already moving to pick up one of the sets of little jam jars. She wrapped it in paper to keep anything from getting broken and took it to the till to ring up Erin's order. "Would you like anything else?"

Erin put her box down on the counter and looked around, but couldn't think of anything else that she might conceivably need for the police department or the bakery. She was well-supplied with everything else she needed. "No… I guess that's all. I just wondered… how you're doing."

"Me? I'm about the same as ever." Mary Lou brushed off the inquiry.

"No, really. I want to know how you are. I know it's been tough on you since Roger's… accident. And now with Campbell being out on his own and it just being you and Josh… how's his school going? I worry about how hard it must be, them talking about his dad and teasing him… kids can be so cruel. And even if they're not teasing him, he's probably still distracted… just because of everything that happened. People talk about their teenage years being so ideal, but I remember being a teenager… and it wasn't much fun."

Mary Lou gazed at her for a moment. Her eyes were suddenly shiny, reflecting the light of the room. She turned her face away from Erin, busying herself with putting the jam jars into a bag and punching the price into the till.

"Thank you, Erin. Yes… it's been hard on Josh and I worry about him all day long. I miss the days when he was little and he was at home, and I could look after him. I could make sure that he was safe and keep him happy just by opening the big bin of Lego bricks for him. He was such an active little boy; I didn't know how I was going to last until he was old enough for school. And now… I wish for the simplicity of those days again."

Erin nodded. She wondered whether to mention to Mary Lou that she had seen Campbell or Josh with Beaver the other day, but decided it would probably just make her worry more. But Mary Lou's brain seemed to shift in that direction anyway.

"Josh's marks at school are abysmal. He was always a good student, even after Roger's accident. The boys both worked so hard to keep things normal.

But when Roger was arrested... everything changed. Josh has dropped out of all of the sports teams. I have to keep reminding myself that at least he's still going to school. Campbell, on the other hand... I wish I had some clue what he was up to."

"He doesn't tell you anything?"

"Nothing of any substance. He was out with this friend or that friend, at a party or hanging out or doing whatever kids do when they're not out working or doing something constructive. Drinking, I'm sure. Hopefully, nothing worse than that... but he wouldn't tell me if he was. He doesn't want me to have to worry."

"Like you don't worry when you have to imagine it."

Mary Lou nodded her agreement. "Sometimes I think that the things he is really doing couldn't be any worse than what I am imagining... and then I imagine what would be worse than what I was already imagining..."

Erin laughed, nodding. Poor Mary Lou. "But you know he was helping out Beaver, so that must be some reassurance... whatever it is that he's up to, he was at least helping law enforcement. Maybe he'll decide he wants to be a cop."

"He'd have to finish school if he wants a career in law enforcement. But whenever I suggest that he should be going back before it's too late and he's lost too much time... he always tells me that I'm getting too stressed out about it, and he can go back whenever he's ready. And he just isn't ready yet. He's still finding himself. He wants to have some fun while he's still a kid."

When Erin had been Campbell's age, she'd still been going to school but, knowing that she wouldn't be able to get any education past twelfth grade, she had also been trying to build up her work experience so that she would have some chance of supporting herself when she aged out of foster care. Just wanting to have some fun being a kid hadn't been in the cards for her.

"How can he afford to do anything? Is he working?"

Mary Lou shrugged. "Another of the things I can't get pinned down. I think he does some casual labor, maybe some panhandling, whatever he's doing for Beaver... these kids get together in groups to cover the bills, but he doesn't have a place of his own. I wouldn't exactly say he was homeless, but he doesn't have a permanent address."

"Does he come to see you when he comes home to Bald Eagle Falls?" Erin asked, thinking about seeing Cam or Josh talking to Beaver.

"He hasn't been back in town. I don't know if he'll ever come back here. Not to live, for sure. For a visit... I'd like to see him. I assume I will sooner or later."

Mary Lou handed Erin her bag, holding on to it for an instant after Erin took it, both of them connecting in a small way.

Mary Lou's eyes welled with tears again. "When I think about what could have happened if it had been one of my boys that Officer Piper arrested..."

"Oh! Oh, no, don't think like that. Terry didn't do anything wrong. Biggles resisted arrest, and... well, Cam or Josh wouldn't do that. And they're not big guys like Biggles. Terry wouldn't have to... it would be easier for him to control one of them."

Mary Lou just shook her head.

"Terry wouldn't do anything to hurt one of your boys," Erin said urgently. "You can't think that."

"The police will do what they have to... and if they think that someone is a danger..."

"Mary Lou..."

"That could have been one of my boys," Mary Lou said fiercely. "You think it's okay because he was a drug dealer, but it's not. He's someone's son too."

Erin walked the rest of the way to the police department, thinking about Mary Lou's statement. She had thought that Mary Lou would be happy to have Bo Biggles off the street and away from the school; she hadn't thought about how Mary Lou would worry about her boys and how they could end up in trouble like that. Everyone always said what good boys Campbell and Josh were, it was hard for her to adjust her thinking to the fact that they could get into trouble just as easily as any of the other boys Erin had known growing up. Just like Bo Biggles. He'd had to start somewhere. Had he been a nice boy once? Or had he always been a little hood with his fingers in all of the pies?

She felt bad for Mary Lou. Erin was worried about Terry, but she'd never had to worry about kids and about them going off-track. She could remember how she had worried about Carolyn when she was younger.

Carolyn was the one who had inspired her to start a gluten-free bakery, a foster sister who just couldn't be different from her friends and go without the nice treats that they could have, even though she had been told it was killing her. She'd needed so much to be the same and to have what everyone else had.

Clara Jones was at her desk at the police department and raised her eyebrows when she saw Erin, doing a doubletake. "What are you doing here? You know Officer Piper is off."

"I know, but I thought you might be pining for some muffins."

Erin put the box down on Clara's desk and opened it up to display the variety of muffins to Clara. "You get first pick. What's your favorite?"

"Oh…" Clara looked at them and inhaled the fragrant steam escaping the box. "They are all so good." Her hand hovered over the box as she decided on first one, and then another. Finally, she went with a blueberry muffin. "You know, I was telling my sister about how none of your baking tastes like it's gluten free. You would swear that it was just normal baking with wheat flour. I would think that you were cheating, only I know people who can't eat wheat or gluten, and they can eat your baking without getting sick."

Erin smiled. It was rare to hear anything positive from Clara, especially something about Erin or Auntie Clem's. "Well, thank you! I'm really glad you enjoy it. I love being able to bake great treats for people who wouldn't normally be able to have them."

"You do a good job," Clara admitted.

"I'll take these to the kitchen for you."

Clara nodded, and Erin removed the box and walked past Clara's desk toward the little kitchen area to put the muffins where everyone could help themselves. She looked at each of the offices quickly as she walked by. Terry's office, empty until they decided he could get back on active duty. Tom didn't qualify for a full office; he shared with Melissa and other part-time workers who were in and out. Erin wasn't sure where the dispatcher worked from. She must have had a dedicated office somewhere else or worked from home or a cell phone. Erin passed Sheriff Wilmot's office last.

Erin stopped at the kitchen counter and put down the muffin box. No one was paying her any attention. It wasn't difficult at all to walk into the police department and have the run of the place without anyone confronting her. As long as she had a good reason to be there. Someone else would have to use a different diversion to get in, but Erin didn't imagine it would be too hard. It was a small town. People trusted each other. Mostly.

She emptied the dregs of the coffee in the carafe and rinsed it out. Then she added grounds to the hopper and started a new batch brewing. It would be nice for everyone to have fresh coffee to go with the muffins. Erin looked around, scoping out the remaining rooms that she was less familiar with. There were three interview rooms. There was another door that might lead to a supply cabinet. There was a small commode so that they didn't have to leave to use the public restrooms in the main part of the Town Hall. Erin took a glance around, then walked toward the interview rooms. No one stopped her or paid any attention.

She looked in the narrow window of the first room. Like the window in a school classroom, it had wires running through the glass to make it stronger and prevent anyone from putting their fist through it. Erin tested the door handle. It turned easily in her hand and she swung the door open. It gave only a small squeak, easily missed with the bustle of a busy office, especially with the coffee maker burbling and a printer spitting out papers on Clara's desk.

Erin took a glance around the room, empty but for a table and chairs. She pulled it shut and went on to the next room. Very similar to the first, but with the chairs upholstered in a dark blue, rather than with plastic seats. The walls were a gross green color that was either supposed to be soothing or to camouflage stains. The third room was smaller, with a camp cot in the corner. It was bare, with no blankets on it. Erin imagined they had all been sent away as evidence. There was a smaller table with just two chairs. Erin thought at first that it would be dangerous to leave a convict in a cell with chairs that he could throw around and use as a weapon, but when she took a closer look, she saw that they were anchored to the floor. Maybe King Kong could pick them up, but not Erin and not, she didn't suppose, Bo Biggles. The cot was the only thing in the room that was movable.

"Miss Price."

Erin jumped and gave a little squeal. She whirled around to face Sheriff Wilmot. She could feel all of the blood rushing to her face.

CHAPTER 19

𝒰h… Sheriff. Hi. Sorry, I was just…"

"Having a look at our crime scene?" He shook his head, brows down. "You don't have any reason to be in here. This is off limits to the public."

"I'm sorry. I brought some muffins, and I just realized as I was putting them out that this must be…"

She didn't know why she couldn't finish her sentences. The look on his face was so forbidding that she just kept trailing off into silence, unable to complete her explanation.

"I can see what you were doing." He waited, looking at her. "Have you seen everything you needed to now?"

Erin looked down at her feet. She knew that she shouldn't have been snooping around. She was supposed to be at the bakery, making and selling her wares, not at the police department poking her nose where it didn't belong. She swallowed. She'd left Vic to take care of all of the customers and had just paraded off to investigate, even though she knew she shouldn't.

"Uh. Sorry. Yeah." Erin looked toward the back door of the suite. "Could I go out this door? I wanted to check on something. I just… I think I can get to…"

Sheriff Wilmot's skepticism was palpable. Erin blushed furiously. She motioned toward the door again. "I'll just be going…"

He didn't make a move to stop her. Erin swallowed hard and walked down the short hall to what looked like an outside door with a crash bar. She pushed it open. No alarms sounded. Erin walked through the doorway and let the door close behind her, taking a glance behind her to see whether the sheriff was following her. He watched her go but did not pursue her.

It led, as Terry had said, to a shared corridor with some pipes, mops, a couple of doorways to utility or storage rooms. Erin didn't open the other doors, worried about opening the door on one of the janitors and having to explain herself again. She'd done such a wonderful job with the sheriff, after all.

Someone could hide in one of those rooms, provided they weren't in use. They could wait there until all was quiet and they could sneak into the police department and access the interview rooms.

Someone would have to be pretty gutsy to do that. Erin felt like throwing up after being caught by Sheriff Wilmot. He'd always been kind to her in the past, even when she was a suspect, and she didn't like to give him a reason to think that she was a nut-job. Or a snoop.

Erin looked around. There was no evidence that anyone had been there and had propped the door or left anything behind. Erin reached back and pulled on the door she had just closed. It was locked.

It could only have been someone who had a key. Or else it had been left unlocked that day, and the fact that it was locked now was just evidence of locking the barn after the horse was gone. Erin pulled on it one more time to make sure that it wasn't just stuck. It was definitely locked.

She walked briskly to the next door, another metal door with a crash bar. She opened it, and there were no alarms. She found herself in the parking lot where she had seen Jack Ward a couple of nights previously.

Was that the first time that Jack Ward had been by? Was there any possibility that he had visited the police department when he heard that Biggles had been arrested? He would know the layout of the police department from previous visits. He'd know that he could probably walk right in without being seen. And if he was seen, he was a law enforcement officer and had good reason to be there. Bo Biggles was from his jurisdiction, and no doubt there were warrants or at least complaints or suspicions that Jack Ward could claim to be following up on. If his department did transport for Bald Eagle Falls regularly, maybe he had a key. He could let himself in the back, into that detention room, and... what? Attack Biggles? If he spent time interrogating Biggles, he would surely have been spotted by the Bald Eagles Falls staff. If he were the one who had choked Biggles, he would have to have been in and out in a couple of minutes, and Erin couldn't think of a scenario where that behavior made much sense.

Erin looked around. There wasn't anything to see in the parking lot.

"Miss Price!"

Erin looked around to see who had called her. It wasn't Sheriff Wilmot's voice this time. Not an adult and not an accusation. Erin spotted a young boy waving. She waved back and, as he got a few steps closer, realized that it was Peter Foster. She strode toward him, happy to leave the police department behind and to see her little friend.

"Peter! How are you?"

"Good! Just going home for lunch!" He made a motion to indicate the crescent behind the Town Hall. Erin wasn't sure which house was his.

"You're nice and close to the school. That's great."

"Yeah. But my mom says that being so close makes me late. People who are farther away are more careful to leave early. I can still run over when I hear the first bell, if I'm really fast, and get to my desk." He smiled, proud of himself and getting pink with embarrassment at the same time.

Erin nodded. "I can see why you wouldn't want to leave until it was time."

"Sometimes I like to go early, so there's time to play with my friends on the playground. But sometimes, I want to see the ending of a show or I don't feel good… and then I'm bad, and I don't go until it's almost too late."

Erin chuckled. "You're not bad, Peter. Just… a little late sometimes."

He smiled and nodded. "Okay, I got to run. I'm not supposed to stop and talk to people on my way home." He rolled his eyes dramatically. "Even if I know them," he said, as if it were a catechism that had been drilled into him.

Erin waved as he hurried away. "See you later!"

Erin served Terry his dessert, some leftover cookies from the bakery, and sat down to help him eat them. The animals were happily munching on their own treats, though Orange Blossom had already gobbled up his and was eyeing K9's biscuit in hopes of getting some of the crumbs.

"So you had a good day working with Willie?"

Terry shrugged. He looked pleasantly fatigued instead of anxious like he had the past few days. At least whatever they had been working on had helped him to forget his troubles for a while. Maybe there was some hope that he could be happy even if he could not get back onto active duty. Maybe he could find something else and be satisfied with it.

"Willie is a good guy," Terry said slowly. "Not always above-board as far as the law is concerned... but still good-hearted and always eager to help a friend."

Erin chuckled. "I guess being brought up in one of the clans, you couldn't expect him to always toe the line as far as the law is concerned. But I think he tries."

"He seems determined to only take honest work," Terry said slowly, pondering it, "but as far as keeping to the letter of the law... he's not so concerned about that."

Erin nibbled at a chocolate chip cookie, hoping to make it last until Terry had cleared the rest off of the serving plate. "As long as he's only taking honest work, why worry about it? Those other little things aren't that much of a concern, are they?"

"Those little things can turn into big things. If you're not going to let the law determine what is right and wrong, and you're not following prescribed religious principles... then what you're doing is deciding for yourself what is right and wrong, setting up your own system of morals... and that can be dangerous. You can justify anything if it benefits you."

"But Willie..." Erin didn't like it when Terry talked about Willie like he was a criminal. He wasn't. He was a good guy like Terry had said, and he took good care of Vic, and he had helped Erin out at times when she had needed it. He wasn't running with the clans or dealing drugs or doing anything else that made him a hazard to Erin or anyone else in Bald Eagle Falls. Terry made it sound like everything he did was shady, and like he was a psychopath who would take out anyone who got in his way. She didn't like to think of Willie that way. "Willie wouldn't do anything to harm any of us. You know that."

Terry polished off another cookie and his hand hovered over the plate for a few seconds before he picked up a ginger snap. "I would trust Willie to take care of you girls and not to do anything to put anyone innocent in physical danger. But who knows what he did while he was a soldier with the

Dysons? Trust me; they are not going to allow anyone who has been inducted into their ranks to get away with penny-ante stuff. If you're a soldier with the Dysons, you're all-in."

"But he's out now. He served his term and then he was released. He's not working for them anymore. Or if he does, it's just for things like computer security."

"That's what he says. And I'm not saying that he does anything else for them. But once you have lived that kind of life, I'm not sure I believe you can just turn it off again. Once you've crossed those lines, you're not going to hesitate to do it again just because it's against the law. I'd be a lot happier if I knew exactly what the limits of Willie's personal morality were. But I'm not sure it's a constant. I think he takes every situation as it comes and weighs the personal costs and benefits. And that's a dangerous way to live."

Erin used her finger to wipe up a bit of melted chocolate from the plate and licked off her finger. Orange Blossom was creeping toward K9. He normally stayed as far away from K9 as possible and hissed and puffed up if K9 paid him any attention. But that did not hold true if K9 had a treat and Blossom didn't. Then he would put his usual sensitivities aside and get close enough to lick the crumbs from K9's face. Like Willie, he was flexible in his standards. "You don't think that Willie had anything to do with Biggles's death, do you?"

Terry pressed his lips together. "Willie was with the Dysons. If he's still doing jobs for them, then it is possible he would want to take Biggles out. But why wait until he was in custody? Unless Biggles had information on Willie or could rat the Dysons out for something. It would have made a lot more sense for him to deal with Biggles when he was in town last time, or when he was in Moose River."

"So you don't think Willie had anything to do with it."

"No." He met her gaze. "I don't think *anyone* killed him. I think it was just one of those things. A weird coincidence. Inexplicable. Natural causes. Whatever the medical examiner decides to call it. I don't think anyone intentionally killed him."

Erin nodded. She knew it was a long shot. The only reason she wanted it to be murder was so that they could prove that it hadn't been Terry's fault.

Terry pulled his phone out and put it on the table beside him, tapping the screen. "Sorry. Got a message."

As he looked at the screen, his expression darkened and his mouth turned down.

"What is it?"

He shook his head. "Sheriff wants to see me."

"Why?"

"He says he wants to ask me some questions."

Erin's stomach twisted into a knot. Was the sheriff calling Terry in to talk to him about Erin and her poking around at the police department?

"Did he say what about?"

"There's only one thing he'd be calling me in to talk to him about. And I am not looking forward to being on the other side of the table."

"Couldn't he just talk to you on the phone? You could tell him whatever he needed to know."

"It's not the same as having a face-to-face interview with someone. You miss out on body language; you can't control the environment. The person knows that they can just hang up at any time. It's much more efficient to talk to someone directly."

Erin bit her lip, trying to decide whether to bring up her visit to the police department. Terry misinterpreted her expression. He put a hand over hers and attempted a reassuring smile.

"It will be okay, Erin. I can deal with the sheriff's questions. He's just clearing up loose ends."

"It might be... because of me."

"What?" His frown swiftly returned.

"I took some muffins over to the police department."

The crease between his eyebrows deepened. "The day Biggles died? I don't remember seeing any muffins."

"No. Today."

"Okay...?" He cocked his head.

"It's been a while since I sent anything over, and I thought they might like a treat."

Orange Blossom, sitting just inches in front of K9, looked over at Erin and yowled plaintively. He knew what a treat was, and if someone else was getting one, why wasn't he? Erin laughed, though she was still anxious about explaining to Terry what had happened.

"You thought they might like some muffins," Terry said, deliberately avoiding repeating the word *treat*. "And that you might look around while you were there."

Erin cleared her throat and nodded, looking down at a crumb on the table.

Terry chuckled. "Nothing is going to stop you from investigating this, is it? You are tenacious."

"I just want to show everyone that it wasn't you."

"So you think the sheriff wants to rake me over the coals for sending you over there to snoop around?"

"I guess so."

"So someone must have realized what you were doing there."

"Yeah… he might have happened by when I was checking out the interview rooms."

Despite the stress of the situation, a dimple appeared in Terry's cheek. "I guess that was a little awkward. What excuse did you give for poking around the interview rooms?"

"I didn't… just stammered a little… he knew why I was there."

"I would guess that was pretty obvious. So did you find anything useful? Satisfy your curiosity?"

Erin scratched her ear and looked at him, trying to decide if he really wanted any details.

"I didn't find out anything that you don't already know. But I wanted to see it for myself."

He nodded. "And what did you conclude?"

"It wouldn't be that hard for someone outside the police department to get in through the back and into one of the interview rooms. He wouldn't have to go by anyone's desk. If he was quick and quiet, he could get in and out without being seen."

Terry's brows climbed higher. "Really. How would someone get in through the back?"

"The police department's exit door isn't alarmed. It really should be."

"It's locked, and so is the outside door."

"But anyone who has access to that utility hall could get into the police department. It's just that one door, if someone picked the lock or left it propped open."

Terry shrugged. "But who would do that?"

"Whoever wanted to eliminate Bo Biggles."

"I think you underestimate how easy it is for an amateur to pick a lock. It may look easy on TV, but this is a heavy, well-constructed door. Not something that you could jimmy with a credit card."

"But someone experienced with a pick and a wrench could."

Something else occurred to Erin. She remembered the bump key that Jeremy had used to get into her house not so long ago. He had scared the heck out of her when he had set off the burglar alarm in the middle of the night, and she had been furious with him. He had sworn he would never use it at her house again.

But she hadn't taken it away from him and he hadn't promised never to use it anywhere else. Even if she had confiscated it, that wouldn't stop him from making another one.

She caught Terry looking at her quizzically. "What?"

"Just how much do you know about picking locks?"

"Oh." Erin cleared her throat and took the last cookie from the plate to distract him from her face. "Well… I'm no cat burglar, but I know the basics."

"Could you pick a lock like that?"

Erin inhaled a cookie crumb and started coughing. It wasn't just to cover up her answer; she really couldn't stop the spasming of her muscles as they tried to dislodge the irritant. Terry nudged her glass of milk toward her and, when she kept coughing, got up and patted and rubbed her back until she could stop coughing and take a drink.

"You okay?"

Erin nodded.

"Could you?" Terry asked.

"What?" Erin asked, still coughing weakly.

"Could you pick a lock like that?"

Erin nodded, gulping. "Yes," she admitted. "It wouldn't be that hard."

CHAPTER 20

$\mathcal{E}$rin's assumption that Terry's visit to the police department would be quick was wrong. When he'd been gone for an hour, she started checking the time every few minutes and looking out toward the street, watching for Terry's car. But he didn't come, and as the time dragged on, he still didn't come.

She couldn't stay up late, knowing that she had to be up early in the morning. But even if she went to bed in good time, she wasn't sure how she was going to get a good night's sleep worrying about what had happened to Terry.

She could drink some of her sleepy tea and maybe have a valerian pill, but she knew that if she took anything stronger, she'd be sluggish and dopey in the morning. Too little sleep was a problem, but so was overmedicating, and she knew from experience her body did not like sleeping pills. Vic had no problem taking them and could be off to sleep quickly and still be fresh as a daisy in the morning. Erin envied her that.

Orange Blossom rubbed against Erin's feet, tickling them, and then jumped up into her lap. He nosed at her and purred loudly, clearly wanting to know what was wrong and trying to comfort her. She petted him and cuddled him close.

"Oh, you're a good kitty, aren't you? I'm so glad you're talking to me again."

He purred and chattered and rubbed against her until Erin squashed him down, telling him to be still. He finally settled into a ball on her lap, purring away cozily as she continued to pet him and watch out the window. She knew she should do something productive. Make her lists for the next day, or even just read through some of Clementine's genealogical files. But she wasn't going to be able to focus on anything but Terry and when he would be back.

Time passed slowly. Could she call him? It might be a silly thing to do, but she wanted to know that he was okay. He could growl at her and tell her that he'd be home soon. Or that the sheriff was keeping him later and he didn't know when he'd be back. It wouldn't matter, as long as he told her something to allay her fears.

It was dark outside when she saw a tall, slim figure making its way down the street. She was worried at first, wondering whether it might be someone from out of town. Another drug dealer. Or someone who was friends with or family to Bo Biggles and wanted to get revenge on Terry for what had happened to him. She didn't like the idea of someone lurking out there in the dark, watching her house or getting too close.

She had armed the burglar alarm, as Terry and Willie always drilled her to do. So no one could break in without alerting the neighborhood.

The dark figure turned and made its way up Erin's sidewalk. At first, her stomach clenched, but then she relaxed. If someone was coming to her front door, then she didn't need to worry that they were trying to sneak up or break in. And as the figure got closer, Erin could see that it was Adele.

Erin got up. She shifted Orange Blossom onto the couch, trying not to disturb him, but he opened his eyes and stretched and watched her to see what was going on. Erin opened the door and motioned Adele in.

"Hi, Adele. How are you?"

"You're not usually up this late. Don't you have work tomorrow? I saw your light was still on and thought I'd check in…"

"I'm okay. Just… waiting for Terry. I thought he would be back by now."

"Where is he? I thought he wasn't on duty this week. Because of the… unfortunate incident."

"The unfortunate incident. Yeah. I wish Biggles had never died. Who knew it would cause so much trouble? You would think that when someone like that, a career criminal, happened to pass away, it wouldn't be such a big deal. I mean, yes, he was a person, and you still treat him with respect, but... I didn't think there would be such a fuss."

As soon as she said it, Erin thought about Mary Lou and her anxiety that it could have been one of her sons. What if one of them had gotten himself arrested and Terry had tased him or had hit him to get him under control, or if someone had choked him? Bo Biggles had a mother somewhere, Erin assumed, and maybe brothers and sisters. Maybe a girlfriend. People who cared that he had died. Because he was a person, not just a piece of junk to be disposed of.

Adele sat in one of the easy chairs, her expression pensive. "Much of what happens in the universe is beyond our control, and we'll never know why it happened. We are like little ants here on the earth, scurrying around thinking that we have control over our lives, and it couldn't be further from the truth."

Erin didn't like the sound of that. She was someone who liked to control everything she could. Her practice of making lists and trying to plan everything out had evolved from her lack of control over her life when she was growing up. She couldn't control anything, so she tried to control everything. And she was still trying.

"I guess you're right," she said, not wanting to argue with Adele that she did have some control when she clearly didn't. She couldn't protect Terry from the accusations against him. She couldn't stop people from being killed in Bald Eagle Falls. The best she could do was follow her recipes and hope they came out of the oven looking and tasting good. Even then, things could happen that would sabotage her results. Bad ingredients, cross-contamination, a malfunctioning oven, getting distracted or sick or forgetting to set a timer. She couldn't prevent someone from reacting to it, as Trenton had when Joelle gave him cupcakes she knew he would be allergic to.

All Erin could do was try her best and see how it all came out.

"So is he already working again?" Adele asked. "That seems awfully quick."

"No, he's not working... Sheriff Wilmot called him in to ask him some more questions. I thought he would be back pretty quickly, but it's been hours. I haven't even heard from him."

"It may be that he hasn't been allowed to use the phone."

"But he has his own phone. And why would they stop him from using the phone?"

Adele didn't answer. Orange Blossom jumped off of the couch and went to greet her. After some ear scratches, he jumped up into her lap and settled there.

"You think… that they've arrested him?" Erin asked as Adele's reticence registered. "That's why he hasn't let me know what's going on?"

"I have no way of knowing. I just wondered… why else he wouldn't call to tell you goodnight, that he'd go back to his own house tonight and catch up with you in the morning, so that you could be calm enough to go to sleep."

"He might have just gotten busy. Wrapped up in something and forgot the time."

"Perhaps," Adele agreed.

But Erin had a lump in her stomach. She knew that wasn't why Terry hadn't called her. He'd been concerned about her health and her sleeping patterns since Mr. Inglethorpe's death. He knew that she wouldn't be able to sleep without knowing where he was and that he was okay.

"Do you think I should call him? I was wondering whether I should… just to check in and find out what his plans were for the night. He was going to come back here, but like you say, if he isn't going to be done until late, he'll probably go back to his own house."

"You could call him."

Erin nodded, but she didn't. She looked at her phone again, sitting on the side table, and didn't pick it up.

"This must be a hard time for Officer Piper. And for you."

"Yeah. It is. But… it could be worse. I mean, the sheriff knows that he didn't have anything to do with Bo Biggles's death. He knows Terry didn't do anything wrong."

"How would he know that?"

"Because he knows Terry. He's worked with him forever. He knows that Terry wouldn't hurt someone. He couldn't kill anyone. We were just talking about morality earlier today… I know Terry believes in upholding the law. All of the law, he doesn't pick and choose. And I know that even though he doesn't talk about it very much, he is a Christian and believes all of those commandments, and that includes not killing."

"Accidents still happen. The arrest of that man was… quite violent."

Erin leaned forward, looking at Adele. No one had mentioned having seen what went down that day. Erin had only Terry's sparse description of picking Biggles up near the school, of having to tase him to get him under control. He hadn't wanted to tell her any more than necessary about what had happened.

"Did you see?"

Adele hesitated. "Didn't Officer Piper tell you all of the details?"

"No. Hardly anything."

"I don't think it's my place..."

"As my friend, I think it is absolutely your place. How am I supposed to figure out the truth and to protect him if I don't know what happened?"

"Is it your place to protect him?"

"Yes."

Adele raised her brows and nodded slowly, accepting Erin's assertion. "The school is not far from your woods; the school field abuts your property line. So for Mr. Biggles to stay off of the school property, he was actually on your property."

"Why would he do that?" Erin shook her head, not understanding. "Wasn't the whole point to deal to the school kids?"

"There are more serious charges if he's caught dealing on school grounds."

"Oh. Who knew? Okay. So he was in my woods. How did Terry know where to find him? Did K9 track him? I gather it was Beaver who told him that Biggles was in town and that's why Terry was looking for him."

"It was probably a combination of witness reports and K9's nose. I didn't see the whole process. I was gathering some berries when I saw Mr. Biggles. I kept out of sight because I didn't want to have to deal with him." Adele paused. "I know I'm supposed to keep trespassers off of the property, but there are times when..."

"Of course, you need to take your own safety into account," Erin agreed. "Don't confront some gangland drug dealer. You stay out of the way. Call the police if you think there is something they can do."

Adele nodded. Her shoulders dipped, relieved by Erin's understanding. "I was keeping an eye on him, and I would have called the police if I saw him actually dealing drugs or doing something illegal. But he was very cagey."

"He must have been good at what he did."

"Yes. I think so." Adele shrugged one shoulder. She scratched Orange Blossom's ears, looking like she was concentrating on a difficult problem.

"Then Officer Piper showed up. It was just like on TV; telling him to put his hands up, and then going after him when he didn't obey. Biggles threw something away and tried to run. For a big man, he moved very fast. But Piper was faster, especially with K9. K9 brought him down but didn't hurt him. I know they can. Sometimes people get injured when K9 units take them down."

Erin nodded. "They've got teeth, and they dig in when someone struggles."

"Biggles started fighting again when K9 released him and Officer Piper was trying to cuff him. Piper fought with him, then used his taser."

"And when he did that, then Biggles stopped fighting? That's when Terry got him under control and... put the handcuffs on him and took him in."

"No. Even though he had been tased, he was quite combative. He was hitting and kicking, trying to get away, even with the taser claws still in him. Officer Piper was... well, hitting him with his nightstick. You know how they do. Just smacking him and smacking him, trying to get him to stop fighting, or to let go of his weapon... I couldn't see very well. Biggles was on the ground; there was lots of grass and undergrowth so that I couldn't see everything."

Erin nodded. She didn't know what to say. She imagined it all from Adele's perspective, crouched over a patch of berries or hidden behind a tree. Watching in horror, but not wanting to get in the way or to interfere with the arrest. Just wishing that they would finish and she could be alone again and not have to witness any more violence.

Even though Adele was a witch, she wasn't the kind of witch that Erin had grown up seeing on television or hearing about in fairy tales. She was a peaceful person, not someone who wanted anything to do with any type of violence. Not to people, or to animals, or even to plants or anything else on earth. She tried to live in harmony with nature and not to harm any living thing or part of the earth.

Erin sniffled, finding her throat suddenly hot and swollen. "And then... what happened?"

"That was all... he just kept hitting and wrestling with Mr. Biggles until he could get him under control and into a pair of handcuffs. He got him to his feet and took him to his squad car." Adele let out a deep sigh. "That's all I know. That's everything I could see. He sat in the car for what seemed like a long time and then left. To the police department, I assume. I didn't follow him to find out."

"But he didn't choke Biggles."

Adele hesitated.

Erin raised her brows and nodded her head with certainty. "He knows it's against policy, that it's too dangerous."

"I couldn't see very well, Erin. They were both on the ground, Officer Piper trying to wrestle him around and get him under control. I couldn't tell whether he hit or grabbed him by the throat. It wasn't movie violence, where you can see every detail of every punch that's thrown. It's... more like the Tasmanian devil, all a whirl of arms and legs, with both of them grunting and yelling. That's what I saw. I couldn't say whether he ever touched Mr. Biggles's throat or not."

"He didn't."

"You weren't there, Erin. And if you were, you wouldn't be able to say any better than I can."

"I know Terry didn't choke him. I know it one hundred percent."

"Maybe not. I'm not saying he did. I'm just saying; I can't say he didn't."

Erin sat back, feeling exhausted, like she had wrestled with Bo Biggles herself. "I'm going to call Terry."

*A*dele went on her way to give Erin some privacy. Erin was relieved to find that Terry still had his phone on him and was allowed to answer it when she called. So Adele was wrong. He hadn't been arrested. He hadn't been kept from calling her or communicating with her. He had just been too busy to call her.

"Hi, Erin. I'm so sorry I haven't called you. I keep thinking that I'm going to get out of here, and then... there's more. I'm sure I won't be much longer. But... maybe you should go to bed. I'll head home after I'm done here and we'll touch base tomorrow."

"I'll try. I was hoping you'd be back here tonight."

"You don't want me to wake you up. You might not be able to get back to sleep again."

"I don't know if I'll be able to sleep if you don't come. Are you... is everything okay?"

"I'm still here... I haven't been arrested." Terry gave a long, exhausted sigh. "But things are not looking good, Erin. I'm not sure how much longer I'll be able to stay on this side of the bars. They are... stacking up a lot of evidence against me."

"But you didn't do it. You didn't cause Biggles's death."

"I hope not."

"You didn't, Terry. It wasn't your fault."

"The more they say and the more tired I get, the less certain I am. I might have to... plead to a lesser offense. To avoid having to spend too much time in jail. A police officer in the prison population... it's not a very good thing."

"Don't plead it out," Erin begged. "Don't tell them that you did something wrong when you didn't. I know you didn't cause Biggles's death, and I'm going to prove it. You just have to give me time."

"You can't prove it, Erin. Even when the medical examiner comes back with a cause of death, there's still going to be some question about it. They are going to come after me with everything they have."

"Why?"

He sighed. "I'll talk to you about it tomorrow... when I see you next."

"Will you be home soon?"

"I'll be going home soon. To my house. You go to sleep. Get a good rest. I'll talk to you tomorrow."

"It will look better in the morning," Erin promised him. "Things always look worse when you're tired. So don't plead to anything tonight. Don't let them wear you down. If you're not under arrest, you can leave whenever you want. Just tell them that you're going home."

"Just who is the cop here? I think I know what my rights are."

"But you're thinking about it from a cop's perspective. You need to think like an innocent witness. An innocent witness doesn't have to stay there all night to get it settled. Just come home now. Come here. I need you."

She hoped that appealing to his protective side would help.

Terry clicked his tongue, trying to make a decision. Erin's chest hurt. She had to get him out of there before he did something he would regret later. Her heart was breaking for him, accused of a crime he wasn't guilty of. No matter what had caused Biggles's death, she knew it wasn't Terry's fault.

"Come, please."

"Okay."

Tears sprang to Erin's eyes.

"I'll be there soon," he promised.

Erin put on the tea kettle. She searched the fridge for comfort food that wouldn't be too heavy before bed. They'd already had cookies, so she didn't want to give Terry anything too sugary. She settled on some rolls from the bakery and started to assemble a couple of sandwiches. Complex carbs were good. Dairy. Turkey. They would both be ready to nod off within half an hour of the snack.

She walked into the living room to look out the front window but didn't see his truck. Had the sheriff kept him for longer? Was he still sitting in his truck in the parking lot with his face in his hands having a breakdown? Or had he been too tired and distressed to drive safely?

The kettle began to whistle, so Erin returned to the kitchen to turn it off. She got out mugs and a basket of assorted teas and put them on the table. The rolls were on the table, ready to eat. All she needed was a man to eat them with her.

She walked back out to the living room to look again and saw his truck at the curb. Relieved, Erin hurried to punch her code into the burglar alarm and open the door.

She didn't even let Terry into the house before enfolding him in a tight embrace. "I'm so glad you're home. Are you okay?"

He held her close for a few minutes. She could feel his breathing, tense, shallow breaths. Hopefully, talk, tea, and a bite to eat would help him to relax and decompress.

Terry finally drew back, taking a breath and looking back over his shoulder. It wasn't until then that Erin saw the figure slouching against a beaten-up station wagon. "Beaver? What's she doing here?"

"She's just... making sure everybody's safe."

Erin frowned. "What do you mean? She drove over to make sure you weren't too tired to drive? I *was* a little worried..."

Terry nodded. "That... and to make sure that there's no one suspicious hanging around."

She looked at him, not asking the questions she was sure he was expecting.

"Do you mind if Beaver comes in?"

Erin frowned. She didn't want Beaver there, but she wasn't going to turn her away if Terry thought that she needed to be there for their protection.

"Why would she need to come in? Is there something going on, Terry?"

His eyes slid away from her and he didn't answer.

"Okay, sure," Erin agreed, shaking her head.

Terry turned slightly and made a large motion for Beaver to come in. Beaver straightened and approached the house. She nodded to Erin as she reached the door. She wore a smile, as usual, but her eyes were hooded. Erin wasn't sure why she was there or what she was thinking.

Erin led them into the kitchen and looked at the cups and sandwiches she had prepared. Obviously for only two people. She got another cup out of the cupboard and placed it on the table. "Do you want a sandwich?" she asked Beaver, starting to get a third one prepared before waiting or an answer.

"That would be awfully nice," Beaver agreed. "I've had nothing but junk this week, with everything that's been going on. Switching between sugar and salt isn't exactly what they mean by a balanced diet."

Erin nodded and didn't look at either of them as she prepared the third sandwich. K9 lay down at Terry's feet with a deep sigh. He sprawled on his side, stretching his feet out, and made a drawn-out groaning noise.

"Doesn't sound like he had much fun today," Erin observed. "Grab him a cookie."

Orange Blossom made himself known, winding around Erin's legs and yowling, and before long, Marshmallow joined them as well so that the whole menagerie was present.

"Terry, do you want to...?" Erin gestured to Orange Blossom in frustration. Normally, she was happy to get them each their treats, but she was tired and at the end of her rope. It was time for bed, and she'd thought she would have some time to unwind with Terry, but now she had a third party to deal with.

Terry obediently got the other animals treats to get them out of the way while Erin finished putting together a sandwich for Beaver. She sat down at the table and made herself some tea. She rubbed her eyes and cupped her palms over them.

"So... what's going on?"

Terry and Beaver were silent at first. Erin peeked at them around her hands before closing her eyes and resting her palms on them again.

"What aren't you telling me?"

Terry shifted restlessly. "Certain facts have come to light that... make me look more guilty."

"What? I don't see how there could be anything else. You just performed an arrest. And then questioned the suspect at the police department. Most of that was right under the sheriff's eyes, so how can they say that you're guilty of anything?"

"For one thing, Davis Plaint."

Erin dropped her hands from her face and stared at him. "Davis Plaint? What does Davis Plaint have to do with anything?"

"Having heard about Biggles's death through the prison grapevine—"

"Or from Melissa."

Terry nodded. "Or from Melissa. He's now decided to claim that I brutalized him after he was arrested."

"What?"

Terry shrugged. "That's what he says."

"And no one else happened to notice this?"

"Well, obviously, everyone else in the department was complicit, so they looked the other way. Davis is only coming out now because there is now evidence to support his story. If I roughed up one person, it probably wasn't the first time. There will probably be convicts coming out of the woodwork for the next three years claiming that I beat them up when I arrested them."

Terry's voice was bitter and defeated. Erin shook her head. "Oh, I'm sorry. But that's ridiculous. And anyone with a head on their shoulders will know that he's just trying to get attention, won't they? It isn't like he filed any complaints about it back then."

"People will believe what they want to. It makes a much better story if there is a suggestion that this isn't the first time I beat up a detainee. That I have a history, but it was covered up."

"No one here is going to believe it."

"Maybe not. But there still has to be an investigation."

"Into whether or not you beat up Davis? It's pretty easy to prove, isn't it? He didn't have any bruises."

"I could have abused him in a way that didn't leave bruises. Of course, the story falls apart there, because if I made a habit of beating people up without leaving bruises, then why was Biggles bruised?"

Erin nodded vigorously. "Exactly! It's obvious that Davis is just making up a story."

"But it doesn't really matter. People like to hear stories, even if they're fanciful."

"It's not like you had any reason to beat Biggles up. You had a lot more reason to beat Davis up, and you never left a bruise on him."

Terry didn't answer. Beaver silently worked her way through her sandwich, the only one of them who was actually eating.

"Terry?" Erin persisted. "Davis was the one who just about burned my house down with me in it. If you didn't beat him up for that, why would you beat up Bo Biggles?"

Terry didn't answer. He just stirred his tea, looking like he would climb into the mug and disappear if he could.

Beaver wiped her mouth with the back of her hand. "Because of what I told him."

CHAPTER 22

$\mathcal{E}$rin looked at Beaver. "What?" She looked from one of them to the other. "What's that supposed to mean? What could you tell Terry that would have any bearing on this?"

Beaver looked at Terry. He didn't look back at her, but kept staring down at his tea. There were fatigue lines around his eyes, dark and sunken. He looked like he hadn't slept or eaten in days. It was shocking how quickly he had gone downhill. A few hours at the police department, and he had been beaten down, almost broken.

"Because I told Officer Piper that I had seen Biggles lurking around your house," Beaver revealed. "The day that you got back from your cruise... I saw him. He was trying to stay out of sight. So, I let your Officer Piper know."

"And I went looking for him the next day," Terry finished.

Everyone went quiet. Erin tried to process what they were telling her. Suddenly Terry had a motive for beating Biggles up, choking him, even killing him. Suddenly he wasn't just an officer pursuing his duty anymore. It was personal. His girlfriend was being threatened. He wanted to make sure that Biggles would never show up at her house again. Whatever it took.

Erin felt like she'd been spinning on a playground merry-go-round. Her head spun and she felt nauseated.

"Excuse me a minute."

She lurched to her feet and headed for the commode. Orange Blossom followed her, meowing inquiringly. It wasn't normal behavior for Erin and he wanted to know what was going on. Erin pushed him back with her foot before shutting the door, shutting him out. She should have known that he wouldn't put up with that. In a minute, he was yowling like she was beating him.

It wasn't like he needed his cat box urgently. He hadn't been trying to get to it; he just wanted to know what Erin was doing. And like any self-respecting two-year-old, he wasn't going to let her shut the door to the bathroom and have a moment of quiet time to herself.

Erin leaned on the counter. She took a few long, steadying breaths to try to get her body under control. Nothing had changed. Everything was as it had been before; she just knew more. How many more secrets were left?

Had Terry gone after Biggles intending to beat him up and run him out of Bald Eagle Falls once and for all in order to protect Erin?

She ran the cold water tap and soaked a washcloth, then used it to sponge her face and the back of her neck. She shouldn't be having such a dramatic reaction to the revelation. So Terry knew that Biggles was in town and went looking for him. Erin had already known that. She had even guessed that it was Beaver who had told him. The only part she hadn't known was that Biggles had been outside the house that day.

She remembered how large and menacing Biggles had looked the day that she saw him on Main Street arguing with Beaver, having fits because Beaver had rear-ended him at the one stoplight on Main Street. He had been lurking outside of her house. He probably carried a gun. Of course he carried a gun. And he knew who Erin was and where she lived.

Beaver had said that the clans would stay out of Bald Eagle Falls for a long time. They would be scared off by the big drug sting and they wouldn't want to go anywhere near the little town. They no longer had any assets to protect there, so they wouldn't be after Erin or any of her friends.

But she had been wrong. Biggles had come back. He had ignored whatever sage advice the clan leaders had given him about staying out of sight. Or maybe they had sent him back to scope things out and see how easy it would be to target Erin.

So Terry knew that simply warning him off wasn't going to work. He knew that Biggles was too stupid or too cunning to stay away.

What could Terry do?

It was too much for Erin. The nausea swelled up, overwhelming her, and she dropped to her knees in front of the commode to throw up. It was a good thing she hadn't eaten her sandwich. Beaver could have hers too. Beaver could have all of the sandwiches. And go home. Erin didn't want her there any longer.

Beaver was a troublemaker, and she knew it. She loved to stir things up and then see what happened. Was that why she had escorted Terry home? To see what kind of fallout would come from the revelation that Terry had gone after Biggles for revenge?

After a few minutes, there was a tap at the door. Erin could barely hear it over the yowls of the cat.

"Blossom," Terry said in frustration. "Get out of here. Scat!"

There was a scuffle, and then the yowling stopped. Terry tapped the door again.

"Erin? Are you okay? Can I come in?"

"No."

Erin tore off a piece of toilet paper to wipe her nose and mouth, gagging again at the sight and smell of the vomit. She flushed the toilet and leaned against the bathroom counter.

"Erin...?"

"I'll be out in a while. You guys finish visiting and then Beaver can go home."

There was only silence in response, and then a couple of minutes later, Erin heard Terry walking away, down the hall toward the kitchen again. Clementine's old house creaked and protested, making it easy for Erin to follow Terry's progress away from the bathroom door.

Erin leaned her head in her hand, trying to get past the nausea and worry. Sheriff Wilmot hadn't arrested Terry. That meant that they didn't think they had enough evidence to build a case against him yet. That was good news. Terry was still walking around free and, as an officer that the sheriff was familiar with, he had some level of protection from wrongful prosecution. But who knew how much pressure the sheriff was getting from the public and the other town and state authorities who wanted to make sure that if there was a dirty cop, he was prosecuted to the full extent of the law.

He wouldn't cave.

Not without a lot of evidence.

Erin hoped.

Maybe that was why the sheriff hadn't had anything to say when he had caught Erin snooping around. He was hoping she *would* find something to give him an excuse for not charging Terry with murder, or at least police brutality.

To think that she had been worried that the reason he had called Terry in was to dress him down for allowing Erin to poke her nose in where it wasn't wanted. Sheriff Wilmot didn't care that she'd been getting in the way. He was more concerned about the suggestion Terry had targeted Biggles for personal reasons.

Erin rose unsteadily to her feet and sponged off her face again. She listened at the door. There was a murmur of voices. Then a couple of minutes later, the front door closed and Erin knew that Beaver was gone.

She opened the door as Terry walked down the hall toward her again, his eyes dark and concerned. She pushed him away when he tried to hug her, worried about smelling like puke, and turned toward her bedroom. Terry stopped in the hall, unsure what to do.

"I'm going to lie down," Erin told him. "Come in with me."

He seemed relieved to be told what to do and followed her into the bedroom. "Are you okay?"

"I guess I'll be fine. I was just... surprised."

"I'm sorry I didn't tell you sooner... but I couldn't."

"You could have."

But she knew how hard it must have been for him to admit how much trouble he was really in. He wanted to be her protector, but he might have to go away and leave her to her own devices. It was so bad that he was considering pleading to a lesser charge.

Erin shook her head and closed her eyes as she rested her head on the pillow. They had to get some rest. Neither one of them would be able to think clearly and logically until they were well-rested.

"How does it make any difference?" Erin asked, without turning to him. "You made a good arrest. He was dealing drugs by the school and you arrested him for that. He resisted. There was a witness to that. And once you got him to the police department, you were under supervision. You weren't in the interview room whaling on him. You were asking him questions, and the rest of the department wouldn't look the other way while you beat him."

"The case isn't turning out to be as cut-and-dried as I would like it to."

"But that's the way it happened."

"They need more than just my statement. The fact that I went looking for Biggles because he was hanging around here... that's a big problem. Maybe I should have gotten Tom or the sheriff involved instead of handling it myself. It was an emotional decision. But it was also in the usual line of duty for me... if I'm aware someone is acting inappropriately and breaking the law, it's my duty to go after them. That's my job."

"Yes," Erin agreed. With her eyes closed and Terry lying down behind her, cuddling her close, she felt warm and protected. She could work out all of the details in the morning. If she could just get a good sleep, the pieces would begin to fit together.

She was dozing off when Terry moved away from her and got up. Erin was too tired to even open her eyes. "Come back."

"Need to get out of these sweaty clothes," he whispered. "And I need to check the alarm system. I'll be back."

"Is Beaver still out there?"

He paused by the bedroom door. "Yes," he admitted.

"To make sure that none of Biggles's friends show up?"

"Yes."

Erin breathed out slowly. "Okay."

CHAPTER 23

*W*hen she climbed out of bed in the morning, Terry got up as well.

"You need more rest," Erin told him. "You did too much yesterday."

"I didn't do anything yesterday except answer questions. I need to get out and do something active today."

"Maybe see what Willie's up to?"

"I don't know. I want to do something..." He trailed off, not finishing.

"Something to do with Bo Biggles?" Erin suggested.

Terry rubbed his eyes and looked at her, eyes squinted. "Are you reading minds now?"

"No... I just figured... that's what I would want to do. I know you're probably not supposed to have anything to do with it, but I don't know if I could help myself if it was me. I would want to get out there and start turning over stones and figuring out what had happened."

"We both know very well that there is no way you would stay out of it if it were you."

Erin couldn't help smiling. She had really tried to be good at the time and to do what Officer Piper had told her and to stay out of the investigation and let him and the police department do their jobs. But somehow... things kept coming up, and even when she wasn't asking questions and poking around, things tended to *happen*. People told her things or misinterpreted her questions or… things just happened.

"It wasn't really my fault. I wasn't even trying to investigate…"

"Uh-huh." Terry took in a deep breath and let it out. "The alternative is sitting around doing nothing and letting someone else have control over my fate, and I'm getting tired of that. I need to do something. Assemble my defense."

Erin nodded. "I know. I've been hoping that it would all just come together, but I haven't had a lot of luck yet. If we can prove that he died because of something else or because of something that someone else did, then we can prove that you are innocent, and you can get back to work where you belong."

"But only if that's true. If it wasn't someone else or some other cause… If it was the taser or something that happened while I was trying to get him under control and into handcuffs…"

"It wasn't," Erin assured him. They both knew that she couldn't be sure of the fact, but she needed to reassure him. He had to know that she had faith in him and that it would all work out somehow. "Adele said that we really can't control fate and that we have to let the universe sort itself out."

"If I believed that, I wouldn't be a cop."

"I always thought that Christians figured God was in charge of everything and he is the one who will work things out."

Terry grimaced. "Difficult philosophical question," he admitted. "I believe that God is in charge… but I believe that I need to do my part and that I can affect the outcome… sort of."

"If God is in charge, then how can you change that?"

"I can't change it… I can… work within his plan to make things work out the way they are supposed to… in a way that's best for me."

Erin tried to wrap her mind around that. "So you can work against God's plan? Make things go wrong for yourself?"

"Err… I can cause pain and trouble for myself by trying to work against his plan. Things are easier if I work with him than against him."

Erin spread her hands apart. She needed to use the bathroom, so she couldn't very well continue the philosophical discussion. "So what does God want you to do about this case? About your defense?"

Terry looked at her, brows raised, and shook his head slowly.

Erin dashed to the commode. She'd let Terry sort that question out for himself. As an atheist, Erin didn't have to worry about making the choice that God wanted her to make, or even about aligning herself with fate or the universe. She was the one who made choices about her own life and the way it would turn out, and she wanted that life to include Terry.

And not visiting him in prison.

She had a shower and dressed and found Terry in the kitchen ahead of her, preparing toast and tea. After emptying her stomach the night before, Erin found herself much hungrier than she would typically be in the morning and the aroma whet her appetite.

"That smells good."

"My specialty."

"Good choice."

Terry had already let K9 out of his crate and the animals were milling about waiting for their breakfasts. Erin fed them all. She looked toward the front door.

"Is Beaver still out there? Should we offer her something?"

"It would be a nice gesture. Do you want her here, though? You weren't too thrilled with her last night."

"I'm a little less emotional this morning. We can feed her. How long has she been up?"

"I didn't ask. Just accepted her offer to keep an eye out last night. I knew I couldn't be the one to keep watch."

"Did you get enough sleep last night? You don't usually get up this early."

"More than I have the last few nights. I don't usually go to bed as early as I did."

"But you didn't go to sleep when I did; you were up changing, and I heard you in the shower."

"Not long. I was asleep pretty soon after you. I can have a nap this afternoon if I need to… I don't plan on going in for any more police interviews."

"Even if they call you?"

Terry nodded. "Even if they call me. I'm thinking… if they want me back in again today, I might have to get a lawyer."

Erin nodded as she started to butter slices of toast. "I think that would be a good idea. Are there any good criminal lawyers in town? Is there a union lawyer? Or do you have to go into the city to find someone?"

"I've never had to look before. I know some of the guys in town... but I don't know that I would go with any of them. If they've represented criminals in cases that we've investigated... it kind of feels like a conflict of interest. Like they might not put their best efforts into the case."

Erin had to admit he had a point.

CHAPTER 24

She left Terry to the toast and other goodies and walked to the front door. She looked up and down the street. Beaver's car wasn't in sight. But a moment later, Beaver walked around the side of the house and nodded to Erin.

"Hey."

"Hi. You want breakfast?"

"Breakfast would go down real nice about now."

Erin made a gesture inviting her in. Beaver walked across the front of the house, took a good look around, and then joined Erin inside.

"Are you okay?" she asked, chewing on the omnipresent gum. "You were in pretty rough shape last night. And I don't know if... well, you and I. I know we're not best friends or anything, but I hate to have you mad at me because I told Terry about Biggles or because I didn't tell you right at the start that he had been worried you were in danger." Beaver shrugged. "I don't know. It just didn't seem like the right thing to do at the time. I'm used to playing things close to the vest. That can cause relationship problems sometimes."

"We're okay," Erin assured her. She didn't want to get into it any more deeply than that. Beaver had done what she thought was right, and Erin probably would have reacted the same way whether they had told her right away or told her when they did. She couldn't change the past or the choices that any of them had made.

Erin put a few jars of jam on the table, along with butter and honey, plates, glasses, knives, and juice from the fridge. Together with the tea and the toast, the table was pretty full. For someone who usually didn't have any breakfast other than a cup of tea, it was a feast. Beaver sat down, making pleased noises.

"This is gonna be great. Your baking is always the best, Erin."

"How do you know this isn't store-bought bread?"

"First, because it's obviously handmade. And also with the amount of leftovers from the bakery, why would you buy bread at the store? You can't afford to run out of bread at the bakery, so you have to make just a bit too much, and then someone has to eat it."

Erin laughed. "And we've been making plenty of donations to a homeless shelter in the city, too. But there always seems to be more to eat."

"Good thing for me."

They all sat down and began to spread their choices of condiments on the toast.

"So… what other things do you keep close to the vest that causes you relationship problems?" Erin asked. She wasn't usually so nosy about other people's problems, but for once it would be nice not to think about hers or Terry's. She knew that Beaver probably wouldn't answer the question anyway. She was good at deflecting.

"Well… sometimes you find something out that affects someone you know and, being in law enforcement, you can't say anything. When people find out later that you withheld something… they tend not to be too happy about it. Not just surprised and upset, but…" She shrugged with one shoulder. "Breakup mad. Or shoot-you-in-a-fit-of-anger mad."

"Ouch!" Erin stared at Beaver in horror. "You're not serious, are you? You said before that you had been shot, but I thought that was in the line of duty. You're not telling me that you had a boyfriend who shot you because you hadn't told him something in the course of an investigation?"

Beaver took a couple of bites of toast, reflecting on her answer. "Well… that's accurate, but not a complete description of what happened. Sometimes something can be in the line of duty *and* personal at the same time."

Erin frowned, trying to figure that one out.

Terry looked at Beaver; head cocked to the side slightly. "Like when you have a relationship with someone you are investigating?"

"It can happen," Beaver admitted.

Erin thought about how Beaver had taken up with Jeremy after the drug investigation was complete. She *had* waited until after the investigation, hadn't she? She had to be talking about some other case, because Jeremy hadn't shot Beaver. He'd known from the start that she was law enforcement. If Beaver had started a relationship with someone she was investigating, though, Erin could see how that could go very badly very quickly.

"Sheesh, Beaver. You should be more careful."

"I *am* more careful. Now."

They all laughed.

There was a knock at the back door and Vic let herself in. She looked around at the group of them. "Things are as busy in here as a cat with puppies! What's up? Did I miss a memo? Is it a party?"

"No one is partying this early in the morning," Terry asserted. "It's just breakfast. Throw a couple more pieces of bread in the toaster and pull up a chair." Terry eyed Beaver and the stack of toast on her plate. "I think we're going to need a bit more than I had calculated."

Vic nodded and put four more pieces of toast into the toaster. She sat down and picked up a single piece of toast for herself.

"So I get why Terry is here," she drawled, with a wink in his direction. "But why Beaver? What are you doing up so early?"

"Actually, I'm not up early. I'm up late."

"You haven't been to bed? You weren't out with Jeremy, were you? I'll have a talk with that boy about keeping his date up so late."

Beaver shook her head, chewing a large mouthful of toast. She swallowed strenuously. "No, ma'am, don't blame your brother for that one. I was on surveillance."

"Oh." Vic took a dainty bite of her slice of toast, spread thinly with marmalade as she considered this. "Anything I should know about? I didn't think that there was anything for you to investigate in Bald Eagle Falls. Things have been pretty quiet here. Other than..." Vic shrugged, tilting her head toward Terry and looking apologetic, "...you know."

Beaver glanced around the table at Erin and Terry. Terry sighed and nodded.

"There is some concern that there could be retaliation by Biggles's clan. As you can imagine, they are not too happy about his unexpected death."

"Biggles is Jackson clan," Vic said. She fiddled with the handle on her teacup. "You think they're going to send people here to Bald Eagle Falls to get revenge?"

"It's a possibility," Beaver agreed, sitting back in her chair. She was watching the three of them carefully. "There have been some rumblings."

Vic looked sick. Erin thought about her own race to the bathroom the night before and was sympathetic. Vic didn't need to be reminded of her family and their criminal enterprises. She didn't need to be wondering if one of them were going to come to town to deal with Terry. Her brothers had been sent out once before to handle things in Bald Eagle Falls—though the police hadn't been able to prove their involvement in anything that had happened.

Erin reached across the table and touched Vic's arm. "It's okay, Vicky. Nothing is going to happen. It's just… preventative. Being extra careful."

"Nothing is going to happen while I'm on watch," Beaver asserted.

"But you can't be on watch all the time. And you can't be everywhere. It isn't like you can put a tail on Terry twenty-four hours a day. And watch his house, and Erin's, and the bakery, and anywhere else they might attack. Even if you could, how long could you justify it? A few days? A week? They'd just wait for an opening."

"We're not just going to sit back and wait for something to happen. We do have people in place and are managing the situation."

Did the feds have people planted in the clan? High up enough to be able to control some of the decisions being made by the gang? Erin shook her head and let her breath out in a heavy sigh. "Well, it's not like we haven't been here before. We've faced the clan and other criminals before and things have worked out okay." She looked at Terry. "If you believe in God or fate, then you need to have some faith that things will work out the way they are supposed to."

Terry's eyes narrowed. He obviously thought she was mocking his beliefs.

Erin put her hand on his leg under the table, giving it a little squeeze. "Really. I mean it. With Beaver on the case and the universe working for our good, it will all turn out, right?"

His expression relaxed and he nodded, putting his hand over hers briefly, warm and comforting. "Yeah."

Vic looked at them. She nodded, but didn't look reassured. "The whisperings you are hearing about clan activity… you don't know any names, do you?"

"Like whether Joseph and Daniel are involved?" Beaver asked baldly. "No, not that I've heard. But I wouldn't assume anything. If you see either of one of them, don't be too eager for a family reunion."

Vic nodded. She rubbed her palms along her pants. She swallowed. "And Jeremy? He's out, right? He's safely away from the clan and its influence."

Beaver didn't answer.

Beaver had said that she had been involved with people she had been investigating before. Was her relationship with Jeremy merely a front to monitor his involvement with the Jackson clan? Or did she want to help keep him safe from the clan, as she had said before? Erin had never sensed any duplicity about her relationship with him. But Beaver was a professional. She was very good at what she did.

"We'd know if Jeremy had anything to do with the clan," Erin told Vic. "He wouldn't be able to keep that from us for this long. He's not exactly an expert. We knew something was going on before. We'd know if he still had contact with them."

"Maybe." Vic shook her head. Her toast sat on the plate half-eaten. "I thought when I left that I wouldn't have anything else to do with the clan. Leaving home was not exactly in my plans, but it was kind of a relief when I did, and I knew I didn't have to be involved with them. I didn't know how hard it would be, knowing that the boys are still part of that scene. I don't want to believe that Jeremy is still mixed up with the clan. But I'm not sure. He hasn't always been… forthcoming."

"Everybody has secrets," Beaver said around another mouthful of toast. "Even you, Miss Victoria."

Erin blinked at this. Of course she didn't know everything there was to know about Vic. She knew the broad strokes, and she knew Vic's personality and the kind of person she was. Erin would trust Vic with her life and knew that Vic would never do anything to hurt her. But that didn't mean Vic didn't have secrets she'd rather no one knew.

Erin herself had a past and hadn't revealed the details even to Terry. He knew whatever he had turned up when he had investigated her background, and he knew what she had told him about her background and growing up in foster care. He knew everything she did about what had happened to her parents. But everything about her... there were still plenty of things she would rather not talk about, even to him and Vic.

Beaver cut her eyes toward Erin and smiled, clearly guessing where Erin's thoughts had gone. She didn't accuse Erin of having secrets too, but she knew. Beaver probably had a clearer picture of Erin's background than even Terry did. She had more resources at her disposal than a small-town cop.

"But you don't think he's involved with the clan? You don't think he's a danger to any of us?"

"I don't think Jeremy is a danger to you or Erin, no," Beaver agreed.

CHAPTER 25

There wasn't time for a lot of discussion before heading off to the bakery. Normally, Erin just had a quick cup of tea before she and Vic drove over to Auntie Clem's, so she felt a little rushed cleaning up after the breakfast in order to get on her way.

"You go ahead and I'll clean up," Terry ordered, motioning Erin and Vic away from the table. "I'm not going anywhere. I'll make sure it's all ship-shape."

"You don't need to—"

"I'm the one who made breakfast; you wouldn't have eaten before going to work otherwise. Let me clean up my own mess."

Erin nodded and left him to it. She wondered by the sharpness of his answer if he was thinking about more than the dishes when he referred to his 'own mess.' Vic headed out to the car.

"Have a good day today." Terry caught Erin by the arm and tugged her gently to him for a goodbye kiss.

"Okay. You too."

He nodded, holding her for an extra second and then releasing her. He walked her to the door and as she was stepping out, stopped her, frowning. "Erin."

"What is it?"

"Last night, you said there was a witness to Biggles's arrest."

"Yes."

"Who did you mean?"

Erin raised her eyebrows, surprised. "Adele."

"Adele saw it? Where was she?"

"Picking berries. You didn't know?"

"She didn't come forward."

"Oh." Erin considered this, starting down the sidewalk. Terry followed her. "I assumed she had been questioned."

"No. As far as I know, no one has talked to her."

"Then I guess... someone should."

"I'll give the sheriff a call and let him know."

"I guess she won't be very happy about being called in, if she didn't let anyone know she was there. She's pretty reclusive."

"She should have reported it herself, reclusive or no. Once she knew Biggles died, which I assume she did."

"She did." Erin gave Terry a quick peck on the cheek before opening the car door. "Call me if you need me."

"I'll be fine. Have a good day."

"You could come by and bring K9 in for a cookie like you normally would. It's strange not having you stop in."

"I don't know. I'm not exactly welcomed with open arms in Bald Eagle Falls public right now."

"No one would say anything, would they?"

"Not to my face, maybe, but there has been plenty of talk behind my back. And the looks... you would think that I was the one dealing drugs at the school, the way they pull their kids away from me."

"Really?" Erin started to walk away, knowing she had to get to the bakery or she would be late opening. "I was surprised at Mary Lou's reaction... but I guess she's worried about her boys getting arrested... what would happen if one of them got in trouble." Erin waved one last time and pulled out.

It was only a couple of minutes to get to the bakery. When they got there and got started on preparations, Vic spoke.

"I didn't know Mary Lou felt like that about the boys."

Erin nodded. "She was pretty upset. I thought she would be happy, like Terry said, about getting a drug dealer off the street. It wasn't Terry's fault that he died. But she was imagining what would happen if it was one of her boys. How even if they were in trouble, she wouldn't want one of them dead like that." She shrugged. "Gives you a different perspective on criminals, thinking about their moms."

Vic was solemn. "I never really thought… I mean, I know my mom doesn't like my dad and the boys being involved with the clan, but she never really said anything about it. She grew up in a clan family, so to her, that's what's normal. But even though she doesn't say anything about it… she must worry about them when they are out on Jackson business."

Erin and Vic had to boogie to make sure that they could get everything prepared and arranged in the display case by opening time. They didn't discuss Bo Biggles, only the baking in each of the ovens and what still had to be done. By the time they were ready to open, Erin felt like she had spent two hours running through sniper fire, and was ready to go back home and go to sleep. Instead, she pasted a pleasant look on her face and greeted her customers, making sure that everyone felt welcome and cared for. Auntie Clem's was more than just a bakery. People went there for gossip and fellowship and to find out what was going on in town. Erin made it as warm and inviting a place as possible so that people would keep coming, even when they weren't out of bread.

Mrs. Foster and the children traipsed in soon after opening time. Erin marveled over how big the kids were getting, how independent little Traci was. When Erin had moved into town, Traci had still been a baby in a sling. Now she was running everywhere. Mrs. Foster had put on weight around the hips lately that Erin strongly suspected indicated another little Foster was on the way.

"How are you? What can I get you today?"

The kids demanded their little stamp cards from their mother to claim their kid's club cookies, and Erin waited patiently while they looked through the glass and discussed which ones they wanted. She smiled at Peter, presiding over the little group as if he were their guide.

"So, have you settled on your Halloween costume yet?" She was curious as to whether he had succeeded in wearing his mother down with his negotiations yet. While Mrs. Foster had good reasons for not allowing Peter to wear a mask, Erin suspected that Peter would get his way, through one argument or another, before October 31 rolled around.

Peter looked at his mother, then turned back to Erin and rolled his eyes. "I want to be a monster," he said. "A werewolf or something scary like that, with lots of fur and a really scary, realistic face." He looked over his shoulder at his mother again.

"Won't fur be too hot?"

"No. It will be the end of October. The end of October is chilly, so it will be just like wearing a jacket," he told her with authority.

Erin nodded her understanding.

"No mask," Mrs. Foster said. "You can find someone to do realistic makeup for you, but not a mask."

Peter shook his head in despair. The girls distracted him by indicating that they all wanted chocolate chip cookies, which Peter insisted was not practical. They should select different flavors and share. But they all insisted that they had tried all of the flavors and knew what kind they wanted. Peter would have to pick something different if he didn't want chocolate chip.

Erin made a mental note that she would need to add a couple of new flavors to mix things up a little.

She hadn't made turnovers or tarts for quite a while, but wasn't sure she could yet. Not with fruit filling, anyway. Maybe she could make some little quiches and pumpkin pies for the grown-ups. They could do cutout cookies and fancy cupcakes for the children.

"Erin…"

Erin snapped back to attention, realizing that her mind had been drifting into Halloween plans, and she had to wait one more day before making any decisions on those. She handed cookies out to the children and looked at Mrs. Foster to see what else she wanted. Vic was already getting her order together and listed off the items for Erin to ring through the register. Erin smiled at Mrs. Foster as they exchanged money.

"You'll have to come by here when you have your costume on," she told Peter. "We won't be open when you are out trick-or-treating, but maybe you can come by after school. You'll be allowed to wear them to school on Halloween day, right?"

Peter nodded. "Yes. I'll have to check with Mom about coming over. I'm not supposed to go anywhere else or talk to anyone on my way home from school." He looked over at Mrs. Foster, raising his eyebrows in query.

"We'll talk about it and sort it out," Mrs. Foster agreed, moving to break up a squabble between Jody and Traci.

Erin opened her mouth to mention to Mrs. Foster how good Peter had been when she'd seen him behind the Town Hall on his way home for lunch. Then something occurred to her.

"Peter... you said that you saw someone in a mask. A really realistic ape mask."

Peter nodded emphatically. Mrs. Foster looked like she was ready to have a meltdown over Erin bringing up the forbidden topic again. But Erin had to know.

"Where did you see that?"

Peter looked at her for a minute, frowning as if it had been too long ago to remember. Then his face lit up. "Where you were," he said. "Behind the... the place where the police station is. That's where."

"What was he doing? Was there a party? Was he hanging out with friends? Was it a whole ape costume, or just a mask?"

"It was just him," Peter said with a shrug. "I don't know what he was doing. Just a guy with an ape mask."

"Sitting back there in a car...?"

"No. Going in the door. Where you came out."

"What day?"

Erin was sure she knew the answer. Peter would probably not even be able to remember what day it had been, but Erin was sure she knew.

"Monday," Peter said brightly. "The day we came to see you."

The day Bo Biggles had died.

Peter had seen someone going into the police department's back door wearing a mask the afternoon Bo Biggles had died in custody.

CHAPTER 26

*A*t first, Vic wasn't sure what to think about Peter's story of a man in a monkey mask. But after Erin talked it through with her, Vic agreed that it was something they would at least have to pass on to the sheriff and whoever was investigating Bo Biggles's death. It wasn't something they could ignore. Terry's future was on the line, and if it was possible that a masked man had been in the police department and had something to do with Biggles's death, then it could be just the break they had been looking for.

"You'd better let him know," she agreed. "Do you want to call him or go over there? You could go over during lunch if you want to."

They usually took their meal before the official lunch hour, so that they could be available to serve customers during the lunch rush. They got up early so they were ready to eat again earlier than the rest of the town. "If I go during our lunch and I get held up, then you are left with the rush. I'll go over midafternoon before school lets out."

"You're going to run into the same problem with the after-school crowd if you get hung up. You may as well go early. The sooner he knows about it, the sooner he can investigate and prove that Terry didn't do anything wrong."

Erin looked at the time on her phone. "Do you think he'll be questioning Adele right now? I don't want to interrupt her witness statement. If he decides this is more important, then she'll have to wait over there half the day."

Vic shook her head. "I doubt it. She's up late at night. I doubt he could get her over to the police department this early."

"Okay. Yeah, you're probably right. I'll just…" Erin wiped her moist hands on her apron. "I'll just go over there right now. I'm sure it will only take a few minutes, and it should be quiet here until lunch. I'll get back as quickly as I can. I'm not the witness, so he's not going to want to spend time interviewing me."

"But you might need to spend some time convincing him that it's a legitimate lead. He might not think so."

"Yeah." Erin took a breath and prepared herself mentally to go over to the police department once more. She would look even more suspicious this time, going over there when Terry wasn't around. And she wasn't going to take another box of muffins over to smooth her way, or they would start thinking she was guilty of something. She wasn't going there to snoop this time. She was going to give the sheriff a legitimate tip, not to check it out herself. She wasn't doing anything she wasn't supposed to.

Still, when Clara saw Erin's approach, she shook her head, looking forbidding. "He's pretty busy today, Erin, and you know you're not supposed to be poking around here. I got in trouble the other day for letting you past the desk with those muffins. You can't have the run of the place."

"I'm not. I'll stay out here with you until he's free. But I need to see Sheriff Wilmot. I may have found something out. A break in the case."

"What kind of a break?" Clara demanded, her penciled eyebrows drawing down. "What could you know, other than pillow talk?"

Erin's face got hot with a combination of anger and embarrassment. "Just let him know, would you?"

Clara stared at Erin. She wasn't an easy person to get along with at the best of times, and the fact that she'd been reprimanded after Erin's last visit meant that she wasn't about to give Erin anything easily.

Erin went over to a visitor chair and sat down. "I'll just wait here until he's ready."

She sat still and stared straight at Clara, waiting. She didn't get out her phone or her lists or rummage around in her purse for anything. She just sat still, staring, waiting.

It didn't take long before Clara was uncomfortable. She shifted around, pretended not to look at her, tapped furiously on her keyboard, and made several unimportant phone calls to show Erin how low on Clara's list dealing with her was. But she was clearly rattled. Erin kept staring, blinking now and then and remaining focused tightly on Clara.

Eventually, Clara turned away, punching a single button on her office phone and talking into the receiver with her hand over her mouth so that Erin couldn't hear what she was saying or read her lips. She hung up the phone with a crash.

"He'll be out to see you when he has a spare moment."

"Thank you."

It wasn't long before Sheriff Wilmot asked Erin into his office. She sat down on the uncomfortable couch while he sat on a chair close to her. A cozy arrangement that indicated she was a friend rather than a suspect, not relegated to a hard chair in a bare interview room. She wasn't sure what she would have done if he had taken her into one of those rooms. She might have had a panic attack and not been able to handle it.

Maybe the sheriff guessed as much.

He listened to Erin's somewhat meandering story about how she had found out about the man with the mask from Peter, being sure to tell him that she had only asked Peter a couple of questions and had not suggested the answers. She had let him come up with those on his own, and his recollections put the masked man at the back door of the police department before Biggles's death.

Wilmot rubbed his chin, thinking about it. He pulled a pen out of his pocket and fidgeted with it, not writing any notes, but clicking the top and trying to decide what to do with the information.

"You're sure about all of this?" he asked. "You're sure that it was the day that Biggles died."

"That's what Peter said. You'll have to check the details with him. He said it was Monday after school."

"But this story… it's a bit of a tall tale. He saw a man with a monkey mask? I don't know what to think of that."

"You don't think it's suspicious?"

"You really think that someone broke into the police department, came into one of the interview rooms, killed Biggles, and walked back out of here, and no one saw a thing?"

"Except for Peter. Yes."

"That door isn't flimsy. Someone would have to unlock or pick it. And right in the middle of the day when everybody was here? When he could have been seen at any time? Who would do that?"

"I don't know. That's for you to investigate."

"I just don't know, Erin. It's not a very believable story."

"But Peter wasn't trying to make us believe that he'd seen a murderer. He was just talking about a cool mask he saw. He didn't connect it with Biggles's death or any other criminal activity. He just liked the guy's mask."

"It could have been completely innocent. If it was even the day that he thinks it was."

"Was there a day that there *was* someone here wearing a monkey mask? Was there a pre-Halloween costume party somewhere in the Town Hall? Why would anyone be wearing a mask in the middle of the day, except to avoid being identified?"

"If someone wanted to kill Biggles, it would have made a lot more sense to wait until night, when I would be the only one here, in my office. To do it before everyone had left for the day and might walk in on him? That's too bold. No one would do that."

"If they thought that he was being transported back to Moose River that night, then it was their only chance. They had to get in here and do it before he was moved. This is the weakest part of the chain, security-wise." She grimaced. "Sorry."

"Anyone who had anything to do with the case knew that he was going to be kept here overnight. Even an outsider could have guessed that we'd want him for another day to question him. We can't always get same-day transportation due to the county schedules."

"Then that goes to show that it was an outsider. Or someone who was really desperate. Maybe they wanted to keep him from talking. He could have spilled the beans on other criminal enterprises. Someone might have been desperate to stop him before he could tell you about their part in the drug dealing. A bigger fish for a lighter sentence."

"Biggles wasn't going to talk. He was a professional. He knew to keep his mouth shut. Mob guys know that. They know that no matter what kind of protection we offer or how much lighter the sentence is, they're still going to end up in prison at the mercy of the clan boys who are already on the inside. There isn't anywhere safe in the pen. Not even in isolation."

"If the clan could get him in isolation at the prison, then why couldn't they get to him here in an unguarded room? No armed guards or security cameras. All he needed was a lock pick, stealth, and a bit of luck. And a mask to hide his identity."

The sheriff sat still, gazing off into space, before finally nodding. "Alright," he finally agreed. "I guess I'd better call Mrs. Foster."

CHAPTER 27

*E*rin filled Terry in on the latest news when she got home. She didn't want to be overheard at the bakery, especially when it involved Peter Foster. She didn't want him or his family being harassed by gossips who wanted to know the details of the investigation. Word of a masked intruder would spread like wildfire. She had promised the sheriff she would keep it under wraps, but had told him that she was going to talk to Terry about it. Wilmot grimaced, but didn't tell her that she couldn't. He knew she could have lied to him and said she wasn't going to. She was being honest about it, and he didn't have any authority to stop her. She had told him what she knew, and she was free to tell anyone else she wanted to.

And Terry had the right to know.

He nodded and looked thoughtful, but didn't have much to say about it. Vic seemed much more enthusiastic about the news than he did, bouncing on her heels, eyes bright and excited.

"This is good news," she insisted. "It proves that there was foul play; it wasn't just an accident or natural causes. There was someone at the police department who shouldn't have been. It will clear you!"

Terry was cautious. He shook his head. "We'll see. It might not go anywhere. It might have been someone on their way to a costume party. Someone who worked somewhere else in the Town Hall and just chose to use that hallway and door."

"It wasn't a costume," Vic maintained.

Erin tended to agree, but she understood Terry not wanting to get his hopes up too much. "The sheriff is going to look into it. He thinks it's worth looking at."

"That's good," Terry said without emotion.

Erin sighed and picked up the stack of mail and flyers Terry had put on the coffee table. Mostly junk. A couple of bills. She frowned at one with a handwritten address on the front. "One here for you, Vicky."

Vic snagged it from her hand while Erin was still looking at it. Usually, the mailman managed to sort their mail into the two separate mailboxes, but sometimes one ended up in the wrong box. Erin opened her mouth to ask who the letter was from but, seeing Vic's face, something made her stop. Vic was pink and didn't meet her eyes. She folded the envelope in half and tucked it into her jeans pocket. She turned her wrist to look at her watch.

"I want to shower before Willie gets in, and I'm not sure when that will be, so I guess I'll see you later."

"Sure," Erin agreed. "No shift tomorrow, but don't forget we're having a business meeting after the ladies' tea."

"I won't forget. I'm eager to get started on some cute cookies. It's time for our harvest and Halloween treats to make an appearance."

"Well, once we talk through our strategic plan for the next couple of months, we'll be good to go. After Halloween is over, we need to be thinking about Thanksgiving and Christmas."

"Awesome," Vic agreed. "I can't wait. I love Christmas."

"I'm not sure we'll do quite as much as we did last year for our Christmas dinner…" They had been eating Christmas treats from the freezer for months.

Vic laughed. "No, maybe not quite so much this year."

⁓

Erin watched Vic leave through the back door to go to her loft and get ready. She brushed the sweaty hair back from her own face. She needed a shower too. It was hot work, even in the fall. But she wasn't in a hurry.

"What do you make of that?" she asked.

Terry considered for a moment. "She did seem in a bit of a hurry to get out of here."

"And the letter?"

"Who was it from?"

"I don't know. There wasn't a return address. It was handwritten. Looked like a woman's handwriting."

"Could it have been from her mother?"

"It looked like a younger person's writing. Older people, their writing is tighter, sometimes shaky. This looked… more like a school kid."

"Ah." Terry gave a slow nod.

"What does that mean?"

"It means… she's been getting calls and texts from some of those people on the cruise. You know, that LGBT group she was hanging out with."

"Oh. Okay. So maybe it's one of them."

"Probably," Terry agreed.

Erin looked at him sideways. "How do you know she's been getting calls and texts from them?"

"Willie mentioned it when we were working the other day."

"Is he worried about it?"

"Worried… not exactly. But he's… a little uncomfortable. He's not used to her having these other friends. They're outside of Vic and Willie's normal social circle and he doesn't have anything in common with them."

"So he's jealous." Erin nodded, remembering how she had felt on the ship when Vic was spending time with her new friends. Like she had been abandoned. She had been there when Vic hadn't had anyone else, and to suddenly have Vic spending time with a whole different group of friends, laughing like they knew each other and understood each other without the need for a shared history, had been disconcerting and had made her feel uncomfortable and out of sorts. Of course, there was no reason Vic shouldn't have her own friends. And she needed friends who understood her feelings and shared life experiences with her.

But Erin hadn't liked it, and neither had Willie. They had both suddenly felt like outsiders, castoffs, while Vic had forged new relationships.

Terry shrugged. "He's feeling uncomfortable," he repeated.

"Does Vic know that?"

"It's up to the two of them to talk it out. I'm not a relationship counselor."

That sounded like a good policy, though Erin wasn't sure she'd be able to stick to it. She didn't like to get involved in other people's disagreements or problems, but she also didn't want to see problems between her friends. Maybe with just a little nudge, Vic would see how Willie was feeling and reassure him that she wasn't going to leave him in favor of her new friends. She'd helped them see each other's points of view before...

CHAPTER 28

*E*rin was in the shower when Terry knocked and entered. Usually, he waited until she was done, knowing that she wasn't going to be in there for long but just wanted to rinse away the sweat of the workday. It was different when she had a bath before bed and might be soaking in the tub for an hour.

"Hi. What's up?"

"Uh… I was planning to have dinner with you, but I got a call…"

Erin's stomach lurched. "From the sheriff? You know what we talked about. If he's going to keep calling you in for questioning, you need to talk to a lawyer. You don't have to go in."

"No, it wasn't the sheriff."

"Oh." Erin ran her fingers through her short hair and scrubbed her scalp with her fingertips, trying to erase the fatigue of the day with the warm water and light massage. "What was it, then?"

"It was Jack Ward, from Moose River."

"Ward? What did he want?" Erin wasn't sure she wanted Terry to go talk to Jack Ward any more than she wanted him to talk to Sheriff Wilmot.

"He said there have been some things going on in Moose River. Rumors. He's been talking to friends and business acquaintances of Biggles. He wanted to fill me in and see if we could put our heads together and…"

"I don't know if you should go."

"He's not going to arrest me, Erin. Biggles didn't die in his jurisdiction. The investigation he's doing is a favor for Sheriff Wilmot and the staties."

"Then why is he sharing it with you? Shouldn't he be talking to them? I don't like you going all the way out there to talk to him, just to find out that he's trying to build the case against you."

"He's not going to do that."

"Do you think it's worth the risk, though?"

"It's not a risk." Terry was still and didn't say anything for a minute.

Erin stuck her head around the curtain to look at him.

"I'm not asking you if you think it's a good idea," Terry explained, scratching the back of his head. "I'm just letting you know where I'm going to be. And that I probably won't be home until late. If it's raining hard or I'm tired, then I won't try to drive. I'll stay at the hotel and come back tomorrow. So... you don't need to worry about me."

Erin withdrew and stood once more under the warm spray of water. "Okay."

"It's okay?"

"You said you weren't asking permission."

"Well... I'm not. I just want to make sure that you're not upset. Don't stay up waiting for me. I don't know how long I'll be."

"Tomorrow is a sleep-in day. You and I usually... make time for each other."

"I know." His face was pained. "I wouldn't duck out on you normally. We'll get together tomorrow for sure. I'm sorry. It wasn't planned, but I think I need to go."

"Can't he wait until tomorrow? Surely he has to go to bed sometime too."

"He's making the time for me. I don't want to quibble over schedules."

Erin sighed.

She didn't tell him that it was okay. She just stood there silently in the warm stream of the shower until he decided to go.

Vic was out with Willie, Terry was on his way to Moose River, and Erin didn't want to stay home alone. The animals were good company, but she didn't get the same kind of feedback when she talked to them that she got from her friends of the two-legged variety. Erin considered going to see Mary Lou and taking her over some treats, but she knew that the treats would all just go to Josh and she already knew that Mary Lou was stressed out by Biggles's death and didn't want to have to deal with talk of Terry and if he'd done the right thing.

She decided instead to go out for a drive. Maybe she would go see Adele at the summer house. Or maybe she'd just enjoy the outdoors for a little while and then turn around and go back home. Being out in the fresh air and beautiful autumn leaves was probably just what she needed.

Erin found herself drawn to the place Adele had described when she told Erin about seeing Terry's arrest of Bo Biggles. She parked and walked around the perimeter of the school, sticking to Clementine's woods. Now Erin's woods. She always thought of them as Clementine's or Adele's, finding it hard to believe that she owned all of that land. Circumnavigating the school grounds, she felt like she was doing something wrong and needed to make sure that no one saw her. But she wasn't trespassing. In fact, she was going out of her way to stay off of the school property. Just like Biggles had.

She could see the wild strawberry patch that Adele had probably been picking berries from in a little clearing in the trees. In the shadows of the trees, with her slim figure and dark clothing, Adele might not be noticeable unless she made a sudden movement or did something else to draw attention to herself. And Biggles had been... where?

Erin mapped it out in her mind. Where Terry would have been able to pull up in his car. Where Adele had been watching from. Where Biggles would have been able to see what was going on in the school grounds and anyone approaching him, and yet still be able to claim that he was not dealing drugs on the school property. She scanned the ground, looking for footprints and torn-up vegetation. They'd had quite a struggle, from what Adele had described and what Terry had been careful not to say. They had both been down on the ground, hitting and wrestling. Biggles was not a small man. And K9 had been there too, employed by Terry to take Biggles down. But then Biggles had tried again to get away. Terry had tased him. Terry had wrestled with him.

She found the trampled vegetation. It was not easy, having been nearly a week since the incident had taken place. The grasses and vegetation had all sprung up again, and any footprints that might have been there initially had been obscured. Had anyone bothered to look at the footprints while they

166

were still fresh? Would they be able to tell anything to either verify or refute Terry's story? Probably not. Prints wouldn't show how hard Terry had hit Biggles, how many times he had tased him, and whether he had employed a chokehold.

Hopefully, Adele had been able to confirm all of those things to the sheriff and the state investigators that afternoon when they had taken her statement. Adele was a good person, an honest person. She didn't like to get mixed up in police matters or other people's business, but she would tell what she had seen straightforwardly and wouldn't try to obfuscate anything.

There was one trampled area where the grass had been scuffed away to the bare earth, and there were cigarette butts scattered around. She imagined it was the place where Biggles had stood, watching the school and peddling his wares.

Erin ran the scenario through her mind. Terry approaching. Biggles trying to run. Throwing something away. Getting taken down. The ensuing struggle. She played and replayed it, listening to Adele's words.

He'd thrown something away. Drugs, undoubtedly. Get rid of the evidence. Make sure it wasn't found on him. Claim that the cops planted it wherever it was found. And had Terry found it? Or had he been so occupied with getting Biggles under control that he had been distracted from it? He might not have even known that Biggles had thrown something away. She moved her feet slowly through the long grass and underbrush, not about to use her hands and end up finding a snake or spider or even just poison ivy or thistles. It would be very easy for a small item to become lost forever.

She heard cawing overhead and looked up at the crow perched on a branch, watching her while tilting his head this way and that. Very intelligent eyes.

"Skye?"

Erin wasn't sure whether it was Adele's crow or not. He didn't fly away at the sound of her voice, but he didn't get any closer or beg for peanuts either.

"Is this where they were?" she asked aloud. Of course he didn't understand her or answer her, but it was comforting to have an animal to talk to, even away from her house. "This must be where Terry arrested Bo Biggles. And he threw something away. Something incriminating. Were you here with Adele? Did you see?"

It was a large area to search, even if all she did was look a foot or two into the vegetation around the disturbed area. And what exactly did she expect to find? Something that would exonerate Terry? Like what? A hand-written confession?

There was another caw, and the crow flew over Erin's head and landed in the low branches of a tree just outside of the area she'd been searching. He tipped forward, looking down at something on the ground. Erin knew that it was impossible that the bird could have found what she herself was looking for, but she pushed her way carefully through the brush anyway. If she didn't look, she'd never be able to stop thinking about how she could have broken the case if she'd just followed the darn bird.

She couldn't see anything at first. Nothing that she was interested in, and not even anything that would interest a crow, like a termite mound or discarded sweet bun. She moved around the area, trying to put herself at the same viewing angle as the bird, looking down and from the side. There was a glint of light off metal. Erin moved slowly closer, trying to keep her eye on the spot even when the glint disappeared again. She pushed back the yellowing leaves of a rosebush, trying to avoid scratching and pricking herself too much. And then she saw the gun. Shiny silver and lethal-looking. Erin pushed back more vegetation for a better look. It was certainly not a hunting gun or a toy. Nothing that there was an innocent explanation for. As much as she wanted to pick it up for a closer look, she knew better. She mentally mapped the landmarks around it so that she would be able to find it again, and started to work her way out from the gun in a tight spiral, looking for anything else that Biggles might have disposed of. If he knew he was about to be arrested, then getting rid of his gun was a good choice. But he might have had other incriminating items on him as well, things that were equally important to dispose of. He hadn't had much time, so they weren't likely to be scattered far and wide—one toss, and then dealing with Terry.

She was right. There was a billfold with cash inside that had fallen unfolded a few feet away. Anything light had probably blown away. She didn't find any baggies of white powder or pills. Hopefully, that meant that any drugs Biggles had been dealing had been scooped up with him, and had not been found by kids on their way home from school.

Erin figured she had found everything she was going to and, before long, night would start to fall, and she had best get someone out there who could take care of the evidence before it was too dark. She sat in the Y of a stunted tree and pulled out her phone.

CHAPTER 29

S he showed Tom Baker and Sheriff Wilmot both the gun and the billfold. After marking the locations with evidence flags and taking pictures, they put on gloves and picked up the gun and the wallet.

"That's a nice gun," the sheriff observed, turning it back and forth to look at every surface. "That's brand-spanking-new. Nickel-plated. A gun you're going to show off. Drug dealers and pimps, they like pretty guns like this."

"We already know Biggles was a drug dealer," Erin agreed.

The sheriff shrugged. "And how about that there wallet, Tom? Anything in there that would indicate who owned it? We're working on the assumption that it was Biggles's, but we want confirmation. There was a struggle out here. If Office Piper happened to drop it while he was making the arrest..."

"That's not Terry's," Erin objected.

The sheriff just looked at her and didn't argue. He knew very well that it wasn't Terry's; he was following procedure. Wearing gloves, Tom opened the billfold pocket gingerly, as if he expected it to be full of rattlesnake eggs. He whistled.

"Nice big wad of cash in here. Someone was making good money."

"I would expect so," Wilmot agreed.

"There's no I.D." He thumbed through the cash to look at the denominations and see if there was anything else folded in with it. "There's a card. A picture or somethin'."

Erin had been trying to stay back out of their way but, at Tom's words, she couldn't help stepping forward to get a look at the picture as Tom tugged it out. Tom looked at it blankly.

It was faded. It had been exposed to the moisture of the grass for almost a week. And maybe it was faded even before that. It looked like an inkjet printing on subpar photographic paper. Better than just printing on copy paper, but it wasn't thick or glossy and didn't hold the ink well.

A boy and a girl. Dressed up for a dance or nice restaurant or even church. Posed stiffly in a position that said, 'this is my boyfriend/girlfriend,' even though they seemed awkward and not quite sure how to hold each other. Erin squinted at it, trying to make out the faces. The boy certainly wasn't Bo Biggles. And Bo wasn't old enough to be a parent to a teen. So maybe a brother or uncle? Why would he be carrying their pictures around unless they were family?

Then Erin gasped as the light shifted and the faces morphed. She knew one of them. While the picture was unclear, she was almost sure she knew the boy.

Wilmot looked at her. He looked down at the picture, studying it thoughtfully. "You know who they are?"

"I'm not sure... the boy... it could be... but I'm not sure..."

"Who?"

"Jeremy. Jeremy Jackson."

Jeremy hadn't been in Bald Eagle Falls for long, so it was understandable that the sheriff and Tom didn't immediately recognize him in the picture. And it was a bad picture, so that even knowing Jeremy as she did, Erin still couldn't be sure it was actually him. But she directed the sheriff to Jeremy's home, a basement suite not far from Erin's home, which he shared with Rohilda Beaven when she was in town. Since it was a weekend and she didn't have any cases that demanded her attention out of town, Beaver was there when Jeremy answered the door.

Sheriff Wilmot turned to Erin. "You don't need to be here, Erin. Now that you've shown me where Jeremy lives, you can go on home."

Erin shook her head resolutely. "No. I'm staying."

Jeremy looked from the sheriff to Erin and back again. "What's going on? Is it something to do with Terry? Is everything okay?"

"This is not anything to do with Officer Piper. Perhaps tangentially, but not directly. Can I come in, please?" The sheriff angled his body forward so that his arm was already through the door and he was ahead of Erin, preventing her entrance. He didn't want her there, and he couldn't stop her if she was determined, but he was making it obvious that he didn't want her there.

"Uh, yeah. Come in." Jeremy opened the door the rest of the way and the sheriff entered, seeming to expand to fill the room. Erin had usually seen him as a bureaucrat. Someone who was required to do the paperwork and keep the town happy, but who wasn't directly investigating cases and making arrests. He wasn't a cop on the street like Terry, and usually let Terry take the lead on things, even though he was Terry's superior. But without Terry there to take charge, Sheriff Wilmot rose to the occasion. He looked confident and competent.

He nodded to Beaver and selected a kitchen chair, turning it around to straddle it backward to face where Jeremy would be when he sat back down on the couch with Beaver. Jeremy was still at the door, though, looking at Erin as if he didn't know what to do about her. Finally, he motioned for her to enter as well.

"What's this about, Erin? What's going on?"

Erin selected an easy chair and sat down, sitting forward rigidly rather than sinking back into it. She might have identified Jeremy in that picture, but she wasn't about to turn Jeremy over to the sheriff without at least trying to help him. Jeremy was too young to be left to handle an interview by someone like the sheriff on his own. With Beaver there, Erin probably wasn't needed, but she still worried that Beaver might have motives other than Jeremy's welfare.

Jeremy shut the door and returned to the couch with Beaver, sliding his arm around her and looking curiously at the sheriff. "Now maybe you can tell me what this is all about."

"You come from Moose River."

Jeremy raised an eyebrow. "Yes."

"And you are part of the Jackson family."

"Obviously. My name is Jeremy Jackson."

171

"And as part of the Jackson family, you were expected to take part in clan activities."

"I'm not in Moose River anymore. And I'm not taking direction from the clan. I left the family and the clan. I came here to be on my own, independent."

Erin knew that Beaver had helped him out significantly, with the bills and getting his apartment, if nothing else. She suspected there had been plenty else. Warnings to the clan to leave Jeremy alone. Finding him a job. Making sure that he was doing all the things he needed to do to keep himself safe and healthy. She was older than he was. Erin didn't have a problem with that. There was a lot more difference in age between Willie and Vic. But she felt it did create an imbalance. Beaver was so much more experienced and mature than Jeremy was and she probably helped him a lot more than was good for him.

"So you haven't had any contact with the Jackson clan."

"No."

"Did you know Mr. Biggles?"

"Did I know him?" People often repeated questions in order to give themselves longer to answer. Erin did it herself when she was stalling for time. "I knew... he was a member of the clan. I knew of him. Were we friends? No, never."

"You didn't do any jobs together?"

"Jobs? No. I didn't do any jobs with Biggles."

"What did you think of him?"

"I didn't think anything of him. He was a guy I knew of. I didn't spend any time thinking about him."

"You and he both came to Bald Eagle Falls at around the same time."

"I've been here a lot longer."

"When you left Moose River, he came here about the same time. Around the time Mr. Inglethorpe died."

Jeremy shrugged. "I wasn't exactly present for that. It was around then, I suppose."

"Which was the same time as Bo Biggles showed up."

"If you say so. I wasn't aware of what anyone else in the clan was doing at the time. That was the whole point in leaving Moose River. To leave all of that behind."

"So you claim you haven't had any interactions with Mr. Biggles."

Jeremy's eyes slid over to Beaver. She chewed on her gum, looking back at him and not giving him any advice on his answer.

"I don't think I said that," Jeremy said slowly.

"What interactions have you had with Biggles?"

"I… we weren't friends. And I wasn't in the clan."

"What interactions have you had?"

"I don't think I should answer that."

Sheriff Wilmot took the evidence bag containing the billfold out of his satchel and placed it on Jeremy's coffee table. "Is that your billfold, Mr. Jackson?"

"Jeremy. I don't like being called Mr. Jackson."

"Is that your billfold?"

"No. I've never seen that before."

"Do you mind showing me your billfold?"

"Well, I don't use one like that." Jeremy worked a wallet out of his back pocket. "There's mine. I don't really carry cash, you know. Just a few cards. I don't need a billfold."

"Your wallet only has cards in it."

Jeremy flipped it open, indicated the cards, opened the money pocket to show that it was empty, and shoved it back into his jeans pocket.

"Have you ever seen this picture before?" The sheriff had put the bad picture into an evidence bag and now placed it in front of Jeremy.

Jeremy peered at it, the color draining from his tanned face. "I don't know. It's pretty blurry."

Sheriff Wilmot was silent for a long few minutes, waiting for Jeremy to volunteer more. Cops were good at using silences. People liked to fill the void. They didn't like to sit in silence, thinking their own thoughts, facing their accusers, and not say anything. Jeremy did well to stay silent.

"Do you want to know what I think, Jeremy?" Sheriff Wilmot leaned forward, resting his arms on the back of the chair. His voice was friendly and nonaccusatory. Personable and inviting. "I think that something happened between you and Bo Biggles. I think that you went to meet with him. To confront him. And I think the two of you fought. A knock-down, drag-out fight. And I think you lost your billfold in that fight. The money is yours, the billfold is yours, and the picture is yours." The sheriff nudged the picture forward a little. "That is you, isn't it? So this was your billfold. And you lost it in that fight with Mr. Biggles."

Jeremy shifted. He squeezed Beaver tightly as if he were afraid she was going to get up and go somewhere else. And then he let her go and moved away from her an inch. He stared at the picture on the coffee table.

"I knew Biggles was here. And I wanted to protect my family. Vic and her friends here. Erin is family. And Terry. And Willie. I didn't want him expanding the drug trade in Bald Eagle Falls. If people want the hard stuff, they can go into the city. There are enough problems here with just alcohol and pot. I didn't want Biggles anywhere near my family. So I confronted him, told him to get out of town or I would make him leave."

"And how did you propose to do that?"

"I didn't have a plan. I mean, I just thought… if I told him I knew he was here and that I didn't want him in town, he'd go. And if he didn't, I'd… encourage him."

"You think he was going to listen to a teenage dropout of the clan? That you were going to be able to force him to leave town? That seems a little naive."

"Well, you ask Vic. I don't claim to always make the best decisions. Sometimes I… overestimate my abilities."

"So did Biggles agree to leave town?"

"Hell, no."

Beaver chuckled. Erin couldn't help smiling herself. Sheriff Wilmot nodded, showing not a crack in his facade.

"And when he said he wasn't going to leave, then what happened?"

"I swung for him. Figured I'd get in the first punch; that would give me a chance of beating him or at least convince him I was serious. But he was… well, he's bigger than me, and stronger, and I didn't exactly make out like a bandit. Before I knew what was happening, he was sitting on my chest laughing at me. I was embarrassed. He'd whipped me like an unweaned kitten. So when he let me up… I booked it out of there. I didn't realize I'd lost the billfold until later. I went back to look for it, but the vegetation is so dense out there…"

Erin nodded. She wouldn't have had much luck if it hadn't been for the crow spotting the shiny gun.

"Why didn't you come forward?" the sheriff asked. "You knew that Terry was being accused of beating Biggles up. And you knew that you'd had an altercation with him. You knew very well that at least some of those bruises might be attributable to your fight with him."

"Terry didn't beat Bo up. I knew he'd be cleared without me ever having to say anything. And my fight with Bo wasn't exactly successful. I didn't land more than a punch or two. So the bruises he had... maybe I gave him a black eye with that first punch, but after that? No."

"And what about the bruises on his throat. You put your hands around his neck? Tried to choke him either during the fight or while he was on top of you, trying to get him off? Or did you get an arm bar on him at some point during the struggle? People don't know how easily those blood vessels in the neck can be damaged."

"I didn't choke him."

"I'm supposed to believe that?"

"Maybe you don't. What's that to me?" Jeremy shrugged indifferently. But his life and liberty were in the balance, so of course he cared.

"What happened later?" Sheriff Wilmot asked.

"Later? Nothing happened later. Like I said, I realized I'd lost my bill-fold, so I looked for it. But I couldn't find it."

"There's a lot of money in this billfold. You're not making that kind of money acting as a security guard on the farm."

"So I do a few other jobs on the side. And I'm careful with my money." He made a gesture indicating his surroundings. "I don't spend a lot on my comfort."

"Maybe when you couldn't find your billfold, you decided to see whether Mr. Biggles had picked it up. You needed that money back. Maybe you owe someone. So you were desperate."

"I don't owe any leg-breakers."

"So you weren't at all upset about losing the billfold."

"Obviously I was upset. I went and looked for it. But I couldn't find it. And why would I go looking for Bo? If he had it, he wasn't going to give it back, and it wasn't like I could take it from him or convince him to give it to me."

"Maybe you went home to arm yourself. You planned to get the drop on him this time around. Not to rush into things quite so recklessly."

Jeremy shook his head. "He was arrested after our little dust-up. I'd have to wait until he was out of police custody before I could do anything."

"Or you could put on a mask, pick the back door, and confront him right in the police department interview room."

Jeremy raised his eyebrows. "What? Why would I do something like that? That's crazy. What, I'd go in there, start fighting with the guy, somehow get him into a chokehold, and no one would see or hear me? He wouldn't shout and attract attention? He'd just sit there quietly while I offed him?"

The sheriff looked over at Erin, bouncing those questions back to her. How likely was it that someone could have broken into the police department and killed Biggles without anyone having heard?

It made sense if it was a police officer who could do something while Biggles was still in cuffs. Everyone knew Terry was in the interview room with Biggles and would think nothing of it if they heard Biggles shouting. He'd resisted arrest, so a certain amount of combativeness would simply be ignored. Anyone who was concerned could look through the window, and there would be nothing unexpected about Terry questioning him or even manhandling him back into his chair. An outsider, though, would be a different story. They would have to get into the room without being seen. Choke Biggles out—or inject him or whatever it was that had actually killed him—and then get out of there without being seen. With no apparent protest or ruckus from Biggles.

It wasn't the most logical explanation. In fact, it sounded more and more farfetched, even though Erin had been convinced of the story. Peter had seen a man with a mask going into the Town Hall. It had to be someone who was trying to hide his identity. Was it one of the officers or staff? She shook her head, trying to wrap her mind around it.

"Did... the witness... have any description of the person who came out of there, other than the mask?" she asked Wilmot. "Like, size, clothes, that kind of thing."

Wilmot leaned back and stretched, turning his attention to Erin. He had, Erin suspected, decided that Jeremy was not a viable suspect in the murder of Biggles. It would have been too hard for him to do what Erin had suggested. Too dangerous. "Average height, slim build, blue jeans and t-shirt. Could be almost anyone. He couldn't say for sure whether it had been a man or a woman. He was focused on the mask."

"How soundproof are those rooms?" That, at least, could explain why the police hadn't heard a fight between Biggles and an intruder.

"They're not soundproof. The concrete construction and the door deaden some of the sound, but yelling and screaming; you would still hear something from our desks."

Jeremy looked at Erin. "You know it couldn't have been me, Erin. Why would I do something like that? I'm not that kind of guy. If I lost a stack of money during a fight… you really think I would sneak into police custody and kill the guy for it? Or out of revenge? That's not me."

No, but to protect his sister…?

"I never thought it was you. I never said that. The sheriff is just following up on leads."

He shook his head and leaned back, snuggling closer to Beaver again. "It wasn't me. Yeah, I lost my billfold, but that doesn't make me guilty of whatever conspiracy the police department is cooking up to cover their butts."

CHAPTER 30

*E*rin was glad that the sheriff hadn't had enough evidence to arrest Jeremy. She didn't think Jeremy had any reason to kill Biggles. As much as she sometimes wondered what Jeremy was up to, she didn't think he had it in him to sneak in and out of the police department like that. Something else had happened, and Erin wasn't sure what it was. She was trying to formulate a scenario in her mind that made sense.

She might be able to explain away the others in the police department not hearing any altercation between Biggles and his attacker. The room deadened the sound. Sheriff Wilmot said that they would still be able to hear any shouting at their desks but, with the tapping of computer keys, talking on phones, running the photocopier or printer and the coffee machine, there could definitely be enough noise to cover it up. Someone might have gotten a chokehold on him before he had a chance to shout.

But who would have the nerve to slip in and out of there?

Erin was distracted driving home. It was a good thing there wasn't any traffic to speak of. She arrived home safely and let herself in. She'd only been there for a few minutes when there was a knock on the back door. Erin was used to Vic and Willie using the back at will, and wasn't concerned when she heard a key in the door.

"Erin?" Vic called out. "You home?"

"I'm here." Erin walked down the hall to the kitchen and looked in at her. "What's up?"

"Oh, okay. I thought you were over at Terry's, because both your vehicles were gone earlier. Then when I saw the lights come on…"

"Yeah, it's just me."

"Where did Terry go? Did you have a fight? I thought you'd stay over there the weekend."

"He had to go to Moose River."

Vic frowned. "Moose River? Why?"

Willie came in the door behind her. "Everything okay?" He spotted Erin and nodded a greeting. "I told you she was back."

"Terry had to go to Moose River," Erin explained, catching him up.

Willie put his hand on Vic's waist to draw her closer, but she jerked away from his touch. He stood there looking at her in surprise. Erin stared into Vic's alarmed expression, unable to understand what she was worried about. "Everything is okay. He'll be back tonight or tomorrow. Jack Ward wanted to talk to him."

"About Bo Biggles?"

"I guess, yes. Something about him. He said there was some chatter about what had happened."

Vic looked at Willie. "I think… we should go talk to him."

"To Terry? He'll be back tonight, Erin said."

"To Terry… to Ward… I need to… I think…"

Willie raised an eyebrow. "If you want to, we can," he said agreeably. "But do you want to tell me what's going on? Do you know something that we should know?"

"You might want to stay here tonight," Erin cautioned. "You can always talk to Terry in the morning. Or call Jack Ward. But Jeremy—"

"Jeremy? What does he have to do with anything?"

"The sheriff was over there tonight. To find out what he'd had to do with Biggles. He's not there anymore, and he didn't arrest Jeremy or take him in for questioning. I just think… you might want to stick around just in case anything changes. Or maybe you should call Jeremy first to make sure everything is okay."

"Jeremy didn't have anything to do with Bo Biggles."

"Well, as it turns out, he and Biggles had a fight that day. Jeremy ended up dropping his wallet, with a picture of him with a girl in it, so the sheriff could trace it back to him." Erin didn't explain her involvement in the evening's events.

Vic opened her mouth. She looked at Erin, shaking her head. "What are you talking about? Jeremy had a fight...?"

Erin explained it the best she could, but Vic didn't seem to believe a word of it. Erin focused on the picture, trying to describe it to explain to Vic how everything had happened and how they had figured out that Jeremy had been there with Biggles. Vic sat down on one of the kitchen chairs, as white as a ghost.

"We have to go to Moose River."

Willie tried to calm her, rubbing her shoulders and back. "We can go to Moose River if you want," he assured her. "It's going to be a bit late to talk to Jack Ward, though. By the time we get there, he's going to be home in bed."

"I don't understand," Erin told Vic, trying to read her face. "Why do you think Jeremy is lying about the fight with Biggles? He lost his wallet there."

"It wasn't his wallet. Jeremy doesn't carry cash, especially like that. Where would he get that kind of money?"

"He didn't explain, but he confirmed it was his. And he had a picture of him and a girl in it."

"That wasn't a picture of Jeremy."

Erin and Willie both just stared at Vic, trying to understand how she could know that and why she was so upset.

"I know because it wasn't a picture of Jeremy. It was a picture of me."

CHAPTER 31

*E*rin blinked slowly, comprehension dawning. Not a picture of Jeremy, but of James, Vic's identity before she had transitioned. The boys in the Jackson family all had a strong family resemblance. Erin couldn't yet tell Joseph and Daniel apart.

"That was you," Erin repeated.

Vic nodded her agreement.

"But that wasn't your wallet."

"No. It was his. Biggles's."

Willie's massaging hands stopped moving. "Why would Biggles have a picture of you in his wallet?"

"I don't know why he had it in his wallet. It was Theresa's."

"Who is Theresa?" Erin asked.

"The girl I was with. Bo's cousin. Crazy Theresa Franklin."

"You dated Bo's cousin. But why would he have a picture of the two of you?"

"He had a thing about her. It was Theresa's picture. He must have taken it when she wasn't around. Because you can bet that if she had been there, she would have killed him for even touching it."

They all just looked at each other. None of them put their thoughts into words.

Finally, Vic said, "We need to go to Moose River. I need to talk to her."

"You should call Jack Ward, give him a heads-up," Willie advised.

"I need to talk to her first."

"I don't think that's smart. Tell him first. Even though I can't see how she could have had anything to do with her cousin's death, you don't just go talk to someone you think might have been involved in another person's death. That's like some too-stupid-to-live character on TV."

Vic covered her face with her hands. Erin didn't say anything, waiting for Vic to work it through and make a decision. She understood Vic's wish to confront Theresa, but Willie was right; if Vic thought that Theresa had anything at all to do with Bo's death, they needed to be smart about it.

"Fine," Vic agreed. She pulled out her phone and tapped through several screens. "I don't have his number. And there's nothing on the website but a general number. Their switchboard is going to be closed, and no one is going to agree to wake him up because some girl in Bald Eagle Falls thinks she knows something about Theresa Franklin."

"I think I've still got it." Erin checked her contacts and found Ward's cell number. She handed her phone over to Vic.

Vic tapped the number and waited. It rang and rang and, eventually, Erin heard the tinny sound of Jack Ward's outgoing voicemail message. Vic sighed and shook her head. "Detective Ward, I don't know if you remember me. I work with Erin Price in Bald Eagle Falls. This is her number. I wanted to talk to you about Theresa Franklin; I think she might have had something to do with Bo Biggles's death here... maybe. Or maybe just knows something about it. I don't know. She knows him. I'm going to come out there. Give me a call, and we can meet, or I can give you some more details. Okay."

She hung up and handed the phone back to Erin. Erin decided to see if Terry was still meeting with Ward or could give them any information about where he was. If they were still meeting, then Erin would have expected Ward to answer his phone when he saw her number, but he hadn't. She tried Terry's cell phone, but it rang through to voicemail just as Ward's had.

"Hi, Terry. Listen, Vic needs to talk to Jack Ward, so I'm just wondering whether you are still meeting, or if you have a way to reach him. It's about someone who might have had something to do with Bo Biggles's death... but I'm not sure how. Anyway. Call back. Me or Vicky."

She also hung up. They looked at each other.

"Let's go," Vic said. She put her hand on Willie's arm. "We'll use your truck."

~

"So…" They were on their way, and it was Willie who broke the silence, eager to find out more details about Bo Biggles and Theresa Franklin and why she needed to talk to Theresa so urgently. "How long since you've seen this Theresa?"

Vic stared out the window into the blackness of the night and the glittering stars overhead. Erin could see Vic's reflection in the glass and saw her biting her lip.

"I haven't seen her since I left home."

Willie nodded. "Heard from her at all?" he asked casually.

"She started sending me letters. A couple of months ago. She's still… she's been through some stuff and is feeling nostalgic about when we were together." Vic shook her head, still not looking at Willie. "We weren't even together for very long, and it was pretty… awkward and innocent. Kids going out to the movies together. Listening to music. Walking to the ice cream store. I was still trying to figure out how to deal with my gender identity. How to live with myself. What kind of relationship I wanted. We were both just experimenting."

"But now, what… she wants to get back together?"

"I don't know what she wants. She wants to see me, yes. Maybe to see if there are any sparks. But I don't know exactly what. If she's expecting things to be like they were back then." Vic gave a sharp laugh. "I'm not even the same person as I was."

"Does she know about your transition?"

Erin remembered the letter Vic had received earlier in the week. It had been addressed to Victoria, not to James.

"Yeah. She knew before she started writing. I don't know who she talked to; my folks are doing their best to keep it a secret. They just tell people that I ran away. I think Mom is still hoping that one of these days I'll have an epiphany and realize that I want to go back home and live out my life as a boy. And then I'll be able to slide right back into my old place in the community."

"But this Theresa is still interested in you."

Vic turned her head to study Willie. "Is that such a surprise to you? She likes me for myself, not for my gender."

"I didn't mean it that way. Just that… it would be hard for a lot of people to make that shift. Not just about you, but about herself and what attracts her."

"Like you did?"

"Yes. Like I did." He put his hand on her knee. "Sometimes, life surprises us."

Vic turned back away from him, but she put her hand over his. "Yeah, she's still interested. But I'm not interested in a relationship with her. Things weren't good the first time around and I'm already in a committed relationship."

Erin waited a few minutes before breaking the silence. "What went wrong the first time around? I know you were just kids, so it's understandable that it wasn't a long-term relationship. But you make it sound like… maybe Theresa has some issues."

"She wasn't called Crazy Theresa for nothing. She's not exactly stable."

And they were going to meet with her. Not the smartest thing Erin could think of to do. But they would first talk to Ward and Terry.

"Do you think that Theresa had something to do with Biggles's death?" Willie asked.

"I wasn't there, so I can't say. Maybe she had nothing to do with it, and it was just an accident or natural death. But him having her picture… the possibilities just make me cold all over." Vic shuddered. "I don't know Bo. I never met him. But she's mentioned him in her letters, and I remember her talking about her cousin when we were together. How mean he was toward her. I thought at the time… he must have a crush on her. But she didn't like him. She's not one of those girls who's attracted to someone who bullies them."

"Do you think Biggles knew who you were?" Erin asked. Bo had the picture with him for a reason. Had he recognized Vic as the former James Jackson? If he saw Vic as a rival, then showing up in town and especially his hanging around outside of Erin's—and Vic's—property took on an even more sinister meaning. Maybe he wasn't there for revenge against the women who had brought down the clan's drug trade in Bald Eagle Falls or to start up his own business dealing to the high school students. Maybe his whole reason for being there was to get rid of a romantic rival.

"I think so. This guy… I never met him, but I remember Theresa telling me the crap he would pull. If he was twisted enough to think that he had a better chance at Theresa if he got me out of the way… he would."

Erin thought about Jeremy and Terry. Both of them had been involved in an altercation with Bo Biggles, if Jeremy had been telling the truth about his encounter and not just making it up to protect his sister. If one of them had thought that Biggles was a threat to Vic or Erin… the idea that Terry or Jeremy might have had something to do with Bo Biggles's death was suddenly not so far-fetched. They had a solid motive.

Erin found herself hoping against hope that Theresa *had* been the culprit.

~

It seemed like the trip to Moose River took much longer than it should have. But they were finally there. Vic gave Willie directions through the semi-rural area to Theresa's family home. It was not quite a farmhouse, but not quite in town either.

Erin tried several times to reach Ward or Terry, but neither of them would answer their phones. Erin's stomach was getting tighter, forming a heavy, solid ball that ached and pulsed with her heartbeats.

"I don't think this is a good idea," Willie opined again. "We should wait until the morning. After we have a chance to talk to Jack Ward or Terry."

Vic shook her head. "Theresa isn't going to do anything to hurt me," she pointed out. "That would undo everything she's been trying to build up between us. If she wants me to be interested in her, she can't do anything to push me away. That means she can't do anything to either of you. I'm not going to ask her whether she killed her cousin. Or any other questions that are going to get her wound up. Just casual chit chat with an old friend."

Willie shook his head. He left Erin and Vic in the truck, telling them to stay put, and got out to reconnoiter. But as he got closer to the house to peek in the windows, motion-triggered floodlights came on, turning the darkness into midday and making them all cover their eyes.

Vic swore. Erin held her palms over her eyes, waiting for them to stop burning. It was a minute or two before she was able to scrub away the tears and squint around at the others and their surroundings.

Theresa stood in the doorway of the house, looking down at them from three steps above them, with a big weapon cradled in one arm. It looked like something that a soldier would carry. She was a young woman, like Vic, with a generous mouth and mouse-brown hair. She wasn't unattractive, but not a memorable beauty either.

"Identify yourselves," she ordered in a tough, flat voice.

Willie held his hands above his head, still pushing his face into his arm to shade his eyes from the blinding light. "We're friends," he said gruffly. "My name is Willie."

"Well, Willie, since I have no idea who you are, I highly doubt you're my friend. Plan on keeping your hands up nice and high."

Erin looked over at Vic, waiting for her to introduce herself. Theresa wouldn't know Erin from Adam. The only person she was likely to recognize or care about was Vic. It didn't matter who the rest of them were.

Vic was looking directly at Theresa, no longer covering or shading her eyes. She didn't introduce herself, and it dawned on Erin that she was waiting for Theresa to recognize her without prompting.

"What are you doing coming onto my property in the middle of the night? You get lost?" Theresa demanded.

"We're not lost," Vic said. "Why don't you show us some of that famous hospitality, Tess?"

Theresa stared at Vic. "Get out of the car."

Both Vic and Erin got out of the car, moving slowly, keeping their hands visible. There was no sudden exclamation of recognition. Maybe Theresa had known who they were all along. She motioned them into the house with the barrel of her gun. Erin wished Theresa would stop waving it around and just put it down. She didn't like having guns pointed at her.

Willie entered the house first, his hands still up, looking around carefully. Erin knew he would be thinking about means of escape, analyzing all of the ways in and out and what was on hand that they might be able to use. Having Theresa holding the gun on them was not conducive to getting friendly or running away. So much for not being in any danger from the woman.

Crazy Theresa, indeed.

CHAPTER 32

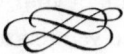

$\mathcal{E}$rin paused, waiting for Vic to enter the house ahead of her. But Theresa motioned Erin forward with the gun, impatient for her to get inside. Erin turned to look at Vic, and Vic nodded that she should go in next. Vic would bring up the rear.

Did Vic have her gun? She was almost always armed, even when she popped over in her pajamas to see Erin. Erin couldn't see a holster, but that didn't mean that Vic wasn't wearing one somewhere. And Willie? Erin didn't think he usually carried a gun, but had he decided to slip one into a hidden pocket or holster before they got on their way? Erin would feel better knowing that they had more guns on their side.

Erin entered the house and, instead of making herself at home in the living room, turned to watch Vic and make sure she was safe. When Vic got to the doorstep, Theresa stepped in front of her, blocking her, the big gun held between the two of them and her body uncomfortably close to Vic's.

"Hello, Victoria," Theresa said softly.

"Long time, no see, Tess."

"What are you doing here?"

"I just wanted to talk. You said you wanted to see me again, didn't you? So… here I am. Are you going to let me in?"

Theresa remained there for several long seconds before finally stepping back far enough for Vic to enter. Theresa kicked the door shut, the slam making them all jump.

Theresa motioned for Erin and Vic to take seats on a worn couch draped with a hand-stitched quilt, which they did. Willie sat in an easy chair. Erin remembered Sheriff Wilmot interviewing Jeremy on his couch not many hours previous. She wished that he was the one standing over them instead of the unstable woman with a big gun.

"To what do I owe the pleasure of your visit?" Theresa demanded.

"Just what I said. You said you wanted to see me again."

"A normal person calls and sets up a time. They don't just show up in the middle of the night."

"There seems to be something wrong with our phones tonight. Maybe the satellites are having some technical problems. Everything seems to go through to voicemail. Did your phone ring?"

Theresa just sneered.

"So…" Vic looked for an appropriate conversation starter. "You mentioned your cousin in your letters. Bo Biggles. Remembering how he used to treat you. I wondered whether…"

"*Used* to treat me? Not used to. Treated me every day of my life." She smiled, showing teeth gritted tightly together. "Until he died."

That answered the question as to whether she knew Bo Biggles was dead. They at least didn't have to break the news to her. Finding out whether she'd had a hand in it was another story. Erin let her shoulder brush against Vic's, trying to show her moral support. But Theresa's eyes picked up on even the very slight contact.

"So this is the new girlfriend I've been hearing all about."

Erin's jaw dropped and she couldn't collect the words to protest Theresa's categorization of their relationship. Vic's eyes got bigger, maybe not as shocked as Erin, but still surprised. She looked automatically over to Willie. Theresa followed her gaze.

"All three of you?" she sneered. "Whatever happened to your good Christian values, Victoria?"

"No." Vic shook her head. "I told you. Willie and I are together. Not Erin. We're just friends. We work together."

"Yeah, I didn't believe you when you told me then, either. You like girls, not boys. I remember. You can't wipe out all the time you and I spent together."

"I was…" Vic swallowed and tried again. "I was trying to do what everyone expected. What everyone said was the right thing. I wasn't… living true to myself yet. I'm sorry… if that hurts you. I didn't want to make you feel bad."

"Bo told me about the two of you keeping time. Laughing and calling me names because you decided to start dressing like a girl. Making all kinds of disgusting comments about you and her, or about me."

Theresa's eyes burned brightly with fury. She didn't seem to be aware of the gun in her hands, handling it as casually as if it were a toy or book. Erin watched every time the gun shifted. Willie too had his eyes fastened on it. Vic wasn't paying any attention to the weapon, caught up in the memories Theresa brought back and the accusations she made. Erin hated the pain that recounting the past always brought to Vic's eyes. But it had been Vic's choice to confront Theresa. Maybe she needed to face her to put that part of her past behind her. Whether Theresa was going to let that happen or not, Erin didn't know.

She had a sneaking suspicion that Theresa didn't have plans to allow any of them to leave the house.

Ever.

"There's nothing wrong with you," Vic told Theresa. "It doesn't matter what Bo said. You know he's been like that since you were a kid. Always saying stupid, hurtful stuff to you, trying to get your attention because he liked you. He's one of those guys who always has to be mean to get a reaction."

"You have a filthy mind, you know that? You think I wanted to get together with my cousin? He was vile. We were like brother and sister. I wouldn't have touched him with a ten-foot pole."

"I didn't mean you wanted to get together. I just meant Bo hurt you with all the stuff he said. But there's nothing wrong with you. None of the stuff he said was true."

Theresa shifted the gun in her hands restlessly. Erin wished she would fidget with something other than the huge weapon.

"And what if I liked you?" Theresa asked. "There's gotta be something wrong with me if I liked you."

Vic dropped her eyes. "You didn't do anything wrong. We were both trying to figure things out. I'm sorry for hurting you."

"You kicked me to the curb. You led me on. Acted like you liked me.

And then you didn't want to be with me anymore. Wouldn't return my calls. Wouldn't even look at me when we passed in the halls at school. Why?"

Erin expected Vic to try to explain to her again how she had been trying to sort out her own feelings about herself and her relationships. But Vic chewed on her lip, not answering.

Willie coughed. Everyone jumped and looked at him. Willie covered his mouth. "Sorry. Just came out of nowhere." He cleared his throat and coughed a little more. "You must have a dog," he said to Theresa. "They always get me choked up. Could I help myself to a glass of water? I think I have an antihistamine." He patted his pockets.

Erin and Vic stared at him. Willie was not allergic to dogs. He wasn't allergic to anything and certainly didn't carry antihistamines around with him.

Theresa made an impatient motion toward the kitchen, which flowed into the front room of the little house. It was more of a galley, not a big kitchen like the one in the farmhouse Vic had grown up in, where her mother could do all of the cooking for a big family, as well as canning and putting up preserves.

Willie got to his feet and shuffled into the kitchen. They all watched him as he got a glass out of one of the cupboards. He managed to find the fictitious antihistamine pill in his pants pocket and mimed popping it into his mouth, washing it down with a couple of gulps of water. Theresa decided he wasn't trying to rush her or get away, and her eyes went back to Vic.

Willie made a motion to Erin, commanding her attention. He walked from the kitchen back to his previous seat, dragging one foot a little as he walked. Was he hurt? Had his leg fallen asleep while he sat there or was the recently healed break bothering him? Erin was looking down at his feet, and when he stepped from the tiled area to the rug, she realized that he'd slid something across the floor with his foot. Something small and shiny, like a quarter.

He settled into his chair and didn't look back at it or her. He wiped his forehead like he was sweating excessively. "Dogs will do it to me every time."

Oddly, Theresa didn't confirm or deny whether there was a dog around. Erin looked down at the little silver circle. The size of a dog tag. Like K9's.

CHAPTER 33

*E*rin didn't gasp aloud, but she was sure it was clear to Willie that she had just made the connection.

Ward had asked Terry to go to Moose River to talk to him about rumors and developments. Neither of them was answering his phone. Theresa had been expecting Vic, ready at the door with her big gun. And there was something that looked like a dog tag on the floor.

Had Terry and Ward ended up going to Theresa's house to talk to her about Bo Biggles? Maybe they thought that she was just a family member, someone good to bounce ideas off of, not realizing that she might be complicit in his death. If she had taken them by surprise, was is possible that she could have subdued Terry, Ward, and K9 all by herself? One woman against two trained cops and a dog?

She had a bigger gun. She probably had the element of surprise. Vic called her Crazy Theresa, suggesting she might just try something as reckless as attacking two police officers without provocation.

Erin tried to look casual and unemotional about the discussion. As if she weren't threatened by Theresa's weapon. She looked around what she could see of Theresa's house for any sign of blood or a violent confrontation. She couldn't see any blood, bullet holes, or overturned or damaged furniture. Just the broken dog tag, which could have belonged to any dog or cat and didn't prove that there was anything out of place.

She sniffed the air, trying to ignore the dust and farm smells. Was there a whiff of dog? Of Terry's cologne? It could have been her imagination, just the power of suggestion. They might have been there to talk to Theresa and then left. Their cars were not parked in the driveway in front of the house. K9 might have lost a tag there innocently, just a loose ring that had snagged on something.

"Why did you come here?" Theresa demanded, casting her eyes around the room in agitation. "I asked you before and you wouldn't come. So why now?"

Vic shifted in her seat, her knee knocking against Erin's. "Bo had your picture in his wallet. Our picture." She rubbed her forehead and looked at Theresa. "You know, the one of you and me."

Theresa swore. She paced across the floor, looking down at the hallway toward the back of the house. "I knew he had something to do with it disappearing. He must have broken into the house while I was out on a job. And of course, the clan wouldn't do anything about it because it's an old boys' network and they protect their own. Who cares about a woman, even if she is an asset to the clan? Some two-bit drug dealer is more important than a woman, even one who—" Theresa cut herself off. "Why did you leave Moose River and the clan? You should have stayed."

"I couldn't stay there. Not the way my parents reacted when I came out."

Theresa shrugged. "Your parents. Big deal. It's not like they're high-ranking. You could still have stayed. The clan would have taken care of you, even with your…" Theresa made a gesture toward Vic, "transformation."

"I wasn't interested in being part of the clan."

"You always talked about it when we were together. How you were going to be one of the top guys. You were better with a gun than any of the other boys."

"Yeah, but you gotta do a lot more than shoot targets if you're going to be a soldier with the clan." Vic glanced fleetingly at Willie, who had lived to regret signing on with his clan. "I was scared. I was trying to figure things out, find my own place. And the clan… wasn't it."

Theresa snorted. "You should have stayed." She paced back and forth across the living room again. "You should have stayed with me and the clan and not changed who you were."

"I didn't change who I was. I stopped pretending to be someone else."

"You and me could have been together. Bo would have left me alone if you had stuck around. But since I'm not with anyone, he still thought he had a chance." She growled to herself. "Breaking into my house! Stealing that picture! Why would he take it away? It didn't mean anything to him."

Vic shrugged and shook her head. Theresa scowled at Erin and kicked her foot as she paced across the living room again. "What's your problem, milquetoast? Cat got your tongue? If you've got something to say, then say it!"

Erin sat bolt upright, startled and instantly defensive, holding up her hands against a further attack. "I... I thought maybe he had the picture to compare it to Vic... to see if it was really her."

Theresa nodded jerkily. She bared her teeth at Vic in a crazed smile. "Well, now you don't have to worry who he might show that picture to, do you? He can't show it to anybody anymore."

"Uh..." Vic swallowed and nodded. "No."

"We can do whatever we want. It doesn't matter what anyone else has to say."

"Bo was never in control of that. He wasn't the one making the decisions."

"No. That was you, wasn't it?" Theresa's voice was a hard, angry growl. "You were the one making that call!"

She raised the gun up over Vic suddenly, butt down like she was going to use it to bludgeon Vic in the head. Erin shrieked and dove over Vic, trying to block the falling blow and to knock the gun away or wrench it from Theresa's hands. The stock of the weapon hit her in the shoulder, causing a blast of pain that made her see stars. Erin cried out, but kept her body between Theresa and Vic.

"Leave her be!" she shouted, ripping her throat raw with the force of it. "You don't have any right!"

"I knew you two were lovers!" Theresa accused, as if Erin protecting Vic were proof of their relationship. "Bo said you were, and I denied it, but I knew it was true! It was the only reason you would stay away from me, the only reason you wouldn't come back to me when I *begged* you!"

She raised the gun to hit Erin again, her face red and contorted with rage. Erin flinched, trying to keep her eyes open to avoid the worst of the blow, but bracing for the pain.

Something stopped the descent of the gun, and then it was jerked out of

Theresa's hands. Willie held it in both hands and used it to shove Theresa down, so she toppled into a heap with Erin and Vic.

Erin tried to untangle the three of them, to get Theresa sitting between her and Vic. A couple of times, Theresa tried to bounce to her feet, only to be shoved roughly back down again by Willie. She finally stopped and sat there, simmering, staring up at Willie with hate-filled eyes.

"Why don't you get out of here? You're trespassing. Get out of here and don't come back. And you!" Theresa looked at Vic. "I can't believe you'd let him treat me that way! You think that's any way to treat a woman? These clansmen are all the same! Old goats who think they've got the right to trample over women. You were better. At least, one time I thought you were. Now you're..." Theresa's face twisted in a snarl. "Now you're just going to sit there and pretend to be a lady."

Vic's eyes blazed. Erin hadn't ever seen her so angry. "And you're just the same as *you've* always been. So full of violence and hate... I couldn't deal with it. Even while I was struggling to figure out how to live my life, I knew how I didn't want to live it. I didn't want to live it like you! Or with someone like you."

"You loved me! You said so!"

"I was fifteen! That's what I was supposed to say. But it wasn't love. It was just the thrill of having a pretty girl pay attention to me. Just like you never loved me. You wanted the rep of dating one of the Jackson boys. It never worked between us. It never felt right."

"You're lying! You just don't want your new girlfriend and boyfriend to know the truth."

Vic took a deep breath and let it out. She looked at Willie, but didn't turn her head to look at Erin; to do so would mean she had to look at Theresa.

Willie was the one holding the gun so, for the first time, they had the upper hand. He wasn't pointing it at Theresa, but he wasn't relaxed, either. He held it balanced in his arm as if he were intimately familiar with it. Erin closed her eyes and tried not to think about him working for the Dyson clan. That was in the past. He was no longer a soldier for them. And his experience was beneficial to them. If they had all been as inexperienced with guns as Erin was, they would have been in big trouble. Erin would never have dared to grab the weapon from Theresa.

Theresa was breathing hard. She stared up at Willie, seething. "I told you to get out of my house."

"First, you're going to answer a few questions."

"I don't have to answer your questions."

He raised one eyebrow. None of them moved. Theresa looked back and forth at Vic and Erin, sitting on either side of her, like an animal trying to avoid being trapped. But they already had the upper hand. Willie was the one with the gun.

"You don't want to tell us what happened with Bo?" Willie asked. "I thought you would want to brag about pulling that off and getting away with it."

CHAPTER 34

*T*heresa considered this, eyes glittering. She started to smile again.

"You want to know about Bo?" she repeated. "I can tell you all about Bo. Everything you want to know. First, you put down the gun."

"I don't think so."

"Then I'm not going to tell you."

Willie shrugged. He stood there like a statue. He didn't fidget. He didn't pace as Theresa had done. He was like a rock. Granite. Theresa licked her lips a few times. She looked around the room. She couldn't keep still and keep her mouth shut.

"Bo's been calling me ever since he went back to Bald Eagle Falls. Calling me every day. Ten times a day, sometimes. Telling me all about what he sees in that stupid little town. About all the whispers and rumors about the two of them." Theresa jerked her head in Vic's direction. "Always ragging on me about how James switched teams, and now I'm in love with a girl, calling me all kinds of disgusting names. And of course, telling me how I need a real man in my life again, and how he can show me..."

She made a face and shook her head, looking absolutely revolted. She swore.

"Like I've never been with anyone else." Theresa looked at Vic. "I've been with plenty of other guys. All of them better than you."

"Good."

Theresa jabbed at her with an elbow, angry. Willie touched the muzzle of the gun to her shoulder and pushed her back. Theresa stopped trying to hurt Vic and was still, lapsing back to a simmer.

"So he's been harassing you," Willie summed up. "And you just took it."

"I didn't just take it!"

"I didn't see you in Bald Eagle Falls doing anything about it. You didn't call the police or get a restraining order. You just took it."

Theresa's jaw clenched. "I did not." She leaned forward slightly. "He keeps talking about how he's going to tell everyone about it. He's going to tell everyone in Bald Eagle Falls that *Victoria* is really a boy, and he's going to tell everyone who knows me that I'm crushing on a girl." Theresa was spitting the words out in staccato. "He's going to tell my parents. The clan. He's going to spread it all over Moose River. He's going to tell any guy I want to get together with. He's gonna mess things up so bad for me that I'll have to leave."

She shook her head, throat working and lips quivering. Erin couldn't help feeling sorry for her. She might be crazy, she might even be a killer, but Erin empathized with all that Bo Biggles had put her through.

"He's been after me since I was a little girl! The guy's ten years older than me and when I was little—" A stream of tears leaked from the corner of one eye.

Theresa suddenly jumped to her feet, going straight for Willie, crazed, heedless of the gun. Erin gasped and tried to grab her, worried about what would happen if Willie reacted too quickly. Vic also tried to grab Theresa to pull her back, managing to catch the back of her shirt and to slow her down. Between the three of them, they managed to throw her back to the couch and pin her there. Willie stared down at her. "Do we have to tie you up?"

"You think I care? You're nothing. You think you're a tough clansman? You're just like all of the other men around here; you haven't got a clue what I can do! You haven't got one inkling of what I could do to you!"

Willie shook his head. He jerked his chin at Erin. "Go see what she's got in the kitchen. String, duct tape, wire, whatever. I don't want her going after one of us every thirty seconds."

Erin nodded and went into the kitchen. She looked through the drawers for anything that would be helpful. She couldn't help inventorying Theresa's kitchen as she did so. Theresa didn't do much cooking, and probably no baking at all. It was evident by the paucity of tools and dishes in the kitchen that she mostly got take out or warmed food up in the microwave. The oven had probably never been used since she had moved into the house.

She shook her head at herself for being distracted by kitchen implements—or the lack thereof—and kept looking through the drawers until she found twine from a hardware store. She took it back over to where Theresa was sitting on the couch.

"Do her up tight," Willie warned.

Erin did her best to tie Theresa's wrists and ankles securely, using the entire ball of twine. She got back to her feet and looked around.

"So, what did you do to Bo, Theresa?" Willie prompted again.

Theresa laughed darkly. "The dog calls me after he's been arrested. He needs to get a message to the clan. He needs to make sure they know where he is and what's going on so they can get him out. They can send a lawyer, or they can break him out when he gets transported, or find some other way to get him loose so that he can get out of Bald Eagle Falls. He's decided he doesn't really *like* it there," she said with heavy sarcasm.

"He called you to get him out," Vic said in disbelief.

"Not me, because what am I? I'm just a girl. A little girl he's been messing around with. He wants me to be his messenger and get the big guns on the case. He thinks he's hot stuff and the clan won't want to lose him. He's *nothing*. Nobody cares about him. His own mother never cared about him. Why was he always staying with us? She didn't want him around, and she took off after some out-of-state slimeball by the time he was fifteen. Didn't care, just left him behind."

Erin did not want to feel sorry for Bo Biggles. No matter what had happened to him in life, he hadn't tried to stay on the straight and narrow. He hadn't tried to make the right choices and to treat people around him with respect. He'd decided to do the opposite, treating everyone else with the same hate and neglect that he'd been treated with.

People could still choose.

There was a noise outside. Everyone froze. Willie lifted the gun and pointed it in the direction the noise had come from. Erin was at the door in an instant, not sure what she was going to see or what she was going to do about it, but how much worse could it be than crazy Theresa Franklin? Unless it was the big guns in the Jackson clan. That might not be such a good thing either.

"Erin!" Willie warned in a whisper.

She looked back at him as she reached for the doorknob.

"Be careful. Stand to the side of the door when you open it." His eyes flicked to the living room window. "The floodlights are still on, so you won't be blind and backlit, but be careful. We don't know who's out there."

"It could be Ward or his men. Or it could be nothing, just an animal."

Willie gave a nod of agreement. Erin turned the handle and gave the door a gentle tug open. Vic was out of the couch as well, ducking below the level of the window and making her way toward Erin.

They all waited. Erin didn't hear anything else, so she took a quick peek around the wall and through the open door to catch a glimpse of the intruder. Maybe it was just the wind. All she saw was Willie's truck, still sitting in the floodlit yard where they had left it. She didn't see any movement. No other vehicle. She stayed pasted against the wall where she was and looked at Willie, who had a better viewing angle but was farther back. He shook his head. Crouching and moving to the side, he approached the door as well.

"I don't see anything."

"Something blew over and made a noise. That's all. We're just all jumpy."

Erin peered around the doorway and took a longer look outside. She shook her head. She looked at Willie. "If Terry was here with K9 and maybe with Ward... where are they now? Did they just leave?"

"If she didn't give away that she knew anything about Bo's death, then maybe they did. Left here, stopped at a diner to eat. Somewhere there isn't good cell reception."

"We should call them again. Now that we know..." Erin looked over at Theresa, sitting tied up on the couch. "We *do* know, don't we? She did it. She's the one who killed Bo."

"We still don't have proof, but I think it's a foregone conclusion."

"She hated Bo," Vic said. "And now he's gone. She was the one who knew where he was. He probably told her all about the layout so the clan would know how to get in and out. He never thought she would come after him."

Erin shuddered. Would Theresa really have been that gutsy? Or that careful? She hadn't shown herself to be someone who had the best judgment or control of her feelings. Erin could see her killing Bo in a fit of anger, filling him full of holes with that big gun of hers, but a cold-blooded, planned attack?

"We should call Terry again," she suggested. The air coming in the door was cool, and she tried to rub away the goosebumps that popped out on her skin. "If they were just out of range for a while, maybe they're back now and we can get them."

"Yeah, try again," Vic agreed.

Erin took out her phone and tapped on the icon for Terry's cell phone. A picture of K9.

Somewhere in the back of the house, a phone started to ring.

CHAPTER 35

*E*rin couldn't breathe. Her throat swelled up so suddenly, with such a hard lump in the middle of it, she was sure she was having an anaphylactic reaction to something and was going to die. She and Willie and Vic all looked at each other in horror.

Erin slammed the front door shut. Even though Willie was closer to the back of the house, she dashed past him toward the bedrooms like he was standing still.

"Erin, no. Someone else could be back there. We don't know if Theresa was alone!"

She ignored Willie, following the tug at her heart. If anything happened to Terry while they were sitting there in the house talking with Crazy Theresa, she would never forgive herself. There was no way that he would have just sat quietly in the back of the house while he knew she was there and wouldn't try to help her. Only if he were incapacitated, hurt, or dead. And she couldn't bear to think of that.

She opened the first door she came to and groped for the light switch. There was nothing out of the ordinary there. Just a bedroom, no Terry and no Frank Ward tied up with the same twine that Erin had found in the kitchen drawer. She moved left to the bedroom at the end of the hall. That would be the larger one, the master bedroom.

It was a mess. Clothes draped over every piece of furniture, even over lampshades, all kind of clutter and junk on every dresser, side table, and dressing table. But no bodies. She turned to double back and check the other rooms, but Willie had turned right, so he was there ahead of her. He stood in the third bedroom door, frozen. Erin hurried after him, bumping into Vic in her rush to get there. She squeezed in beside Willie, afraid of what she was going to see, but she had to see it anyway.

But as with the other two rooms, there was no one there. No Terry, No Ward, no stranger holding them at gunpoint. Erin followed Willie's eyes and the sound of the ringing phone. There were two phones on a messy desk along with keys, wallets, and other pocket litter. Erin swallowed and looked around.

"Where are they?"

Willie shook his head. "I don't know. Not in here. But they were here." Willie turned slightly and grasped Erin's hand, turning it slightly to look at the face of her phone and tap the red button to hang up the call. "Try 9-1-1. I don't know if they have 9-1-1 service out here, but that's the first recourse. Stay here."

He checked the bathroom at the end of the hall, but there were no bloody bodies stowed in the dirty white bathtub. Erin tried to get a connection to 9-1-1 on her phone without any luck. She tried accessing the internet for a police phone number, but couldn't get internet access either.

She could hear Willie moving through the house again, making a more careful search the second time. He murmured a few words to Vic. Erin followed the sounds of their voices as they met up in the front room again.

"There's no basement or cellar," Willie advised. "That means we're going to have to check outside, and it's pitch black beyond the floodlights. You didn't get anything?"

"No."

"Do you know the number for the police department?" Willie asked Vic. They had both grown up there, but apparently, neither one of them had been forced to memorize the number for the police department. Maybe they had 9-1-1 service in the houses they had grown up in. Or maybe they had just had the phone numbers written beside the wired phone for reference.

Erin turned to her contacts. She had Jack Ward's cell number, but did she have a landline? A switchboard number? Something that would be monitored after hours so that units could be dispatched? There were two other numbers. Erin tried the first one as she followed Willie and Vic to the door. Vic flipped on a series of other switches, lighting up the entire perimeter of the house as bright as noonday.

Erin blinked at the bright lights. Grass rustled and eyes reflected in the darkness past the circles of light the floods created as wild animals fled.

"It's like Neyland Stadium," Vic said in wonder, shading her hand against the brightness of the lights. "Talk about security lights."

Erin almost forgot the phone she was holding to her ear until it rang through to voicemail and she heard Jack Ward's gruff voice telling her to leave a message and he would get back to her.

If he could.

If he were still alive.

Erin stepped out the door with Willie and Vic. Willie had the big gun to his shoulder and swiveled around like an army scout on some thriller movie. Back and forth, searching the brightly lit yard for anything that shouldn't be there.

"Where are they?" Erin murmured.

"Shh," Vic cautioned. She had her gun out. Erin hadn't seen her take it from the concealed holster. She thought about sitting so close to Theresa back in the house. They were lucky that Theresa hadn't searched Vic and hadn't pulled Vic's gun when they had been wrestling on the couch. Erin shuddered. She did not like guns.

As if Vic had heard this thought, she looked back at Erin, at her lack of a weapon either to defend herself or to attack someone else. Who knew if there was a nest of clansmen somewhere close by, guarding the prisoners and just waiting for the visitors to leave or for Theresa to signal to them that everyone had been secured.

"Stay in the house," Vic whispered, motioning Erin back.

Erin ignored the instruction. She could see a hundred yards in every direction. There was no movement. No one was going to be able to sneak up on them with so much light shining from the house security lights. Erin tapped the final number she had for Jack Ward and held the phone to her ear, holding her breath as she listened for any sounds in the night while the ring tone repeated over and over.

As they approached a big barn or garage behind the house, there was suddenly a voice in Erin's ear. "Moose River dispatcher," a bored woman announced.

"Moose River! This is… my name is Erin Price. We need police dispatched to this location…" Erin looked around, trying to find something that would identify where they were. A house number? Crossroads? The name of the farmhouse? There wasn't anything that identified where she was. She looked up at the sky, trying to tell which direction Moose River lay from them, but she couldn't see the lights of the town.

"What is the nature of your emergency?" the dispatcher responded.

"There's… a murderer. And we think Jack Ward has been… abducted or hurt, or maybe killed. We're looking for him. There was a noise out here, but I don't know where he is…"

"Ma'am, did you say a murder? Can you tell me what happened, please?"

"There was a murder in Bald Eagle Springs, but the woman who did it, she's in Moose River, and Jack Ward was investigating, but we found his phone and not him…"

"Jack Ward is there? Would you put him on the phone?"

Erin shook her head in disbelief. She stayed a few paces behind Willie and Vic, not wanting to be separated from them, but also not wanting to be in the line of fire if something happened. She didn't want her voice to alert anyone of their presence, but Willie had told her to call the police, and he wasn't turning around and waving at her to be quiet. So she persisted, trying to stay close but not too close and to explain to the dimwitted dispatcher just what was going on.

"We haven't found Jack Ward yet. She might have done something to him. We're looking for him."

"Ma'am, can you tell me your location?"

"No… I… I don't know where this is. Can't you ping my phone or something? Won't it give you GPS coordinates?"

"We don't have an integrated system yet, ma'am. How did you get where you are? Can you tell me what buildings you see around you?"

"I wasn't driving. I didn't pay any attention when we left the highway. All that's out here is a farmhouse and barn and some other little buildings…"

Willie had found the big doors of the barn padlocked, and hammered away at it with the stock of the gun. Erin didn't know why he didn't just shoot it off like they did on TV.

"Do you know whose farm it is?"

"Uh… Theresa… Theresa…? I can't remember her last name… She's a young woman with the Jackson clan."

"Crazy Theresa?" the dispatcher asked in disbelief. "Theresa Franklin?"

Erin almost burst into tears of relief. "Yes. Yes, Crazy Theresa Franklin."

The dispatcher muttered something that Erin couldn't make out. "And you think Jack Ward was out there?"

"He was. We're just trying to get into the barn," Erin explained. "He might be locked up in there."

"I'll get all the units I can out there," the dispatcher promised. "We're not very big, but we'll be out in force in ten to fifteen minutes."

Willie's hammering with the gun succeeded and the padlock and latch fell to the ground.

CHAPTER 36

$\mathcal{E}$rin hurried after Willie and Vic as they wrenched the doors open and slipped in, sticking close to the walls of the barn. She stayed as far back from them as she dared, not wanting to lose track of them or to be a target. The barn was full of junk. Some of it old stuff that had probably been part of the farm since before electricity was invented. And some of it pallets of neatly boxed goods with the Amazon logo plastered to the sides. Willie and Vic went in opposite directions, forcing Erin to decide which of them she was going to stay with. She elected to stay with Willie, who had better firepower and was, therefore, better equipped to protect two people than Vic was with her handgun.

He turned his head toward her, aware that she was with him, and continued without a word. She tried to step exactly where he had, though her stride was smaller, not wanting to set off any booby traps or to kick a metal dog dish or something else that would give their position away.

Erin startled at every sound, from the wind pushing branches against the outside of the building to birds in the eaves and the pings and creaks of the old structure. She prayed that they would find Terry there safe, not believing that her prayers would reach any mind but her own, yet hoping beyond hope that there was some way to influence fate with her fervency. Terry's words came back to her. *I believe that God is in charge... but I believe that I need to do my part and that I can affect the outcome...* She hoped that she could help control that outcome.

Willie suddenly dropped into a crouch. Erin's knees bent of their own accord, mirroring his movement within a split second. She stayed frozen, watching Willie. He peered through a metal shelf of paint cans, gun barrel resting in the space between them. He watched for a long minute or two and then started moving again.

Erin tiptoed after him. He walked purposefully toward his goal, alert but no longer as cautious as he had been. Erin closed the distance between them and was almost abreast of him. Willie rounded the corner, looked around for any guards or other dangers, and then hurried over to the two men tied up and lying in a pile of junk and rags. Willie went to Jack Ward and Erin hurried to Terry's side. Ward was kicking and struggling. When Willie managed to pull the gag from his mouth, he let out a blue streak of curses and tried to turn to look at both of them at the same time. When his eyes met Erin's, his head fell back, expression relaxing. He swore a couple more times.

"Erin Price. What happened? How did you know where we were?"

"It's going to be okay," Erin said, turning her eyes back to Terry, whose eyes were not open. "Your troops are on the way."

"Good." Jack Ward cleared his throat and spat to the side a couple of times. "Crazy woman! Not you, Erin. Theresa."

"I know."

Willie worked at the bonds immobilizing Ward. "Is Terry okay?"

Erin was touching him, feeling his cheek, watching for the rise and fall of his chest. When she moved his collar to feel for his pulse, she saw bruises across his throat, and her breath caught.

"Oh, no..."

Willie looked over. He abandoned his efforts to free Ward and moved over to Terry. His fingers were quick and competent as he felt Terry's wrist and looked at the bruises Erin had revealed.

"He's alive," Willie confirmed. "It's okay."

"She took him down with a chokehold and smashed his head on the table," Ward said, unable to turn to get a good look at Terry. "He hasn't come to, but I could still hear him breathing."

Willie continued to monitor Terry's vital signs. "Will your department have sent EMS?"

"I'm sure Geraldine would."

Erin took her phone out again, but the service indicator that had previously been there was gone. She slid it back into her pocket. Vic joined them, having completed her circuit around the other side of the barn. "Erin? Are they okay? What did she do to him?"

Erin ran her fingers through Terry's hair, studying his face, willing him to wake up. "They'll be okay," she said, hoping it was true.

Vic walked over to where K9 was tied up and made use of a utility knife laying on a nearby workbench to cut him free of the rope. Once free, K9 dashed over and nosed at Terry, whining, then barking. Terry didn't stir. Erin petted him and murmured to him, trying to reassure herself as much as him. He lay down beside Terry and put down his head, waiting for his master to wake.

Vic approached Ward. She nodded a greeting. "How are you doing? Just hold still, and I'm going to get you free."

"Yeah." Ward was still as Vic worked on his bonds, a combination of ropes and zip ties, with the utility knife. "You must be Victoria."

"That's me," Vic said cautiously. She glanced over at Terry, silent and unmoving. Erin wondered how much Terry had told Ward about Vic. How much Ward knew about who she was and where she had come from. And Ward must have told Terry about Vic's former relationship with Theresa.

Ward suddenly flinched away from Vic. She put one hand on him to hold him still while she cut through a tie.

"You okay?" she asked him again.

"She came at me with a knife," Ward said. "It was out of nowhere. We were talking to her about Biggles, about what had happened in Bald Eagle Falls and who would have had the motive to kill him, and she just grabbed a Ka-Bar knife and came at me."

Erin turned her attention to Ward. Vic's eyes were wide. Her hands froze in position.

"Are you hurt?" Erin asked.

"Durn thing hurts like the dickens," Ward complained.

Vic and Erin looked him over, scanning for any injuries. Erin moved around him and checked his side. Together, she and Vic rolled him toward Vic so Erin could check his back for any injuries. Ward was lying on an uneven pile of junk. When Erin shifted him, she felt something wet. She straightened the folds of Ward's jacket and first saw several puckered holes soaked dark with blood.

Then she saw the knife.

CHAPTER 37

*E*rin fell back, staring in horror at the knife.

Jack Ward wriggled uncomfortably, and Erin pressed her hand down on him. "Stay still. Don't move."

Vic was straining to look over Jack Ward and see what Erin could see. Her mouth dropped open and her face went sheet white. "Willie, you'd better come over here."

"I need to see to Terry. He's in rough shape."

"I'll watch Terry," Erin said, having difficulty speaking with how dry her mouth had gotten. "We need you here."

"Ward is fine," Willie grumbled, leaving his place to walk around them and return to his first patient. He stared down at the Ka-Bar protruding from Jack's back and stopped protesting. "Okay, Erin, go look after Terry. Monitor his pulse and breathing. Talk to him and if he comes to, keep him calm and don't let him move around. Jack," Willie raised his voice slightly and spoke to Jack Ward in a stern voice. "I want you to stay as still as you can."

Jack squirmed slightly. "Is it bad? Hurts like heck. Woman is mad as a hatter!"

"It will be fine if you do what I say," Willie said calmly.

Erin went back over to Terry and immediately checked his breathing. Time was dragging so slowly it seemed to be standing still. The dispatcher had said that the police would be arriving in ten minutes, but it seemed like an hour had already passed. She worried about what would happen if Terry stopped breathing. She could do CPR, but her previous experience with that had not been good. At least then, Terry had been at her side as they took turns.

K9 whined. Erin scratched his ears. "It'll be okay, buddy. Everybody's going to be fine." She split her attention between Terry and Ward. Even though she was only in charge of Terry, she couldn't help being concerned with Ward and how he was doing. Despite his blood-soaked jacket and the knife buried to the haft in his back, he stayed alert and vigorous, talking with Willie and complaining only occasionally about the pain.

At long last, she heard the first thready notes of sirens. She breathed a sigh of relief.

"Why don't you go flag them down, show them where to go," Willie said to Erin. "Vic, you take over on Terry, just keep an eye until Erin gets back."

Erin got quickly to her feet and hurried outside. The barn was much smaller than it had seemed when they were inching their way in, afraid there would be more Jackson clansmen lying in wait. She jogged into the brightly-lit driveway to wait for the emergency vehicles to pull in off the highway. There was a blur of motion from behind Willie's truck, and something solid crashed into Erin, knocking her off her feet. She tried to right herself and figure out what had happened. She realized a split-second before the forearm pinned her to the gravel by her throat that it was Theresa, somehow loose of her bonds. Erin struggled, but it was too late, Theresa squeezing hard to cut off both her breath and the flow of oxygenated blood to her brain. Even before Erin's lungs began to hurt, blackness started to gather around her. Theresa was screaming at her, but Erin couldn't sort out the words.

Then the chokehold was released and Theresa was gone. Erin gasped for breath and tried to get up. The sirens were on top of her, doors were slamming, feet were running in every direction, and someone knelt at her side.

"Are you okay? What happened?"

Erin tried to sit up and nearly passed out. "The barn," she croaked. She motioned in the direction she thought she had come from. "The others are in the barn."

There were orders shouted back and forth, more running feet, more sirens, and eventually, Erin's head stopped whirling in dizzy circles and she was able to sit up with the assistance of one of the Moose River police officers.

"Are you okay? Feeling better?" He cracked a water bottle open and handed it to her, keeping his hand close in case she needed help. Erin took a sip of the soothing cold water.

"Yeah. I'm okay. It was just a few seconds... did you get her?"

He shook his head. He was young, with a round, boyish face that made him look like a teenager. "She ran back there somewhere," he waved in the general direction, "had a motorcycle, rode off into the trees. We can't get through in our cars, can't keep up on foot, too dark for any pursuit. She knows all the backroads here, how to get back out to the highway without being spotted. She's long gone."

Erin's head was pounding. She closed her eyes for a moment, leaning back against the boyish officer, trying to get a handle on it all.

"The others? Is everyone okay?" She opened her eyes again.

"Got paramedics taking care of Jack Ward and the other one. Your friends are all fine. Just being debriefed separately before you all get together again."

"I can't believe..." Erin was at a loss for words. It had all happened so fast; she was still trying to process it all.

The young man nodded. "We're not exactly sure what happened here. Someone will talk to you in a few minutes."

Eventually, another policeman knelt beside Erin and let the young man go on to other duties. Erin did the best she could to sit up and focus on what he was saying, distracted by her pounding head, all of the activity around them, and trying to sort out what had happened.

"Is Terry Piper okay?" she asked.

"Everybody is stable. The injured officers are being taken to the hospital where they'll be treated. We have no reason to believe they won't both fully recover."

Erin nodded very slightly, trying not to move her head too much.

"And how about you, ma'am? Have you been checked out by a medical professional?"

"I... don't know. The police, but I don't know if a doctor did..."

"Okay. We'll have someone check you out in a few minutes." He pushed her collar back to look at her throat and nodded. "You're breathing okay? You don't feel like your airway is closing?"

Not until he suggested it.

Erin took a few deeper breaths and nodded. "Yeah. Just sore, I guess."

"You've got a pretty good bruise. Can you tell me what happened here today?"

Erin did her best to relate the evening's events, though she kept getting things out of order and having to go back to explain something.

"You tied Miss Franklin up?"

"Yes… she was dangerous. She was threatening, kept trying to hurt us."

"Don't get me wrong; I'm not criticizing. Just trying to get the whole story."

"Yeah… I found some twine in the kitchen. Heavy-duty stuff. I don't know how she got out of it. I tied the knots pretty tight. I was afraid I was going to cut her circulation off, but I figured for a little while, it would be okay, and it was more important that I didn't let her slip out…"

He nodded his agreement.

"How *did* she get out?" Erin wanted to know.

"Knife. Cut the string."

"Oh." Erin blinked. "I didn't see a knife."

"That girl is pretty cunning. It's not the first time she's slipped through our fingers. She probably had it hidden on her body somewhere."

None of them had checked. They had just assumed that the big gun was her only weapon. They had thought that if she was securely tied, she couldn't get into any mischief.

"Can I get up now? And see my friends?"

He stood up and offered his hand to help Erin to her feet. She took it and leaned on his arm for a moment while waiting for her head to stop spinning. Once she was able to stay upright on her own and walk, he escorted her over to Willie's truck, where Vic and Willie were talking with the other cops. Casual, finished answering questions. K9 was at Vic's side, looking out of place. Willie and Vic turned toward Erin, worried looks in their eyes, and reached out to help her.

"It's okay. I'm fine. I can manage. Can we go to the hospital? See Terry?"

"You bet," Willie agreed, "We were just waiting for you to finish up. Are you sure you're alright?"

"A bit shaken. But I'll be okay."

"She'll be right as rain once she sees her beau," Vic declared.

Erin had to agree. She would feel much better when she saw Terry and knew that he was okay. And even more so when he woke up. She needed to know for herself that nothing was going to change. He would recover and be able to go back to active duty, and everything would return to normal.

"Was he okay? You're sure he's going to be alright?"

"You can never be one hundred percent sure with head injuries," Willie cautioned. "But he was breathing on his own. I'm sure he's probably taken knocks on the head before."

Erin wished he had just said that Terry was going to be perfectly fine. Even if it was a lie, she didn't want any prevarication.

"And how about Jack Ward?" Erin shuddered when she remembered the instant she saw the handle of the knife. "I can't believe... he was still talking and acting just like everything was fine. He had to be the one who caused the noise we heard outside. Trying to get someone's attention."

Willie raised his brows and shook his head. "Never seen anything like it," he admitted. "I've heard about stuff like that but never seen it myself. Best thing is to leave the knife in there, where it's putting internal pressure on the wound. Do whatever else you can to stop bleeding and treat for shock, but... don't mess with it. You never know what damage you're going to do when you pull it out. Leave a surgeon to do that part."

"He shouldn't have survived. Being stabbed that many times. How could he?"

"Today was his lucky day," Vic said with a chuckle. "He had an angel watching over his shoulder. So did Terry. I guess we all did. Theresa could have just opened up on us when we got there."

"Which is why we shouldn't have gone in before the police," Willie reminded her. "You said she wouldn't hurt you."

"Well... she didn't."

"She would have if Erin hadn't gotten in the way and I hadn't taken the gun off of her. That was no love tap."

"Yeah. I guess," Vic admitted, looking sheepish. "I'm sorry about that, Erin. Are you okay? She hit you pretty hard. And then getting attacked out here..."

"Should have searched her properly," Willie grumbled. "I should have stripped her down before hogtying her. No excuse for being so sloppy."

Vic made a shocked face. "Willie, really! I had no idea you had such proclivities."

Willie chuckled. "Let's get on our way. Erin wants to make sure that Terry's okay, and they'll need to check her out at the hospital too."

"I'm fine."

"You still need to be checked out. Theresa wasn't fooling around." Willie looked at Vic as he opened the truck door for the girls. "Just what's the deal with that woman? She thought she could take us all down? That she could get away with killing Bo Biggles? How does a girl that age have the combat skills she does?"

Vic motioned Erin into the truck ahead of her. "You go ahead. I want to make sure you're not going to get dizzy or pass out."

"I'll just sit in the back. You go ahead."

"Not this time. We need to keep an eye on you."

Erin looked for a way to convince Vic otherwise, but neither she nor Willie looked inclined to agree. Erin stepped onto the running board and grasped the inside of the truck to pull herself up. Willie gave her a quick boost with his hands on her hips, practically tossing her into the truck. In a moment, they were all in the cab of the pickup and headed toward the hospital.

"In the Middle East, they train kids to be soldiers," Vic said to Willie, addressing his unanswered question. "It's the same in the clans... if you have an aptitude for violence or some other part of the business, they're happy to teach and train you. Theresa's always been..." Vic searched for words. "A good prospect. Even when we were together, she was... unstable... angry, moody... a bit sadistic."

"I'm glad you got away from her," Erin told her.

Vic stared out the window at the darkened landscape. "I never realized the bullet I dodged there. It was just... a teenage crush, break-up, move on. Not something that stuck with me. Not something that affected the direction of my life—other than that I knew I didn't want to be with someone like that. And that I wasn't attracted to her the same way the boys were." Vic's lips pressed together and she shrugged.

Erin thought that was all she was going to say on the matter. But then Vic went on after a few more minutes had passed in silence.

"When she started writing to me again, I thought it was my chance to still have a friend in Moose River. Someone from my old life who would accept me. In her letters, she seemed okay with my identity. Not like what she said today."

"A little easier to say all the right things in writing," Willie observed. "When you're not actually confronted with reality. She thought that things could go back to the way they used to be."

Vic chewed on her nail, something that she never did. "She killed Bo because of me."

"No," Willie said sharply. "She killed Bo because of Bo. Because he was constantly harassing her. And unless I miss my guess, he had abused her in the past, when she was too young to do anything about it."

"And that's what was eating her up inside. Why she was so angry and violent."

"And the clan trained her to kill," Erin added.

"So it's Bo's fault? And the clan's fault?"

"It was still Theresa's choice," Willie said. "But there were... certain influences."

CHAPTER 38

*A*s much as Erin wished to avoid an examination at the hospital, Willie was adamant and Vic backed him up. It was two against one, and the nurse they talked to in triage nodded solemnly and agreed that Erin needed to be examined.

"Being choked like that, and there's no telling what vascular damage there could be… better safe than sorry. Sometimes it takes a few hours before someone shows negative aftereffects. Why, there was a case in the papers just the other day of a man who died in custody. You hear about it all the time. Someone gets restrained and everything seems fine, and then a few hours later, or when someone goes to wake them up in the morning…" She trailed off delicately.

Erin couldn't believe she'd cited Bo Biggles's death as an example. But it did convince her that she needed to do as everyone was saying and at least have a cursory examination.

After providing all of her information and waiting what seemed like forever in the waiting room, a nurse took Erin to a curtained bed. "Just take off your shirt and put that on," she told Erin, providing her with a hospital johnny. "The doctor will be right with you."

Erin doubted that anyone would be 'right with her.' Hospitals operated on a different timetable from the rest of the world. She unbuttoned her shirt and attempted to pull it off as the nurse finished making notes on the clipboard, so the nurse was still there to hear Erin's gasp as a bolt of pain shot through her shoulder.

"What is it, dear?" The woman was instantly at her side, pushing her to the bed so that she wouldn't fall down. She examined Erin gently. "Good heavens!"

Erin managed to pry her eyes open again. Looking down at her throbbing shoulder, she saw the big, black bruise. Her fingers were tingling and when she touched the injured shoulder with the opposite hand, she found it swollen and puffy.

"You didn't even mention this," the nurse chastised. "You're supposed to tell me everything. Who did this to you? A boyfriend?"

"No! No, there was a woman. She was attacking my friend and I... got in the way," Erin finished lamely, realizing it didn't sound too heroic.

"What did she hit you with?"

"A gun. The butt of a... a big gun."

"Let me get you some ice to put on that. You're going to need an x-ray. First, let's finish getting you changed." She helped Erin to change into the hospital gown and to lie down before going to get an ice pack. Erin sighed. It was going to be a much longer night than she had thought. It was going to take even longer to see Terry and find out how he was doing.

Despite all of the testing and delays, Erin was beside Terry's bed when his eyes finally opened and he looked around to try to figure out where he was. He stared at Erin for a few minutes with vague, clouded eyes before he finally blinked and tried to speak.

Erin offered him a sip of water from the cup beside the bed. The doctor had warned that he would probably have a sore throat, something Erin could attest to. Terry drank the lukewarm water through the straw and cleared his throat.

"What happened?" he asked. "Why am I here? And what happened to you?"

Erin sat with her arm in a sling to help ease the pain of her bruised collarbone, and she imagined he could probably see the darkening bruise across her throat that matched his.

"Theresa Franklin happened."

He stared at her, trying to access his memories and make sense of every-thing. Erin took his hand and intertwined their fingers. K9 looked up and whined.

"He's okay," Erin told him. "You can come see."

He stood and looked up at Terry's hand and arm, then stood on his hind legs to see Terry lying on the bed. He couldn't jump up onto the bed with the sides up, but thrust his nose as close to Terry's face as he could, and stretched out his long tongue to lick Terry's face.

"Get down," Terry ordered, laughing. "You know better than that! Lie down and behave."

K9 stood there, not lying down immediately as he usually did. He stared up toward his master, his tail waving back and forth slowly.

"He's okay," Erin repeated. "Lie down, now. You don't want to get kicked out of here for being too rambunctious."

K9 lay down again. Erin squeezed Terry's hand.

"We were going out to talk to a witness," Terry remembered. "A young woman in Bo Biggles's family. Jack Ward said that he had lived with her family."

"Theresa. She and Vic were friends. Back... before."

"I can't remember what happened."

"It might be a while before you do," Erin said, repeating what the doctor had told her. "Don't try to force it."

"Do you know what happened?"

"Theresa is the one who killed Biggles. She snuck into the police depart-ment to break him out... only she didn't break him out."

"She killed him? Ward just thought she was a background witness."

"He didn't know about their... personal issues, I guess. You guys went over there, and she attacked you. Ward first, I think; stabbed him with a knife, and then went after you. Choked you, like with Biggles... only she didn't kill you... she hit you on the head to knock you out."

He looked at her, bemused, and she wondered how much of what she was saying he was actually understanding and going to remember later. "What happened to you?"

Erin sighed. She gave his hand a squeeze and tried to summarize it succinctly. "Vic and Willie and I went to see Theresa. We got her tied up and were looking for you and Ward. But she got away. Cut the ropes. So then when I went back outside to flag down the police, she attacked me."

Terry shook his head. "They got her?"

"No… she got away on a motorcycle. They're still looking for her, but the police department here isn't that much bigger than the one in Bald Eagle Falls, and they don't have enough people for roadblocks and that kind of thing. They probably won't find her unless she does something stupid to give herself away."

〜

Jack Ward came through surgery with flying colors. All four of them were not allowed to see him at the same time, and they had to wait until his wife was willing to leave his side to go down to the cafeteria. Then Erin and Vic were allowed in, as long as they promised not to get him excited.

Ward didn't seem like he was going to excite too easily. He had been calm and lucid when they had found him in the barn and, even though he'd only been out of surgery for a couple of hours, he looked like he was ready to get up and go home, rather than to convalesce after being stabbed multiple times.

"Here are a couple of rays of sunshine to brighten my day," he commented, his creased face breaking into a smile.

Erin remembered meeting him when Charley had been arrested. He hadn't seemed like such a friendly person that day.

"Hey. How are you feeling?" Erin asked him.

"Better than I have any right to, by all accounts." His eyes went over the two of them. "Well, you don't look too bad," he told Vic. "But you look like you met our lovely Theresa Franklin." His eyes rested on Erin.

"Yes," she admitted. "We sort of… had words."

"I hope they've got her in a jail cell in shackles by now."

"No." Vic shook her head. "She got away."

He swore. "She's a durn slippery one. You don't know how many times we thought we had her on something, and it's gone away. When her folks disappeared, I was sure we had her dead to rights. But…" He shrugged with one shoulder and shook his head. "No such luck. Couldn't seem to get her on anything."

"Her folks?" Vic repeated.

"Yes. Maybe a year ago now. They just… dropped off the face of the earth. According to her, they're traveling. But of course, there's no sign of them anywhere. But we don't have any proof of foul play. Can't get a warrant for their bank accounts or to take cadaver dogs onto the property. Other people in the clan have confirmed that there's nothing to be concerned about, they've just left town."

"So they're covering for her."

"For some reason... yes. You wouldn't think that anyone would want to cover for someone who was—if you'll excuse my French—so bat-crap crazy. But for some reason, they are."

Vic grimaced. "We were kind of talking about that. How she could be so... skilled. Breaking in and killing Bo while he was in police custody and all. I think they've spent a lot of time training her. So now they're protecting their asset."

Jack nodded his agreement. "They protect their own. We have a backlog of unsolved clan-related killings that I think I'm going to need to take another look at. Never would have thought that they would use a woman. And one so young. They must have had her killing before she was even out of school."

CHAPTER 39

*E*rin was glad to be home, back in Bald Eagle Falls where she belonged—keeping a regular schedule, baking at the bakery with her regular employees. Even taking time off to spend at home with her animals, genealogy, and Terry.

Terry wasn't back on active duty yet, but that was because he was on short-term disability, no longer under investigation. The doctors said it might be a few weeks before he felt like himself again, and that he shouldn't push it to be back at work too quickly.

So he was at home when she got there, eager to spend time with her, help around the house, and occasionally even have dinner on the table—takeout or frozen pizza—when she got home. She felt relaxed and comfortable once more.

But the nightmares were still bothersome, sometimes waking her up several times during the night. It helped when Terry was there, but didn't stop. At some point, she might have to break down and follow his suggestion to see a therapist.

Erin had been in the bakery kitchen to take some bread out of the oven, handling the trays carefully so as not to aggravate her still-sore collarbone. She could hear that there were a number of customers out front and hurried out to help Vic once she had the bread on the cooling racks.

She was carrying a tray of pumpkin-shaped sugar cookies to put into the display case and reached out to set them on the counter for a moment. By the front door, she startled at the sight of a slim figure with a rubber ape mask. Her hand trembled and the cookie sheet hit the top of the display case with a clatter. She tried to brace herself, but her legs were like jelly.

"Erin! Erin!" Vic caught her by the arm and tried to hang on to her. "What's wrong, are you okay?"

"It's…" Erin's vision blurred as she stared at the masked figure.

"Trick or treat!"

Erin recognized the voice as that of Peter Foster. He jumped down from the chair he was standing on.

"Do you like my mask?"

Erin took a couple of deep breaths and forced a smile. "Wow, it's very realistic."

Peter took the mask off and beamed at her. Jody danced and reached for it. "My turn, my turn!"

Peter reluctantly gave it to her and she pulled it on over her head. Jody danced around, making screechy monkey sounds. Erin leaned on the counter, her legs still shaky.

"What a funny little monkey!"

It was good to be back. And hopefully, there would be no more masks or surprises in the near future.

TAI CHI AND CHAI TEA

AUNTIE CLEM'S BAKERY #11

For those bending over backward for others.

CHAPTER 1

$\mathcal{T}$his time, it was Terry who woke Erin up, rather than the other way around. He was gasping hard like he was running or maybe even having a heart attack. She reached for him beside her and found his body rigid as he fought for breath.

"Terry. Terry!" She shook him, trying to rouse him, her mind jumping to all kinds of possibilities. Maybe he was having a heart attack. Maybe he had suffered some sort of damage in Theresa's attack on him that the doctors hadn't discovered. He had thrown a clot, and it had gone into his lungs or heart. Or something had happened in his brain and it was a seizure.

He'd been hit on the head as well as choked out, and either one could have caused neurological damage. Maybe damage that the doctors hadn't seen or predicted. They had warned that his road to recovery might not be smooth.

"Terry!"

He gasped one last time and sat bolt upright in bed, shoving her away. Erin was hurt even though she knew that he wasn't conscious of what he had done. He was always gentle with her, and being pushed away like that sent her sense of danger into hyperdrive. She was sure, as ridiculous as it was, that she was going to be attacked.

Terry looked around. There was just enough light in the room to see his shape, not the expression on his face.

"Erin? Where are you? Are you okay?"

Erin breathed deeply, trying to slow her racing heart.

"It's okay," she soothed. "You just had a dream. Lie down, and come here."

It took a minute before he reacted, still looking around him as if there might be some danger lurking. He drew in a long breath and let it out slowly.

"It was just a dream?"

"Yes. Come on." She wrapped her arms around him and molded her body against his. She could still feel his rapidly-beating heart as well as her own. "Do you want to talk about it?"

She needed to get up early, so both of them were usually careful to avoid conversation late at night, but she wanted him to know that if he needed a listening ear, she was right there. If it would help him to calm down, then it would help both of them get back to sleep sooner.

"No." He let out a few more quick puffs of breath. "I don't even remember what it was. Not really. I wasn't dreaming something was happening. Just… a feeling."

"Mmm-hm." She cuddled close against him. She'd had plenty of night terrors herself. There wasn't always any narrative to go with the feeling, just that crushing anxiety, that sense of danger. "Do you need anything? A drink? A back rub?"

"No. I'll just go back to sleep."

She knew that he worried about her getting enough to sleep with her early-morning baker's hours. His first instinct would be to protect her rather than to deal with his own needs. She rubbed his shoulders in spite of his answer.

"Are you sure? I can get you something. Milk or tea…?"

"No," he assured her again. "It was just a dream. I'll be able to go back to sleep."

"Okay." She was still again, cuddled up against him, eyes closed, soaking in the warmth of his body and his musky smell. Despite being woken out of a sound sleep, she felt safe and comfortable with him there, the two of them intertwined. It helped to soothe her own nighttime fears.

"Should I get up and check the burglar alarm?" Terry asked, rousing Erin. "Are you sure that it's armed?"

Usually, he didn't worry about the burglar alarm when he stayed over with her. He was more concerned if she was by herself. If he, an experienced police officer, was there, he didn't think anyone would be stupid enough to break in.

But his squad car wasn't parked in front of the house anymore. Since he had been taken off of active duty, it had been parked in the police department's parking lot. And since Stayner had been contracted to cover Terry's duties, he was the one who had been driving it. He wasn't a full-time hire, so he didn't get to drive it home at the end of his shift as Terry had, but Erin knew that Terry still didn't like the idea of someone else driving 'his' car when he wasn't there.

"I set the alarm," she assured him. "You don't need to check. Besides, if there were a burglar, Orange Blossom would be letting us know. And probably K9 too."

Hearing his name, Orange Blossom gave a soft meow and jumped up on the bed next to Erin. He sniffed her ear, investigating why she wanted him. Erin giggled. K9 was in his crate, but she was sure he would be making noise if he had heard or sensed an intruder in the house. And Orange Blossom, her little attack cat, was very territorial and had raised the alarm in the past when someone had managed to bypass her burglar alarm.

"Blossom, lay down," Erin ordered. She turned away from Terry to deal with him. She scratched his ears and kissed him on top of the head, then pushed him down to lie beside her. It took a few times before he was content to curl up against her, purring loudly in contentment.

"Do you think you could get him to turn the engine down a bit?" Terry asked dryly, putting his arms around Erin from behind her and holding her close again, so that she was sandwiched between the two of them, cozy and warm.

"It doesn't work. The more you ask him to be quiet, the louder he gets."

Terry knew how loud Orange Blossom could be, so he accepted this. They both just lay there, listening to his rumbling purr. It was a comforting sound, and Erin soon found herself drifting off again.

CHAPTER 2

*M*orning came too soon. It seemed like she had only been asleep for another five minutes when her alarm sounded. Erin reached over to shut it off. She pushed Orange Blossom out of her way and slid her feet out of the bed. She knew better than to hit snooze. If she fell back asleep for even just five more minutes, she would be even more groggy, and she wouldn't have the time she needed to get her engine running before work. She'd be draggy and grumpy all morning.

She would never have considered herself a morning person before starting the bakery. But once she managed to wake herself up, she found the extremely early hours of the morning exhilarating. She loved getting the gluten-free baking into the ovens every morning, working side-by-side with Vic or one of her other employees. The smell of the baking bread and muffins and the quiet of the early morning made her feel calm and peaceful at the beginning of the day, something that she desperately needed with everything that had happened since she had first arrived in Bald Eagle Falls to open Auntie Clem's Bakery.

She used the commode, splashed cold water on her face, and started the kettle heating in the kitchen. Looking across the yard to Vic's loft apartment over the garage, she could see it was still dark. Vic hadn't managed to pry herself out of bed yet. But she would. Despite her youth, Vic was very responsible, and Erin had never had to harass her to get her out of bed in the morning. She loved having Vic just across the back yard from her and hoped that Vic wouldn't move away any time in the near future. The two of them worked well together and were good friends, and it was convenient living so close together. They each had their separate spaces, but even when off work, could often be found in the kitchen together.

It wasn't long before she saw the light go on across the yard. Erin was at the kitchen table drawing up her list of tasks for the day when Vic made her way in the back door, yawning and pulling her long, blond hair into a pony-tail behind her head.

"Morning, sunshine," she greeted around the yawn.

Erin laughed. "Good morning. You slept a little late."

"No," Vic yawned again, covering her mouth with the back of her hand. "I think you're mistaken. This is what the rest of the world calls early."

"The rest of the world doesn't run a bakery."

"Good thing, or we'd have too much competition."

Vic went to the kettle and checked the temperature before pouring herself a cup of tea. She sat down to join Erin. Orange Blossom meowed for attention, rubbing against Vic's legs. She bent down to scratch his ears. Marshmallow, seeing that the cat was getting attention, hopped over to Vic to get his long ears scratched too. Vic smiled at the brown and white rabbit and gave him some love as well.

K9 was stretched out on the floor beside Erin and looked up at Vic but didn't bark or go over to her. Orange Blossom didn't like the big shepherd. While K9 would have been perfectly happy to make friends with the ginger cat, Blossom had steadfastly refused to have anything to do with the dog. Unless he was eating a treat. Then the cat was right there to steal whatever crumbs he could snatch or lick off of K9's face.

"Do you know what I found when I was looking for the Christmas ornaments yesterday?" Erin asked, looking back down at her task list.

"Didn't you know you're not allowed to get out Christmas things until Thanksgiving is past?" Vic teased.

Erin ignored her. She hadn't gotten the ornaments out; she had just been inventorying to see what she would need to add or replace. There was nothing wrong with being prepared.

"I found a huge box of chai spices."

"From Clementine's tea shop?"

Erin nodded. Her aunt Clementine was the one who had left her both the house and the retail space that had been her tea shop, having no other kin after the death of Erin's mother years before. The bakery would never have been anything more than a distant dream if Erin hadn't inherited the little shop on Main Street. She'd barely been able to keep her head above water up until then, working whatever jobs she could find and never able to stick with something for very long. It was hard to believe how fast the months had gone and everything that had happened since she had moved to Bald Eagle Falls. Bald Eagle Falls, Tennessee was now home, even though she had spent most of her growing-up years in Maine.

"So I guess we're going to be drinking chai and nothing else for a while?" Vic suggested.

"I think I'd get tired of it before long," Erin said. She liked variety, and for the brief time that she had known Clementine and "helped" with the tea shop when she was a young child, she had developed a wide-ranging taste for teas. "And I don't think we'd be able to sell that much at the ladies' tea each week. People like their traditional teas. I suspect that's why Clementine ended up with a big box of spices in the attic."

"Strange foreign tea," Vic agreed, sipping her English Breakfast. "What will people think of next?"

"So I was thinking… Thanksgiving is a great time for nice warm, spicy baking. Pumpkin pie, gingerbread, all of those other great spice blends…"

"And how about using chai spices in something?" Vic suggested.

Erin nodded eagerly. "We have them, we might as well use them for something. We can offer chai tea at the ladies Sunday tea as well, but I don't think we'll be able to move more than a cup or two a week."

Vic pursed her lips. "But what can you put it in? People don't really bake with it, do they?"

"Actually, I was looking at some recipes online." Erin looked down at her lists, warming to the topic. "There are a ton of different recipes that you can use chai spices in. Cookies, muffins, apple pie, oatmeal raisin bars… really, anything that you might put cinnamon or pumpkin pie spice in. Just a little twist on some old favorites."

Vic raised her brows. "Well, that might work. Just don't expect everyone to be enamored with the idea. You might not have noticed, but we have a few rednecks around here who are a mite suspicious of anything... different."

Erin laughed. Her gluten-free baking and atheism and Vic's transgender identity had already raised more than a few eyebrows and attracted comments, lectures, and even threats. "Just a mite," she agreed.

CHAPTER 3

*A*t the tinkling of bells, Erin looked at the front door to see who had just entered the bakery. The woman's slim, well-tailored figure and neat ash-blonde hair shot with gray were instantly recognizable. "Morning, Mary Lou."

Mary Lou's smile seemed brighter than it had been lately. She nodded to Erin and Vic in turn. "Good morning Erin, Vic." She took a long sniff of the air. "It always smells so good in here. I'm not sure I would have enough willpower to work here and not eat the inventory."

Erin knew very well that Mary Lou had iron willpower, so she didn't believe it for a moment. But she smiled at the compliment. "Thank you! How are you today?" She tried to guess at what might have put a genuine smile back on Mary Lou's face. "How is Roger?"

The smile dimmed. "Oh, he's about the same. They're changing his medications around again, hoping that he'll be more stable on a different cocktail." She shrugged. "I'm not sure how they can expect him to stabilize when they keep changing things around. I think he would be better if he was at home in familiar surroundings... but I know that's not an option. They're doing the best they can to help him, but I don't know if anything they do will make a difference."

"Oh, I'm sorry." Erin felt terrible for bringing up Mary Lou's husband. "You looked like you'd had good news, so I hoped..."

"We must have hope, but no." Mary Lou's eyes crinkled a little at the corners. "But you're right; I did get some good news."

Erin brushed a trace of flour from her apron and smiled in relief. "Great! What is it?"

"Campbell is going to come home for Thanksgiving dinner."

"Oh, that *is* good news! It will be so nice for you to have him home. I'll bet you're looking forward to that."

"I am. I was not looking forward to it just being Joshua and me for Thanksgiving. It's a little tough to do with just the two of us, and I was waiting for him to say that he was going off with friends for Thanksgiving to avoid it. But now that Campbell is coming, Josh will stay for sure. And Campbell said he will be bringing a friend along as well. So even though it's only four of us... it feels like an event. An actual celebration instead of just Josh and me trying to figure out what to do with ourselves to make it not so depressing."

"That's wonderful," Vic contributed. She leaned forward. "So what are you planning to do for treats?" she asked in a conspiratorial tone.

Mary Lou chuckled. "You have a very astute employee there, Erin. We are definitely going to need to do something special. I can't just pick up a pie from the grocery store, and Roger won't be there to make anything."

"We've been discussing some ideas for Thanksgiving," Erin offered. "One idea that I had was to make a lot of tiny one-bite treats. Fairy cakes, tiny tarts, mini cookies, maybe some mousse or ice cream in little shot glasses. That way, people can have a taste of everything, instead of having to choose one big piece of pie at the end of the meal. And they would work well for get-togethers where people weren't having a full meal too. It would work for casual dos like an end-of-day party in the teacher's lounge, or a fancy-dress party."

"What a good idea," Mary Lou approved. "Then there is no fight over who gets their favorite this year. Everybody can have their favorites. And if they're small... maybe I'll even allow myself an indulgence this year, while I have both of my boys home."

Mary Lou was always a strictly no-sweets person, so that was a real coup.

"Why don't you text or email me their seasonal favorites," Erin suggested, "then I can make sure that I have something that they like. We'll probably do the same at Christmas too."

Mary Lou nodded her agreement. She looked into the bakery display case. "Of course, we'll also want some white rolls to go with dinner and to make turkey sandwiches for the next week."

"Of course," Erin agreed.

"Can you believe that a couple of years ago, I would never have considered getting gluten-free baking for my boys. If Auntie Clem's had been the only choice in town back then, I would have made the trip into the city for my baking."

A couple of other customers entered the bakery behind Mary Lou. She blushed a little and patted her hair. She wasn't usually so complimentary. But the last few months had been hard on her and she had discovered that many of the women she had thought were friends had not stood by her through her challenges.

"For this week, just a loaf of rustic rosemary… and a few of those pizza pretzels that Joshua likes so much."

"Coming right up," Vic agreed, and started on Mary Lou's order. Erin rapidly tapped the entries into the till. Mary Lou was soon on her way, and Erin turned to the next customers.

"Are you and Willie doing anything together tonight?" Erin asked as she drove home with Vic at the end of the work day.

"No, I don't think I'm going to see him. He's been kind of… busy with other things lately."

Erin frowned. She didn't like to think that Vic and Willie weren't getting along very well together. They had been through plenty of ups and downs, with their gender issues, age difference, life views, and each being from old Tennessee clans who were at odds with the other. Not just feuding, but organized crime syndicates that were constantly at war with each other.

Willie had been sensitive about the friends that Vic had recently made on their Alaskan cruise, and if he'd decided now that he wasn't going to be there for her…

"You don't need to look quite so protective," Vic laughed. "He's not out chasing after women." She chuckled. "Or at least, he's only chasing after one woman."

Erin frowned. "What?"

"Theresa Franklin. He thought he might have gotten a lead on her in the city. So he's doing a little investigating to see if he can find her."

"Oh!" Erin let out a pent-up breath she hadn't realized she was holding. Of course Willie wasn't out fooling around. He and Vic hadn't broken up. He was trying to find the crazy woman who had injured Terry Piper and Detective Jack Ward during the course of an investigation. Erin wasn't sure whether or not she wanted Willie to find Theresa, but she supposed it was probably better if he did. As long as he didn't turn his back on her. "Terry will be glad to hear about it if Willie can track her down. He's pretty sore about her getting away."

"Willie will let Terry know if he finds anything. Right now, it's just rumor."

Erin nodded. "I think Beaver is still looking for her too. No one was too happy about her escaping after everything she did."

"Crazy Theresa," Vic sighed. "I'm just glad I haven't heard anything more from her."

"Do you want to come over for supper with me and Terry? It won't be anything fancy, unless Terry has taken up cooking to fill his time."

"I'm not sure. Okay if I see what I feel like after I've had a chance to shower and relax?"

"Fine with me. You know where to find us."

CHAPTER 4

*E*rin told Terry about the news that Campbell Cox would be home for Thanksgiving dinner, and went on a little more than was necessary about the treats that she and Vic were planning on cooking up for the holidays. She was excited about putting her plans into action and was so happy for Mary Lou, knowing she would be able to have both of her sons with her for Thanksgiving Day.

"That is good news," Terry agreed. "I hope everything works out for her."

Erin shrugged. "As long as Campbell gets there, she'll be happy."

"That may be what she thinks right now, but we're talking about human beings here with real frailties. Campbell might be planning to come home, or he might just be saying that to make her happy. Even if he plans to come home, a lot of things could happen to prevent him. And if he does make it... I'm sure you know that not all happy family dinners end up being... happy family dinners."

Erin could attest to the fact that many family celebrations she had attended had not ended up going well. Especially where teenagers were involved. Some of them had been pretty disastrous.

"Well... I guess you're right. But we're going to do everything we can to help make it a successful event. And Campbell and Josh are good boys. Everybody says so. I'm sure they'll try to make it nice for her."

Terry nodded. "Just don't get your hopes up that this is going to be a happy reunion. It may not be. Don't get too invested in someone else's perfect day."

"Yeah. But we're going to have a good day too." Erin smiled at Terry and met his eyes. This year, she knew for sure that Terry wouldn't end up working on Thanksgiving Day. They would have a feast, and there would be lots of baked goodies for their table. Whatever didn't sell out at Auntie Clem's.

Terry smiled back, but the expression didn't quite reach his eyes and the dimple didn't make an appearance in his cheek. She still loved his ruggedly handsome good looks, but she wanted to see real joy in his expression. He had been happy and fulfilled when he was on duty. Convalescing did not suit him.

"Vic might come over for dinner tonight."

Terry nodded. He went to the fridge to see what was on hand. Erin wondered whether he had eaten anything during the day. He had been worried about putting on weight while he was recovering, since he wasn't walking a beat all day like he normally did. But his face had lost some of its fullness and she didn't think it was just his nightmares and restlessness that were making him look so gaunt. He'd lost the few pounds that he had gained on their cruise, and a few more.

"Did you get out for a walk today? How are you feeling?"

"Took K9 out a couple of times." Terry sighed. "Didn't go very far, though."

"Because you weren't feeling well? Is it your head?"

He knew that she was worried about his head injury, even though the doctor said that he would likely make a full recovery. That was what they said, but she couldn't help thinking about Mary Lou's husband, Roger, and how he had been damaged by his *accident*. Terry had taken a double-whammy, with Theresa choking him out and hitting his head. He might have had damage from both oxygen deprivation and the insult to his brain. The doctors said that his tests were promising. But they had told Mary Lou that her husband didn't need any specialized testing or supports, and that had turned out not to be true.

"My head was okay," Terry reassured her. He knew how worried she was about it. "I just... didn't have the motivation to go very far. It's different just going for a stroll. It's not like walking a beat."

"But you could set a goal, make a plan to walk a certain route... I know it wouldn't really be the same, but you could still get out there..."

"It isn't just a matter of not having a plan or something to do. I don't want... well, the way that people look at me now..."

Erin felt irritation—not at Terry, but the townspeople of Bald Eagle Falls. As much as she liked living and working there and felt like it was home now, as much as she enjoyed visiting with the friends she had made in her time there, she hated how small-minded and prejudiced some people could be. They had proven that Terry didn't have anything to do with Bo Biggles's death, and yet people still regarded him with distrust, as a policeman who had committed brutality, when all he had done was to arrest a dangerous criminal. He hadn't been found guilty of any wrongdoing, and everyone knew now who the real culprit had been.

But people still acted like he had done something wrong.

And the sad part was, they had both known that was the way it was going to end up. They knew that even if they proved Terry's innocence, there would still be people who thought that he had just gotten away with murder.

"Most people are not going to treat you any differently than before."

"I don't know about most. There may be a few who don't see me any differently than they used to... but the sideways looks that I get, and the whispers, and people turning away from me and blocking their faces when they talk to each other... I'm not imagining that, Erin. That's the reality. I've been marked. And people are not going to forget."

"We could go somewhere else. We could move somewhere people wouldn't have preconceived notions about you."

"And leave Auntie Clem's? What would you do? You've made a life for yourself here. This is where your friends and employees are. This is where your home and your bakery are. What would you do if we went somewhere else?" He shook his head. "It's not even worth considering, Erin. You know that. This is where we live, and I won't be run out by people who are... stupid and backward."

"Okay." Erin breathed out. She didn't like arguments or confrontations, and the conversation was getting too emotional for her. She felt trapped. She needed to back off and get some air. But she didn't want to walk out of the room and make Terry feel like he had said or done something wrong. He was expressing his feelings, and that was precisely what she wanted him to do. She just didn't want him to feel so bad. She busied herself with getting out plates and the rest of the things they would need for dinner.

"It's okay, Erin. It isn't you."

She glanced over at him. He could read her way too well. He was watching her with concern and regret on his face, ashamed at having upset her.

"I know that," she said. "You're upset at the people who are mistreating you. I'm upset about that too. It's one thing when people say stuff to me… I can handle that. It's when people attack my friends… you or Vic or anyone. Mary Lou, Adele. I hate it when my friends are treated badly. I want to fix it all and make everyone behave themselves."

"You're a nurturer."

He came up behind her and massaged her shoulders. His grip hurt, and she pulled away from him. "Ow."

"You're all knotted up." He caught her again, and his fingers were gentler this time, kneading the muscles and seeking out the sore spots, trying to loosen them up. "You're concerned about me going out for a walk and feeling better, but you need to think about yourself, too. You need to find a way to let some of this tension go."

"I know. It isn't that bad. It will be fine. I'll feel better when we sit down and eat. And cuddle after dinner."

He continued to massage her tense muscles. "Your job is physically demanding, and when you worry about me and Mary Lou and everyone else, it affects you."

He wasn't just talking about her knotted muscles. That was only one of the ways that the stress was affecting Erin. He was talking about the dreams and the other problems too. But those weren't caused by worrying about whether people were talking behind her back. Those were the product of the other things that had happened since she had moved to Bald Eagle Falls. Unexpected deaths, accidents, and threats to her house, her livelihood, and her life.

Terry was the police officer; Erin was the baker. She had never signed up to deal with dead bodies.

She knew that the next thing Terry would suggest was therapy. He was just as concerned about her as she was about him, and while he had avoided suggesting she see a professional for a while, she could always see it in his face.

Of course, if he suggested it to her, she would kick it right back at him. He had been injured in the line of duty. The department would want him to see a professional before he was allowed back on active duty. They would need doctors not only to sign off on his physical ability, but his mental and emotional state as well, certifying him as well enough to return to duty.

"I'm going to do something," she told him, heading off the suggestion of therapy. "I *am* taking care of myself. I'm going to try some meditation and see if that helps."

His hands relaxed, and he just let them lay on her shoulders for a few more moments, warm and reassuring.

"That's good. I'm sure it will help."

The next week when Mary Lou came by the bakery, she had a gleam in her eyes that told Erin she was still expecting Campbell to make it for Thanksgiving. Erin hoped against hope that Terry was wrong and that Mary Lou would get her special dinner with her sons and that things would go well for them. It could be the next step to healing their family. They needed some good news, a nice time together, sharing happy feelings and good food and enjoying one another's company without pressure or stress. Erin wanted them to be the happy family they had once been.

Even when Erin had first moved to Bald Eagle Falls, she had sensed that there were problems. While Mary Lou was always calm and collected, perfectly turned out, Erin had sensed the stress behind the mask. Mary Lou smiled coolly and was open about the challenges her family had been through, but had made out that everything else was fine. They were getting along alright. The boys were doing well in school and Roger was, if not recovering, at least in reasonable health. She didn't let the cracks show. The looks and comments that she had to endure from other members of the community. The real struggles that Roger was having at home or the boys were having at school. They continued to be leaders in the community, to get good grades and play on the school teams and to work in their spare time to help Mary Lou make ends meet, since they had lost the family breadwinner's earning ability.

And despite Roger finding solace and some ability to contribute to the family by making the Jam Lady jams, his mental state had been worsening, his anxiety and confusion building and leading to violence that Mary Lou had never expected.

It was a lot to expect one family to deal with. And then to be ostracized by most of her friends... Erin felt like it wasn't fair what Mary Lou had been forced to go through. Vic maintained that God didn't give any person more than they could deal with, but Erin was pretty sure that even if there was a God, that much was not true. She had seen people who had been given more than they could bear. Roger was one of them. She hoped that Mary Lou could rally and her family could heal, and she would not be another example of someone broken by the challenges of life.

Mary Lou gave Erin a reserved smile, but her eyes shone more than usual, giving away her excitement.

"How are things going?" Erin asked. "Are you ready to place your order for Thanksgiving Day?"

"Everything seems to be coming together," Mary Lou confirmed. "Campbell promises he'll be there. Josh doesn't say much, but he's excited about having his brother back, even if it is only for a day or two. He wouldn't go anywhere else and miss the opportunity."

"That's great. It will be so nice for you to have the whole family—to have both boys home."

Mary Lou's face blanked for a moment, but then she lifted her chin, gave another determined smile, and nodded her head. "It will be a good day. I'm not going to overplan it. No program or games or anything enforced, just a meal and spending some time being with each other."

"Yeah. They're getting to be more independent. It's not like when they're little kids, and you need to keep them entertained."

Mary Lou nodded her agreement. She leaned forward a little. "And it turns out that the friend Campbell is bringing home for Thanksgiving... is a girl."

"Oh!" Erin grinned. "Well, I guess now you know what's been keeping him away. That's wonderful. Do you know anything about her?"

"No, nothing. He only let it slip accidentally that she was a girl. I haven't drilled him for details, however much I want to know them. I'll just let him bring her, and introduce her, and..."

"Then you can grill her over dinner," Vic supplied. She was standing in the doorway behind Erin, drying a bowl with a red-striped towel.

Erin rolled her eyes. "Vic!"

"You'll have to, won't you?" Vic asked Mary Lou, giggling. "You need to find out everything about her!"

Mary Lou let out a chuckle. "You may be right. But I'm going to make sure I have her there at my table before I start asking questions. I don't want Campbell to change his mind and stay away because he thinks I'm being too nosy."

Vic and Erin nodded their agreement.

Mary Lou cocked her head slightly. "And how is Officer Piper doing? He is recovering well, I hope?"

She clearly felt that since Erin had been inquiring about her family, she needed to ask about Erin's. Erin wished that she hadn't.

"Yes... I'm not sure when he'll be back on duty, but the doctors say he'll make a full recovery."

"That's good news. I'm glad to hear it. He's been a good policeman in our little community. It's an important job."

Erin nodded. Mary Lou frowned, eyeing her. Maybe detecting that everything wasn't quite as rosy as Erin would like her to believe.

"He's having a tough time," Erin admitted, before Mary Lou could ask her anything more intrusive. "He has headaches and can't concentrate on things the way he wants to. He has nightmares. I'm sure he'll be fine, but it's hard for him. And not everyone is so keen on him getting back on the street. Some people are acting like he really did do something to Bo Biggles, in spite of all of the evidence to the contrary. I don't understand people being so stupid and... ignorant."

"We do have some... stubborn people in the community. I'm sorry that he's had to learn that the hard way."

"I think he's always known it... he grew up here, so he must know the way people think and gossip. But still, that's not the same as actually facing it."

Mary Lou sighed. If anyone had learned that, it had been her. Erin didn't know for sure what she had thought of the community and her friends before the tragic turns her life had taken, but she knew that Mary Lou had been sorely disappointed in the way that people had reacted to Roger's arrest.

Erin opened her mouth to tell Mary Lou not to pay attention to what any of those people said. Erin knew that Roger wasn't responsible for his behavior. But they weren't talking about Roger; they were talking about Terry, so she closed her mouth and left it unsaid.

"You must really be looking forward to Thanksgiving. I guess since you don't know anything about this girl, you don't have any idea what she's going to like or not like at the table. That makes it a little more challenging. But as long as we provide a variety, there should be something she likes."

"And they're small, so even if she is watching her figure, she can have just one or two bites and not be worried that it is all going to go to her hips." Mary Lou smoothed her blouse over her hips as if worried that she might have put on some weight herself. If she had, Erin couldn't detect it. The combination of stress and an iron willpower kept Mary Lou looking as slim and svelte as a schoolgirl.

CHAPTER 5

*E*rin ventured out into the backyard as the air cooled and the sky started to darken. She was a little nervous about being seen, but Terry had gone out with Willie, and Vic had gone out with Beaver and Jeremy. Erin had begged off spending the evening with anyone, telling them that she was just going to rest and work on plans for the bakery.

She straightened her clothes and assumed the start position.

She had watched several videos on her phone, but even though she had no audience, she felt awkward and self-conscious.

She closed her eyes and focused for the first few minutes on her breathing, trying to calm her mind and be aware of her body. She slowly started moving through the forms that she had seen in the videos, trying to remember everything she had read and watched. She had practiced a few of the movements inside while watching them, but the various sites she had read had all advised on performing her practice outside in nature. She didn't buy any of the woo-woo stuff about aligning herself with natural forces, but she knew that it did help to calm her to be outside, and that was good enough. The whole point was for her to meditate and relax and to start to heal her brain.

She needed to let go of all of the nightmares and be able to find her center again. She'd always been an anxious person, but she hadn't always suffered from the nightmares and jumpiness and poor focus that she had been dealing with ever since Mr. Inglethorpe's death. Maybe even before that.

She could remember her foster sister Reg's nightmares. Erin didn't know all of what had happened to Reg, but she remembered the nightmares. Even during the day, Reg had been hypervigilant, paranoid about someone or something following her. She had confided in Erin about the presence that she believed followed her from place to place. She had sworn Erin to secrecy, not wanting to be sent back to the hospital for treatment.

Erin took long breaths in and out, focusing on her final pose, wondering whether the practice had done her any good. She didn't feel much different, and she hadn't exactly been able to stop her racing thoughts. She was a bit tired. Maybe a teensy bit calmer than she had been before she started.

She opened her eyes.

Vic was sitting on the stairs to her loft apartment, watching. Erin let out a startled cry.

"What are you doing here?"

"I live here," Vic advised dryly.

"I mean…" Erin tried to catch her breath and to slow her racing heart. So much for being calmer. "I thought you were out. You said you were going out with Jeremy and Beaver."

"Beaver ended up running late. Jeremy is going to drive out to the city to see her, but I don't feel like being out that late. I was going to come in and see if you wanted any company."

Erin blew out her breath noisily. "Come on over." She motioned to the house. "Let's go in."

"Are you done?"

"Yes."

"Didn't seem like very long."

"You're not supposed to do too much to start with. All of the sites say to start slow, with just a few minutes."

Vic stood up and started to descend the stairs. "So, what is this?" She waved her arms around randomly. "Yoga?"

"No, it's tai chi."

"Tai chi? Like martial arts?"

"I guess it is, but it's not like jujitsu or karate. It's not for fighting. It's for… health and meditation."

"How long have you been doing this?"

"I just started." Erin's cheeks heated. "This is my first time… going outside to do it. I thought you were out."

"Why? You don't have to hide it from me."

"I'm just self-conscious."

They walked into the house together. Erin automatically put on the tea kettle. Vic sat down at the table. Orange Blossom wandered in to see what they were doing and rubbed against Vic's legs.

"Well, now I've seen you, so you don't have to be self-conscious anymore."

"I don't know." Erin shrugged. "It's something different. I didn't know how you would feel about it."

"You could just ask."

"Well…" Erin slowly got out the mugs and tea tray and arranged them on the table. "How *do* you feel about it?"

"I think it's weird that you'd take up some foreign spiritual practice when you're an atheist. If you're curious, why don't you go to church? The ladies would be happy to have you attend over at First Baptist. Or one of the other churches, if you're interested in the competition."

"It's not a spiritual practice," Erin objected. "It's just… standing medita-tion. Something to help to calm me down. Get me centered. So maybe I can get rid of the nightmares and anxiety."

"Prayer," Vic said. "So why don't you just try a prayer or a psalm?"

"That's not what it is. It's like exercise. Except for the brain."

"Your brain or your mind?"

The kettle started to whistle. Erin poured it into each of their mugs. She wanted to argue that there was no difference between her brain and her mind, but she wasn't sure it was true. Was her mind, the person she was inside, just the function of a properly or improperly functioning organ? Or was her individuality more than that? Was it just the sum of electrical connections inside her brain, or was consciousness something separate? She sat down and stirred her tea.

"I don't know. It's all the same, isn't it?"

"Is it?" Vic raised one eyebrow.

"This is too philosophical for me. I'm just doing meditation. Something that might help me to feel better. To get over… these problems."

They were silent for a few minutes.

"I couldn't sleep after what happened with Alton," Vic reminded Erin. "I had a really tough time after that. Couldn't get to sleep at all without taking something."

"I remember. But you're doing a lot better now. So what did you do?" Erin figured they spent so much of their time together, she would have known if Vic were seeing a therapist.

Vic stared down at her tea. "Prayer. Talking to a priest. Just... getting it sorted out in my mind. That's why I say, you know, it could help."

"I don't think prayer works if you don't believe in it."

Vic opened her mouth to argue the point, then smiled and shrugged. "You do what works for you. If this Eastern meditation thing works for you... then I guess you go for it."

"I don't know if it does yet. I'm just trying it out to see."

"Because you don't want to take the next step."

They had talked about it enough; there wasn't really anything left to say. "I've seen enough psychologists before. I never really felt like they helped. I don't think they're the magic pill that Terry seems to think they are. Or that they have the magic pill. I'd rather do this my own way."

CHAPTER 6

$\mathcal{E}$rin looked around the laden Thanksgiving table at her friends, her adopted Bald Eagle Falls family. It seemed like it had been a long time since they had all been around the table together. Since Theresa's attack on Terry and Jack Ward, it seemed like everyone had been going in different directions. She would see one or two of them, but they weren't together as often as she was used to. Maybe because Terry was not working during the day, people felt like they could drop in whenever they wanted to, rather than waiting until the evening when Erin would be home as well. Or maybe people like Adele didn't feel as comfortable dropping by when she knew Terry would be there as well. She was strongly introverted and preferred to meet with Erin one-on-one rather than in a group.

Willie and Beaver had each been investigating Theresa's disappearance, seeing if they could track her down and, although neither Willie nor Vic had said anything about going through a rough patch in their relationship, Erin sensed that Willie was still feeling uncomfortable about Vic's expanding circle of LGBT friends, people who shared experiences with Vic that Willie didn't relate with.

Or maybe that was just Erin's own anxiety, worrying that things weren't going to work out as they should. She found herself obsessing every time she and Terry disagreed about something or she found him to be irritable or out of sorts, terrified that he was going to break up with her or do something drastic.

But they were all there for Thanksgiving. Everyone had put aside their investigations and work schedules and had made the time to be there.

Vic and Erin had prepared the turkey, since they were used to being up early and could get the big bird started in time for a noon dinner. The herbs were from Adele's garden or wildcrafting. Beaver and Willie had each brought a store-bought dish with them. Beaver brought enchiladas, and Willie, a more traditional dish of roasted brussels sprouts. There were sweet potatoes and mashed potatoes with gravy, sweet peas and corn. And there were, of course, plenty of desserts from the bakery.

"This is really nice," Vic proclaimed, when Erin found herself tongue-tied, unsure of what to say for the occasion. "Our family is getting bigger all the time. I'm thankful for that. And for all of this plenty." She bowed her head and said a few words praising God. Erin wasn't sure whether it was an official prayer or not. Some around the table bowed their heads briefly, but most didn't. Then Vic smiled, looking around at them all, eyes sparkling. "We're going to be as stuffed as hogs on their way to the market. So dig in!"

There were exclamations of appreciation all around the table. Everyone grabbed the nearest serving dish and started dishing up.

"Everything looks and smells so good," Erin said appreciatively, drinking in the smells that were nearly as thick as the gravy. Now that the formal welcome was done and the spotlight was off, she found herself able to talk again.

"Sure does," Willie agreed. Almost twice Vic's age and with skin always stained dark from his mining and processing activities, he didn't look like a likely match for the beautiful and graceful Vic, but the unlikely couple usually got on well.

Terry carved the turkey and served everyone their preferred cuts, with Beaver adding an enormous drumstick to her plate. Erin would once have thought it impossible that the lean Rohilda Beaven could possibly eat that much and still have room for all of the side dishes too, but Beaver had proven her appetite in the past and Erin had no doubt the drumstick would be gone before Erin was even halfway through her own meal.

Jeremy, Vic's older brother, with shaggy blond hair falling to his shoulders and an expression that was always right on the edge of a laugh, had his plate piled as high as Beaver's. The two were a couple, with appetites to match.

There was a comfortable lull in conversation as everyone dug in. Silverware clinked and there were occasional comments and general approval, but the conversation lagged for a few minutes as the meal was enjoyed.

After a while, the conversation started to pick up again as everyone shared updates on what they had been doing. Since they had all been going in different directions, there was news from pretty much everyone. Erin kept her eye on Terry, whose thoughts seemed far from the table and his friends sharing the meal with him. Normally, he would have plenty of stories to share. News about Bald Eagle Falls, funny things that had happened while he had been on patrol, some new trick or skill that K9 had learned, complaints about politics or personality conflicts in the police department. But he kept quiet, listening to everyone else, or maybe not hearing a word they said.

Beaver was entertaining as always. While there wasn't much she could share about her government job, she still regaled them with stories of past investigations. People doing stupid things, trying to get away or to lie about what had happened. Parts she had played while undercover. Descriptions of people and their traits and flaws that were so colorful, Erin could picture them clearly. Beaver had a long nose and generous mouth, and had a knack for portraying the expressions of the subjects she told tales on.

Then Beaver switched to childhood memories. Thanksgivings past, family trips over holidays that always seemed to end with someone throwing up somewhere inconvenient, and even dinners celebrated in soup kitchens with the street people she worked with, masquerading as a junkie or someone else down on her luck.

Beaver looked around the table, eyebrows up, waiting for someone else to volunteer their Thanksgivings past.

Things were awkward and quiet for a few minutes. Beaver shook her head. "Now I know y'all have celebrated Thanksgiving in the past. Maybe it was good, and maybe it was terrible, but everybody here has something to share."

Erin could remember a few childhood Thanksgivings, but not a lot. Sometimes she had been with a foster family, and sometimes she had been sent to respite care while the family traveled or had a big family celebration without her. Once she had aged out, she had ceased to mark the holidays, preferring to continue as if they were regular days and not time to be spent with her nonexistent family or with friends who felt sorry for her. She would beg off, saying that she wanted to celebrate it her own way, and then have a sandwich and read or do something else that wouldn't make her feel unwanted or depressed.

Vic and Willie had both had traditional Tennessee celebrations with their big families, but since they were both estranged from their kin and were from rival clans, they might have felt awkward talking about it.

"We used to play football on Thanksgiving," Jeremy said, giving Vic a light punch on the arm. "You remember that? Always a family football game in the afternoon. Pretending we were all pros and knew what we were doing. Very serious. The kind you always end up getting covered in mud and grass stains from."

Vic smiled. "Yep. The family fight."

"Always," Jeremy agreed, grinning. "And you and me, we were determined to beat Joseph and Daniel one year. We figured we were catching up with them in size; we should be able to beat them. But it never happened."

"Almost," Vic said. "But Daniel cheated."

"Daniel always cheated!"

They both laughed.

Erin looked around the table. Willie was dishing up another serving of sweet potatoes and also snagged some turkey from the platter. He gave his meal great attention, projecting the impression that he was clearly too busy to contribute a memory of Thanksgiving past.

"How about you, Adele?" Beaver prompted. "How did you celebrate when you were a kid? Did you have a big family?"

Adele didn't look pleased to have been singled out. She looked at Erin and glanced swiftly toward the door as if measuring whether she could make a dash for it without being tackled by the retired football players. She shook her head.

"Just regular Thanksgiving dinners like any other family," she said. "Nothing special."

"And when did you become a witch? Did you start celebrating it differently then?" Beaver prodded.

Everyone shifted uncomfortably. Erin and Vic had always been careful to say nothing to anyone about Adele being a practicing Wiccan, as she had been run out of other small-minded rural communities in the past. Erin didn't know if Adele herself had told Beaver this detail, whether she had heard it from someone else, or figured it out for herself. But Beaver didn't have the best social graces and often made people uncomfortable.

Adele looked at the remnants of the food on her plate. She was normally unflappable, and Erin felt sorry for her being put in the spotlight, but didn't know what to say to make it easier for her.

"How about you, Terry?" Vic chimed in. "What's the weirdest holiday crime you can think of?"

Terry was far away. It was a few seconds before he realized that everyone was looking at him and that Vic had asked a question. He looked at Erin, then Vic, wetting his lips and opening his mouth to ask what he had missed.

He startled, putting his hand over his chest, and Erin's first thought was a heart attack. That was it. He'd gone from being active to sedentary, had filled up on a big, heavy meal, and now she was going to lose him.

But he slid his phone out of his shirt pocket to look at it, unaware of the scare he had caused. While he tried to remain impassive as he looked at the screen of his phone, it was clear that something had happened. He half-turned to look at K9 and get to his feet before remembering that he was no longer on active duty. Then he just sat there, looking at Erin, not sure what to do with himself.

"What is it?" Erin asked.

He looked at the phone again, trying to come to a decision.

Erin swallowed, nervous in anticipation, worrying about what could possibly have gone wrong now. He was apparently still on the police distribution list despite being on leave. A break-in at the bakery? Another fire? Someone else hurt or killed, and he didn't know whether to act as a first responder or stay out of the way and let someone else take it?

"I think... you should go by and see Mary Lou."

CHAPTER 7

*E*rin covered her mouth.

If there was anyone who didn't deserve one more blow, it was Mary Lou. How much could one woman stand?

"Is it... did something happen to Roger? Is he okay?"

People got killed in prison. Or hung themselves in mental facilities. Something could easily have happened to Roger in his facility. Something horrible that his family would never recover from.

"No. Not Roger."

Terry flashed a look at Beaver.

The Thanksgiving dinner turned into a rock in Erin's stomach. Campbell? What could have happened to Campbell? He had made it home for dinner, Erin was sure of it. He'd arrived the night before, and all kinds of speculation were flying around Bald Eagle Falls about him and his girlfriend.

Not just a city girl, someone whose pedigree and history they could not explore, but a black girl. Tennessee might have legislated mixed-race marriages decades before, but the old prejudices still lingered. The whispers were flying thick and fast around Bald Eagle Falls.

For a few seconds, Erin was rooted to the spot. She wanted to ask all of the questions, to find out everything that Terry knew or didn't know. But he had already told her what she should do. She needed to go over to Mary

Lou's house and see if she was okay. Mary Lou didn't have a lot of friends left in town, and if something had happened to Campbell, she needed Erin's support.

Erin leaned on the table, making the dishes rattle, and pushed herself to her feet.

"I don't know how long I'll be. Can someone make sure that the turkey doesn't get left out? We don't want to have to worry about food poisoning."

"We'll take care of the food," Willie assured her. "Vic, are you going to go too?"

Vic nodded. She was on her feet half a second after Erin. "Yeah. We can have dessert later. It will be better to have it after everyone's dinner has settled anyway. We'll enjoy it a lot more if we aren't all stuffed. Just make sure everything is covered so it won't dry out…"

Erin looked around for her purse, quickly made sure that everything was in it and that her phone was charged, and fished out her keys.

Vic was right behind her. "What do you think happened?" she asked, as she and Erin climbed into Erin's car and Erin crossed her fingers that the engine would start.

"I don't know. Campbell was home… I don't know what could have gone wrong. What could have gone wrong? I thought… Roger… but it wasn't Roger."

Nothing was very far away in Bald Eagle Falls, so they reached Mary Lou's house in just a few minutes. Fast enough that there were still police cars in front of the house. Erin looked at them, feeling ill. There was no ambulance, but that didn't necessarily mean anything. The police were first responders. And the volunteer fire department. A fully-equipped ambulance would have to come from the city, which could take an hour or more, depending on what kind of Thanksgiving Day emergencies had happened there.

Erin pulled into a vacant spot against the curb, and she and Vic got out quickly. As they headed toward the front door, it opened, and a uniformed police officer exited with Campbell Cox in handcuffs, escorted firmly by the arm. Erin knew Officer Stayner by sight, but she didn't know him personally. He had been hired on contract to help cover for Terry's position while he was off of active duty. He hadn't come from Bald Eagle Falls, but had been sent over from one of the other counties. A rookie, low man on the totem pole, with plenty to prove.

"What happened?" Erin asked. "What's going on?"

"Private matter, ma'am," Stayner said stonily. "Excuse me, please."

Erin and Vic weren't exactly blocking the sidewalk, but they each moved a little farther away. "Campbell?" Erin asked. "What's going on?"

She didn't know him well. They had only met once or twice. But Campbell knew who she was, knew that she was a friend of his mother's.

Stayner continued to hustle Campbell on, not letting him stop to talk to explain what was going on. He called out to her frantically as Stayner dragged him on toward the car.

"It wasn't me," he told her. "Tell her that it wasn't me. I'm sorry, I can't believe this happened! On Thanksgiving Day! Tell her I'm sorry!"

Stayner opened the door and shoved him into the back seat with a terse warning to watch his head.

Erin looked at Vic, her eyes wide. They turned back toward the door and continued to walk up the sidewalk. Erin felt removed from reality. It felt like a movie screening, like it was a drama or a joke or part of a bizarre family tradition and soon everyone would be talking about it and laughing about how she was naive to have believed that it was real.

"What's going on?" she asked Vic, even though she knew that Vic didn't have the answer.

"I don't know."

They mounted the stairs to the door and stood there, unsure what to do. The door was still open a few inches and there was a lot of activity inside. They hadn't been invited and Erin had no idea what the etiquette was for barging into someone's house when a member of the family had just been arrested. Was it like a funeral? Did one knock and go in? Ring the doorbell and wait to be invited? They hadn't brought a casserole or cookies.

Vic eventually knocked sharply on the door and pushed it open a few more inches, sticking her head in and yoo-hooing to let Mary Lou know that she was there. She paused for a moment, then pushed the door open the rest of the way and stepped in, motioning for Erin to follow.

They walked into the living room. The feeling of being on a stage set continued. Mary Lou was sitting on the couch, her eyes wide and her face pale, looking around her in distress. The turkey and fixings were still on the dining room table, barely touched. The chairs were pushed out around it. Josh sat next to Mary Lou, his arm around her shoulders, speaking to her in low, urgent tones. He looked up at Vic and Erin, relief flooding his features.

He was only sixteen and needed another adult there to take over. Sheriff Wilmot stood in front of Mary Lou, notebook in hand. His look was one of compassion, but his lips were tight and his stance rigid and unbending. Erin could hear Tom Baker talking to someone else outside the room. The girlfriend, Erin supposed. He was trying to get her side of the story, whatever it was.

Vic swooped in and sat down on Mary Lou's other side, also putting her arm around the woman.

"Mary Lou, what happened? What's going on?"

Mary Lou just looked at Vic and shook her head. She and Vic looked at the sheriff, who flipped a page back in his notebook as if he had to refresh his memory on what had taken place there in the past ten minutes.

"Campbell Cox has been arrested for possession of illegal narcotics," he informed Vic.

Mary Lou was shaking. There were no tears in her eyes, but she had clearly been pushed past the point of being able to bear the news. Josh tightened his grip and leaned to press his head against his mother's as if trying to transfer strength directly from his brain to hers.

"It's okay, Mom. It's a mistake. It's just a stupid mistake. Please don't cry."

But he was the one with tears in his eyes. He let go of Mary Lou's shoulders to stroke her short, neat hair.

"It's okay. It's all going to be okay."

"But I don't understand. How could this happen?"

"Ma'am," Wilmot sounded like he was repeating something to Mary Lou for the third time. "We are impounding the boy's car. He will be taken to Moose River to be arraigned. It's a holiday today. He might be held for a few days before he can get bail. Okay?"

Josh nodded his understanding. "Yeah. Okay. He'll get out on bail, Mom. Everything will be okay. They just made a mistake."

The sheriff left the room to talk to the girl Tom Baker was with. Erin could hear the girl's tones getting more strident, but couldn't make out what she was saying.

Erin stood there, looking at Mary Lou helplessly, knowing there was nothing she could do, but longing to be able to help. After a while, Wilmot and Tom Baker left, and it was just the four of them.

Mary Lou looked toward the table, all set for the family's Thanksgiving meal. It looked like they had just started to serve up.

"What are we supposed to do now?" Mary Lou asked. "I suppose we still have to eat." She looked at Josh, trying to be the responsible adult but at a loss for what to say or do. "You must be hungry."

"No, Mom. Not really."

"But we have to eat." Mary Lou looked at Vic. "What about you? Have you eaten? We can't let it all go to waste."

"We ate. But we can sit with you while you have your dinner. Come on," Vic coaxed Mary Lou to stand up. "You might not feel like it, but at least have a taste. You need some sustenance to keep going."

Mary Lou shuffled like a zombie to her seat at the table. She looked around at the other empty chairs. "Brianna. She'll need something too. Where did she go?"

"I'll get her," Erin offered.

She went to the other room, a parlor at the back of the house, where she had heard the voices. She looked in the room. A young woman was sitting on a chair, her face in her hands, elbows on knees. Her face was smooth and unlined, very young, and streaked with tears and mascara.

"Brianna?"

Brianna looked up. "Who are you?"

"I'm a friend. Come on and eat. You'll feel better if you have something in your stomach."

Erin wasn't sure that was true. She was feeling rather nauseated and wishing that the Thanksgiving dinner wasn't sitting like a lead weight in her own stomach. But Vic said that they should eat, so Erin was following that script.

"Come on."

Brianna eventually rose from the chair. She had a round face and a body hidden under several layers of clothing. Her black hair was braided back from her face, quite dark-skinned. She picked up the backpack at her feet. They walked together back to the kitchen, and Brianna moved to her seat. She looped the arm straps of the backpack over the chair. She sat and stared at the empty chair at the place setting where Campbell had obviously been sitting.

CHAPTER 8

To begin with, they all just passed the dishes around and ate food mechanically. It wasn't like the dinner at Erin's house where everyone had been enjoying the food and saying how good it was. Erin supposed that they barely even tasted it.

Mary Lou swiped at her eyes a few times, sniffling.

"It will be okay, Mom," Josh told her again.

She sniffled, trying to force a smile. "I'm sure it's all just a misunderstanding," she agreed. She swallowed and looked around the table at her guests. "It will all be straightened out. It wasn't..." Her eyes settled on Brianna. "Campbell doesn't take drugs, does he?"

Brianna avoided her eyes. "I don't know, Mrs. Cox. I don't know what's going on."

"You don't know where these drugs came from? I don't understand how there could have been drugs in Campbell's car. And how the police knew they were there."

Brianna shook her head, staring down at her plate. She poked at the food, not eating.

"It wasn't anything to do with me," she insisted. "I don't do drugs. I wouldn't let them arrest Cam if they were mine."

Erin looked across the table at Vic. Their eyes met. Vic didn't believe it either. Neither of them knew Cam very well, but they were more inclined to believe him over the stranger. Yet Campbell was the one who had been arrested and Brianna had not been taken into custody.

Erin glanced over at Joshua and found him staring at Brianna, his expression openly hostile. Did he know something, or just resent the stranger for whatever her part might have been? It was easy to blame someone you didn't know and love when things went sideways. A lot harder to believe that it could be your brother.

"I'm sure it will all get straightened out," she said, lamely echoing what had already been said.

In the meantime, it was going to be a miserable few days for Mary Lou and Josh.

Mary Lou pushed her plate away from her. She had hardly made a dent in the modest amounts she had dished up, but clearly wasn't able to stomach it. She rubbed her temples, worry lines deepening across her forehead. She looked at Joshua's and Brianna's plates and could see that they weren't eating either.

"I guess we may as well clear up. When people get hungry, they can warm something up in the microwave or have cold turkey sandwiches."

The phrase *cold turkey* rang in Erin's ears, an unfortunate pun that Mary Lou had definitely not intended.

"Let us help with that," she offered, standing up and reaching for a couple of serving dishes after checking to make sure that Joshua and Brianna were in agreement and weren't going to want any more. As she took them to the kitchen counter to pack away, she saw the platter of one-bite desserts covered with plastic wrap. "Do you want dessert? Something sweet might go down a little easier?"

Mary Lou shook her head. Brianna and Joshua looked slightly interested.

"Would you like anything?" Erin addressed the two of them. "You can take a few, and then I'll rewrap the rest so they stay nice."

Brianna nodded and, seeing that he wouldn't be the only one, Joshua agreed as well.

"Yeah, just a little," he agreed. "Chocolate makes everything better, right?"

Erin took the platter and dessert dishes to each of them and Josh attempted to compliment the dishes.

"These are yours from the bakery, right? You've single-handedly kept us in desserts since you moved into Bald Eagle Falls."

Erin smiled and nodded. "We wanted to make sure you had a nice Thanksgiving."

After it came out, Erin wasn't sure that had been the right thing to say. Their chances at a nice Thanksgiving had gone down the tubes.

"Wow, it all looks so good," Brianna murmured, helping herself to a few of the bite-sized treats. Erin took them over to Mary Lou, but she waved the platter away.

"I'm sorry, I can't right now. You two have some. No point in them going to waste."

"We've got some at home," Erin laughed. "There are plenty to go around. I'll just make sure these are covered. You might feel like some later."

Mary Lou pressed a knuckle into her forehead. Standing beside her with the tray, Erin felt she should be doing something more to comfort her. She put her hand on Mary Lou's shoulder and gave it a little squeeze. Mary Lou patted Erin's hand, then she pulled away slightly and Erin let go.

"I'm so sorry. Is there anything else we can do?"

Vic was working quietly, helping to put the Thanksgiving dishes away.

"No, no. We'll be fine. There's nothing you can do. You should go home to your own families."

"We'll just get this cleared up first," Vic said.

Erin returned to the counter to help with the effort. Mary Lou stood up with a sigh.

"I'm sorry we're not very good company right now. I think... I may lie down."

Joshua nodded. Brianna looked quickly around. "What am I going to do?" she demanded. "Is there a hotel? I don't have any money. Where am I going to go?"

Her words hung in the air. Erin wasn't sure what to suggest. She had a free guest room, but she wasn't eager to invite a stranger over to stay, especially one who might be involved in illegal drugs.

"You will stay here, of course," Mary Lou said. "I'll make up the spare room."

"You go lie down, Mom," Joshua instructed. "I can do that."

"Josh, you don't need to do that..."

"My mother taught me how to make a bed properly," Josh told her firmly. "I know how to take care of guests."

She gave him a faint smile. "Okay. Thank you."

Mary Lou nodded vaguely at Vic and Erin and mounted the stairs.

Joshua popped his last bite of dessert into his mouth and rose to his feet. "Why don't you have a seat in the living room," he suggested to Brianna. "You can have a cup of tea while I get the room ready."

When he headed for the tea kettle, Vic shooed him away. "I'll do that. Erin and I will keep Brianna company while you do the real work."

Josh lifted his palms and shrugged, then followed Mary Lou up the stairs to get the bedroom ready for Brianna.

Brianna took her backpack from the back of her chair and went into the living room with it. She sat in one of the upholstered chairs, holding the backpack against her chest and looking at them with wide eyes. She had wiped most of the mascara and tear tracks from her face.

Erin didn't think it would be polite to ask for a recounting of what had happened and what the police had said to her that the rest of them hadn't heard. She sat looking at Brianna, unable to think of what to say to put her at ease. Vic bussed the tea over.

"Here you go. So where did you and Campbell meet, Brianna?"

Brianna looked awkward holding the teacup and her bag at the same time, but didn't seem inclined to put it down, looking as if she expected one of them to grab it. Erin understood Brianna's need to keep her possessions close. She knew what it was like to have little to call her own and the constant fear that someone else would get into it and steal or mess with her stuff.

Brianna sipped at the scalding hot tea, looking over the rim at Erin and Vic. "I don't know. Cam and I just… knew each other from parties. Same group of friends. We saw each other different places and just started talking."

"I don't really know Cam at all, but Mary Lou is a good person. She's had a lot to deal with, but seems like she's really devoted to her family. I think she's a good mom to them."

Brianna nodded. "Yeah. Cam doesn't complain about her. So I guess."

"For a family to go through everything they have had to, they have to be strong."

Brianna just shook her head. "What do you mean, what they've gone through? They seem like they've got it pretty good."

Vic and Erin exchanged glances. "Well, they don't own this," Vic pointed out. "It's a rental. They lost their house."

"They're not hurting. It's not like there's rats."

Vic kept her voice low, glancing toward the stairs to make sure that Mary Lou and Joshua were not within earshot.

"They lost all their savings and their house. Then Campbell's dad tried to commit suicide."

"Tried to? Because he didn't have enough money? Plenty of people worse off than this."

"He ended up with brain damage," Vic explained further, ignoring Brianna's comment. "He couldn't work anymore, so Mary Lou and the boys had to try to take up the slack."

Brianna considered this. "Cam never said anything about any of that." She scratched at a spot on her jeans. "So that's why he's in the hospital, or whatever that place is?"

"Well, partly." Vic looked at Erin, asking with her eyes whether she ought to say anything else. It wasn't like it was a secret. Everyone in Bald Eagle Falls knew. It had been in the papers. Even if Campbell hadn't told Brianna, it wasn't like she would remain in the dark once he brought her home. He would have to explain to her what had happened sooner or later.

Erin nodded and shrugged, hoping it conveyed her opinion that it wouldn't matter, Vic could tell Brianna if she wanted to.

"He went there because he killed a woman," Vic said gently. "And he tried to kill Erin too."

Brianna's eyes widened.

"He wasn't in his right mind," Erin hastened to add. "He wouldn't have done it if it wasn't for the brain injury."

"He tried to kill you? What did he do? Shoot you?"

"No. It was just spur of the moment. He didn't have a gun, he was afraid, and he tried to choke me."

"After he poisoned you," Vic reminded Erin.

Erin wriggled uncomfortably. Maybe they should not have opened the door to that conversation.

"Good thing they locked him up," Brianna declared. "Imagine having someone like that living in your house." She shuddered.

"I don't think he was a danger to Campbell and Joshua," Erin hurried to assure her.

But how could she know that? Just because Mary Lou and the boys hadn't chosen to share any incidents of Roger hurting or threatening any of them, that didn't mean they hadn't ever been in danger from him. They might have brushed off intentional poisoning as accidental food poisoning, or might have chosen not to share his more violent moments for fear of what would happen to him when it came out. Or how they would be treated in Bald Eagle Falls if people knew everything there was to know.

Mary Lou had said she didn't have any secrets. But no one was that transparent. Everyone held something back. Mary Lou had certainly never let Roger know she was aware of his infidelity. Maybe saying she didn't have any secrets was evidence in itself that her life was overflowing with them.

As Beaver said, everyone had secrets.

Vic sipped her tea. She didn't offer any more details. What more was there to share? Their knowledge of Campbell's experiences ended with when he had dropped out of school and left his mother's home. They had seen him once or twice since he had left Bald Eagle Falls.

There was nothing else to tell.

It was time for Brianna to reciprocate with what she knew.

CHAPTER 9

*I*t was suppertime when Erin and Vic got back home. There had been nothing left for them to do, and they had left Mary Lou, Joshua, and Brianna, telling them to call if they needed anything, but knowing full well that they wouldn't. Erin's stomach eventually relaxed and she started to feel hungry. She eyed the dessert platter but didn't help herself to anything, knowing that she had a pile of treats back at her own house to dip into.

Terry and Willie were visiting in the living room, the TV playing the NFL football game. Terry stood as Erin and Vic entered.

"How are they?" he asked immediately.

"It's pretty tough, but they're hanging in there."

"What a thing to happen on Thanksgiving Day!" Vic exclaimed. "Poor Mary Lou."

Terry nodded. He hugged Erin and searched her face.

"Come sit down," Willie told Vic, indicating the space beside him on the couch.

Vic instead sat in his lap and put her arms around him. Startled, Willie returned the embrace to hold her steady. "It was so sad," Vic told him. "I just don't understand what happened."

"What exactly is unclear?" Willie asked. He had obviously managed to break down Terry's defenses to find out what had happened. "Campbell was caught in possession of illegal drugs. It's a pretty common story."

Erin loosened her hold on Terry, turning toward Willie. "Campbell was just here for a day. How would the police know he had drugs? It's one thing if they pull him over in a traffic stop and see something suspicious. But why were they looking in his car? How did they know he had any drugs to look for?"

Willie had no answer. Erin looked at Terry to see if he would explain. He might not be on active duty, but someone in the police department had sent him that text and might have given him details. Or he might have a guess based on his experience.

"I suppose they had a tip."

"Who could have tipped him?"

No one answered. Erin looked around the room. "Where's Beaver?"

Of all of them, Beaver was the one with the most intelligence on Campbell. He was her informant.

"She wouldn't have said something to the police, would she?" Erin asked. "She wouldn't have wanted him to be arrested."

"She's gone to Moose River to see to things," Terry said. "She was caught just as off-guard by this as any of us."

Erin nodded, but wasn't convinced. Maybe Beaver hadn't known what was coming down the pipe. But Campbell was her CI, wasn't he? Maybe she had known more than she let on.

"Did Jeremy go with her?"

There was noise in the direction of the bathroom and Erin turned to see Jeremy coming down the hall. He joined them, nodding a greeting to Vic.

"How is everyone over there?"

"Pretty rough shape."

"You didn't go with Beaver?" Erin asked, though the answer was patently obvious.

"You think she would let me go with her on business?" Jeremy shook his head. "I'm not an agent."

"You could go as a friend."

"I don't know Campbell. And Ro wasn't going as his friend. Or not entirely."

"They'll let him go if she tells them to, won't they? She can get him out."

Jeremy raised an eyebrow at Terry. Terry shrugged his shoulders. "I don't know what their exact relationship or Campbell's involvement was. If he's an important informant and the amount of narcotics wasn't too high, then she can probably talk them into dropping the charges and letting him go so that she can continue to build her case. Better to get the big fish than little guppies. But is he an informant? I don't even know that."

Erin considered the question. "I'm pretty sure he is. He's helping her with something. What else would it be?"

～

When they finally got around to getting out the desserts, Erin realized that they were also missing Adele.

"She didn't stick around for long after you left," Terry advised. "She likes you, but I don't think she's very comfortable with the rest of us. Or with too many people in the same room. It was probably an effort for her to come, and once you were gone, she made her apologies and headed for the trees."

"I'll take her some desserts. I don't want her to miss out, just because our meal was interrupted."

"Not tonight," Terry said, looking out the window at the gathering darkness. "It's not safe to be wandering through the woods at this time of night. You can catch up with her tomorrow."

Erin didn't like being told what to do. She had been in the woods after dark before and had been perfectly safe. But she had to admit to herself that she hadn't liked it and had been pretty freaked out by the experience. Walking through the dense woods in the daytime was one thing. At night, it became a totally different place.

"Adele goes out at night," she grumbled.

"Yes. And I'm sure that if she had a boyfriend in the police force, he would warn her that it wasn't a safe practice too. In fact, I have suggested that she not go wandering like that... but Adele has a mind of her own. And she's pretty good at getting around in the woods without being seen."

"Whereas I bumble around like a baby elephant?" Erin suggested.

"Well... not an elephant." Smiling, Terry looked at Vic for help. "What's smaller than an elephant?"

Vic had grown up hunting, fishing, and camping, and when she walked through the woods, Erin could hardly even hear her. Vic shook her head and didn't answer.

"A buffalo?" Erin tried.

Terry took a tiny pumpkin tart from the platter and hugged Erin around the shoulders. "I would never compare you to a buffalo. But will you wait until tomorrow? For me?"

"Yes," Erin grudgingly agreed.

"If not, I could go with you. Then at least I wouldn't be wondering if you were okay."

But Erin knew that Adele wasn't particularly comfortable with Officer Terry Piper. They'd had several encounters before and Adele had always been on the wrong side of the investigation. It didn't make her well-disposed to Terry, no matter how many times Erin tried to tell her what a sweetheart he was.

"No. That's okay. I'll wait until tomorrow."

It was a long day, and Erin was exhausted before it was over. After dessert, everyone went their separate directions. Only Terry stayed behind. He made sure that everything was cleaned up and the floor swept so that Erin wouldn't feel like she had to keep working. He suggested that she change into her pajamas and get started on her lists so that she could settle in and her mind would be quiet when she went to bed.

"Will you stay with me?" Erin asked.

"I'm here. I'm not going anywhere."

"I mean in bed. Not get back up and go watch TV until morning."

"I don't want to keep you up if I'm restless."

"I just want someone there with me."

Terry considered. "I'll stay until you're asleep," he promised. "But if you're asleep and I can't get to sleep in good time, I'm going to leave you alone so that you can get a sound sleep. Once I'm tired enough, I'll come back."

Erin knew that was as good as it was going to get, and that it was as much as she could ask for, so she nodded.

Hopefully, he would fall asleep at the same time as she did, and they would both sleep soundly, without any nightmares, and neither would wake the other up.

CHAPTER 10

*B*ut the day had been far too eventful for either of them to sleep soundly. Erin was restless, worrying about a dozen things even though she had written down her thoughts and made her lists for the next day before going to sleep. Sometimes, she hated to admit, even making lists didn't help to calm her anxiety. Terry seemed to get to sleep quickly for once and lay snoring beside her. But he had only been down for an hour when he awoke with a jump and was immediately out of bed looking for a threat.

"You just had a dream," Erin whispered. "It's okay."

"I heard something. Is the burglar alarm armed?"

"Yes. And I was awake. There isn't anything to worry about."

"There was a noise. I heard…" he couldn't seem to remember what it was that had alarmed him. "I heard something."

"I was awake. There wasn't anything. Just you snoring. You had a dream."

Terry wouldn't be convinced. He pulled on his pants and toured the house, gun in hand, looking for any threats. By the time he finally decided that no one had broken into the house or was lurking around outside, Erin was so wound up she wasn't sure she would be able to sleep at all.

"Maybe it was just a car backfire," Terry reasoned, sitting on the edge of the bed to pull his pants off again, and then sliding into bed beside Erin.

"It was just a dream," she repeated.

"Okay. It was a dream," he snapped.

Hurt by his tone, Erin didn't say anything else. She lay there, facing away from him, and waited for him to go back to sleep.

"I'm sorry," Terry apologized after wriggling around several times to get more comfortable. "You didn't do anything wrong. I'm just anxious."

"I am too."

"I know. I'm sorry. I should have better control. Okay?"

Erin nodded. "Okay," she mumbled into her pillow. Terry's arms tightened around her and he kissed her neck gently.

"I am sorry."

"I know. We should try to get back to sleep."

But there was no way either of them was ready to settle in to sleep, both thinking about the possibility of an intruder, about bad dreams, about the increasing number of sharp words and hurt feelings between them.

Erin was tired and knew that it was the worst time for them to have any kind of relationship discussion. Things would look better in the morning when they were both fresh and feeling better. At night when she was tired, things always looked their bleakest. She sniffled, tears running into her pillow, and she didn't talk to Terry, waiting for him to go back to sleep.

After another twenty minutes, he got up from the bed and left her there, sitting down in front of the TV to try to distract himself until he was too tired to stay awake any longer.

Morning came too soon and, although Auntie Clem's was closed for the day, Erin couldn't sleep much after her usual rising time, even if she had only gotten a few short hours of sleep. She felt the empty space in the bed beside her, and couldn't get back to sleep without knowing that Terry was okay. She slid out of bed as quietly as she could, but Orange Blossom heard her up and immediately started meowing and chatting with her about all of the things that he had done while she had been sleeping.

"Shh, shh. You're going to wake Terry up. Be quiet," Erin whispered to him.

As she walked past the spare room, she peeked in to see whether he was in the extra bed, somewhere he could sleep without worrying about kicking her or waking her up with his dreams. But the spare bed was empty, the coverlet unwrinkled. Erin used the commode before venturing out to the living room, where the TV was on, tiny voices from a peppy morning show playing to a sleeping audience. Terry sat slumped on the couch where he had fallen asleep watching some late-night movie.

There was no possibility of him staying asleep with Orange Blossom's maddeningly loud meows. He awoke as she moved past him into the kitchen, hoping to quiet the cat with a couple of treats. Terry scratched his whiskery chin and rubbed his eyes.

"What time is it?"

"Too early for you to be up. Go on back to bed. You need more sleep."

He grunted and groaned, moved around trying to get comfortable again. He scratched and groaned some more.

"Can't you shut that cat up?"

"I'm doing my best. Come on, Blossom."

"He needs a crate like K9. But soundproof."

"That would be something," Erin laughed. She skidded a few kitty treats across the floor for Orange Blossom to chase and eat. "Have you ever actually tried putting a cat in a cage?"

Terry grunted and cleared his throat. "Probably a lot more times than you have. I always had cats as a kid. They don't take to it quite as well as dogs…"

He finally got up off of the couch and shuffled toward the bedroom.

"I'm just going to knock off for a couple more hours."

"Sweet dreams."

He grumbled something else that she didn't catch, but she didn't need to hear it to know that sweet dreams probably were not on the program. He shut the bedroom door so that he wouldn't be able to hear the cat—or at least, not as well. Erin sighed and petted Orange Blossom.

It was early enough that Erin hoped to be able to catch Adele before she headed to bed after her night-time wanderings, so she packaged up an assortment of treats and went out immediately without putting the kettle on and having her usual cup of tea.

The morning was cool enough for a jacket, brisk and refreshing. Erin hurried across her property into the woods beyond the fence. Erin's woods, though she always thought of them as Clementine's rather than her own. Or even as Adele's woods, even though Adele was her tenant and groundskeeper. It was wildland, not groomed with walking trails and fire pits and picnic tables. Erin frequently saw deer as well as the birds and squirrels that twittered and hopped through the trees, and occasionally other animals, which scurried through the underbrush or froze at her approach, hoping not to be seen by her.

The pathway to Adele's cottage was becoming well-worn, with their trips to and from each other's houses, and it wasn't long before Erin was in the clearing that just a year before had been unfamiliar to her. She crept to the door and listened, trying to discern whether Adele was still up or whether she had gone to bed. She couldn't hear anything. She tiptoed to the window and tried to see past the curtains, looking for light or movement.

The door opened, making Erin jump. Adele stood looking at her, a slightly amused expression on her face.

"I thought I might have a burglar," she commented. "It's been a while since I had to run anyone out of the woods."

"Sorry. I didn't want to disturb you, but I thought you might not be in bed yet…"

"You were right." Adele opened the door wider. "Come in."

Erin entered. She presented Adele with the plate of goodies. "You missed dessert yesterday."

Adele took them without protesting that she was trying to lose weight or didn't eat carbs. She set them on her kitchen counter but didn't open them. "Things were a little busy yesterday. I didn't know how long it would be before you were able to get back."

"Yeah. We were at Mary Lou's for a few hours."

"Is she alright?"

Erin shook her head. "As okay as you can be when your kid is arrested in the middle of Thanksgiving dinner. I can't imagine what she must be going through right now. I wish there was more that I could do."

"She knows that. You're a good friend to her. You've stood by her and she won't forget that."

"It's so sad. She was excited about Campbell being home for their celebration, and them all being together again for a bit. And Campbell brought a friend with him, and she was tickled to be meeting this new… girl."

"Girlfriend?" Adele prompted.

"He says not, but I don't know. I don't think boys want to admit to their mothers when they are getting serious about someone. Not at first, anyway. He said they're just friends, but…"

"You got the feeling that they were close?"

Erin frowned, thinking about it. Campbell had brought Brianna home for the holiday, but he hadn't told her about any of the trials their family had gone through. Brianna had known nothing more than that Campbell's dad was in the hospital. If they were boyfriend and girlfriend, wouldn't he have at least told her a little more about his father's problems?

"I got that feeling that they were… involved with each other. But I'm not sure that they are…" Erin grimaced, trying to put it into words. "Emotionally close…?"

"Just sex, you mean."

Erin coughed. "Uh. Maybe. Yeah."

Adele nodded and didn't make any further comment. She motioned to the chairs and table for Erin to sit down, and put the kettle on the stovetop, bending down to light the kindling already in the stove. It would take a little longer for her kettle to warm than Erin's.

"I hope, for Mary Lou's sake, that it is all a mistake," Adele said. "But there are so many temptations for teenagers these days. For a boy Campbell's age, off on his own, without adult supervision… who knows what he might have gotten himself into."

"You think they were his drugs?"

"They were in his car."

"They could have been planted there. They could have been Brianna's. Or… someone else's. A friend's. Maybe Campbell didn't even know they were there."

"Because kids often store their drugs in other people's cars?" Adele asked wryly. "And planted by who? Not the police, surely, after all the time you spent recently arguing that the police department in Bald Eagle Falls would never break the law."

"I don't know. I don't know much about the new guy, Stayner. Maybe he thought if he could get a good drug bust, he could get a promotion. Be considered for a permanent position instead of just filling in until Terry can get back. I don't know him at all. Or maybe… someone planted them there and then called it in to make sure that Campbell got arrested. The police didn't just happen to walk by and see drugs in his car during the few hours Campbell was in Bald Eagle Falls. That doesn't make any sense."

"I'm not sure your story does either."

"Well… no. But I haven't really figured that part out. I'm just saying… I hope that there's some other explanation."

"An innocent reason for having illegal narcotics in his car."

"Yeah." Erin sighed. "Exactly."

CHAPTER 11

*E*rin wasn't working as many Saturdays as she had in the past, but a number of her workers were taking an extended long weekend for the Thanksgiving holiday to spend time with their families, so she had agreed to work both Saturday and Sunday.

As she had suspected, Saturday was a quiet day. She worked by herself, promising to give Vic a call if things got busy. Erin didn't think there would be enough work to justify them both being there at the same time, and she was right. A few people popped in for pastries or extra one-bite desserts to round out their weekend meals, but it was very quiet.

She worked in the kitchen on new batches of gluten-free doggie biscuits, and some softer treats she was developing for cats. Not that Orange Blossom didn't like K9's biscuits, but they were a little large and unwieldy for a cat to gnaw on. She had plenty of leftover turkey to experiment with.

The bells on the front door jingled. Erin wiped her hands on her apron and walked out to the front to see who it was. Melissa smiled and nodded at Erin, her dark curls bouncing.

"Hello, Erin. Did you have a good Thanksgiving?"

"Well, it was a little disrupted," Erin said cautiously. She didn't know how much the news of the arrest had spread through Bald Eagle Falls. It didn't usually take very long for gossip to make its way around the small town.

"Is it true that you were over at Mary Lou's when it happened?" Melissa asked in a low voice, looking around as if someone might overhear her. But she was the only one in the shop. No one was going to hear unless they had the place bugged.

"No, I wasn't there when it happened, but I heard and went over to see if there was anything I could do." Erin shrugged. "There really wasn't. I stayed over for a few hours, but I don't know if I was any help or comfort."

"Oh, I'm sure Mary Lou appreciated it," Melissa assured her. "She has a hard time showing her feelings. She's very reserved. But that doesn't mean she doesn't feel them. She just—doesn't show it."

As someone who was used to masking her own feelings when they were inconvenient, Erin could understand that. It wasn't easy for her to let herself be vulnerable, even to her closest friends. It was easier for her to mother Vic than to explain how she was feeling deep down. Easier to comfort Terry after one of his nightmares than to tell him about her own and the feelings of dread they always left behind, like an oily residue on her consciousness. And easier to wrap up Mary Lou's Thanksgiving dishes and put them away than to tell Mary Lou how concerned she was about Terry and his state of mind.

"I know. She was pretty shaken up. I wish there was more I could do for her."

"I can't imagine what Stayner was thinking," Melissa said, shaking her head. "The Coxes are such a pillar of the community. Whatever would possess him to search Campbell's car?"

Erin leaned on the top of the bakery display case. "I thought you would know whether the police got a tip. I can't see how Stayner would just stumble across something like that. Campbell's car on the street in front of Mary Lou's house. He surely wouldn't have left drugs in full view."

"I'm off work for a few days, so I don't know." Melissa helped part-time with administrative work at the police department and frequently let information slip when she should have guarded her tongue. But the Thanksgiving weekend was working against Erin. Melissa wouldn't be in the office until at least Monday. There was no way for her to know whether there had been an official tip called in unless Clara or someone else in the department told her.

"It has to be the girl," Melissa suggested. "Nobody knows anything about her. Who knows where she came from or what kind of history she has?"

Erin didn't like to throw around accusations, but she too had her suspicions about Brianna. It would make far more sense to her if the drugs were Brianna's than Campbell's. Brianna had just been too afraid to admit that they were hers. Campbell either didn't know where they had come from or wanted to protect Brianna. He had told Mary Lou that he and Brianna were just friends, but it was more likely that they were boyfriend and girlfriend. So, of course, Campbell would want to protect the one he loved.

"I don't know anything about her," Erin told Melissa. "She seemed like a very nice girl. But I didn't talk to her very much."

"Can you believe that Campbell would be going out with a black girl?" Melissa's eyes were wide. She shook her head. "I know that may not be such a big deal where you come from. Or even in Nashville. But around here? The courts may have passed *Loving* in the sixties, but that didn't have much effect on people's opinions on interracial marriages in these parts."

"There's nothing wrong with Campbell dating or marrying a black girl," Erin asserted. "But bringing her home for Thanksgiving dinner doesn't mean he's getting ready to marry her. He says they're just friends."

"So he says. He's got to know what folks around here would have to say about the matter."

Erin agreed, but she wasn't going to let Melissa think that she had anything against Campbell dating or marrying a girl of another race, which she did not. "Best we don't judge."

"Oh, I'm not judging. But if I had to pick which one of them is on drugs, it wouldn't be Campbell. And that's not because of the color of her skin, or his. That's just because I know Mary Lou and I've known those boys since they were babies. I just can't see Campbell getting into something like that. He has too much good sense."

Erin shrugged uncomfortably. It was hard to see anyone you had known since they were a baby taking up drugs or any other dangerous or criminal behavior. That was only natural. But it didn't mean Melissa was right. Erin knew from what Mary Lou had said in past months that she was worried about what Campbell might be getting into, and she was more likely to know than Melissa.

"So, what would you like today?" she asked, directing Melissa's attention to the display case. "Are you interested in some of our bite-sized Thanksgiving treats? Or are you looking for something for dinner today or tomorrow? Or one of your favorites?"

Melissa looked over the displayed treats, moaning about how good they looked. "I swear, you're going to make me gain ten pounds! Everything is always so good; I can't stop eating it."

"Maybe some of the little bites, then. You can have a few different ones, and it's like you've had one treat instead of three or four."

"Okay, how about a variety of those? Make sure you get some chocolate in there."

Erin knew that chocolate was one of Melissa's weaknesses. She nodded and got out a small box to put them in. "So do you have any plans for the rest of the weekend?"

"I'm planning on going out to Moose River—for a visit—this afternoon." Melissa avoided saying that she was going to see Davis at the penitentiary, but Erin knew what she meant.

She just smiled and nodded. She couldn't understand what it was Melissa saw in Davis, other than the fact that they had been friends when they were young. Erin never could see why women were attracted to men in prison. Those who became prison pen pals, especially to men on death row, made no sense to her. Why would they want a relationship with a murderer or some other criminal? And why have a relationship with someone they could never see except through bars or bulletproof glass?

"He's not as bad as you think," Melissa said. "I know that your experiences with him were not good, but he really isn't like that. He's just—that's how it's made him, the way that Angela treated him. Having to grow up like he did, without a father, knowing how he had died. He didn't have the kind of home life and opportunities that you or I did."

Melissa should have remembered that Erin's background was nothing like hers, and that having grown up in foster care, she hadn't had the home life and opportunities that Melissa referred to. Yet she hadn't found herself compelled to kill anyone she knew or to burn down any houses. Davis was where he belonged after making the choices he had, not as a result of something his mother had done decades before. He had still made his own choices to break the law and cause harm to others.

Melissa looked away from Erin and fussed with her wallet. Erin finished packaging the desserts and ringing them up on the register. She supposed that if she didn't want to hear Melissa was going out to see Davis, she shouldn't ask what her plans were.

~

After work, Erin decided to stop by Mary Lou's house. Mary Lou hadn't asked her to, and Erin hadn't said that she would, but she felt like it was the right thing to do. Mary Lou had a lot to deal with and if Erin could do anything to help her get through it, she wanted to do it.

Probably Mary Lou would assure her that everything was fine and they could get on without her. She had two other people in the house, not necessarily grown adults, but close enough to it.

But Erin felt she should check, just to be sure.

She had second thoughts while standing on Mary Lou's doorstep with her finger poised over the doorbell. Maybe it would be better if she just went home. Or if she called before showing up on the doorstep. She thought that the neighborly thing to do was just to go because, of course, if she called, Mary Lou would say that she didn't need anything. It was a friend's job to figure out what she needed and offer it. Something specific, not just an 'if there's anything you need, call me.'

She should have taken Mary Lou a casserole. Or at least rolls. She could go back to the bakery and get the day's leftovers out of the freezer. She'd hardly sold anything,

The door opened and Mary Lou looked at Erin. She raised her brows.

"Erin?"

"Oh, I'm sorry… were you just going out? I wanted to see if everything was okay. If there was anything I could do for you."

"Come in; I didn't know why you were just standing there without ringing the bell."

"Oh." Erin entered, her face burning. "I realized I didn't have a casserole…"

Mary Lou laughed. "You don't need a casserole, Erin. Heaven help me, I'm going to have a freezer full of casseroles. I never knew that a drug arrest was a 'casserole' event."

They sat down in the living room. Erin glanced around. It was very quiet. As if they were the only ones in the house.

"Where are Josh and Brianna? Are they… resting?"

Mary Lou rubbed her forehead, looking pained. "I don't know. What I mean is... no, they're not sleeping. We got up this morning and Brianna was gone. She left sometime in the night, just walked out of the house. No message or note, she was just gone. I don't know whether to tell the police she is missing or just to be glad I don't have to look after her. She said she was stranded here without a car... but I guess she found some way around that."

"She didn't take your car, did she?"

Mary Lou looked at Erin for a long moment as if she were considering the question, then finally shook her head.

"No. My car is still here. And if she's taken someone else's car, no one has informed me of the fact. I just assumed... that she must have called a friend from the city to pick her up. I was just glad that I didn't have to do it. She made it quite clear that she didn't have a way to get around on her own."

Erin remembered how Brianna had whined about needing somewhere to stay on Thanksgiving. Like somebody owed it to her. But what else was she going to do? With no way to get around and no money, the only other option would be to live on the streets, as Vic had when she had first arrived at Bald Eagle Falls, trying to keep under police radar and remain invisible. Not so easy in a small town like Bald Eagle Falls. Not like it would be in the city. When a person didn't have any home or money, she had to learn pretty quickly to speak up for what she wanted or to take what she needed. There was no other way to survive.

"I guess that's a good thing, then. Joshua didn't know where she had gone?"

"If he does, he isn't telling anyone. He's gone out... I think he might be looking for her, but I'm not sure. I'm... not looking for her."

"No, I think you have enough on your plate right now."

Mary Lou nodded.

"Have you heard anything from Campbell today? I know that because it was a holiday, the sheriff said not to expect anything for a few days, but did you get a chance to talk to him or hear that he was settled...?"

"I'm told he's fine but that I can't speak to him. I'll have to wait until he's arraigned and they decide whether he will be able to get out on bail or have to stay..." Mary Lou's voice broke and, for a moment she didn't speak, trying to regain control. "Or whether he will have to stay there until his case goes to court. It can take a long time for cases to be heard, so I am hoping that he can make bail."

"I hope so too. I'd hate to see him having to wait for that long."

Mary Lou nodded. She looked around the room. "Can I get you some tea?"

"No. I just stopped in to see if you were okay. I should be bringing you something."

"As I say, I don't need any more casseroles. And there are still all of the Thanksgiving leftovers. We barely touched anything. And now it's just down to Joshua and me again."

"I could help you get some of it packaged up and put in the freezer. You don't want to have it going bad."

Mary Lou closed her eyes and leaned back in her chair. "That sounds like a good idea. I don't have the energy to do it myself, but it really should be done."

"Okay. Why don't you rest there for a few minutes and let me take care of that."

"I should get up." Mary Lou put her hands on the arms of the chair to push herself up.

"No. I can find my way around a kitchen. You just stay put. That's an order."

The other woman settled back into the chair again. "You can't give me orders in my own house."

"I certainly can. If I was a doctor, I could give you orders, couldn't I?"

"Perhaps... but you're not."

"Hush."

Erin opened the big fridge to look over the contents, most of which she had packed away on Thanksgiving. It didn't look like anything had been touched. She looked quietly through the drawers and cupboards to see where all of the necessary supplies were, and started running water to fill the sink so she could clean the dishes she emptied and not leave them for Mary Lou to do. The noise of the water running helped to cover up the clinking of dishes as she proceeded with the work. Mary Lou's eyes remained shut and, in a few minutes, Erin was sure she was dozing, if not flat-out asleep.

Erin finished getting everything put away for Mary Lou, transferring most of the food into the freezer and leaving a couple of plates for Mary Lou and Joshua ready for microwaving, and left while Mary Lou was still asleep. She probably hadn't slept much during the night and had been worrying herself all day with Campbell's arrest. It wasn't fair that she wasn't even able to talk to him on the phone to reassure herself that he was alright.

She headed for home, thinking that there was still plenty of food left over from her own Thanksgiving dinner, so she didn't have to make anything new, either. She could also just warm up some turkey and gravy and the other fixings and microwave them. Done and dusted.

Terry wasn't able to tell her any more than Mary Lou had about Campbell. He wasn't on active duty, but Erin had thought that he would at least have gotten word from the sheriff or someone else in the department and would know a few details. Likewise, he hadn't heard anything on whether the police department was looking for Brianna or wanted her as a witness for the drug charges against Campbell. Erin suspected that was exactly why Brianna had disappeared. She wasn't going to want to appear in court to testify against Campbell or to take the chance that they would decide the drugs were hers and turn around and charge her as well.

"Do you at least know whose idea it was to arrest Campbell? Or to look at his car? They must have had a warrant to search his car, right? They couldn't have looked at it otherwise."

"Unless he had the drugs in plain sight," Terry agreed.

"But he wouldn't have them in plain sight. That would be stupid."

"There are plenty of stupid drug dealers and users out there. How do you think we manage to get the arrests that we do?"

"Well, I suppose. But I don't think Campbell is stupid. I don't think he would leave them where anyone walking by could see them."

Terry shrugged. "I wish I could tell you something, but I'm not involved in the investigation, so I don't know."

"And if you were involved in the investigation, then you wouldn't be able to tell me."

"Exactly."

"What good is having a police officer for a boyfriend if he can't give you all of the details of a current investigation?"

Terry grinned. "Darned if I know."

"Well, at least you can make dinner!" Erin observed. She hadn't even had to microwave the turkey dinner herself. Terry had everything ready on the table. When she got home, she felt bad for a moment for having gone to Mary Lou's house after work and being held up there. It meant that Terry's timing had been off, as he'd expected her home half an hour earlier than she was. But the turkey was still warm, and nothing was dry or congealing. "Everything is great. Thank you so much for getting it all on. That was a nice surprise."

"Well, you and Vic made everything. All I did was warm it up. The least I could do."

Erin pushed Orange Blossom away when he stood up on his hind legs and tried to reach the plates of turkey with one of his forepaws. "Blossom! No! You'll get your own. Stay back from the table."

He dropped back to his feet and sat looking at her.

"No need to sulk, you'll get some."

"I probably should have fed him before dinner. Then he wouldn't be bothering you."

"He knows better. K9 is behaving himself. Why can't Orange Blossom be polite like him?"

"Because Orange Blossom is a cat, and cats are allowed to behave however they want."

"Not however he wants. I told him to get down."

"And he's going to do it again anyway," Terry pointed out.

Erin used her toes to push the cat down again. "If you do that again, I'm going to lock you in the commode," she warned.

Orange Blossom slunk away, his ears down.

CHAPTER 12

Sunday was a sleep-in morning, since all they had to do at the bakery was the ladies' tea after their Sunday services. Erin told Vic that she could handle it, but even if she couldn't, then Charley was going to stop by and would pitch in.

As she parked her car in the lot behind the bakery, she eyed the unfamiliar vehicle behind her. Customer parking was in the front and no one else should have been parked in back when Erin was the only employee scheduled to be there. She didn't recognize it as an employee's vehicle.

She got out of her car and, after taking a glance around, sidled up to the unfamiliar black car. It had out-of-state plates and was a lot nicer than what most people in Bald Eagle Falls drove around.

The windows were tinted, and she leaned in close to peer into the car for any clues as to who it might belong to.

Erin jumped when she realized there was someone inside, looking back out at her. "Oh! I'm sorry, I was just looking to see if…" Erin sputtered, trying to explain herself. "I didn't recognize the car, so I wanted to see…"

The man inside did not move. He didn't change his position or say anything. Erin stood there, frozen, looking at him and waiting for his response.

As she stood there, it gradually dawned on her that no one could stay that still for that long. Not if they were awake. The man had clearly fallen asleep. Maybe he had pulled off the highway because he was tired and had found his way into a quiet private parking lot so that he could sleep without being approached by a highway cop.

She knocked on the window to wake him up. There was still no movement from within. The man stayed just as still as if he were unconscious. Maybe he was sick. Maybe he had diabetes and had gone into a coma from low blood sugar.

Or maybe…

Maybe he'd had a heart attack. Or something worse.

Erin knocked a few more times, more and more loudly, with increasing anxiety over the lack of response.

Finally, her heart pounding hard in her chest and a knot tied in her guts, Erin slid her phone out of her pocket and dialed the police dispatch number.

In a few minutes, Officer Stayner was on the scene. Erin hated that it wasn't Terry, or even one of the other people in the police department that she knew. She wanted the comfort of it being someone she knew.

Stayner wasn't at all comforting. He climbed out of his car slowly, eyeing her, his body language projecting that he thought she was a hysterical female who was panicking over nothing. About the only thing missing was an eye-roll, and she was sure he had done that when he had initially answered the call.

Stayner was probably around her age, late twenties or early thirties. New on the police force, without very many hours under his belt. Perhaps just enough to let him operate on his own without a partner babysitting him. Just enough to be dangerous.

"Miss Price," he greeted.

"Hi, Officer Stayner. Sorry for bothering you…"

"Not at all. That's what I'm here for. To serve and protect. Or whatever the Bald Eagle Falls version is."

She could just hear the snide remarks he was making in his head about the little town, and how boring it was to be a policeman there. Nothing exciting ever happened in Bald Eagle Falls. Well, if he'd been policing there for longer than a few weeks, he wouldn't be thinking that.

"So what have we here?" Stayner asked. He looked in the window of the unfamiliar car and tapped on the glass with his big flashlight. "Buddy. Time to get up."

When there was no response to his initial knocks, he pounded harder. "Hey! Are you drunk or stoned in there? Wake up! Let's see some ID."

There was still no response from the man. Erin watched Stayner, waiting for the moment when it would finally occur to him that there was something wrong. Something was very wrong.

Stayner stood there for a minute. He looked at her. He looked back at the unmoving man. Then he finally did what Erin hadn't dared to do and lifted the door handle.

CHAPTER 13

*E*rin braced herself. But she still wasn't prepared for what she saw.

The man's skin was white. That hadn't been obvious from viewing him through the tinted window. In fact, his skin was shockingly white. As if all of the blood had been drained out of him. Vampire white.

But not everything was white. His shirt was red. A nice dark red. It was, Erin thought, a white t-shirt originally, with a band logo stenciled on the front in black. It had been stained a deep, dark blood red, and Erin didn't think it was a fabric dye. There was a faintly sweet smell. His deodorant or the beginnings of decomposition.

Stayner reached out to shake or steady the driver, but stopped with his hand an inch away from the man's shoulder.

"Uh…"

"You should probably put on gloves," Erin said in a small voice.

Stayner cleared his throat. He seemed unable to move or to act. While Erin wasn't happy about the situation, she was just a little bit pleased to see his superior attitude disappear. He had answered the call thinking that she was panicking over nothing, but when it came down to it, he was the one who had frozen up.

"Gloves?" Erin suggested again. "Or maybe you should call the sheriff?"

Bobbing his head, Stayner finally reached for his shoulder-mounted radio and clicked the button. He placed the call in a calm voice, but Erin suspected it was more the consequence of shock than of feeling collected and in control.

"Are you okay?" Erin asked him. It was much easier to focus on Stayner and his reaction than on the man in the driver's seat. Her eyes stole back to him. He had on a black ball cap and dark glasses, so she couldn't see his eyes. He appeared to be in his early thirties. Well-built. She couldn't tell how tall he was sitting in the car, but his seat seemed to be pushed back, so he was probably a good height.

"I'm a cop," Stayner snapped. "I'm fine."

"Okay."

"Did you touch anything?"

"Just the window. I just knocked on the window to wake him up. Like you did."

Except that he hadn't used his hand and left prints on it. Erin tried to remember whether she had leaned on the car. Had she left prints on the top or the side when she was bending down, peering in the window?

"I don't think I touched anything else. I didn't open the door."

Stayner had been the one to open it. His prints would be on the handle, maybe obscuring the prints of whoever had last opened the door. Unless that person had been wearing gloves and had not left prints.

Erin didn't get close enough to see how the driver of the car had been injured. She didn't want to add whatever bullet hole or stab wound might be visible to the catalog of images in her head. Her brain already had plenty there to keep her up at night.

Sheriff Wilmot pulled into the parking lot in his squad car. Once out of his car, he met Erin's eyes, raising an eyebrow.

"Miss Price... what have you done now?"

Erin gave a laugh that was more of a sob. "It's not my fault that bodies keep showing up. Can't these guys find somewhere else to die?" She laughed again, feeling a little giddy.

The sheriff glanced in the open door of the strange car, but didn't get close.

"Let's get you out of here first. Have you opened up the bakery yet?"

"No."

"Where are your keys?"

Erin looked down at her purse. She knew she must have just put them away and they should have been sitting right on top, but they weren't. She dug down deeper into the purse, shifting things around. She didn't hear the jingle of the keys. She patted her pockets and found a lump. She handed the ring of keys to the sheriff. He took her by the arm and escorted her to the back door of the bakery, looking through the keys to find the one that would unlock the back door. He opened the door and took her into the kitchen.

"Have a seat, Miss Price. Have you had anything to eat this morning?"

"Yes." Erin pulled one of the stools back from the counter and sat. The muscles in her legs started to twitch. She hadn't even realized how she had been shaking until she sat down.

"Good. Can I get you a drink of water? Do you want to put on the kettle?"

"I need to make tea for the church ladies. I have a boiler." Erin indicated the tall, stainless steel electric boiler.

Sheriff Wilmot eyed it. "I'll just get you a glass of water for now, and you can operate that thing. But only when you're sure you're steady." He found the coffee mugs and filled one with cold water from the tap. He handed it to her.

"Sit for a while and sip that. Will you be okay here for a few minutes while I go deal with that?" He made a motion toward the back.

"Yes."

"You're not going to faint?"

"No. I'm okay."

"Don't try to do anything yet. I'll have someone check on you in a few minutes and take your statement. Until then, stay put."

She stayed put. She knew that she needed to get things ready for the ladies' tea, but she didn't know if the sheriff would even let them go ahead with it, or if he would keep the whole place closed down until he had finished their initial crime scene review.

Erin wanted to call Terry and tell him what was going on. But the sheriff probably wouldn't like her talking to anyone until she had told them everything she knew—which was nothing. But he still wouldn't want anyone else talking to her about it.

Eventually, she got bored with sitting on the stool without doing anything else. She got down and started puttering around, getting things prepared for the ladies' tea in case it was allowed to go ahead. There wasn't a lot of preparation that had to go into it; they often had leftover treats from the freezer rather than her making anything specially for the event. Desserts and hot water for the tea were the only things that were needed. Though she might make coffee for the sheriff and the other officers too. She knew they preferred coffee over tea.

"We have a few questions for you now, Miss Price."

Erin startled at the voice behind her. She hadn't heard the door open while she'd been rattling dishes. She turned quickly and saw Officer Stayner. She wished that Tom Baker or the sheriff had been assigned to question her instead. At least she knew them and that they would be fair to her.

"Uh, okay."

"How do you know the victim?"

She looked at him, blinking. "I don't know him. I've never seen him before in my life."

"Are you sure of that?"

"Of course. He had out-of-state plates. I didn't recognize the car. I knew it was out of place as soon as I got here."

"You're from out of state."

"Well… yes. I guess. But I don't know him. I've never met him before."

"Then what was he doing in your parking lot? If he was waiting for someone, why would he be behind the bakery? He was waiting for you, or for one of your employees."

"I don't know him," Erin repeated.

"It can be difficult to recognize someone… in that condition."

"Dead, you mean?"

"Yes. People's faces look different when they aren't… animated."

"I have seen dead people before."

He lifted his eyebrows. "So I understand."

"I didn't mean that. I meant… funerals and things like that. I've been to funerals and seen open caskets before. People look different, but not that different. I don't know the guy. I swear."

"So you don't have any explanation of why he would be here in your parking lot."

"As far as I know, he just randomly pulled in there to rest."

"And someone just happened to come by and kill him while he was resting there. If Bald Eagle Falls had a night stalker serial killer, I might believe that, but there isn't exactly a history of random murders here."

Probably more than he realized.

"I don't know him or why he stopped here. That's all I can tell you."

"Start at the beginning and tell me how you found him there and what you did."

Erin sighed. She moved around the kitchen, making preparations and walked him through the sequence of events from pulling into the parking lot to calling the police and Stayner's arrival.

"And that's it. All I did was try to wake him up, and when he didn't wake up and I thought there might be something wrong, I called the dispatcher. That's what I'm supposed to do, isn't it?"

Stayner was making notes in his notepad. He nodded grudgingly. "Yes, that's what you're supposed to do. You know the drill. Been here before, haven't you?"

Erin just looked at him. She couldn't see how he could think it was her fault that someone had been killed in her back parking lot. She hadn't had anything to do with it, and if she had been out to kill someone, why would she have done it right there on her own property? Wouldn't it make more sense to do it somewhere farther afield? Maybe where they wouldn't connect it with her? Unless she was some lunatic who liked getting the attention of the police and being put under the microscope again and again.

"We would like you to come to the police department to make an official statement and sign it."

"I just made a statement. I have the ladies' tea soon. It will have to wait."

"Are you being obstructive?" he challenged.

"No. I'm running my business."

Stayner glared at her. Erin made a motion to indicate the kitchen and what she was doing. He couldn't be that blind. He knew that it was her bakery. She couldn't just drop everything.

The man wasn't going to get any deader.

"Did you identify him?" she asked. "I assume he must have had some ID On him, or the car registration, maybe…?"

"He's been tentatively identified by his ID, yes. We'll have to get that confirmed through fingerprints or medical records."

Erin waited for more information. The man had died in her parking lot, after all; she deserved to know something about it. But Stayner didn't look like he was going to offer any more information without prompting.

"Was he someone known to the police? Did he have family around Bald Eagle Falls?"

"We'll have to follow up on all of that," he snapped.

That told Erin that the victim wasn't known. Stayner would have been more likely to tell her it was none of her business if he knew but didn't want to share it.

"So nobody knows him? That's pretty weird."

"I suspect your friend Campbell Cox knows something about it."

Erin opened her mouth to object. Campbell Cox? What did the stranger have to do with Campbell Cox?

"Awfully coincidental, don't you think, that we have this sudden crime spree when he gets in town?"

"Crime spree? You arrested him for drug possession and someone we don't know shows up dead? That's a spree?"

"It's pretty unusual around here, wouldn't you say?"

"No... I wouldn't. We've had several unusual deaths, and they didn't have anything to do with Campbell. And I don't know if I believe that he was in possession of drugs, either. I think that smells like a set-up."

Stayner advanced toward her, his expression grim. "*What* did you say?"

Erin took a step back. She looked toward the back door, hoping Sheriff Wilmot would appear. "I'm saying I think someone set him up. How did you know there were drugs in his car? Were they in plain sight? Did someone call in a tip?"

"Listen, Miss Price." He continued to advance until he was right inside her personal space. "I don't like these accusations. Do you think I would act without due cause? That I go around arresting whoever I feel like? Campbell Cox was arrested because he was in possession of a large amount of illegal narcotics. Not because of any personal feelings I may or may not have toward him."

"Okay." Erin held up her hands, trying to keep him from advancing any farther or touching her. "I didn't mean to imply that you had done anything wrong, just that there might be someone who had an axe to grind. Someone else could have called in a tip and set him up."

"Do you think that I'm not qualified to investigate something like that?

I'm just some backwoods inbred cop who just got the job because no one else wanted it?"

"No."

"I have the training. I have the experience. They wouldn't have put me in this job if I hadn't."

"No, of course not."

"You think that your sweetheart is the only one who can investigate anything around here? You think he's God in these parts and no one else can possibly measure up to what he does."

"Officer Stayner…" Erin protested, tears of frustration springing to her eyes as she tried to stop the verbal assault.

He just looked all the more enraged by her attempts to stop him. There was a sound at the door, and Stayner whirled around.

Tom Baker touched his cap in greeting at Erin. "Miss Price." He turned to Stayner. "Sheriff wants us to do a canvass of the block, see if anyone saw or heard anything last night…"

"No one would have witnessed it. Bald Eagle Falls shuts down at nine o'clock. There wouldn't have been anyone in any of these stores."

"Some of the stores have residences over top," Tom pointed out. "Or they might have stayed late to do their books or inventory. You never know what people might have been doing."

Stayner grumbled and headed for the door to go out to do the canvass with Tom. After he was gone, Tom nodded to Erin and left, pulling the door shut behind him.

CHAPTER 14

*T*he ladies' tea went ahead as scheduled. Erin had everything ready and hadn't been told by the sheriff that she would have to remain closed or shouldn't have anyone into the shop.

By the time the women got into the bakery, they knew most of the details about the death already. More than Erin could have shared with any degree of certainty.

"We pigged out at Thanksgiving," Cindy Prost said as she selected a couple of treats from the platter of goodies. "I really shouldn't be having more sweets today! Christmas is still coming, and I don't want to put on extra pounds before that. It's hard enough to lose the Christmas weight in January."

"They're so small," Erin assured her. "And the tea is hardly any calories. That's not enough to cause any weight gain."

"I don't know how you can bake all day and stay so slim."

"Do you think Mary Lou is going to come today?" Melissa asked.

Erin was shocked by the question. "Oh, I don't think so. She's having a hard time holding it all together. If I was her... I certainly wouldn't be making it to tea."

"She didn't make it to church," Melissa confided. "I thought she would at least do that. Where can you go for solace if not to church?"

Erin smiled and shook her head. If she were looking for peace and quiet, a place where she could really heal the hurts, it wouldn't be to church where everyone would be whispering about her and talking about her behind her back.

"Maybe I'll stop by there after the tea," Melissa offered. "A few of us could go, give her our regards, let her know that we were there for her whenever she needs us." Melissa looked around at the other ladies and got nods and murmurs of agreement from a number of them.

"We should take something over, though," Lottie Sturm reminded them. "I can't imagine she's up to making meals, and she has a teenager. That poor woman. I can't believe Campbell would put her through all of this after all she has been through already. It's like a stab to the heart."

There was a sharp intake of breath and everyone looked at her.

"Oh!" Lottie covered her mouth dramatically. "I didn't mean it that way!" She let out a high-pitched giggle. "A stab to the heart! Oh, my goodness. It must have been because I was already thinking of…"

They all looked toward the back of the bakery, though of course there was no way for them to see what was going on through the walls. They had all seen cop shows on TV. They could imagine everything that was going on.

"Do they know anything yet?" Cindy asked Melissa. "They must at least know the identity of the man who was…"

"I won't know anything until tomorrow! This is one long weekend when I wish I hadn't got the whole time off. There has been so much going on, and I don't get to hear any of it because I'm just sitting around at home. I even asked at the penitentiary yesterday, but they weren't letting anyone see Campbell. I can't imagine what he's going through, the poor boy. He can't even see any visitors!"

"Why not?" Cindy demanded. "Even criminals are allowed to have visitors!"

"They said no one could see him," Melissa reiterated. "I even told them I was with the Bald Eagle Falls PD, and they just shook their heads and said there were no exceptions! I was shocked. If one of them wanted to come and see one of our detainees, I would let them."

"You don't exactly make the rules for the police department," Lottie pointed out. "I don't think it would be up to you! Besides, why would they want to see one of your inmates, except to transport them to Moose River? You wouldn't exactly stop them from doing that!"

Melissa's cheeks turned pink. "I was just saying, we would never treat them that way. Like they were just a name on a list. We would consider the circumstances. In a little place like Bald Eagle Falls, we don't just rubber stamp everyone and treat them the same way. We understand that circumstances vary. And someone like Campbell... well, it isn't like he's a dangerous criminal. He's just a boy. And not one of those violent psychopaths that you see on TV, up for murder before they're eighteen. He's just a nice young man. They should take that into account."

Erin worked her way around the room with a teapot to see if anyone needed more hot water. It was a smaller crowd than usual, and if they were planning to visit Mary Lou before heading home to make their families' suppers, then it would be a short day at Auntie Clem's.

"So we don't even know who it is yet?" Cindy asked. "It wasn't anyone from Bald Eagle Falls. Some outsider. That's what I heard."

"Clara couldn't make it," Melissa observed. "She's almost always here for the tea, but they called her in to work. On a Sunday! She'd be able to give us the details, but with everybody busy over there right now, she's not going to be able to give us any information." Melissa shook her head grimly. "Sheriff doesn't like to think that people are gossiping about the cases."

And yet, the gossip always got out anyway. Erin looked the ladies at the tea over, wondering which of them would manage to pry information out of Clara first. Clara might be worked within an inch of her life at the police department, doing all of the administrative work demanded by the three policemen, and Sheriff Wilmot might hover nearby making sure that she didn't spill the beans over the phone, but one way or another, Clara would still get the information out just like a town crier. Everyone would know what had happened long before the weekly paper was circulated.

The bells on the door jangled, and Charley burst into the bakery. She always had to have a dramatic entrance. To make it look like she was over-worked and just barely keeping it all together. One would think that she was the one running the bakery instead of Erin. Charley liked to think she ran the bakery, but it was all for show. She really didn't have a clue about most of the day-to-day running of the business.

"Oh, Erin. I'm sorry to be so late getting here! You would not believe what a day it has been! If it's not one thing, it's another! I meant to be here in time to help you get everything ready to go, but there has been no end of interruptions today! I was wondering if maybe we should arrange to take some things over to Mary Lou Cox's house. You heard about her son, right? I couldn't believe it when I heard that he was arrested. That poor woman."

"I was there," Erin said. "On Thanksgiving. And yesterday. To help her out with a few things. You can talk to Melissa about what arrangements the ladies are making. I'm sure you would be a big help to her."

Charley's nose wrinkled. She did not like being told what to do. If there were a rescue mission, she wanted to be the one leading it, not the one following orders. "Oh, of course," she agreed. "Do let me know what you're doing, Melissa, and what you need."

"Come sit down and we'll talk about it," Melissa said, inviting Charley into the circle of women and their discussions about what would need to be done for Mary Lou and Joshua, and about the latest word on the man who was stabbed.

"What?" Charley's voice rose above the rest. "Who was stabbed?"

They all looked at her, and Charley immediately knew she had made a mistake.

"I didn't make it to services today," Charley explained quickly. "You know how it is when you're planning for an event like this; I needed to be here. I had a list of things that Erin would need…"

She glanced at Erin, hoping that her big sister wouldn't give away the lie. Not that anyone believed her anyway. If Charley had needed to prepare anything for the women's tea, then she would have been there before it started, not halfway through.

"There was a man in a car in the back parking lot," Erin told her.

"And he was… stabbed? By who?" Charley looked around at the other women as if expecting one of them to jump forward and explain their part in it. Maybe that was the way it had worked in her old life in the Dyson clan, but that wasn't what happened in Bald Eagle Falls. The man had probably been stabbed by another outsider. It was a crime that had just happened to take place in Bald Eagle Falls. It didn't actually have anything to do with anyone who lived there.

"We don't know that," Erin told her. "They're investigating. It just happened this morning. It wasn't like someone was standing over him with a knife or who confessed to it already."

"Who was stabbed? Was he injured? Killed? Did he know who had done it?"

"He's dead," Melissa said. "Discovered by your sister."

"By Erin?" Charley shook her head at Erin. "How is it that you keep stumbling across bodies? You're bad luck!"

"I just... he was in the parking lot. It isn't my fault that whatever happened had to take place in my parking lot. I didn't plan it that way, I can assure you!"

"I hope not!" Charley agreed. She shook her head in mock dismay. "She looks like such a quiet, harmless little thing. But under the surface... still waters run deep."

Melissa laughed, tossing her head of bouncing dark curls. "You're always so funny, Charley."

Charley frowned, maybe deciding that 'so funny' wasn't the image she wanted to project. She was supposed to be a tough chick from a crime family. An entrepreneur and business owner. Not a clown. She looked around at the little group.

"Where is everyone today? Is Vic in the kitchen?"

"Vic is off with Willie today," Erin reminded her. "That's why you were supposed to be here to help in the kitchen."

"Oh right, I forgot she was off this weekend. I'm just so used to seeing her here all the time. And Terry? Does he know yet that you found another body?"

CHAPTER 15

I t was a question that Erin didn't know the answer to. She suspected that if Terry knew about her latest discovery, he would have been there at the bakery to at least make sure she was okay. But he was also off of active duty and might have thought it was best to stay away so that the on-duty officers could take care of the investigation, knowing that he would be in the way if he were there. It was a weird feeling, not having him and K9 on duty, making their rounds, always there at the end of the ladies' tea to help Erin to clear up so that they could spend the rest of Sunday afternoon and evening together.

The ladies' tea was not interrupted by the police canvassing the neighborhood. They probably wanted to catch each of the women alone. But since they were going to Mary Lou's to check on her, they broke up a little earlier than usual, and Erin was left to tidy up herself.

Charley, of course, had gone with the others to Mary Lou's. Hopefully, she wouldn't make a nuisance of herself.

The bells on the door rang, and Erin looked up, expecting to see one of the policemen there. Or maybe Terry, there to help as he usually did. But it was Rohilda Beaven.

"Oh, Beaver. I'm afraid you're a little late. The ladies' tea wrapped up early. They headed over to Mary Lou's house to see if she needed anything."

Beaver chewed on her mouthful of gum, nodding. "I know. I saw the convoy."

"I hope they don't stay there too long. They'll wear her out."

Beaver said nothing. Erin paused in her work, wondering what to say. Beaver was clearly not there for the ladies' tea. So what was she after?

"Guess you had some more excitement this morning."

Erin nodded slowly, wiping a few crumbs from the tables. "Yeah. You heard. Did you know anything about it? Is he... one of yours?"

"One of my what?" Beaver laughed. "I didn't leave a dead body in your backyard, if that's what you're asking. I wouldn't be so messy."

"No... I guess I mean, was he a drug dealer you knew of? Or an informant? Anybody... from your world?"

Beaver chewed for a few more minutes, considering Erin's question. Erin didn't think that it was that complicated a question.

"We might have a line on him," she said slowly, "but I can't say that I know for sure who it was yet. For one thing, the police department has not asked for my assistance."

"That doesn't mean you can't go in, does it? Can't you ask, if you think it's related to a case of yours?"

"A person has to be careful of politics between departments and organizations. I don't want to step on any toes. I wouldn't be surprised if the sheriff asked for help, but so far he seems to think this is something he can take care of on his own."

"Can he?"

"I don't have any reason to tell him he doesn't. Unless, of course..."

"What?"

"Well, if it is someone who is known to us... then that could put a different spin on things."

"But how will you know he's known to you unless they identify him and pass that information on to your organization?"

"It's a bit of a Catch-22," Beaver agreed, chewing.

"Do you think you know who it is?"

More chewing, no response.

"Do you think I can tell you something about him?" Erin tried.

Beaver gave a wide smile. "Well, if you're offering..."

"You know I'll always help you out if I can."

Beaver leaned forward. She looked around the bakery and apparently changed her mind. She flipped the front door sign over to 'closed' and turned the bolt to lock it.

"Back door locked?" she asked.

"No, I think it's still open. The police were in and out."

"After all that has happened, I would think you would be more careful about securing doors."

"The police were here. What's anyone going to do?"

"You don't know until it is done, and then it is too late."

"I don't want to become completely paranoid. I already have to fuss with the burglar alarm at home, even if I'm in. I don't want to be the town crazy lady."

"Oh, I think that position is already taken."

"By who?" The thought gave Erin pause. Erin herself, because she kept stumbling over dead bodies? Beaver, an outsider, who was aloof and knew things that no one else did? Mary Lou because her husband was crazy, so she must be too? Adele? Charley?

Beaver shrugged. She pulled down the blind that covered the window.

"Let's go in back. Less chance of being seen or overheard there."

"No one is going to overhear us out here."

But there was no point in arguing about it. Beaver walked around the counter and into the kitchen. Erin followed her, wondering what was going on.

"Tell me everything you can about finding the stabbing victim," Beaver instructed.

Once more, Erin went through the story. She didn't remember anything significant that she hadn't told the police. She was going to have to go into the police department to tell it once again and to sign her statement, so it wouldn't hurt to practice telling it one more time to Beaver.

Beaver didn't interrupt, listening carefully to every word. Erin finished with her call to the dispatcher, looked at Beaver, and shrugged.

"Can you describe him?" Beaver asked.

"White guy. Thirties. He looked well-muscled. Can't exactly tell how tall he was. T-shirt with a band name or something on it. Blue jeans."

"Any identifying features?"

"No... I don't think so..." Erin tried to replay the moment in her mind. She had seen the man pretty clearly. She hadn't been standing far away. "He had... like a black, patterned bandana around his neck. He had on dark glasses and a cap, a black cap, so I couldn't see much of his face."

"Long hair, short?"

"Short. Maybe buzzed."

"Tattoos?"

"Uh… yes." Erin closed her eyes and tried to picture the areas of skin she'd been able to see. "I think there was something on his neck, under the bandana, but I couldn't see what it was. And he had one on his arm."

Beaver nodded. She waited while Erin tried to remember what the tattoo had looked like.

"It might have been a homemade tattoo. A little fuzzy."

"All black?"

Erin nodded.

"Colors are harder to cook up in prison," Beaver said.

"You think it was a prison tattoo?"

"Do you remember anything else about it?"

"I'm trying."

"Was it a word or a symbol? Or a picture?"

"There might have been a word under it. But I don't think it was English. Maybe Greek or Russian, those kinds of letters."

"Cyrillic."

Erin thought for a minute, then shook her head. "I can't think of what it was. I was… trying my best not to look at him. I have enough nightmares already; I didn't want anything else to add to them."

"Sure," Beaver agreed. "That's fine. I'll ask the police department. See if they mind telling me what they know. The guy's identity should be released within a few days. It's just nice to get a head start on it if it happens to be related to one of my cases. Since the big drug bust, I'm the person who is sort of responsible for… keeping an eye on things in Bald Eagle Falls. Making sure that the bad elements don't start creeping back in."

"Well, this guy looked…" Erin fished for the right word. "He certainly could have been one of them—a drug dealer or organized crime. But I don't think he was from around here. Not from one of the clans."

"Not with a Russian prison tattoo," Beaver agreed.

"Are they gone yet? Have they taken him away?"

Beaver went to the back door and cracked it open to peer out. "Still here. From what I understand, transport gets a little tricky out here. And on a Sunday… they probably have to call someone in who wouldn't normally work today."

"With Bo, they had to wait longer than twenty-four hours. You don't think we'll have to wait that long, do you?"

"We could always strap him into a seatbelt and do it ourselves," Beaver suggested. She laughed at Erin's alarm. "The medical examiner wouldn't like that. Chain of custody and all. Let me see what they have to say."

Beaver opened the door the rest of the way and walked through the parking lot to where Stayner was positioned to guard the scene until the victim could be transported to the medical examiner's office in the city. Erin could hear her inquiring tones. "Erin wants to know when…"

Erin figured Beaver was probably happy to have an excuse to get closer to the scene and see what she could find out from the officers. Erin looked out the door to see how Beaver was being received, but she didn't want to see any more of the body, so she only took a quick look and then went back to cleaning up. Stayner didn't appear to get aggressive toward Beaver like he had been to Erin. He'd have a shock if he did antagonize her. Beaver was more than capable of defending herself. She wouldn't put up with any nonsense from Stayner.

When Erin got home, she was expecting Terry to be watching anxiously for her. He would have heard about the dead man in her parking lot and would want to know if she was okay. But he didn't come to the door as she walked up to it, not watching out the window for her. He wasn't in the living room when she walked in. Erin frowned.

"Hello? Anybody home?"

There was no answer. The house was quiet. Quiet enough for Erin to hear Orange Blossom jumping off of the bed and coming down the carpeted hall toward her.

"Hey, Blossom. How are you doing?" She bent down to scratch his ears, and saw Marshmallow watching her from behind a chair. "Where's our friends? Where are Terry and K9? Did they go out?"

The cat meowed, which didn't help Erin at all. She straightened back up and looked out the front window. Terry's truck was still parked against the curb, so he hadn't gone out for a drive. He was probably just taking K9 out and would be back soon. It was such a change for them to be at the house most of the day, instead of out on patrol, always moving.

Erin didn't know what to do with herself. She had anticipated having to tell her story and answer all of Terry's questions. Instead, she was in an empty house with no one to talk to.

"I guess… I'll work on my plans for next week," she told Orange Blossom. "It's nice and quiet, so I should take advantage of that while I can." Soon enough, she would be hearing from Terry and Vic and everyone else who learned about the demise of the unknown man in her parking lot.

Blossom rubbed against her encouragingly. It was comforting that he didn't care about the dead man. As far as he was concerned, it was a perfectly normal day.

CHAPTER 16

*E*rin was starting to get worried about Terry not getting home. He knew what time she usually got finished at the bakery, and she had expected him to be back. They liked to spend time together Sunday afternoon and evening; it was a special time that they tried to set aside for each other.

Maybe he thought that since he was at home all the time now and they had more time to spend together, she wouldn't expect him to make time for her Sunday night.

But he wasn't usually out for so long without letting her know where he was.

She couldn't help but think of Mary Lou's Roger, wandering away, getting lost, how the whole town had turned out to search for him. But that was different. There was nothing wrong with Terry. At least, the doctors said there wasn't. They said he would fully recover. There was nothing to worry about.

Erin looked out the window, hoping she would see Terry walking toward the house with K9 at his side. There was no sign of him.

An anxious knot in her stomach, she finally pulled out her phone and texted him. A text would be less intrusive than a call. She wouldn't sound like a nagging wife. He would know that she was home and waiting for him, but he wouldn't have to give excuses or explain where he was.

She watched anxiously for his reply.

~

Eventually, Erin gave up on waiting for Terry or anyone else to get home. She was her own person with her own life, and she didn't have to wait around for Terry to finish having a beer with the guys or whatever he was doing. Since there was no one else around, it was a good time for her to practice her tai chi.

There were a lot of thoughts she wanted to clear out of her mind.

She padded out to the yard in her bare feet, keeping a lookout for any stray offerings from K9. He was good about using the run that Terry had built along the fence for him, but she didn't want to get sloppy and end up putting her foot into something she would regret later.

She found a nice flattish area in the grass under a shade tree, and stood still for a few minutes just breathing and grounding herself. She could do it. She could heal her brain and stop having dreams and distressing thoughts, could quit jumping at every little thing, and could get a good night's sleep and be a support for Terry rather than his having to always come to her aid. All it took was a little self-discipline, a few minutes of standing meditation every day. Just like she had to eat and sleep to nourish her body, she needed some quiet time to meditate for her brain. Then she would be able to banish the effects of the traumas.

She focused on the forms she had learned from watching videos. She was, she was sure, not doing them quite the right way. If she had a trainer who knew what he was doing, he would correct her posture and tell her the right way to do each form, but she didn't, so her imperfect move- ments would just have to do. She didn't believe that there was any magical alignment of her body's energy fields that she needed to achieve. It was just a matter of quieting her mind and relaxing her body. Meditation would slow her heart rate and breathing, and that in itself would bring benefits.

Erin was nearing the end of her practice when she heard the back door of the house open. It slammed shut again.

"She's out here!" Terry called back into the house.

Erin opened her eyes and turned as he hurried across the yard toward her.

"I came home and you weren't there, I was worried sick that something might have happened to you!" Terry told her, his voice edgy and irritated.

Erin pulled her arms in and rested her feet flat on the grass and looked at him. "I was worried about you too. You didn't leave a note or tell me you were going out. We always do Sunday afternoon together, so I thought you would be here."

"Willie needed a part, and asked if I wanted to go into the city with him for a change of scene. I did message you."

"I guess I didn't get your message," Erin said calmly. She thought she was doing very well not to get upset by the conversation, by his panicky and accusatory tone.

"I wouldn't just leave without letting you know what I was up to!"

Erin raised her brows. "And I didn't either."

"You weren't in the house!"

"I was still in the yard. I would have been back inside in a minute, I was just finishing up. It wasn't like I left for hours on end."

"I sent you a message," Terry grumbled. He stood there for a minute, looking at her, his face a confluence of mixed emotions. Worry, irritation, relief, defensiveness. Everything but the smile and dimple that she liked to see there. Things just hadn't been the same since he'd been injured.

Erin put her arms around him, and he hugged her back fiercely, squeezing just a little too tightly and rocking her side to side. He kissed her head and neck and she felt his body start to lose some of its rigidity.

"Hey, if you guys are done out there…"

Terry released his hold on Erin, and she looked past him to Vic, standing at the back door grinning at the two of them.

"Looks like everybody is home. Did you go into town for parts too?" Erin asked her.

"I had some other things to take care of while the men did their manly shopping. Maybe we should have waited for you. I didn't think about taking Terry away from you. We just thought he might like to get out."

"I didn't need to go into the city. But it would have been nice to at least know where everyone was."

Vic grimaced. "Sorry. You're right. It was just spur-of-the-moment, because Willie's auger broke, and he needed it if he was going to—well, you know. It was an emergency. I didn't think we'd be so long, but apparently there aren't a lot of auger shops open on a Sunday."

Erin walked back across the yard and into the house, with Terry behind her, Vic withdrawing into the house and leading the way to the living room where Willie was already sprawled on the couch, his legs stretched out in front of him and a beer in one hand. He smiled and nodded at Erin. "So, any excitement at the ladies' tea today? I imagine there was a lot of chatter about Mary Lou's problems."

"Yes, that and the dead guy in the parking lot."

CHAPTER 17

*T*he room went utterly silent. Erin held back a self-satisfied smile. She had been waiting to tell them all about it ever since she had left the bakery, and it was reassuring to see that she had not misjudged the situation. They hadn't heard about the appearance of Mr. Dead Guy because they had been out of town. They were in Willie's truck, so they didn't have Terry's police scanner along. And apparently, no one had bothered to call or text them. Probably everyone assumed that Terry would be the first to know, and the police department preferred to get their tasks done without his interference while he was off-duty.

Terry was standing behind Erin. He put his hands on her shoulders and turned her around to face him. "What?" He searched her face. "Is this some kind of joke?"

Erin shook her head. She couldn't find the words to say immediately, halted by the expression on his face. She shook her head again, blinking her eyes to avoid the tears that threatened suddenly. "No. Not a joke."

She had been strong all day. She had not fainted. She had called the police. She had reported to the police and held the ladies' tea and talked to Beaver about it, all without any show of excessive emotion. But in Terry's arms once more, looking up into his concerned face, the emotions welled up in her and her throat was hot and tight. She cleared her throat and shrugged.

"Come sit down."

Terry took her over to the couch. Willie sat up straighter so that she had enough room, and she and Terry sat down together, cuddled close. He encircled her with a strong, protective arm.

"What dead guy in the parking lot?"

"When I got to the bakery today, there was a car parked back there. It's private parking, and no one is supposed to be there except for me and my employees, but sometimes people pull in there because it's convenient to somewhere else they want to go."

Terry nodded. He knew that as well as she did. Who did she call when there was someone parked there illegally?

"It had tinted windows and I could see that there was someone inside, but I couldn't see any details. That he was... not just asleep."

She gave them the details of realizing that there was something wrong and calling the dispatcher, of talking to Stayner and the sheriff and Beaver. She only touched briefly on the ladies' tea; there wasn't really anything in that part of the story that would interest Terry or Willie.

"Have they identified him yet?" Terry asked.

"I don't know. You'd have to talk to the police. I don't think they had yet when I came home. But that was a few hours ago."

Terry shook his head. "I'm so sorry I wasn't here. I had no idea!"

"I know. I didn't think there was any point in calling or texting you, since you couldn't be involved in the investigation."

"But I still would have liked to know what had happened to you. You're the one that I'm concerned with."

Erin felt warm. She snuggled against him. Orange Blossom decided that he was missing out on all of the cuddling and jumped up onto Terry's lap and started kneading with needle-sharp claws. Terry winced and repositioned the cat, eventually managing to get him settled, half on his lap and half on Erin's.

"I'll check with Beaver," Vic declared. "The police department might not like you getting involved when you're not on active duty, and they for sure won't tell one of us anything. But I think Beaver will."

Erin nodded her agreement. Vic pulled out her phone and tapped in Beaver's number.

Beaver didn't have a delicate, ladylike phone voice. Vic's volume was turned up high enough that even a few feet away from Vic, she could hear Beaver's voice clearly.

"Evenin' Miss Victoria. I'm not far away. Do you want me to come over?"

"Yes," Vic laughed. "We're just at Erin's."

"I expected a call long before this."

"Well, we just got home. Erin's been here alone all afternoon."

"Be right there."

Vic slid her phone back away, shaking her head.

They mostly just looked at each other, not sure what to say, as they waited for Beaver to get there. As she had said, she wasn't far away, so they didn't have long to wait. She gave a quick rap on the door and let herself in.

Erin studied Beaver as she slouched into the room, lazily chewing her gum and looking around at them. Beaver always looked lazy and relaxed, but Erin was starting to recognize little tells. She looked around at them, not with the expression of someone who was bored with the situation, but with the interest of someone who was excited and had news to share. Her excitement was hard to detect, but it was there.

"So, you solved it yet?" she drawled.

"We don't even know who it was yet," Erin pointed out. "Have they identified him?"

"I have," Beaver said smugly.

"You have?"

Beaver looked around at the rest of them, as if expecting someone to jump in and say that they already knew. But nobody else knew what she had found out.

"Well?" Vic said impatiently. "Who was it?"

"I think Miss Erin has more of a right to be impatient than you do," Beaver pointed out. "You just barely even found out there *was* a victim."

"Just tell us what you know," Erin insisted.

"Volkov."

"What?"

"That's who it was. The victim's name. Valerie Volkov."

"Valerie?" Vic giggled.

"He's Russian," Beaver said, allowing a small smile of amusement. "Valerie is not an uncommon man's name."

"Valerie," Vic repeated again. "So, what do you know about Valerie Volkov?"

"He's a pretty unsavory character." Beaver nodded to Erin. "Like you and I thought, he has spent time in a Russian prison. That was a good catch."

Terry turned his head to look at Erin, frowning. "You figured out he had been in a Russian prison?"

Erin laughed. That had been Beaver's observation, not her own. Or Beaver had deduced it from what Erin had told her. And she would have figured it out quickly enough when she saw the body and saw the tattoo for herself. "It was a joint effort," she said. "He had tattoos, Beaver figured out that they were probably prison tattoos. And there was Russian lettering. So…"

"So Russian prison," Terry said. "And he was?" He turned the conversation back to Beaver.

"He was. In and out a few times. Maybe not Russian mob, but definitely a gangster. And then he shows up in the United States."

"And continued his life of crime," Terry suggested.

"Yes. Involved in all kinds of unsavory practices here."

Erin was sinking into the couch against Terry. She leaned away from him slightly. "What kind of things? What was he doing in Bald Eagle Falls?"

"What he was doing here. That's the question." Beaver looked off into the distance, her eyes unfocused. "That's the ten million dollar question."

"If he's Russian, than he's not one of the clans, right? So what was he up to?"

"He's into the drug market. Human trafficking. Prostitution. I've just barely identified him, so I can't tell you what he was doing yet. Just where he has experience."

"We got rid of the drug dealing. So it can't be that."

"Well…" Beaver trailed off.

"You busted that big drug network," Erin maintained.

"We did that. But that doesn't mean all of the drugs are gone from Bald Eagle Falls. There will always be drugs for sale, no matter where you go. You're not going to get rid of them all. You know that Bo Biggles came back here to deal drugs. At least, that was part of his reason for coming back. And then... there's Campbell."

"Campbell wasn't dealing drugs," Erin said with certainty. "And since he's your informant, you know that. Maybe he's here posing as someone selling drugs, but you know that he isn't really dealing."

Beaver tried to shrug it off, but Erin held her gaze. "You *know* Campbell isn't selling drugs."

Beaver sighed. "And *you* know I can't talk to you about that."

"You're the one who brought it up. I'm just saying... he's not really dealing drugs."

Beaver said nothing.

"So..." Terry cleared his throat. "Maybe this Volkov was here to scope things out. Or maybe he was here to... see someone? Not Campbell, surely. He's just a little fish."

Erin opened her mouth to protest, then just shut it and shook her head.

"It might have been something to do with Cam," Beaver agreed. "What... I'm not yet sure. I don't know how Cam would have attracted a big-time scumbag like Wolf. But sometimes there are things happening underneath the surface that you don't see."

"Wolf?"

"Volkov means wolf. That was what his tattoo was a picture of," Beaver advised.

Erin suddenly remembered the tattoo.

"Not a very good one," Beaver said. "I can understand you not even being sure what it was a tattoo of, but that's his name and that's his tag on the street. You know, it's supposed to strike fear into the hearts of his enemies."

"Of course," Vic said.

Beaver nodded.

"So he didn't have any known associates in Bald Eagle Falls?" Terry asked. "I don't ever remember hearing his name before. There are not a lot of Russian mobsters around here, so I think I would have remembered that one."

"We don't know yet who he was here to see. I assume that he was here to see someone—which is why he was in Erin's parking lot when he was killed. It's a good place to rendezvous. It's quiet and out of the way, but close to Main Street and a quick route out of town. Easy to find, easy to stay out of sight, easy to get out."

"See? It's not anything to do with *me*," Erin said.

Everyone looked at her. None of them responded.

"I don't think anyone suggested that it was anything to do with you, Erin," Willie reminded her.

Erin rubbed at her ear, her cheeks getting hot under their scrutiny. "Well, that's not what Stayner thought. He figured it had to be something to do with me. Thought I should know who the victim was and what he was doing there."

Beaver rolled her eyes. "Give him a break, Erin. He's still green."

"Give him a break? Tell him to give me a break!"

Erin felt tears threatening again. Not because she was upset about Volkov being killed in her parking lot, but because she was angry with Stayner. Furious, in fact. And no one else had been there to see how he had treated her. She swallowed a couple of times and rolled her eyes up to the ceiling, trying to head off the tears.

"Erin...?" Vic asked.

"He was acting like I orchestrated the whole thing," Erin complained. Maybe it was an exaggeration, but not much of one. Stayner had acted as if she'd had something to do with it. When the only connection she had to the man was that he had died in her parking lot. That had been his bad choice, not hers. "I didn't even know the guy. Why would I have killed him?"

"You wouldn't," Vic said. "We know that, Erin. If Stayner was acting like you did, he doesn't know anything. You wouldn't have anything to do with it."

"I didn't," Erin agreed.

"Of course not!" Terry agreed. "And if it had been one of the others of us talking to you about it, you wouldn't have been treated like that."

"I know," Erin agreed. "I was wishing that it was the sheriff. But he was busy with the crime scene."

"Probably a good thing, too. I don't know how many crime scenes Stayner has processed. You don't want to get it wrong in a case like this. End up with contaminated evidence or things being thrown out because chain of custody wasn't properly preserved... you can lose a whole case. And when it's murder..." He looked at Beaver. "It was murder, wasn't it?"

Beaver nodded. "It was homicide," she agreed. "Of course, there's no ruling yet; it will be days before the medical examiner confirms anything. But the guy was stabbed in the chest. That's pretty clearly homicide to me. It wasn't in the middle of a fight. Not when he's sitting inside his car. Not like it was a fight, heat of the moment."

Erin remembered the dark red stain down Volkov's shirt, and closed her eyes for a minute, trying to erase the image from her mind. She didn't want to be seeing that in her dreams. She already had Mr. Inglethorpe's bloody death scene in her nightmares. She didn't need another.

Terry rubbed her back. "It's alright," he soothed. "I'm sorry you had to see that... again."

"I didn't see much," Erin dismissed. Not like with Mr. Inglethorpe. That had been completely different. It was understandable that she would react to such a gruesome scene. But Volkov's death hadn't been nearly so gory. She could get over that, push it to some corner of her mind and not think about it.

"So, if I had to choose between assigning Stayner to question a witness or process the crime scene, I would have made the same decision," Terry went on. "If there is a problem with a witness statement, you can always get it straightened out later. But once you get physical evidence thrown out... that's the end of the case. You can't recover from that. Not unless there's a lot of other evidence that you can still use."

"He didn't put on gloves before he opened the door," Erin remembered. "He might have messed up any fingerprints under the door handle."

Beaver shook her head. "Stupid rookie mistake. Underneath handles is prime real estate in a scene like that. Whoever stabbed him probably did open the door. And you'd be amazed at how many people don't think to put on gloves before they kill someone."

Terry chuckled. "There's just no pride of workmanship these days."

Beaver grinned. "You said it," she agreed. "So... maybe he already destroyed some of the evidence at the scene. Best to get him away from it and keep him from destroying anything else. But I am sorry that he upset you, Erin. That wasn't professional."

Erin realized that she had been pretty lucky up until that point. With the number of murders that she had been connected with since coming to Bald Eagle Falls, she hadn't been railroaded or abused by the police. She'd certainly been a suspect, but even when she was the chief suspect in a case, the police had not bullied her. Terry, Tom, and the sheriff had always been courteous and careful. Even Jack Ward in Moose River had been gruff but not pushed her around.

"I guess there was no harm done. I told him I'll go in later to sign a statement. He thought I should go in and do it right away. But I had the ladies' tea to deal with."

"Of course." Terry smirked. "The ladies' tea has to take precedence over a little thing like a murder in your parking lot."

"He wasn't going to get any more dead," Erin shot back.

Vic giggled. "I can just see you telling Stayner that. I'll bet he just loved that."

"He wasn't too happy, but what's he going to do? Arrest me for saying I'll do it later?"

"He could have threatened arresting you for obstruction."

"He might have said something like that. But they were the ones who were obstructing me, not the other way around. I called them, gave them my statement, and said I would sign later."

"It's not like it's going to have any material effect on the investigation," Beaver said, shaking her head. "Since Erin isn't the one who stabbed him and didn't see whoever it was that did… She can't really tell them anything that she didn't already—that she found the guy in her parking lot, already dead."

"You didn't stab him, right?" Vic teased.

"I didn't see anyone around," Erin said, looking at Beaver. "Not that I remember. But what if I passed someone on the street and didn't even realize it? Just walking or driving down Main Street wouldn't have been suspicious… I wouldn't even notice."

"You didn't. The blood on his shirt was dry. He wasn't stabbed right before you arrived. It would have been hours earlier."

Erin was relieved. "Good. So it was probably sometime in the night, while it was still dark."

Beaver nodded. "That kind of thing is much easier to do under cover of darkness. Most stabbings don't happen at ten o'clock on a Sunday morning."

CHAPTER 18

*S*unday was a restless night. Erin was glad that she'd slept in Sunday morning. She at least had some reserves in the bank. She was exhausted by the excitement of the day, but her brain was still busy trying to process all that she had learned about Volkov's death.

She had the morning shift with Bella, who Erin hadn't spent a lot of time with since coming back from the Alaskan cruise. Bella was back in school. That meant she couldn't put a lot of time in at the bakery, but she still scheduled shifts in when she could. It was a week off at school, so she had a few shifts to cover while she was off.

"It feels great to be back here," Bella enthused. "I forget how much fun it is when I'm at school."

Erin laughed. "It is work," she reminded Bella, "It's not all fun and games. But I do enjoy baking."

"I do too. And getting money for it, too. And I want to be in business and run my own company, so it's good to have the experience and to see how you're doing things and how it all works."

"So you know all the things not to do?" Erin teased.

"You shouldn't put yourself down! You've done really well in getting the bakery off the ground and making money. It's hard for a specialty shop like this to be profitable, especially in a small town where there isn't a big population of people who are gluten-free."

"I don't know if I would be able to if there was still a traditional bakery here, a lot of the customers are a captive audience because it is a small town. If they want freshly-baked bread, they have to go into the city."

"But they wouldn't buy yours if it wasn't any good."

Erin shrugged. "Well, I'm glad you're in today too. I've missed working with you."

Bella smiled. She was an attractive young woman, heavier than society's ideals, but in a way Erin thought was pleasing. Her round face, surrounded by curling locks of shoulder-length blond hair was attractive and made her seem approachable. Erin noticed that customers spent more time talking with her than they did other employees.

"I really do enjoy it."

They were quiet for a few minutes as they worked on getting everything arranged for the morning rush.

"It was so sad to hear about Campbell," Bella said, shaking her head. "I can't believe that he would have anything to do with drugs. He was never with that crowd in school. Neither of them was."

Erin rested for a moment, nodding. "I know that you can never know what people are like in their private lives... someone who looks perfectly normal can be capable of all kinds of horrible stuff... but I'm with you, I never would have thought it of him, and I still don't think they're right."

"But Officer Stayner really did find drugs in his car? I mean, they didn't just misinterpret something he said or believe something that someone else had said about him, they actually found drugs?" Bella frowned and sighed.

"I guess so. It's pretty hard to believe."

"If they weren't his drugs, then they must have been the girlfriend's. And she took off? Just disappeared in the night?"

"Yes. Mary Lou doesn't have any idea where she went. Back to the city, I guess. We can't accuse her when we don't know anything about it... but I don't know what else to think."

"The police must not be too happy that she's gone. Isn't this one of those cases where they tell you 'don't leave town'?"

"I don't think they can actually do that. That's just TV. They can ask you questions, but if they're not arresting you, they can't make you stick around."

"Huh. Well, there you go. I guess if I got in trouble with the police more often, I'd know that."

Erin found herself blushing, and hoped that Bella didn't notice. It was always hot in the kitchen with the ovens on, no matter how hard they ran the AC, so she had an excuse to be flushed.

"Have you been over to see Joshua?" she asked Bella. "I know a bunch of the church ladies went over to see Mary Lou, but I don't know if anyone has really focused on Joshua. I gather things haven't been very good at school."

Bella considered this. "No. I haven't seen him. It's not like we were great friends, though; it might be kind of awkward for me to go by there. I wasn't ever very popular. He was nice to me, but…" She shrugged.

"It's up to you. I just thought he might be able to use some support."

"I'll think about it. Maybe I'll take some leftover cookies to him at the end of the day."

Terry texted Erin partway through the afternoon that Campbell had been granted bail and Mary Lou had gone to pay it and bring him home. She and Bella decided to go by the house after work together to see if the family needed anything. Then it wouldn't just be Bella and Joshua trying awkwardly to make conversation. With luck, Mary Lou and Campbell would be back from Moose River by the time the bakery was closed and cleaned.

Erin had rearranged the cookie tray at least three times, anxious about possibly intruding on the family when they just wanted to be left alone. But they didn't need to stay if they got the feeling that Mary Lou or one of the others wanted them to be on their way. Bella cocked her head at Erin and gave her a knowing look.

"They don't care how the cookies are arranged, you know. Stacked or overlapping, all of one kind together or in a random assortment; they really aren't going to even notice."

"I know."

"Are we ready?"

Erin nodded. She took a deep breath and let it out. "Okay. Let's go."

They each had their own cars, but wanted to arrive together. Erin paused as she opened her door to get into her car, looking at the spot where the Russian's car had been parked the day before. It was an odd place to park. Had he been hiding? Napping?

"Erin?"

"Yes, I'm coming," Erin agreed hurriedly. She slid into the driver's seat and pulled the door shut. She was flustered and managed to stall the engine once before reversing out of her parking space. She swore under her breath. Terry kept telling her that she had enough money to get a new car, and she should get one before hers broke down and left her stranded somewhere. But Erin was used to not having money and had a hard time with the idea of spending money on a new car before she had driven the old one into the ground. He was right, of course. Getting stuck in the middle of the city where there were cabs and buses was one thing. Getting stuck in the middle of Bald Eagle Falls, she'd be able to walk home from wherever she was. But if she got stuck on the highway or in some remote area one day, that would be another story. She really should listen to him and replace the car before it gave up the ghost.

She got to Mary Lou's without incident. Bella pulled her car in against the curb behind Erin's. Erin was glad to see that Mary Lou's car was at the house, so she knew Mary Lou and Campbell were back home.

Erin rang the doorbell and, when Mary Lou answered, presented her with the plate of cookies.

"Oh, Erin." Mary Lou looked tired. "You don't need to bring any more food."

But she stepped back to allow them to enter, and led the way into the living room and dining room area. A meal was spread out buffet-style across the table.

"It's a repeat of Thanksgiving dinner," Mary Lou said, as if embarrassed by the fact. "But with paper plates this time. I can't bear to even think about clean-up. We will be using disposable until further notice."

"Nobody cares, Mom," Campbell said. "And anyone who does, can go—"

"Campbell!"

"—jump off a cliff," Campbell finished, grinning at her. He looked happy and relaxed. Erin admired his ability to bounce back. It was clear that he was glad to be home with his family and going about normal activities like teasing his mother.

"We're not going to tell anyone you're using paper plates," Erin agreed. "Why would anyone even care?"

Mary Lou shook her head, unable to explain. "It's just… what people must think…"

Campbell was standing by the table and heaped a plate high with food. "I don't think people are going to be criticizing the paper plates. I think it's the fact that your son is going to prison that they're going to be talking about."

"You're not going to prison," Mary Lou said firmly.

Campbell snagged an extra piece of turkey from the bowl on the table and popped it in his mouth. "You wouldn't believe the kind of food they serve there. If I had to eat like that for ten years…" He shook his head. "I'd waste away to nothing. I wouldn't feed that… crap to a dog." He sat down at the table to eat. "Guess I'd better get used to the idea."

"You are not going to go to prison," Mary Lou reiterated. "We're going to figure this out."

"I hope so."

Campbell began to eat. Erin's eyes slid over to Joshua. He had stopped filling his plate, watching his brother, but now that Campbell was sitting down and eating, he started to move again, as if waking up from a dream. Bella moved toward him, awkward and uncertain.

"Hey," Joshua greeted, acknowledging her.

"Hi. We just came by… to see how you were doing. All of y'all. I can only imagine… it must be tough."

"Nothing happened to me. I guess I'm fine."

"But it still must be stressful." Bella looked over at Campbell. "Having something like this going on over the holiday, when you thought you were just going to have a nice family meal together…"

Campbell snorted and continued to shovel food into his mouth. Erin could see Mary Lou restraining herself from criticizing his table manners. Of course all she wanted to do was enjoy a family dinner together, to celebrate having her son home again, for however long it might last. She didn't need anyone else there poking their noses in and asking questions.

"Well, we don't want to keep you. Just wanted to make sure you got home safe and to see if there's anything you need."

Mary Lou shook her head. "Nothing that time won't cure," she said without enthusiasm.

Campbell was watching Bella as he ate. They were close together in age. Erin wasn't sure whether they were in the same grade or a year apart. They both seemed so young and so mature at the same time. Had she ever been that young and naive? And yet mature and knowing everything?

"Miss having you around school," Bella said, noticing his attention. "It's weird, you not being there."

"Yeah." He chewed more slowly. "Maybe I should have stuck around. Wouldn't have gotten in this trouble."

Erin didn't look at Mary Lou. How many times had she told Campbell that he should be going to school and not going off on his own? How many times had she begged him to come home and to stay away from whatever trouble he was getting into in the city? Erin didn't know if she'd be able to handle having kids. Not when they got to be independent and you couldn't stop them from getting in trouble by sending them to their beds anymore.

"Maybe you could come back now," Bella suggested. "Are you going to stay around here? You could show the judge that you were back in school and being a good citizen, maybe that would help your case."

"I have to stay here," Campbell said. He stuck his leg out and pulled his pant leg up, showing off an ankle monitor. "I go anywhere else, and they revoke my bail."

"So you could go to school."

"I can't go more than two hundred yards from the house, so I don't think so."

"You could do home study. They have that."

Campbell shook his head. "Yeah, I don't think so."

Mary Lou put a few bites of food on her paper plate and walked away from the table, toward Erin. "Why don't you sit down and visit for a few minutes, Erin. Let the kids… talk."

Erin obligingly sat down across from her. Mary Lou poked at her food, obviously not that interested in it. Erin searched for something to say.

"Have you seen Brianna?" Campbell asked Joshua.

Mary Lou cocked her head slightly, not turning to look at the boys, but clearly listening in.

"No. Don't know where she took off to. I looked around a bit, but she's not around here. I figure she must have gotten back to the city. Called someone or hitchhiked."

"Stupid. She should have stayed around here."

"She probably figured she was next. The cops would pick her up as soon as they had something they could pull her in on."

Campbell shook his head. "What's wrong with girls?" He looked over at Bella. "No offense. I know you're not like her. But why can't they just be sensible? We wouldn't be in this mess if it weren't for her."

There was silence in the room as everyone considered this statement. It was Bella who finally spoke. "So the drugs were hers?"

"They weren't mine. I didn't know they were there, so you tell me how the cops would know? The whole thing stinks. I don't think Bree put them there. Doesn't make any sense. If she had drugs with her, they would have been in her backpack and she wouldn't have let it out of her sight. She wouldn't leave a crap-ton of drugs in the car. Even she wouldn't be that stupid."

"Well, if you were set up, then she could be set up just as easily," Bella pointed out. "I'd probably run too. Get as far away from this as possible."

"She can't run away from it," Campbell muttered.

There was another period of silence. Campbell was making good headway in cleaning all of the food from his plate. Erin wouldn't have thought it was possible with the amount he had taken, even if he hadn't had anything to eat from the time he was arrested until the time he got home. But it had disappeared in short order. Teenage boys had an amazing capacity.

"You could call her," Joshua suggested. "Find out what's going on."

"I already know what's going on."

Erin waited, wishing that she could ask him to explain further, to unfold the whole thing for them, but knowing that the minute she gave any indication she and Mary Lou were listening in, he would clam up completely. She glanced at Mary Lou, who shook her head slightly, and Erin knew she was thinking the same thing. It must have been killing her to be so shut out of her son's life. To only hear these things because she happened to overhear him. She had always seemed close to her boys.

"What are you going to do, then?" Joshua asked. "It's not like you can go into the city and find her."

"Nope," Campbell agreed. "I just have to sit here and do nothing."

"Could I ask you for a favor, Erin?" Mary Lou asked as Erin and Bella prepared to leave.

"Of course, I'd be happy to help out any way I can."

"I have a casserole dish that belongs to Rohilda Beaven. I know she usually stays with Jeremy when she's in town, and I wonder if you could drop it off there…?"

"Sure. No problem."

Erin waited while Mary Lou retrieved it. It was the only casserole dish on the counter, and Erin remembered Mary Lou saying how many they had in the freezer. Maybe everyone else had used disposable pans so that they wouldn't be without them while waiting for Mary Lou to eat the casserole and return them.

Mary Lou handed it to her, flushing pink. At Erin's look, she blurted out an explanation. "It was fried chicken. Not homemade, you could tell it wasn't actually cooked in the dish, and I know she just got it at the family restaurant and put it in her own dish. To tell the truth… I dumped it all out. After her involvement in getting Campbell into this trouble, I didn't want her peace offering. And I don't want to return it in person."

Erin nodded and took it from her. She felt her own cheeks warming at Mary Lou's explanation. She liked Beaver and hated for Mary Lou to think that Campbell's trouble was her fault.

"I don't claim to know all of what happened… but I think Beaver was trying to look after Campbell and keep him out of trouble. I don't think it's her fault that Campbell was arrested. She wouldn't have… put drugs in his car or told him to do anything to break the law…"

Mary Lou looked at her for a minute. Erin looked down.

"Like I said. I don't know."

"She should not have had anything to do with him. He's not even an adult. She didn't have any business getting him involved in her investigation."

Erin nodded. "I'll run this by Jeremy's apartment," she promised.

When she got into her car, Erin called Vic. "I need to go by Jeremy's. Do you want to come along?"

"Sure," Vic agreed. "Always happy to have a reason to check up on him and harass him a little for his housekeeping. Are you going now?"

"I think I'd better, because once I get home, I'm going to crash. I'm not going to want to go out again."

"Okay. Just pull in front, and I'll be right out."

They headed over to Jeremy's together. Erin didn't tell Vic the details Mary Lou had confided about throwing the fried chicken out and blaming Beaver for what had happened.

Jeremy was surprised to see them, but didn't seem upset about the unexpected visit. He opened the door wide and invited them in, with a caution that he wasn't prepared for visitors.

The apartment was disorderly, but no more than any other bachelor's basement suite. Erin imagined Beaver probably ensured it didn't get too messy when she stayed over.

Erin and Vic made space for themselves in the living room area, moving a newspaper, laptop, and stray charge cables out of the way.

"I guess Beaver probably isn't too happy about all of this stuff with Campbell," Erin suggested, wondering whether Beaver or Jeremy knew anything of Mary Lou's animosity toward Beaver for the way things had turned out.

"Ro doesn't talk much about the things that bother her," Jeremy said.

"But don't think that means that she doesn't worry just as much as the next person."

"She always seems so cool and unaffected by things," Erin said. "I'd love to be like that. To just be able to go with the flow and not be bothered."

"She's like that about some things," Jeremy admitted. "She's been through a lot of difficult stuff, so the little things aren't a concern. She knows that in the big picture, they really aren't going to matter, so why worry about them? But the big stuff...? It still bothers her just like anyone else."

"And she's worried about Campbell?" Erin asked.

"Of course. She took him under her wing and was helping him out, and now look at the trouble that he's in. He could end up in prison. And for a long time, not just probation or a few months in some minimum-security place. She feels responsible for that."

"But it's not Beaver's fault," Vic pointed out. "She's not the one who got him in trouble."

"No..." Jeremy said uncertainly. "But she's not saying how much he was already involved in and how much she might have nudged him forward so that he could feed her information for her investigation. You know he's been acting as an informant."

"But she's not the one who put him into the situation," Erin said, feeling her way along. "He was already involved with these people in the city. Mary Lou said that she didn't know what he was involved in and who he was staying with. She knew he didn't have a job or any money, so he was obviously involved in something... shady. Or he was living off of someone else. That's not Beaver's doing."

"I don't know what he was already involved in and what Ro might have gotten him into. And now she's taking flak from her bosses. They are not happy about her involving someone so young in her investigation."

"Didn't they know?"

"I guess when you're an agent, you don't always pass all of the details on to your superiors... you tell them what they need to know and keep the rest to yourself. So they might have known that she had an informant, and what kind of information he was giving her, but not that he was still a minor."

"And she's not supposed to use a minor?"

"I don't know if there are hard and fast rules. But I guess once that minor gets arrested and accused of serious trafficking charges… they might question your judgment."

Erin nodded. She hadn't ever been comfortable with the idea of Beaver using Campbell to get what she wanted. Campbell had seemed happy to work with her and for the sense of accomplishment and maturity that it gave him. But teenagers, especially teenage boys, had immature brains. Their judgment was impaired. Had Beaver taken advantage of Campbell's youth, getting him into something that he wouldn't have been involved in otherwise? Was he involved with drug dealers, and that was why drugs had been planted in his car?

Or was it even worse than that? Erin had seen a lot of the nastier elements on the street when she was younger. She had never been entirely homeless and on the skids, but she had been close, and her closeness to that life had taught her a lot of lessons that she would rather not have had to learn. Kids on the street were vulnerable. They thought that they were in control of their own lives. They thought that they were invincible. But they were easy victims.

"So… is Beaver in big trouble?" Vic asked. "Or is she just being asked to justify what she did?"

"She doesn't say much about it. You know, she can't give me any details, so she's pretty careful about what she says. But I gather… it could be a career-ending mistake. If Campbell goes to prison or they decide that she was out of line in using him as an informant… her job could be down the toilet."

"Oh, no…" Erin tried to imagine Beaver in some other job. She was made to be an agent. It was a job that fit her like a glove. She was a treasure-hunter as a hobby, but what would she do for a job that would fulfill those needs? Erin couldn't picture her as anything else.

"She'll be okay," Vic said. "You know Beaver. She'll come out of it smelling like a rose."

Jeremy nodded, but his eyes were distant. "I hope so. I don't know what she would do if she lost her job."

CHAPTER 20

*I*t had been a long day. Erin was relaxing on the couch watching TV and dozing on Terry's shoulder when the back door slammed open, and Erin just about rocketed out of her seat. Terry was on his feet right behind her.

Vic strode through the kitchen and had started her tirade before she even reached the living room.

"What is wrong with men?" she demanded. She saw Terry. "No offense, Terry, but why do men have to be so thick-skulled? Is it in the rule book? Can't they listen and be sensible? Why do they have to always be right about everything?"

Erin's heart was still racing. She tried to calm herself down. Whatever was bothering Vic, it wasn't a real emergency. She wasn't being chased or attacked. She was just riled up about something that Willie had done. She swallowed and tried to answer Vic calmly.

"What happened?"

"Nothing happened. And nothing is going to happen if he is going to keep being so hard-headed and acting like he can't trust me! What have I ever done to make him think I would be unfaithful to him? I've never given him any reason to think that I would wander!"

"I know," Erin soothed. "I don't know what happened, but it will blow over. The two of you are just... passionate. You're going to butt heads sometimes. But you love Willie, and he loves you, the two of you can work it out..."

"I'm prepared to be reasonable. He is the one who isn't! I'm perfectly happy to talk things through and work them out."

"What exactly is bothering him?" Terry asked. He sat back down on the couch where he had been before Vic's dramatic entrance. He put his feet up on the coffee table, and Vic shook her head at him.

"What?" Terry demanded. "I don't have my shoes on and this isn't your coffee table. It's Erin's, and if it doesn't bother her, you don't need to act like I've committed a capital offense."

"It's not that." Vic shook her head, rolling her eyes at her own response. "I'm just wound up. It's not you. I need to talk to Erin. Someone who understands."

"Come to the bedroom," Erin invited. "You can say whatever you like without being overheard." She glanced over at Terry. "As long as you lower your voice. You are... a mite loud."

Terry snorted. He didn't offer to be the one to leave the room so that they could talk in private. He was in the middle of watching a show, and there wasn't a TV in the bedroom, so Erin couldn't very well insist.

"Come on," she repeated, motioning to Vic.

Vic followed her down the hall to the bedroom and, once she was in, Erin shut the door. Vic threw herself down on the bed, sprawling on her back, and groaned loudly.

"Can I go back to being a kid again? I'm tired of dealing with relationship crap. I want to go back to just... making mud pies and shooting squirrels."

"I don't think you'd better be shooting anything while you're in this mood." Erin thought about the fact that Vic was almost always carrying a concealed weapon since the house had been broken into, and that it was within reach when she was so angry during her argument with Willie. The thought made her queasy. All it would take was Vic losing control once... She had never given any indication that she would, but it was a frightening thought. "You need to calm down."

Vic sighed. "I'm just blowing off steam. I'm not going to do anything. I just get tired of being reasonable and patient and answering the same questions over and over again."

"You're okay?"

Vic nodded. "I'm okay."

Erin sat down on the edge of the bed, sighing. "So tell me all about it. If you want to share, I mean."

"He's just… you know, everything used to be good between us. I never had to worry about Willie getting jealous. I think… for the first little while, it just took so much to get used to me being transgender, that he didn't think about me being interested in anyone else, or anyone else being interested in me. It was just working out whether we could be compatible or not."

"Or you were just in the honeymoon phase."

"Maybe that was it. I don't know. But the last little while… you'd think that he caught me stepping out on him. Every little thing sets him off. I talk about one of the friends that I made on the cruise, and he thinks I'm going to run off with them or start sneaking around behind his back. And heaven forbid I should mention Theresa."

"Well," Erin said reasonably, "you can see how Theresa might be a sore spot with him. She is an ex, after all. You have a history."

"But I broke up with her. I'm not interested in getting back together. I'm not the one who started writing to her; she started writing to me. And I haven't had any contact with her since the whole thing blew up. But just mention her name and Willie…" Vic shook her head and blew out her breath. "I asked him if he'd found any trace of her. You know both he and Beaver have been trying to track her down. And…" Vic drew her hands out expressively, "you'd think that I said I wanted to get together with her. I didn't ask him because I want to see her. I asked because I want her to be brought to justice just as much as anyone else. I don't want that crazy chick running around all over Tennessee, and I especially don't want her in my backyard. What happens when she decides she wants to see me again? What if it's me with her arm around my neck in a chokehold next time? I don't want to be with her; I want her behind bars."

"Did you tell Willie that?"

"No. I blew up. Freaked out. Tore up one side of him and down the other." Vic closed her eyes, shaking her head. She held the heels of her hands over her eyes, groaning. "And now he's going to think that he struck a nerve. That the reason I'm protesting is that I'm secretly in love with her. When I'm just tired of him thinking I'm interested in other people when

I'm not. Maybe he's the one who is attracted to someone else. Maybe he's just looking for an excuse to break up because he wants out."

"I don't think so."

Neither of them said anything for a while. Vic sighed.

"I don't want to lose him. I know he thinks that I've got better prospects with the LGBT crowd, but that's not the way it is. I like talking with them, sharing life experiences, things that Willie can't really understand, but I want to go home to him. It's nice to have friends who can understand what I've been going through. That part is great. But I really am happy with him. I'm not looking for someone new."

"So tell him that."

"I have. A hundred times."

"Men are hard-headed," Erin reminded her. "It might take a few hundred more."

Vic uncovered her eyes, stretched, and sat up. "What makes you so wise?"

"I'm not. It's just easy to give advice when it's someone else's problem."

Vic looked at her and laughed. "I can relate! Do you need advice about anything? Any problems of yours that I can solve?"

"I wish there were." Erin was thinking of her continuing nightmares and Terry's unhappiness. There wasn't anything Vic could do about either issue. And then there was Campbell... It was nice to try to solve someone else's problems instead of her own, but she had no idea what to do for Mary Lou and her family. She hated the thought of Campbell going to prison. He was a teenager. Prison would eat him up. Guilty or innocent, they would change him from a good kid with some family trouble and who was testing his limits into a bitter, hardened criminal. If he went to prison, he would be a different person when they let him out, whether it was two years or twenty. *That* kid would be gone.

They had to figure out who had set him up. If it was Brianna or Stayner or someone else, Erin had to figure it out and keep Campbell out of the system.

~

After a bit more girl talk, Vic and Erin left the bedroom and went back out to the living room. Vic had intended to apologize to Terry for blowing up

334

and treating him like he was part of the problem when she was just upset with Willie, but when they got out to the living room, they saw that Terry wasn't alone. Willie, his skin darkly stained as always, sat at the other end of the couch, watching along with him.

"Oh. Hey." Vic swallowed and looked down at Willie. "Umm… sorry for going off the deep end. I guess I just lost it."

"It was my fault," Willie offered, sitting forward as a precursor to getting up. "I know I've been overly sensitive about you… being interested in other people lately. That's on me, not you."

"It's okay for me to have other friends."

"I know. You're right."

"I'm not seeing anyone else. I'm not looking for anyone else. I just have some friends that you don't know very well. I'm not running away with anyone."

"Of course not," he agreed, voice gruff. "It's just that… I'm so much older than you are, and I don't fit in with that crowd in any way. I don't want to lose you to them."

"You're not going to."

Willie stood up. He offered Vic a hug, and she stepped into his arms. Her next words were muffled.

"And you're not losing me to crazy freaking Theresa, either, okay? I want to know where she is so that I know she's not going to show up at my door someday. Not because I want to see her again."

Willie chuckled. "Yeah."

"Good. So no more jealous boyfriend?"

"I'll… do my best. No promises."

Vic drew back to look at his face. She shook her head and looked over at Erin. "Why do men have to be so hard-headed?"

She and Willie headed back toward the back door and Vic's apartment. Terry waited until he heard the door close, and turned to Erin.

"Maybe because he has to be strong enough to survive butting heads with *her*."

CHAPTER 21

$\mathcal{E}$rin and Vic made a trip into the city to do a supply run for the bakery and, after getting everything they needed, headed over to the food court to grab a bit to eat before driving back to Bald Eagle Falls. Looking across the bustle of the food court at the mall, Erin saw a couple of familiar faces.

"Erin? Erin!" Vic tugged at her sleeve. "I was just asking you—" she followed Erin's gaze and saw the two boys. "Oh. There's Jeremy and Campbell."

"Joshua," Erin corrected. "Campbell is on house arrest."

Vic studied them across the milling lunch crowd. "Yeah. You're right. It's Joshua. What are they doing here? I didn't think they even knew each other. Jeremy is still new to Bald Eagle Falls, and he wouldn't have much opportunity to run into Joshua, when Jeremy's working and Joshua's at school."

"I don't know," Erin said slowly. The two young men had their heads together and were looking around surreptitiously. It was a good thing they weren't the ones working with Beaver, the way their furtive looks drew attention. "Something is going on."

"Shall we crash the party?" Vic suggested, grinning.

Erin wouldn't have dared if it weren't Vic's brother, but she figured Vic knew what she could get away with. They worked their way through the tables and throngs of people, and Jeremy and Joshua were so thick in conversation that they didn't notice the two women until they were only a few feet away.

"Vic!" Jeremy's face flushed instantly. "Hey, what are you doing here?"

"Erin and I needed to pick up some supplies for the house and the bakery. And what are you two up to? You've got to be the worst spies ever. You stand out like a strawberry in a bowl of peas."

"We're not doing anything," Jeremy protested. "Just happened to run into each other and were discussing the Cowboys and their chances at—"

"Oh, give me a break," Vic interrupted. "You were not talking football. I can read you like a book. Fill us in. What are you up to?"

Jeremy and Joshua exchanged looks.

"Are you going to get something to eat?" Erin suggested, figuring that maybe once everyone relaxed, she and Vic might have a better chance at getting the truth from Jeremy and Joshua.

Vic flashed her an irritated look, but Erin ignored it and continued to look at the boys for their response. Jeremy and Joshua eventually nodded.

"Great. I'll grab us a table before they all fill up."

She gave Vic a bill and her order, and everyone split up to get their food. Vic brought back a tray laden with both her lunch and Erin's and divided it up accordingly. The young men joined them with their fat burgers and supersized fries, and everyone settled in.

"So," Erin said after a few bites. "What are you guys up to?"

Jeremy rolled his eyes. "I should have known this was just a ploy. You," he pointed at Erin, "are devious. Much subtler than my sister here."

Erin just raised her brows. "We all needed to eat, didn't we? Why sit at different tables?"

Joshua looked at Jeremy, and then at the women. "Okay... I wanted to see if I could find Brianna. Get the story out of her. Find out what she knows about what happened."

"I see." Erin had suspected as much. She chewed slowly on her sub sandwich. "So... does Beaver know what you guys are doing?"

"I don't think she'd approve," Jeremy contributed. "I didn't tell her."

"Easier to get forgiveness than permission?"

"I don't need her permission to take a look around and ask some questions. I'm just showing some concern for a missing girl. If you were missing, you would want me to look for you, wouldn't you?"

Thinking of the times that she had been in trouble, Erin nodded. But

Brianna wasn't in the same situation as Erin had been. She hadn't been attacked or kidnapped. She had run away out of fear of the authorities.

"I would, but that's not exactly our job, is it? You should leave it to Beaver and the police department."

"Do you really think they're looking for her?" Joshua asked. "I don't think anyone is looking for her. She's a runaway, not the victim of a crime. Police don't look for runaways. Especially when she's not even in town. If we try to report her missing in Bald Eagle Falls, the sheriff knows they're not going to find her there. If we try to report her missing here… they'll say the last place she was known to be was Bald Eagle Falls. And if she did come back here, then she's home, and she's not missing. People like her don't get the attention of the police. Not as missing persons."

"People like her?" Erin repeated.

Joshua looked around. He apparently didn't see anyone that concerned him, so he answered. "She doesn't have a permanent address. She moves around, so the cops are just going to say that she's moved on somewhere else. They don't look for homeless people. There's no indication of foul play. And she doesn't want to get arrested, so she's going to stay away from any cops she sees."

"How much do you know about her?" Vic demanded. "She's Campbell's girlfriend. What did he tell you? Did he tell you where to look for her?"

"He doesn't… exactly… know that I'm here."

"Not exactly," Vic repeated dryly.

"Okay, maybe not at all. I didn't exactly tell him. Just like Jeremy didn't tell Beaver. Campbell has said enough that I know a few places to look, people to talk to. I knew he wouldn't want me getting involved."

"But you got involved anyway."

"You think I want Cam going to prison?"

Vic shook her head, her expression softening. "I don't want him going to prison either. I don't think he's done anything bad enough to be sent to prison. But I don't want you getting hurt, either. What exactly are you guys poking your noses into out here? Drug dealing? You talk to the wrong person or say the wrong thing, and you could end up with a bullet between your eyes."

"I'm not going to let that happen," Jeremy said with certainty. He patted his side where, Erin had to assume, he had a concealed firearm.

"Going after drug dealers with a gun isn't exactly safe!" she protested.

"Shh." Jeremy frowned fiercely and looked around. "Watch what you say. We don't want to attract people's attention. I don't exactly have a permit for a concealed carry."

"Then what do you think you're doing? You think this is a good idea?" Erin shook her head and looked at Vic. "What about you? Tell them that's just stupid."

Vic shrugged. She didn't comment on the issue of weapons. She *did*, Erin knew, have a concealed carry permit, so at least she couldn't be arrested for that, but she had to believe that the boys going after potentially violent criminals was a bad idea.

"How much do you know about where she might be or who she might be with?" Vic asked. "If we can talk to her alone, without alerting anyone else, I don't see how that could be a bad thing." She gave a little grimace in Erin's direction, knowing that Erin was not going to be happy with her answer.

"We've got a few places to look," Jeremy said cautiously. "Between what Ro has said and what Campbell has said, we have a pretty good idea where to find her. But as far as talking to her alone without attracting anyone else's attention... that is a bit of a problem. And the fact that she probably won't want to talk to us or to have anything to do with us."

"Then, why are you here?" Erin asked, exasperated. It didn't seem like they had thought their plan through very well.

Jeremy fixed Erin with a penetrating gaze and raised one eyebrow. "Because you wouldn't ever consider doing something on your own, would you? *You* wouldn't investigate a crime without the police. Ask a few questions here or there to try to solve the crime?"

"I don't do that. I've just gotten... mixed up in things before. I wasn't really *investigating*."

"Uh-huh. And when Terry was facing charges? You didn't investigate that? Try to get him off, even though the police were already involved and told you to stay out of it?"

"I just..." Erin tried to think of some excuse or explanation. "That was different."

"Because it wasn't a drug dealing?"

"It wasn't... it wasn't dangerous..."

"No. Terry and Jack Ward just happened to fall down and get tangled up in some rope, and to injure themselves in the process. And Bo just happened to die in custody, nothing to do with no one."

"But it wasn't organized crime, that was just crazy—"

"As far as you knew, it could have been one of the clans. You didn't know whether it was an official hit or a revenge killing or what. You knew it wasn't an accident, that it wasn't Terry."

Erin looked down at her plate, wishing that she could argue with his analysis, but it was impossible. She didn't think it was the same as looking for Brianna when she might be in the company of drug dealers or some other criminal element. Erin hadn't ever gone looking for trouble. She had just been following the clues.

"So where do we look first?" Vic asked.

Jeremy looked at her. "Not you. This is just Joshua and me. We're not getting... a couple of women involved."

"That doesn't stop a couple of women from joining you. You think it's okay to involve a teenager in this but not a couple of grown women? You know my skills are just as good as yours."

Vic's skills with a gun were considerable. But Erin hoped that those skills would not be required.

"Maybe we should rethink this," she suggested.

Jeremy rolled his eyes. "Look. Vic and I know how to protect ourselves. We're not going to run into anything dangerous, just see if we can find Brianna and talk to her. If she wants to come, then fine." He shrugged. "And Joshua knows more about this than anyone, so he's coming too. She's more likely to talk to him. He's less threatening, and Brianna knows him. She doesn't know me from Adam, and she's only seen Vic once. If you don't want to come, don't feel like you have to. We didn't plan on going in with a whole group. You get what you need and head back to Bald Eagle Falls."

There was no way Erin was going to leave them to find and confront Brianna by themselves. Jeremy, the oldest of the three, had just turned twenty-two. They might know how to handle firearms, but their brains weren't fully mature. Not the part that governed judgment and impulse control, which was exactly what they were going to need if they ran into trouble.

"I'll come... but you have to promise that you'll be careful and won't do anything dangerous. Those guns don't come out... unless we're in mortal danger. Everyone needs to stay calm and not overreact."

"Of course," Jeremy agreed, and the others nodded. "We're not expecting any gunplay. We're just taking precautions."

"I still don't like it."

"Then like I say… go home. There's nothing wrong with that."

"No. Someone has to keep an eye on you guys."

CHAPTER 22

hey didn't discuss it any further as they ate. They talked about other things and laughed and didn't address the fact that they might be going into a dangerous situation and properly prepare for it. Once everyone was finished eating their meals, they discussed vehicles, deciding they should all go together in one car rather than splitting up. They could leave Erin's beater at the mall and return for it after they had talked to Brianna.

"Unless she's coming back with us," Erin said. "Will there be enough room for all five of us?"

Jeremy shook his head in disbelief. "First, she's not going to come back with us. We'll be lucky if she says anything at all that will help us. She's not going to go back to Bald Eagle Falls now that she's put it behind her. And second… you can put more than four people in a car."

"I just wasn't sure whether you had enough seatbelts…"

"I do. Not that it would kill anyone not to have a seatbelt on driving back to the mall."

Erin thought about the rollover that had killed her parents and put her in the hospital. "It could," she said. "That's the whole point."

Jeremy looked at her for a moment, then shrugged it off. "Doesn't matter. It's not going to be an issue. So. Are we ready to go?"

He and Joshua discussed where to go first, and they were soon on their way. Erin watched the streets they drove through change from clean, upscale commercial buildings and homes to rougher, dirtier, darker streets. There were more people out and about, walking or biking from place to place rather than driving cars, panhandling, talking, and conducting various transactions right out in the open. She swallowed and looked over at Vic.

"It's okay," Vic assured her, though her eyes were a little wider than usual. She was farm born and bred, and her only exposure to street life had been the short time she had been homeless in Bald Eagle Falls before Erin took her in. Bald Eagle Falls had little to no street crime. "We'll be just fine. In and out. We're just going in to talk, nothing else."

Erin wondered if she would say the same thing if she knew where Theresa was. They had walked into Theresa's web once; it wouldn't do to step into the nest of someone as bad as or worse than she was.

"You think Brianna's here?" Erin asked Joshua. "We're getting close?"

Joshua was looking down at his phone. Erin assumed he was trying to navigate where they should go rather than playing Pokémon or checking Facebook.

"Yeah. If we turn into the alley up here," Joshua pointed, "we should be able to get in and out without any trouble."

Erin looked around as Jeremy followed Joshua's instructions and pulled off of the main street, parking as close as he could to the building, behind a cluster of garbage bins. "You think this is a safe place to park? The car will be here when we get back?"

"It will be fine, Erin," Jeremy laughed. "You're being melodramatic."

He, like Vic, had no experience with the seamy underbelly of the city. The two of them might think that they had learned everything they needed to from their father and the rest of the Jackson clan, but operating under the protection of an organized crime family was utterly different from having to fend for oneself on the street.

Joshua led the way into the apartment building through the back entrance, up the stairs instead of the elevator, to a door that he counted off, since there were no numbers attached to them. He rubbed his hands on his jeans to wipe off the sweat.

"Are you sure this is the right one?" Erin asked.

"Sure… no. As sure as I can be. Campbell just mentioned it once. I wasn't taking notes or planning on coming here myself then."

Erin nodded. "Is this where she lives?"

"Sometimes?" Joshua's voice went up, making it a question. "There are a few places she could be; I'm just hoping… that we'll hit it lucky the first time." He glanced around the hallway, the dingy walls scarred by graffiti, and a thick, sweet smell in the air that Erin knew was rats. Along with the cooking smells of everything that had ever been heated over a hot plate in the place.

"Let's go," Jeremy encouraged, motioning for Joshua to knock on the door.

"We're going to make him do this?" Erin asked. "The youngest one in the group?"

"The least threatening," Vic reminded her.

Erin shook her head. She raised her fist and rapped on the door. Not a quiet, tentative knock, but the sharp, authoritative kind that said they meant business. Vic looked at her in surprise, an eyebrow raised.

"I'm not very threatening either," Erin said. "But if I act like someone's mom, maybe they'll show me some respect."

She was hoping that everyone inside the apartment was as young as Brianna was. Erin wasn't old enough to be the mother of anyone over the age of ten, and she didn't have the experience. She'd had enough foster moms that she hoped she could get the attitude and the look right. If they believed the act, maybe Erin could find something out.

She was raising her fist to bang on the door again when they heard the sound of a bolt sliding, and the door was opened a crack. Someone around Erin's height, her face darker than Brianna's, put her eye to the crack.

"Who are you?"

"I'm looking for Brianna," Erin told her in a strong, authoritative voice. "Is she here?"

"She don't live here."

"Maybe not, but she stays here. Open this door. I want to see her."

The girl on the other side of the crack didn't move. "Who are you?"

"I'm here to talk to Brianna."

"You a cop?"

"Do I look like a cop?" Erin demanded.

There was no reason she couldn't have been a cop. Beaver was a federal agent. There were plenty of female police officers. Most were probably taller and more muscular than Erin, but she still *could* have been. But most cops wouldn't be surrounded by a cadre of young adults, either. Eventually, the door opened wider, and Erin could see the girl who had answered it. She was a dark-skinned black girl with tightly-braided hair, wearing a halter top with nothing underneath it and short shorts. The spindly legs that stuck out from under the shorts were scarred, and she had a black eye and lump on her cheek that probably kept her from seeing anything out that side. She was wearing makeup, an orangy lipstick, and the mascara on her good eye had run down her face. She'd probably washed away the mascara on the other side with cold compresses.

"Who are you?" she asked again, looking over the group.

"I'm Cam's brother, Josh."

The girl's eyes went to him, and she nodded. The boys looked very similar, and she would have to have both eyes blackened shut not to recognize the resemblance. She backed up and let them in.

"Is she here?" Erin asked.

"I haven't seen her."

"You haven't seen her today?"

"Haven't seen her since she went home with Cam. She never come back."

"She didn't stay in Bald Eagle Falls. She didn't call you for a ride? Say she needed someone to pick her up, that she needed somewhere to stay?" Erin asked.

The girl shook her head. "She never called me." Her eyes went to Jeremy and Vic, then back to Joshua. "She wouldn't call me for a ride no-how. I don't have a car."

"How do you get around?" Joshua asked, looking concerned.

The boy had never seen that kind of poverty before. He had no idea how the world worked for people who didn't have all of the advantages that he had.

"I walk," the girl said, with a laugh of disbelief. "I get rides with someone. Sometimes. I never had a car."

"Oh." Joshua stared at her with open curiosity. "What's your name?"

"What's it to you?"

His eyes stayed on her. Erin wondered if that was how it had been with Campbell and Brianna too. That he'd been so fascinated with the novelty of her life that he'd been drawn in. He wanted a different experience from the one that he'd been living, and there it was. As different from him as if she came from a different country, all the way around the world.

"I'm Kim," the girl finally said, apparently deciding that Joshua wasn't going to come up with a good reason for asking, but there was no reason not to give it to him. "So what do you want with Brianna?"

"Campbell is looking for her."

"They have a fight?"

Joshua pursed his lips. He apparently didn't want to lie to her, but he didn't want to tell her the whole truth, either. If he told her that Brianna had run away and that the cops might be trying to get her on a drug charge, or that Campbell might change his mind and decide to testify against her, then Kim wouldn't have any reason to help them out. She'd know why Brianna had run. "They had... a misunderstanding. He had to go out, and she left in the middle of the night. He's worried about her. Something might have happened to her."

Kim studied him suspiciously. "He hit her?"

"No! Campbell wouldn't do that! He's not that kind of guy."

"Everybody is that kind of guy, sooner or later." Kim pinned Vic down with her gaze. "Mark my words," she warned. She looked again at Jeremy, distrustful. She had determined that Joshua wasn't a threat, but she wasn't so sure about Jeremy. Older, wiser, bigger, and more of a threat.

"Not everyone," Vic said softly.

Kim rolled her eyes. "Who do you think knows more about it? You or me?" She indicated her black eye. "I know what they're like."

"Can I use your bathroom?" Joshua asked. "I'm sorry, I wouldn't ask, but the gas station down there," he indicated the way they had come. "I didn't think that would be the safest place to stop."

"You'd be right," she agreed with a snort. She shrugged. "Go ahead. But mind your own business. Keep your nose out of mine."

Joshua nodded and went in the direction she indicated. Not that there was anywhere else to go. They stood in the combination kitchen/living room area, and the bathroom and bedroom could only be through the hall on the other side of the living room. The living room was filled will all kinds of trash. There were clothes and old bags of fast food, flies buzzing around the bags and bouncing against the glass of the dirty window. Erin deduced that other people were living there. Not just

Kim. Not just Brianna. Probably a few more of them, sleeping on the couch and the floor as well as whatever mattress or bed was in the bedroom.

Erin heard the bathroom door bang shut. There was the noise of the handle turning and jiggling, and the door banging against the doorframe a few times. Then Joshua apparently figured out that it wasn't going to latch properly, and quickly attended to his business before someone could barge in on him. He was back a couple of minutes later, sweat on his face, complexion pale. He nodded to Kim.

"Thanks. So… you know when Brianna will be back?"

"I told you she wasn't here." She gave him a knowing look. Of course she knew that Joshua's only reason for going to the bathroom had been to provide him with an opportunity to check out the rest of the apartment that he couldn't see from the doorway.

Joshua shrugged in embarrassment.

"I don't know when she's coming back or if she's coming back," Kim said. "Your guess is as good as mine."

"Do you know where else she would go? Is there somewhere else she can stay?"

"I don't know where she would go. She doesn't report to me."

"Does she have a friend? Someone other than Campbell or you? Who would help her out if she was in trouble?"

"What trouble?"

"Nothing. Just if she was in trouble? Where would she go?"

"She wouldn't come back here. She'd go away. Somewhere you couldn't find her."

"She'd have to go to someone. Someone who could help her out."

Kim shook her head. "She wouldn't have to. She knows how to look after herself. She could get herself some cash and a fix and be all set."

Joshua looked at her for another minute, then shrugged, unsure of how to proceed. He looked at Jeremy for help. None of them had any suggestions. Eventually, Joshua led the way back out the door, and Kim closed the door and slid the bolt behind them. Joshua led the way back to the car in silence, and Erin was relieved to find that it was still there and in one piece. They all piled back in.

"So there wasn't anyone else there?" Vic asked.

"There were some others in the bedroom. Not Brianna." Joshua shook his head slowly. "I can't believe people live that way. Why would anyone choose to live like that?"

"Not everyone has a choice," Erin said. "You make do however you can."

"But they could go to a shelter. Salvation Army. Get help from social programs. There are lots of social programs, lots of people out there to help."

"Most of them won't take addicts. And working girls take pride in being able to help themselves. Even if they've got a pimp taking most of the money and controlling everything in their lives. Not everyone has a choice."

"Campbell was out here by choice. Why would he do that? This can't be the kind of life he wants to lead."

"I don't think it is," Erin agreed. "I think he just wanted something different. He wanted to get away. He's probably not living somewhere like that. He's got friends with jobs who can make the rent on a decent place. He couch surfs. Crashes here or there for a few days. He probably saw the way Brianna was living, and…"

"And brought her home for Thanksgiving," Joshua finished. "He wanted to save her." He thought about that for a few minutes. "He kept saying that she wasn't his girlfriend. Maybe he just wanted to get her out of there. To show her a different kind of life. To try to help her."

Jeremy shifted the car into drive and cleared his throat. "You said you had a couple of other ideas. Where else?"

Joshua hesitated. "I don't know. We should probably just go home. If they're all like that…"

"We came all the way out here. Might as well do the job right. If Brianna knows what's going on, if she can help get Campbell out of trouble…"

"I don't think any of her friends are going to be able to help. Not people like her."

"They won't all be like Kim," Erin said. "She probably has a few people she can touch when she needs something. People who feel sorry for her and give her a bit of help now and then."

"I don't know…"

"Give me the next place," Jeremy said firmly. "We're going to check."

CHAPTER 23

*T*he next place Joshua knew about was a second-story flat over a dilapidated bar. No matter how many times they knocked or called out, they couldn't get anyone to answer the door. Jeremy tried to peer in the windows.

"I'm sure there's someone home. We could break the glass..."

"We're not breaking any windows," Erin told him.

"I might be able to do something about this lock," Jeremy said doubtfully, studying the hefty-looking bolt. Erin had caught him using a bump key before, and doubted that he had much experience or skill with a pick. That security bolt would need more than a little skill. It would be simpler to break the door through the unreinforced wooden frame than it would be to pick it. But they weren't going to do that.

"Let's just go," she said. "If there's someone home, they aren't going to let us in, and they aren't going to stay put while someone breaks the door down. You'll get a shotgun blast in the chest if you try. I don't think Brianna's here."

"She could be," Vic disagreed.

Erin wasn't sure why she was arguing. Erin was pretty sure Vic wasn't going to stand for breaking into someone else's house either. So what were they going to do? Wait out there until someone decided to come out or go in?

"If Brianna saw Joshua out here, she would come out to talk to him," Erin told Vic. "She'd come tell him to get lost, or to tell Campbell to stop harassing her. She's not here. Probably another girl like Kim, cowering in there, waiting for us to go away, so she knows she's safe again."

An apartment over a bar like that—there were probably several girls living there, providing cheap entertainment to the patrons. Working all night and trying to sleep during the day.

"Let's go. Is that the last place?"

"No... I got one more." Joshua sighed. "Ten minutes, and we'll be done."

Joshua and the others looked relieved when they saw the next place Joshua directed them to, but Erin got a tight feeling in her chest. It was a nice place, an upscale hotel with a manager at the desk who watched them like a hawk. The carpet in the lobby was plush, with no stains or burn marks. The elevator appeared to be modern and fully operational—nothing like the abject poverty of the first two places.

Erin eyed the suspicious manager. "Do you know which floor?" she asked Joshua in a murmur. She didn't want to have to ask the staff. They would just run them out. They needed to act as if they knew exactly where they were going and had been invited. Anything less would end up with them out on their butts on the street. Maybe the police would be called as well, just to make sure they hurried on their way.

"Yeah, fourth floor," Joshua said, looking at the plaque beside the elevator. There were meeting rooms, a business center, and a fitness room on the first couple of floors. Nothing was marked for the fourth floor, just regular rooms.

They got on the elevator and Vic punched the button. They were silent as it rose to the appointed floor.

Everything was quiet. No shouting. No noise from behind the corridor of closed doors. Erin shifted anxiously. Everything looked perfectly fine. Clean, well-appointed, no foul smells. So completely opposite from any of the other places that Brianna might have run to. Erin was afraid of what they were going to find.

She didn't knock on the door. Jeremy gave her a questioning look, then stepped forward and knocked himself. They didn't have to hammer on the door and call out this time. Within a minute, the door handle turned and the door whispered open. This door was also opened by a young woman, but one who looked a lot better than Kim had. She wore a kimono dressing gown, but her hair and makeup were immaculate. Erin could smell the fresh scent of soap and shampoo, but no heavy perfumes. The girl looked over the visitors and raised an eyebrow.

"How may I help you?"

"Uh…" Jeremy cleared his throat. He put his hands behind his back, awkward and unsure what to do with them. "We're looking for Brianna?"

Her brows drew down. "Brianna?" She paused, thinking about it. "You'd better come in."

She led them into the living room of a large suite. She called toward the bedroom. "Mickey? We have company."

There was a muttered curse, then the squeak of a desk chair, and in a moment, an older man entered the room.

The smell of his cologne hit Erin like a punch in the gut. She looked back toward the door they had entered through, measuring the route to escape. She grasped Vic's arm. "We've got to go."

Vic resisted, giving Erin a puzzled frown. Erin turned to Joshua. "Come on. Let's get out of here."

He shook his head. They all looked at her as if she had just sprouted two heads. Erin's heart was racing. She couldn't understand why they didn't feel it too. The man was dangerous. She had known something was wrong going into the apartment, and her senses were all ringing alarm bells with the man's entrance.

"What is all this?" he asked. He looked at the four of them, and then at the girl, snapping something at her that Erin didn't understand. Erin was still holding on to Vic's arm. She dug her fingers in, hanging on for dear life.

Mickey was a medium height and build, giving the impression of compact efficiency. His neatly trimmed hair was graying around the temples. He was dressed in business attire, not a hood like Volkov, but he spoke with a Russian accent.

Jeremy was only then starting to get an inkling of the danger they were in. He licked dry lips and addressed Mickey.

351

"We're looking for Brianna. Someone said that she might be around here. That she came here sometimes."

"Brianna." Mickey looked at the girl. "Which one is she?"

The girl in the dressing gown looked at them, then back at the Russian. "The black girl. With Wolf. The one who—"

"Why are you looking for her?" Mickey cut across the girl's words. His gaze fixed on Erin. "Why would she be here?"

"She might have thought she was in trouble," Erin said, stammering for an explanation. "She disappeared and we just wanted to make sure she was okay. That nothing happened to her. Someone thought that she could have come here. I don't know; maybe she does some work for you…"

His eyes drifted away from Erin, discounting her. He took a step closer to Joshua, studying him carefully.

"You are the boyfriend."

"No. No, that was my brother. I mean, he wasn't her boyfriend, but he's the one who knows her. We look a lot alike."

"Where is your brother now?"

"There was some trouble. He couldn't come. But he was worried about Bree. I thought… I'd help him out."

"You go in the bedroom," Mickey told the girl. "Leave us alone."

She didn't argue. She walked out of the room, and Erin heard the bedroom door click behind her. She pulled on Vic's arm, desperate for them to get out of there. Vic used her other hand to pry Erin loose. It was clear from her expression that she was starting to get uncomfortable with the situation as well. Mickey ran his eyes restlessly over the group.

"Brianna is not here. You can see that. She doesn't live here. She does not…" his words were overly precise, "hang out."

Erin nodded and moved an inch closer to the door.

"It was a mistake to come here," Mickey advised.

"We're sorry," Erin said. "We'll go now."

"You," Mickey pointed at Jeremy. "And you." He pointed at Vic. "Remove your weapons slowly and put them on the table."

Jeremy and Vic looked at each other. Erin didn't know whether she wanted them to obey the Russian or to pull their guns to cover the group as they tried to leave the hotel room. Mickey didn't have a weapon trained on them, but Erin had felt threatened from the instant he walked into the room. He was probably armed. There were probably others close by—if not in the hotel suite, then in one of the rooms next door or across the hall. Mickey might have already given them a signal. They could be listening to what was going on in the room through a bug or an earwig. There could even be video surveillance. It would be impossible to spot the tiny spy cameras that were available to anyone who wanted one, certainly to the Russian mob.

But there was no one else in sight; it might be their last chance to make a break for it and get out of the hotel room. Erin watched to see what Jeremy and Vic would decide to do. The instant they made a move, she would be ready to act.

Jeremy first raised both hands to chest height, palms toward the Russian to show that he wasn't a threat. He pulled his jacket aside and then his shirt up to display the concealed carry holster at his hip. With the other hand, he slowly reached across his body and used two fingers to pull out the handgun. He bent over and laid it gently on the coffee table. Erin breathed a sigh of relief that he hadn't tried to shoot Mickey and that Mickey had not done anything to him.

Yet. Once Jeremy and Vic were both disarmed, he would have the four of them at his mercy.

Jeremy straightened up. He lifted his shirt and spun in a full circle to show that he didn't have a second holster in his waistband.

"And yours," Mickey told Vic.

Vic followed Jeremy's example, carefully removing her gun from a holster snugged up to her bra. Erin wondered how Mickey had seen either one of them. Even knowing that the two were armed, she hadn't been able to see either holster. But the Russian probably had a lot more experience in the matter than Erin did.

The four of them exchanged glances. They were now defenseless, at Mickey's mercy. Best case scenario, he would send them on their way. Erin wasn't expecting the best. She closed her eyes and tried to regulate her breathing.

Her thoughts went to Terry. Was she ever going to see him again? If Mickey killed them, would Terry even know what had happened? Or would they just disappear and he would always be left wondering what had happened in those final moments?

"Sit down," Mickey ordered. Erin opened her eyes and saw him pointing to the couch and chairs in a conversational grouping. He bent down and picked up the two guns and casually moved them across the room, leaving them on top of the minibar out of everyone's reach.

As they nervously sat down, Mickey looked over his shoulder toward the bedroom that the girl had retreated to. There had been no sound of the door opening, and likewise no noise from the TV or shower to indicate what she was doing. Was she lounging on the bed reading a book or having a nap, unconcerned with what happened to their 'guests,' or was she perched there, knees drawn up to her chest, tensely awaiting the sound of gunfire or cries for help?

Mickey went over to the window and looked out, his back to them. Erin glanced at the others for their reactions. Should they make a break for it while his back was turned? Or was that what he was waiting for them to do? Then he would whirl around and shoot them, or his goons would be waiting outside the hotel room door waiting for them?

No one made any move.

Mickey turned around and looked them over, leaning against the windowsill behind him.

"What happened to Brianna?"

They all looked at each other, trying to figure out how to answer him. His voice was neutral, his face an impassive mask. He wanted to know how much they knew. Or did he really want to know about Brianna?

He could have shot them all when he'd picked up their guns. There were enough bullets in those two guns to shoot them all several times over, making sure that he had done a thorough job. If he were a Russian mobster, he could probably put a bullet into each of their foreheads before they knew what was happening.

Those guys didn't play games.

"Tell me," he prompted. "You come here to find her, so you tell me what you know."

Joshua was the first one to give in. "She was staying at our house. She came for Thanksgiving. When Campbell got arrested, Mom told her she could still stay there. Until he got out on bail and they could figure out what to do. Brianna said she didn't have a car or any money. And there are no hotels in Bald Eagle Falls. A couple of B&B's, but she couldn't have afforded them even if they agreed to take her, and they wouldn't."

Mickey was watching Joshua intently. "Because she was black?"

"Black, homeless, an addict. The whole package. No one would want her in their house."

"Except your mother."

"She would do that for Campbell. She'd do anything for him. It wasn't anything for her to put up Brianna for a couple of nights. She just wanted Campbell back, and if she helped his friend when she was in trouble, that would go a long way to convincing him that she just wanted him to be happy."

"Then what?"

"That was it. When we got up Saturday morning, Brianna was gone. She didn't leave a note, but she didn't steal anything either. Just managed to find a way out of Bald Eagle Falls. She must have called someone or hitchhiked."

"Why do you say that?"

"She wasn't anywhere in Bald Eagle Falls. I looked around. It isn't like living in the city; there's nowhere to go. Nowhere she could be overnight. And she didn't have any friends."

"Did she know anyone? Meet anyone?"

"Just us. Me and my mom. Erin and Vic came over when Cam was arrested, so Brianna met them, but she didn't go to their house."

Erin and Vic shook their heads in unison.

"And where else? Did she know where you worked? She could not just disappear without help."

"We work at the bakery," Erin explained. "My bakery. She wasn't there." She rubbed her temples, trying to soothe the pounding.

Mickey paced back and forth across the room, slowly, deep in thought. He turned around and faced Joshua.

"What did Beaver say?"

CHAPTER 24

*J*oshua's mouth hung open, shocked. Erin was sure she looked pretty much the same as he did. She tried to adjust her thinking. Mickey knew Beaver?

"What does Beaver say?" Joshua echoed.

Mickey leaned in slightly. "What did she think? That Brianna ran? That something happened to her? Is she looking? I don't understand what you are doing here, looking for her. A bunch of kids. Isn't she already in enough trouble for using Cam?"

"How do you know about that?" Jeremy asked.

Mickey shrugged. "It is my business to know. Everything that goes on here."

"Are you an informant?"

"I... have information," Mickey said cagily.

"And you know Ro? Beaver? You give her information?"

"You are getting off track. Why is *she* not here? Why has she not called me? What has happened?"

"You know about Volkov," Erin said, finding her voice.

Mickey looked at her. "The baker," he said flatly. "Would Brianna go to you? No. She did not know you. But maybe she knew where the bakery was. Maybe Cam pointed it out to her. So she told Volkov to meet her there."

356

"And...? Then what?"

"You tell me the rest of the story." He folded his arms and leaned back slightly, adopting a casual stance. "Go ahead."

"I don't know. None of us know. Was Brianna connected to Volkov? Was he her drug dealer?"

"He was... many things to her."

Erin swallowed. She tried to read Mickey's face, but it was impossible. He didn't twitch. Didn't give anything away.

"*You* were there," she said finally. "Why don't *you* tell us what happened?"

"Erin!" The cry came from Vic, a yelp of protest. A warning.

"Mickey was there?" the Russian gave a chuckle. "What would Mikhail be doing there? There is no reason for me to be in Bald Eagle Falls."

"Maybe *you* were the one she called. Not Volkov. Maybe you went to meet her. Or maybe Volkov called you, because he figured you would want to know that something was up. Maybe there was a reason you would want to know that Brianna had left Campbell's house and was trying to get out of Bald Eagle Falls."

"Why would I care? She is nothing to me. Just a used-up junkie."

"Then why were you there?" Erin asked.

Mickey chuckled. "I like this one," he said to no one in particular. "And you knew the minute I walked into the room. I could see that. How?"

"The smell. Your cologne or aftershave. I could smell that when Stayner opened Volkov's car door. Just for an instant."

"So he uses the same cologne. It is Russian. Why not?"

Erin shook her head. He had as much as confirmed that he had been there. Had he seen Volkov before he died? After? Had he been the one to kill him?

Mickey gazed at her steadily, his face still expressionless, and she wondered if he were trying to think of the best way to kill her and dispose of her body.

"Where is Campbell?" he asked.

"He's at home." Joshua was the one to answer. "He's on electronic monitoring; he can't leave the house, or go more than two hundred yards, anyway. If he came here, they'd put him back in jail."

"So he told you to come here? Told you where to go, that you might find Brianna here?"

Joshua looked around at the others. He hadn't been very forthcoming up until then about how he had gotten the information from Campbell. But it was no longer a matter of just looking around in the city to see if they could discover where Brianna had disappeared to.

"I talked to him before. Sometimes. While he was in the city. He'd call late at night or early in the morning, when he was mellow, and he'd talk about what he was doing. Who he saw and where he'd gone, what things had happened. He didn't always remember what he'd talked about the next time. I guess maybe he was a little buzzed."

"So he didn't tell you where to look. He said that he'd been here," Erin said.

Joshua shook his head. "He said that Brianna had come here. Not him. He'd followed her to see what she was doing. But he didn't get inside."

Unsurprisingly, Mickey did not jump in to tell them what Brianna had been to his hotel room for. Erin thought about the things that Beaver said the Wolf had been involved with. Drugs, prostitution, other human trafficking. Who knew what else. She suspected by Mickey's demeanor that he was not just a street soldier, low down on the totem pole. He was one of the bosses. Pricey hotel room, girls at his beck and call, whatever else he wanted. Had Brianna been there to entertain him? To run drugs? Maybe the drugs in Campbell's car *had* been her delivery, and she just hadn't had a chance to pass them on to whoever they were supposed to be going to. Volkov, waiting behind the bakery? Falling asleep because he'd had to wait for so long without any sign of her? And then…? Who had killed him? Mickey? Erin couldn't connect it up.

Mickey sat on the edge of the arm of the couch Jeremy and Vic were sitting on. He reached into his pocket, and Erin couldn't help holding herself tense, waiting for the inevitable weapon. Now that he had their story, now that he knew everything that they knew and whether he was safe or not, he could dispose of them.

But he pulled out a phone. Propped there on the arm of the couch, he tapped in a number and held it up to his ear. It didn't ring for very long. With the length of time that it sometimes took cellphones to connect, Erin suspected that it probably hadn't rung more than once on the recipient's end.

Looking at Erin, Mickey spoke into his phone. "We have a problem."

CHAPTER 25

ime stood still. Not entirely still, but it ground down to such a slow speed that Erin could feel every one of her heartbeats and the space in between, even though her heart was thumping fast in anticipation of danger.

The voice that answered the other end was loud enough to hear across the room, and it was a voice that Erin recognized.

"What's up, Mickey?" Beaver asked.

"Got some kids sneaking around here. Asking questions, poking their noses where they don't belong. You know I don't like people poking their noses in my business."

"What are you worried about? What kids?"

"That's just it. One of them looks like the one you were running. Cam."

They all looked at Joshua while they waited for Beaver to answer. She didn't respond immediately. Several long and painful heartbeats passed before there was any response from Beaver. A little quieter this time, the first sign that she was concerned.

"A kid that looks like Cam? Maybe his younger brother?"

"Yeah. How do you want me to get rid of them?"

"Don't say anything to them. Just tell them to mind their own business and get out of your way," Beaver suggested sensibly.

"They're asking about Brianna. I thought you said she didn't have anything to do with Wolf's death?"

"She didn't." Beaver cleared her throat.

"You're sure?"

"There's no evidence that she was at the scene. No fingerprints. No one saw her. No one who has connected the two of them."

"She called him."

"If she did, they were both using burners. And he didn't have it on him when he died."

"Because she took it."

"Mickey…" Beaver's voice was reproachful. "You're paranoid. I told you, there's no evidence that she called him. Where would she get another phone? She had no money, and any she did have went straight into drugs."

"He give it to her." Beaver couldn't see his shrug. "He decided he wants to keep her on the hook. So he gives her a hit. Gets her a phone. Tells her to call him if she needs anything. Your boy gets arrested for drug possession, so she calls. *Help me get away from this place before they arrest me too.* So Wolf goes. And…"

"And what?" Beaver repeated. "She kills him? Why would she? He's her meal ticket. He gets Brianna her next job, her next fix. She has no motive to kill him when he shows up to help her. And she needed a car, so why didn't she take his car?"

"Where is Brianna?"

"Where? How am I supposed to know? She took off. She's in the wind."

"I don't like these kids showing up."

"No," Beaver agreed. "Neither do I. They shouldn't be interfering. They're going to put themselves in harm's way, just by being around there. Tell them to go home if they know what's good for them. I'll talk with Joshua. Tell him to leave this alone or he's going to end up in a cell next to Campbell."

Joshua swallowed, looking green.

"I have to go," Mickey said. He tapped the phone screen to end the call.

～

For a few minutes, Mickey just sat there looking at them. He slid his phone back in his pocket.

"You coming here was stupid. If others had been here… there is only so much I could do. You do not want to end up killed," he said baldly. "You do not want these ladies," he indicated Erin and Vic, "to end up in the game. You think it cannot happen? One taste of China Girl, maybe two, and they will do anything to get another dose. A-ny-thing," he said it as if it were three words. "Beaver has been on this for months. You think you can come in here and blunder around and not screw everything up? She will not thank you for ruining a case they put hundreds of man-hours and millions of dollars into."

Erin put her hands over her burning eyes, the headache that had started in her temples banging behind her eyes. Everyone was deathly quiet.

"So go home," Mickey said finally. "Now I have to figure out how to clean up this mess."

He looked toward the bedroom, scowling. The girl who had let them into the hotel room had seen all of them and could put them together with Mickey. She had heard them inquire after Brianna. She hadn't witnessed anything beyond the initial introductions, but Mickey was going to have to figure out how to keep word of their visit quiet.

They got up, all moving slowly, still worried that anything they did could set Mickey off and make him change his mind. Just because he had told them to go home, that didn't mean he wouldn't do anything if he decided they were too big of a risk. He might be helping Beaver out, but he would still be running his illegal business operations as well. He had to stay involved to give her any help.

Jeremy took a short step toward the minibar.

"No," Mickey snapped. "Leave them where they are. Do you know how stupid it is, coming in here armed? You think you are Magnum PI? Maybe you lose your guns, you think twice about where you take them next time."

Jeremy looked toward his gun, then looked at Vic. She sighed and shrugged. It wasn't worth the risk for either of them to disobey him to see how serious he was. They all walked single-file to the door.

"Have a nice day," Mickey told them.

They let the door shut behind them and left the building without speaking to each other.

CHAPTER 26

They were a subdued group as they drove back to the mall to get Erin's car. They agreed to drive back to Bald Eagle Falls separately, in the same configuration as they had arrived, so as not to arouse any suspicions. Jeremy would drop Joshua at home, and then he would meet the girls at Erin's house.

Erin and Vic drove back to Bald Eagle Falls with little discussion of what had just happened. Erin wondered whether Vic understood what kind of an organization Mickey and Wolf and Brianna and Campbell were involved with. Vic had been on her own for only a very short time before Erin had rescued her, and before that had grown up on the farm, which Erin had to assume was sheltered from the type of street life that went on in the big city. She might not have understood as well as Erin, who had seen more of life on the streets, what kind of danger they had put themselves in.

Vic wiped at her face and sniffled, looking out the side window. Erin realized she was crying and swerved momentarily, looking for a tissue or some other way to comfort her friend.

"It's okay," she assured Vic. "We're going to be okay. If he was going to do anything to us, he would have done it while we were there. As long as we stay out of the way, he'll leave us alone. And anyone else… Beaver's already got an eye on it, and we'll set the burglar alarm, and Terry is right there if anything goes sideways…"

"I'm not worried about him coming after us," Vic sniffled. She searched in her purse and found a tattered tissue, which she dabbed at her eyes, trying not to mess up her carefully applied makeup. "It's just... I guess it's just hitting me, how close we came..." She took a deep breath and let it go. "If he hadn't been working with Beaver... or like he said, if there were other people there and he couldn't do anything to protect us... We were unarmed and totally at his mercy."

Erin nodded.

"And Brianna?" Vic asked, her voice going up questioningly. "Do you think... do you think she's dead too?"

"I don't know." Erin exercised all of the willpower she had to keep Vic's tears from making her break down too. She was driving, trying to keep up with Jeremy's reckless highway speeds, and she couldn't afford to let her eyes blur. "I don't know if she left on her own, or if something happened to her..."

"What if she's the one who killed Wolf?"

"Like Mickey said... why? If he was the one who supplied her with drugs and helped her, why would she kill him?"

"Because it happens all the time, Erin. Lovers get into fights. Pimps beat up their girls, and maybe she tried to defend herself. People on drugs do crazy things that don't make any sense logically."

"Well... yes. But Beaver doesn't think that's what happened."

"Neither of them knows where she went."

"Maybe that's good. Maybe it means she's safe somewhere, where no one knows where she is."

Vic sniffled and nodded. By the time they got back to Mary Lou's house, everyone was dry-eyed and appeared calm. Vic had managed not to wash away too much of her makeup, so that her moment of tears was unde-tectable. "And don't you dare tell Jeremy I cried!" she warned Erin.

"Why would I tell Jeremy?"

"I don't know. Just don't."

They dropped Joshua off at home. They watched him in to make sure that he was safe. And then they drove on to Erin's house.

$\sim$

Erin was glad to be home. It was getting late and the street lights were starting to come on. The lights inside the house were bright and warm and inviting. Erin was looking forward to a warm bath and hot cup of tea, and then to a long, undisturbed night's sleep.

She could wish, couldn't she?

She led the others into the house, feeling the tension fall away from her. She was home, and she was safe. She could cuddle with Terry and fall asleep in his arms. No more thinking about Mickey and what he might have done.

She was expecting to find Terry sitting on the couch, watching TV and waiting for her to get home. He would be wondering why they had been held up for so long in the city when they had just gone to look for a couple of things. Erin had texted on the way back that they had been held up but were on their way, but she would need to think of something to tell him to explain the delay.

But it wasn't Terry sitting on the couch; it was Beaver. And for once, she wasn't grinning and cracking her gum.

CHAPTER 27

*V*ic and Jeremy entered behind Erin. They had both been talking in lowered voices, but stopped when they saw Beaver.

Beaver sat on the couch, one foot up on the coffee table and one foot on the floor, knee jutting out at an angle. On one hand, she looked completely relaxed and comfortable, but on the other, she was intense and serious, so far from what was normal that they knew they were in big trouble.

"Did y'all have a nice day shopping?"

Erin swallowed. The others didn't answer either. What were they going to do? Lie to Beaver? She clearly knew what had happened already.

"Doesn't look like you bought very much," Beaver noted. "Day ended up being a bust?"

"Yeah," Jeremy agreed, trying to force humor into his voice. "Looks like we're busted."

"And not just by me, either."

Jeremy shifted uncomfortably. "I'm sorry, Ro. We didn't mean to get in the middle of anything. I hope… we didn't screw up your op."

"Sit down."

Her nod indicated that the instruction was to all of them. Jeremy sat on the couch beside Beaver, but he didn't cuddle up to her like he normally would, looking awkward and uncomfortable.

"Joshua made his curfew?" Beaver asked lightly.

"We took him home first."

"Does Mary Lou know what happened?"

"Not unless Joshua decides to tell her."

"He didn't tell her he was in contact with Campbell while he was in the city; I don't think he would tell her about… this," Erin said.

"I'll touch base with him later. What exactly did Cam tell him?"

"It sounds like… pretty much everything where Brianna was concerned. Joshua had a list of places to look for her."

"And no luck?" Beaver asked, looking at each of them and meeting their eyes. "No sign of her?"

"No sign of her. I would guess… she got on a bus and kept going."

"Except she didn't have any money," Vic pointed out. "So how could she buy a bus ticket?"

"Turn a few tricks," Beaver said with a shrug. "Or she hitchhiked or took off with a friend. I hope that's what happened."

"What do *you* think happened?" Erin asked.

Beaver looked at her for a minute. "That would be for me to investigate, Miss Erin. Not you."

"Don't bust her chops," Jeremy said, rubbing his forehead. "She's the one who was trying to talk us out of looking for Brianna. And who got a whiff that something was wrong at Mickey's."

Beaver nodded slowly. "At least someone's got some sense. You should pay more attention to her."

Erin's cheeks got warm.

"There are a lot of heavy hitters involved here," Beaver said. "Wolf getting killed is not a good sign."

Erin was tired and shaky, coming down off of the adrenaline rush brought on by the danger they had faced at Mickey's.

Beaver chewed slowly, looking at them. "You were actually *at* Mickey's? He didn't just get word that you were asking questions?"

"We didn't know," Jeremy protested. "We thought… it was just somewhere a friend lived. She'd crashed there, like Cam was crashing with friends."

"Really. You thought she had a friend who could afford a place like that."

Jeremy looked at Vic and then at Erin. "I guess… yeah. I didn't think anything of it. I mean… Campbell was hanging out with this crowd, and he wasn't homeless. He could go back to Bald Eagle Falls anytime, and his mom's got a nice place. I mean, I know they lost their money, but they still live in a nice house. So maybe… Brianna's folks lived in a nice place. Or some other friend or relative that she hoped would help her out."

"And you?" Beaver looked at Erin.

"I didn't feel good about it. I didn't want to go in. The kind of people that operate out of a hotel, with young girls coming and going… she didn't go there looking for a handout or a couch to crash on."

"No, she didn't," Beaver agreed. "You should have listened to that warning voice."

Erin nodded. She had only been one of four, but she had been the oldest and most experienced and should have been more assertive about not going in. She should have put her foot down and told them no. But she didn't know if they would have listened. If they had gone in without her, would the results have been any different?

"We're really sorry," Jeremy repeated. "Are you going to be in trouble for this? I wasn't acting on anything you said, it was what Cam had told Joshua…"

"You know my head is already on the chopping block for Cam's part in this. If he's telling Joshua this stuff when he was clearly instructed to keep his mouth shut… who knows what else he might have said to other parties. Who he might have accidentally tipped off. I thought he was a good bet, but this is turning out to be a disaster."

"You couldn't have known that he would say something when he wasn't supposed to," Jeremy commiserated.

"It's my job to know. I'm supposed to be able to judge when someone is ready and when they're a bad risk. I should have known that he was too young and impulsive." Beaver's words clearly encompassed Jeremy and Vic as well, and they both looked shamefaced. Beaver had picked Jeremy to be her partner, even knowing that he was so much younger than she was, and had been involved at some level with the Jackson clan. Jeremy agreeing to go with Joshua to the city to help him find Brianna had clearly been a poor choice.

Erin wondered whether Beaver's words were true of her too. Was she any better than the teens, sure that they could just rush in and rescue Brianna?

"What's done is done," Beaver said briskly, and cracked her gum so loudly it made Erin jump. "No way to go back and change it now. But going forward... I'm going to have to see what can be done to salvage the situation."

They all sat around the living room, not sure what to do or say next. Beaver slapped her hands down on her thighs.

"I've got my car, so you don't need to wait for me," she told Jeremy. "I'll catch up with you."

Jeremy took the dismissal well, looking relieved. He had probably been wondering, as Erin had, whether that would be it for their relationship. "Okay." He stood up, giving Beaver a swift peck on the cheek on the way to his feet. "I'll see you tonight."

"If I get there," she said. "Don't know for sure what the night will bring."

"Okay. Then... whenever."

Vic decided it was time for her to go too. "Don't know if Willie's back yet or not. You'll be okay?" she asked Erin.

Erin nodded. "Yeah. Thanks. I'll be fine."

Beaver pretended to be gathering her things as Jeremy and Vic said goodbye and departed. She straightened and looked at Erin when they were alone.

"I'm sorry too," Erin told Beaver. "I should have been... more insistent."

"What did you think of Mikhail?"

It took Erin a minute to remember that Mickey had referred to himself once as Mikhail. A much more Russian version of the name.

"He scared me. We were all surprised to find out he was working with you. I'm worried... he might be involved in Brianna's disappearance and Wolf's murder."

Beaver nodded briefly. "What did he say?"

"Not very much... he wanted to know what had happened, why we were looking for her. He said she and Wolf were involved... I don't know any details, but I guess you know that already. He didn't say that much more to us than he did to you."

"You have good instincts. I think you read people well."

Erin thought about how many time she had been mistaken about who had committed a crime. Who had been guilty and who had been innocent. Who had been safe and who was dangerous. She couldn't agree with Beaver's assessment.

"Sometimes, maybe. I miss a lot."

"We all do. Hundreds of signals every day. What's really surprising is that any of us can get along and communicate with each other, considering how little we understand about human interaction."

Erin laughed. "Well, that's comforting."

"Why do you think he was involved with Wolf's death?"

"Were they rivals? Partners? Did they work together, or was Brianna playing two different sides against each other?"

"Probably all of the above. Alliances change. You've heard that there's no honor among thieves? It's true. And no honor among murderers, mobsters, pimps, or any other classification of criminal. Wolf and Mikhail are similar in a lot of ways—passionate, changeable, egotistical, greedy. They may look different, try to brand themselves as a different class of criminals, but they're still cousins. They're still very similar under the skin."

"They're cousins?"

"I didn't mean it literally, but these Russians all are, if you go back far enough. So… you didn't answer the question. Why do you think he was involved in Wolf's death? Just because they're the only two Russian mobsters you've run into lately? Because he was connected to Brianna?"

"No. It's silly. I shouldn't even mention it."

"Mention away."

"You're going to think it's nothing."

"So what? It takes hundreds of infinitesimally small clues to build a case. It's not like on TV where they know who did it, and all they have to do is go through his drawers or his car or run his DNA, and then they can prove it. Building a case is hundreds and hundreds of pieces of information that you fit together like a puzzle."

Said the treasure hunter. Erin could see why she enjoyed her job and her hobby so much. They were mirror images of each other. She loved to solve a mystery.

"Okay, but I warned you. When we opened the car door, Wolf's door… I caught just a whiff of a sweet smell. A cologne or deodorant."

"Yes…"

"And when Mickey came in to the room, he was reeking of the same scent."

Beaver raised an eyebrow. "So they use the same deodorant? That connects them?"

Erin shook her head. "Mickey was there. He was there with Wolf. He admitted as much when we were there."

Beaver chewed her gum slowly. "Okay," she agreed. "Mickey was there. He had contact with Wolf. Did he kill him?"

"I don't know."

"What motive would he have?"

"That's why I asked how they were connected. Whether they were friends or enemies. Because I don't know."

Beaver nodded. "It's one more puzzle piece. Don't worry. I'll put it to good use. And you… stay away from gangsters."

CHAPTER 28

$\mathcal{E}$rin looked toward the bedrooms. She hadn't heard a sound from that end of the house since she had gotten home. She had thought at first that Terry had just gone to the bedroom to read when Beaver said that she wanted to talk to the rest of them in private. But Terry would have heard the others leave. And he hadn't as much as moved enough for the bedsprings to squeak. "Is Terry home?"

It was strange, not only to find Beaver sitting in the living room by herself, but also not to have heard from Terry and to find him absent once more. Had he let Beaver into the house? And then left? Had she let herself in?

"He went out," Beaver said vaguely. "I'm sure he'll probably be back before very long."

Erin opened her mouth to say something, and then wasn't sure what. Beaver wasn't in charge of Terry. She wasn't his mother or his wife. He had told her he was going out, and had gone out. Erin had no idea whether he knew that Erin and the others had run into problems, or if Beaver had been just as vague about Erin's whereabouts as she now was about Terry's. She had probably just told him they were on their way back from shopping and she wanted to catch Vic and Erin before she went home.

And Terry had gone… for a walk. Or to visit with a friend. To help Willie out with something. Or for a drive to clear his head.

"What's wrong?" Beaver asked.

"I'm worried about Terry. It's been so hard on him, having to be at home all day. Not being able to go back to work yet. It's not like the department is keeping him home when he feels like he's well enough to go back. He knows he's not ready to be back on duty again, and that's even more frustrating. You can't fight with your own body."

Beaver nodded. "I'm always restless and angry when I have had to wait for my body to heal. And that's without a head injury. Painkillers make you fuzzy enough; I would hate to have a concussion or other brain injury on top of that. The days are too long."

Erin nodded. "I'm like that too, when I'm off work. When we were between bakeries… I drove everyone around me crazy."

Beaver smiled widely. "I remember." She pulled on her jacket, with lots of pockets to store the equipment she liked to carry. Some of it lethal, some of it less so. "He's worried about you too, you know."

"I know. But I'm doing okay. And I'm working, so that I at least have a distraction during the day. If I wake up at night and can't get back to sleep, I can plan out my week. Work on the next advertising campaign. Whatever. There's always something to do, even if I'm not baking."

"Speaking of baking…" Beaver tilted her head toward the kitchen.

"You know you can help yourself to whatever is in the freezer. It's not like I'm going to run out."

Beaver ducked into the kitchen to go through the leftover baking that Erin kept on hand for dinner and treats. She put a few things in a bag and gnawed on a frozen chocolate chip cookie.

"You need to talk to each other," she advised. "You could probably help each other more if you weren't both trying to avoid upsetting the other."

"We talk…"

"About…?"

Erin thought about the last few weeks with Terry. How often had they had a real conversation? About something that mattered to one of them? Beaver was right; they were both tiptoeing around the real issues, anything that might trigger flashbacks or nightmares or an angry mood. They kept pretending there was nothing wrong, watching TV or cuddling, having meals together and, while that was nice, it wasn't helping.

"Maybe you're right," she sighed.

"Keep doing your tai chi."

Erin was surprised. "Really? No one else thinks it will help. They say it's just mumbo jumbo, or it's spiritualism, and I should pray to their god, or whatever."

"You're the one who knows your body and what the trauma is doing to you. You're the one who knows your brain and what fits in your belief system. It isn't up to anyone else to tell you what is the right or wrong thing to do."

"But you're telling me to do it?"

Beaver grinned. "That's because you chose it. You're doing what's right for you. And you should keep doing it, despite any flak you might be getting from anyone else."

"They think it's a religious thing. That alienates people, and I don't want to lose customers because they think I'm... worshiping the devil in my meditation."

"Where else are they going to go? Into the city? To the grocery store? They know your product. I don't think it matters that much what they think of your private life."

"I don't know." Erin shook her head, remembering what it had been like when rumors had gone around that she was a witch. Business had dried up very quickly. For a few days. She didn't know how long it would have gone on if she hadn't sorted things out with Adele so that people wouldn't see any sign of her rites in Erin's woods. Then, the trickle of customers had started up again and things had gone back to normal. "Maybe you're right. I mean, they were buying bread from Angela, and even if she was a Christian, a lot of them thought that she'd killed her husband."

"People get over ethical conflicts pretty quickly when they're hungry and just need a dozen rolls for company dinner."

Erin smiled. "Thanks. That makes me feel better. I was going to skip it today, but maybe while I'm waiting for Terry, I'll spend a few minutes connecting with my body."

"Attagirl," Beaver agreed. "And you know, I can help you with some other martial arts too. Ones that can be useful during a physical confrontation, not just for meditation."

"Meditation is what I really want. I'm not that well-coordinated, so I like the slowness of tai chi."

"You can learn the others slowly as well. They can be very relaxing." Beaver's eyes closed slowly, almost all the way, like a cat having its back stroked. She opened them again and nodded. "Take care of yourself."

CHAPTER 29

*E*rin had just finished her tai chi and was walking back toward the house when Terry got home. Erin was relieved that Beaver had been right and he hadn't been too long. She hesitated whether to ask him where he had been or what he had been doing. She'd been trying to give him his own space. But maybe space wasn't what he needed.

"Hi. I was worried about you," she told him.

Terry held out his arms and hugged her close when she stepped in.

"I'm a little sweaty," Erin apologized. "You wouldn't think that moving that slowly could raise a sweat, but…"

"You're just fine." He buried his nose in her hair and breathed warm air into her scalp. Erin squirmed.

"That tickles."

"You smell good."

"I don't; I'm sweaty."

He bent closer, the short whiskers of his chin rubbing against her face as he leaned in to kiss her. Erin returned the kiss, then looked into his eyes.

"Are you okay?"

"Fine. Why? A man can't kiss a pretty lady without something being wrong?"

"No. I just wanted to make sure that everything is okay."

"Everything is fine."

They turned together and started walking back to the house, up onto the porch, in through the back door, into the kitchen.

"What did you do today?" Erin asked him.

"Not much, just puttered around the house. Fixed that sticky window in your attic room. Took K9 out for a walk."

"I just wondered, since you weren't here when I got home, but Beaver was."

"I told her you wouldn't mind her waiting here for you." He looked at her curiously. "Was I wrong?"

"No. Of course not. I don't mind any of our friends hanging around here. I like it that people feel comfortable here and like they can come over when they want to." When she had been young, she had envied the foster sisters who had been more popular, who had friends who would come over to the house, and they would always have something interesting to do. Erin had rarely had friends who were close enough to invite over for no reason. She needed to have a birthday or a party, an event that she could invite people to. People didn't just want to be around her.

"Good. You... worked things out with her?"

Erin wondered how much he knew. Was Beaver able to tell him more because he was a law enforcement officer, even though he wasn't on active duty? Or did he have an intuition that something was wrong? Erin was sure Beaver hadn't told him that their lives had been in danger. Terry wouldn't be nearly so calm and relaxed if he knew that. He'd be lecturing her about staying safe and he'd want to go confront Mickey, which wouldn't be a good idea. It was better if he didn't know everything.

"Yeah, I think so," she said vaguely.

He studied her, eyes quick and calculating. Trying to decide if he was going to push for more details. Did he know that it was about Campbell's case or related to the murder? He had to know that was what Beaver was focused on.

"So, you had a good day?" she asked him.

"Sure. Just fine."

Erin ran her hand down his arm. "Are you doing okay? We should talk more."

"We're talking."

"Really talk."

He stared into her eyes. "You don't want to *really talk* about it."

"I know. But we should anyway."

They walked into the living room. Terry looked for a moment at the couch, where they had spent many hours lately watching TV and comfortably not communicating. He took her hand and pulled her toward the bedroom.

Erin's stomach clenched. He was right. She didn't want to talk about it. As soon as she thought about sitting down and discussing her feelings and the dreams, flashbacks, and other emotions she had been feeling, her body clenched up and all of the benefits of the tai chi disappeared.

They walked into the bedroom and, when Erin stopped, Terry bent down, swept her off her feet, and dumped her on the bed, falling down beside her.

Erin was on the wrong side of the bed, and she immediately felt anxious about being trapped, penned in by him lying on the side of the bed nearest the door. Terry leaned in close. He kissed her cheek and stroked her hair back.

"I'm here."

Erin nodded. Her throat was hot and her breathing labored, like all of the air had been sucked out of the room. Her eyes immediately filled with tears.

Terry put his arm around her and bumped his forehead against hers. For a few minutes, they both just lay there, breathing on each other and not saying anything.

"I was scared," Terry said softly.

Erin pressed closer to him. She closed her eyes and nodded. She hoped he understood that she wasn't trying to shut him out, but just needed to block out the extra sensory input. There was only so much she could handle at once, and she was at her limit.

"When Theresa hit you?"

He didn't answer at first. Erin could feel a slight tremor in his body as he held her. "When I realized... what was going to happen. Going in there, neither of us realized that she was the one. We just thought she could give us some background. Jack knew that Biggles had lived with her family for a while. But he didn't know about... the history between them."

Erin sniffled, struggling to keep her emotions under control. "I was scared for you. When we found your phone."

"Yeah."

"Before that, even… that was the worst moment because I knew for sure… she had done something. Before that, I only thought that… you had been there. That it was K9's dog tag on the floor. I didn't know for sure. And I thought that you had just come and gone. Or I hoped that you had just come and gone and that you were okay. You were on your way home or had stopped for a burger or a beer with Jack. But when I saw both of your phones there, there was no way for me to make up a story anymore… I knew that she had done something to you."

Terry cleared his throat. Erin opened her eyes briefly to see the tears shining in his eyes and starting to run down his cheek.

"She took us both off guard. We didn't know. We just… didn't have any idea. I don't know what happened… it's all a jumble in my mind. Not like a memory where you can walk through it sequentially and remember each of the steps. Instead… it's everything at once, like an avalanche. I can't tell you what order anything happened in, and if I told it to you ten times, it would be a different story each time, because different things come to the surface. But the fear…"

Erin nodded.

"I've never felt like that before. I've been in plenty of dangerous situations before in my life. Most of them, I didn't know I was in danger until it was over. Or I knew, but I didn't feel it at the time because of the adrenaline rush, or because I knew that I had a job to do and I just had to do it, and I didn't let myself feel it until it was all over. But she had me around the throat. I couldn't breathe. She cut off the carotid and my brain couldn't get enough oxygen. That's what happens. But what it feels like is… dying. I knew I was dying. All she had to do was to keep holding me in that position and I would be dead. I was terrified about leaving this life with things undone. Leaving you behind. Never having the chance to…"

He couldn't talk for a few moments, sobbing and trying to catch his breath. Erin stroked his short hair, wishing she could take it all away from him.

"Never have a chance to grow old together. To have a family. A home that belonged to both of us. It was just all wiped out in that one moment. She could erase it all forever."

"But she didn't," Erin whispered.

"I don't know what made her stop. I can't remember. Jack said that she let go and I hit my head on the table. You know that. You know as much as I do. I can't remember that part."

"And then she attacked Jack."

"I think… she must have attacked him first."

"But he saw her attack you."

"I saw… I saw her stab him. Not just once. That knife." He shuddered.

Erin remembered it. She hadn't seen the blade. Only the hilt, sticking out of Jack's back. While he talked to her like there was nothing wrong. Her stomach lurched, and she was worried about what would happen if she were sick and couldn't get out of the bed fast enough with Terry blocking her exit to the door. She managed to calm it again and stayed where she was.

"You saw? And then what happened?"

"There is no 'and then.' I told you, it's all at once. It's not in sequence. I was… I was trying to help him, to treat him and to find a way to get help… and she was there. I didn't see her coming. I don't know where I thought she was. Did I think she had run?" He shook his head, impatient with himself. "I don't know. I can't remember. Why would I turn my back on a crazy killer like that? I wouldn't do that!"

But he clearly had, somehow, assumed that Theresa was no longer there and that he could do something for Jack Ward. So he had done what any cop would do and stopped to help his fellow officer rather than pursuing the culprit. But she had not run away. She had circled around and caught him from behind.

Erin ran her fingers through Terry's hair, now damp with sweat, starting to stand up in little points when she touched it. She just kept stroking him, letting him know she was there.

"I'm so sorry," Terry said hoarsely.

"Sorry? Sorry for what? You didn't do anything wrong!"

"But… I did. I let down my guard. I did the wrong thing. And because of that, you almost lost me. We almost lost each other."

"No. No, it wasn't your fault. You can't always do the right thing. There isn't always a right choice. What else were you supposed to do? You had to take care of Jack. He could have died."

"We could have both died. I should have made sure that she was gone. Or gone after her. Or dragged Jack out of there. Something."

"You didn't do the wrong thing. You had to help Jack."

"I know."

Erin ran her hand down his rough cheek, his five o'clock shadow sharp against her fingers.

CHAPTER 30

*Y*our turn," Terry said.

"Hmm?"

Erin opened her eyes and looked at him. She had been starting to drift. She felt exhausted, as if she had been there beside him, fighting for his life and Jack Ward's. She felt physically and emotionally drained, and her body was ready to shut down and go to sleep.

"You need to talk too. Not just brush me off and tell me that you're okay. I need you to talk to me."

Erin swallowed. She rubbed her eyes with one fist. "Not tonight. I'm too tired."

"Don't keep putting this off. You said it. You said that you needed to really talk."

"You can't force me," Erin protested.

"I'm not forcing you. I'm not telling you that you have to go into therapy. I'm not giving you an ultimatum. I'm telling you it's time to talk. You said so."

Erin rested with both palms over her eyes, her body stretched out along his. She was still on the wrong side of the bed and desperately wanted to switch places with him to reassure herself that she wasn't trapped. She knew in her mind that she was safe with Terry and he wasn't going to do anything that would make her run. And he wouldn't force her to stay if she needed to get up. But she still felt anxious and trapped.

She cleared her throat and tried to figure out what to say to him. He already knew her problems. He knew what she dreamed and why she dreamed it. There was nothing left to tell; it would just be a repetition of what he had heard before.

"I don't know. When Mr. Inglethorpe died, it was different. Different than any of the others."

He was silent, waiting and listening, not asking questions and demanding that she explain herself better.

"The other deaths bothered me. I hated to think about them and I did dream about them sometimes, but it was different. When I saw Mr. Inglethorpe, I couldn't even take it in. I couldn't understand what I was seeing. My brain wouldn't accept it."

She stopped talking. She didn't think she could go on. She didn't think there was anything else she could say. He knew it all.

"When I came in, you were frozen," Terry said. "You were standing there, with the rolling pin in your hand, just frozen in the middle of the scene."

Erin nodded. She couldn't remember it all. It wasn't like he had described his experience, with everything happening at one time. It was like she was stuck in time, in another reality. It was too much for her brain to take it in, so she had removed herself from the situation. She had seen it all, but at the same time, she had refused to see anything.

"I dream about it every night," she admitted. "Not just the nights you wake me up. Sometimes... all night long, over and over again."

He cupped his hand around her cheek. Her eyes were closed again and she didn't open them to look into his. She let the warmth of his hand soak into her skin. He didn't tell her that if she was that broken, she needed to go to the hospital or had to see someone.

"I'm afraid if I talk about it, that it will get worse."

"It's not getting better by *not* talking about it," he pointed out.

Erin nodded. She wasn't saying that she wasn't going to talk about it anymore, but why it was so hard for her—one of the reasons.

"I think about it during the day too. I have flashbacks. I'm jumpy."

"I know," he murmured. His tone told Erin that he hadn't just noticed these things in her, but that he was struggling with them too.

And why wouldn't he? What he had gone through had been horribly traumatic.

When she thought about him lying in that garage, bound, waiting for someone to find him, she remembered her own experiences. It wasn't only dealing with the crime scenes that she had seen. She had nearly died in that cave. And that hadn't been the only time her life had been in peril. She'd had some very close calls. And so had her friends.

"I'm scared of caves."

Terry's chuckle came out as a snort. He gave her a squeeze, brief but heartfelt. "Of course you are!"

"I never, ever want to ever go underground again."

"And I'll never force you to," he promised. "That isn't going to happen."

"Sometimes I dream of that, or of other things that have happened. Vic and the others getting caught in the mine collapse." She swallowed. Her mouth was as dry as a desert. "But mostly, it's Mr. Inglethorpe."

He rubbed her back in slow circles.

"That's all I can do right now." Erin sniffled. "Even though I don't want to dream… I just want to go to sleep now. I can't talk about it anymore."

"Okay. You go to sleep."

"Will you stay with me?"

"Yes. But I don't want to keep you awake with my tossing and turning."

"I just need you here."

"If I have to get up for a while, I'll come back."

Erin snuggled against him, but the anxiety was a yawning pit in her stomach.

"Terry…?"

"Mmm-hm?"

"I have to sleep on the other side."

He laughed. "You are a creature of habit."

"It's not just habit. I need… to be close to the door."

He didn't argue or demand an explanation. Wrapping his arms around her, he rolled over, flipping her from the side of the bed closest the wall back to her side, on the very edge, where she could get out the door in a heartbeat. Erin giggled at his maneuver. She was so tired, but it felt good to have something. Terry backed up to give her a little more space, and she cuddled against him once more, telling her brain it was time to be quiet and to let her get to sleep.

CHAPTER 31

The after-school crowd was starting to dwindle when Erin saw the Fosters approaching. She smiled, happy to see one of her favorite customers, young Peter Foster. He led the pack, his younger sisters and mother following close behind. Mrs. Foster was getting slower, her tummy larger. The girls went straight to the display case to look at the goodies and discuss what kind of cookie they wanted to get with their kid's club cards. Peter stood behind them supervising, looking very grown-up.

"We got lots of treats for Thanksgiving," he advised her.

"I remember. How did it go? Did you like them?"

He nodded. "Most of them. I remember when I could only have one kind of cookie, from the store, when we had treats. That was before you came here."

"That's right. It's a lot nicer to have some choices, isn't it?"

He nodded vigorously. "It's so much better!"

Vic returned from the kitchen and waved cheerfully at the Fosters. "Afternoon, y'all!"

"So what didn't you like?" Erin asked curiously, having noted Peter's 'most of them.'

"Oh…" Peter glanced over at his mother, probably having been told it would be rude to say he didn't like something. "Mom said lots of kids don't like pumpkin pie. Or gingerbread. Because they use strong spices."

"She's right. A lot of times we don't learn to like them until we've had them a few times. And as our taste buds get older things don't taste as bitter as they do to kids."

"Then maybe when I'm older, I'll like them."

"Maybe. I didn't like them when I was little, but I do now."

Peter nodded again. "Yeah." He looked at the little girls and edged around the display case to get closer to Erin. She leaned closer to see what he wanted. "I heard about what happened," he said in a whisper. For a moment, Erin didn't know what he meant. "About that guy," Peter clarified. "They were talking at school about how he died back there!" He motioned toward the parking lot.

Mrs. Foster swatted him. "Peter!"

He jumped and looked at her guiltily.

"I told you not to bring that up!"

"I was quiet," he protested. "They didn't hear." He indicated his sisters.

They were now looking at Peter and their mother, wide-eyed, trying to figure out what was going on.

"Did you decide what kind of cookie you wanted?" Vic asked, trying to distract them.

They were reluctant to be pulled away from the family drama, but Vic coaxed them until they were engaged once more in getting their cookies.

Mrs. Foster rolled her eyes at Erin and shook her head. "I'm sorry. It's so hard to teach boys social graces! He won't just obey me when I tell him something. He has to know why, and if I tell him why, then he thinks he can argue and get around it." She fixed her gaze on Peter. "If you aren't going to be polite, then I will not come here when school is out. I'll go while you're in class, and you won't get to see Miss Erin or get a cookie."

"Why isn't it polite to talk about it? Erin knows what happened." He widened his eyes at his mother. "She *saw* him."

"You don't talk about it because it's upsetting. You don't make people talk about upsetting things."

"She's not upset."

"She doesn't look upset," Mrs. Foster countered. She looked at Erin. "What did I tell you? Going to grow up to be a lawyer, that boy!"

"He's very bright. I'm sorry, Peter, but it is upsetting for me to talk about, and you wouldn't want me to cry on your cookies, would you? And you wouldn't want the girls to get nightmares."

"I wouldn't get nightmares."

"Maybe not. But I do."

"Oh." This seemed to bring his more sensitive side back out. "I'm sorry. I didn't know it would bother you."

Erin nodded. "Now, pick out a cookie, or the girls are going to get all of them."

While he joined the scrum, Mrs. Foster stepped forward, nodding at Erin. "Sorry about that. Mom can tell him a hundred times, but until he hears it from someone else, he just doesn't believe it."

"Yeah." Erin recalled how she had been much quicker to believe trusted school teachers than any of her foster parents, and could relate. "So, what else do you need?"

When the Fosters were gone, there was a lull. Erin wiped the fingerprints and nose-prints from the display case and tidied up. There would be one more influx of customers who needed things for supper or for breakfast the next day, and then it would be time to close up.

The doorbells tinkled. Erin was surprised to see Joshua. He slouched into the bakery, looking at his feet. He raised his eyes to look at Erin.

"I just wanted to say… that I'm sorry for everything yesterday. I didn't mean to put anyone else in danger."

Erin shrugged. "I know you didn't mean to. You were just trying to help find Brianna."

"Campbell and I both got in trouble with Beaver." He gave a low whistle. "Let me tell you; you do *not* want to get on her bad side."

Vic laughed. "I can imagine. Well, I don't have to work that hard to imagine it, since she was waiting for us after we dropped you off last night."

"Yeah, but it wasn't your fault. It was mine."

"And Campbell's. He wasn't supposed to be telling anyone about it."

"But I knew that. I should have gone to Beaver instead of looking for Brianna myself. I just thought… we'd have better luck."

Vic nodded. "Less threatening. I know. There was a chance it would work."

He was looking down at his feet again. "Not as good as I thought it would. I guess this Mickey… he's a real gangster. Not someone to mess around with. If he wasn't working for Beaver…"

Vic looked over at Erin, aware that she was the only one in the group who had seen him for what he was. Who had known before they even walked into his hotel room.

"It's over," Erin said. "Over and done. You can't change anything by going over it."

Of course, the same was true of the things that her brain insisted on hanging on to. Could she go back and stop Mr. Inglethorpe's murder? Would anything change what had happened in the past? By that logic, she should be able to leave it behind, but it still had a pull on her. It still affected everything she did.

"Well, thanks," Joshua acknowledged. "I just wanted to let you know how sorry I was."

After a couple more apologies, he was on his way. Erin watched him go. She noticed an unfamiliar car parked across the street and watched it for a minute, trying to figure out who it belonged to, but nobody got in or out. Someone who was visiting town or who had just purchased a new car. She turned her attention back to her work.

CHAPTER 32

*V*ic and Erin were both glad to be heading home at the end of the day.

"I didn't get much sleep last night," Vic admitted. "I was so wired that even with my Ambien, I couldn't shut my brain down and get some sleep."

"Did you tell Willie what happened?"

Vic looked at her sideways. "Well, no. Not really. Said that we went into the city... did some shopping... ran into Jeremy... Did you tell Terry?"

"No. But we talked about some other stuff."

Vic raised her brows, waiting for more information.

"Stuff that we've been avoiding talking about," Erin explained. "About... when Terry got hurt, and emotional stuff..."

"Good. You needed to. I'm glad. Did it help?"

"I think it helped us... but it didn't help my sleep. I was exhausted, but I kept waking back up again, and I think I kept him awake too." Erin glanced at the clock on the dashboard. "I haven't heard from him all day. Hopefully, he got more sleep after I left. It makes me nervous when he doesn't call at all during the day. I worry that he's sitting at home depressed all day. He doesn't want to bother me at work or bring me down, but I'd rather know if he's having trouble."

"Did you tell him that, during your talk last night?"

Erin sighed. "No. I guess we've still got a lot of ground to cover."

"We all do. You know, I look at the relationships of some of the couples that I know that have been together twenty or thirty years, and they're still working out the bumps. I don't know if you can ever truly know someone else one hundred percent."

"Huh. I guess. But I wish I knew a little bit more… or that it wasn't so hard to tell him things or figure things out. It looks so much easier when it's someone else's relationship. You don't see all of the little things that don't quite match up, or how many different ways you grew up, or think about one thing or another. You think, when you're looking at it from the outside, that everything just goes smoothly."

"I lived with a bunch of different families growing up," Erin contributed, "It wasn't easy for any of them."

"Great." Vic rolled her eyes dramatically. "That means I'm going to have to keep working at this for the rest of my life. It doesn't just start getting easier after a year, or whatever the cutoff is."

Erin looked in her rearview mirror, frowning at the car behind her.

"What?" Vic asked.

"Nothing. I was looking at that car earlier this afternoon, trying to figure out who it belonged to, and now I see it again. Someone bought a new car."

"Could be." Vic looked at it in her wing mirror, then turned around in her seat to get a better look. The car turned at the intersection before she'd gotten a good look. "Gone now. I guess we'll find out sooner or later."

"Well…" Erin pulled up to the house. "Here we are. Time to practice getting along with our… guys again."

"What's wrong with boyfriends?"

"I don't know. It feels… juvenile. We're partners, not kids going out to the movies."

"We should go out to a movie," Vic said brightly, getting distracted from the point.

"Okay. You pick one, and we'll work it out. We'll make it a double date with our *boyfriends.*"

"Well, when you say it in that tone of voice it sounds silly," Vic agreed. "But I mean it. It sounds fun. We'll go to a movie in the city when neither of us works early the next morning. Right?"

Erin nodded. "It's a date. Have a good night!"

Vic agreed and headed around back to her apartment. Erin turned her key in the lock and looked around once the door was open. "Terry? Are you home?"

Once again, the house was quiet. The animals greeted her, Orange Blossom meowing loudly about something important in his life. He must have been happy that K9 had been out during the day and he had his domain back. Erin petted the cat and the rabbit and followed Orange Blossom into the kitchen to give him one of the homemade kitty treats she was testing. He happily gobbled it up. Marshmallow ate his treat of apple and carrot more sedately.

Erin decided that since Terry was out, she would do her tai chi immediately, rather than waiting until later. Then they could spend what time they had once Terry got home with each other. She removed her shoes and socks at the door and went out into the grass in her bare feet to the spot that had quickly become her practice area.

She had barely started her tai chi when alarm bells started going off. Erin tried to calm her brain, reminding herself that she was in a safe place, she was working on her body-mind connection, and that occasionally that would mean something uncomfortable came to the surface.

But telling herself that she was safe and trying to focus on the forms didn't work. She heard her own voice again, telling Terry how jumpy she was all the time. That was perfectly normal. She had been through some traumatic experiences. It was normal for her to be affected by them.

She couldn't keep her eyes closed, so she opened them and tried to focus on the forms she was practicing.

An engine stopped nearby. An engine that didn't sound familiar to Erin. Everything she was hearing seemed out of place. Like she was standing in someone else's yard instead of her own. Or in a different time, her world out of sync. She shook her head, trying to shake off the feelings of alarm, and focused on her practice. She needed to start again, unable to remember what she had already done and where she had stopped.

A door slam, again in an unfamiliar pitch. Parked close to her house, but she wasn't expecting any visitors. But when had that stopped people from coming over? Erin turned around, looking at the gate to the yard. If she had company, she wasn't going to get her tai chi done.

There was silence. She couldn't hear a knock on her door or the doorbell ringing. Maybe it was someone visiting a neighbor rather than Erin. But she stood there frozen, still unmoving. Something was wrong.

The gate opened, and standing there was the Russian named Mickey.

CHAPTER 33

*E*rin's heart pounded so hard in her chest that it hurt.

Mickey?

What was he doing there? How did he know where she lived and why had he come? To check her out and see if the story they had told him was true?

To return the two guns to her and tell her that she could give them back to Jeremy and Vic if she thought they had learned their lessons, but not to come around his territory again?

He had to be there looking for Beaver. He knew that they knew Beaver, so he stopped by to ask her where Beaver lived. She wasn't listed, after all, she just roomed with Jeremy when she was in town.

"Mickey?" Erin couldn't think of what to say to him.

"Miss Erin Price, specialty baker," the Russian said.

"Yes, that's me. I told you I had a bakery."

"I saw you there today. You do good business."

Erin nodded. "It's been a good location. We get pretty good business from Bald Eagle Falls. Sometimes even from other towns nearby."

All the time she was talking, she was wondering what to do. What an inane topic it was. He didn't care what she did. Whether her business did well or not. He was trying to keep her occupied while he walked closer, watching her carefully. He knew that she hadn't been carrying a gun when she had shown up at his hotel. He had spotted Jeremy's and Vic's weapons without a problem, so he knew that she wasn't armed, that she couldn't do anything to stop him from whatever he had in mind.

Mickey's eyes went to the stairs up the side of the garage to the loft apartment over it. Had he asked around? Did he know that Vic lived there? Maybe he'd even been watching them.

The unfamiliar black car. That was who it had been. Mickey staking out the bakery, watching them and then following them home. And of course, Terry wasn't home. Mickey had probably already checked out the house and knew there was no one else there. Maybe he knew that a policeman was living with Erin, and maybe not. But for the moment, it didn't make any difference. Terry might as well have been on the other side of the world.

She swallowed. "What are you doing here? Are you looking for Beaver?"

"No. Not looking for Beaver." His eyes flicked around the yard, looking for any dangers. "Why don't we go into the house, where it is more private?"

"I'm… not ready to go in yet. I was doing my tai chi."

He blinked at her, clearly not expecting that response. He reached under his jacket and pulled out a gun. He pointed it at her, making sure she understood that she was being threatened.

"You come in the house now," he suggested again.

"No, I don't think so." She stood her ground. Inside the house, no one would be able to see or hear what was happening. At least outside, there was some chance of someone noticing that something was wrong. Vic and maybe Willie in the loft apartment. Neighbors who might hear something. Walkers through the wood behind her house. Bald Eagle Falls was a small town and people weren't afraid to walk the streets. They were friendly and dropped in on each other. Maybe today would be the day that someone dropped in and saved her from a gangster with a gun.

If it were a movie on TV, then Erin would be able to put her recent tai chi training into action, kicking the gun out of his hand and gracefully punching him in the face, all with perfect tai chi form.

Only she hadn't learned any gunman-disarming moves, and she was still just as uncoordinated as she had been when she started.

Mickey stood looking at her, stymied. He didn't want to stay outside, but if he were going to force her inside, he was going to have to use physical force. Which might be witnessed by neighbors. Or he could shoot her right there and beat a hasty retreat. Either option had a reasonably high likelihood of being seen.

"Instead, why do you not tell me," Mickey said in a precise voice that didn't entirely wipe out his Russian accent, "where is Brianna?"

"I don't know where Brianna is! Why would we drive all the way into the city and spend the afternoon knocking on doors and facing... unhelpful people... if I knew where she was? If I knew where she was, I wouldn't be looking for her."

"Maybe you are not looking for her. Maybe you are only pretending to look for her."

Erin shook her head in exasperation. "Why?"

He kept the gun pointed at her. "Someone knows. Maybe you. Maybe Beaver. But someone knows the truth. She did not just disappear into the thin air."

"She ran away. I don't know where. I don't know who helped her. She probably hitchhiked or caught a bus. And she's hundreds of miles away from here where she is safe."

"Someone would know. Someone would still see. Would catch her on camera."

"Then where do *you* think she is?"

Mickey took a couple of steps closer to her. "I think Beaver has her. I think she has Brianna stashed somewhere."

CHAPTER 34

*N*ot a bad guess."

Erin knew the voice without even looking. How could she not know her boyfriend's voice? Terry stepped out of the house, K9 at his side, his gun trained on Mickey. The weapon could have been on a tripod, it was so straight and steady. Erin breathed through her mouth, feeling like she wasn't getting enough oxygen. Terry kept sighting Mickey down the barrel of his gun, taking a few steps out of the house and down off of the porch.

"How about you put the gun down, Mikhail?"

"Who are you?"

"I'm a friend of Erin's. And I don't like you pointing a gun at her. So why don't you drop it? Right there. And put your hands behind your head."

Mickey grinned and shook his head. "Oh, you talk big, cop, but if you shot me, Erin would get hurt. Maybe killed. You don't want to risk that."

K9 was bristling at Terry's side, eager to do his part in bringing down the villain. Erin breathed shallowly, hoping that neither of them would be hurt. Mickey's gun wasn't pointed at them, but that could change in half a second.

There was another whisper of sound at the gate, and Mickey whirled around, gun hand automatically moving to point at the figure at the gate. Erin was no longer at the wrong end of the barrel, but Officer Stayner was.

He stood there, grim-faced, and didn't back down. He also already had his sidearm out, so it was two against one. Mickey could see things starting to fall apart, and his head moved on a swivel, looking for an opportunity to escape. His gun stayed pointed steadily at Stayner, but he was nervous, no longer in the position of power he had hoped to be in.

"Drop it, Mickey," Stayner said. "You heard him."

"You don't know me. You don't call me Mickey."

"We haven't been formally introduced," Stayner said slowly, "but I've heard all about you. I feel like I already know you."

"You don't know anything about me. None of what you are hearing is even true."

"You killed Wolf, and now you're here to take out any witnesses. Brianna. Erin. Anyone you think might know too much. Maybe you've even got your eye on taking out Rohilda Beaven. But you're not going to do it."

Erin was a little surprised that he knew who Beaver was, and knew her legal name. Stayner hadn't been around town for that long and didn't work directly with Beaver.

"Are you trying to impress me? Make me think that you know Beaver? You don't know her. Maybe you met her once or twice, but it takes a lot more than that to know a person like Beaver, someone who has so many false faces, someone who always lies about who she really is."

Stayner was not distracted by Mickey's chatter and threatening manner. Mickey took a step toward Erin and the back of the property. Erin didn't know whether he intended to grab her and use her as a hostage or make a break for it through the woods. Maybe he thought he could do both, grab her and then hold her hostage while he worked his way through the woods to safety.

But he didn't know his way through the woods. He didn't realize how dense they were. Or who he might find there.

Terry and Stayner were still pointing their guns directly at Mickey, and he was moving more quickly, gliding across the grass toward Erin like he was on wheels. Erin took a couple of steps back. The last thing she wanted was for him to grab her and use her as a shield. She wanted to leave Terry's and Stayner's lines of sight unobstructed. Mickey still pointed his gun at Stayner, but he was getting farther away, and before long he would be choosing a new target.

"You don't want to come this way."

The woman's voice was quiet and firm. Erin thought for a moment that it was Beaver because they had been talking about her. But the voice was not Beaver's. It was Adele. Erin could barely see the shape hidden behind a tree, barely a shadow, but the shadow definitely had a long gun, and Mickey might not want to run directly into that.

"What is all this?" Mickey demanded. "Some kind of set-up? What is going on here?"

"You weren't set up," Terry told him, chuckling. "No one made you come out here. That was your own idea, your own choice. But we're not going to let you threaten citizens of Bald Eagle Falls."

Mickey's eyes were still on the woods, his best avenue of escape. He shuffled another step or two closer to it, trying to make out the shape behind the tree and to see if he had any chance of getting past her.

"Just try it," Adele said. "Let's see if I still have the skills."

Mickey's jaw clenched. He looked over at Erin, but to bring his gun around to point at her now, he would have to swivel around and bring it across his body. The three opposing gunmen would know in an instant what he was trying, and they would put a stop to it. With two handguns and a rifle pointed at him, he knew he wouldn't stand a chance.

Flushing with fury, Mickey bent slightly and reached as far away from himself as he could before dropping the gun.

"Hands behind your head," Terry prompted.

Mickey slowly obeyed. None of the three guns dropped; they all remained trained directly at him. Erin wondered whether she should pick up Mickey's gun so that he could not dive for it in one last escape attempt. But she figured if she wasn't prepared to use it, she shouldn't pick it up.

"Take two steps backward, toward me," Terry instructed.

Mickey obeyed, distancing himself from the gun.

"Now, down on your knees."

"No one does this to Mikhail," Mickey growled. "No one!"

"Then you shouldn't come hunting my family."

Mickey lowered himself to his knees. He was not a young man, and his knees appeared to give out as he got lower, ending up with him landing much harder than any of them expected. But he didn't manage to get close enough to his dropped gun to pick it up again and put it to use. Terry next had him lie down, then approached carefully. He stood there over Mickey and nodded to Stayner, who also approached. Then while Stayner kept his gun trained on Mickey, Terry pulled his hands behind his back to cuff them and patted him down for any other weapons. He pulled Mickey's jacket partway down his arms to hamper his movements further, and took his time checking all of Mickey's pockets and anywhere else he might have secreted a weapon.

Erin found herself breathing more easily once Mickey was in handcuffs. She could finish her tai chi now that he was in custody.

But she knew she wasn't going to. She found her legs were weak as jelly and, before she could get to the porch where her lawn chairs were, her knees gave out, and she ended up sitting on the ground. Terry twisted his head around to look at her. "Erin? Are you okay?"

"Yeah. Just... resting."

"Okay. You're not hurt? He didn't touch you, did he?"

"No."

"Good thing," Terry said, giving Mickey a shove. "It's a very good thing that we caught you before you could do anything you might regret later."

"You are lucky you got here when you did," Mickey retorted, pushing back against Terry. "Things might have turned out very differently."

"Put out the word to stay away from Bald Eagle Falls."

"How about I put out the word about your snitch? We see how long Cam Cox lasts when *that* gets around."

"That wouldn't be very good for your health. How are you going to fare in prison if people know you've been working for the feds?"

Mickey sneered. "You do not have anything on me. I get a walk. That's the deal. I don't go to prison while I'm working with Agent Beaven."

"Attempted murder is not one of the charges they will let slide. You overreached."

"Attempted murder? I just talked to Erin Price. I never try to kill her."

"We caught you here with a gun on her. You don't think a jury will interpret that for exactly what it was?"

"I was holding a gun." Mickey shrugged. "Minor weapons charge. I walk. I never said I was going to kill her. I never pulled the trigger. I did not even resist arrest." He smiled smugly. "You don't know how it works. You'll see."

"Erin is a personal friend of Beaver's. She's not going to let it slide."

"She has bosses. They will decide."

Terry pushed Mickey toward Stayner. "I'll let you take this scum in. It's your arrest."

Stayner brightened, clearly pleased that it would be his arrest rather than Terry's. As green as he was, he could probably benefit from the mobster's arrest being attributed to him. He took Mickey's arm.

"Check him one more time before you put him in the car, and don't let him talk you into anything," Terry advised. "Treat it like any other arrest."

Stayner nodded and escorted the Russian out of the yard, poor Mickey still complaining about how he was being mistreated and would be released once the authorities found out what was going on.

Terry offered his hand to Erin. "Can you get up?"

She grasped his strong hand and let him pull her to her feet. She stayed on her feet, breathing slowly. Her muscles were still quivering, but she wasn't quite as weak as she had been. Terry put his arm around her and held her close. Adele crossed the fence line and approached them.

"How did you know?" Erin asked, trying to grasp it. "How did you all know that he was here?"

"Stayner saw the car when he was on patrol, thought it looked suspicious. He ran the plates, which rang all kinds of alarm bells, and both Beaver and I got calls. The sheriff is out of town and Tom is down with the flu, so I agreed to help. Stayner was keeping an eye on the car, so he knew when Mickey followed you here."

"I saw the car, but I thought I was just being paranoid… it turned down another street, and I thought everything was okay…"

"He probably realized his car would stand out as not belonging in the neighborhood, so he fell back to give you a false sense of security."

Erin shuddered. "And you called Adele?"

Terry shook his head. "No, Adele showing up was a pleasant surprise."

Adele reached them. "I was going to stop by and say hello to you. Then… it seemed like you could use a little help."

Erin shook her head. "You deserve some kind of bonus. That's going above and beyond what a groundskeeper should have to do."

"Not at all," Adele said with a shrug. "I'm supposed to be watching and keeping intruders and unsavory characters away from your land."

"Well, thank you. You were there at just the right time. Three guns to one were just too many for Mickey."

"And Mickey is…?" Adele asked.

Erin looked at Terry, realizing that she hadn't told him the story, yet he wasn't asking her who Mickey was or why had had come after her. She cleared her throat.

"He's… uh… someone that might be involved in Campbell Cox's case. We ran into him in the city… and I guess he decided we might know something about someone he's looking for."

"You and Terry?" Adele asked. "Why would he come after a cop? And why would the two of you…"

Terry was shaking his head, and Adele stopped. She raised one eyebrow.

"You know Erin," Terry said simply.

Adele looked back at her. "But who is 'we'?"

"Uh…" Erin looked at Terry, wondering if he already knew the details. "Joshua Cox, and Jeremy, and Vic."

"And you were lucky enough that he picked you to go after first."

"I guess so. He knew I was a baker, so he followed me from Auntie Clem's." A thought occurred to her. "Joshua came by while the car was there… he didn't go after Joshua or Campbell, did he? Before he came here?"

"Stayner was following him," Terry reassured her. "He came here first. He probably already knew where to find the Coxes. Their address is listed. Or has been, in the past. It would only take a two-minute internet search to track them down."

"Maybe someone should go by there to make sure everything is okay."

"Mikhail came here."

"But he could have sent someone else to the Coxes. He could have sent someone to each house."

Terry considered this for a moment, then nodded. "Okay. Give me a minute and I'll make a couple of calls. That's easier than running all over the place." He let Erin go, his movements slow. "Will you be okay? I'm just going to go into the house."

"I'm fine," Erin told him, managing to keep her feet. "I'll be in in a few minutes."

She knew that Adele preferred to talk in private.

As she was about to thank Adele again for her serendipitous appearance, Vic's apartment door opened. Vic stepped out and looked down the stairs at them. "Hey, what's up? I heard voices."

"You missed the excitement," Erin told her, laughing.

"Excitement? What happened?"

CHAPTER 35

*E*rin had told Vic the story, Adele had visited briefly and then gone on her way as darkness fell. Vic and Erin moved into the house and talked until Terry was finished his phone calls. He approached Erin from behind while she chatted with Vic and wrapped his arms around her in a hug. Erin leaned back into him.

"Beaver would like to see you," Terry said, leaning down close to her ear.

Erin looked over her shoulder at him. "Why would Beaver want to talk to me? We got Mickey; she can talk to him at the police department. Does she not believe that he was threatening me? She can't let him off."

"She's not going to let him off. She understands what happened, and the only one she is upset with is Mickey. But she would like your assistance."

"My assistance."

"Yes, ma'am."

Erin frowned, thinking about that. "I can't think of anything she would need my help for."

"Can't you? Well, why don't I take you over there, and we'll find out."

"Um... okay." Erin looked at the clock. "Does it have to be tonight? I should be getting ready for bed."

"Any way you could get someone to cover for you tomorrow?"

"I suppose. Vic, could you see who is available?"

Vic nodded. "Yeah. No problem. You didn't have anything special planned, did you?"

"No. Nothing out of the ordinary. All of the plans and recipes are in the binder for the week."

"We'll take care of it, then. Don't worry about anything. You and Terry can sleep in." She winked.

"Okay, I guess I'm free," Erin told Terry.

"Good. Get your handbag, and let's go."

Erin could have just grabbed it and put on her shoes, but she was still feeling off-balance from the events of the evening and was unsure why she had to talk to Beaver right away. She dragged her feet, feeling like Terry was rushing her.

He had been too remote lately, not telling her what he was up to, where he was going or when he would be back. She felt like he was holding back from the relationship. When they had talked the night before, she thought it had heralded a change, that they would both be able to be more open and vulnerable to each other, but Terry was still not keeping her apprised. At one time, it would have been unthinkable for him to disappear for a few hours without telling her what his plans were.

Of course, she hadn't told him about going to see Mickey, either, and Beaver had filled him in on at least part of the story. So he knew that she had still held something back. Why should he tell her everything?

"Erin? Are you ready?"

Erin focused on Terry, standing by the door with K9, waiting for her to get herself together.

"Yeah. I know. I just feel like… are you sure we couldn't do this tomorrow? I don't feel like going out. I just… want to cuddle and go to bed. Beaver can wait."

"Let's get it over with. You'll feel better once we're done."

Erin sighed and followed him out to his truck.

They didn't drive in the direction of Jeremy's apartment, which was where Erin had assumed they would be going. And it wasn't in the direction of the police department. Erin looked at Terry, confused.

"Where are we going?"

"Safehouse."

"A safe house? A safe house for who? Campbell?"

"Be there in a couple of minutes."

Erin didn't think that Bald Eagle Falls would be a very good place to have a safe house. Everybody knew everybody else's business. How could they hide someone there?

She watched out the window, intrigued. A couple of minutes later, they were out of the town limits, not yet at the safe house. A few more minutes down the highway, Terry turned off onto a gravel road, then took several other twisting turns in the dense trees, until she wasn't sure she'd be able to find her way out again if left to her own devices. She would have to leave a trail of breadcrumbs to find her way home.

It was dark when they reached the cabin in the trees. There was a light on inside, but no lights outside that would act as a beacon to anyone trying to negotiate the rabbit trails that twisted through the woods. Terry parked the car and opened his door. K9 jumped out after him. He leaned down and looked into the vehicle at Erin.

"We're here."

"This is a safe house?"

"Yep."

Holding her purse on her lap, Erin looked at it. She didn't want to get out of the car and walk through the dark into the isolated, unfriendly-looking shack.

"It doesn't *look* safe."

"I promise you, it is. Do you think anyone could find it without being given directions?"

"I don't know. Maybe a helicopter with one of those heat-sensing cameras."

"Exactly. And then all they would see is a couple of people in a cabin. Nothing to give away that it's any different than any of the other remote cabins around here. And it isn't the only one. There are plenty of people who don't want to live right in town." Terry stood with his thumbs in his pockets, staring up at the starry night sky. "Some people like to be out in the wild, at one with nature."

Erin had been trying to achieve some kind of Zen state with the world around her with her tai chi, but living in a place that was so isolated would be way too much for her.

"Come on. Beaver's inside. With her and me there, you couldn't be much safer."

"I want to see her first."

Erin didn't know why she was being so stubborn about it. It wasn't like she thought Terry was lying or was going to lead her into a dangerous situation. She was perfectly safe with him by her side. With Beaver there too, she was that much safer. But it wasn't her logical brain dictating her actions; it was the same primitive instinct that had been troubling her since finding Mr. Inglethorpe.

Terry said something under his breath that she couldn't make out and walked up to the cabin. He spoke at the door for a minute, and then the door opened wide and Beaver stepped out. She stood there on the doorstep where Erin could see her, and Erin finally relented. Beaver was there. With both of them insisting it was safe, she couldn't really argue.

She opened her door and walked reluctantly up to the cabin. Beaver nodded and went back inside. Terry stood on the doorstep and motioned Erin in ahead of him. He stood for a moment longer after she was inside, looking and listening for any sign of trouble.

Erin was sure that no one had followed them. It would be impossible for someone to know which turns they had taken without keeping them in sight, and there had been no one behind them.

Erin looked around the rustic cabin. It looked friendlier inside than it did out. There was a fire burning in the fireplace, old furniture covered with handmade blankets and quilts, and various boating and fishing equipment and memorabilia on the walls.

The girl sitting close to the fire looked up as Erin came in. Erin's jaw dropped.

"Brianna!"

CHAPTER 36

*B*rianna didn't say anything in response, dropping her eyes and then turning her head to the side, as if there were something far more interesting to see in the dark corner beside her.

"Come on in and sit down," Beaver encouraged.

Erin followed Beaver's motion and sat down on the couch adjacent to Brianna's. She shifted, looking for a comfortable position. The couch itself was comfy enough; it was Brianna who made her restless and self-conscious. Erin looked at Beaver.

"Did you know where she was all along?" She couldn't quite make herself believe it. Maybe Brianna had run, and Beaver had followed her trail. Or someone else had brought Brianna out there.

Beaver chewed her gum. "Yep."

"You knew? Since when? Since she left the Coxes' house?"

Beaver pursed her lips. "Pretty much, yeah. Since Saturday night, or early Sunday morning."

"How?"

Beaver raised an eyebrow, not answering.

Erin looked at Brianna, trying to connect with her. Why had Beaver wanted Erin? Why hadn't she made the trip into town, if she wanted to talk to Erin? That would have been less risky than letting someone else know about the safe house. The more people who knew about it, the more dangerous it became.

Terry walked over from the door and sat down next to Erin. He put one arm around her shoulders and held her hand in her lap with the other. Much more intimate than she would expect him to be in front of strangers. K9 lay down at his feet with a sigh. Terry turned his body slightly to look at Erin, studying her face as if she were the only one in the room.

"I've been taking guard duty to allow Beaver time to deal with other parts of the investigation."

"This is where you've been?"

"Yes. I'm sorry I didn't give you any explanation. I didn't want to lie to you, but I didn't want to have to bring you in on the secret either. It was better if you didn't know anything."

Erin nodded. "Yeah. Okay. That makes sense." She hesitated for a moment before asking, "How has it been? Have you felt…"

"Back to normal? Not exactly. I can only take a few hours at a time, with the headaches and fatigue. It's better here than in town, where there are so many distractions pulling me so many different directions. Being… jumpy and anxious all the time. It's a bit easier out here to relax and just watch and wait."

Erin nodded.

"I was talking to Brianna about our talk yesterday." Terry's cheeks were a little red, but it might have just been the firelight. "Just about… how you have felt since Mr. Inglethorpe's… death. Like you were telling me."

Erin looked over at Brianna, who still wouldn't meet her eyes.

"I thought that maybe Brianna would like to hear about that from you. Maybe share something about her own experience."

Erin wasn't sure what to say. She looked at Terry and then at Beaver, who was standing back out of the way, clearly trying to stay in the background so that Brianna wouldn't feel like they were all ganging up on her.

Erin looked down at her hands. "I don't know how much Terry told you. I've had… some kind of awful experiences since I moved to Bald Eagle Falls. I mean, I love the town, and the people are great, mostly, but the things that have happened while I've been here are… challenging."

Brianna made a noise that could have been a sob or a grunt of disgust.

"When Mr. Inglethorpe got killed…" Erin looked at Terry, and he nodded, encouraging her to continue. "It was… very violent and… I was the one who found him."

Erin swallowed. She glanced toward the girl. Brianna was looking toward Erin, out the corner of her eye, without turning her head toward her. Like a trapped animal trying to figure out if she were a danger.

"When I saw him, I just froze up. I couldn't believe what I was seeing. My mind kept making up other explanations for what I saw. I couldn't function. I couldn't do anything. When Terry came, that's how he found me, in the middle of the scene, holding my rolling pin… just… paralyzed."

Erin stopped for a moment to swallow and try to slow her breathing. It had been one thing to talk about it to Terry. She had told him that she didn't want to talk to therapists about it, and telling it to Brianna with Terry and Beaver listening in was not easy either. It wasn't something she could talk about dispassionately.

Brianna nodded and looked in Erin's direction. Her face was still pointing down, but she raised her eyes in swift glances to look at Erin.

Something that Erin had said was getting through to Brianna and she wanted Erin to go on. She didn't say anything, but her body language was clear. Erin took a long breath in and let it out.

"I remember Terry telling me that I fainted, but I don't know… I don't remember that part. And I don't think I actually fell down, but I can't remember a lot about what happened. He took me out of there… they had to collect evidence. Get the blood and any evidence from my hands and clothes. I had to tell them what I had seen and done, but I don't know if I was very coherent."

Erin looked at Terry, expecting him to comment, but he didn't. He just nodded at her, encouraging her to go on. The fire snapped and crackled in the fireplace but, other than that, the room was silent, waiting for her to continue.

"That's all, really."

But it wasn't. That wasn't all that she had told Terry and, even if she hadn't told him anything else, he still knew that wasn't where the story ended. She had been different since finding Mr. Inglethorpe. It had affected her more deeply than any of the other deaths. Or maybe they had all built up over time, and Mr. Inglethorpe's was just the one that had pushed her over the edge.

"Since then… I've been really jumpy about everything. If someone moves too fast, or there's a loud noise... anything can scare me. Being in a room where there is someone else between me and the door so I can't get out quickly. I've been... emotional... crabby without any reason..."

Terry squeezed Erin's hand. She swallowed and nodded her appreciation for his support. It was silly for the next part to be so hard. How were her dreams a sign of weakness? It wasn't like anyone could be expected to control their dreams. It was just the way her brain was trying to deal with all of the stress. If she could just calm her body and brain down before bed, like she'd been trying to do with the tai chi, then maybe she could get some control over her sleep again.

"I have trouble sleeping. I'm too restless and anxious to get to sleep. And then when I do... I have nightmares. It isn't just now and then, like I tell people. It's every night. Sometimes all night long. It's... terrifying. I dream about people I know dying. I see them in that murder scene over and over again. I dream different people I know are the killer, or victim, or even trying to kill me. I don't know how many times I've dreamt about someone trying to kill me since it happened."

Erin wiped at the corner of her eyes, trying to stay in control. She looked at Brianna and saw the tear tracks down her cheeks.

She was just a kid. Sixteen or seventeen. Maybe she was eighteen but, even if she was, that didn't make her a grown-up, able to deal with grown-up problems. *Erin* couldn't deal with all of her grown-up issues, so how could she expect a teenager to? She went to Brianna. She sat down beside her and put her arms around Brianna, holding her tightly.

"It's okay, honey. It is. It's okay, Brianna."

Brianna shook her head. "I'm so scared," she whispered.

"I know. I would be too. I *am* scared too. Even when I'm not in any danger, I still feel it. Like someone is watching me, just waiting until I'm vulnerable and distracted. Waiting until it's my turn... you know."

Brianna clutched Erin's hand. She was sobbing openly. Erin stroked her braided hair. "Tell me about it."

Brianna scrubbed at her eyes with both fists, and attempted to get herself calm and under control once more. But the dam had burst and there was no stopping the flood.

"I was there," she blubbered. "I was there. I saw it all."

"You were where?"

"I was... I called Wolf. I wanted him to get me out of there. I told him

I'd do whatever he wanted, I didn't care. I'd do whatever he wanted if he would just get me out of there. I was scared that they would be coming after me. The cops. Because they had taken Cam, and I know those weren't his drugs. He'd never leave them in the car like that. He didn't deal. He'd never have that much on him. I knew he was being set up and that... it wasn't going to stop. I didn't know for sure who was behind it, but... I had to protect myself. I had to go back."

"Go back where?" Erin held Brianna, rocking slightly, trying to give her some comfort. She was a stranger; what kind of comfort could she provide to the girl? But she did her best anyway.

"Back to the old life. It was too hard. Cam was so good to me. He was always so kind, and he'd talked me into getting out of the life, into trying to... do something else with my life. Get free. I knew it wouldn't work." She shook her head despondently. "I knew it wouldn't, but he kept saying... he could help. He could help me to get clean, to get my own place, an honest job, all of those things. But he wasn't that much older than I am. He didn't have any money or job himself. He couldn't get a place of his own, so how could he help me?"

Erin nodded, not sure what to say, just encouraging Brianna to keep talking, to get out all of the feelings that she had been holding in.

"I wanted to believe him, so I did. I told him that Wolf and the others weren't going to like it. I told him that. They wouldn't let me. They'd keep me there. They just... wouldn't let me leave. There are ways to keep girls from leaving. I didn't want them to hurt me, or Cam, or someone else I was friends with. And they would. Those Russians, they're nasty dudes. When they talked about stuff they saw in prison..." Brianna rolled her eyes upward and held both arms across her stomach. "It would make me sick, just hearing them talk about it."

"But Cam talked you into leaving."

"I wouldn't say yes. I said I would have Thanksgiving dinner with him. That's all. Just... go home with him for turkey day. I never told anyone I was leaving the life, that I wouldn't work for them anymore. But I guess... they knew."

"And you think that Wolf, or one of the others, set Campbell up. Planted drugs so that he would have to go to prison, and then if you didn't fall in line, they would get you too."

"They've got guys on the inside. There are plenty of Russians in the prison. I was so scared that they were going to kill Cam. I thought… he wouldn't ever get out. They'd kill him as soon as he was transferred."

"He's out on bail. He's on house arrest, but he's back home, and he's okay."

Brianna wiped at her eyes. "Beaver said that. But I didn't know if… that was true."

Of course not. How could she trust a cop to tell her the truth?

"So… then what happened?"

CHAPTER 37

rianna sobbed aloud, covering her face. "It was… I can't tell you. I can't tell you."

Erin pulled Brianna's face to her shoulder, sheltering her protectively like a mother with a child afraid of monsters.

"It's okay. It's okay. Wolf is dead and Mickey has been arrested. You're safe. This is a safe place."

"It can't be. Nowhere is safe if I tell."

"It's okay," Erin repeated soothingly, rubbing Brianna's back. "You called Wolf," she recapped. "You told him that if he would come to get you, you'd do whatever he wanted."

Brianna nodded. She sniffled. "I begged him. He said he would come. But I was his. I would be his forever. I didn't care. I didn't want to go to prison. I didn't want to get killed."

She gulped and cried into Erin's shoulder.

"I told him to meet me at the bakery. I didn't want him going to Cam's mom's house. I know he could have found out where they lived anyway, but I thought if I didn't meet him there, he would leave them alone."

"Yeah. That was good. You were looking out for them."

Brianna was quiet. Erin rubbed her back. "And then what?"

She was afraid herself. She didn't want to hear what happened. She had seen the results, and she was doing everything she could to keep it from taking root in her brain, where it would keep coming back in her dreams like Mr. Inglethorpe's death. She didn't want to visualize what had happened.

And she was afraid that Brianna was going to say that she had done it. And what would happen to her then? Would Beaver put her in prison? It would be Erin's fault if she did. She was the one who was encouraging Brianna to talk because that was what Terry and Beaver wanted her to do. Not because it was best for Brianna.

They would tell her it was good for Brianna to talk about it and get it off of her chest, but that wasn't why they had brought Erin there.

"I was late getting there. I got cold feet and didn't want to meet him. I didn't want... my life to be over. I didn't want to give up on what Cam had tried to get me to do. But I was hungry and tired of hiding. I knew it was the only way. I had to."

Erin stroked Brianna's hair, her heart breaking for the girl and the choice she was faced with. It wasn't fair that her choice was between Cam being murdered in prison and giving herself over to the man who would continue to pimp her and feed her addiction and probably end up killing her anyway. Cam had tried to help her to find another way, and they had taken him out of the picture.

"I got myself out of there. Made myself go. I thought maybe if I went back, they'd leave Cam alone, at least. It didn't matter what happened to me."

Erin remembered Brianna's face after the Thanksgiving dinner and Cam's arrest. The mask of indifference. The hopelessness in her eyes.

"Wolf was still there, waiting in the bakery parking lot."

Erin saw his car again in her mind's eye. The unfamiliar vehicle parked in the back lot, waiting for Brianna. Forever waiting for Brianna, until Erin got there and called the police and Stayner opened the door so they could see what had happened.

"He didn't see me. He was talking to someone else in the passenger seat."

She swallowed.

"Mickey?" Erin asked. He had left his scent behind. She was sure it couldn't have been anyone else. And if Brianna had seen Mickey with him, then she wasn't the one who had killed Wolf.

Brianna didn't move or say anything for a long time. Then she finally nodded.

"Mickey's door was open so that I could see in. He and Wolf were arguing. I couldn't hear what they were saying. Mickey pulled a knife and he pounded it into Wolf's chest. Like he was trying to drive a stake into a vampire's heart. Really hard. And Wolf made this awful noise. But he didn't fight back… he just went still."

CHAPTER 38

$\mathcal{E}$rin could feel everyone in the room relax. Once the words were out of her mouth, the tension went out of Brianna and she sagged in Erin's arms. She had fought herself so hard not to tell what she had seen, and now that she had told, a weight had been lifted from her shoulders. Her breathing changed from frantic, shallow breaths to longer, even respiration. Erin continued to rub her back.

"I was so scared," Brianna said softly. "I didn't know what to do. I just wanted to run away from there, all the way home, and never look back. But there wasn't anywhere to go. No way to get out of town. Wolf was my one way out. It's like you said… I couldn't believe what I had seen. After Mickey left, I kept watching Wolf, waiting for him to move, to be okay. I don't know how long I stayed there. Then I started walking. I don't know… where I went or how long I walked…"

"She was lucky I came across her," Beaver contributed, speaking for the first time. "She was in a state… shock, fugue, whatever you want to call it… it was before you found and reported Wolf's death. I didn't know what had happened, but I knew I couldn't leave her on the street like that."

Erin turned her head to look at Beaver. "So you brought her here and pretended you didn't know where she was."

Beaver chewed for a minute. "Well, it was a little more complicated than that. I didn't have this place yet, so I had to move her a couple of times without being seen, which is not easy in a place like Bald Eagle Falls."

Erin could imagine.

"What am I going to do?" Brianna sniffled. "I got nowhere to go now. No way to get anywhere."

"You're not going anywhere yet," Beaver told her. "We're going to need a signed statement and more details from you. Once everything is in place, we can talk about options. I'm sure we can help you get to where you want to go, make sure you have a starting point."

"What about the witness protection program?" Erin suggested. "You could give her a new name and everything."

"It doesn't work like it does in the movies," Beaver advised. "WITSEC is very rare. It's used for high-level targets. Someone like Brianna… she's low profile. She can get a new start anywhere. Use a new name if she wants. No one is going to put any amount of time and effort into looking for her. Mickey was a danger, but he's in custody. If he's the one who killed Wolf, Brianna isn't a danger to anyone else. As long as she doesn't go straight back to the same neighborhood, she'll be safe."

Erin looked at Brianna, stroking her hair. The girl seemed so vulnerable. But once she got her equilibrium back, the tough front would reappear. Erin had moved to avoid trouble more than once. Brianna was a little younger than Erin had been when she'd been forced to make it on her own, but she could do it too, if she had a few breaks and could stay away from drugs and the street life.

"The biggest thing is to get clean and stay clean," Beaver told Brianna, as if she had read Erin's mind. "If you want a new life, then you have to leave the old one behind. No one is going to give an addict a job. A real job, not turning tricks or couriering contraband."

"I'm not an addict," Brianna snapped. "You're just assuming that because I'm black and on the street. That doesn't mean I'm an addict."

Beaver gazed at her, expressionless, giving nothing away. "It's interesting that Wolf didn't have any drugs or money on him. He's a drug dealer, known to indulge himself, and he's picking you up, knowing he's going to have to give you something to calm you down and keep you on the string. It's surprising that there was nothing on him, don't you think?"

Brianna pulled out of Erin's grip. She sat back, a few inches away from Erin, the walls going up. Her tears had washed away all vestiges of makeup from around her eyes, and she looked both young and worn by experience at the same time. How long had she been on the street and how many people had used and betrayed her in that time?

"I don't know what you're talking about. He'd know better than to be caught with drugs on him. Someone like that makes sure other people are holding for him."

"But there was no one with him. And he knew you would be jonesing. You'd already talked to him on the phone, so he knew what kind of shape you were in."

"I'm not the one who killed him." Brianna wiped her nose with the back of her hand. "If he had something, then I guess Mickey took it."

"And if I search your bag and this cabin, I wouldn't find anything?"

Brianna stared at her; challenging and defiant.

"I could use the dog," Beaver said, with a nod toward K9. "He could find drugs no matter how well you think you've hidden them."

Brianna's mask slipped. She glanced uncertainly toward the dog, lying next to Terry's feet but watching her intently. "He's not a drug dog."

"You think he couldn't find them? Are you willing to stake your future on that?"

Brianna clenched her teeth, the muscles in her jaw and neck standing out. "Fine. He'd find drugs. Wolf hardly had anything on him. It wasn't hardly anything."

"But even in your state of shock, you weren't too scared to go through his pockets and car to relieve him of it. And it's been enough to get you through four days."

"Because I'm not an addict. I don't have to be high all the time."

"There are plenty of people with addiction issues who don't use every day. It's not a requirement. Are you the one who planted the drugs in Cam's car?"

Brianna stared at Beaver, her face tight. "Why would I do that? Cam was my friend. Maybe my only real friend. The only one who cared about me as a person."

"You would do it because Wolf told you to. Maybe he threatened you. Or maybe Mickey did. You put the drugs in Cam's car. You were there. No one else was. Wolf didn't show up until Saturday night."

A tear escaped Brianna's reddened eyes and ran down her cheek. Brianna didn't admit it, but Erin realized with a sinking feeling that Beaver was right. Brianna didn't offer any other explanation, didn't point to anyone else. It wasn't Stayner; he hadn't been working with the gangsters. One of the Russians could have sent someone to Bald Eagle Falls to plant the evidence, but why do that when they already had a puppet on the scene who they could control?

"And Cam knew it was you, but he didn't say anything," Beaver suggested. "He just let them arrest him."

"I couldn't let him go to prison."

"But you did."

Brianna shook her head. "I tried to stop Wolf. I told him he didn't need to do anything to Cam; I would go back to him. I'd do what he wanted."

"But that was *after* you'd already set Cam up for him."

"I tried to stop him," Brianna insisted, voice cracking.

"Did you?" Beaver took a couple of steps closer to Brianna. "Was it Mickey who killed Wolf or was it you?"

"It was Mickey! I couldn't. I was too scared of him. If I tried... he'd kill *me*."

Erin tried to picture Brianna meeting with Wolf. Erin hadn't known Volkov in life, but she'd met Mickey and didn't imagine that Wolf would be any less threatening. She pictured Brianna getting into the car with him, shaking, terrified, desperate.

Would Brianna's concern for Cam be enough to overcome her fear of Volkov, the man who had been controlling her with threats, violence, and her addiction? Erin thought Brianna was telling the truth. She wouldn't have had what it took to kill the Russian.

"Where's the phone you contacted Wolf on?" Beaver asked.

"I dumped it." Brianna snuffled loudly, gulping. "In some creek I walked past that night."

"And where is his phone?"

"That one too. Both of them."

"Together?"

Brianna nodded.

"And if I was to recover them, would I find Mickey's number on your phone?"

"What?" Brianna's eyes got wider.

"After you arranged for Wolf to pick you up, did you call Mickey?"

"Why would I do that?"

"To get Wolf out of your life. Because he wouldn't leave you alone. He made you set Cam up and just laughed at you when you told him that Cam was a nice guy and to leave him alone. You were mad at him, but you were too scared to do something yourself, so you called Mickey. What did you tell him?"

Brianna's jaw worked. She dragged her eyes away from Beaver to look at Terry and Erin. "I didn't tell him anything."

"There's no point in lying to me. We have Mickey in custody, and you didn't have a burner number for him. Your number is going to show up as an incoming call on his phone Saturday night."

Brianna sank back. "You can't open his phone."

"You wanna bet? Are you going to bet the next ten years on that? If you want to stay out of prison, you need to tell me the truth."

Brianna stared at her with hollow eyes. The seconds ticked by. Finally, Brianna leaned forward, elbows on knees, and covered her eyes. "Yes. I called Mickey."

CHAPTER 39

hat did you tell him?" Beaver asked. Her tone was flat and without inflection. No accusation. No disappointment or thrill that she had been right. Nonjudgmental, seeing what Brianna had to say about it.

"I told him…" Brianna swallowed. She looked sideways at Erin, then away again. Maybe regretting that she had opened up to Erin. Or that she had to disappoint Erin by admitting what she had done. "I just told him about Cam getting arrested."

"He didn't know yet?"

"No. It was the weekend and I was the only one there. The only one connected to Mickey."

"But Campbell wasn't working for Mickey," Erin said slowly. "So why would he care?"

Brianna gnawed on her lip.

"He didn't care about Cam," Beaver explained, working it out. "He cared about the drugs."

Brianna nodded.

"Why?" Erin was still lagging behind, not seeing what Beaver could. But Beaver had been involved with these people. She knew what they were like, what was likely to happen. She wasn't out in the cold like Erin was, trying to see her way in.

P.D. WORKMAN

"Because she didn't set Campbell up with Wolf's drugs. She set him up with Mickey's."

Terry let out a whistle. "No... is that what you did?"

Brianna rubbed her eyes. "I did what Wolf told me to. He said to tell Mickey I had a line on a really good prospect in Bald Eagle Falls. That I could get him to buy from Mickey. Wolf told me that he was going to arrange it and Mickey would be real grateful when we got it all set up. I could get a share of the money."

"Why use Mickey's drugs? Why wouldn't Wolf use his own?" Terry asked.

"I don't know. He had his own chain all tied up. Mickey was bigger; he had more product free. He said Mickey would be happy when he found out what we had done."

"But there was no buyer," Beaver said.

Brianna shook her head. "No," she whispered. "There wasn't anyone. He tipped off the cops to search Cam's car, where he'd told me to leave the drugs. So the cops got it all."

"How did Wolf plan to explain that to Mickey?"

"He didn't. He was gonna leave me flappin' in the wind. Leave me to take all the heat. Maybe tell Mickey that I had planned it myself. Or me and Cam." Brianna dug her knuckles into her eyes so hard it made Erin wince. "He wanted to break me and Cam up. I thought if I just did this one more job for him, he'd leave me alone."

"But Wolf stabbed you in the back," Beaver summed up. "So you called Mickey and told him that it had been Wolf who had lost him the drugs. And Mickey got his revenge."

Brianna sniffled. Erin stared at Brianna, trying to reconcile the picture of the vulnerable, weeping girl in front of her with that of a person who had intentionally had the double-crossing gangster murdered.

"It wasn't fair," Brianna said. "He shouldn't have done that to me."

Beaver nodded. "He didn't realize he was putting a plan in motion that would result in his own death."

"I didn't want to go to prison. I wasn't going to let him put me there. Or let Mickey kill me."

"I assume you were supposed to meet Mickey, once the deed was done."

"Uh-huh. I was watching the whole time. He hung around, calling my name. Telling me it was safe to come out. But I knew better. I was the only one who knew what had happened, so he'd kill me too."

"So you waited until he was gone. You took whatever drugs and money Wolf had on him and the burner you had called him on. And then there was no one left for you to call."

"It was like she said," Brianna explained, nodding to Erin. "It seemed like it wasn't really real. None of it. From the time the cops came and arrested Cam. I was in shock. And seeing Mickey kill Wolf like that…" Brianna screwed her eyes shut, but Erin knew from experience that wouldn't shut the images out. "I never saw nothing like it. I didn't know what to do then."

"Other than rifling the body and covering your tracks."

"It wasn't like that," Brianna insisted. "I had to take care of myself. If you don't take care of yourself, no one else is going to."

Beaver let Brianna go to bed when she'd finished squeezing as much information from her as possible. She waited until she heard the bedroom door shut, then walked across to the bookshelves and pressed the button on a black box sitting on one of the shelves. A red light that Erin hadn't previously noticed winked out. Erin hadn't realized that the whole conversation was being recorded.

She looked at Terry. "So you used me to get information out of Brianna. So you can throw her in prison."

"You helped to get information vital to a murder investigation, yes." He hesitated for a moment. "But it was your choice to talk to her. I didn't force you."

"You kind of did."

Terry sat there for a minute, thinking about it. Then he nodded. "I'm sorry… I didn't tell you what was going on, and just expected you to do what I said."

"Is she going to prison?" Erin asked Beaver. "After you get me to convince her to spill her guts, are you going to send her to prison for drug trafficking or conspiracy to commit murder?"

"No. I don't think so. I'm not in charge of all of that, but my input will be considered. And I would like her to be protected. Get her into rehab and try to give her a second chance at life."

Erin looked toward the back of the cabin, where Brianna had retreated to go to bed.

"There are bars on the windows," Beaver said. "She can't get out."

"I was more worried about drugs. She could overdose. If she thinks she's going to prison…"

"I'll check on her in a minute. Managed to keep her alive until now."

"Yeah, but you hadn't wrung the truth out of her then. Forced her to incriminate herself."

"She wasn't forced. That will be clear in the recording."

"She's just a kid."

Beaver nodded, her expression softening. "Yes," she agreed, "a kid, an addict, and someone who essentially put out a hit on her pimp."

"And someone Campbell Cox cares about."

"I told you, I'll do my best to get her the help she needs."

CHAPTER 40

$\mathcal{E}$rin was sipping a cup of hot chai tea and eating one of the leftover miniature pumpkin tarts from Thanksgiving on a quiet Sunday morning when she heard footsteps and voices outside. She peeked out the window to see who it was and saw Mary Lou and the boys coming up her sidewalk. She brushed crumbs from her lap and got up to open the door for them.

"Hi! How is everyone?" Neither she nor Mary Lou were normally huggers but, after all the family had been through, Erin didn't feel like a wave or a handshake would be enough. She gave Mary Lou a brief hug and cheek-touch as she entered, and gave Campbell and Joshua more vigorous hugs.

She put a plate of treats out on the coffee table and pointed out the tea kettle for anyone who wanted to help themselves.

"You're off of house arrest," she observed to Campbell.

He lifted his pants to show off his bare ankle before sitting down. "Yes. Thanks to you and everyone else who helped."

"It isn't anything I did," Erin said with a modest shrug. She hadn't been the one to make the arrest or to do any of the other paperwork required to ensure that Mickey would be going to prison for a long time and that Campbell would be able to go free.

"You were the one who talked Brianna into telling what happened,"

Campbell countered. "If she hadn't talked, I don't know whether I would have gotten off."

"You were innocent. We would have gotten you off somehow."

"Well, thank you anyway," Mary Lou said firmly. "I know who my friends are in this town."

"You have a lot of friends. So many people were concerned when Campbell was arrested. Everyone wanted to do something to help you."

"Most of them were just vultures. They wanted a good look at the carcass."

"No... a lot of people care, Mary Lou. But there wasn't a lot anyone could do. You said you had a lot of casseroles."

"Oh, heavens," Mary Lou rolled her eyes. "Fewer casseroles and more sincere prayers. That's what we needed."

Erin felt a little pang at Mary Lou's need for prayers. That was one thing that she hadn't done, and didn't think she would ever do. Hopefully, Mary Lou would understand that and accept a plate of cookies or whatever support Erin could actually offer.

"I'm sure people did what they could." Erin looked at the boys. "So... what are your plans now? I guess you've had a chance to think about what you want out of life."

Campbell shifted uncomfortably. "Lots of time to think," he agreed, "but I'm not sure I got any further on it than I ever did before. My life... just doesn't go the way that I plan."

"If you had better plans—" Mary Lou started, and then she stopped herself. "You can still set goals, and the rest of us will help you all we can."

Campbell nodded. "I just don't know. I get why Mom wants me to come back here, and to finish school, and I know that's the only way I'm going to be able to get a decent job. It's just... I don't want to do that right now. I want to have some fun while I'm still young enough to enjoy it. I can finish school later. And then get a good job. I've only got so much time to be a kid."

"You're lucky," Erin said. "I knew I had to finish high school before I turned eighteen because, after that, I'd be out on my own. I had to get a job lined up, figure out where I was going to live... there wasn't any safety net."

Campbell nodded. "We have it pretty good. I know that. I'm just... not ambitious that way. All of these years..." His eyes focused off in the distance. "We worked so hard for so many years. And Mom's worked really hard too. But I just… burned out. I can't do it anymore. I can't keep pretending that everything is okay and that I want to do well academically and get a job or go to college. I don't want any of that. I don't want any responsibility. I've done enough and I just need to be able to stop and think for a while."

Erin glanced over at Mary Lou, whose face was tired and worn, despite perfectly-applied makeup. Mary Lou would love a break too, she was sure. But she wasn't going to get one.

"I hope everything works out for you," she told him. "I know you've had a tough time."

He nodded.

"And… what about Brianna? I haven't heard much about how things worked out for her. Whenever I ask Beaver, she says that there are privacy issues and she can't tell me about it."

"I don't think Bree would mind. She's in detox. A twelve-week program and, hopefully, that's long enough for her to get clean and develop some new habits and ways to cope. They'll help her with job hunting too, but I don't know what she's going to find. Nothing that's going to bring in very much money. So how is she supposed to support herself? That's why I wanted us to… share resources. Maybe then, she can stay out of trouble."

"I sure hope so. I think she really cares about you."

"I care about her… but we'll see what she thinks when she's out of rehab. I don't know if she'll want anything to do with me then."

"Why wouldn't she?"

"I was trying to get her out. I talked her into Thanksgiving dinner, but that's about all I could manage and that didn't turn out real well. If she's clean and has a job… then I don't have much to offer her anymore."

Her company was gone by the time Terry's truck pulled back in front of the house. Erin was glad to see him and hoped he wouldn't be too worn out after spending so much time at the police department. When he stepped in the door with K9, Erin studied his face, looking for signs of fatigue and any other indicators of whether things had gone well or not.

Terry smiled. Tired, but he seemed to be satisfied.

"You had a good meeting?" Erin asked.

"It was good."

There were a few bits of desserts left on the tray on the coffee table, which Erin hadn't bothered to clean up yet, and he picked up a small gingerbread cookie and a chai apple tart and ate them without a plate to catch the crumbs as he settled on the couch beside her.

"They're going to keep Stayner on," Terry said. "He's done pretty well here, and they've managed to work his salary into the budget with me being off, so they said he might as well stay if he wants to."

"And does he?"

"I guess so. I figured he'd want to go into the city once he was finished his temporary assignment here. But the place grows on you." He smiled at Erin. "Or so I've been told."

"But does that mean… they can afford both of you? And Tom? No one is going to lose their job if he stays on…?"

"They've apparently worked it out. That's good enough for me. He's green, but he's trainable. He's already showing progress."

"He's the one who noticed Mickey was out of place and followed his car and took action on it."

Terry nodded. "Exactly. Good instincts, as long as we keep refining them. He's had a couple of blunders, but who hasn't? We all make mistakes. Some big, some not."

"It's just that his mistakes could cost lives. Or convictions. They're pretty vital."

"Which is why we're working on him. He's not going to replace me, and it will be nice to have one more person on the squad. We get spread pretty thin sometimes."

"It will be nice to have you home more."

"You're not tired of me yet? I'd think you would have had enough of me while I've been on leave."

"That's different. And I'm not here the whole day, so I don't really notice that. It has been nice having you here evenings and nights, when you aren't sneaking off to guard safehouses or buy emergency crankshafts for Willie."

"It was an auger."

"Whatever."

Terry used his finger to try to pick up the crumbs left on the platter. Erin watched him. "There's more in the freezer, you know. If you're still hungry…"

"I know. I have to watch the desserts, though. Don't want to put on weight."

"You're not putting on weight. You're dropping it."

"Because I'm being careful."

Erin knew that wasn't the reason he'd been losing weight, but she didn't pursue it. While they needed to share more with each other and to be open about their feelings, she didn't need to keep picking at sores that were starting to heal. If Terry was happy with the way things had gone at his meeting, then his stress level would be lower, and maybe he would eat more. She didn't want to raise his stress level by harping on him how he needed to eat more.

"You didn't get very much. I can get a few more out for you."

"No." Terry put his arm around Erin and pulled her closer. "Let's just cuddle."

Erin took long, deep breaths, staying still and focused for a long time, before releasing her last pose. With both feet flat on the ground and her arms hanging loosely at her sides, she breathed in a few last practice breaths through her nose.

She heard Vic's door open and the footsteps and low voices of two people trying to be quiet, but not doing a very good job of it.

"Don't interrupt her," Vic whispered. "She needs to stay focused."

"I'm done," Erin said.

"Shh," Willie advised. "We're supposed to be quiet."

Erin grinned at him. Vic smacked his arm lightly. "Are you making fun of me?"

"I'm laughing with you, not at you."

"But I'm not laughing."

"Maybe you should be."

Vic rolled her eyes at Erin. "Somebody's in a silly mood today."

"Enjoy it."

Vic wrapped an arm around Willie. "I am."

"Where are you guys going tonight? Out on a date?"

Vic made a show of examining her clothes. Not a dress or an outfit that showed off her slender figure. Baggy cargo pants like Beaver often wore. A rain jacket. A ball cap and her hair pulled back in a ponytail. Willie was dressed similarly grungy, but she never could make any judgments as to what he was planning from his clothing.

"Okay, not a date," Erin amended. "What are you doing?"

"We're going fishing tomorrow."

"Oh. Right. I remember that. But isn't it… cold? Don't the fish… I don't know… hibernate during the winter?"

Vic shook her head and ignored Erin's ignorant questions. "Tonight, we're out to get some bait."

"Who sells bait here in town?"

Another pronounced eye roll. "We're not buying it. We get our own," Vic told her patiently. "Earthworms, grubs," a shrug, "whatever."

"Ick. Not my idea of a fun date."

Willie chuckled and squeezed Vic. "Some people just don't know how to have fun. See you tomorrow, Erin. We'll bring you back some fish for supper."

"Just don't bring me back any bait."

Erin awoke slowly. It was light out, which meant that she'd slept much later than her usual baker's hours. She stretched, feeling warm and comfy and relaxed. She was feeling something elusive that she couldn't quite put her finger on. She rolled over and looked at Terry. He was awake, his face relaxed, watching her.

Erin smiled. "How long have you been looking at me? How late is it?"

"You're not working this morning, so it's not late."

Erin started to turn back toward her nightstand to check the time on her phone, but Terry caught her shoulder before she could. "It's not late," he repeated. "It's just right."

Erin relaxed and stayed facing him. She closed her eyes and opened them again in a long blink. "I feel…"

He traced a light finger down her arm, waiting for her to finish. He smiled, the dimple appearing in his cheek. "Did you have a good sleep? I didn't hear you wake up last night."

Erin thought about it. "I don't think I did. I think I slept through."

"That's good."

"So I guess I feel… rested."

He cupped her cheek. "Good. Hopefully, the first night of many."

"Don't jinx it."

"Sorry."

But Erin couldn't help hoping that he was right. If she could start sleeping again, she could go back to a normal life in Bald Eagle Falls. And there would be no more dead bodies or missing persons to investigate.

SANTA SHORTBREAD

AUNTIE CLEM'S BAKERY #12

For all of the nurturers

CHAPTER 1

*E*rin spoke to young Peter Foster as he bent close to the bakery display case, examining the newest gluten-free treats with his younger sisters.

"What are you going to make for Christmas?" he asked. "You made lots of really good cookies last year."

"We will again this year," Erin assured him. "I just met with Charley, my partner, on the weekend. We have a nice list of what we are going to have for you this year. We're going to do some of the little one-bite desserts like we had at Thanksgiving."

She saw the disappointment chase across his face.

"I know you didn't like the pumpkin tarts and gingerbread, but that won't be all that we have. And there will be lots of different kinds of cookies. I'm going to make some cutout shortbread cookies. You'll like those, and we can do all kinds of fun shapes."

"Christmas shapes?"

"Yes, of course. Stars and trees and gingerbread men and snowmen. All kinds of things."

"Santa?" one of the little girls asked, bouncing up and down. Her sticky fingers were on the glass of the display case and either Erin or her assistant Vic was going to have to clean it again after they left, but Erin didn't mind. She loved her littlest customers, the Fosters especially.

Erin looked at Vic and glanced at Mrs. Foster to see what they thought. Vic had warned her against using too many secular symbols of Christmas. Bald Eagle Falls was in the Bible belt, and they had to be careful not to offend the customers who didn't want to see pagan symbols or a lot of commercial crap around their religious holiday.

"I'm sure we can do some Santas," Vic agreed and, after a moment Mrs. Foster nodded too. The kids had won that round. They were so inundated through the media that they couldn't be expected to be completely blind to Santa and the other commercial offerings.

"And the Grinch?" Peter demanded. "You have to do the Grinch!"

Erin laughed. "Hmm. I'll have to see what I can find. We're going into the city to look for some new cookie cutters, and I'll have to see if I can find a Grinch. I haven't seen any around."

"That would be cool. We'd buy them."

"The Grinch is green," Karen contributed.

"Yes, I would have to make green cookies or frosting," Erin agreed.

"Green cookies! You can't make green cookies!"

"I certainly can."

"How?"

"Magic," Erin teased. Then, thinking better of the comment, changed her mind. "Just with green food coloring, Karen. It's really easy."

"I haven't had green cookies before."

"Then I'll have to make some for sure, won't I? What did you guys want today?"

They made their choices for the kids' cookie club and Vic handed them out. Mrs. Foster ordered the baked goods she would need for the week and stood with her hand on her slightly-protruding belly while she waited for it all to be wrapped up and totaled.

"I know I've said it before, but I can't thank you enough for all of the lovely gluten-free baking you do. I used to have to do so much extra baking to make something safe for Peter so that he could have something other than the packaged baking from the city. And half the time it didn't even turn out. I always felt bad that he didn't have any choices and just had the same kind of cookies and bread over and over again. Now… it's just so nice to come here and know that he can have anything in the bakery, and it's all so good!"

Erin flashed a look at Peter. "Even if he doesn't like pumpkin pie!"

"Mom says lots of kids don't like pumpkin pie."

"But I do," Mrs. Foster assured Erin. "And I much prefer yours to the ones at the grocery store!"

～

When the Fosters had gone, there was a lull. Vic went around the display case to wipe down fingerprints.

"I'll be right back," Erin told her. "I need to fix my hair."

Several dark strands had escaped her hairpins and baker's hat, so Erin ducked into the commode to look in the mirror while she took care of it all and then washed up again. Vic, with her long, blond hair, seemed to be able to manage to keep hers tidy and out of her face all day, but Erin frequently had to take a break at some point to get hers back in order. Maybe she should grow hers longer so that she could pull it into a ponytail or bun rather than trying to keep the shorter locks pinned back.

She returned to the front of the bakery, looking presentable again, and smiled at the approaching customers. It was getting noticeably busier as Christmas approached and people were buying more baking for parties, presents, and preparing ahead for their Christmas meals.

Melissa was one of the latest customers. She gave Erin a broad smile and stepped up eagerly to look into the display case. While she lived alone, Erin knew that she would be hosting a dinner for some of the other single women in her church group, and later on Christmas day would be off to the penitentiary to see her friend, Davis Plaint. Melissa never referred to him as a boyfriend or in a romantic way, and wouldn't mention him in front of the other church ladies. Erin often found herself puzzling over their unusual relationship.

"What would you like today?" Erin asked. "Need anything for the department?"

"I think it would be nice if someone other than me sprang for muffins for the police department now and then," Melissa said with an irritated shake of her head that set her dark spiraling curls bouncing. "I only work there part-time, so my paycheck is lower than anyone else's. Maybe Clara or the sheriff could buy them sometime."

Vic's eyebrows climbed. "I always thought you got reimbursed for those."

"No, it's just out of the kindness of my heart. Seems to me it's time for someone else to buy them this time."

Erin nodded uncomfortably. She had taken muffins over to the police department herself occasionally but like Vic, she had always thought that Melissa's purchases were covered by her employer. She would mention it to Officer Terry Piper when she saw him later in the day. She was sure they didn't mean to take advantage of Melissa; probably no one had ever thought twice about it. "Something for you, then?"

"A person can only do so much," Melissa muttered. "With all that I do for the department, they could show some appreciation."

"Yes," Erin agreed. "Everyone likes to be recognized for what they do. Anything interesting going on lately?"

Erin didn't usually encourage Melissa's gossip about the police department or crimes going on in Bald Eagle Falls, but she felt the situation called for a little distraction.

Melissa leaned forward. "Actually..." She looked dramatically left and right to see if anyone were listening in. There were customers behind her, but they were waiting patiently and didn't appear to be eavesdropping. Though Melissa put on a show of being discreet, she preferred an audience. "Have you heard of the Grinch?"

"We were just talking to the Fosters about the Grinch," Erin laughed. "They want me to make green Grinch cookies for Christmas."

"No, not the Dr. Seuss character. The *real* Grinch."

Vic leaned on the display case. "There is no real Grinch."

Melissa nodded vigorously. "There is. At first, we didn't think it was anything more than the usual holiday thefts. You know, there are always a few cars broken into, usually in the city. People leave newly purchased gifts in full view and then are surprised when someone breaks into their car in the parking lot. But Bald Eagle Falls has had an unusual rash of thefts the past couple of weeks."

"What counts as a rash of thefts?" Erin asked.

"I don't know for sure how many have been reported; I haven't filed all of the reports. But there have been house and car thefts, with some pricey items stolen."

"More than normal."

"There are always some. But there have been a couple of families..." Melissa frowned and shook her head. "They've lost all of their Christmas gifts. Folks in this part of Tennessee are not wealthy; some families really have to scrape to get a few things together for the little ones. And when someone like the Grinch comes along and takes everything away... there's nothing they can do. They can't afford to replace them."

"Oh... what about their homeowner's insurance—can't they make a claim?"

"Even if they can, if their deductible isn't too high and it's worthwhile to make a claim, they're not going to get the money in time for Christmas."

"That's so sad!" Vic exclaimed. "Who would do something like that?"

"The Grinch," Melissa said, giving a nod. "You see? Whoever it is, they're stealing Christmas from the children of Bald Eagle Falls."

Erin and Vic shook their heads. Bald Eagle Falls was a small community, close-knit, and it was hard to believe that anyone would want to hurt their neighbors that way. Especially little children.

"That's just terrible." Erin looked down at the products on display. She was mindful of the fact that there were other people lined up behind Melissa, so they couldn't gossip for long. "What do you think you would like today, then? We have chocolate chip muffins." She knew Melissa's weakness for anything with chocolate in it.

Melissa frowned, examining the various possibilities, and then returned to the chocolate chip muffins that Erin had pointed out and decided, "I do think it is a chocolate chip muffin kind of day."

CHAPTER 2

*E*rin knew that Officer Terry Piper was working a modified afternoon shift, and watched to see if he would stop in at Auntie Clem's Bakery while he was on patrol. He and K9 were happy to be getting out of the house after Terry had been sidelined with a head injury and been choked out by an assailant. Neither one of them liked being cooped up all day with nothing to do. But Terry was still suffering from headaches and wasn't yet able to put in a full shift.

Under his old routine, Terry would stop in for water partway through the afternoon on a hot day, and for a cookie and doggie biscuit around closing time. The weather was chilly so close to Christmas, so they didn't need the extra water, but she was still hoping for a visit at the end of the workday, when they would be getting off work as well. But as she turned the sign on the door over to 'Closed,' there was no sign of her boyfriend and his furry sidekick. Vic wiped down the display case.

"No visit from Officer Handsome today?" she teased.

"Doesn't look like it." Erin let out a sigh and left the door unlocked, just in case he came by before they were finished. "Hopefully, that means he went home and not that he's stuck at the office or dealing with a case."

"The sheriff said they'd make sure he didn't work too long."

"Hopefully," Erin repeated.

They fell into the usual rhythm closing out the till, cleaning up, and mixing up batters that would soak overnight for the next morning's muffins and breads.

"Grinch cookies," Vic recalled with a laugh. "I wonder if we'll be able to find some cookie cutters."

"Even if we can't find one that's specifically The Grinch, we could make Santa cookies and give him a green face. It wouldn't be perfect, but people would know what they were supposed to be."

"Perfect," Vic declared. "Great idea."

Erin drove herself and Vic home as usual. Vic lived in the loft apartment over Erin's garage, so when they were on the same shift, they almost always drove together. Vic didn't have a car of her own and was constantly getting after Erin to replace her old clunker. But Erin didn't like to spend more money than she had to, an attitude that had carried over from her lean years, even though she finally had money in the bank from cashing in on a crop of wild ginseng.

"One of these days, it's not going to make it," Vic commented, shaking her head at Erin's car. "It sounds worse than ever."

"I'll take it in for an oil change. That's all it needs."

"It needs a lot more than that," Vic said with authority. "Timing belt. New transmission. The electrical is all screwed up…" She had probably fixed up a lot of cars with her brothers on the farm before she had come out as transgender and been forced to leave home.

"It still runs."

"Until the day it doesn't."

"If I only use it for tooling around Bald Eagle Falls, I'll be safe. If we go out to the city, we can use Terry's or Willie's truck."

"Or you could get a new car."

"Not yet."

Vic shook her head. They walked up the sidewalk together. "Looks like Terry's home. Say 'hi' for me."

"I will. You and Willie going out, or are you going to come over for dinner?"

"We'll do something together. You can have Terry to yourself today."

"Okay. Have a good night, Vicky."

Vic walked around to the back and Erin let herself in the front door. Despite the fact that she had a perfectly good garage, it currently held

Clementine's old Volkswagen, so she and the others always parked in front of the house instead.

She gave a mental shrug and walked up to the house. She opened the door and checked the burglar alarm and saw that it had already been disarmed.

"Terry?"

She heard the bathroom door open and Terry walked out of the hall. Orange Blossom darted past him with a yowl. Marshmallow hopped sedately out from behind the couch.

"Hi, guys." Erin bent down to scratch the rabbit's ears and Orange Blossom practically climbed into her arms, complaining loudly. Probably about the presence of K9, who he'd had plenty of time to get used to.

Erin made understanding noises to Orange Blossom, acknowledging his chatter, and looked at Terry with a smile, rolling her eyes.

Terry shook his head. "I think you might be thirty seconds late getting home; he's been pacing around here making a racket."

"Oh, is that the problem?" Erin pressed her cheek against Orange Blossom's head and squeezed him. "Well, I'm here now, so stop complaining."

He instead started with a rumbling purr. Erin scratched his ears. "That's better."

Erin studied Terry's face. "How are you doing?" There were lines around his eyes and he seemed pale. "Are you in pain? Do you want something for your head?"

"Mostly I'm just tired out." Terry thought about it. "Actually, I guess I might need a painkiller too. It's hard for me to tell, sometimes." He pressed his fingers to his temples. "I start feeling tired and foggy, and it takes a while to figure out I've got a headache."

"Let me get one of your pills."

"I can do it."

Erin shook her head. "No, sit down and relax, I'll get you one." She put Orange Blossom down and ignored his renewed complaints as she went into the bedroom and retrieved one of Terry's prescription pills. She got him a glass of water from the kitchen and returned to where he was sitting in the living room. Terry passed his hand over his face, looking slightly gray.

"I don't like to take too many of these," he said, taking it from her and swallowing it down with the water.

"You are allowed to take them when you need them. It doesn't help you to be in pain."

"But it doesn't help me to be dopey either. I don't want to spend the days in a haze."

"If they're too strong, then you can ask the doctor to prescribe a lower dose. But he won't know unless you tell him."

Terry nodded once. "Yes, you're right," he agreed. He went back to rubbing his temples. "I was going to have something ready for us to eat. Or at least to get started on supper."

"Don't worry about it. I can get something ready. You must be hungry."

"Not really. More nauseated than anything."

He had obviously waited too long after his headache had started. Once that nausea had set in, it tended to stay the rest of the evening. He had wanted to lose a few pounds after their cruise but, since the attack, he'd lost more than he should.

"What could you eat? Could I make you a smoothie? Some yogurt? What wouldn't bother your stomach?"

"I don't know. Give it a little while; maybe it will feel better after the pill kicks in."

Erin knew very well that it wouldn't. But he was a grown man and needed to be in control of his own body and life more than he needed her to mother him.

"Okay... but try to have something later. Don't just skip eating."

Terry grimaced, not looking at her. "I'll try. Later."

"And if you want me to go out and get something..." Erin offered. "If there is something you think you could eat..."

"No, you don't need to make a special trip for me."

Erin left him sitting on the couch. K9 was in the kitchen waiting for her, standing close to the cookie jar and looking her way with pleading eyes. He was very well-behaved, but he seemed put out that it had taken her so long to get there.

"Aren't you being patient," Erin crooned. "And such a gentleman. Unlike some animals around here..." She looked pointedly at Orange Blossom, who meowed loudly in exasperation that he hadn't yet received a treat.

Erin got all of the animals treats and checked the fridge for dinner inspiration. Her usual fallback was leftover bread or rolls from Auntie Clem's with some locally-sourced jam. But she was making an effort to take care of her body better and eat something other than straight sugar and carbs, so she made herself look at the vegetables to see if she could put together a salad.

Vegetables were really not her thing, except for the ones that Vic had made at Thanksgiving, with lots of buttery sauces or nuts in caramelized sugar. Those had been really good. But she suspected that the benefits from the vitamins they contained would be counteracted by all of the fat and sugar, which would go straight to her hips and, with her small frame, every extra pound showed.

CHAPTER 3

$\mathcal{S}$he returned to the living room with a good-sized bowl of salad and a cold pack for Terry's head. She handed the ice pack to him. Terry looked at it dolefully. He always hated putting it on his head, even though it did seem to provide some relief. He watched her sit down, balancing the bowl on her knees to eat.

"That looks like a particularly virtuous supper."

"Yes, it is," Erin agreed. "If I can fill up on the veggies and not eat bread and jam or ice cream afterward as a reward."

Terry chuckled, the dimple appearing on his handsome cheek. For an instant, the lines on his face smoothed. Then he winced and put the cold pack on the back of his neck.

Erin ate for a few minutes without saying anything, watching him worriedly for some sign that the painkiller and the ice pack were having the desired effect.

"Don't just look at me," Terry complained. "Talk to me. I can still listen."

His eyes were closed, but he could still tell she was looking at him.

"Sorry. Melissa stopped by today."

"Ahh, Melissa. Carrying more news, I assume."

"Did you know she pays for those muffins and everything for the police department out of her own pocket?"

Terry didn't say anything at first. His tone when he spoke again was noticeably different. Not the irritated, slightly sarcastic tone, but more concerned. "No... I didn't know that. I never really thought about it. I always just assumed that it came out of the department's budget."

"It's all her own money. And she's getting kind of annoyed that no one else ever springs for it."

"Well, I guess so. It's not her job to keep us supplied with goodies. Especially not out of her own pocket. She's only a part-timer." He was silent for a minute. "Why doesn't she stop doing it? Sooner or later, someone would either figure out that it was time for someone else to chip in, or that we didn't need them. I don't think anyone ever told her to bring muffins to the department. It was just her own thing."

"Maybe put a bug in Sheriff Wilmot's ear. Have him reimburse her or bring in something himself some time."

"Yeah. I'll try to remember to mention it to him. I'm sure he has no idea that she's getting resentful about it. She may be loose-lipped, but she does her job well and none of us would want her feeling like she wasn't appreciated."

Erin nodded, then remembered he wasn't looking her way. "Yeah. That would be good. I think it would help if she knew it was appreciated and that you weren't all just taking advantage of her kind heart."

"She *is* a kindhearted person."

"Yes." Erin thought about Melissa's relationship with Davis Plaint, currently incarcerated for murder. Was it just that she felt sorry for him? Was there anything else to it? Erin didn't know if she had romantic feelings toward him, or if it was just as Melissa said, a friendship. They had known each other when they had both been in high school and Davis's addiction had kept her from ever having a serious relationship with him then. Did she wish she could rekindle those days? Or was she just being kind to a man she used to know who was down on his luck?

"So, what else did she have to say?" Terry asked. "Or did she just come to gripe about the insensitive jerks that she works for?"

"Oh. She was telling me about your Grinch."

Terry sighed. "Did she tell you that no one knows if the same person is perpetrating these thefts? There is no proof at this point that we have a serial burglar."

"No, she didn't mention that. She sounded like… it was pretty much a foregone conclusion."

"It's not. She's jumping ahead of herself. It has been suggested, but not by any means proven. We may just have a higher rate of theft this year. Bad elements that moved in with the drug problems. Or people who have hit hard times this year. It isn't necessarily just one person."

"Okay. So maybe we don't have a Grinch. Or maybe we have a flock of Grinches."

He chuckled. "A flock? What's the appropriate collective noun for Grinches? A grunt of Grinches?"

"A grouch of Grinches?" Erin suggested.

Terry nodded. "Or maybe some families are just looking for sympathy or handouts. There isn't always proof that they had these gifts in the first place. They could be using theft as an excuse for the fact that they couldn't get anything for their kids this year."

Erin wrinkled her nose and thought about it. She had lived with families who hadn't had very much around Christmas time, but none of them had ever tried anything like that. Approaching agencies to ask for something, maybe when they didn't deserve it or qualify for it, but not flat-out lying and saying that the presents they bought had been stolen.

"I don't know. That sounds a little far-fetched. Did something happen to make you think so?"

"No. It's just another possibility. The claims haven't all been processed yet. If people pay with cash that they've been socking away all year and leave the receipts in the bags with the merchandise, how do they prove what they bought in the first place?"

"But you must be able to tell whether the cars or houses have been broken into, though."

"Not always. A lot of them seem to be opportunistic, taking advantage of an unlocked door. We've had a couple of broken windows, but in other cases, nothing. They're not all the same MO."

"Hmm." Erin nodded. "I guess that's why you don't want to call them serial burglaries."

"There hasn't been anything that appears very violent or personal about any of them. No graffiti or wanton destruction of property. Nothing that would suggest it was addicts or ex-boyfriends."

"And has it all been high-priced items? Things that are worth stealing?"

"In most cases... it has been everything. High-priced and low-value items, everything just swiped at once."

"Like The Grinch."

"No. Not like The Grinch," he said firmly. "We don't have a Grinch. We have a *burglar*. Or burglars. Don't romanticize it."

"Oh, I didn't mean it that way. Yeah, okay. I won't do that. Peter Foster and his sisters want us to make Grinch cookies this year. So it was already on my mind when Melissa came by. I didn't mean to encourage her."

"It's not your fault; someone had already suggested the nickname. But we're trying to keep it under wraps until we decide whether it is one burglar or several people acting independently."

"Okay. I'll make sure I don't repeat it in front of anyone." Erin put the remainder of her salad to the side, unable to finish it. Orange Blossom promptly jumped up into her lap and tried to shove his head into the bowl. Erin pushed the bowl farther away. "You don't want that, silly. Come here and cuddle."

He settled into her lap and started kneading with his paws, his rumbling purr starting up again.

CHAPTER 4

$\mathcal{E}$rin didn't have to say anything to anyone about the possible Grinch; it soon became apparent that the word was spreading quickly through town. Erin wasn't sure whether that meant that more people had been talking about it than just Melissa, or if her gossip had caught fire and was spreading that fast. It seemed like within a day, everyone was talking about the burglaries and the missing presents.

"Who would do such a thing?" Bella asked when she was on for her weekend shift. "Stealing presents from families, from little kids... that's really dirty. How are they going to have Christmas without something for their kids?"

Lottie Sturm, friends with Bella's mother, was close enough to hear Bella and shot her a disapproving look.

"You know that Christmas doesn't have anything to do with gifts. It's about the birth of Jesus. Without him, there is no Christmas."

"I know that," Bella said, a red flush rising from her neck. She was fair-haired and fair-skinned, and the blush was immediately noticeable. "I just meant that... it's what kids look forward to, and for a lot of them, that's the only time they get something really nice. Because it's such a special time of year. So if they don't get anything... it's just sad."

"It is," Erin agreed. She never had been able to understand the connection between the birth of the babe in the manger with Santa Claus and giving wrapped gifts and eating turkey for dinner. "Families that spend all year scraping by to be able to buy something nice for their children shouldn't have to face losing them and not having any way to celebrate the season. No matter what their beliefs are. It isn't fair to the children."

"There are children all over the world who don't have Christmas gifts," Lottie said dismissively. "It is not a part of worshiping Christ."

Erin rolled her eyes and didn't try to explain her position any further. It was hard enough dealing with Bible bashers the rest of the year. They seemed to be all the more zealous as Christmas approached. Erin had never been one to be insulted by anyone wishing her a Merry Christmas, even though she did not believe in any god or religious tenets. But some of the evangelists in Bald Eagle Falls had been getting on her nerves lately. She let everyone else live by their religious beliefs; she didn't see why they had to be so pushy just because she didn't share them.

"It's just not right," Bella agreed.

"It isn't any more wrong to steal Christmas presents than it is to steal the rest of the year or to steal from a corporation instead of a family," Lottie pointed out. "Either way, they are breaking the same laws and commandment. It's the same thing."

"But it seems a lot worse when children are being hurt, don't you think?" Erin asked.

"I don't know if I would say that," Lottie maintained. "It's a sin either way."

"I thought Jesus said it was worse to commit sins against children."

Lottie opened her mouth to argue, then closed it again. "I don't know," she said stiffly.

Erin handed her the bag of bagels she had ordered. "You enjoy those, now. And let me know what you want for Christmas dinner, if you're having anything special. I'm trying to make sure that I have everything prepared that people are going to need. It's not a preorder, you don't have to commit to anything; I'm just trying to ballpark what we are going to need so that we don't end up with too much of one thing and not enough of another."

Lottie nodded briefly and took the bagels. "I'll think about it," she agreed.

When she was out of the store, Bella gave a little giggle. "I think you know more about Christianity and what it says in the Bible than you let on," she told Erin. "You pretend that you don't know anything about what our beliefs are, and then you come out with something like that."

"I wasn't exactly quoting scripture," Erin said, her face getting a little warm. "I don't know exactly what Jesus said about little children. I just remember learning some story in Sunday School... and there are lots of paintings of him with kids. I don't remember the details."

Bella nodded. "Yes, 'suffer the little children to come to me' and talking about not offending them. Better to be thrown in the sea with a millstone around your neck... something like that."

"See, that's pretty drastic," Erin said, nodding.

Bella adjusted the spacing of the baked goods in the display case. "I think that was the point."

"So then the person who is stealing from kids is doing something worse than if they were shoplifting or stealing copper wire."

Bella nodded. "If you believe those scriptures, yes."

Erin nodded, satisfied.

The next morning, Willie walked into the kitchen of Erin's house and looked around at the flour and cookies covering every horizontal surface. He smiled.

"This looks like fun."

Erin wiped her sweaty forehead with the back of her arm. "We're working," she corrected. Then she gave a shrug. "But yeah, it is fun."

"You've got a little smudge..." Willie told Vic, indicating her chin.

Vic put her hands on her hips. "I've got a little smudge?" she repeated. "This from the guy so stained you'd have to remove the first three layers of skin to find any pink?"

Willie's mining and processing work always left him looking grubby, even though he was good about washing. Whatever methods he used in processing his own minerals left his skin stained dark, which probably contributed to the Bald Eagle Falls opinion that he was the equivalent of a homeless bum, when it was actually a testament of his dedication to his work.

Willie looked at his hands as if he'd never noticed this fact, and grinned proudly. "So, which samples are ready for testing?" he asked, looking around at the various batches of cookies.

"We're experimenting with the colors," Erin said, "they'll all taste the same."

"I think somebody had better test them anyway. Just to be sure." He grinned.

"You'd better save room for supper," Vic warned.

"Why, what are you making?" Willie feigned innocence.

"You're in charge of supper tonight and it better be more than just canned soup!"

"What's wrong with canned soup?"

"Nothing, if you're making lunch for your ten-year-old. When you're making dinner for your girlfriend, something more sophisticated is expected."

"Then I'm going to need enough energy," he pointed out. "A man needs calories after a long day's work, if he's going to have enough energy to make a nice dinner."

Vic rolled her eyes at Erin.

"There's a plate over there," Erin motioned to the counter by the fridge. "Those are the freebies. Everything else is necessary for our scientific endeavors."

Willie strode over and grabbed a couple of green cookies before Erin could change her mind. He took a small bite of each and nodded his head. "Definitely edible."

"They'd better be more than edible," Erin told him.

"I'll have to think about it." Willie took another bite as he headed toward the back door. "Dinner at seven?" he suggested to Vic.

Vic wiped at the smudge on her chin. "Yeah, that sounds good."

He exited and walked across the yard to Vic's loft apartment above the garage. Erin shook her head. "Edible!"

"They're delicious," Vic agreed, "but some of them look pretty disgusting."

"Yeah. It's one thing to offer a lime green cookie. It's quite another to make them puke green."

Vic giggled. They continued to work, making careful notes of the amounts of coloring in each small batch of dough to come up with just the right color in the finished cookies.

CHAPTER 5

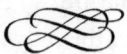

$\mathcal{I}$t was dark when Vic headed home for supper, and Erin puttered around the kitchen tidying away the last few bowls and implements. There was a tap on the back door. Erin looked through the narrow window in the door and let in Adele, the tall, slim redhead who acted as Erin's groundskeeper in the woods behind the house and, in exchange, was allowed to live in the summer cottage on the property.

"Adele, come on in."

Adele still seemed to be avoiding Vic as much as she could. They had all been together for Thanksgiving dinner. Adele had been visibly uncomfortable, but had done her best to be a gracious guest and not show it. Vic, who had been the victim of Adele's estranged husband, was not at all awkward about being with Adele, which seemed to Erin to be a little backward. But Adele was keenly aware of her husband's misdeeds and self-conscious around Vic.

"Evening, Erin." Adele looked around the kitchen. She went to a tray displaying a series of different cookies in varying shades of green and looked down at it. "There seems to be something wrong with your Santas. I think they might be ill. Is it flu season already?"

Erin laughed. "Yes, he's looking rather green around the gills," she agreed. "What do you think of our Grinch?"

"Is that what it is? Yes, I can see that. Once they are decorated. Not bad."

"It was Peter Foster's request. I think all of the kids will like it, anyway. Have you heard about our real-life Grinch?" Erin bit her lip after saying it, remembering that she was not supposed to be spreading gossip about the Grinch around. But Adele was her groundskeeper. She was like a security guard. She was Erin's eyes and ears in the woods and should know about any crimes being committed in the area so that she knew what to look for.

"Your Grinch," Adele repeated blankly, looking around as if Erin might have a new pet she was referring to as the Grinch.

"He's a burglar in the area," Erin explained. "Stealing Christmas presents. So… the Grinch, stealing Christmas, you know."

"Oh. Yes, I might have heard something about that. Have they identified it as one person, then? It's not just the usual holiday thefts?"

"No, the police haven't come out and said that it is a serial burglar. Terry says they haven't been able to figure out whether it is all one person yet."

"So it could just be the usual opportunistic thefts."

"Yes."

Adele nodded. "Well, I haven't seen anything in my neck of the woods. But then, there are not a lot of Christmas presents lying around under those trees."

Erin smiled, nodding and putting away the last few utensils. "I guess not." She turned back toward Adele. "I guess you don't celebrate Christmas, do you?"

Adele kept her affiliation as a practicing Wiccan under wraps, having already been run out of at least one town for being a witch, something that was not well-tolerated in the small Bible-belt towns. She kept to herself and was regarded by the townspeople as being a wise woman knowledgeable in the use of herbs, but kept her actual identity a secret.

"I observe Yule. Winter solstice. It shares a lot of symbology with Christmas, since the Christians chose to borrow the older pagan traditions and repurpose them."

"Do you get together with anyone else to celebrate? It must get kind of lonely living here and not having anyone who shares your beliefs."

Adele studied Erin for a moment, her eyes shrewd. "It can be isolating when you don't have others who share your beliefs… or your lack of beliefs."

"Yeah." Erin let out a stifled sigh. She did sometimes feel rather alone in her own beliefs.

"I maintain a network of friends and practitioners I keep in contact with remotely," Adele explained. "Phone calls, texts, emails. These old-school communications called letters. I am comfortable with keeping my practice personal, for the more part. There are gatherings that I can travel to, if I want to. Maybe sometime I will. But not this year, I don't think."

"That's good. I know you don't want to… *come out,* if that's what you would call it. But maybe you would be able to find more people around here who share your beliefs, if they knew what they were."

"Is that what you have found?"

Erin hadn't exactly found atheists to be popping out of the woodwork to make friends with her because of their shared outlook. Most people in Bald Eagle Falls seemed to either profess Christian values or to keep their mouths shut. Maybe Erin ought to have done the same and not made it known that she was an atheist. But she couldn't imagine trying to live under false pretenses. It would bother her too much to pretend that she was something she was not. Or just to let people think that she was.

"No. I guess not," she admitted.

Adele nodded. "I know Terry is around, so I'm not going to monopolize your time and stay for too long. You've obviously been working hard and you should take some downtime now and spend some time relaxing with him. But I just wanted to mention that I've had… a couple of interesting calls from your sister recently."

"Charley?" Erin tried to think of what Charley would have been calling Adele about. The two didn't exactly run in the same circles.

"Reg Rawlins."

"Oh, Reg."

Reg was one of Erin's former foster sisters. She had made an appearance in Bald Eagle Falls which wouldn't be forgotten any time soon. Her act as a medium who was able to speak with the dead was one thing. Erin didn't approve of the scam. But the disappearing act that she had pulled along with the heirloom jewelry of several clients was quite another thing. The woman had no shame.

"What exactly did Reg want to talk to you about?"

Adele shook her head slowly. "It's a little difficult to follow, sometimes. She seems to have gotten involved with some of the paranormal community out there… I don't know if she's playing them, or they're playing her. Or maybe she's…" Adele looked upward, trying to put her thoughts into words tactfully. "Maybe she's a little bit… different…?"

"Reg has always been different," Erin sighed.

That was an understatement. Reg had driven their foster mother, her social worker, and a myriad of medical professionals crazy trying to figure out how to deal with her. Sometimes she seemed like any other long-term foster child, resigned to the uncertainty of life, doing her best to put on a show of being a good, responsible kid. Testing the limits and chasing new schemes to make money and figure out how she was going to survive once they aged out of foster care. And dragging Erin into her schemes.

And on the flip side, Reg could do magic tricks that freaked Erin out, talked to the air, and acted out so bizarrely that Erin was sometimes sure she was out of her mind.

Adele cocked her head, waiting for further information. Erin sighed. Like Adele, she was trying to be sensitive and politically correct about Reg's more unusual behaviors.

"She has had issues in the past. It's hard to know how to take her sometimes, whether she is putting on a show for you or is… having an episode." Erin shrugged. "I've only heard from her once or twice since she was here, and both times, she sounded kind of… excited."

"Right," Adele agreed. "Quite excited." She put her palms up in a gesture of surrender. "Anyway… she has some kittens that she is trying to find homes for, and she wondered if I wanted one of them."

"Isn't she in—" Erin broke off, remembering that she didn't want to give away where Reg had run to. "She isn't even in Tennessee. If she's trying to give away kittens, she should do it locally. What's she going to do, ship one here?"

"She says they're very special kittens. She's trying to match their personalities up with the people she thinks they would get along with best, and she and the owner of the mother cat are willing to ship one of them here if I want it and they think I would be a good match."

"Don't do it," Erin said immediately. "I don't know what kind of a scam she has cooked up, but don't step into her trap. It will not turn out well."

Adele considered this for a minute, then nodded. "I'll take your word for it. It… didn't feel right, but I thought if she needs help with these kittens and I was thinking about getting a cat anyway…"

"Don't let her talk you into it. You can get a kitten from any of a dozen farms around here, or a stray like Orange Blossom or one that Doc is trying to find a home for. Whatever Reg is up to, it's bound to be some new moneymaking scheme of hers. Maybe she's insuring them and then they get lost in transit, or she's transporting something illegal in the cat carriers. I don't know. She's got something up her sleeve. Believe me, she is not doing this just for the good of the kittens or their owner."

Adele nodded. "Good to know. Thanks for that. I won't get involved, then."

"Do you want to stay for a cup of tea?" Erin offered as Adele started to turn back toward the door.

"Oh, no. You go ahead and take some time with Officer Piper. I am going to walk my rounds."

Erin smiled. It was good to know that someone was keeping an eye on things in her woods, making sure that there weren't teenagers lighting fires or leaving beer cans and other litter behind. She didn't like Adele wandering around alone at night, but that was what Adele wanted, and she was a grown woman capable of making her own choices. Erin felt safer knowing that she was on the job, just like she did with Terry doing his police rounds.

"Okay, have a good night, Adele."

CHAPTER 6

*E*rin tossed and turned restlessly. She tried just to stay still and let sleep overcome her, but Terry had been in and out of bed several times, and it was hard to turn off her worry for him and whether he was still up, pacing restlessly and trying to get his own demons under control, or whether he had fallen asleep in front of the TV and she was the only one still awake and restless.

When she finally drifted off to sleep, her dreams were soon overtaken by visions of Mr. Inglethorpe, one of the most disturbing murder cases she had been exposed to. She relived the horror and disbelief that she had felt when she had seen his body, combined with the terror and despair that had flooded her brain and body when she had realized that Terry had been kidnapped by a crazy woman and could already be dead in a shallow grave or lying injured with his lifeblood draining slowly away. She woke up suddenly, a scream strangled in her throat. She saw a dark shape hovering over her.

She tried to hit, to cry out, to call for help. It wasn't the first time her bedroom had been invaded, and she knew she had to fight for her life if she were going to escape.

"Erin, Erin! It's me. It's okay. You were having a dream. It's Terry."

Erin stopped fighting him off and Terry sat beside her and enfolded her in his arms, holding her close and waiting for her to recover.

Erin broke into sobs, her voice finally released, able to express all of the fear and horror that overwhelmed her. She put her arms around Terry, sobbing into his chest, melting into him.

"It's okay," Terry soothed. "Why don't you tell me about it? Get it out into the open."

She knew that she should; it was the only way to integrate the nightmares with her logical daytime thoughts. The therapists she had seen in the past talked about exposing her fears to the light of day, desensitizing herself so that she could handle the feelings and work through them.

But that operated on the assumption that she could talk about it, that talking about it wasn't just as painful as the nightmares themselves. Talking about it meant not allowing herself to heal from trauma, but continually ripping off the scab that had started to form and making it bleed all over again.

"I'm sorry." Erin tried to wipe her eyes and to stop herself from sobbing. "I didn't mean to wake you up. You had probably just gotten to sleep."

"Don't worry about that." He rocked back and forth slightly and rubbed her back, trying to soothe her. "That's not an issue at all. I'm not working full days. I can have a nap if I need to. I just want you to be okay."

"I'm... I'm okay," Erin sobbed and sniffled.

"Tell me about it." He stroked her hair back from her face.

"Nothing new. Just the same things... the bakery. All of the..." She couldn't bring herself to describe it in detail. She clutched herself to him. "I was so worried when we didn't know where you were." He had heard this often enough to know she had jumped from one story to another. No longer talking about discovering Mr. Inglethorpe, but realizing that Terry was in danger and trying to do something to help him.

"I know you were. I was scared too. It's okay to be scared."

"But not now. Not over and over again. It's over and done."

"It was so big that you weren't able to process it all at once. You're still trying to get through it. To allow yourself to feel it all."

"Is that what you're doing?"

Terry rested his chin on the top of Erin's head and breathed into her hair. "No, I'm trying as hard as I can to avoid feeling it," he said honestly.

Erin giggled. "You're trying to process it too."

"My brain is trying to process it. I don't want anything to do with it. I want to block it all out and not have to feel it anymore."

"Yeah," Erin agreed. She was glad that he could joke about it and be honest with her about what he was feeling. It made her feel just a little bit better about the struggle she was still having.

She wasn't the one who had been hurt. She hadn't been attacked like Mr. Inglethorpe. She hadn't been attacked like Terry and Jack Ward. She had only seen and been a part of the rescue effort. Even then, there hadn't been much she could do but sit and hold Terry's hand or to keep Jack Ward still while they waited for the real professionals to arrive.

Her sobs started to slow and her heart began to beat more normally. The tense muscles of her stomach started to relax, leaving her feeling just a little bit empty and nauseated at the same time. Terry kissed her head, and then pressed her down gently, back into the warm spot in the blankets where she had been sleeping. He continued to rub her back after she was lying down.

"We'll get through it, Erin," he promised. "I don't know how long it's going to take, but we're going to get through it. I don't care if you have to tell me the same dreams a hundred times. Just keep telling me, just keep getting through it. Someday..."

Someday, she'd be able to talk about it and to describe it without the sick feeling in her stomach and the feelings of panic and despair. Eventually, it would just be a story, something she had witnessed, and not a memory that ripped the breath right out of her.

"Will you cuddle with me?"

He moved to the other side of the bed and she knew he was preparing to lie down with her. She always felt better when he was in bed beside her. Except when she knew she was keeping him up with her restlessness. Or when he was swearing under his breath as he tried to find a comfortable position and convince his body that sleep was possible. The doctor had prescribed both of them sleeping pills, but Erin never took hers because she knew they would leave her feeling dopey in the morning, and Terry didn't take his because of some macho feeling that he should be strong enough to force himself to sleep. And he worried that he might be needed at night at some point, even though he wasn't yet back on call.

He cuddled up behind her, molding his body against hers, enfolding her in his arms and breathing in her ear.

"It will be okay. You're going to have a good sleep for the rest of the night. You're not going to have any more nightmares. You will be able to wake up in the morning relaxed and refreshed for the day ahead."

She hoped that the affirmations would have the desired effect on her brain, giving it his 'marching orders' for the night. But she was afraid his words would have no effect at all.

Erin was starting to relax and let her thoughts drift again when Terry's body suddenly jolted. She thought at first that he'd had a 'sleep start,' one of those jerks that she sometimes had as she was starting to fall asleep and then had the sensation of falling and startled back awake. But he turned over and she heard him pick up his phone from the nightstand.

"What is it?"

Terry swore as he read the message that had been sent to him. "There's been another burglary."

"You're not on call."

"No… but they're having everyone available go out."

"Tell them you're not available." She reached out like she could physically hold him back. Like if she just touched him, he would agree to stay with her and not go to the burglary scene. But she knew that he had already made up his mind. He missed the late-night calls, the way that the police department needed him and the citizens of Bald Eagle Falls relied on him. Maybe it was what he needed to do to get his confidence back. Maybe going out to a crime scene was better than staying at home trying to go to sleep when his brain wouldn't quiet down. Maybe it was just the adrenaline rush pushing him into action. A lot of first responders were addicted to that rush. So much that they would make their own excitement if there weren't an actual emergency.

"I can go, Erin. I'm fine. You go back to sleep. You don't need to stay up or worry about me. You have the bed to yourself; I won't be keeping you awake with how restless I am."

He was looking for excuses. Erin slept better when he was there with her.

Most of the time.

Some of the time.

Sometimes she needed him there and nothing else would help her to get to sleep.

"Don't stay for hours. Just long enough to sort things out. Someone else can worry about all of the paperwork and follow up."

"I'll be back as soon as I can," Terry promised. His weight lifted from the mattress and she could hear him pulling on his pants and his duty belt.

"But I don't know when that will be. You might be up already before I get back. Just get some sleep and don't worry about me."

He walked around the bed while he slipped his arms into the sleeves of his shirt and started to button it up. He leaned over and kissed her on the cheek.

"It will be okay. I'm not going into anything dangerous. You know that the crime has already been committed and I'm just helping process the scene and get the case moving forward. Nothing is going to happen to me."

"Okay." She didn't argue with him. Her mind immediately went into overdrive, running through the scenarios of all of the things that could happen to him. All of the different ways that things could go terribly wrong on his way to the scene, while he was there, when he was at the police department offices in the Town Center, or on his way home afterward.

Or maybe they would ask him to put in a shift while they investigated the burglary.

She never knew what things might happen while he was away from her. He had a dangerous job and had nearly lost his life the last time. Who knew how many more times he had been in danger that he had not told her about? Who knew how many more he would face before his number was up?

"I'll see you later," Terry promised. "Sweet dreams."

CHAPTER 7

*T*he day dawned, but Erin was already up by that time, at the bakery, working away on their Christmas offerings. There was plenty to be done as the season approached. The children were getting more and more eager and, throughout the town, there was a rising tide of excitement that surprised Erin.

It had never occurred to her that adults—some adults—anticipated Christmas just as much as the little children. She'd never been big on Christmas herself, and when she had aged out and was no longer forced to attend church masses, bickering family dinners, or respite care while the family and their 'real' children went on a nice vacation, she had ceased to mark the day as anything more than a day off of work. When she had been doing home care for seniors, she had often taken extra holiday shifts to cover for someone else who wanted Christmas off to celebrate with their own family.

But in Bald Eagle Falls, the adults often seemed just as eager to buy their children special gifts, arrange big celebratory meals, or plan other holidays to enjoy the time together as a family. It was kind of nice, making Erin think of old movies with snow and sleighs with bells and Christmas trees that reached to the ceiling. People just didn't do Christmas like that anymore. Or maybe in Bald Eagle Falls they still did, a little pocket of tradition amid commercially catered parties and spoiled brats trying to one-up each other on the best high-tech Christmas haul.

Terry texted Erin just before noon to inform her he was going home and would see her at the end of the day. Erin was glad that he hadn't let the sheriff talk him into working a full day to stay on top of the latest burglary. Or maybe it wouldn't have been Sheriff Wilmot, but Terry talking himself into putting in a full day when his injured brain still wasn't able to do that much work yet. And then he would have a setback and be angry that he couldn't put in the time that he wanted to, and the bitter and disappointed feelings would build until he was impossible to be around.

By the time she headed home, she knew a lot of the details of the latest burglary. It just wasn't possible to keep news from spreading around a little community like Bald Eagle Falls. She hurried home to discuss it with Terry. He might not want to give any details to her, but if she knew them already, he couldn't be blamed for that.

"Can you believe that he had the nerve to steal the Christmas gifts for needy families?" Erin demanded, almost before she was even in the front door. "What kind of a person not only steals families' Christmases, but also steals presents for children who don't have anything else? Who does that?"

Terry was on the couch in front of the TV. He startled at her entrance and rubbed his eyes, blinking at her owlishly. Marshmallow jumped down from his lap and Orange Blossom hurried into the room to get in on the conversation, giving his own input in a loud voice at regular intervals.

"What was that?" Terry asked groggily.

"The children's gifts. Why would anyone do that?"

"I don't think our burglar particularly cares about whose gifts he is stealing," Terry said. He rubbed his eyes. "It seems to be nothing more than where he can get the best haul. And what's better than a charity collection like that? Just load it all into a truck, and head into the city to pawn it or to hawk it on a street corner. Besides, it doesn't exactly belong to anyone. Not yet."

"And you think now that we are dealing with a serial burglar?" Erin asked, noticing that there had been a change in his language.

Terry hesitated. He wasn't revealing the inner workings of the police investigation. He hadn't told Erin anything about suspects or how the burglaries had been committed. He was just answering a general question, one that parents all over Bald Eagle Falls would also want to know the answer to.

"I think," he said slowly, "that we can probably conclude that at this point. This isn't just the normal level of crime seen around this time of year in Bald Eagle Falls from year to year. There is something more sinister at work. Someone who thinks they can get away with this. It's not just opportunistic… it is planned. Carefully orchestrated."

"Who would do something like that?"

"We're going to have to develop a list of suspects. Who knew about the gifts and how to get access to them for each of the burglaries. Any enemies of the families. Who knew their plans at the times the burglaries occurred."

"Because they were all done while the house was empty."

Terry nodded. "Either someone was watching for the houses to be empty, or they knew when the families were going to be away. It's not as easy as you might think to surveil a house for any length of time without people getting suspicious about your activities. People watch out for the neighbors. They don't like strangers sitting in cars for no reason or walking up and down the block somewhere they don't belong."

"So you think it was someone who knew all of the families."

"Or a service provider that was in their homes or had access to their schedules. A cleaner, a dog walker, a carer. People used to pose as telephone repairmen, but cell phones are so ubiquitous now that you don't often see anyone who has anything to do with physical lines. Except maybe in a business. But someone knew when these victims were going to be out."

"And how to get into the Center where the needy children's gifts were being held. They were at the Community Center?"

"Yes. And they're pretty good about not giving out keys without proper documentation. Everyone signs in and signs out. Keys are provided face-to-face, not left in a mailbox. And they have to be returned immediately upon the end of an event. And there is an electronic keypad alarm which they change the code to regularly. It wasn't tripped."

"Was it set?"

"The woman in charge of hall rental swears that it was. But it wasn't set when the police were called. Either it wasn't set, or it was disarmed."

"Or maybe someone cut one of the sensor wires?" Erin suggested, remembering the problems they'd had when her system had been installed.

"We made a thorough check of all of the wiring and sensors. Everything was intact."

Erin rubbed the back of her neck, right below her skull, and thought about that.

CHAPTER 8

*E*rin headed for the front door of the bakery carrying a tray of goodies. She gave Vic a little wave.

"Back in a few minutes, just taking some treats over to Naomi for the book club."

"No problem."

The Book Nook was just a little way down Main Street from Auntie Clem's new location. Erin stepped out into the cool, crisp air of the Tennessee winter, savoring the chance to get away from the warmth of the bakery ovens. The winters in Tennessee—or the one she had experienced so far—had not been nearly as bad as the biting cold of the Maine winters.

The Book Nook had been decorated with garlands and lights, a toy train running in the front window display with various children's books arranged to tempt parents and grandparents to buy books for the kids instead of just the latest electronic gadgets. It was pretty and festive. Vic had put up decorations at Auntie Clem's as well, and while Erin liked them, she did find them a little distracting and would be glad when it was time to put them away again. She preferred the uncluttered lines of the shop to the busy-ness of Christmas.

"Hi, Erin! Merry Christmas!" Naomi greeted in a pleasant voice, clearly enjoying the season, and maybe the extra money that came in from Christmas shoppers. She didn't sound stressed out by the season, anyway.

"Merry Christmas," Erin returned. "I come bearing sweets."

Naomi approached and looked over the tray of Christmas goodies as she took them from Erin.

"These look just great! Oh, and look at your Grinches! Those are wonderful! Perfect for our discussion today." Naomi motioned toward the chairs that had been set up for the book club.

Erin saw the famous Dr. Seuss book set up together with some other classic Christmas books for children. "That's great! Everyone will think we coordinated it. Very professional of us."

"Hopefully, we'll still get a good group today. Things always slow down a little this time of year with people out shopping, going to kids' recitals, parties, all of the other rush and chaos of the season. How about you—are you all ready for Christmas?"

"Uh..." Erin's face heated. She looked away from Naomi, focusing on the titles of the books in the Christmas display. "I actually don't do much for Christmas. I'll be helping Vic to get Christmas dinner together for us, but... I don't do anything special other than that."

"Oh. That must be a bit of a letdown. You don't do anything?"

Erin shrugged. "I'll take the day off. Auntie Clem's will be closed. But other than that... just the dinner with Vic and the others."

"You don't give gifts? What about Officer Piper? Or Vic? Not even to your closest friends?"

Erin bit the inside of her lip. The year before, they had focused on the dinner and other things that Vic wanted to do. Watching some of the cheesy old Christmas movies on TV. Decorating the bakery and the house. The cookies and treats they had made, which ended up populating her freezer at work and at home for several months. Willie had arranged for Jeremy to visit from Moose River, the first person that Vic had seen from her family since leaving home, and Vic had been over the moon.

There had been the trouble with the dognapping ring and returning animals to their families, which had ended up taking most of the day and had distracted people from the fact that they weren't exchanging gifts. But now that Vic and Willie and Erin and Terry were established couples, would it be different? Would they be expecting Erin to conform and spend her time trying to find the perfect gift for each person in her life?

And if she gave a gift to Vic, would she need to give one to Charley, her sister and business partner? And what about her employees? It had mostly been just her and Vic the previous year and Erin hadn't considered giving Christmas bonuses or a white elephant exchange or special gifts to her other employees. She hadn't planned a Christmas party or even just end-of-year celebration for the bakery workers. They were so busy with making sure they had all of the special Christmas treats customers would be looking for to mark the season; it seemed crazy to be trying to plan a Christmas party too.

"Sorry!" Naomi said. "I didn't mean to upset you. I didn't realize that you didn't do anything for Christmas. I don't know why, but I thought…" she trailed off and gave a helpless shrug. "A lot of people who aren't religious still give gifts and participate in the other traditions of the season. We're always complaining that it's too commercial, too secular. So I hadn't really thought about… what people like you do."

"I never really wanted to get into all of that," Erin explained. "Growing up, Christmases were just so awkward, and I never believed in the 'reason for the season,' so… then I was on my own, and it was just a day off. Or a day I put in extra shifts so that others could get it off."

"Well, you're certainly not required to observe it," Naomi said, putting the tray down and straightening it as if getting the edge perfectly parallel with the counter was vitally important. "I imagine you get enough flak about it from the more… devout ladies."

That was one way of putting it. Maybe Erin had set herself up by agreeing to restart the ladies' tea after church services each Sunday, a tradition that Clementine had started when she was running her tea shop. Erin had thought that it would help the ladies who attended First Baptist to accept her in spite of her atheism. And it had; but it also opened her up to a certain amount of evangelism as they tried to 'encourage' her and Vic to attend church services.

Vic was Christian, but had a pretty good idea of how she would be treated as a transgender woman if she were to attend church in Bald Eagle Falls. She and Willie sometimes went into the city over the weekend and, while Erin had never asked, she suspected that Vic occasionally snuck into a church service where her background was not known.

"I should be getting back to the bakery," she observed, preparing to leave.

"Oh, wait for a minute. Don't run away," Naomi protested. "I wanted to ask for your help with something."

Erin hesitated, hovering between staying to see what Naomi needed and returning to her shop rather than facing the awkwardness of the situation.

"I've been talking to some of the other ladies about doing something for the children," Naomi said.

Erin stopped. "What children?"

Naomi took a step closer to establish a more intimate conversation. "There are several families who have been affected by... the thefts this Christmas. Families that aren't going to be able to recover themselves and give their kids a happy Christmas. And maybe it wouldn't be your thing, seeing as you don't observe Christmas..." Naomi hesitated.

"What are you thinking of doing?" Erin prompted.

Naomi's shoulders dipped in relief. "Well, we're looking at doing some fundraising. Or maybe a toy drive. I'm going to donate some books. Some of these families are really hurting. The kids will just be devastated if they don't get anything for Christmas. How do you tell your children someone stole Christmas and you can't get them anything? We may not be able to replace the electronics that got stolen, but we can give them some of the traditional toys—cars, puzzles, board games, books..."

"Those are probably better for their brain development anyway."

"Yes," Naomi agreed. "So... you're not offended by me asking? Whether you're interested in being involved?"

"Of course not. I remember what it's like to be a kid at Christmas when everyone else is getting special presents, and I was sort of... forgotten or a second thought."

"Oh?" Naomi frowned. "I'm so sorry to hear that."

Erin shrugged. "Obviously, I survived it. It doesn't bother me. Mostly the families I lived with did the best they could. Not every child has an ideal upbringing. But if I can do something to help out some of these little guys to at least feel like someone cares this Christmas, I'll do what I can."

"Thank you so much. We're going to have a meeting over at the school tomorrow night if you can make it. Not until seven, so you have time to close and get a bite to eat. And there will be cookies and refreshments at the meeting." She laughed. "I was going to pick up a bag of store-bought, but maybe I could impose on the baker to bring some day-olds?"

"You can have whatever is left in the case at the end of the day. I always have leftovers."

"Awesome." Naomi's voice squeaked. "I'll see you there!"

CHAPTER 9

hey met the next day in one of the classrooms at the school.

Erin hadn't been inside the school before and looked around in interest. It was strangely familiar; a high school room filled with desks and tables much like the ones she had attended, but modernized with technologies that had been developed since she went to school, posters about putting phones away to study, anti-bullying messages, and health messages that were more explicit than anything she had been exposed to at school.

Since it was a high school classroom, the desks were big enough, and though the grown-ups might be uncomfortable sitting in desks once more, they were at least physically accommodated. Most of the adults there had grown up in Bald Eagle Falls and had probably attended classes in that very room.

Erin's platters of cookies and other baking were set up at a station with coffee, hot water for tea, and what was supposed to be cold water for drinking but had been left to sit out for too long. Erin circulated, not hungry and not wanting to be corralled in one of the desks until she had to be, and she visited with the other adults, business owners, the church ladies, and some parents from the PTA, who had come to the meeting.

"If we could all sit down," a middle-aged man with graying hair instructed. "The sooner we can get started here, the sooner we can get done and let you folks get back home."

It was a few minutes while everyone broke off from their conversations and found seats. Then the whispering and scraping of chairs ceased and everyone was still.

"For those who don't know me, I'm Vice Principal Fitzroy. I have been asked to coordinate the efforts from the school's point of view. We can help in identifying which families have the greatest needs and share some information on the children—ages, gender, what some of their interests may be —so that we can get them gifts that are targeted instead of just generic toys thrown in a bin."

Erin nodded, having been on the receiving end of generic charity gifts as a child. Cheap stuff usually, a baby doll or some toy that was intended for a much younger child. Nothing that she was genuinely interested in.

"Naomi from the Book Nook has generously offered to donate some books, and we would like to raise some money to pay for some more, and to get some toys, games, clothes, or other gifts as well. We are looking for ideas for some quick fundraising activities since we don't have much time before Christmas and need to start buying the gifts within a few days. Luckily, it's not Christmas Eve, but we're still going to have to be quick and efficient."

"A bake sale?" one of the women suggested.

"A bake sale," Fitzroy echoed, and he turned around to write it messily on the whiteboard. "Do we have volunteers who could contribute something to a bake sale? We want to catch people before they have done all of their shopping for Christmas treats or we're not going to sell much."

A couple of people turned and looked toward Erin, and she nodded. "We can do a few extra batches of cookies to contribute to a bake sale," she agreed.

"Great. And is there any chance you could be in charge of coordinating others? Gathering everything to a central location, arranging for when and where the sale is supposed to be?"

Erin winced inwardly at being put on the spot. She might not have Christmas shopping to do, but she was already pretty busy with the bakery.

"Uh, let me think about it."

He nodded and wrote her name beside 'bake sale' on the whiteboard. They went on to the next suggestion without further discussion, as if that were all settled. Erin frowned and fished a notepad out of her purse. As they talked about other ideas, she started a list of things that she would need to do if she were in charge of the bake sale.

If she were going to refuse the assignment, then she would need to do it by the end of the meeting so that they could pick someone else. She didn't hear much else that was said as she worked through the logistics of running a bake sale but, in the end, it wasn't too bad a job, and Erin figured she could probably fit it into her schedule with a little help from Charley and the employees at Auntie Clem's.

Eventually, she looked up from her list and at the whiteboard to see the column of other fundraising ideas and names that had been suggested. If they all went ahead, the town would be pouring a lot of resources into those families that had had their gifts stolen or who would have been the targeted recipients of the toys in the needy children's donation bin. But they wouldn't all be able to get off the ground in such a short period of time. Some of the ideas didn't have any names next to them, which meant no one had been volunteered to spearhead them.

She was getting tired as the meeting drew on. Looking at her phone, Erin decided she would give it another fifteen minutes. If things weren't winding down, she was going to have to sneak out anyway. She needed to be up early for the bakery. Other people might not be going to bed until midnight, but she needed to have a few hours of sleep under her belt by that point.

Others were moving around restlessly, feet starting to tap and desks to scrape the floor as people got tired of sitting. Fitzroy nodded and clapped his hands once. "Okay, please contact the people whose names are on the board to coordinate efforts. We won't be able to get all of these things done, but it should be obvious pretty quickly which ones have the most interest and the best potential. I will be the contact point for the school, for both internal and external communications." He looked around at the room. Everyone nodded. Fitzroy smiled. "Class dismissed."

As everyone got up, the room filling with chatter and movement, he turned around and wiped the ideas off of the board that didn't have any names beside them. Erin quickly jotted down the other fundraisers that might be going ahead and stuffed her notepad back into her bag.

"You're the baker," a big man next to her commented. Erin turned and looked at him. She had seen him around Bald Eagle Falls before, but she didn't know who he was.

"Yes," she agreed, giving a nod of confirmation. "Erin Price. Auntie Clem's Bakery."

"I'll have my wife give you a call. She makes a mean banana loaf. Always sells out at the Founder's Day sale."

"Great, thank you, Mr...?"

"Coach Hadrian."

"Oh, you're the coach of one of the teams here?"

"The coach of *all* of the boys' teams," Coach Hadrian corrected. "That's right. It's a big job, even in a town this small."

"It must be. So you know the families of some of the kids who have been the victims of these thefts?"

Hadrian looked grave. He nodded solemnly. "I've been teaching here for a few years, so I know just about all of the families who have teenagers. I think I know most of those who have been targeted. Sad business."

"It is. I don't think that whoever is behind it understands what it is like for a kid who doesn't have anything... how you handle Christmas when all of your friends are getting presents, some of them really expensive, but you aren't getting anything. Or you're getting new socks and underwear. It's tough on kids."

"That sounds like the voice of experience."

Erin shrugged it off. "I met a lot of other families and kids in foster care. You see how it is."

"I can sympathize with those kids."

"You must, or you wouldn't be here today, right?" Erin agreed. "If you didn't care, you wouldn't bother to show up for this meeting."

"That's right. I feel like these kids are my own, I'd do anything for them. And if I have to eat a few extra cookies and banana loafs, well then..." He patted his stomach, which lapped his belt by a couple of inches, and grinned.

"You'll take one for the cause." Erin laughed.

"Exactly."

Vice Principal Fitzroy approached them. He smiled and slapped the coach on the shoulder and nodded to Erin. "Thank you for your help on the bake sale, Miss Price. It's good to have someone with baking experience and good business sense to take control of that."

Erin's face warmed. She usually thought of herself as a blue-collar worker, someone without any education who provided what services she could with elbow grease and not much else. She wasn't used to being complimented for her business acumen.

"I don't know how much business sense I can claim," she said with a nervous laugh. "It's just what I've learned in running Auntie Clem's Bakery."

"That's exactly what I mean. You run a successful niche business that anyone would have told you would fail here in Bald Eagle Falls. You've got feet-on-the-ground experience, not just book learning or some fancy university; you've done whatever it took to make it work, and you've been successful."

Erin started to sweat, embarrassed at the compliments. She nodded again. "Well... thank you. I appreciate that."

"And we appreciate your help on the bake sale. Your contribution will be invaluable. I see you've met the coach."

"Yes, he was just telling me about his wife's banana loaf."

"Excellent. I hope Shirley will send a few our direction."

"Of course she will," Hadrian assured him.

"It's so sad about the families that have had their presents stolen," Erin repeated to the vice principal. "I'm glad that you're doing something to help the families out. Though it will be hard for a lot of families to donate to the drive, won't it?"

Fitzroy nodded. "This is not a wealthy area, so there are many who are already stretched to the limit. But people are remarkably generous, and will still give their widow's mite."

Erin stared at him, trying to translate his words into something that made sense. "What?"

"The widow's mite."

Erin glanced over at Hadrian to see if he understood the reference, and he apparently did. "It's a story from the Bible."

"Oh. You'll have to tell me about it; I don't know that one."

"Jesus watched people donating money at the temple, and many people were giving huge sums of money and showing off how generous they were with their offerings and, consequently, how rich they were. The widow, though, gave one tiny coin, worth very little. But it was all she had."

Erin nodded. "So she gave the most, percentage-wise."

"Exactly," Fitzroy agreed. "And our indigent families are likely to give more than the wealthier individuals. They know what it's like not to be able to give their kids what they want to, and they will give whatever they can, and more."

CHAPTER 10

*E*rin broke away from the classroom as quickly as she felt was polite. A lot of parents and townspeople were still talking and visiting, but she didn't know a lot of them and wanted to get home to bed in good time.

It was dark outside the school, but there were lights on in the parking lot and kids playing basketball nearby, so she didn't feel like she was alone or in any danger. The boys' voices and the echoing bounce of the ball seemed familiar and soothing. The air was cold. Not as cold as Maine, but winter had definitely hit Bald Eagle Falls. There was no snow, and likely wouldn't be, which made Erin a little homesick—just a very tiny bit—for the north. There would be a white Christmas in Maine.

"Hey, Miss Erin!" one of the kids called out.

Erin smiled and turned to see who it was. "Oh, hi Harold." Erin nodded a greeting.

Harold Melville was the son of a family that had recently moved to Bald Eagle Falls, all the way from Nashville. Erin hadn't heard their reasons for moving, but didn't think it had been for Mr. Melville's work. He seemed to be still looking for something steady, taking some early shifts at the grocery store and doing some yard work for local families. Maybe they had wanted to get away from bad influences in Nashville, getting their boys away from the drug culture and other temptations until they were older.

Harold was tall and skinny, a celiac like Peter Foster, who had to avoid gluten to stay healthy. He didn't often shop with his mother and, unlike the Foster children, did not participate in the kids' club for free cookies, but he did stop at the bakery after school some days to grab a muffin or granola bar to hold him over until after a game or practice.

"This is Miss Erin," Harold told the other boys. "She's the baker. She makes awesome food."

"At that bakery that burned down?" one of the others asked.

"Yes. We have a new location now, but the old one did have a fire."

The boy nodded. "My mom says that's for people who need another kind of food. I couldn't eat it, or it would make me sick."

Erin rolled her eyes. "Are you allergic to something? It wouldn't make you sick unless you reacted to one of the ingredients."

"No. But she said it was only for sick people, and that if I ate it, I would get sick."

"Oh, I see. Well, I think she's mistaken about that, but she would know what makes you sick better than I would. It is for people who have celiac disease or some other sensitivity or allergy. But eating it wouldn't normally make you sick. You can eat rice and corn?"

"Yeah."

"Well, I use a lot of rice flour and corn starch, and alternative flours like that. It doesn't give you celiac disease. It just helps people who have celiac disease. Like Harold."

Eyes turned to Harold. Harold spread his hands apart. "I don't want to get sick, and she makes the best ever gluten-free baking. All of her stuff tastes just like it was made with regular wheat flour. Or better!"

Erin smiled. "Thank you for the endorsement, Harold. You are all welcome to come by the bakery when it is open. First customers always get a free cookie."

The way to a teenager's heart was his stomach, and the boys immediately exclaimed over the offer of a free cookie and high-fived each other. Erin smiled.

"Good, you all come by, then. I'll be looking for you."

She turned to find her car.

"I'll walk you to your car," Harold said importantly, striding forward to escort her.

"You don't need to do that. I'm not worried about the security of the parking lot. There's no one hanging around."

"You never know. I wouldn't want anything to happen to you. Then you wouldn't be able to make any more baking."

"Hey, yeah, that's right," the others agreed immediately, and suddenly Erin had an entire vanguard to walk her to her vehicle.

She laughed. "Well, thank you. You are all gentlemen."

"You have to be careful," Harold warned. "You know about all of the burglaries lately? Something could happen to you. We don't want that."

Erin slowed her pace a little, interested in hearing what he had to say. "It's just terrible about the burglaries, isn't it? Do you know some of the families that were affected?"

"Sure. Everyone goes to school here. And even if the families don't have teenagers, we still meet the little kids when we do mentoring or reading buddies. Or we go to church together."

"It's very sad for the little guys especially. You boys, you're almost grown up, so you could understand if your parents couldn't afford to replace the gifts that got stolen. But the little kids, how do you explain to them that Santa isn't coming this year?"

The boys looked at each other. They kicked rocks and elbowed each other as they walked across the parking lot. Erin drew her jacket to herself, feeling suddenly chilly.

"Do you know who the police are looking at?" Harold asked. "I know you and Officer Piper are..." he ducked his head, "you know, a couple... Do you know who they are investigating?"

Erin shook her head. "He hasn't said anything to me. He can't really talk to me about it. Why? Is there someone you think they should be looking at?"

Harold shrugged and looked at the other boys uncertainly. Erin waited to see if they had something to tell her. They dropped their gazes and didn't answer. They reached Erin's car. Erin unlocked it, then stood there, looking at them.

"Do you boys know something?"

"Maybe they should look at people from out of town," Connor Walker said finally. "People who come here to work over the Christmas season... you know... or who have just moved here recently."

"Not me!" Harold said hotly.

"Did I say you, man? I just mean, there are people that you can trust, and there are people who are outsiders… people who ain't from around here and aren't part of the community."

"I'm from Tennessee. My roots go back to these mountains."

Connor rolled his eyes dramatically. "I know, man. Just cool your jets. I'm saying *outsiders.*"

Erin looked at them, wondering, as Harold did, whether they considered her an outsider. She had been born in Tennessee and had lived there in her early years. But as far as any of the young people or those who hadn't known Clementine knew, she was an outsider too, someone who had just shown up in Bald Eagle Falls the previous year and didn't belong there. It took a lot longer than a year for the backwoods Tennesseans to recognize a person as one of their own. But Erin too had the pedigree to prove that she belonged there.

"Is there someone in particular you are thinking about?" she asked Connor.

The boy didn't seem to want to accuse anyone straight out. Erin thought about what he had said.

"Who would come to Bald Eagle Falls for work? It seems like there are enough people in Bald Eagle Falls who are looking for steady employment. It's pretty hard for us to support anyone from outside the community."

They nodded their agreement, faces grim. They had probably all felt the pinch of hard times. Erin studied them. The boys were tall and gangly, adolescent frames that hadn't yet filled out. Fourteen or fifteen years old, maybe. One of them had the shadow of a mustache above his lip. She didn't know any of them well except for Harold. Teenagers didn't come into the bakery very often. Mothers dragged the younger children in and out, but teenagers who were old enough to be left at home or to come and go on their own didn't make it into the bakery. Unless, like Harold, they wanted to grab a muffin between classes. And then they didn't talk to her, didn't identify themselves or tell her what family they belonged to. They just pointed or grunted what they wanted, tapped their bank cards or tossed a few bills on the counter, and were gone again before they could be missed at school.

"*Who* comes to Bald Eagle Falls to work?" Erin repeated.

She wanted an answer. She waited for them to either give in or to sneer at her and walk away. Harold seemed to be the thread holding them to her. He knew and trusted her, so they were willing to talk to her.

"Harold? Is there someone specific you are talking about? Who comes from outside to work in Bald Eagle Falls?"

"Just over the holiday season, you know? There are other jobs created around the holiday, and sometimes people come from out of town."

Erin looked at him.

"Like the Santas," the boy with the mustache contributed.

"The Santas?"

There were Santas. Erin hadn't stopped to think about where they had come from. She assumed that they were Bald Eagle Falls residents like everyone else. But they wore beards that obscured their faces, so she hadn't recognized them or even taken a second look at them. There were always Santas at Christmas. On the street corners ringing bells and collecting charitable donations. In the stores for children to tell their wishes to and to have pictures taken with to send to grandmas. She'd even seen one playing the violin on Main Street a few days before, busking for change.

"They come from outside Bald Eagle Falls?"

"Some of them," Harold agreed.

Erin pondered that and nodded slowly. They were anonymous, practically invisible. They could watch the shoppers coming and going and identify who might have a particularly good haul of electronics or higher-priced gifts. There could be a second person tailing such targets home to see where they lived so that their houses could be burgled later.

"I'll have to ask Officer Piper whether he is looking into them," she told the boys. "Is that what you want?"

They looked down at the ground and their feet and cast furtive glances at each other. They didn't want to tell her outright that they knew something, or to tell her whether they suspected someone. They wouldn't go to the police, and if questioned by the police would undoubtedly deny knowing anything at all about the thefts.

But she was sure they didn't want the burglar to get away. Didn't want him to keep ripping off the families in Bald Eagle Falls and making people unhappy. Especially the children. Especially if he wasn't even from Bald Eagle Falls.

Erin couldn't tell Terry that the boys thought it might be one of the Santas, but she could ask him if he was investigating them. Plant the seed. She wouldn't tell him she had gotten a tip, she would just let him consider the idea and then pursue it on his own.

Harold nodded at Erin, looking at her sideways as if he were embarrassed. "Yeah, maybe you could ask him that," he agreed.

One of the boys tapped the roof of Erin's car twice, and at that signal, they left her there and returned to the basketball court to resume their game.

CHAPTER 11

When Erin got back home, she was ready to cuddle on the couch with Terry for a few minutes to find out how his day had gone, and then to go to bed. It had been a long day and she just wanted to get to sleep.

But when she opened the front door, she could hear voices in the kitchen. She stopped for a moment and listened. It wasn't that she didn't often have people stopping in to visit, and Vic and Willie came and went as they pleased, but she hadn't been expecting anyone, and people generally knew that she retired to bed early and wasn't available to chat past the early evening.

She recognized Terry's voice, but not the other male voice that answered him. She listened for a moment, but couldn't make out their words to get a clue as to the visitor's identity.

But it was her own house. There was no point in waiting at the door or trying to hide or pretend she wasn't there. She walked into the living room and then through the doorway to the kitchen.

"Hi, I'm home."

Terry was leaning against the counter with a can of beer in his hand. He smiled a greeting and looked quickly at his watch. "I didn't realize it was that late. I'm sorry." He turned to his guest. "Erin and I will want some time together before she has to go to bed, so…"

The other man was Stayner, the new deputy who had joined the police department temporarily to cover for Terry's position as he was recovering from his injuries. They had managed to find room in the budget to keep him on permanently as Terry transitioned back to work. Bald Eagle Falls had needed another deputy for some time. Terry had worked a lot of extra hours keeping the town safe and responding to calls. Having Stayner on permanently would allow them to split up the police work and let Terry work a more normal schedule.

Erin smiled and nodded to Stayner, but she wasn't exactly happy to see him there. He was very different from Terry. Not as experienced as Officer Piper, he tended to be a bit of a bully and to rush into things without thinking, assuming that he was always right and making snap judgments that may or may not be correct.

Terry thought that he would eventually wear down the rough edges and Stayner would become steadier and less inclined to make assumptions about people, but Erin wasn't sure it was a matter of his inexperience. It might just be his personality and would remain no matter what his training was.

"Hello, Officer Stayner. Nice to see you," she said politely. She didn't ask him how he was or what he was doing there. She didn't want a conversation with him. Terry had indicated it was time for him to go and Erin didn't want to delay his exit.

"Miss Price," Stayner acknowledged. "Hope you're having a good Christmas season."

Erin looked at Terry. He didn't correct Stayner and point out that Erin was an atheist and didn't observe the season. They just both looked at him.

"Just fine," Erin said finally, feeling that some response was necessary. "And you too, I hope."

"Well…" Stayner drawled the word out, "it's been an interesting one so far. I wasn't expecting quite so much action in Bald Eagle Falls. The theft of the donations for needy children has been a big deal. We're getting a lot of pressure from the community to figure out who stole the toys and is responsible for these burglaries. And they want it solved now, not after Christmas has come and gone."

"That makes sense," Erin agreed. "They all feel vulnerable. They don't want to think that they could have their Christmas stolen away too. Like in the movie."

Stayner looked at her blankly.

"The Dr. Seuss story," Erin clarified.

He still wasn't getting it. Erin cleared her throat uncomfortably.

"The Grinch," she said. "You know how in the Grinch story, he steals away everybody's presents, and trees, and turkeys, and decorations. Every last thing. And even though the people in Whoville still had Christmas and were happy about it, the people here are afraid that their families will be sad and the kids will be traumatized by Santa not bringing them presents this year... you know..."

Stayner nodded slowly. "The Grinch," he repeated.

Surely he had read the story or seen the cartoon or the motion picture. He hadn't lived under a rock. Everyone knew the storyline.

Stayner rubbed his chin, just starting to darken with five o'clock shadow. "Yes, I can understand the comparison," he agreed. "But this isn't a cartoon and people aren't going to get up in the morning and sing in delight if they discover all of their presents stolen."

"Exactly," Erin agreed. "That's just... a fairy tale and people know it. They know that their kids wouldn't be singing on Christmas morning if everything was gone. They'd be crying and complaining, and there would be nothing they could do about it."

"The police department is going to do a toy drive," Terry contributed. "We're going to try to replace as many of the stolen needy children's donations as we can. We might not be able to raise enough in the short time that we have, but we can try. We'll get more than if we don't do anything."

"That's good! I'm doing a bake sale too. And they're organizing some other fundraisers to try to help the families who have had their gifts stolen."

"Might do better collecting donations in the city," Stayner suggested. "They don't have the same connection with the families as Bald Eagle Falls residents do, but then we wouldn't be asking the same people to donate as who couldn't afford to get Christmas gifts in the first place. People are going to get tapped out pretty quickly, between their own Christmas donations and giving what they can to the fundraising efforts. Having ten different fundraisers isn't going to bring in any more money than two if people just don't have the money to give."

"Yeah," Erin agreed. "That's what I was thinking too. Now not only do people have to prepare for their own Christmases, but they have to do extra baking for the bake sale, then buy other people's baking when they don't need it; we're just adding to people's time and asking for more of their money."

"What we need to do is to find the burglars and put them behind bars, and to salvage what we can of whatever they haven't fenced. That's how we get people's' Christmases back."

Erin had to admit that his arguments made sense. But then, that was precisely what he said the people of Bald Eagle Falls were pressuring him to do. Get the burglaries solved, and do it before Christmas. It was a pretty tall order.

It didn't look like Stayner was heading out the door, despite Terry's comment that it was time for him to leave. He seemed instead to be settling into the conversation. Erin glanced at Terry to see if he were going to make another effort to kick Stayner out and, when he didn't, decided to ask her questions and go to bed whether Stayner was still there or not.

"Do you have any suspects?"

Terry pursed his lips and didn't answer. He was always careful about involving Erin in a case or giving her information that was not already public. Stayner didn't seem to have any such reservations.

"We have a few," he offered. "But if you're asking if we have any evidence as to who did it, that's another story. He has been pretty careful not to leave any fingerprints or other hard evidence for us to analyze."

"For burglaries, they've been remarkably clean," Terry agreed. "Very professional. And no broken doors or glass."

"Do you think they were let in? Or that they picked the locks?"

"Can't find anything to suggest that they were let in. The victims have been pretty broken up. I can't see any reason they would have been involved in the break-ins. It isn't like they are putting in huge insurance claims. They're pretty devastated. I don't think that any of the victims let them in."

"So they must have picked the locks."

Stayner nodded. "And the burglar alarms disarmed, if there are any."

Erin couldn't help looking at the control panel for her own burglar alarm. She'd had it bypassed once before, and didn't like to think that there was someone in town who had special expertise in getting around alarms.

Not that anyone would be targeting her. Anyone who knew anything about her would know that she wouldn't have any Christmas presents around or any pricey electronic equipment. She had a computer and a tablet and, of course, her phone, but she wasn't the type of person who bought high-end gadgetry. They were all budget purchases. Things that the boys playing basketball at the school would roll their eyes over.

"Are you looking at people from out of town?" She tried the question that the teenagers had suggested.

Stayner's brows drew down. "Out of town? It isn't like there are a lot of people here who are from out of town," he pointed out.

It wasn't until he said it in that defensive tone that Erin thought about the fact that *he* was one of the most recent arrivals. Surely the teens hadn't thought that Stayner had anything to do with the burglaries...

Though, of course, he *would* have the professional skills needed.

"I just thought... there are a few people who aren't normally here, and maybe they could have been involved."

Stayner shook his head, scowling more deeply. "People here are so insular. They think that it couldn't be anyone they know. All of the crime must have been committed by an outsider."

"No..." He was uncomfortably close to the truth.

"You need to be thinking about some of your friends. William Andrews. Jeremy Jackson. These are men known to be involved in organized crime. They would be just the kind of people to be involved in something like this. Did you ever think of that?"

Erin took a moment to process his comment. Willie or Jeremy? She trusted them both completely. Or almost completely. In the past, she might have wondered whether they were involved in the goings-on in Bald Eagle Falls, but she knew them better now. She didn't believe that either of them would be stealing from the families of Bald Eagle Falls. Not from little children.

In her mind, she saw Willie's dark, stained face, and Jeremy's easy manner and wide grin. Jeremy was always up for anything, and she knew that he had lied to her in the past. And she'd caught him with a bump key which he had used to unlock her door. Could he be supplementing his income through burglary?

And Willie, though he had always treated Erin with kindness and consideration, was involved in all kinds of schemes. Were all of them legal? Terry had often expressed suspicions about Willie's sense of morality. They knew he had worked for five years as a soldier for the Dyson clan. He would have all of the knowledge and training needed for something like the Grinch burglaries.

But would he do something like that? If he saw it as a source of easy income and wanted to supplement what he was making with other ventures?

"It couldn't be either of them…" she murmured in protest.

"Oh, couldn't it?" Stayner challenged. "They don't have solid alibis. You have no idea what they might have been doing at night when you thought they were home in bed. No one can know."

"Well, they have partners. They're not sleeping alone."

Stayner gave a shrug. Erin tried to read his expression. Did he think that the men had snuck out at night without their bedmates knowing about it?

"You don't think that Beaver and Vic are involved too, do you? Beaver is a federal agent!"

"It wouldn't be the first time that a federal agent broke the law or had a… sideline."

"Beaver would never do something like that!"

"You don't know her that well," Stayner challenged. "And even if you think you do, she is trained in deception, in pretending to be something other than she is. So what makes you think that you would know anything about her true personality and motivation?"

Erin stared at him. Erin knew the showy Beaver, the one who made a point of facing off against a drug dealer after rear-ending his car in the middle of Main Street. She knew the Beaver who joked about anything serious and made fun of herself with self-deprecating wit. She had been with Beaver when she was off duty, when her guard was down. And she had seen Beaver relaxed and knew her dry sense of humor and the loyalty she had for her friends. She knew the Beaver who was anxious about Jeremy or Campbell Cox.

But maybe all of those were fronts. Perhaps *none* of them was the real Beaver.

Erin shook her head. "I know Beaver. And Willie too. They wouldn't do anything to hurt a child. Neither one of them would."

"No child has been hurt. It doesn't injure a child or even traumatize them not to get a Christmas present. So they have a quiet Christmas with their family at home and don't get to open a present. How is that going to hurt them?"

"It does. I know what that's like."

Stayner stared at her for a moment, not blinking, then slowly nodded his head. He looked at Terry, who didn't say what he thought of Beaver and Willie or whether the burglar had done anything to hurt anyone.

Terry looked again at his watch. "I'll see you tomorrow, Rod."

Stayner took the hint this time. He shrugged dramatically and headed toward Erin and the kitchen door. Erin stepped back out of his way. He didn't pause or give her any extra space, just barreled by as if she weren't there.

"I'll see you again, Miss Price," he said gruffly.

Erin didn't answer. She watched him leave through the front door. Terry followed and locked the door and armed the burglar alarm.

"Sorry. He was supposed to be gone by the time you got home. Are you okay?"

"Sure." Erin rubbed her eyes tiredly. "I'm fine. He's… you don't believe that Willie or Beaver was involved in these burglaries, do you? That's ridiculous."

"Unfortunately, it's not as ridiculous as you would like to think. I can't talk to you about the details of an investigation. I wouldn't have said as much as he did, but that was his choice."

"You don't think that Beaver could have anything to do with the burglaries."

"What I think doesn't have anything to do with the investigation. That's not my judgment to make. I have to investigate anyone who is identified as a suspect. And as Officer Stayner says… it is possible to get around their alibis."

"But you can say the same thing about anyone. Most of the population would have been sleeping when the burglaries happened. So how could anyone prove that they were in bed asleep when everyone else was in bed asleep?"

"Some people don't sleep soundly enough for their partner to sneak out. But again, how do you prove that? Establishing alibis is only one part of the process. We will be investigating motives, where the suspects were at the time of each of the burglaries, not just one. If they have been seen doing anything suspicious, making unusual purchases, or seem to have more money or high-priced items than normal. Investigating."

"But you don't think it's either of them."

Terry didn't move or speak for a minute, his lips pressed together in a thin line as he considered his answer. After a while, he shook his head. "No.

I don't think it's Willie or Beaver. But that's a gut feeling, a feeling that I have because they are our friends. I can't go by that. I have to remain unbiased."

"I know." Erin took a couple of steps to close the space between them and wrapped her arms around Terry. She was glad to know his opinion, even if he weren't allowed to rely on his feelings. He didn't think it was Beaver or Willie either. And he had to be right. He was a good cop.

"You need to go to bed," Terry said, rubbing her back in firm, soothing circles. "You must be exhausted."

"I am. Or I was. I'm not sure I am anymore." The discussion with Stayner had gotten her wound up. She wasn't sure she was going to be able to quiet her brain if she went straight to bed. "Maybe we can have a cup of tea and relax for a few minutes first."

"Sure." He kissed her forehead gently. "Why don't you get your jammies on and I'll start the tea?"

He wasn't much of a cook, but he was certainly qualified to start the water heating. "Thanks. That sounds really nice."

CHAPTER 12

*E*rin was clumsy in her morning duties and nothing seemed to be coming together the way it was supposed to. Erin had been working at the bakery for long enough that her hands knew what to do without her brain, yet she just couldn't seem to get it together.

"You look tired," Vic commented.

"I am tired, I guess."

"Get to bed late last night? How long did that school meeting go? I'm sorry I didn't get there, but Willie and I had some errands to run in the city, and they really couldn't wait."

"No need for both of us to be there. I don't think you would have provided any additional benefit. You might as well have gotten done what you needed to."

"I guess. But I don't like to see you having to take everything on. How did it go?"

"Fine." Erin stifled a yawn. "It didn't really run that late, but then when I got home, Officer Stayner was talking with Terry, and then I couldn't settle down right away…"

Vic made a sympathetic noise. "You should have said something. We could call someone else in. We have enough people on staff now that you don't need to take it all on yourself, you know."

"I'm not. And I wouldn't have been able to sleep late anyway. Once I hit my usual wake-up time, my body is just too disrupted to get any more rest. I might as well be up and baking."

She bent down to get a better look at the batter the mixer was swirling around and banged her head on the arm of the mixer.

"Oof. Okay, maybe there are some things I shouldn't be doing." Erin rubbed the spot she had hit. "Ouch. That hurt."

Vic was trying to suppress her giggles but wasn't having much success. "I'm sorry! I'm not laughing at you. Really."

"You're laughing with me."

"Exactly."

"I'm not making change today. You'd better be on the till."

"I think so, or we might be bankrupt by the end of the day."

They worked together in silence for a while.

"We're supposed to be making extra cookies for this bake sale thing?" Vic inquired.

"Yes. A few dozen should do it. I'm thinking of doing more Grinch cookies, packaging them individually. Buy a Grinch to fight the Grinch."

"Oooh, good idea."

"I don't know how much money it is going to bring in, though. It's like Officer Stayner was saying last night. People don't have the money. It isn't that we need to be clever and think up more ways to persuade them to give. They just don't have the money. It doesn't matter whether it is a cookie or a book."

"Well… we'll pray it's enough."

Mary Lou Cox was by for her baking that afternoon. Erin smiled, happy to see that the neat, trim woman with ash-blond hair was out and about and looking like herself. She had been very worried about Mary Lou since her son had been arrested at Thanksgiving dinner for possession of illegal drugs. It had not been an easy time for her, even when they had managed to prove that the drugs had been planted in Campbell's car. Some people would always believe the bad about people. Even if their opinion was proven wrong, they could never quite let it go.

"Hi, Mary Lou. How is it going?"

Mary Lou smiled and smoothed her pantsuit. "I'm well, Erin." She hesitated before offering, "You're looking a little worn."

"Oh, does it show?" Erin rubbed her eyes, hoping to erase any trace of puffiness.

"Have you been doing too much? With Christmas coming, you must be very busy with your baking."

"Yes, it's busy. And I don't always sleep the best. But it's been manageable." She stifled a yawn. That was the trouble with thinking about being tired. Just the suggestion was enough to make her start yawning. "I was just up a little late last night. We had that meeting at the school…" Erin had seen Mary Lou there, but had not stopped to talk to her. Mary Lou had seemed occupied in discussions with others, and Erin had been impatient to get home, not realizing she would end up not being able to sleep anyway.

"Of course," Mary Lou agreed. "It was nice of you to volunteer for the bake sale."

"Well, I didn't exactly, but it was fine. I guess I'm the most obvious choice."

"Volunteering at the school isn't like volunteering in other places," Vic put in. "If you don't object loudly enough, you just accepted."

"Yes, that's exactly what happened." Erin laughed. "I was volun-told."

"If it is too much, then you can say so," Mary Lou advised. "People do drop out of assignments."

"I'll manage. We're going to do some Grinch cookies. You know, so people can help fight off the Grinch."

"That's clever. You always have such interesting ideas."

Erin wasn't sure it was a compliment. *Interesting* ideas rather than good ideas.

"How are you guys doing?" she asked. "And how's Campbell?"

"We're hanging in there. Campbell will be home for Christmas… I don't know for how long, but…" She shrugged, trying to look like it didn't matter to her. Of course it did. She would want Cam to spend at least a few days home. Since his arrest had ruined their Thanksgiving, it was only right that he try to make it up by spending some quality time with his mother and brother. And they would, Erin assumed, make some time to visit Roger in the facility where he was incarcerated.

"And Josh…?"

"He's still in school, that's about all I can say. He doesn't say much to me about how he is doing. I haven't had calls from the school saying that he's failing or missing classes. But he's not doing any of the things he used to do, the sports and after-school activities. He doesn't bring friends home. I don't know who he's spending time with at school, if anyone."

Josh had seemed like such an honest and caring person when Vic and Erin had spent time with him in the city. It was hard to believe, with his level of maturity, that he was still a teenager. The two boys had been through a lot in their young lives, and it showed in the way they behaved, Campbell falling apart and abandoning his old life for something fleeting and uncertain in the city, and Joshua trying the best he could to keep it together, but clearly struggling. He wanted his brother to come back, or at least to know that he was safe. And he tried to protect his mother and not make her unhappy. But he couldn't keep doing everything he had previously, being an all-star and honor student and working to contribute to the family income.

"I wish I could help," she told Mary Lou. "He seems like such a great kid."

The lines in Mary Lou's face softened. "He really is," she agreed. "He's not perfect. None of us is. He's no angel. But he's a good kid, caring kid, and I hate to see him drifting."

Erin decided she would try to talk to Joshua. Maybe there was something she could do or say that would make a difference. Or perhaps she could ask Beaver for suggestions. Beaver had been in contact with Cam, and she'd talked to both boys after the ill-fated trip to the city, so maybe she would have some insight into the best way to help Josh.

"At least he's still in school. You don't have to worry about where he is or what he's doing during school hours."

Mary Lou sighed. "Hopefully. You never know how well they are keeping track of the kids. Not all of the teachers take attendance regularly."

"I'm sure you'd hear about it from someone if he was getting into trouble."

CHAPTER 13

*E*rin arrived home and tiredly put down her purse and greeted Terry. K9 jumped to his feet to nose at her hand and get ear scratches, and Marshmallow hopped over to get his share as well. Erin frowned, looking around.

"Where's the other critter? Is Blossom pouting because of K9?"

Terry looked around, thinking about it. "I haven't seen much of him today. He was yowling this morning, but he must be in the bedroom sleeping, I think."

It was unusual for Orange Blossom not to meet her at the door unless he was upset about something. Erin tried to think of what it might be as she walked down the hall to the bedroom and peeked in, expecting to see him sleeping on mussed-up blankets on her bed. But he wasn't there. She looked around the room and under the bed.

"Terry? He didn't get out, did he? I don't see him."

"I haven't been out or had the door open. He has to be here somewhere."

Erin looked under the bed again with her phone switched to flashlight mode, just in case she had missed him. But he wasn't there. She checked the closet in case he had been shut in there. Then she headed for the bathroom. Blossom had shut himself in there before, and Terry might not have noticed the reason for his meowing to be let out, thinking he was just being vocal.

But the bathroom door was open a crack. Erin glanced in and didn't see him there.

A search of the rest of the house and calling to him turned up no results. Erin returned to the bathroom to check it again, and realized that her furry friend was hunched up behind the commode.

"Terry? There's something wrong."

Erin made calling noises to Orange Blossom and put out her hand, expecting him to come to her. But he just looked at her with glazed eyes and didn't move. Erin dragged him out.

"Oh, Blossom. What's wrong? What's wrong, baby, huh?"

She petted his too-dry fur and examined his face, mouth, and belly, looking for any sign of what was wrong. He had feces caked on his backside, and just lay there listlessly as she poked and prodded him.

Terry appeared in the doorway. He immediately looked concerned.

"What's wrong?" he asked, kneeling down and squeezing in beside her.

"I don't know. He's sick. How long has he been like this?"

"I haven't seen him most of the day. He was okay when you left, wasn't he?"

"Yes, everything was normal this morning."

Terry did an examination similar to Erin's, but she was more confident in his. He had grown up around cats and other animals and she had not.

"Wrap him up in a towel and let's get him over to Doc's."

"He'll be closed."

"I'll call him. Get Blossom ready to go."

"Okay."

He got up. With tears in her eyes, Erin pulled one of the towels down from the rod beside her and carefully wrapped the cat up like a burrito. He didn't struggle and only made one low moan of protest. For a cat who was usually so loud, his silence was the scariest part.

She could hear Terry making a phone call. By the time she got to the door, he was hanging up. He scooped up her purse and led the way out to the car.

"I'm so sorry, Erin. I should have noticed that something was wrong. It didn't even occur to me that he hadn't been underfoot all day."

"It's not your fault. I'm his owner, I should have known he was sick. What do you think it is? He hasn't been around any other cats to catch something. I couldn't see any injuries. Cats don't just get sick for no reason, do they?"

"They can get sick just like any other animals. Just pray it's nothing serious. Doc will sort him out."

In a few minutes, they were at the vet's office. Doctor Edmunds was there to let them in. He looked at Orange Blossom's face sticking out the end of the towel wrap and led the way to one of the examination rooms.

"Bring him right here. Let's have a look at this little fellow and see what's wrong."

Erin put her bundle down on the examining table. Orange Blossom felt light and frail.

The doctor unwrapped the towel and began his examination, palpating the cat's stomach, using his stethoscope to listen to his heart and respiration. He checked Blossom's eyes, ears, and mouth, and used some wipes to clean off the cat's backside and check for problems there. Erin watched anxiously, waiting for his diagnosis.

"Has he been outside?" Doc asked.

"No, not lately. I take him out sometimes just into the yard, but he hasn't been out for a few days. He hasn't been around any other animals, just Marshmallow and K9."

Doc's eyes went to the open examination room door, where he could see Terry and K9 waiting. "K9 looks like he's fine."

"Yes. He and Marshmallow both seem perfectly normal."

"Has he changed his diet? Litter box habits?"

"I didn't know anything was wrong until I got home from work. That's the first sign that he was sick. He was okay this morning."

"Energetic this morning?"

"Yeah. He was just the same as any other morning. Talkative, playful, demanding to be fed."

He nodded. He petted Orange Blossom gently as they talked. "Could he have gotten into household cleaners, antifreeze, weed killer, or rodent poison?"

Erin shook her head. She was always careful to put such things out of reach. "No, I don't think so."

"You're a baker."

"Yes."

"But you probably don't do much baking at home, just at the bakery?"

"I experiment at home, developing new recipes."

"Could he have gotten into chocolate or another baking ingredient?"

Erin hesitated. While she didn't feed him people food other than a bit of whatever meat she was cooking, she never worried too much about him eating something that had fallen to the floor, and more than once had found him nosing around in the pantry between meals.

"It's possible. I didn't see anything he'd gotten into, but I rushed him straight over here without checking the kitchen or pantry."

"Let me know after you go home if you can tell what he might have eaten. I'll treat him the best I can, give him fluids and try to neutralize whatever might still be in his digestive tract, though it looks like whatever it was has probably already moved through and he's absorbed whatever toxins were present." He stroked Blossom's head. "His heartbeat is still strong, but he's feeling pretty rotten. This is probably as bad as he'll get, but we'll keep an eye on him and do whatever we can to help him recover."

Erin nodded, her eyes brimming with tears.

"Now, I can do some tests on liver and kidney function, but unless you're willing to do dialysis or other extreme measures, that's just an extra expense."

Erin swallowed. "Let's see how he does before spending a whole lot." It was not an easy decision to make. She wasn't sure whether it was the right one. Should she do everything she could no matter what the cost?

The vet nodded his agreement. "Okay. Why don't you say goodbye to him for now, and I'll take him back and get an IV going. Just getting fluids into him will make a big difference, he's quite dehydrated right now."

Erin bent down over Orange Blossom, giving him a gentle hug and snuggle and kissing the top of his head. "I'm sorry I have to leave you, buddy, but the doctor is going to help you to feel better." She scratched his ears and chin and gave him one final pet. "Okay," she told Doc Edmunds.

He scooped Orange Blossom up and held him cuddled against his body. "We'll take good care of him, mom. I'll give you a call in the morning to let you know how he's doing."

Erin returned to Terry, tears spilling down her cheeks.

CHAPTER 14

$\mathcal{V}$ ic walked into the kitchen in her usual familiar manner, already chattering about something she had heard or maybe something about what she and Willie had done the night before. She got a good look at Erin and stopped mid-sentence.

"Erin? What's wrong?"

"It's Orange Blossom."

Vic immediately cast her eyes around and, not seeing the cat, looked back at Erin, her face pale and mouth partly open. "What happened? Did he get out?"

"He's sick. Terry and I took him to the vet last night. I won't know how he's doing until later this morning." Erin sniffled. "It's just really hard to wait."

"Sick? Sick how?"

"Doc thinks maybe he got into something. Chocolate or a household chemical. But I'm pretty careful about things like that. He might have gotten into something in the pantry, but I don't see anything spilled or knocked over. Nothing that he's gotten into. Maybe I let him eat something that had fallen to the floor while I was baking and it ended up making him sick…"

"Oh, honey!" Vic stepped forward and enfolded Erin in a soft hug. "Hey, It's not your fault. Don't blame yourself. You know how cats are;

they're curious about everything. They get into things. He'll be okay, won't he? What did Doc say?"

"He thought Blossom would get better. He was really dehydrated, Doc was going to give him an IV and wait and see…"

Vic released Erin and patted her on the back. "I'm sure he'll be okay. They'll have him fixed up in no time. I'm so sorry, I didn't know he was sick."

Erin forced a smile. "Yes, he'll get better. I'm sure everything will be fine."

Erin was keeping a close watch on the clock as she worked at Auntie Clem's. What time would Doc be at the clinic and call her back? Eight o'clock? Nine? If there were an emergency or a desperate case, he might forget to even call her.

At least if he didn't call her, that at least would suggest that Orange Blossom was doing well. If he were in dire straits, Doc wouldn't forget to call her with an update.

Vic noticed Erin's frequent looks at the clock, but just raised an eyebrow and didn't make any comment.

Finally, at about five minutes past nine, Erin's phone vibrated. She pulled it out and looked at the face.

Veterinary clinic.

Erin swiped to answer the call and held it up to her ear. "Hello?"

"Miss Price, Doc Edmunds here. Did you get any sleep last night?"

"Not much," Erin admitted. "I was pretty anxious."

"Well, your little friend is feeling a lot better this morning. Not one hundred percent; I'd still like to keep an eye on him until at least the end of the day, but I am encouraged."

"Oh, good." Erin blew her breath out and gave Vic a thumbs up. "Thank goodness for that. So you think he'll be okay?"

"It's quite an improvement over last night. I'd like to see him eating and having normal elimination to show that everything is in working order. Then the best thing for him will be to be back home in his familiar environment."

"Maybe tonight?"

"Hopefully, yes."

"I'm so glad! Thank you for calling me."

"All right. We'll talk later. Give me a call when you're getting off work."

The day had dragged on incredibly long. Erin had felt like she would never get to the end of it. They managed to get the last few customers out of the bakery a little before the time that they would normally close, flipped the sign over to 'closed,' and did their usual tidying up and preparation for the next day. Erin felt like she was fumbling with everything instead of working smoothly as she normally did. She just wanted to be out of there and to get to the vet's to see Orange Blossom.

"We can probably leave it at that," Vic said, looking around. "If there's anything else, we can catch it up tomorrow."

"I don't know, I should probably..." Erin trailed off. She wasn't getting done the tasks that she knew she needed to get done; what was she doing trying to add to the list? Vic was right. Everything else could wait. They had the essentials done. "Okay. Let's go."

Vic smiled. They gathered their purses, phones, and keys, and headed for the door. Erin hit the crash bar on the back door and, when she reached the car, looked back to see where Vic was. Vic came through the door shaking her head.

"What is it?" Erin asked.

"Just arming the burglar alarm, boss."

The blood rushed to Erin's face as she looked back and realized she'd just bolted out of the bakery without even thinking of the burglar alarm. "You'd think that after all that has happened around here, I would remember about the security!"

"Your mind is on other things right now. It's called mommy brain."

"Well... I'm not sure if I can claim that, but I certainly am worried about my 'baby.'"

It was a good thing that they didn't have far to go to get to the vet's. Erin was rattled by forgetting to arm the burglar alarm, and kept making simple mistakes in operating her car, which she'd had for three years, so it wasn't like she didn't know how to drive it. She hit the windshield wipers instead of the turn signal, hit the brakes too hard, and was generally jittery.

Vic didn't say anything about it, but Erin was sure she was wondering if her boss were losing her mind.

They pulled into the empty parking lot and Erin urged the car gently into a parking space and shifted it into park.

"He knows you're coming, right?" Vic asked. "He was going to wait for you?"

"Yes. It's closed, but he said he'd be here waiting for me."

They approached the doors and found them still unlocked. Doc Edmunds strolled into the reception area when he heard the door, and smiled at Erin.

"Right on time, Miss Price. Ready for your furry friend?"

"Am I ever! I've been on pins and needles all day. Or is it on tenter-hooks? I can never remember which is right."

He chuckled and motioned her into the same examination room that she had taken Orange Blossom into the day before.

Blossom was already there, lying on a clean towel, curled up in a ball. At Erin's entrance, his head popped up and he looked at her with an expression of affront. Erin didn't know if he was upset because she had awakened him, or because she had left him there all day. He certainly did appear to have his nose out of joint.

"Hey, Blossom! How are you doing? Are you feeling better?" She petted him and gave him a gentle hug. "Are you ready to go home?"

He let out a groan that sounded like an old man's, then slowly straightened his body until it was all in a line. He stretched his hind legs out and spread his toes, a shudder running through his body as he got everything ready to go. Erin bent over and kissed him on the top of the head.

"It's good to see you looking normal again." She looked over at Doc. "Though, he'd normally be scolding me and pacing, yowling to go home."

"Yes, he's not one hundred percent, but he's on the mend. He'll prob-ably sleep a lot over the next few days and not have all of his usual energy for a while yet. He needs a chance to recover. But he can do that at home and doesn't need to stay here."

"Good. Thank you so much for helping him. I don't know what I would have done if…" She couldn't even finish the thought out loud. She'd grown very attached to her furry baby.

Blossom pawed at Erin, then reached up and put both of his front paws onto Erin's chest, standing up tall to bump her with the top of his head. Erin scratched his ears.

"Yeah, good to see you too. Shall we go home?"

He allowed Erin to pick him up and cuddled against her. Erin looked at the vet. "What do I owe you?"

"I'll email you and you can e-transfer. Sarah has gone home, and I always mess up with the point-of-sale machine."

"Okay, thanks."

"I sent some samples off to the lab to see if we can identify what he ate. You didn't discover anything that he had gotten into?"

"No, I checked the pantry and everywhere else I could think of, but I couldn't find anything open or spilled. I don't know what it could have been."

"We may find out, or we may not. It will be a while before the results come back."

"Okay. Let me know... I'll get rid of it, whatever it is."

"Of course."

Erin and Vic walked back out to the car. Orange Blossom looked around, but didn't struggle or make any attempt to jump out of Erin's arms. He seemed completely content to stay with her, wherever she was going.

Once in the car, though, Vic held her arms out. "You can't drive with him in your lap. Give him here."

Erin reluctantly relinquished the cat to her friend.

"It's only for a few minutes, and then you can have him back again."

"I know." Erin concentrated on driving, even though tears were blurring her vision. She'd been doing too much crying lately, and it bothered her. Vic either didn't notice, or didn't see the need to draw attention to the fact.

Then they were home. Erin gathered Orange Blossom back up in her arms and took him into the house. The cat kicked to be free as soon as she got him into the house, unlike his sedate behavior at the vet's office. Erin released him, putting him down on the floor.

He immediately started sniffing around to make sure that everything was as it should be and that she hadn't moved furniture or gotten a new cat while he was gone. Marshmallow hopped over to smell him and Orange Blossom gave him a few licks, something that he rarely did.

"Yeah, we're glad you're home," Erin murmured. "So glad that you're feeling better."

CHAPTER 15

*E*rin stopped at the grocery store to pick up a few necessities for the next batch of Christmas treats. It was bustling with shoppers and energy; she could feel the excitement of the holiday building as people tried to get everything together that they would need for their Christmas celebrations.

There were Christmas decorations up at the store. Garlands around the checkout stand poles, painted windows, and various other little touches that Erin knew she wouldn't see at one of the grocery stores in the city. It was nice to be in a small town. They really did go all out to make it nice for people.

As she waited for the cashier to check her items through the checkout, Erin's eyes landed on a Santa outside the store. The beard and body suit obscured the man's identity. She didn't know whether it was someone she knew or not. It would be pretty easy to get around town without anyone ever knowing who you really were in an outfit like that. She watched the man ringing his bell for donations. He watched the people coming out of the store, wishing them a Merry Christmas and angling for a donation to his pot.

Did he seem just a little too interested in what was in people's carts? Was he looking for some high-priced items that would be worthwhile stealing later?

Erin shook the thought off. People coming out of the grocery store? It wasn't like they were buying electronics or expensive children's toys, clothing, or jewelry at the grocery store. They were buying food. Turkey, stuffing, potatoes, and whatever else they wanted for their tables this year. And even though she called the burglar a Grinch, she didn't think he was actually interested in stealing every vestige of the Christmas spirit. He only wanted the high-value stuff.

"Erin?"

"Hmm?" Erin realized that the cashier was waiting for her. "Oh, sorry. Lost in my own little world. Who is your Santa this year?" She entered her PIN on the keypad.

The cashier looked out the front window. "He's not actually one of ours. Salvation Army, I think. They have them everywhere, you know."

"But he's on your property."

"No one minds. They can pretty much set up where they want. I know there are rules about business licenses and busking and all that, and where you are allowed to ply your trade, but it's for charity. Nobody really cares where the Santas set up at Christmas."

Erin nodded absently, thinking it through. She put her packed groceries into the shopping cart and pushed it out the doors, keeping an eye on the Santa.

She couldn't see his face well behind the beard, but he seemed to be a fairly young man. He gave her a hearty 'Merry Christmas' and rang his bell, watching to see if she would donate. Erin slowly took out her wallet, examining him.

"Who's under there?" she asked him. "Do I know you?"

"No ma'am." He took a step to the side to allow her to reach the donation pot, but she thought he was also doing it to distance himself from her. "I'm not from around here."

"Oh… do you do this every year, or…?"

He 'Merry Christmas-ed' a couple of other shoppers, shooting Erin an irritated look. "Times are tough. I'll take work wherever I can get it."

Erin nodded sympathetically. "Do you have a family?"

"I'm just trying to work, here, ma'am."

"I just thought maybe…" Erin pulled another bill from her wallet and held it out to him. "For you. For your little one."

He stood frozen for a moment, looking at her. "We're not allowed to take tips. All donations have to go into the pot."

But he reached his hand out, fingertips extending toward the cash.

"I already put money in the pot," Erin said. "You're not taking from the Salvation Army. This is for you and your family."

He took it from her, shoving it into his pocket and glancing around to see if anyone was watching.

"It's so sad," Erin said, "about all of the burglaries, isn't it? I feel bad for those families."

"Burglaries?"

"Our Grinch," Erin said, forcing a little laugh. "Stealing Christmas presents from families around here and from the needy children's collection."

He poked at his pocket, making sure that the money was going to stay there and was out of sight. "I don't know anything about that. I drive in, I do my bit, and drive home."

"Oh. Right." Erin couldn't see any way to draw the conversation out any further, and started to push her cart toward her car. "Well, Merry Christmas. I hope you make enough to have a nice time with your family."

"Merry Christmas," he repeated. He turned away from her and rang his bell vigorously at the next person coming out the doors.

Erin packed her groceries thoughtfully into her car.

How would anyone from out of town know which houses to hit and when? Whoever had been stealing from families appeared to have known their schedules. They hadn't just been crimes of opportunity; they had been carefully planned. She couldn't see how someone from out of town would be able to do that. Unless they had an accomplice inside Bald Eagle Falls to feed them information.

CHAPTER 16

*I*t was a few days before Erin saw Beaver. A few days and a couple more burglaries later. Terry's mood was not good; the police department wasn't getting much further ahead on the case. He was getting dark circles around his eyes, and his answers when Erin tried to engage him in conversation were getting more terse.

Erin and Vic had Saturday off and had made arrangements for morning brunch with Beaver at the family restaurant. The restaurant always put on a nice brunch buffet. It was a more relaxed morning than Erin was used to, a nice break from her usually busy pace.

Vic looked from her plate with an eggwhite omelet, one buttermilk pancake, and berries, to Beaver's plate heaped with food, and shook her head.

"Where do you put it all?"

"I'm a very active person," Beaver said with a wide grin.

"Wow. You must be, to burn all of that off."

"It's also probably the only real meal that I'll have today. Jeremy is off doing his thing, and when I'm on my own, I tend just to graze. There's not much around the apartment. I'll pick up some fruit and granola bars, and that will do me the rest of the day."

Vic nodded.

Beaver turned to Erin. "So how is the investigation going?"

"What?" Erin was momentarily confused. She wasn't investigating anything.

"The Grinch. Have the boys in blue made any progress?"

"Not much," Erin admitted. "Not that Terry would tell me about it if they had; it's not any of my business. But from his mood… no, they're not getting anywhere."

Beaver started to work her way through her heaping plate of food. She chewed thoughtfully.

"There have been daytime burglaries as well as the evening break-ins. That says something about the burglar."

Erin considered. "Not someone who works all day."

"I would say not. Of course, it could be someone on shift work who is off some mornings, or someone could call in sick in order to commit a burglary. But my gut says not. This is someone who only works sporadically, if at all."

"That narrows it down a bit." Erin didn't say anything to Beaver about her being a suspect. Or Jeremy or Willie. Other people in Bald Eagle Falls fit the profile. Or it could be someone from outside of Bald Eagle Falls or someone who had just arrived recently. She didn't like to consider the possibility of one of her friends being involved. "What about someone like… someone who is just visiting Bald Eagle Falls? Someone who got some seasonal work for Christmas. Maybe a retail store or Santa Claus or Salvation Army."

"Possibly, but I think that's less likely. A stranger would be noticed. You are looking for someone who knows people's habits—when they are likely to be home or away. Someone who would know about the charity toy drive and where the donated items were kept. Someone new in town or visiting… I can't see that working."

"Unless he also has a Bald Eagle Falls contact," Vic suggested. "Someone who could give him that information."

Both of these conclusions matched Erin's thoughts on the subject.

"Right," Beaver agreed. "That would, of course, be a possibility as well. We may be looking at a group of perpetrators." She ate some more, then tapped her fork on the table as she thought. "A group of people would be a real possibility, based on the facts that I'm aware of."

"Do you want to suggest it to Terry?" Erin asked. "If I say something about it, he's going to think that I'm sticking my nose where it doesn't belong."

"And he won't think that about me?" Beaver asked with a chuckle.

"Well, at least you're law enforcement. I'm not, and he always gets irritated about me getting mixed up in things that the police are supposed to be investigating. And besides—you don't live with him."

"No, thank goodness."

Erin raised her eyebrows. "What is that supposed to mean? You like Terry."

"Officer Piper does a fine job. He is very conscientious. But he's not my type."

The comments that other women in Bald Eagle Falls usually made about Terry were envious comments about his good looks and how admired he was in the community. And then there was K9. The combination of a handsome officer in uniform and his cuddly-looking companion was enough to set most of the women swooning. They all told her how lucky she was. It was startling to hear a dissenting opinion.

"Too old for you?" Vic suggested to Beaver.

Her question made Erin wince. While Vic had not said much about it, Erin suspected that she had some issues with the older woman dating Vic's brother. Though Vic couldn't really object, considering that the disparity between her age and Willie's was considerably greater than that between Beaver and Jeremy. But dating an older woman was still not quite as acceptable in society as dating an older man, at least not in rural Tennessee.

Beaver was unfazed by Vic's comment. She smiled her usual wide, lazy grin, looking Vic in the eye. "No reason I have to date someone my age, is there, Miss Victoria?"

"No, of course not. I'm just wondering what you have against Terry. Most women in Bald Eagle Falls think he's a pretty good catch."

"I'm not most women. He's fine for someone like Erin, but I prefer someone a little less... uptight."

Erin bit the inside of her cheek to keep from responding. She paid close attention to her brunch. She couldn't deny the fact that Terry was strait-laced. She still didn't feel comfortable talking with him about everything that had happened in her life before moving to Bald Eagle Falls. There were a lot of things in her past that he probably wouldn't approve of. He knew some details of her former life from his previous investigations, but she had kept others to herself.

She cleared her throat and decided it was a good time to change the subject. "Hey, have you talked to Joshua Cox lately? I haven't seen him since... the thing in the city... and I was wondering if you'd had anything to do with him."

"Why?" Beaver asked baldly.

"Well... I worry about him. He's a nice kid, but I worry about what's going to happen without Campbell around, and with all of the stress on the family. Mary Lou worries so much about those boys..."

"Maybe it is time for her to let go and give them a bit more independence."

"She has... but that doesn't stop her from worrying."

"Or you, apparently. Or is this just Mary Lou's roundabout way of getting to me?"

"No. She doesn't know I'm asking. I didn't know whether you'd had anything more to do with Joshua. So I thought... there's no harm in asking."

"From what I can tell, Joshua is fine. He doesn't say much about his personal life. I don't imagine he is enjoying school, but what teenage boy does?"

Erin sighed. "Do you think I should talk to him? Maybe he'd tell me..."

"What would he tell you? Everything that's wrong with his life? I'm not sure why he would tell you that, unless you have some connection with him that I'm not aware of."

"No."

Vic studied Beaver. "Is Joshua doing work for you, like Campbell? Is he an informant?"

"I wouldn't tell you if he was."

"I guess not." Vic laughed. "You wouldn't be much of a handler if you did."

"I suggest you leave the Cox boys alone," Beaver told Erin. "They don't need another parent."

CHAPTER 17

*E*rin headed over to the school to meet with Vice Principal Fitzroy to report on the progress of the bake sale and coordinate timing. She checked in at the office and was directed to a meeting room where Fitzroy was to join her. Erin looked around at the room. Lots of posters on the walls addressing teen social problems, just like in the classroom she had attended at the first time.

Before Fitzroy put in an appearance, Coach Hadrian stuck his head in the door. "Hey, Miss Price, I heard you were here. How's everything coming together for the bake sale?"

"It's coming. I talked to your wife the other day, and she's making those banana loaves like you said she would. We're very grateful for all of the support the bake sale is getting. I think it's going to be very nice. As long as there are as many people to buy the food as there are to make it."

"We usually have a pretty good response to fundraisers. I'm sure we'll have enough people."

Erin cast about for something else to talk with the coach about. "And… how are your teams doing? I didn't get a chance to ask you the other night. Do they play against teams in other towns, or just internally?"

"Most of the year we're just playing intramurals. But toward the end of the season, we'll join in some tournaments."

"So you're not doing that yet.... do you have good teams this year?" Erin looked toward the door to see if the vice principal were there yet. He had arranged for the time to meet, so he should have been there on time.

"They're pretty good. We've lost a few players since last year, so they'll have to play hard to make up for it."

"Do you know Joshua Cox? And his brother?"

"Yes. They were good players. I've talked to Josh a few times to try to convince him to play. I don't know why he had to drop the teams. He wasn't as good at sports as Campbell, but we're still missing him."

"Maybe Campbell will come back next year. His mom is still trying to get him to come back to school. Finish his last year."

"Kids are so shortsighted. Can't he see that he's going to need to finish school if he's going to get anywhere in life? What kind of a job is he going to be able to get if he doesn't even have a high school diploma? But everything has to be immediate for this generation. Instant gratification. He can't see a year or two down the line. He has to have his fun now and isn't farsighted enough to see the consequences."

"It's hard for them." Erin remembered how it had been as a high school student, trying to structure her life so that she would not end up homeless on the street. As much as she would have liked to have dropped out of school and crashed with other friends and not had to worry about money and a place to live, she had known that she had no safety net. She wasn't going to have a home. She wouldn't be able to go back to high school in the future if she didn't finish by the time she was eighteen. Unless she got a scholarship or apprenticeship, she wasn't going to get any more education. "Cam and Joshua have been through a lot lately. It's been very stressful for them. It's hard to concentrate on work or sports when there is so much traumatic stuff going on."

Coach Hadrian rolled his eyes. "Too much coddling. If these kids were not coddled and babied so much, they would be able to withstand more of the hard knocks."

Erin stared at him. Either he had no idea of what the Cox boys had gone through—and she didn't know how he could not be aware of it—or else he didn't have any understanding and compassion for them. She turned away from him and looked for the vice principal. Facing the door, she looked down at the clock face on her phone. If the vice principal was not able to break free from whatever was occupying him, she could leave and reschedule it for a better time.

Fitzroy appeared in the doorway at that moment, catching her looking at the time. "Sorry, Miss Price. The work of a vice principal is never done," he told her jovially. "Seems like there's always something to take me away from where I have planned to be."

"I don't have a lot of time," Erin said, giving Hadrian a quick look to encourage him to be on his way.

"Thanks, Coach," Fitzroy said. "I'll catch up with you later."

Erin waited for Hadrian to go and, eventually, he nodded to Fitzroy and left the room. Fitzroy sat down at the table and smiled at Erin. "Okay, then, let's sort this out."

When Erin got out of the meeting with Fitzroy, school was about to get out. She looked around, wondering whether she would be able to spot Joshua Cox. Beaver was right, of course; she couldn't expect him to tell her all of his problems just because she wanted to help, but they had shared the experience of looking for Brianna, and maybe they had bonded a little over that and Joshua would feel like he could tell her about his problems.

She walked slowly as she left the school. If she saw him, she saw him, and she would say hello and see where the conversation led. If she didn't see him, then she wouldn't pursue it any further.

As she watched, she saw Joshua come out of the school with a couple of other boys. She tried to get close enough to get his attention and wave to him.

"Miss Erin!"

She was confused at first, thinking that Josh had called her, but he didn't call her 'miss.' She turned and looked around, and again saw Harold and one of the other boys who had been playing basketball.

"Oh, hi Harold. How are you doing?"

"What are you doing here? I thought the bake sale wasn't until Tuesday."

"No, just ironing out some details with your vice principal."

"Oh, okay."

Erin looked over at Joshua, but it was too late to catch up and get his attention. He was moving quickly away from them with his buddies.

"You know about them?" Harold asked.

Erin looked at him, feeling her brow furrow. "Do I know about them?"

"Joshua and them? You look like you know them."

"Yes, I know who Joshua is… I know his mother. Do you know him?"

Harold shrugged, his hands held wide. "He's like tenth grade. I don't *know* know him."

Erin smiled. She remembered how that was. Knowing who the older kids were, admiring them from afar, but not being part of their circle. Everyone knew who the older kids were, especially in a small town like Bald Eagles Falls.

"He seems like a nice guy," she told Harold. "It's too bad about Campbell. They've both had a lot of trouble in the last few years. I hope things will go better for them now. Maybe Campbell will come back to school. And Joshua will stay in school and be able to get back on track."

Harold scratched behind his ear. "Coach would really like to be able to get Campbell back on the sports teams. And Josh, I guess. But he wasn't ever a big star."

"Yes, I talked to Coach Hadrian, and he said he's tried to get Josh back on the team a few times, but he won't do it. And he'd love to get Campbell back, but I suspect Campbell won't be coming back to school. If he did, he would probably do some other kind of program. In the city, maybe. Continuing education or some outreach program."

"Did Coach tell you that?"

"No, just that he wished that Campbell were still here. Do you play on any of the teams? Basketball? You seemed like a pretty good player when I saw you the other day."

Harold blushed. "I'm not that good. We were just messing around."

"You didn't look too bad to me."

"Maybe when I'm older, I'll be able to get on one of his teams. But I'm still too young for the high school teams."

"I bet you won't have any trouble getting on."

He shook his head, still red-faced. His friend grinned and nudged him, some private joke between them.

Harold pushed him away, embarrassed. He looked back at Erin.

"Well… I guess I'll be seeing you around," he said.

Erin nodded. "Come by the bakery later on; we've got pumpkin muffins with chocolate chips on today."

"Oh…" Harold grinned. "Maybe I'll go by there now."

They separated, and Erin went on her way.

CHAPTER 18

$\mathcal{T}$here was plenty to occupy Erin's time, even on a day she was not on shift. She still had business records, accounting and advertising, and employee payrolls to be processed. And she had to look at the schedules for the coming week, both for herself and the other employees.

Aside from bakery work, she had a house to maintain and needed to keep food in the fridge and have something on the table at mealtimes. Or at least once a day.

She chopped vegetables, her hands on autopilot and her mind far away. Orange Blossom wound around her feet, waiting for something edible to fall from the sky. He seemed to be back to his normal self and she still had no idea what had made him sick.

Terry had put in a short shift and was already bouncing around the house looking for something to keep him occupied. Erin was aware of his location in the house at all times, even though she wasn't consciously trying to track him. He came into the kitchen behind her and put his hands on her waist.

Erin let him nuzzle her neck for a moment before pulling away to continue making supper.

"How was your day?" Terry asked...

"It was fine. Getting the final arrangements made on the bake sale. I hope it brings something in. I'd hate to go to all of this work for nothing."

"People will donate what they can."

"I know. I'm just worried about how much that will be."

"Melissa has been working on the toy drive. I'm glad she took it and left the rest of us to deal with police work."

"Toy drive isn't your thing?"

"I like kids, and it's a worthy cause. I'm glad we're doing it. I'm just... grateful that it isn't part of my job."

"How is she doing with it? Does she need any help?"

"As far as I can tell, she's doing just fine."

"Good."

Erin worked quietly on the vegetables.

"You seem very far away," Terry commented.

"Oh... yeah. Sorry. I keep thinking... about something one of the boys at the school said."

Terry massaged her shoulders. "What?"

"When we saw Joshua, he said, 'Do you know about them?' Not 'Do you know them?' but 'Do you know *about* them?'"

He considered. "Like they were doing something?"

Erin nodded slowly. "Yes. You know how it is when you're at school, and there's a group of kids that everyone knows about except the adults. They're drinking or cheating on tests or harassing girls. Do you know *about* them? Do you know what they're doing? What kind of people they are?"

"Hmm." Terry sat down at the table to rest. He motioned for K9 to lie down beside him and watched Erin. K9 flopped over onto his side with a thump and a groan. He almost seemed more tired on the shorter shifts than he had been when Terry had been putting in long hours. Or maybe it was boredom rather than tiredness.

Terry himself looked tired, but he was also interested in Erin's thoughts. "Do you think Joshua is involved in drugs?"

"I don't know. Beaver wouldn't say whether he was working with her as an informant, but I feel like she's keeping an eye on him, and why would she do that unless she was either worried what he was getting into or he was someone she was handling?"

"After the trouble with Campbell, maybe just because she feels guilty and wants to make sure the family doesn't suffer any more problems."

"But she would know that you can't stop kids from getting into trouble if they decide that's what they're going to do. If Joshua is going to get into trouble, he's going to get into trouble. If he's drinking or doing drugs or dealing, he's not going to stop because she warns him to."

"No, but she could threaten to arrest him. You never know, that might scare him straight."

Erin nodded slowly. "Oh, I sure hope he isn't interested in anything really bad. I really hope I'm just jumping to conclusions and there's nothing to worry about."

"You could ask your friend for more information."

"I would... but he's pretty... anxious. He's fairly new here in town, and I think he's worried about staying on the good side of the group of boys that he hangs out with. He wants to tell me things, but he's afraid that they'll think he's a rat."

"What makes you think that?"

"Just... the way he talks, the way they treat each other. I think they know something about the burglaries, or have some guesses, at least, but they don't want to come out and say it."

"You think they know about the burglaries?" Terry asked sharply. "And you're just telling me about this now?"

"Well, I don't know what it is they know about," Erin defended herself, "because they're afraid to tell me. I'm trying to find out what I can, but if they won't talk to me, I don't have anything to pass on to you."

"Except for the fact that you might know of witnesses to the burglaries and you haven't bothered to mention it. They may not be willing to say anything about it to you, but put them in separate interrogation rooms, and we would probably have everything they know in pretty short order."

Erin's stomach tightened into a knot. Harold in an interrogation room with Stayner or someone determined to scare him into talking? She couldn't do that to him. He was already nervous, not sure what to say. It would be cruel to report him to the police and let them interrogate him.

"Who is it?" Terry asked. His voice was quiet and even, carefully controlled so that he would not come across to Erin as being angry or bullying. But she knew that didn't mean anything. He still expected her to give him the names.

"I don't know if they know anything," she protested again.

"It's not your job to investigate it. It's the responsibility of the police department. You give me the information I need, and then I can talk to them to find out what they know. If they know something about the burglaries, then it's important for us to find out. That's the only way we're going to be able to figure out who this is."

He waited. Erin put the vegetables into the soup pot and put on the lid.

"Come sit down," Terry suggested.

Erin sat down and let him take her hand across the table.

"Look, you want to find out who has been targeting these families, don't you?" he asked reasonably. "These children? You said you know what it's like not to get anything special at Christmas. You want to put a stop to the burglaries so that no more children will wake up to an empty stocking Christmas morning."

"Yes," Erin agreed, "of course. We all do."

"The police department is doing everything we can to find out who it is. We're gathering as much physical evidence as we can, but there hasn't been a lot left behind. We need witnesses. People who have seen or heard something. Maybe these boys have just heard some rumors going around. It may be totally unconnected with the burglaries, or it may just be gossip. But we can't determine that until we get a chance to talk with them."

"I'll try to talk to them again," Erin suggested. "See if I can find out some more… they haven't actually said that they know anything about it. They just said that maybe it's someone from out of town. Like someone who's here to play Santa Claus during the Christmas season."

Terry nodded. "That could be important information. If they've actually heard something. If it's not just 'it can't be one of us, so it must be an outsider.'"

"I'll talk to them."

"No. You just need to give me their names, and I'll talk to them."

"Terry, I can't."

"You need to. How else are we going to solve this case?"

"I owe it to them to talk to them first."

"No, you don't. You owe it to me and the rest of the police department and Bald Eagle Falls. You know where investigating on your own has gotten you before."

Erin stiffened. She knew what he was saying, but she didn't want to hear it. "Sometimes it's led me to the truth," she pointed out. "How many times have you not believed what I had to say?"

"I believe you. That's why I want to follow up on it. But so far, all you've given me is maybe Joshua and his friends could be wrapped up in something and maybe someone who is here for temporary work."

"So look into that to start with. See where it leads."

"We will. But we need to know what the boys know. So many crimes go unsolved not because there aren't any witnesses, but because the witnesses won't come forward."

Erin shrugged and looked away from him. "I'll tell you when I can."

"Are you serious?" Terry's tone changed from the patient, encouraging one he had been using to disbelief. "You aren't going to tell me? You think you can investigate this yourself?"

"Not investigate. Just talk to these boys. See if there's anything there."

"I can go to the school and start interviewing all of the kids."

"That's a lot of people."

"Erin. Be reasonable. You know it's my job to protect Bald Eagle Falls and its residents. That's what I'm going to do."

"Yes. You're very good at your job."

Terry got to his feet abruptly. Erin shied away, even though she didn't believe he would ever do anything to hurt her. She was already anxious, and the sudden movement startled her. Terry stared at her for a minute, frustrated, then headed for the front door. K9 looked up, then jumped to his feet to follow.

"Where are you going?" Erin's voice squeaked higher.

Terry looked over his shoulder briefly. "Home. I think I need some space."

The door banged shut behind him. Erin stood and watched him walk down the sidewalk to his truck, get in with K9, and drive away.

CHAPTER 19

*E*rin was finding it too cold in the evening to do her tai chi outdoors, so she had switched her practice to the living room until it got warm enough to take it back outside. She worked her way through her usual routines. Despite the improvement she had made in achieving a focused and meditative state, the house felt very empty. Orange Blossom and Marshmallow watched her exercise, always a bit bemused by her actions. She knew she wasn't completely alone, but she couldn't forget Terry leaving in anger either.

They hadn't ever had a real fight before. They sometimes disagreed with each other. They got impatient and got short with each other like any couple. But she couldn't remember either of them walking out on the other before.

She had thought that he would come back. He would take a walk or a drive, blow off his steam, and come back to her, embarrassed by his actions. But he didn't. There was no sign that he was coming back.

Erin called Vic. "You want to come over for a while? I could use the company."

"Did Terry have to go out? Sure. I'll be right over."

"Okay, thanks."

Vic was in the back door a few minutes later. She joined Erin on the couch, picking up Orange Blossom and cuddling him.

"Everything okay? How's Blossom feeling?"

Erin shook her head. Her eyes filled with tears and she didn't know what to say or do, embarrassed by the show of emotion. "Oh, brother." She sniffled. "Ignore the tears. It's just… Terry."

Vic did as she was asked and made no comment on Erin's tears and didn't act like something must be dreadfully wrong. "You guys have a fight?"

"I guess. An argument. And he took off. Went home. Said he needed some space."

"Well, that's better than taking your head off or getting physical." Vic looked at Erin, waiting, too polite to ask what it was they were arguing or fighting about.

"I was talking to one of the boys at the school. Someone who might know something about the burglaries." Erin swiped at the tears that leaked down her cheeks.

"Really?"

"I don't know. Maybe. It's just a feeling. They haven't actually told me anything."

"And why was Terry upset about that? Didn't he turn up the same kids in his investigation?"

"No. Not yet, anyway. He says he'll go over to the school to talk to all of them on his own if I won't give him their names. He'll find out who it was I was talking to and interrogate them until they tell him everything they know."

Vic frowned a little. "You don't want him to know who it is?"

"Not until I know if they really know something or not. I don't want them getting dragged into the police department to tell everything they know. I wouldn't want them to be scared and their mothers all worried that they're involved in something. If they do know something, it doesn't mean they're involved, just that they heard about what's going on."

"Terry isn't going to bully them."

"You didn't hear how he was talking… and Stayner might. Or someone else. I just don't think it's fair that they get pressured because they said something to me. I don't want anyone to get in trouble."

"Okay. That's fair. So you're going to try to talk to them? Find out what you can for Terry?"

"Yes. I guess. But he's pretty ticked off about it. You know how he gets about me investigating something, even when I'm not investigating."

Vic rolled her eyes. "Well, there is historically some reason for concern. I mean… things have happened."

"You really think there's any danger in talking to some young teens to find out if they know anything?"

"No. I'm just saying he's not completely off the mark."

"I'm not telling him that someone is a witness when I'm not sure. I need to know for sure."

Vic shrugged and nodded. "That's totally up to you. If Officer Piper doesn't like it… well then, he should go home and think about it for a while. You're free to do what you think is best."

But Erin didn't find that comforting. She had made her bed, and now she had to lie in it.

And lie in it alone.

She went to bed without Terry for the first time in weeks. He had been there every night since he had been discharged from the hospital. She kept waking in the night, reaching out for him, and being disappointed to find an empty space where he should have been. They both tended to wake each other up when they had restless nights, so she had thought that she might get a better sleep with him gone, and not tossing and turning or getting up to watch TV to quiet his anxious brain. But that had not been the case. She felt like she barely slept a wink.

Vic knew better than to ask her whether she and Terry had made up. She could see when she got into Erin's car that Terry's truck was still missing. She gave Erin a sympathetic look and climbed in without asking for any additional details.

"I'll decorate the last of the Grinch cookies today," Vic offered. "Then they'll be all ready for the bake sale."

"Yeah, that will be good. We have a few more people who will be dropping off other baked goods at the school today. If anyone tries to deliver them to Auntie Clem's tell them they *have* to go to the school. I am not going to be storing gluten items at the bakery."

"Roger that."

"Roger," Erin repeated, her brain segueing to Mary Lou's husband. "Do you know whether Mary Lou is going to be able to see him for Christmas? They must allow visitors on Christmas Day."

"I would assume so," Vic said. "She hasn't said anything to me about it." Vic gave a little shrug. "But why would she?"

Erin admitted that there was no reason for Mary Lou to have to tell either of them any of her plans. She deserved some privacy.

Her mind shifted to the Cox boys.

Do you know about them?

Maybe Harold had just wondered if she knew about everything the Coxes had been through. Maybe he'd heard the stories about Roger's attempted suicide and about being committed after Joelle's death.

It could have been something as innocent as that, and she'd gone and told Terry that he thought Josh was involved in the burglaries. Now Terry was going to be looking at Joshua Cox and asking him uncomfortable questions. She felt sick at the thought.

As if the Cox family hadn't already been through enough.

CHAPTER 20

*E*rin's phone rang, and since it was a quiet moment, she pulled it out to see who it was. Mrs. Peach, one of her neighbors. Erin frowned. They normally didn't do anything more than nod and smile to each other if they both happened to be outside their homes at the same time. They didn't socialize. Mrs. Peach was, as far as Erin knew, a very nice old woman with thin, white hair who usually wore a flowered print dress that fell just below her knees. She had probably been one of those to call in noise violations on Erin when Orange Blossom had been yowling too loudly. But she kept an eye on things around the neighborhood, and Erin didn't hold it against her.

"Erin here."

"Is this Erin Price?"

"Yes, it is, Mrs. Peach. Is something wrong?"

"Do you know you have a broken window?"

"What? No, I had no idea! Which window is it?" She thought immediately of the little attic room where she liked to read and do her genealogical research. It seemed like attic windows would be the most likely to be broken, maybe by a bird.

"Your living room window. It's quite a large hole. You should get someone over here to cover it up until it can be fixed."

"Yes, I will. I'll pop home and have a look right now."

"Okay, then, dear. I'll be out for my morning constitutional, so I won't be here."

"Thanks for calling to let me know."

"Of course. It can't just stay like that, can it?"

Erin hung up and started to untie her apron. "Will you be able to cover for a few minutes?" she asked Vic. "It's not too busy."

"Sure. What's wrong?"

"A rock through my window or something like that. Mrs. Peach called to say that it had a hole in it. I'm going to go take a look."

"Oh, goodness. I wonder what happened?"

"I'll find out."

"I'll give Willie a call. If he's not too busy, he can have a look and see about fixing it for you."

"Okay, thanks. That would be good."

Erin pulled on a jacket and hurried out to her car. Bald Eagle Falls was such a small place, and Clementine's house was walking distance from the bakery, so Erin was there in a couple of minutes.

Even though Mrs. Peach had said it was a large hole, she wasn't prepared for it. She had been expecting something an inch or two in diameter; maybe a rock kicked up when someone was pulling out of their parking space on the street. She hadn't been expecting a gaping hole like someone had shot a cannon through it.

"What the heck happened?" Erin wondered aloud.

She hurried up the sidewalk and unlocked the door. She disarmed the burglar alarm as she stepped in the door, muttering to it that it really hadn't done her any good if it wasn't going to let her know when someone broke a window.

In the middle of the living room lay a brick. Erin stared down at it, trying to come up with a reason for it to be there other than the obvious. Who would throw a brick through her window? It had to be a mistake. Some bizarre turn of events. A rock falling out of an airplane flying overhead. Someone trying to throw a brick at an intruder. Kids playing a game.

She knew none of it was true, but she didn't know what else to think. No one would intentionally damage her house like that, would they?

She was still standing there, looking down at it, when Willie arrived. He came up behind her and stood in the doorway.

"Knock, knock?"

P.D. WORKMAN

Erin startled at the sound of his voice. She turned and looked at him. Willie entered the house and looked into the living room. He took a sharp breath in.

"Was there a note?"

Erin looked down at it. "A note?"

"Was it a warning? Did someone tie or wrap a note around it? No?"

Erin shook her head. "No."

"Do you know… what this is about?"

"No."

"Well, if people are going to threaten you, it would at least be a courtesy to let you know why."

"Who would do something like that?"

"I don't know. Have you called Officer Piper?"

"Uh… no."

"I assume he's on duty. If he'd been here, this wouldn't have happened."

"I don't think so. They've only got him on afternoon shifts right now."

Willie frowned, looking toward the street. "Then where is he…?"

"He's at his house. Or at least, I assume he is." Erin ignored his questioning look. There was no reason Terry wouldn't be at his house. He did have a place of his own, after all. Erin hadn't been to his bachelor pad lately, but she knew the little house well and had spent a few nights there. But they had naturally fallen into the habit of Terry staying at Erin's, rather than her dropping in at his place. There were the pets, for one thing.

"Oh… where are the animals? Orange Blossom? Where are you?"

She looked behind the couch, Marshmallow's favorite hiding place, and he tilted his head slightly to look at her.

"Come on out, Marshmallow. Did that scare you?"

"Don't call him out yet," Willie warned. "Unless you want to pen him in the kitchen. You don't want him to get cut on the glass."

"Oh." Erin realized belatedly that there were shards of glass everywhere. "Oh, this is pretty bad. We'll be finding bits of glass for weeks. And if one of them eats it…"

"I don't think they're going to eat it. But we do want to get it cleaned up so that they don't walk through it."

"Come here, Marshmallow," Erin called to the rabbit once more. She liked Willie's idea of penning him in the kitchen. And Orange Blossom too, if she could get him to stay there. Maybe she'd better put him in the bathroom where she could shut the door.

Marshmallow came out to sniff at her and get his ears scratched. He kicked a little when Erin picked him up, then settled down again. Erin put him in the kitchen and put up the baby gate they had for just that purpose. She climbed back over it and went looking for the cat.

He was crouched on the bed waiting for her, his pupils wide and black, clearly spooked.

"Hey, Blossom. Did that scare you? Poor kitty." She picked him up and cuddled him. He started to purr. "Yeah, that was pretty scary, wasn't it? Were you out there when it happened?" The cat liked to sleep in the living room when she was out, finding a sunbeam to snooze in, waiting for her to get back. She looked at his paws to make sure they were okay. No blood or embedded glass. She kissed him on the head. "I know you're not going to like it, but I'm going to put you in the bathroom for a few minutes while we clean up."

He started yowling plaintively the moment she closed the door. Willie was waiting for Erin to get back.

"You're going to call the police department, right?"

Erin hesitated. What was there to report? She couldn't point to anyone or say why it had been done. They would be just as clueless as she was, unless there was a serial brick-thrower as well as a burglar.

"I don't know. Do I have to?"

He gave her a puzzled look. "I'm not sure why you wouldn't. You probably need a police file number to claim it on your insurance."

"But I could just replace it myself, too."

"Yes... you could. Is something going on with you and Terry?"

Erin shrugged. "We have a difference of opinions."

"You don't have to call him. Just call the dispatcher. If he's not on shift, they'll send someone else to deal with it."

Erin thought about Stayner and wrinkled her nose. She'd feel better if she knew it would be the sheriff or Tom taking the report. With a sigh, she pulled out her phone and, with Orange Blossom's cries still ringing in the background, reported the act of vandalism. She hung up.

"They'll send someone out right away."

"We'll wait until they see it before cleaning up. Then we'll get the glass

527

cleaned up and cover the hole. I'll measure the window and get you a new one."

Erin tried to relax the tense muscles of her neck and shoulders. "That's really helpful, thank you. I'm not sure what I would do without you."

"You'd just ask one of your friends or the police who to call, and they'd put you in touch with someone else who could do it for you."

"Well, it's nice not to have to do that. Thanks."

"Happy to help."

It was Sheriff Wilmot who responded to the call, which calmed Erin somewhat. He was low-key and relaxed. He tugged his heavy duty belt up, looking around the living room.

"That's a nasty surprise for you," he observed. "Were you home when it happened?"

"No. A neighbor noticed and called me."

"So, no one saw it happen?"

"I assume if they had, they would have told me."

"I'll ask around just in case. See if anyone was seen behaving suspiciously."

"Carrying around a bag of bricks?" Erin asked with a laugh.

"Scoping out the house, looking nervous, or yes, carrying a brick. Or running away. You never know. It's a small community. It's not easy to get away with something like this without someone noticing something."

"Do you need anything else, or can we start cleaning up?"

"Y'all can start cleaning up, but I'd like to ask you a few questions. Do you have any idea who might do something like this?"

"I don't know. No one I can think of."

"You haven't had any threats lately, any fights or arguments with anyone?"

Erin shook her head, even though she had, of course, had an argument with Terry. That wasn't what Sheriff Wilmot was asking. Terry wasn't the kind of person who would have thrown a brick through a window, especially over something like a difference of opinions. He was a strictly law-abiding citizen and wouldn't tolerate such behavior in himself or others.

"No, nothing."

"Strange phone calls? Hang-ups or heavy breathing?"

"No."

"Ever have anything like this happen in the past?"

"No."

"So there's nothing you can think of that this could be related to? You've had some run-ins with shady characters in the past…"

"Yes… but I don't think any of them are around anymore. Everyone has been caught, been put in jail. Or… they're not around anymore."

"Might be worthwhile to make sure that no one's been released or made bail."

"That wouldn't happen, would it? I mean, we're talking about accused murderers, drug dealers…"

"They still get out on bail regularly. Can't hurt to check."

"Yeah. I guess. You'll do that?"

Wilmot nodded. "All the ones I know. Is there anyone else that I should be aware of?"

"No."

"No one from your life before you came here? Someone who might have tracked you down?"

"You make it sound like there should be!"

The sheriff spread his hands wide. "All I know is what I've seen. And that is that you tend to… attract trouble. So it would not surprise me if you have had some… interactions with unsavory characters before you came here."

"No."

"Nobody in your past who might have been resentful and tracked you down?"

Erin shifted uncomfortably. Of course she'd had disagreements with people in the past. Run afoul of someone, been falsely accused… there had always been something. But no one who would have followed her to Bald Eagle Falls or have known that she was there.

"No."

"Okay. If you're not telling me the truth, you are the one who will suffer from it. I don't want you to be in danger because you were afraid to admit to something."

"You don't think I'm in danger, do you?" Erin clenched her fists, trying to stay calm and in control. "This is someone who wouldn't even talk to me face-to-face."

"In my experience, the type of folks who throw bricks through windows are the same ones as will use a Molotov cocktail or some other kind of violent behavior. He may not want to talk to you to your face, but people who make threats or cause property damage like this do still get violent."

Erin let that sink in. She didn't need someone else stalking her. The burglar alarm was supposed to protect her from crazies.

Terry was supposed to be there with K9 to defend her against any intruders.

They were supposed to be keeping her safe from harm.

CHAPTER 21

*E*rin stayed for long enough to get the glass cleaned up and for Willie to put cardboard over the broken window. Then he was going to order a new window and put it in for her. That would probably take a few days. Her stomach was complaining. Looking at the time on her phone, she realized that she had missed her usual early lunch hour and that Vic had been left to deal with the lunchtime rush herself.

It couldn't be helped. Erin would make it up to her another day, covering for Vic when she needed time off for something else. They were already doing that, of course…

She had a quick bite to eat, standing over the sink to catch any crumbs, then headed back to Auntie Clem's. The lunch rush was already past, and Vic didn't look too poorly for having had to weather it herself. Erin walked into the kitchen and grabbed her apron, apologizing to Vic.

"Sorry to be so long, we had to call the police, and deal with making a report, and we just got everything swept up and covered. I didn't mean to take so long."

"It's fine. I did all right."

"You did take a lunch break, right?"

"I did. So what's the scoop? Was it a bird? A rock?"

Erin looked blankly at her.

"What broke your window?" Vic asked.

"Oh. Sorry, I was thinking about lunch! No birds or rocks for lunch."

Erin told her as much as she could about the brick, which wasn't very much other than that it had been thrown through the window. There wasn't anything about the brick itself that would help the police figure out who had thrown it.

～

It was almost closing time when Terry came by. That was not unusual; he liked to stop by at the end of the day to see how she was, to help tidy up and consume stray cookies that had not sold during the day. It was a relaxed end-of-day ritual that they all enjoyed, including K9, who would lie down nibbling a gluten-free doggie biscuit.

But that ritual had ceased when Terry had been injured and gone off of active duty. And although he was back to acting as a policeman part-time, he hadn't started coming by again.

So for an instant, Erin's heart rose when she saw him coming up to the door. Things were finally getting back to normal. He was going to start coming by at the end of the day again, and she would get to spend some quiet time with him just tidying up and getting ready for the next day.

But when she saw his face, she knew that he wasn't there to help her to clean up and get ready for the next morning. She had become accustomed to seeing the fatigue and worry on his face more often than the dimple that appeared when he was really smiling about something. But that didn't compare to the thundercloud that was over him as he stepped into the bakery.

He didn't slam the door open or send the bells jingling wildly. If anything, he opened it more slowly and quietly than he usually did. But that didn't stop the cold chill that raced through Erin. She looked quickly over at Vic, who raised a questioning eyebrow, also wondering what was going on.

"Why didn't you call me?" Terry demanded without preamble.

"Call you?"

"About the brick through your window. Why didn't you call me and let me know what had happened?"

Erin hesitated, not sure she was willing to answer. Not sure if there was an answer that would soothe him, or if any response would be wrong. "I just called the dispatcher. I didn't think you would be on duty."

"I wasn't. But what does that have to do with it? I would still think that I would be your first phone call when you have something to be concerned about. Especially something like this, where you called the police to make a report."

Erin was silent. It didn't feel right to tell him that she normally would have called him first. That had been her first instinct. But that she hadn't because they had argued and he had left, and she didn't feel right about being the one to call him. She was still waiting for him to apologize for his anger and for leaving her alone.

She poured a finished muffin batter into a bowl to soak and set it to the side. She rinsed out the mixing bowl and started the next batch. She kept her eyes down, waiting for him to finish talking and either leave or lend a hand and go home with her.

"Erin, you should have called. Did you think I wouldn't come?"

He waited. Erin kept working. She was glad to have something to keep her hands and brain busy. She didn't want to think about that. How horrible it would be to call him and not have him come running. Is that why she had been so hesitant?

"I'm sorry," he said softly, but with an urgency behind his words. "I shouldn't have pushed you when you said that you weren't going to tell me the names of your witnesses. I should have just waited until you'd had a chance to think about it and were ready. And I shouldn't have just walked out on you."

"You said you needed space. You're allowed to go home whenever you want to. You're not obligated to stay with me. It's your choice."

"I know that. That isn't what I meant. I'm not dumping you; I just needed to think."

Erin nodded.

"So are we okay?" Terry asked.

"Sure," she said curtly.

Terry looked at Erin, then glanced over at Vic. It was awkward to be having the discussion in front of her, but he had chosen the time and the place. He had known that Vic had work to do there and couldn't just politely excuse herself.

"So... tell me about the happenings at your house today." His voice was casual, but his expression was not. He sat down on one of the stools she kept in the kitchen for when she needed to be off her feet. His eyes were intense and focused. He was in investigation mode.

"Not much to tell," Erin said with a shrug. "I imagine you got it all from Sheriff Wilmot's report. There wasn't much to say."

"An unknown person threw a brick through your window."

"Yes."

"No witnesses?"

"None that I know of. He was going to canvass, ask around."

"But the house wasn't broken into?"

"No."

"Nothing stolen."

"No. It wasn't a burglary. Just a brick through the window."

"But no note warning you to stay away from a certain place or event. No hint of what this might be about."

"No."

"It has to be related to the burglaries."

"Really? Do you think so?" Erin considered, and shook her head. "I don't see the connection. Why do you think that?"

"What is the one thing you have been asking questions about and poking your nose into that people might not like? The burglaries. You're the one who knows that Joshua might be involved. Who got a tip or two from unnamed witnesses. You've rubbed someone the wrong way."

"I haven't been asking questions. All I've been doing when I talk to anyone at the school is getting the bake sale preparations done. If someone is offended by me asking if they'll make some cookies or tarts for the bake sale, then yeah, maybe one of them threw a brick through my window. But most of the ladies I have talked to haven't seemed to be the brick-throwing type."

"If you haven't been asking any questions, then how did you find out that Joshua could be involved? And how do you know that someone might know something that we don't? People don't just walk up to you and tell you things like that."

"No, that's why I need to see if I can get some more information from him. But I didn't *do* anything; I just talked to them casually. A couple of times. He said just enough to make me wonder if he knows anything. But he might not. He might think he does, or he might just be teasing me, trying to show off to his friends."

"Let the sheriff and I work that out. I don't understand what your objection is to this."

"You're not going to talk me into it," Erin said forcefully.

Terry leaned back from her, looking startled.

"You say you're sorry for pushing me, and then you start pushing again," Erin pointed out. "Just stop it."

"You need to come in and at least tell the sheriff about the witness. Even if you don't want to talk to me about it for some reason, he needs to know that there is a witness."

"No."

"Erin. You need to turn over the names of anyone who might be a witness. You can be compelled to tell what you know."

"You can't compel me. Are you really going to drag me before a judge? You can't make me go in and make a statement."

He searched for something to say to change her mind, but Erin just shook her head. She put the last bowl in the sink and ran hot water. Vic gathered up any other utensils or dishes that needed to be washed and added them to the sink.

They worked together in silence, with Terry hovering over them trying to think of a way to force her to tell what she knew. Erin washed up and put everything away.

"Are you coming to the house?"

"Maybe I'd better not."

Erin gave one nod. "Fine. I'll see you later, then."

After he was gone, Vic gave Erin a wide-eyed look. "Whoa. You're really not backing down on this, are you? I've never seen the two of you so at odds with each other, not even at that first case."

"He has some issues. He's still recovering from a head injury, and he's not feeling that great. I think… if he was feeling his normal self, it wouldn't be an issue. So I'll wait… until he's back to himself again."

"But what if he doesn't go back to the way he was? It is possible for people to change, especially after a head injury. What if this is the new normal?"

Erin took a deep breath and let it out again. "Then I'd better either get used to it or move on."

She wasn't going to stay in a relationship where her partner thought he could push her around.

CHAPTER 22

*K*nowing that Terry wasn't likely to be returning to her house until Erin gave him the name of her potential witness, Erin decided she'd better push forward and find out more. She'd been hesitant to pursue it in the pre-Christmas season. Everyone was in such a rush and had so much stress already that she didn't want to push them. Especially when so many families were dealing with the burglaries, wondering how they were going to be able to have Christmas. Erin didn't think that Harold's family was one of the ones that had been targeted, but she wasn't sure.

Either way, if Harold knew something about who had been breaking into people's houses and stealing their presents, Erin had to find out what it was and relay it to the police department. She didn't want to be still fighting with Terry when Christmas Day came around. She'd had enough miserable Christmases in the past.

She looked up Harold's address. She was surprised to see that he lived at one of the farms outside the city. She had thought that, being new, he would be right inside town. She had assumed that they were city people. After studying the map to make sure she knew the way to his house, she drove over, hoping that she would not arrive during their supper hour.

She wanted to get there early enough that his parents wouldn't find it creepy that she was calling on their son. She wasn't sure how she was going to explain that she thought their son might know something about the burglaries if the door were answered by one of the parents. Did she just say, "is Harold available?" or did she explain herself in detail?

With any luck, they wouldn't even be home, but Harold would. She wasn't sure where she was going to find him if he wasn't at home. He might be at the school again, playing a pickup basketball game. Or maybe at a friend's house.

But she was in luck. Harold answered the door himself and his parents were not in evidence.

"Miss Erin?" He stepped back from the door to allow her to enter. "What are you doing here?"

She let him close the door and seat her in the living room before trying to explain.

"I'm glad I found you at home, Harold. I was worried that you might be out with friends and I really wanted to talk to you."

"Well, you weren't actually so lucky. I don't have a lot of friends."

"You were playing basketball the other day, and with another friend yesterday."

"Yeah, I hang out a little with them. But we're not really... friends."

"Oh. Okay. Anyway, that's not the point. What I mean is... I wanted to know... you seem like you know about the burglaries. And I wanted to find out what you do know."

His eyes slid to the side. Erin tried to make him more comfortable.

"I know this is kind of coming out of nowhere... but you said a couple of things and I'd like to know. Do you know who has been stealing people's presents?"

Harold scratched his ear. "No."

"You don't have any idea?"

He tapped his toes and looked around some more, refusing to meet her eyes. "I dunno."

"Harold... whoever it is has messed things up for a lot of families. If you think you know something, you should share it with me. Or with the police."

"I know that, but... I don't really know anything."

"I think you do. Or maybe one of the other boys has been bragging and you were repeating what they said. It doesn't matter how you know..."

"I don't really know anything." He shook his head more vigorously. "Sometimes…" A shrug with one shoulder. "Sometimes, you overhear something. Or like you said, someone is talking about it, but you don't know if it's true or not, you just know that it's interesting. That people are repeating it."

"And you'd like a little attention too, so you start to collect some of these things…"

"I don't want to get anyone in trouble. And I don't want to get in trouble. It isn't anything."

"You asked me if I knew about Joshua. Is Joshua Cox involved?"

"No." Harold shook his head. "Joshua is a good guy. He wouldn't do something like that."

"So who would? Do you know someone who has been involved?"

"No. I don't, Miss Erin, honest."

"You said maybe it was someone new in town, maybe someone here doing seasonal work like one of the Santas. Is that who it is?"

"I don't know. Maybe. I don't really know."

Erin let that sit for a few moments. It didn't sound right. It didn't sound believable.

"How does the burglar know which houses to hit?"

Harold's face started to turn red.

"Harold?"

"I don't know anything."

"Is it someone at the school?"

"I don't know." A pause. A defeated shrug of his shoulders. "Probably."

"It's probably someone from school, or you know for sure it is someone from school?"

"I don't know for sure." But he looked away from her again. His forehead was sweating, and he wiped it with the back of his hand.

"But it is probably someone from school."

Harold nodded.

"Someone you know?"

"I don't know many people. I'm still pretty new here."

"What else can you tell me about them?"

"Don't say 'them.' Say 'him.'"

Erin had meant 'them' as a generic singular pronoun, but Harold had clearly been spooked by it. She cocked her head. "Does that mean it is more than one person? It's a group?"

"I never said that."

"No. But I think it could be. That's what Beaver said too. She thought it was probably more than one person, because of the different times of the day. And she probably knows other facts she couldn't share with me too. I'm not exactly part of the investigation. The police always hold things back from the general public."

"I never said it was anyone. I don't know who is involved."

"But maybe you have heard rumors... that it is a group of kids from school?"

"It could be anyone," Harold argued. His voice climbed a little higher. "I don't know who's doing it. I'm not involved, and I never would be. Everyone knows that. They'd never ask me."

"So this business about maybe it being one of the Santas, that was just misdirection? Trying to throw people off the trail?"

"I don't know. It could be."

"But if it was one of the Santas, he wouldn't be someone going to your school."

Harold looked down at the floor.

"You can tell me more," Erin encouraged. "You look like you need to get it off your chest. How long have you been holding on to this?"

Her sympathy affected him. His eyes became shiny with tears. "Miss Erin, you know I wouldn't be involved in anything like this."

"I know that, Harold. I wouldn't be here if I thought you were. It wouldn't be very smart of me to walk right into the home of someone I thought was involved in the burglaries, would it?"

"No," Harold agreed, giving a little laugh and wiping surreptitiously at his eyes. "It wouldn't."

"I don't think you're involved or have done anything wrong. But you need to tell someone what you know. We want to catch these guys. Everybody who knows something needs to come forward with the information they have so that the police can put them away. Then everyone can breathe a sigh of relief and be able to have their Christmases. A happy Christmas, instead of worrying about their gifts being stolen."

"I don't know anything, though, not really."

"But the little bits that you do know, put together with what others know, could lead to a break in the case."

He stared down at his feet. "Maybe."

"Will you think about it? I don't want to force you, but you know it's the right thing to do."

He shrugged. Erin decided to leave it at that.

For the present.

CHAPTER 23

*D*riving back to town, Erin pondered over what to do. She had asked Harold to think about going to the police, but she was worried he wouldn't make the right decision. He was too nervous about whatever it was he knew. If he decided not to go to the police, what was she to do? Would she go to Terry, forcing Harold to talk to them? She wanted the burglaries to be solved, for everyone to be able to relax and have a good Christmas without worrying about their houses being broken into. With any luck in the fundraising efforts, they would be able to ensure that all those who had been victims of the burglar had presents for their children. If the burglar were behind bars, no one would have to live in fear that they would be the next victim.

Erin was startled out of her reverie by a heavy thud. She tightened her grip on the steering wheel instantly, trying to keep control of the car and assess what had happened.

Her first thought was that something had gone wrong internally. Terry and Vic kept telling her that she needed to replace her car before it broke down at the most inopportune time. She had said she wouldn't use it out of town, and then she had.

Her eyes swept the dashboard for any lights, then looked in the rearview mirror and realized that the truck right on her tail had bumped her and was still only inches from her. Was he having mechanical problems, or had she been driving below the speed limit and he had gotten frustrated and bumped her intentionally?

The road was only a single lane, but there was a wide shoulder, so Erin pulled carefully to the right, giving him enough room to pull past her.

As he pulled forward to pass her, he clipped the corner of her bumper and the car slewed, coming dangerously close to rolling into the ditch. Erin held to the wheel for dear life, swearing at him in her head.

What did he think he was doing?

Erin inched the car left again, trying to avoid the ditch. But the truck was still right behind her, refusing to pass and riding her bumper. What was he was doing?

Erin pressed the gas pedal down gently, increasing her acceleration, trying to pull a safer distance ahead of the menacing vehicle.

Was he trying to kill her? She still couldn't let go of the idea that maybe he was having mechanical problems. Maybe his brakes were not working, or he had some foreign object wedged under the pedal. Or maybe he was having a heart attack or seizure. He could be confused, pressing the accelerator instead of the brake.

But as she sped up, he sped up too, staying right with her and bumping her again. Erin looked over at her purse, trying to figure out if she could get her phone out without losing control of the car.

Speeding up hadn't solved the problem. Now she was going faster, more likely to lose control of the car on a curve or if he hit her again.

She moved her foot back over to the brake and pressed it slowly down, hoping that he would back off as he saw she was slowing. She could feel the truck pressing against the bumper as she braked. The smell of burning rubber filled the air as she was braking, but the truck was shoving her forward.

Then the truck fell back, separating from her car and putting some space between them. Erin let out a pent-up breath, relieved. She continued to slow, looking for a good place to pull over. She would pull off of the highway completely, let him pass her, and call Terry for help. He'd make sure she got home without any further problems.

She heard the rush of a revving engine, and then the blow to the back left corner of her bumper. The back of the car lifted slightly from the road. Erin was helpless to stop the spin of the vehicle and correct its heading. She braced as the car headed through the shoulder and nose-first into the ditch.

Even as she tried to hold herself stiff and still, she remembered that the reason so many drunks survived accidents they had caused while their victims in the other vehicle did not was because they stayed relaxed on impact. But she was scared to death, and there was no way she could relax her body as the car plunged into the ditch, cartwheeling once and coming down on its roof, then rolling over and over until it came to a shuddering stop, wheels down, facing the direction she had come from.

CHAPTER 24

$\mathcal{E}$rin didn't know how much time passed as she sat there in the car. She waited for the driver of the other vehicle to get out and check on her, but he didn't. Maybe he had gone off of the road or been injured as well. Or maybe he had gone on ahead to get help.

She closed her eyes and sat there, waiting, for what seemed to be a long time. A few times, she opened her eyes and looked around, but she didn't feel any compelling reason to move or get out of the car. She couldn't see her purse and wasn't sure where it had bounced to while the car was doing its acrobatics down the embankment.

The water in the ditch wasn't deep. That was a good thing. Erin wasn't sure what she would have done if water had started creeping up her ankles. Or worse.

Her phone started to ring. She looked around for it. It was hard to move. The phone had rung quite a number of times before she was able to find it in the back seat. She managed to unbuckle her seatbelt and leaned around the seat to retrieve the phone. She tapped the screen to answer it and put it to her ear.

"Hello?"

"Erin? Where are you? I drove by your house, and your car wasn't there. I just wanted to make sure you are okay." It was Terry's voice.

Erin blinked, considering. "What time is it?"

"Did I wake you up? Is the car in the shop?"

"No, not yet. Will you call them?"

"You want me to call the mechanic?" Terry's voice was uncertain. "What's wrong with it? Did you get stranded?"

"I guess so," Erin admitted, looking around.

"Where? Are you somewhere safe?"

"I'm not sure where I am. There... isn't anyone else here..."

Terry's voice took on greater urgency. "Erin. *Where are you?*"

"I'm just waiting here. I thought he would get someone to help."

"Who?"

"The other driver. I thought he was getting someone."

"The other driver. Were you in an accident?"

"Yes."

He swore under his breath, but loudly enough that she could hear him. "Do you know where you are? Did you go to the city?"

"No. To see Harold."

"Who is Harold?"

"He's a customer. Comes to the bakery."

"Where does Harold live?"

"Out on a farm. After the Bushman's turnoff."

"What's his family name?"

"Melville. They're new here."

"Melville. Okay, I'm going to come out and find you. Are you in your car?"

"Yes."

"Are you on the highway?"

"Well... sort of..." Erin wasn't sure how to answer.

"What do you mean, sort of?" Terry asked, frustration clear in his voice.

"I mean... I was. But I went off the highway."

"You turned off onto another road?"

"No, I went into the ditch."

"Good grief. Are you hurt?"

This hadn't occurred to Erin before. She looked down at herself. "I don't know. I don't think so. I don't see any blood."

"I'm on my way. Do you want to stay on the phone with me?"

"Sure," Erin agreed. She leaned back, trying to relax. She closed her eyes and rested with the phone still to her ear. She could hear Terry moving around, calling to K9, the sound of his doors slamming. The low rumble of his truck's engine.

"I'm coming. Just hang in there," Terry encouraged.

"I'm okay."

"That's good. Keep talking to me, so I know you haven't passed out. What happened? You said there was another car."

"Yeah. A truck. Like yours."

"How was it like mine? A pickup? What color?"

"Yeah, big pickup like yours. I don't know… dark… maybe black."

"Could you see the driver? Did he talk to you? You said you thought he was going to go get help."

"No… he didn't stop. I just thought he must have gone to get help because he didn't stay here."

"What happened? How did the accident occur?"

"He hit me from behind. Forced me into the ditch."

"Was he following too close? Going too fast?"

"Yeah."

"And then he just takes off after the accident. Coward. I'll have him up on hit and run, you can trust me on that one."

"How will you know?"

"Because he won't be able to get it fixed without the police department being notified. We will get him."

"Okay." Erin was feeling very tired. She didn't know how long it would take Terry to find her and thought she might take a nap while she was waiting. It was night, and she wasn't sure if he'd be able to find her in the darkness. She might have to wait until morning when the sun rose and he could see the car from the highway.

"Erin!"

"Hmm?" Erin tried to rouse herself. "I'm tired, Terry."

"I know you are. But you need to wait until I get there to evaluate you. Keep talking to me so that I know you're okay."

Erin took a deep breath. She was just so tired. "Okay. I'll try."

"Were you going to see the Melville boy or were you on your way back?"

"Back."

"And can you tell me whether you went into the ditch on the right side or the left?"

It took Erin a moment to orient herself and work out which side was right and which was left.

"Off the right."

"That's the passenger side. Is that right? You went into the ditch on the passenger side?"

"Yes."

"Good. I don't know how far out you are. I'm working my way along the shoulder."

"It's dark."

"I know it is," he agreed.

"You won't be able to see me. Maybe you should just come back in the morning."

"I am not waiting until morning to look for you. I'll find you tonight so that I know you're safe and being taken care of."

"Okay."

"I'll find you. I promise."

Erin waited. She couldn't think of anything to say, so she hummed to herself. It was getting harder and harder to stay awake, but she tried to do as he had told her.

A light flashed by the window. Erin thought it must be the first car that had driven down the highway since she had crashed there. It flitted past her and was gone.

"I saw a light," she told Terry.

"You did?" The light stopped moving away from her, then slowly started to move toward her again. "Can you see that?"

"Yes."

"Tell me when it's closest to you."

Erin watched the light approaching, trying to time her answer for when it was exactly beside her. "Now!"

She was a little late. It had overshot slightly, but it stopped. She heard a car door slam.

"I'm here, Erin. I'm going to come down to you."

"It's kind of steep. Be careful."

In a few moments, she could see another light bobbing toward her. There were a few missteps when the light moved to one side or the other, but it kept coming until it was right up beside her. Terry tried the door. No luck. He switched the powerful flashlight to his other hand. "Is the door locked?"

Erin felt blindly for the switch. She knew where it was, but she couldn't quite find it. Then her fingers finally encountered it. She switched first one direction, then the other, not sure which was which. Usually, the car unlocked when she parked it and she locked it with her key fob after getting out.

Terry tried the handle again and this time it clicked as the catch opened. He pulled on the door, and it creaked and protested until he finally got it unstuck and pulled it open.

"Erin."

His fingers went first to her throat, finding her pulse.

"How are you feeling? Can you tell me if it hurts anywhere?"

"I don't know. Not really. I'm getting stiff. It's cold."

"The temperature is dropping and I don't know how long you've been here. The car is pretty beaten up—did it roll?"

"Yes."

"I'm going to get a rescue team out here. I don't want to move you, in case your neck or back are injured."

"I don't think they are."

"If you damaged your spinal cord, you might not feel any pain, even though you were hurt. You might think you were okay."

"But I can move." Erin moved her arms creakily to show him. "The phone was in the back," she motioned to the footwell where she had found it. "I got that okay."

"That's good. But I want to be one hundred percent sure. If the car rolled… you could have a lot of damage you don't know about. You're in shock. It's cold; I don't want to assume you're not hurt and do more damage."

"I want to go home."

"I know. It's just going to be a little longer."

"Can I go to sleep now?"

"I'm going to get some blankets, and then I'll sit with you while we wait for the paramedics. I can wake you up and check on you now and then."

"Okay."

She closed her eyes when he walked away and the light disappeared again, up and over the embankment. He startled her when he got back, reaching in to tuck blankets around her. Erin was grateful for his kindness, tears welling up unexpectedly in her eyes.

"I'm sorry," she apologized. "I don't know why I'm crying."

"It's all right. You're allowed to cry. You've been through something pretty traumatic. Help is on its way. We'll get you out of here soon."

Erin wiped at the tears running down her cheeks. "I don't like crying."

He leaned in, putting one hand against her cheek and kissing the other. "It's okay. You don't need to be embarrassed about crying. I know how strong you are."

CHAPTER 25

*E*rin awoke again to the sound of voices. Not just Terry's voice this time, but several others as well. There were more lights; some stationary lights pointed at the car and some flashlights in hand. Erin rubbed her eyes, but she got a chill and put her hands under the blanket again.

"Can I go home now?"

"You need to let the paramedics check you out. They'll see that you're removed from the car safely and get the treatment you need."

"Ma'am?" One of the paramedics was in front of her. "Can you tell me your name?"

"Erin Price."

"How about the date?"

Erin did her best to dredge it up from her memory but wasn't sure she got it right.

"And how about the President of the United States?"

She wasn't likely to get that one wrong.

"Can you tell me what happened to you, ma'am? How did you get here?"

Erin stifled a yawn and shifted around. "Can I just go home? I'm exhausted. I need to get home and get some sleep."

"We need to check your mental state as part of our examination." He took her pulse. "How did you get here?"

"In my car."

"Yes, ma'am," he agreed with a chuckle. "And how did that happen? You drove down here?"

"Got hit from behind. Rolled down into the ditch."

"Can you tell me if you are in any pain?"

"No. I just want to get out of here."

"I understand that. I want you to follow my finger with your eyes. Don't move your head."

Erin followed his instructions.

"And can you squeeze my fingers tight with both hands?"

Erin squeezed. She closed her eyes, tiring of the paramedic's requirements.

"Stay with me, ma'am. How long have you been here?"

"I don't know. Early evening. It wasn't dark yet."

"You didn't call for help?"

Erin was at a loss to explain it. "I don't know why not," she said finally. "I just didn't think of it."

"We're going to get you out of here now, okay?"

"Okay." Erin leaned forward, ready to get out of the car. But the paramedics had other ideas. She waited again while they discussed the best way to transport her. Eventually, they put a collar on her and two of them removed her and laid her on a backboard. Erin rolled her eyes.

"We don't need to do this. I didn't hurt my neck or back."

"We'll just take all reasonable precautions. Once the hospital has cleared you, they'll remove the collar and get you in a regular bed."

"I don't want to go to the hospital. I want to go home."

"You will. But first, you're going to the hospital to get checked out."

Erin knew that even in the best-case scenario, one where they said she was just fine and could be released from the hospital, it would still be hours before she got home.

"Terry?"

"I'm here, Erin. What is it?"

"Can you call Vic? I'm going to need someone to take my shift at the bakery."

"Yes, I'll let her know," he agreed with a chuckle. "Doesn't sound like there's anything wrong with your head."

~

At the hospital, Erin closed her eyes, finally able to go to sleep. But every few minutes, it seemed like someone new needed to ask her the same questions and to poke and prod her. She felt ridiculous. She was perfectly fine, and everyone was acting like she should be a wreck. There were blood samples taken, her vital signs were continuously monitored and, eventually, she was taken to x-ray so that they could have a look at her spine and make sure there was no damage. It didn't matter how many times Erin said she was okay; they had to verify it for themselves.

She was separated from Terry much of the time. At some point, he had purchased a crossword puzzle book, which he worked his way through while waiting for her.

Finally, a doctor appeared at her bedside who confirmed that she didn't have a broken back or neck and it was safe to remove her collar and the backboard. Erin tipped and turned her neck and rolled her shoulders, trying to work out the stiffness from having them kept in the same position for so long.

"So, can I go home?" she asked the doctor impatiently.

He looked over her chart, reluctant to tell her yes. But eventually, he shrugged. "It wouldn't hurt to keep you under observation for a while, but if you're intent on going home… then yes. You can be released. You might be stiff for a few days but, considering the accident you were in, I am amazed that you don't have any major injuries. You must have a guardian angel."

Erin laughed. A guardian angel for an atheist?

"Do you have a way to get home?" the doctor inquired, ignoring her mirth.

"That would be me," Terry said from behind him.

The doctor turned and nodded at Terry. "Good. I don't want her overexerting herself. She should take it easy for a few days."

Terry raised his eyebrows. "Good luck with that. I'm not sure she knows how to relax."

"You need to," the doctor said earnestly, speaking to Erin. "While we can't point to any visible injuries, you will still have suffered some soft tissue damage and have had quite a shock to your system. I want you to be careful."

"I'll be careful. But I have the bake sale to look after, and we have a lot of work to do at the bakery to make sure everyone is ready for Christmas, and—"

"Don't do too much. Have someone give you a hand. Delegate some of these jobs. What if you had been killed in this accident, who would have taken over then?"

Erin looked at him, startled. She thought about it. If things had gone differently, she could very well have had the opposite outcome. And then who would have taken over? Vic and Charley would have had to take charge. There were enough other employees that they could keep things running while they sorted out the long-term impact of Erin's death. And then what? Would they keep Auntie Clem's open, or would they shut it like they had closed The Bake Shoppe after Angela Plaint's death? She hated to think of anyone closing Auntie Clem's. They had worked so hard to keep it running, despite everything that had happened.

"I'll... I'll try to get some help," she agreed.

"Good. Take the opportunity to enjoy the Christmas season. A lot of people work too hard to enjoy it. Don't be one of them."

"I'm not really big on Christmas."

He shook his head at this answer. "You deserve some time off. Take this as a sign that you need to."

Erin slid her feet off of the bed and got to her feet, holding on to the bed for a moment to make sure she was steady. "I just had a vacation," she grumbled.

"If you want to call being attacked while solving international crimes a vacation," Terry said wryly.

The doctor's eyes widened. "That doesn't sound relaxing," he agreed. "Exactly what is it you do? Are you an FBI agent?"

"No. Just a baker," Erin told him over her shoulder, as she and Terry walked away.

CHAPTER 26

*E*rin slept quite late the next day. She wasn't usually able to sleep much past her usual rising time, but her body obviously knew that she needed it. When she awoke, she found that, as the doctor had warned, she was pretty sore. Not bruised, but like she'd had a tough workout a day or two before.

The bedroom door opened, and Terry peeked in at her.

"Hey, you're awake."

"Yeah." Erin stretched painfully and massaged her muscles and joints. "What time is it?"

"What time it is doesn't matter. The question is whether you've had enough sleep. Everything is taken care of; you don't need to worry about work."

"I'm not. Just wondering how late it is."

Terry opened the door the rest of the way to enter the room. He sat down on the side of the bed.

"It's ten. But you can spend all day in bed if you need to."

"I know."

"How are you feeling?"

Erin stopped massaging her shoulders and allowed him to take over, rubbing them gently.

"Just sore. And tired. Nothing major."

"Good. You'll need to be careful for a while, make sure your body has a chance to recover." He shook his head. "After seeing that car in the daylight... I can't believe that you got through it without any injuries. It's impossible."

"Is it really bad?"

"It's time for you to get a new car. Of course, I have been telling you that for a while now."

"I know... but if I had, then the new car would be wrecked, and I'd have to get *another* one."

Terry chuckled. "That's true. I guess your timing is perfect. Just don't get into any more accidents after you replace it."

Erin nodded her agreement.

"Do you want anything to eat?"

When Erin moved to get up, Terry held up his hands to stop her. "I will bring you breakfast in bed. Whatever you order."

Erin knew she'd better not order anything too elaborate. Terry was an excellent policeman, but his culinary skills were not stellar.

"Well... I'm not sure how much I am up to yet. I don't usually have much to eat when I first wake up. Maybe... tea and toast?"

"Your wish is my command."

He gave a little bow and left the room to prepare her breakfast. Erin settled back into her pillow and closed her eyes while she waited.

She hadn't meant to fall back asleep, but she awoke drowsily to Terry putting the breakfast down on the side table.

"Sorry," he apologized. "Do you want this? I can make more later if you want to go back to sleep."

"No, it's okay. I didn't mean to go back to sleep. I'll eat it now."

He transferred the breakfast tray to Erin's lap as she struggled to sit up the rest of the way. He helped with her pillows and then hovered, waiting to see if there was anything else she needed.

"This is good. Relax."

"Are you sure? Do you want something else on the toast? Some of the Jam Lady jam or some honey?"

"No. I don't think I'm up for that yet. This is fine."

He stood there for another moment, then sat on the edge of the bed again. A bit farther away this time so that she had the room to enjoy her meal.

"So… I know sometimes it can be hard to remember something traumatic like a car accident," Terry offered. "A lot of people can't remember how they got into a wreck. Sometimes it comes back to them again later, and sometimes it never does."

"I remember it. Most of it, anyway, I think."

"You said it was a truck like mine. What do you remember about it?"

Erin pondered while she nibbled a triangle of toast. "It was a big pickup, like yours, with the extended cab. I don't remember much else about it. It was dark, I think. Maybe black."

"Could you see anything inside? Hanging from the mirror? A load in the bed?"

"No… I don't remember. I couldn't take more than a couple of quick glances. I was trying to keep control of the car and to figure out what he was doing. I couldn't understand… why he was right on my tail. I wasn't going that slow."

"Why do you think he was?"

Erin bit her lip. She sipped her tea, not wanting to answer right away. She didn't want to make an official statement. But she supposed it would be required. If it wasn't one thing, it was another.

"I really don't know. At the time, I didn't have time to think about it. I was just trying to get out of his way. I thought maybe he was having mechanical problems with the truck. The brakes weren't working. Something like that."

"And now? What do you think now that you've had time to think about it and consider the possibilities?"

"I guess… that it must have been intentional. I tried to get to the shoulder, out of his way. He didn't pass me, even when he had plenty of room and no traffic coming the other way. When I tried to slow down, he hit me, was pushing me forward. Then I sped up and he dropped back, and I thought that it had worked."

He nodded and waited for the rest of the story.

"But I guess he dropped back to get some momentum. He put on the gas, and then hit me again, hard. Forced me off the road." Erin shook her head. "It was so scary. I knew that I should relax my body to avoid getting injured, but I was holding tight for all I was worth."

"Good thing you were wearing a seatbelt. That's the kind of accident where people get thrown from the car and crushed."

"It was crazy. When he hit me, it cartwheeled." Erin demonstrated the movement with her toast. "Then rolled over going down into the ditch. Everything was flying all over the place inside. I didn't know which way was up. Glad it landed right side up."

"I'm just glad that I could open the door and we didn't need the Jaws of Life. I was relieved to be able to touch you and reassure both of us that you were okay."

"Yeah."

"So... it sounds like it was deliberate. This guy's goal was to run you off the road. It wasn't an accident or a mechanical issue."

Erin's stomach tightened in a knot. "Where's Orange Blossom? I thought he'd be in here with me."

Terry studied her. "You were asleep. He was looking for more attention. I fed him and played with him. He's napping in the sunshine right now."

"Oh, good. He's okay?"

"Who do you think would want to hurt you?" Terry persisted. "This wasn't just to scare you. Someone intended to do you harm."

"I don't want to think about it."

"That's not going to help us. We need to find this guy. Next time, you might not be so lucky."

"I don't think I'm going to feel like driving on the highway again any time soon. Besides, I don't have a car."

"But you don't know how he'll come after you the next time. It won't necessarily be a car accident. Someone threw a brick through your window. They know where you live. Next time, they could attack you in person."

Erin felt nauseated. She pushed the toast away and sipped the tea, hoping it would help to settle her stomach.

"You think this is because of the burglaries."

Terry nodded slowly. He took her hand and held it between his two hands, warm and strong, soothing. "Somebody doesn't like you asking questions. They are worried you are going to find out the truth and expose them."

Erin licked her lips, her mouth dry. *Them.* There were more of them, not just one person.

"Do you think it is a group acting together?" she asked Terry. "Like a gang?"

"We think it is probably a group. They get in and out of houses pretty quickly. Strike at different times of the day or night. We haven't been able to pin down any one person who had the opportunity for every one of the burglaries, they all have alibis for one or two of them."

"Yeah."

"You think so too?"

Erin nodded.

"Maybe not a gang like you are thinking of," Terry went on. "Not like a motorcycle gang or a street gang. But a group of people organized and working in concert. It lets them get away with things that they wouldn't be able to otherwise. But it is also more dangerous for them, because the more people who know, the bigger the chances are there will be a leak."

"I just can't figure it out."

"You don't need to. That's up to me. Up to the police department."

Erin let out her breath in a long sigh. Tears prickled her eyes again. "Harold Melville is one of the boys who I thought might know something."

"I figured as much."

But Terry was there with her, not at the police department offices interrogating him.

"I didn't want him to be treated like a suspect. To be bullied and scared into talking. He's my friend. He's just a kid."

"We know our jobs, Erin. He'll be okay. But we need to find out what he knows."

"He doesn't really know much. Just rumors. Just things going around the school. Probably everyone else knows the same things."

"Then it's time that some of them open up."

Erin covered her eyes, wishing that she were asleep again, not thinking about Harold and how he was going to feel about her turning him in to the police. So much for the happy, friendly kid who stopped by the bakery for a muffin or granola bar after school.

"Think about the damage being done by the burglaries," Terry said quietly. "Not just the financial losses, but how they make the victims feel. Vulnerable. Violated. Despair over the loss of everything they had planned for Christmas, maybe saving all year for it. And one day, they're going to make a mistake and hit a place where the owners are home. And then we could have more than just a burglary to deal with. You already know that they don't have any compunction about committing violence against a possible witness."

Erin nodded.

"Do you want to go back to sleep?"

"No. I think maybe I'll have a bath, see if it helps some of these aches."

"Sure. Are you finished with this tray?"

Erin uncovered her eyes and looked at it. She didn't have any more appetite for the meager breakfast. "Yes. I'm sorry, I'm just not ready to eat much yet today."

"That's fine." He picked up the tray from her lap so that she had the freedom to get out of bed for her bath.

CHAPTER 27

*T*erry was out during the afternoon. Erin ping-ponged around the house, a knot of anxiety in her stomach, looking for something to do, but unable to focus on anything. She cuddled with the animals and tempted Orange Blossom into chasing a string for a while but, eventually, he flopped over on his side, panting, and wouldn't pursue it anymore.

She flipped idly through one of Clementine's genealogy files but was unable to focus on it correctly. The names swam in front of her eyes, names that she was familiar with from Bald Eagle Falls, families who had raised children on the mountain for generations. They were all related, those who had been there for several generations.

Erin had checked the time half a dozen times during the afternoon. The clock seemed to be standing still. But finally, she heard the back door and knew that Vic was home.

"Erin? You up?"

"Upstairs."

Vic climbed the pull-down stairs to the attic. They usually visited in the kitchen or living room, Vic didn't have much occasion to be in the attic. She looked around and smiled. "So nice up here in your little hideaway." She sat down in the window seat, which looked toward her loft apartment over the garage. "So, how are you doing? You look a lot better than I expected."

"Just sore. Nothing particular, just an all-over ache. Like you get when you have the flu."

"You're lucky. Terry said the car was trashed."

"It rolled a few times."

"Sheesh. I'd at least expect a few bruises."

Erin nodded. "I don't know how I managed to get out without a scratch or visible bruises. The doctor said I need to watch out for any concussion symptoms. I guess even if you don't hit your head on something, your brain still bounces around inside your skull. But I've been okay. No dizziness or double-vision. Just sore and tired. A little distracted."

"Very lucky. I'm glad you won't be spending Christmas in the hospital."

"Me too."

Erin thought briefly about Christmas. They would have Christmas dinner together again, just like at Christmas the year before and Thanksgiving a few weeks previous. Aside from that, she didn't have any plans. She hoped she would just be able to relax and enjoy a day off without any expectations. She didn't have to fit in any religious rituals. She and Terry hadn't officially been together the previous year. She didn't know whether as well as their Christmas dinner together, he had also attended any mass or observance. Even people who didn't think about church all year long sometimes attended church at Christmas.

"So, what's your plan for the bake sale?" Vic inquired. "Are you going to be able to make it? We've got it covered, so you don't have to, but of course, you can if you want to."

"I've been going stir-crazy today. So I'd better!"

"Good. Always nice to have the face of Auntie Clem's Bakery there. People associate you with all of the good stuff you bake and will buy more if you're there."

Erin's face warmed at the compliment. She wasn't sure it was true. People knew her employees just as well as her, and maybe even better, since mostly they had been in Bald Eagle Falls longer than Erin had.

"I had really hoped that they would have the burglaries solved by now," Vic sighed. "It would be nice to have the fundraisers without the specter of more thefts hanging over our heads. How can people relax if they think that the new stuff might be stolen too?"

Erin thought about that. It wasn't just an idle worry. What if they raised a bunch of money and, since the burglars lived in Bald Eagle Falls, they knew where the money was kept and could steal that too. Or if they stole the new presents once they were purchased and the toys collected for the toy drive.

"We should do something to ensure that people can't," she said slowly. "I don't know if the police department has the resources to guard everything. Maybe we could set up a citizen's guard to keep an eye on things."

"How do we ensure that none of the guards are burglars? And then once the gifts go to the families they are intended for… even if we wait until Christmas Eve, how do we keep anyone from breaking in and stealing them on Christmas Eve, just like The Grinch?"

"Nobody could break into all of the houses on Christmas Eve. Maybe one or two if people were heavy sleepers, but everyone is going to be home that night. They're not going to find presents in empty houses."

"Except maybe during church services. There's a candlelight service Christmas Eve at First Baptist. I don't know what's going on at the other churches."

What would people choose when faced with the possibilities? Stay home to make sure their children had presents, or go to church services together? In some families, the father could stay home while the mother took the children to services, but not every family had two parents.

"We should talk to Terry or the sheriff about it, I guess. See if they have a plan."

They would have to come to a landing pretty quickly. The bake sale was the next day, and it was only a few days until Christmas.

Terry's eyes were even more tired than usual when he got home. It was late; he'd ended up putting in eight hours even though he wasn't supposed to be working full shifts.

He rubbed at the corners of his eyes, his skin looking thin and yellow. He had clearly done too much. He held up his hands in a 'stop' motion to Erin before she could open her mouth to say anything.

"Yes, I know I was gone too long and you're worried about me. And I'll tell you what I can, but before anything else, I need to sit down and put a cold pack on my head and a cold beer in my belly."

Erin turned and walked into the kitchen ahead of him. "You'll need more than beer. Have you had anything to eat?"

"The department sprang for pizza. So I didn't go hungry, but I've probably had too much caffeine. I needed something to keep me on my feet."

"You'd better not try to go to bed too early, then, but you can at least relax."

He sank into one of the kitchen chairs. "Believe me; I'm not planning to do anything else for the next twelve hours."

"Good."

She went to the fridge to provide him with the necessities and started the tea kettle heating for herself.

She didn't ask him all of the questions that were running through her mind. She wanted to know so much.

But he hadn't called or texted to let her know that they had caught the burglars, so she knew they were still in the same position as they had been at the beginning of the day. Even though she dreaded them interrogating Harold, she had hoped that something good would come of it. He would be able to provide them with the critical pieces of information that they needed to break the case.

Terry popped the tab on his beer and took a long pull. Erin got a doggie biscuit out of the cookie jar for K9. Orange Blossom's treat radar immediately pinged, and he was in the kitchen demanding to be fed. Marshmallow followed more sedately.

"Treats for everybody," Erin agreed, doling out the appropriate snacks to each of them. "Then you'll be quiet so that I can talk with Terry in peace."

Terry watched her, sipping on his beer, lounging back in his chair to stretch his fatigued back and shoulders. Erin finished handing out the treats, poured boiling water into her teacup, and sat down at the table with him.

"So... what happened? What can you tell me?"

"Not a lot, unfortunately. We've done our best with the potential witnesses, but people are not talking."

"Harold?"

"We had him in and did our best... but I think you got more out of him than we did."

Erin couldn't show him her reaction to this news, but she was both relieved that they hadn't broken Harold down and a bit proud that they hadn't been able to get any more information out of him than she had.

"So he didn't tell you anything?"

"No. Didn't confirm that it was anyone at school. Didn't want to tell us anything. Not obstructive, more... scared and shy, I think. Not nearly as easy to confide in a cop as a pretty lady he admires."

Erin's face burned. She looked away, trying to hide her reaction.

"Then his mother showed up and put an end to the questioning. No way I was bullying her child into confessing something he hadn't done."

Erin rolled her eyes. Of course, Terry wouldn't do that, but she herself had been worried about how the police would treat Harold. Not Terry, necessarily, but one of the others... Stayner, for instance.

"Well, I'm glad she was looking out for him, but I'm sorry you weren't able to get anywhere."

"Me too. I had hoped that by the end of the day, we would be able to say we had made some progress. Maybe even arrested some suspects. But as things stand now, we're not much further ahead than we were a day or two ago."

"You don't have anyone who looks good for it?"

"I have plenty of people who look good for it. But no one who fits exactly and no one that we have enough evidence to arrest and press charges against. If we could catch them red-handed with some of the loot, that would be ideal."

Erin nodded. She sipped her tea. It wasn't particularly tasty, but it was supposed to help her to sleep, and she wanted to be fresh for the next day.

"Have you thought about all of the money and gifts from the charity drives? They could be next." She set down her cup. "If it was me, that would be the best target. That's a lot of loot."

Terry stared at her for a minute. "Yeah. I wonder if we can capitalize on that. Make it a really attractive target and then catch them at it."

Erin raised her brows. Maybe there was something they could do other than just protecting the gifts. She hadn't thought about using it as bait.

"It would be really nice to get these guys."

"Yes, it would."

CHAPTER 28

Then it was the day of the bake sale. Erin's baking was all prepared, and everything had been stored in the school kitchens. She opened Auntie Clem's for the morning, but closed at noon and Bella drove her over to the school. A couple of her employees had been sent over earlier to set everything up, so when she got there, there wasn't a lot left to do. She looked everything over, made sure it was all clearly labeled, and set up her cash box so she could make change quickly.

She wasn't as sore as she had been the day after the accident, but she was still pretty tender and wasn't able to stand for long periods. She was given a chair and did most of her transactions sitting down, developing a crick in her neck from looking up at everyone.

It was busy, and sales were brisk. The bake sale, book sale, and a table for the toy drive were all set up in the gymnasium. There were lots of smiles and Merry Christmas wishes going around. Erin saw Harold across the gym, but he didn't approach her table or talk to her. She watched to see if he was there with any of his friends, or if she could catch any interactions—positive or negative—with other boys from the school. But she saw that Mrs. Melville was going to each of the charity tables. Harold was standing there waiting for her to finish, probably with strict instructions not to move from the spot.

When Mrs. Melville arrived at Erin's table, she did not smile. Erin wondered whether Harold had told her about Erin's inquiries, or whether she blamed Erin for Officer Piper's actions, or whether she was just sour-faced and unhappy because of the stress of the season and everything that had been going on in Bald Eagle Falls. It couldn't be easy for the family as newcomers to the area. It was easier to blame the outsiders for the burglaries than it was to blame the people you had lived next door to and trusted for years, so they had probably been under the microscope.

"Hello, Mrs. Melville," Erin said as cheerfully as she could, hoping to pass some good feelings on to the woman.

Mrs. Melville still did not crack a smile. She gave a curt nod but did not answer Erin. She picked up one of Mrs. Hadrian's banana loaves and a plate of cookies. She did not touch Erin's gluten-free Grinches, which meant that Harold would not be able to partake of any of the bake sale treats. She counted out a few coins and bills and managed to come up with exact change for the purchases, which she handed to Erin, then gathered up her goods and walked away without a word.

"Somebody got up on the wrong side of the bed," Bella commented in a low voice.

Erin glanced over at her and didn't answer. Bella knew better than to be making comments about the customers, especially when there were still other customers around. No one wanted to think that people were talking about them behind their backs.

She tried to catch Harold's eye to at least nod to him, but he avoided looking in her direction. Erin sighed and continued to smile and greet people and encourage everyone she could to buy the baked goods and donate to the cause.

There was a sudden increase in chatter, and Erin looked up from her trans-action with Mrs. Peach to see what was going on. She saw a Santa across the gym from them. Erin looked over at Bella.

"I didn't know they were going to do Santa today, did you?"

Bella shook her head. "I never heard it announced. Maybe they decided to do something for the little kids..."

Erin looked around, waiting for an announcement to be made. The school telling the kids there to line up if they wanted to each get a visit with

Santa. But none of the school administrators were coming forward to pick up the mike. They seemed just as surprised as anybody else to find Santa in their midst.

Erin watched the kids crowd around Santa, all calling out and trying to get his attention, tugging on his clothes and speaking over each other.

Santa gave a few 'ho ho ho's' and 'Merry Christmases' and attempted to walk across the gym without tripping over all of the little rug rats trying to get his attention. He moved in abbreviated steps, cajoling them.

"Santa just wanted to have a look around, see how all of the fundraising is going," he told them, trying to shake them all off.

Erin didn't recognize the Santa's voice. She watched him make slow progress across the gym.

"Everybody is being such good helpers to Santa," Santa said. "Can you kids be good helpers too and let Santa go for a few minutes? I want to get a head start on some Christmas cookies. Santa needs to train too, you know. You think I can go all year without eating cookies and then be able to eat all of the cookies you leave out for me on Christmas Eve?"

"I thought you burned it off," one of the kids piped up authoritatively. "Because you have to do so much work all in one night. With magic and going all the way around the world and leaving presents for everyone. That burns a lot of calories."

"I still need to train," Santa insisted, patting his stomach. He made it to the bake sale table and looked at the goodies spread across the table. He nodded at Erin.

She had assumed she would recognize whoever it was, but she still didn't know the eyes framed by the beard and hat.

He gave her a wink with one of his cheerful blue eyes. "There seem to be an awful lot of Grinches around here," he observed, looking at the green cookies Erin and Vic had made.

"We've had a lot of Grinches in Bald Eagle Falls lately," Erin said, studying what little of his face she could see, along with his body language and demeanor. If he was one of the burglars, she would certainly not have guessed it by the way he talked and moved. He didn't seem to be at all concerned about being watched. With every eye in the place on him, he wouldn't be able to get away with anything.

"And how are you feeling, Miss Erin?"

Erin shifted uncomfortably, looking up at him. She pushed herself to her feet so that she at least didn't have to strain her neck to look at him. She didn't like a stranger calling her Miss Erin, acting like Erin should know who he was. She glanced at Vic, trying to get a read on the situation. Was she overreacting to the Santa's presence? Was it expected, or should she be worried about it? Vic raised her brows and didn't seem to have the answer.

"Who are you?" she asked in a low voice. Maybe it was somebody that she ought to know. She was just confused by the beard.

"I'm Santa Claus," he said cheerfully. "Kris Kringle. The fat guy. Whatever you like."

She looked down at the cookies. "So what can I get you today? You don't like the Grinches?"

"I'll take a Grinch. Always wanted to bite his head off. And some banana bread, and..." He surveyed the rest of the table. "Are those tarts yours?"

Erin nodded. "Yes, the pumpkin. Those are ours."

"And you made them yourself?"

"Yes."

"I hear a lot of cats like pumpkin."

The hair on Erin's arms stood up.

Cats?

Was that supposed to be a threat?

Or was he saying that he was the one who had poisoned Orange Blossom, that it wasn't just a freak accident? She was pretty sure that pumpkin was just fine for cats. It wasn't on the list of things that Doc had told her to look for at her house.

"I... don't know. Do they?" she asked uncertainly.

"Yes. Doesn't your cat like pumpkin?"

"I don't know. I never fed any to him."

"You ought to try it sometime."

Was it possible that he had poisoned Orange Blossom? That he had hidden some kind of poison in a pumpkin dish and then coaxed Blossom to eat it? But how would he have gotten into the house?

None of the houses had been damaged in the break-ins. No broken windows or doors. Whoever was doing the stealing knew a thing or two about breaking into a house, even one with a burglar alarm. Erin's system had been foiled once before and, though that weak point had been corrected, there was always the possibility of some other vulnerability.

"Now, don't do anything that would put you on the naughty list," Santa warned Erin. "You wouldn't want to get moved off of the nice list and get a lump of coal on Christmas morning."

Was Santa implying that he would burn her house down? Or was it just some Christmas silliness?

Vic moved closer to Erin and the Santa, her movements taking on a certain wary intensity that told Erin she was now on full alert and wasn't about to put up with any nonsense from the Santa.

The Santa put a Grinch cookie, banana bread loaf, and pumpkin tarts in front of Erin and patted his red suit pockets until he found his wallet. Erin rang it up and told him his total, then took his proffered twenty.

"No change," Santa said, a twinkle in his eye. "We want to help as many kids as we can, don't we?" He picked up the bag of baking and turned to make his way back across the gym, kids starting to pester him again. He boomed plenty of 'Merry Christmases' and 'ho ho ho's' and made his way out of the gym.

"Do you know who that was?" Erin asked Bella, her heart pounding hard.

"I think it might have been Mr. Hopewell," Bella offered. "But I can't be sure. I don't know him really well. He's new here. He's the junior science teacher, so I don't have any classes with him."

After the sale was finished and the doors were closed, Erin and the others gathered their money and donations to total everything and see how they had done. Husbands and boyfriends stood around at the doors to the gym to make sure that no one could take them unaware and make off with the cash. Terry was there, as well as Willie, Naomi's husband, Beaver and Jeremy, the sheriff, and Tom Baker. Everyone determined to make sure that the donations would make it to the intended parties.

"Did you see the Howie boys hanging around in the hall outside the gym?" Vic asked Erin. "Their family was one of those that was hit. I guess at least the older ones know that they aren't getting anything for Christmas unless people are generous at the fundraisers."

Erin had noticed them loitering nearby. Families in Bald Eagle Falls tended to have larger families than those in the city or farther north in the urban areas Erin had lived in. The Howies had at least six boys.

"I hope the younger ones don't know what happened. It would be nice if they didn't know how close they came to losing their Christmas. At that age… it would be nice for them just to enjoy the anticipation of a special day."

Vic nodded, her eyes shiny. "We never had a whole lot for Christmas, but it was always a special time. I guess I knew pretty early on that there wasn't any Santa Claus coming down our chimney. I don't remember a time when I didn't know that the presents came from Pa and Mom. We knew how hard they worked, and anything special was… that much more special."

Erin finished counting and stacking all of her bills and moved on to the coins. "We did really well. I think we'll be on track to give all of the families who were burglarized and all of the ones who were supposed to be getting something from the needy children's fund a nice day."

"Good." Vic breathed out in relief. "And that's just us. With the toy drive and the book sale as well, and whatever other fundraisers are wrapping up today… this town has really come together. Everybody deserves a pat on the back."

"Almost everybody," Erin amended, thinking about the burglars.

"Yeah, everybody except the ones who stole everything in the first place," Vic agreed. "Somehow, I don't see *those* Grinches skiing down the mountain to return everyone's things when they come to understand the true meaning of Christmas."

Erin laughed. "No, I don't think so."

CHAPTER 29

There were more children than usual playing outside the school when Erin left the building, closely escorted by Terry, who was determined to make sure that nothing further happened to her and she was able to deposit the money and get home unmolested. Since school had let out early, she had expected the schoolyard to be quieter. Everyone would be going home to tend to their own Christmas preparations, play with friends, or whatever else they liked to do away from the school.

But children bounced balls in the basketball court where Harold had been playing the night of the fundraising meeting. Others ran playing tag or sat on benches or makeshift seats while they looked at their phones and tapped out messages to each other. There were children with their parents and other friends who tagged along with them while their own parents worked or shopped or ran errands.

She watched them, and they watched her making her way to Terry's truck. Did they all know what had happened to her? That she had been forced off the road and could have died? How many of them knew why or who it was? The way that rumors were flying around at the school, there had to be children who knew.

She didn't see any sign of any Santas in the parking lot.

Terry gave Erin a hand up into the truck, though she was quite capable of climbing up into the cab herself. He took a careful look around, studying the various groups of children and analyzing threats and group dynamics. He looked up at Erin before shutting the door.

"It will all be okay," Erin told him.

His face was grim as he nodded agreement. Like he had to agree because it was in the script he'd been given, but he didn't really buy into it. He was tired. It had been another long, fatiguing day. He was putting in too many hours and he wasn't going to be able to get caught up on his sleep on the holiday.

He slammed her door shut, and Erin waited there while he went around to his side and climbed up into the driver's seat after sending K9 into the back.

"Now is the time to be careful," he warned. "I don't want you to think that it's a home run because we made good money at the bake sale. We need to keep the money safe like you said yesterday."

"I know. That's why I'm here with you. I'm not going off somewhere on my own."

He showed his teeth in a smile. "There might be a good side to having your car totaled. Now that you can't get around on your own, I can keep better track of you."

"I never hid where I was from you."

"And I never tracked you. But I also never expected you to be targeted like that. By someone who fully intended to kill you because you might know something about the burglaries."

Erin couldn't help shivering with the cold wave that washed over her. She wanted to object that Terry couldn't know what their intention was.

Perhaps they had only intended to warn her, to scare her.

But she knew it wasn't true.

The brick through the window had been a warning. She had disregarded it, telling herself it was just some sort of prank or mistake, and had gone on to talk to Harold. Then they had ramped up the consequences and done their best to kill her.

And Orange Blossom? Had that been a warning? And the Santa at the bake sale? Had he been warning her off or just making jokes?

She didn't say anything as they drove to the bank. Terry put his hand on her arm to prevent her from getting out, looking around to make sure there was nothing that triggered suspicions. Then he nodded. "I'll walk you to the door."

"Are you sure you don't want to walk me all the way to the counter? I don't think anyone is going to do anything in the parking lot with you right here!"

"I don't either. But I wouldn't have expected anyone would run you off the road, either, and they did. We haven't yet found the truck that did it. It's got to have some front end damage. But there's no sign of it around town."

"They probably took it into the city to have it fixed."

"Or dumped it in a river somewhere. There are lots of good places to abandon vehicles out here."

"But you'd know from the VIN number, wouldn't you? If you ever found it, you'd know whose it was."

"Could be stolen. Though I haven't had any stolen vehicle reports either. But they don't always come in right away."

Erin climbed out of the truck.

"Why would anyone not report a vehicle theft right away? They'd end up in trouble with the police and their insurance agency then, wouldn't they?" she asked.

He walked around the truck to meet her and take her to the door. "People don't always know when a vehicle has been stolen."

At Erin's doubtful look, he raised his eyebrows. "Where is your other vehicle?"

"At the junkyard." Then she realized he'd said *other* vehicle and had to think about what he meant. "Oh… you mean Clementine's car? It's in the garage."

"When is the last time you saw it?"

"I don't know. It's been a while, but…"

"Would you know if someone had taken it?"

"If someone broke into the garage? I would know."

"How?"

"We would have heard them. The door would be open. Someone would have tipped us off. Like Mrs. Peach calling me to tell me that there was a hole in my window."

"And if it was done covertly? Someone picked the lock on the side door, hit the garage door opener switch, and drove the car out? If they closed everything again when they were done, would you know the difference? How long would it take before you reported the theft of your vehicle?"

Erin paused at the door with him. "I don't think I've been in there for months. Only a couple of times since the garage was built. And then… just to put something into storage."

"It's easy to lose track of your possessions if you don't see them very often. And some folks around here have more cars than they know what to do with. You have a half a dozen kids, and you end up needing more than one or two cars for Mom and Dad. Or you retire and buy a luxury car, but you still have the old beater to fall back on. And farm vehicles. And maybe something that you're holding on to for the collector in the family when he gets old enough to drive or to work on it. One family, out on a farm with plenty of space, might end up with six different vehicles. And if one of them disappears, nobody really thinks anything about it."

"I guess so. I never thought of that." Erin walked into the bank and stood in line, pondering over what Terry had said. The reverse would also be true. A family with half a dozen vehicles might not even notice if another one was added to their stables. Park the car in question on someone else's property, pull a tarp over it, and they might not even notice it in their daily comings and goings. The truck that had driven her off the road could be anywhere, hidden or in plain sight, and all she could say was that it was a big, dark pickup truck. There had to be hundreds of them in the county. Everyone had a pickup truck.

The cashiers were waiting for Erin and the other ladies who had been involved in the charity drives. One of them motioned Erin over as soon as she walked into the bank. "Over here, Miss Price. I'll take you now."

Erin looked at the other people standing in line who had gotten there ahead of her. "I can wait…"

"No, you can't. You have an appointment. Come on."

Erin walked up to the counter and smiled at the young woman who was waiting for her. She didn't know Paige Chesterton very well, but she knew her on sight, and Paige had always been very pleasant toward her.

Out of the corner of her eye, she saw movement and a flash of red, and she knew before she finished turning her head what she was going to see. A man in a Santa suit, of course, though he had a coat pulled on over top of the suit that had kept her from noticing him the minute she walked into the bank.

Her heart raced. She stood there frozen, the deposit bag in her hand, trying to figure out what to do if he made a sudden dash toward her or pulled a weapon.

The Santa turned his head to look in her direction. He wasn't wearing his beard. Probably people weren't allowed to go into the bank with their faces obscured. It was just Willie. Erin hadn't even known that he was doing any Santa gigs. Not that he told her everything he did; she had just never thought to ask.

Willie gave Erin a nod and a little salute, and took a look around the bank. He nodded a couple of times quickly, indicating that everything looked safe.

With Terry watching for trouble outside and Willie inside, Erin was finally able to relax. She rolled her sore shoulders and set the deposit bag down on the counter.

She smiled at Paige. "Okay. I just need to make a deposit for the bake sale funds. I want to make sure that the money is safe until it can be used as we promised."

"We don't want any mishaps," Paige agreed cheerfully. Despite her smile and cheer, she looked around the bank carefully, as if marking each person who was there. Her eyes lingered for a moment on Terry, standing outside the door keeping his eyes open. Then she smiled at Erin again, nodding. "Have you filled out a deposit slip? Good. If you'll wait while I re-count the money and verify the amount…"

She didn't have one of the fancy machines for counting money like some of the big banks Erin had been to. She just carefully counted it up by hand, adding together all of the totals of each kind of bill together, then counting the pile of change. She verified Erin's total with a smile, and carefully put everything into a drawer with a slot in the front.

"All done," she said. "Thank you for choosing to bank with us."

It wasn't like there were a lot of banks in Bald Eagle Falls to choose from. Erin smiled, thanked Paige, and turned back toward the door. Outside, she couldn't help mirroring Terry's actions, looking around for anyone suspicious, feeling anxious that nothing had happened and feeling like the burglars might come in at any moment to hold the bank up at gunpoint.

She laughed at herself for being so dramatic, drawing Terry's attention to her. He smiled and nodded, acknowledging the ridiculousness of the situation. "That's the bake sale money safe. The sheriff will make sure that the book drive money is deposited safely. Then it's just a matter of keeping the toy drive donations safe. And a few smaller fundraisers that won't make very much."

"Do you think they will be safe? Do you think the burglars will attempt to steal all of the toys again?"

Terry sighed. "I know it sounds silly and dramatic, but… yes, I have to say, I don't think they'll be able to resist the temptation."

~

Erin was exhausted at the end of the day. Her body was sore, not yet recovered from the accident. She was used to being on her feet all day at the bakery, but even having sat most of the time at the bake sale, she collapsed on her bed when she was finally home.

"A long day?" Terry suggested.

"Yeah. I feel like a ran a marathon. Or the whole Iron Man thing. I don't know when I've been so tired and sore."

"You did too much."

"Maybe," Erin admitted. "But I'm glad I was there. I wouldn't have wanted to miss it."

"Yeah." Terry nodded understandingly. "Well, nothing bad happened, and you can spend the rest of the day relaxing."

"Oh…" Erin realized she had not yet told him about the strange encounter with the Santa at the school.

"Oh?" Terry repeated.

"I just… before I forget… who knows if I'll remember to tell you later."

She filled him in on the Santa situation at the school, and then about the scare Willie had given her at the bank. Terry chuckled.

"Now you'll be seeing Santas wherever you go. Oh, wait a minute… there *are* Santas everywhere you go."

She pretended to punch him in the arm. "You're a big help!"

"I'll look into him," Terry assured her. "We're screening everyone we can at the school, but it's hard when you know so little about who might be involved. I'll move Mr. Hopewell up the list. Just to be sure."

"Yeah. It's probably nothing. I just… I don't want to ignore any… red flags."

Terry nodded his agreement. He suggested supper, but Erin shook her head. "You go ahead and scrounge up something for yourself. I'm not hungry, just tired. I'm going to go to sleep."

"Are you sure I can't get you something? I'll make you whatever you like."

"No. Thanks. Maybe I'll take you up on the offer tomorrow."

She closed her eyes. Terry stood there looking down at her for a minute, then quietly left the bedroom. Erin could hear his footsteps as he entered the kitchen and then remembered nothing more.

CHAPTER 30

*A*lthough she was tired, she slept restlessly. She kept waking up and turning over, trying to find the sweet spot in her bed and to get back to sleep. Her body was so sore that, like when she had the flu, she couldn't stay in one position for any length of time. The bouncing and stretching as the car had rolled over must have really put a strain on her muscles and joints.

She rubbed her eyes, pounded her pillow, and tried to find a deeper sleep. She felt beside her, but Terry's half of the bed was empty. He was either still up, or had been in bed and gotten back up again. Since he had been attacked, he'd had a much harder time sleeping. He often got up and watched TV until he could drop off, sometimes coming back to bed once he was drowsy and sometimes just passing out on the couch.

Erin thought of calling him. If they were both trying to get to sleep, then maybe they could cuddle and comfort each other and help each other to get to sleep. But she knew that the opposite was more likely to happen, with each of them rousing the other as they moved restlessly and tossed from one side to the other. If he'd fallen asleep in front of the TV, then it was better just to let him sleep there.

As Erin drifted from awake to restless sleep, her mind wandered, her dreams jumping from one time and place to another in a chaotic collage.

"Terry?" she called out, feeling for him again. But he wasn't there. Erin snuggled down, looking for a deeper sleep.

"They're gone! The presents are gone!"

Erin squinted and looked around, trying to figure out who was talking. Her mind was restless and she couldn't quite wake up.

"Which presents?" she mumbled. "I didn't buy any presents."

"The ones that are most needed," a hearty man's voice told her. She tried to figure out who it was. Vice Principal Fitzroy? Or maybe the voice of some actor she had seen on TV. It all felt a little bit like she was in a movie on TV. Removed and surreal. She couldn't remember where she had heard that voice.

"The needy children's donations?" she suggested.

"Need and want. Ignorance and want. Are there no prisons?"

Erin tried to compute this. Something was niggling away there in the back of her brain. She had heard it all before. Why? Where had it come from?

"We did everything we could to replace the toys," she informed the voice. "We've been holding fundraisers to replace what was stolen, and everybody has been contributing, even if they could only manage a dollar or two. People have really come together."

"It isn't enough. We must help the children."

"Okay. I will. In the morning. We don't have much time."

"Time? The time is drawing near. Tonight at midnight."

Erin startled in her sleep and woke herself up. The words stuck in her brain.

Tonight at midnight.

She tried to go back to sleep again, feeling for the dream she had been having. It had been an uncomfortable dream, but at least she had been able to sleep. She wanted to get back to that place again.

Her brain would not cooperate. Erin got up and wandered to the commode. If she just walked for a moment, relieved herself, and had a glass of water, maybe she would be able to return to sleep like she had never left it. She didn't care if it was the same dream or not, as long as she could sleep.

But after the bathroom, she was more wide awake than ever. She traipsed to the living room to see if Terry was asleep. He was either still awake or had been awakened by her wandering.

"Erin? Are you okay?"

"It's okay; I'm just… I can't sleep. I had a dream…"

He straightened up. "Was it *the* dream?"

The dream where she kept finding Mr. Inglethorpe's body over and over again, changing identity every time and appearing there as one of her friends or acquaintances.

"No. It was something different. Not a nightmare, just... confused."

He made space beside himself for her. Erin sat down and cuddled up to him, hoping her body would settle down and figure out that she still needed more sleep.

"Tonight at midnight," she murmured.

"What's that?"

"That's what the man in my dream said. That it would be tonight at midnight. I think he meant that's when the presents will be stolen." She yawned widely, trying to cover her mouth with her hand.

Terry turned his wrist to look at his watch. It lit up. "It's already past midnight," he said. "I haven't had any call that the presents have been stolen or that any attempt was made."

Erin shook her head. "So much for the prognosticating power of dreams. Can't even get the time right."

"If you just had the dream, then maybe it means *tonight* at midnight."

Erin closed her eyes. "Maybe it does," she agreed.

"If it was me, I wouldn't want to wait for long. I wouldn't want to wait until the last minute. Especially not until Christmas Eve when people will be home with their families."

"Yeah."

"And it makes sense to wait until after the bake sale money has been used to buy gifts. They weren't able to steal it before it was deposited, so they missed out on that opportunity. So now there wouldn't be as big a haul. If I were the burglar," Terry paused, considering, "I would want to hit it when it was as much loot as possible. After all of the gifts are bought, but before they are distributed."

"Then we should do something about that. We shouldn't get everything and then wait until Christmas Eve to give them all out. We should start the distribution today. Start putting together the gifts for the family groups that we already have enough for and delivering them." Get the loot split up as quickly as we can.

In the darkness, she could feel Terry nodding his head slowly. "Yes... that's not a bad idea. It makes the families more vulnerable than if we deliver the gifts on Christmas Eve, but spreading the gifts around makes it more difficult for the burglars to target everything. They'll have to prioritize their targets, and it will take longer, give us more opportunities to catch them."

"Right."

"Not a bad idea, Miss Price. Not bad at all."

Erin had fallen back asleep on the couch cuddled up to Terry, which meant that she woke up with a crick in her neck that wouldn't go away. She had known she wouldn't be able to put in a full day at the bakery after her difficulties at the bake sale the day before, so she allowed Bella and Vic to run things at the bakery and went with Terry to the police department in the town center to help sort the items donated to the toy drive and figure out what they still needed to buy. She was able to sit and rest when she needed to and she chatted with Terry or with Clara during her breaks. She and Clara had never gotten along well, but Erin could make small talk and be pleasant, which was all that was required. Clara had no overwhelming desire for them to be buddies.

"Are you up to Christmas shopping?" Terry asked, looking in on Erin while she sat resting, drinking a glass of water.

"If you give me a few more minutes to rest, I'll be fine. I can do things, but just for a little bit at a time."

"Can you rest in the truck while I drive to the city?"

"Are we going all the way into the city to shop?"

"I figure they'll have better selection and pricing than out here. It costs extra to get stuff shipped to Bald Eagle Falls, so you always pay a premium in town."

"Okay. Let's go into the city, then. But I might sleep in the truck."

"Sure. That's fine with me. Maybe I'll have a nap too."

Erin glared at him dramatically. "You better not!"

"If you can, why can't I?" he teased.

"Because your eyes are supposed to be on the road." She faked punching him in the shoulder.

He smiled, the dimple appearing in his cheek. "Oh, that's right..."

Erin was glad that he was in good spirits.

CHAPTER 31

*E*rin slept both on the way to the city to do the shopping and on the way back. Her body ached and the crick in her neck did not get better with sleeping in the truck. But she was happy with what they had been able to buy with the bake sale money, and she and Terry agreed that he would start delivering the completed family packages immediately.

Before Terry took the gifts back to the police department, he dropped Erin off at Auntie Clem's Bakery so that she could check in with her employees and make sure that everything was going well.

Vic and Bella were all smiles, cheerfully relating the various customers who had been in during the day. While she would have preferred to have been there in person, Erin enjoyed hearing the secondhand stories.

"Oh, and here's Mary Lou," Vic said, looking toward the door. Erin turned around to see Mary Lou Cox coming toward the bakery. Erin smiled and nodded a greeting. Mary Lou did not return the smile as she came in the door. Erin felt a little disconcerted. She was at a disadvantage. She should have been on the other side of the counter, serving customers, not chatting from the customer side. It felt strange to be there when Mary Lou came by.

Mary Lou stood just inside the door, not advancing the rest of the way up to the display case and order counter. Erin swallowed, looking at her grim expression.

"What is it? Has something happened?"

Mary Lou pressed her lips together. "That's an interesting question for you to ask."

"Well, I mean, I know about the burglaries of course, if that's what you mean. And I guess you heard about my car accident." She looked for anything that Mary Lou might be upset about. "I didn't see you at the bake sale yesterday. We've already been out buying some new gifts, but if you wanted to make a donation, I'm sure we could—"

"I am not here to donate to the bake sale fund. I'm here because of what you have done, interfering in our lives. After all that we have been through, I thought that you understood."

Erin swallowed. Her chest was tight and there was a feeling of dread in the pit of her stomach. "I'm not sure what you're upset about, Mary Lou, but if you tell me, I'll try to straighten it out…"

"After all that my family has gone through the past few years, I thought that people would give us a break. Instead, you sic the police on Joshua."

"Me? I didn't…" Erin trailed off, remembering how she had told Terry about Harold's question. *You know about them?*

Mary Lou's eyes burned. She took in Erin's sudden silence and how she didn't deny the accusation. She nodded her head. "Exactly. You're the one who accused Joshua. How could you?"

"I didn't. That's not what happened. I didn't accuse him of anything, I just… I repeated what someone else had said, a question, not an accusation. You know that they think the burglars are at the school, that's where the police have been focusing their efforts…"

"Joshua is not one of the burglars."

"I'm sure he isn't. It wasn't an accusation. Just a throwaway comment, but it was bothering me, and I asked Terry…"

"And Officer Piper is part of the police force in Bald Eagle Falls. You can't separate your pillow talk from an official report. For your Officer Piper, it's all the same. You can't say something like that to him without him investigating it."

Erin covered up her mouth, hiding her grimace. "I didn't mean for him to investigate Joshua. Everybody is under scrutiny. I don't think that it was Joshua."

"You think that he's a criminal. That both him and Campbell are mixed up in crime, because of what happened over Thanksgiving. But that wasn't

Campbell's fault. And it was nothing at all to do with Joshua. You should be ashamed of yourself for repeating gossip and throwing accusations around so recklessly."

Erin bit her lip, trying to keep her emotions under control. It had been a hard enough week without Mary Lou accusing her of wrongdoing on top of everything else.

"Erin doesn't think that Joshua is a criminal," Vic piped up. "You know she's been right there to support you all through everything that happened with Campbell. She never accused him of anything and did her best to help prove he was innocent. She put herself in danger helping Joshua. Why would she turn around and accuse him of something?"

Mary Lou frowned and shook her head, her brows drawing down. "Put herself in danger? What are you talking about?"

Erin looked at Vic. Vic's mouth hung open as she tried to figure out how to take back what had slipped out of her mouth.

Mary Lou looked from one to the other. "Erin, what is Vic talking about? When did you put yourself in danger helping Joshua? Why don't I know anything about this?"

"Uh..."

"Tell me what's going on."

"I thought you knew," Vic said, putting both hands on top of her head like she was afraid it was going to explode. "Didn't Beaver...?"

"Beaver?"

"Oh, shoot. Shoot, shoot, shoot..."

Mary Lou put her hands on her hips. "One of you had better start explaining."

Erin rubbed her temples and tried to downplay it. "Joshua went into the city. He and Jeremy. When Brittany was missing. They were trying to find her."

"Oh?"

"Yes..." Vic agreed, "And... Erin and I ran into them, just by accident, and we kind of joined up to help them. Erin didn't want them to search for Brittany. She tried to talk them out of it. But we all said that we were going ahead, so she said she'd come along too."

"And...?"

"And... well... things didn't go exactly the way we had thought they would. And we ended up dealing with some pretty nasty characters. Erin was the only one who had the sense to know that we were doing something stupid. We just thought we would talk to people, and if we ran into any problems, we were armed, so..."

"Armed?" Mary Lou repeated faintly, moving farther into the bakery and putting her hand on one of the chairs to steady herself. "Joshua was armed?"

"No, not Joshua. But... me and Jeremy. And we thought that we could handle any trouble."

"You are children! What made you think you could take on thugs with guns?"

"We're not children," Vic protested, her face turning red. To Mary Lou, they were. They were only a couple of years older than her boys. Even if they were technically adults, she didn't see them that way.

"So... don't get after Erin. She knows Joshua isn't a criminal."

Mary Lou looked at Erin, studying her closely. Erin couldn't hold her gaze. She hoped that Joshua wasn't involved in any of the burglaries, but she knew that other boys at the school were, and she couldn't automatically discount Joshua just because she liked him and had helped him out in the past. She couldn't assume that because she liked Mary Lou, that automatically meant that Joshua couldn't be involved in something criminal. Campbell, after all, had been involved with drug dealers and other bad stuff in the city. She didn't know if he was a user, or just an informant for Beaver, or if he had been more deeply involved in the drug trade.

Mary Lou shook her head. "You stay away from Joshua," she warned Erin. "I don't want you involved with him. Or you, Miss Victoria. And if you happen to see Beaver before I do, you can tell her in no uncertain terms that I don't want her involved with Josh either. It's bad enough that she involved Campbell in her investigations. Maybe he would have gotten involved in that life without her help, but I can't say that for sure. You can all just stay away from him and let him live his own life. He is *not* involved in these burglaries."

Erin nodded. "Yes. Okay."

Vic was still bright red. She indicated her agreement as well. Mary Lou's eyes went to Bella. Erin knew that she and Joshua were not friends, but that they at least knew each other. They both attended the same school and, in a small town like Bald Eagle Falls, the students quickly got to know each other.

Mary Lou didn't say anything to Bella. She turned and walked back out of the bakery.

Bella let out a breath. "Wow."

"I'm sorry," Vic said to Erin, her words coming out in a rush. "I should have kept my big mouth shut. I just made things worse. I'm so sorry."

"Don't worry about it. She should know what's been going on with Joshua. Someone should have told her before this."

CHAPTER 32

The school had involved the students in making cards and some paper decorations for the Christmas packages. They wouldn't know which families their cards were going to, so there were no names on them, but it was a nice way to get the students involved in the project and thinking about others who might be having a tough time during the holiday season.

Erin circulated the gymnasium, helping to supervise the effort and make sure that the finished cards were collected and sorted for them to be matched up with the family packages. She kept an eye out for any fat men in red suits, but there didn't seem to be any Santas around this time. Erin stopped near one of the groups of students, bunched close together to talk to each other while they drew or wrote. Peter Foster looked up from the card that he was working on and grinned at her.

"Hi, Miss Erin!"

"Hi, Peter. How's it coming along?"

"Pretty good." He sat back and looked at the card he had been working on. "It's Santa's sleigh, full of presents. I'm not a very good artist. The reindeer look kind of like dogs."

Erin laughed. "Well, maybe he decided to use dogs like Max in *The Grinch*."

Peter brightened. "Yeah! They can be dogs like Max. The antlers are just tied on." He carefully drew a string from the former reindeer's antlers to his chin and examined it again. "That's pretty good."

"Good job. I'm sure whoever gets it will like it."

Peter nodded. "I like dogs. Do you?"

"Sure. I like most animals."

"But you don't have a dog, you have a cat."

"Yes, that's right," Erin agreed, surprised that he knew this. "Orange Blossom. Isn't that a funny name for a cat?"

"And he got sick. That's what I heard." He looked at her questioningly.

"Yes, he did," Erin agreed. Small town gossip was certainly living up to its reputation.

"I was sorry he got sick."

"Me too. But he's doing better now."

"That's good." Peter continued to color. Then he put his crayon down and looked around at the other students and lowered his voice. "It's really sad about the kids who had their presents stolen. Nobody is telling us whose were stolen, but if they don't just have really little kids, if they have bigger kids like me, then the big kids know if their presents got stolen. So I know who some of them are." He shook his head. "It's very sad," he repeated. "And the needy kids' presents... why would anyone do that? They knew that those things were going to kids whose families couldn't afford anything for Christmas. Why would they steal from people who didn't have anything?"

"I don't know. I don't understand what they were thinking. I guess they just felt entitled to take them and didn't care who they hurt. We've been able to raise enough money that those kids can still have something for Christmas, so maybe they feel like they didn't cause any harm. But it's made things hard for a lot of people this Christmas."

She crouched down next to Peter, looking at his card and getting closer to him so that other people wouldn't hear their conversation as easily.

"A lot of people who have given money and donations to replace the stolen presents didn't have very much to start with, so it's made it really tight. They won't be giving as much to their own kids, because they gave something up to help someone else."

"That's really good. Some people *are* good."

"Yes. Some people are really good."

"I don't like what the burglars are doing. Someone should tell them that what they are doing is wrong, even if the kids do still get presents for Christmas."

"I think they already know that what they are doing is wrong. They knew that from the start. But I wish that the people who know who it is would turn them in. It's not right that they're being protected by the people who know who they are."

Peter looked at Erin, frowning. "But you're supposed to do things that are good for your school, and not talk bad about the other students. That's school spirit."

"It's not school spirit to cover up for people you know are doing something wrong. That hurts everyone as much as the people who are doing the stealing."

"But the coach says if you have school spirit, you support your school and you don't do anything that might…" Peter searched his memory for the right word, "that might *detract* from the school's image."

"Keeping quiet about who is stealing things from other families is not showing school spirit. It's the opposite, because instead of people thinking you come from a school that teaches kids to be honest and good and to stand up for the right, they will think you come from a bad school that condones theft and dishonesty."

Peter nudged and elbowed a couple of the boys in his group. They looked at each other and at Erin, exchanging looks.

"Coach says we need to support our teams."

For what seemed like a long time, Erin just crouched there, looking at Peter and analyzing his words and the looks that passed between the boys. She went over everything Peter had said and then started over again.

"Does the coach know who is doing the stealing?" she asked carefully.

Peter looked at one of the other boys for assistance. Erin remembered the same kinds of looks passing between Harold and his friends as they weighed what to say to her.

Erin's body ached and crouching down was aggravating too many muscles. She abandoned her position, leaning back and landing on her butt and stretching her legs out in front of her. She leaned over closer to the boys.

"Coach Hadrian knows who it is?" she whispered.

They didn't answer, but in her mind, Erin kept hearing what Peter had said about the coach.

We need to support our teams.

Had he been telling them—or been telling someone—that saying who the burglars were would be betraying their teams? Betraying the school? That meant, then, that there were boys on the team who were helping to commit the burglaries. They were known to Coach Hadrian, and he was actively trying to prevent them from being discovered.

Why would he be trying to prevent them from being discovered?

He didn't believe, like the little boys did, that he would be detracting from the image of the school if he didn't reveal who was breaking the law. He had to know that the entire school was going to be painted with the same brush if people came to understand that the burglars were students there.

She pretended to be looking at Peter's Christmas card, but she was scanning the rest of the gym, looking at the teachers and other adults who were milling around supervising. She picked up the card and used it for cover as she looked past it to see where the coach was, if he was there in the gym.

And he was.

He was standing just a few paces away from her.

His dark, intense eyes drilled into her, watching her intently.

CHAPTER 33

*E*rin swallowed. Her mouth was dry.

The toys had not been brought to the school, so there were no police guards close by keeping an eye on things. Just teachers who— she hoped—knew nothing about what the coach was doing. They were just there to keep an eye on the kids and make sure they didn't get too wild. No sniffing markers or sword-fighting with scissors. Other than that, they didn't really care what the students did. It was like a free period. And most of the adults were standing around chatting with each other casually.

Erin felt her pockets for her phone, but it wasn't there. She had left it in her purse, and had left the purse in a locked classroom with other volunteers' purses so that they wouldn't be at risk of being lost or stolen while they worked with the kids.

Erin sat on the floor, trying to catch the eye of a staff member who could unlock the classroom. She tried to keep her movements casual, hyper-aware of the coach's eyes on her the whole time.

"Peter, could you do something for me?"

Peter looked at her, his face open and guileless. Always happy to help his favorite baker. She was the one who had brought the blessing of widely varying desserts and other baked goods into his life, rather than having to forever rely on commercial boxes of cookies and bags of bread. For a kid to have all of the variety that his friends could have was a huge deal. And that was why Erin did it.

"What do you want, Miss Erin?"

"I wonder if you would go over where Vice Principal Fitzroy is. Pretend you are looking for another color or marker, or that one of these ran out and you need the same color to finish your card."

He frowned at her. "Okay… why?"

"Make sure that no one else is listening or watching you, and ask Mr. Fitzroy if he would let me into the classroom to get my purse. Tell him I'm not feeling very well."

Peter nodded, looking concerned. "Are you sick?"

"I'm… well, I'm not feeling the best. You remember I had a car accident? It's been kind of hard on me if I try to do too much. I think I have done too much, and I'd better go home."

"Okay." He frowned again, obviously wondering why he had to go through the charade of looking for a marker and making sure no one was listening. Why didn't she just go over there herself and ask him?

Erin didn't fill him in. She just nodded, encouraging him to go. Peter picked up one of the markers and walked over to the table beside the vice principal, where there was a plastic bin of markers. He pawed through it, pretending to look for something. He looked at Mr. Fitzroy and looked around him to see if anyone else was watching or listening. He looked at Erin to make sure he was doing what she wanted him to. Erin nodded again, encouraging him to keep doing what she had said.

Peter saw Coach Hadrian, and Erin saw sudden understanding flood over his features. He could see the way that the coach was looking at Erin and knew that there was something wrong. Maybe he connected it up with their conversation, or maybe he hadn't made the full leap yet.

He tugged at the vice principal's sleeve to get his attention. Mr. Fitzroy looked down at him, asking a question.

Peter answered him and, after a moment, Fitzroy was looking over at Erin. He started to walk over, one hand going to his pocket to jingle his keys. Peter walked with him.

Erin pretended that she was still looking at the cards of Peter's friends and talking with them about what they were doing. She tried not to do anything that would give away to Coach Hadrian that she had figured out his game and was trying to get away so that she could take action.

Then Fitzroy stopped to talk to Hadrian. Peter's eyes got wide, and he tried to tug Mr. Fitzroy away from Hadrian, over to Erin. He flashed a look at Erin, wide-eyed, desperate.

Hadrian must have seen that look. He glanced from Peter to Erin, and a flush started to spread up his neck. She could see his mouth form the word 'no.' He must have said it out loud, because Fitzroy looked startled and confused. Fitzroy looked around.

Looking for an escape route? Looking for some of his prize athletes to help him out?

Erin remembered Hadrian's words about Joshua.

I've talked to Josh a few times to try to convince him to play.

Did Joshua know about Hadrian's side play? Did he know about Hadrian coaching his students to burglarize homes, not just to win school games? Was that why he had dropped out of sports and refused to go back?

It made sense that it was the coach. He was used to telling the boys what to do. Telling them exactly how to behave and live their lives. She didn't know what he could have said to convince them to steal people's Christmas presents, but he probably hadn't had to do a lot of convincing if he offered them each a cut. A few special video games or consoles. *What do you want for Christmas? All you have to do is what I say, and you can have it.*

He had been unconcerned about the children whose Christmas had been ruined by his plundering.

If these kids were not coddled and babied so much, they would be able to withstand more of the hard knocks.

She tried to gather herself together, pulling her legs in and getting ready to jump to her feet. She didn't know what Hadrian would do, whether he would cut and run now that he thought he was discovered, or whether he would come after her. He had run her off the road or ordered her to be run off the road once before. There was no telling what he would do if cornered.

But she couldn't run. Her purse and her phone were locked up and she had no car. She didn't want to leave with Peter standing so close to Hadrian; what if he decided to take a hostage and reached for the closest kid?

She wanted to call Peter to come over to her but was afraid that if she did so, it would just point Hadrian in her direction. That was the last thing she wanted. She tried to communicate with him with only her eyes. Peter stared at her, his eyes wide, frozen in place.

Fitzroy put his hands down on Peter's shoulders and said something to him, smiling genially. Peter turned and ran from the gym. Several people turned around to look at him, drawn by the sound of running feet amid the murmur of children coloring, cutting, and pasting. Fitzroy spoke to Hadrian for another minute, then continued toward Erin.

She let out her breath. Hadrian stayed where he was, still staring at her with malice, but not making any move to attack her or to take any of the innocent children nearby hostage. If he had any sense, he'd wait until she was out of the room and then run. He could make a clean getaway before she had a chance to report him. He just had to hold it together long enough.

Erin rose to her feet as Fitzroy got within a couple of strides of her.

"Miss Price, you're not feeling very well?" the vice principal asked with a concerned smile.

"No, I'm sorry. I thought I would be able to last the whole time, but I don't have a lot of stamina since the accident. I need to get home to where I can lie down."

He nodded his agreement and took her solicitously by the arm as if she were an old lady who needed to be helped or she might fall down. Erin let him. If he could just extract her from the gym, she would be safe. She could call Terry. She could give him a heads-up that the coach was the mastermind behind the burglaries. They would be able to track and capture Hadrian, and everything would be fine.

She was aware that she was breathing too fast. Her heart was pumping so fast she felt like it would burst right out of her chest.

"It was a shame to hear about your accident," Fitzroy said. "I was very sorry to hear what had happened."

Erin nodded. "I was fortunate. I should have been killed, or at least injured pretty badly. Who would have thought my little beater would stand up to that kind of abuse and I would walk away?"

She watched the faces of the people they passed, looking for anyone who understood what was going on and might interfere. How many boys were on the coach's teams? It had to be a good percentage of the boys in the upper grades. It wasn't that big a school.

How many were firmly enough under his control to take action to keep her from getting to a phone and informing on them? They would want to keep their coach safe from investigation. It was because of him that they could get the loot that they wanted; money, games, and whatever else they had wanted from the homes they robbed. The coach would only want liquid assets. Cash and whatever he could quickly convert at a pawn shop or fence in the city.

Some of the teens were definitely watching her with suspicion. They would have been warned about talking to her. They would have heard about the failed attempt to put her out of action. They would know that she was the girlfriend of one of the town's police officers.

She didn't remember the hallways being so long. The floors were a nondescript white pattern, buffed to a shine. The walls were covered with bulletin boards showcasing student work, posters, and seasonal topics. Very cheerful. How many different schools had she gone to that were exactly the same?

"Here we are," Fitzroy said, stopping her. He pulled out his keys and picked through them to find the right one. "Do you need someone to drive you home?"

"No. I'll be fine to walk."

"I don't like to let you do that when you're not feeling well. It wouldn't be very gentlemanly of me."

Erin swallowed. She glanced at him sideways, trying not to stare or make eye contact as she tried to figure out whether he might be involved as well. He seemed so nice, so charming, but that could be a facade.

She had dealt with enough parents and authority figures in the past who were able to put on a convincing front, but who behind closed doors were completely different people. Fitzroy gave no indication that he thought anything was wrong or out of place.

He unlocked the door and let Erin go over to the table to pick out her purse. Relieved, Erin reached to pick it up.

She thought fleetingly of what might be in the other purses there. If she went straight for her purse, was she giving up the opportunity to arm herself with pepper spray or something more lethal? She was not experienced in using pepper spray or firearms, but it seemed easy enough. Aim and press the button or pull the trigger. Vic had encouraged her more than once to protect herself by carrying a gun and learning how to use it. Erin had refused on more than one occasion, and yet she kept finding herself in circumstances where it might have been helpful to have been able to defend herself.

Except that people were killed by their own guns as often as they managed to kill or hold off their attackers. Any weapon that she used could be turned and used against her if she were not well-coordinated and experienced enough to use it properly. Whose purses were there? Who did she know carried pepper spray? At least that wouldn't kill her if someone turned it against her.

"Can't find it?" Fitzroy prompted.

"It's here somewhere." Erin moved her body in between Fitzroy, who was still standing in the doorway of the classroom and the table. She didn't want him to be able to see what she was doing or to decide to come over to help her out.

It was silly to be worrying about weapons. She had left Coach Hadrian back in the gym, and she would have Terry there in a few minutes.

But every time she had walked out of the school lately, there had been someone there waiting to talk to her. She didn't want to take the chance that the coach could have left the school and might get the drop on her.

Erin grabbed her purse. She looked at the others, but couldn't start going through them to find pepper spray. That would be too obvious. The vice principal would want to know what she was up to.

She opened her purse and felt for her phone. She wanted it in her hand. She wanted to be ready and to get Terry as soon as she could. He would help her. He'd drop everything to be there and be sure that she was safe from Hadrian and his young burglars.

"Are you all right?" Fitzroy asked as she made her way toward the door. "You're very pale. I could call the nurse. You could lie down in the first aid room until you feel better."

"No. I'm okay. Maybe… I'll just use the commode before I go."

He nodded. When she walked out of the room, he didn't leave her side. Maybe he was just careful about school security. Or maybe he was in on it with Hadrian.

Could the coach operate without any of the other adults at the school knowing what was going on? Or were there others, like Fitzroy, who looked the other direction and allowed him to get away with stealing from the people of Bald Eagle Falls? Maybe some of them were getting paid to keep quiet.

Erin let him escort her to the nearest restroom. He would have to wait outside the door.

~

The door closed and Erin looked around, making sure that the stalls were empty and trying to decide how to proceed. There was no way she wanted Fitzroy to be able to hear her through the door. So go into one of the stalls? Would that muffle the sound of her call enough? Or go out the second doorway at the other end of the restroom and try to get farther away from his curious ears?

Erin went to the sinks and started the water running in a couple of them, then went to the far end of the restroom and tapped her screen to call Terry.

The call went to voicemail.

Erin stared at the screen. If looks could kill, that little device would be toast. Of course, it wasn't the phone's fault if Terry rejected the call or had his phone turned to 'do not disturb.' Or maybe his phone battery had died. He was pretty good about keeping it charged, but there had been times in the past when he had been on duty for too long and hadn't had the chance to charge it and didn't have an external battery pack on him. There was already so much weight on his duty belt; the last thing he needed was another heavy piece of electronics equipment.

"Terry..." she whispered. "Come on. I need you."

She texted him an urgent message and pressed send. She watched the screen, waiting for a text back or an incoming call. She tapped her fingernail against the back of the phone, impatient. Every second seemed like an eternity. How long would it be before Fitzroy decided that there was something wrong and came into the bathroom after her? She glanced toward the door. If only he would just stay out there, or get distracted by something else, she could find someone who could help her.

The police dispatcher was the next most logical call. It didn't matter which of the police officers came to her aid, as long as someone did. Someone experienced who could protect her from Hadrian.

But one man against Hadrian was not enough. What if he called on his chosen athletes to help him? How many were there? Was it just a handful of them? A few carefully-selected individuals who he knew would be loyal to him and do whatever he asked? Or was it most of the boys on his teams? Most of the boys in the upper grades? Whoever came to her rescue might have to face multiple attackers. And who would want to fight a kid? Their first reaction would be to protect the children, not to see them as a threat.

She tried the police dispatch number. Hopefully, everyone wasn't off chatting as they finished organizing the Christmas packages. Someone would still be manning the phones. Crime didn't stop just because there were Christmas hampers to be organized.

It rang a few times, and Erin was swearing in her head, biting her lip, and keeping an eye on the door.

"Come on, come on," she murmured urgently.

Finally, a familiar voice answered the phone. "Bald Eagle Falls, emergency dispatch."

CHAPTER 34

*E*rin breathed a sigh of relief.

"It's Erin Price. I'm at the school. I need… help. Is Terry available? He didn't answer his phone."

"Officer Piper is not on call right now; I'm not sure where he might be. What's wrong, Miss Price? Are you in danger?"

"I think… I think I know who the head of the burglary ring is, and he's here. I think he knows I figured it out…"

"Where are you now? Are you safe?"

"I'm hiding in a restroom."

"So he isn't there right now. Does he know where you are?"

"No… but I don't know who else knows and might be in on it. Fitzroy knows where I am. Other people probably saw me come in here. Some of the other students… who knows how many of them are involved, or which ones of them are…"

"Are there any weapons? Are you in immediate danger?"

"No. Not immediate."

"And who is it you're afraid of? Who do you think is heading up the burglary ring?"

"Coach Hadrian."

There was a sharp intake of breath. One brief break in the dispatcher's professionalism, then her businesslike voice was back. "Okay. And Coach Hadrian is at the school right now? Where and when did you see him last?"

"He was in the gym about five minutes ago. Maybe less. But I think he's onto me, so he might bolt. Can you send someone?"

"I already have a unit on its way. I'm going to direct him to the gym first, if you're safe where you are for the moment."

"Yes, okay." Erin gulped. She wished that it was Terry. She wished she knew that he was on his way to get her and that he would come directly to her. "The gym is full of children."

"Thanks for letting me know that. Do you know if he is armed? Have you seen any weapons?"

"No, I haven't seen any."

"Has he made any threats?"

"No. He didn't say anything to me. He just… looked at me. In a threatening way."

"Units are arriving at the school now. You won't hear them; they are not using sirens. Just stay where you are."

Erin was quiet, straining her ears to hear what was going on, even though the dispatcher had said they would be arriving without sirens. She listened for screams, gunshots, heavy police shoes on the run.

But everything seemed quiet.

"Are you still there, Miss Price?"

Erin nodded and swallowed. She licked her lips, wishing her mouth wasn't so dry. She was in the bathroom with the water running but hadn't thought to take a drink. "Yes. I'm here."

"What restroom are you in?"

"I don't really know my way around the school. Close to the kindergarten rooms, I think. Mr. Fitzroy was standing outside the door, but I don't know if he still is."

"Okay, someone will be there in a moment."

The door opened and, even though Erin was braced for it, she still nearly jumped out of her skin. It was Sheriff Wilmot. He looked around the room, taking in Erin and the running water in the sinks. His weapon was still in its holster, so there must not have been any violence in response to their arrival.

"Miss Price. All okay?"

She let out her breath, trying to relax. "Yeah, I'm okay. Did you find him? Coach Hadrian? Was he still there?"

The sheriff's lips pressed together in a thin line. "No, he wasn't in the gym. We'll have to find out whether anyone saw him leave. Do you want to come out of here, and we can have a chat?"

Erin nodded. She walked over to one of the taps and turned it off. Wilmot turned off the other.

"I didn't want Fitzroy to overhear my call," Erin explained. "I don't know... whether he's involved or not. He and Coach Hadrian seem pretty close. He didn't do anything, but some of the things he said... I was just worried that he might be in on it. Even if he wasn't taking part, he could know about it and be taking a cut to stay quiet." She shook her head. "I just don't know."

He led her out of the bathroom into the hallway. Fitzroy was standing a short distance away, looking confused, talking to Tom Baker. The sheriff led her away without any comment. They found an empty classroom and she and Wilmot sat down at a table and Erin explained what Peter had said and the conclusions she had come to. On repeating it, she realized that the connection was pretty tenuous and she had no real proof that Hadrian was involved, but she was still confident that it was true. It made perfect sense.

"We had come to the conclusion that there had to be at least one adult involved," the sheriff agreed. "We've talked to a number of people, but no one pointed to the coach. We didn't have anything to indicate he wasn't telling the truth. I imagine he's gone to lengths to make sure that he has alibis for the actual burglaries. Leave the kids to do the dirty work, and convince them that turning on him or the team would be a betrayal of the school and the town."

Erin nodded. "But we'll need evidence, won't we? You can't search his house for any of the stolen property until you have some real evidence that he was the one leading the burglary ring, or at least knew of it."

"Leave that to me. You don't need to be doing the investigating here."

"I know... I was just talking to Peter. I wasn't investigating."

"Make sure you keep it that way. We'll talk to Peter and to the boys on the teams to see if we can crack them."

"Peter is so young. I would never have thought that someone his age would have known anything about it."

"We certainly didn't interview anyone his age. But I supposed if it's become part of the culture of the school… then even kids as young as him are going to be conditioned to think it's okay for the elite to break the law and that it would be wrong to report them." Sheriff Wilmot didn't seem surprised that the boys on the teams had something to do with the burglaries.

"How long have you known? That the kids were involved?"

"Well… it was obvious when you were talking to the boys that something was going on at the school. The only reason they would know the things they did was if other schoolkids were involved. There was just too much awareness, even if no one knew—or admitted to knowing—exactly who was involved."

"What would make someone do something like that? How would you even think of it?" Erin shook her head. "Was he just sitting grading papers one day or yelling at a football player to complete a certain play, and thought 'why don't I start stealing from families in town?'"

"In my experience, he's probably in debt. Maybe he took up gambling. Suddenly he has a whole lot of money that he has to pay back and needs to come up with it fast. So he's willing to take a risk if there's the chance of a big payoff."

Erin nodded slowly. "Yeah, I guess so. It just seems so… bizarre. I can't imagine anyone deciding to rip people off like that."

"That's because you're a good, decent person who tries to do what's right. Not everyone has been raised that way. Or has decided to live their lives that way."

Erin felt her face flush. She shrugged in embarrassment.

"We would hope that people who we entrust the care of our children to would have high moral standards," Wilmot said, "but that isn't always the case."

"No." Erin had direct experience with that fact.

She wondered fleetingly if she would ever have children of her own. She enjoyed being around kids, especially a friendly little fellow like Peter, but she wasn't sure if she were cut out to be a mother. Owning pets and worrying about keeping them safe and well was challenging enough.

She rubbed her forehead, trying to ease the headache that was settling in. "Do you know where Terry is?"

He shook his head. "He's not on shift. I'm not sure what his plans were. You would have a better idea than I would."

"I thought he would be helping with the Christmas hampers. But I guess you'd know if he was doing that."

"Not as far as I know. It's possible Clara sent him out to pick up something extra. He's not at your place? Having a nap, maybe?"

"I haven't been home. He didn't answer his phone."

"Might have just been asleep. He's had a lot to do the last few days."

Erin nodded. "I guess… I'll head home and find out."

"You're not in the best shape yourself. Can I drive you home?"

"You must have a lot to do here. You're still looking for Coach Hadrian?"

"I can take a few minutes out. I'd rather know that you were safely home."

"Well… okay." Erin hadn't been looking forward to walking home. While she hadn't thought about her aches and pains while the adrenaline had been coursing through her veins, it was wearing off, and she was feeling tired, sore, and shaky. It would be one thing if she had her own car to drive home. She could have managed that. But walking was a bit much.

CHAPTER 35

hey didn't have much conversation on the way home. Erin rested her head against the window, eyes closed, just wanting to be home in bed. With Terry. It didn't matter that it was still early afternoon, that was what she wanted.

Sheriff Wilmot pulled up in front of the house and looked at it. "You'll be okay? Do you want to see if Officer Piper is here before you decide?"

If Terry was back at his own house, it meant that he wanted to be alone. Erin wouldn't go over without an invitation. If he needed his space, she would give it to him.

"No, it's okay."

"Do you want me to clear the house first? I highly doubt that Hadrian would come over here instead of running, but you never know."

Erin looked at the house. "The burglar alarm hasn't gone off."

"Are you sure you armed it?"

"I always set it." She thought about it, trying to recall each moment that morning before she left. She couldn't specifically remember arming the burglar alarm. She always did, but that didn't mean she had. She wasn't feeling well, and if she had been too tired or distracted, it was possible that she had missed that step in her usual routine. "Um, yeah, actually. I'll take you up on that. Just to be sure."

He nodded his agreement and opened his door. "Your key?"

Erin rifled her purse to find her ring of keys and handed it to him.

"And the passcode for the alarm?"

Erin gave it to him.

"Okay. I'll be just a minute; then you can lie down and relax."

She watched him walk up the sidewalk to the door, unlock the door, and go in. She pictured him clearing the burglar alarm, calling out to Terry to alert him if he was home, walking through the house with one hand on his gun to make sure that everything was in order and no intruders were hiding in closets or under the bed. She felt a little like a child demanding that the adult in charge check for monsters before she could go to bed.

Hadrian wouldn't have gone to her house. He would be far away.

But he had tried to run her off the road. He or one of his students. They had been willing to take that step. She remembered the vice principal's words.

I was very sorry to hear what had happened.

Sorry that she had been run off the road or sorry that she had survived? She wished that she had the answers as to who had been involved in or known about the burglaries. It was going to be a long time before she felt safe trusting anyone connected with the school.

There was a tap on her window that made Erin startle.

But it was just the sheriff. She opened the car door.

"All clear," he pronounced, handing her key ring back.

"Thank you so much. I feel like such a coward. I can't even walk into my own house by myself."

"With your record? You're not being a coward. You're being very brave. Now you take care of yourself. I'm hoping you're a lot more bright-eyed the next time I see you."

"I will be," Erin promised.

She couldn't be much worse. She was ready to pass out.

She didn't even remember walking up the sidewalk into the house.

It had been early afternoon when Erin had returned home, but it was dark when she woke up. She didn't remember everything immediately, feeling warm and comfortable and swaddled with sleepiness.

Terry was there, stroking her hair, waiting for her to wake up. "Hey, sweetie. You don't have to wake up if you don't want to, I just want to let you know I'm here."

She raised one heavy arm to touch his hand and clasp it briefly.

"You can go back to sleep," he told her

"No," Erin murmured. "I want to talk. Just give me a few minutes to wake up."

"Okay." He pushed a wisp of hair away from her eyes. "I hear that you've been cracking cases again."

"Mmm. I tried to call you."

"Sorry, I missed it. I was having a nap."

"Mmm." Erin accepted his explanation, but her brain continued to worry at the explanation. He hadn't been sleeping there. Where had he been? His own house?

And she remembered how quickly the call had gone to voicemail.

He'd rejected the call, or been in 'do not disturb' mode, or maybe his phone had been out of juice. But he hadn't just slept through it ringing for several minutes.

"A couple of the boys knew that Coach Hadrian has a fishing shack by the lake," Terry said.

For a long time, Erin just lay there, waiting for her brain to come out of sleep mode, wondering why that was important.

"Wh-what? What did you say?"

"Coach Hadrian has a fishing shack. A little bit bigger than you might think when someone uses the word 'shack.'"

"Did you catch him?"

"Can't say *I* had much to do with it. Stayner was the one who headed out there while I was napping the afternoon away."

"Me too."

"Yeah. A great pair."

"I was so tired." Erin rubbed her eyes. "So Stayner got him? He's in custody? But there's no proof that he was the one leading the burglary ring…"

"Did I mention that he had a lot of loot stashed at the fishing shack? That's why he went straight there when he figured you were onto him."

"Oh, good." Erin pushed herself up a little and readjusted her pillow. If she could get closer to sitting up, she'd be able to chase the cobwebs away more quickly. "And… no one got hurt?"

"Stayner shouldn't have gone in by himself, but he was okay. No gunfire. And he found a truck parked by the shack. In addition to the one Hadrian had driven out there."

"Mmm-hm."

"Do you want me to turn on the lamp?"

"Yes."

Terry fumbled for a moment and then turned it on. Erin blinked painfully in the flood of light.

"You found a truck?" she repeated.

"Yes."

"Was it the one he hit me with?"

"Looks that way. We'll have to test the paint, but it has a dented front end. I'm pretty sure it was the truck that rammed you."

Erin took a deep breath and let it out slowly. "So you got him. You've really got him, there's no question."

"I would say so. We've got him all wrapped up in a neat little package." Terry chuckled. "A very special Christmas present just for you."

"Best Christmas present ever. It's such a relief."

"I thought it would be."

"Do they know if there was anyone else involved? Or anyone else who knew about it and didn't tell? Besides the kids, I mean."

"That is going to take somewhat longer to figure out. I'm hoping that we'll be able to sort that out as we interview the teens who were involved."

"Do you think you'll be able to identify all of the kids who were working for him? And are they guilty, or were they coerced?" Erin sat up the rest of the way, awake and her brain working now.

"That will have to be decided on an individual basis. I imagine we'll have the whole range, from kids who were eager to get involved and suggesting the houses to hit to those who were forced to participate or pass on information."

"They knew which families to hit because they had a pretty good idea what the other kids were supposed to be getting and what their families' schedules were."

"Yeah."

"Did some of them hit their own families?"

"Undoubtedly. And they would get double the loot because they get what they stole and then what the town fundraised to give them a second present." He shook his head in disgust. "Some people have no scruples."

"Yeah."

"And the community center? Turns out that the woman who keeps the keys has a son on the basketball team."

"And he took it to break in and get the needy children's toys."

Terry nodded, rubbing the back of his head. "Like I said… no scruples."

Erin stretched her limbs, seeing how her body felt. "Do you want anything to eat?"

"I can get something out. Are you hungry?"

"Just sort of peckish. But I know I should eat."

"Come on out, then. You can sit while I make you something."

"I can make dinner."

"No, you can't. You can sit at the table and watch me."

Erin laughed and shook her head. "Okay, fine. I'll sit and watch."

CHAPTER 36

$\mathcal{T}$he day before Christmas had been busy as they made sure that the rest of the Christmas packages were delivered so that children would be able to wake up with presents under the tree. Erin was tired, but not exhausted as she had been previously. She was glad to know that everybody would be getting a day off. She wouldn't be missing her shift at Auntie Clem's Bakery and making someone else cover for her; they would all be off and able to enjoy time with their families. And after that, she thought, she'd be able to get back to a regular schedule.

It surprised her how hard it was to be limited by her physical health. She usually had the stamina she needed to get up early and work through the day. It was a big change to only be able to stand for a few minutes or an hour at a time. It gave her more sympathy for Terry, who'd been struggling with his body's limitations since the attack. She'd understood that it was difficult, but not how frustrating it was to be battling against her own body.

Christmas Eve arrived and Erin sat on the couch cuddled up to Terry with the animals all in a happy, relaxed state. Erin picked up Orange Blossom and cuddled him, happy that he was well and back to normal after their scare.

"This is nice," she told Terry. "Just how I wanted it to be."

"But this is pretty much the same as every other night."

"Yes."

He laughed. "Well, Christmas Eve is our time. Then tomorrow… you'll have to deal with company."

"It will be nice to have everyone together again." Erin shook her head. "It's been strange with everyone going in different directions. I feel like we haven't seen anyone."

He nodded.

It had been uncomfortable being at odds with Terry, too. She wasn't used to arguing with him. Not seriously. "Is this okay? Us just being with each other for Christmas Eve?"

"Sure."

"You don't want to… go to Christmas services tonight? There's a candle-light service at First Baptist."

"How do you know that?"

"I hear things."

He considered the question for a minute. "I'm okay just being home with you. I don't feel the need to go to church."

"But would you rather go than not go? If you weren't with me, would you go?"

"I don't know."

"What have you done the last few years, before you met me?"

Terry scratched his ear. "You're quite the interrogator. Other years, I have usually gone to Christmas Eve services."

"You could go this year."

"I know. But I'll stay with you."

"What if I said I'd go? Would you go then?"

Terry raised one eyebrow and studied her face. "It really isn't that big of a deal. I believe what I believe, whether I go to services or not."

"I'll go."

"You said *this* is just what you wanted."

"That doesn't mean we can't do what you want too. It would only be, what, an hour out of our evening?"

Terry nodded.

"Then why don't we go?"

∽

The church was already quiet when Erin arrived with Terry, people speaking in whispers as they distributed candles and herded their families into the chapel. But when they saw Erin, everyone froze. The whispers stopped and for a moment, there was complete silence. Then Melissa jumped forward.

"Erin, isn't this nice! I wasn't expecting you to join us today. Each of you grab a candle," she passed a tall white candle to Erin. "I really do think this is the most beautiful service of the year. Then find a seat in the chapel. There are no reserved spots; you can sit anywhere."

"Thank you."

"I'd suggest a few rows from the front. You want to be able to see the children."

"Okay, thanks."

Melissa patted Terry on the arm and left them to their own devices.

"You still okay with this?" Terry asked, looking down at Erin.

"Yes. It all looks very nice."

Even so, she did feel awkward and uncertain as people around her whispered and eyed her. She had hoped that people would be too excited about Christmas to take notice of her appearance, but she had underestimated people's level of interest in what she did.

The chapel was quieter than the lobby, with just the rustle of clothing as the worshipers found their seats. Terry led her up the aisle to a bench close to the front.

"How is this?"

Erin nodded silently. They shuffled down the bench to the end and sat down. Erin tried to look around and see everything she could without swiveling her head back and forth like a tourist. It was a pretty little church, with some stained glass windows and ornamental carvings. Not too dark. She was glad to see that the cross at the front of the chapel did not display the tortured Christ, but was simple and unadorned. As a child, she'd been horrified and fascinated by the cruel crucifixes displayed in churches she'd been dragged to.

Terry took her hand in his and gave it a little squeeze. He didn't whisper to her anymore, not wanting to disturb the stillness of the place, but he kissed the corner of her forehead, and she knew he was thanking her for joining him for the service.

Erin watched the congregants make their way to their seats, focusing on the families with teens and young children. Most of them were smiling as they looked around and waited for the candlelight service to begin. Maybe they still would have been happy even if they hadn't gotten any Christmas presents, but Erin was glad that they hadn't had to find out.

CHAPTER 37

*E*rin and Vic were up early to get the turkey stuffed and cooking and to put a couple of trays of cinnamon buns in the second oven to start the day properly with a sugar-induced haze. They were joined before long by Adele, who smiled uncertainly at Vic and offered to help with whatever she could. It was a bit crowded for the three of them to work in the kitchen, but Erin made space the best she could and included Adele.

"So, what's this I hear about you going to the First Baptist service last night?" Adele inquired.

"I didn't," Vic said with a frown, turning to look at her. "I know they won't accept me like this, and I'm not going to hide who I am for a church service. Willie and I went into the city; there was an LGBT-friendly service at one of the missions downtown."

Adele quirked an eyebrow and shook her head. "No. Not you. Erin."

"Erin?" Vic put down her spatula and looked at Erin. "*You* went to First Baptist?"

Erin swallowed and stared down at the buns she was icing. She wasn't sure how Adele managed to hear everything that went on in town. She hardly associated with anyone, yet she always seemed to know what was going on.

"Uh, yes. I went with Terry to the candlelight service."

"How did he talk you into that? I'm going to have to have a word with him!"

"He didn't coerce me. He was happy just to stay home together, but I didn't want him to miss out on it because of me. So I offered to go with him."

"That was so nice of you. And so… what did you think?"

"It was nicely done. Very peaceful and pleasant. Lots of families there, so they kept it short. Kind of a nice way to start off the holiday."

"And did you feel…" Vic hesitated and shook her head, trying to put it into words. "Did you feel like it was…"

"I wasn't converted," Erin said, her face getting hot, "if that's what you're wondering. I'm not planning to start going to church services every week. It was just something that I did with Terry. Because of his beliefs, not mine."

"Yeah, okay. I just wasn't sure how it would make you feel. Whether…" Vic was getting a little pink herself. "Whether it would *move* you."

"I'm still the same Erin. Still an atheist."

Vic shrugged. "Okay, just asking. It was nice of you to go."

Erin continued to ice the buns. "And your service in the city? Was it good? You enjoyed it?"

"Yes, it was really friendly. I felt like I belonged there, instead of being an outsider. I like Bald Eagle Falls, but I know what would happen if I attended church here. It would not be fun."

"And Willie? Did he like it? I don't even know if he's Christian or not. I guess he is…?"

"I'd say he probably identifies as Christian, but not as any particular sect, and he doesn't see the need to go to church to worship. He's not against it; he just doesn't see the point when he has so many other things he wants to do. Last night was something special, like with you and Terry. Something that he tagged along for because he figured it would make me happy."

"And did it?"

Vic's eyes cut over to Erin. "I didn't drag him along. I wouldn't do it if I thought he didn't want to. So… yes, it made me happy that he could be there with me too. I didn't want to go by myself, and leave him all alone Christmas Eve."

They went on with the breakfast and dinner preparations, listening to

Terry watching *A Christmas Carol.* Willie wasn't there yet. Jeremy and Beaver were supposed to be joining them.

"It's nice to have a place where we can all gather around the table and be welcome, no matter what our beliefs," Adele murmured.

"Yes, it is," Erin agreed. In the Bible belt, where everyone was expected to be Christian at least in name, it was difficult sometimes to make people understand that being an atheist—or a witch—didn't mean you were an evil person, just that you had different beliefs. It was nice to have a port in a storm, people who were close to her who didn't care whether they shared religious beliefs or not, who liked her for who she was.

Erin was sitting back in her chair, belly fully, contemplating whether she dared have just one more Grinch cookie or whether it would make her stomach hurt for the rest of the day, when the doorbell rang.

"Carolers?" Jeremy asked. "You weren't expecting anyone, were you?"

"No, I wasn't expecting anyone else today." Erin pushed herself up off of her chair and decided it was probably a good idea if she didn't try to fit one more cookie into her full stomach. She made her way to the door and opened it without checking the peephole first. There were plenty of people there to protect her. Who was going to cause trouble on Christmas day? Everyone would be spending time with their own families. Although—Erin had a chill as she opened the door that wasn't from the weather—they still hadn't managed to track down crazy Theresa. And they couldn't be sure that they had identified everyone who had been involved in the burglary ring. Maybe she ought to be more cautious about opening the door without checking first.

It was Joshua. No weapon, of course, not standing there with lasers shooting out his eyes, as Mary Lou's would surely do if she knew he was there. Joshua stood there awkwardly, one foot behind him with the toe digging into the step as if he were trying to drill a hole with it.

"Merry Christmas, Miss Erin."

"Hi, Joshua. It's nice to see you. How is everything?"

Joshua looked past Erin and saw all of the people seated around the table. "Oh, I didn't mean to disturb you. You're in the middle of dinner."

"No, we're done. Do you want to come in? There are still more cookies…"

He shook his head, looking away from her. "I just… I wanted to apologize for my mom. I don't know why she went off on you like that. I mean, she knows how you tried to help us out before, and you were there after Campbell was arrested and you never shunned her like other folks did for what Dad did. And he even tried to kill you."

Erin didn't say 'twice.' That might have been pushing it when he was in mid-apology.

"You don't need to apologize for Mary Lou. I know she was just trying to protect you, and she was afraid I was going to get you in trouble when you hadn't done anything. She's afraid, after what happened to Campbell, that the same thing could happen to you."

"I know… but it was still wrong for her to get after you. You didn't do anything. The cops would have come to talk to me anyway."

"Maybe," Erin agreed. "But as it was, they did come after you because of what I'd said. I never thought you were committing the burglaries, but I was confused about what Ha—about what one of the boys said to me. I didn't think that you would be involved in anything like that."

"I could have been," Joshua pointed out. He cleared his throat. "A lot of the boys were."

Erin stepped out of the house and pointed down at the steps. She and Joshua sat down together to talk. "A lot of the boys were," she agreed. "It's really hard to believe that the coach could talk them into it. Could brainwash them like that so that no one would even report it."

"He really wanted me to join up again. To be on all of his teams. I think maybe he thought that if I did, Campbell would decide to come back. I don't know. It's stupid. But I don't think he really wanted me. It wasn't like I was an all-star. He just thought that if he could get one of the Cox boys, he could get both of us. And Cam was a lot better than me."

"It must have been so hard for you when Campbell left."

"I wish he hadn't gone away. But I know… he couldn't stay. He couldn't keep going on like he was, or it would have killed him. He couldn't take the stress and the expectations."

"You boys have had to go through so much. And I know that you're still struggling. I didn't mean to cause you any extra stress because of what I said.

You didn't need being accused and interrogated by the police on top of everything else."

Joshua pulled up the hood on his hoodie and cuddled up in it, arms wrapped around himself. "It was actually kind of cool," he said with a wicked grin. "You see this stuff on TV all the time, and you wonder how much is real and how much is just made up for drama. And to actually be caught in the middle of a thing like this…"

"You enjoyed it?" Erin said in disbelief.

"I don't know if 'enjoyed' is the right word, but it was interesting. I was anxious, but I didn't really think they were going to put me in jail or that anyone was going to set me up like they did Campbell. So I wasn't really worried that they were somehow going to find some evidence that pointed to me."

"I'm glad."

"Maybe I'll write it all down and make a script or screenplay sometime. My own cop show."

"I didn't know you were interested in writing."

"Well… I don't tell a lot of people. Because of Campbell, they expect me to be a jock and to get honors in everything. And I don't sit around writing in my spare time. It's just… something I'd like to do some time."

"Did you write down what happened when we were looking for Brianna?"

He took a covert look around and then nodded. "In a notebook. I write little things in there sometimes. Just… thoughts… ideas… things maybe I'd like to write about someday. It's not a journal. Just… a notebook."

They sat on the steps in silence for a while. Erin shifted, her tailbone starting to ache from the cold concrete. "Did you know what was going on with Coach Hadrian and the team? Did you know that they were the ones who were committing the robberies and that he was at the head of it?"

Joshua pursed his lips and considered. "No, not really… but there was talk about there being secrets and that the coach was doing something… I was worried at first that he was molesting them or something, but when I talked to Campbell, he said there was never anything like that. The coach didn't ever touch them or hang out in the locker room. Of course, then he wanted to know why I was asking…" Joshua rolled his eyes. "Talk about drama. So I just put it out of my mind. Figured maybe they were throwing games for him. I didn't know that they had anything to do with the burglaries. But I don't hang out with anyone on the teams anymore. When I dropped out of them... the other players pretty much shunned me. No one wanted anything to do with me. And I guess it was a lucky thing that they didn't."

"I'm very glad that you weren't involved."

"That's just not the kind of guy I am." Joshua contemplated a hole worn in his jeans. "You know... I'd rather give up my own presents and see little kids happy at Christmas. I'd never steal from them. I know what it's like to struggle now, like I never did before Dad lost everything... and I'd rather have nothing than put someone else through that."

Erin put her arm around his shoulders and hugged him. "You're a special guy, Joshua."

"Special," Joshua echoed in a mocking tone.

"I don't mean it in a mean way. Really. I like you, and I like the kind of guy you are. You're going to be a great catch for a girl someday."

He chuckled. "Thanks. I wonder sometimes. I don't exactly see myself as the type of knight in shining armor that girls want to sweep them off of their feet."

"You don't need to be a knight. And you don't have to be flashy. One day, they'll recognize what a good guy you are, and you'll have the kind of girl who will support and encourage you."

Joshua nodded, swallowing a few times, and couldn't seem to get any other words out. Erin turned her face away from his to give him a chance to collect himself.

"I'd better get back in there. Don't worry about your mom. I know she was under a lot of stress and she's just worried about you. We'll work it out. Do you want some treats to take home?"

"Well... I probably shouldn't."

"Why not? Do you have any idea how many desserts we end up throwing out around here? We've always got too much to eat ourselves. I'll make you a plate."

"That might kind of give away where I've been."

"You don't want Mary Lou to know that you came here?"

He shook his head.

"Well, just a couple of cookies then. One for each hand."

Joshua grinned. "Well, if you're that set on getting rid of them."

"I am."

"Okay."

Erin returned to the house while he waited on the steps.

"Everything okay?" Terry asked.

"Yes, just fine."

"He's not bothering you?"

"No. He was apologizing. And talking about what happened. I'm just going to get a couple of cookies for him."

She felt like all eyes were on her as she looked over the dessert platter and grabbed two cookies for Josh. She glanced around at her guests, and they mostly looked away. Beaver continued to look at her.

"Do you think I should talk to him too?" Beaver asked.

"Mary Lou was pretty clear that she wanted you to stay away from him, so I wouldn't if I were you. Just stay clear until things have settled down again. Even then... I don't know. She doesn't want him involved in any of your investigations."

Beaver popped a couple of sticks of gum in her mouth. "Too bad. He's very observant. And more discreet than his brother. I wouldn't mind having his insight."

Erin shook her head and took the cookies out to Joshua.

CHAPTER 38

*E*veryone had made their way back to their own homes. Erin and Terry had both had a nap in the afternoon. With how exhausted Erin had been since the accident, she wasn't worried that having a rest would ruin her sleep for that night.

A couple of hours later, they were both up again spending some quiet time cuddling and watching whatever Christmas movies were still on the TV.

Terry muted it and turned to Erin during a commercial. "I have something for you."

Erin looked at him, shaking her head slightly. "What?"

He snaked his hand down into his pocket and drew out a velvet box with the name of a jeweler stamped on it in gold. Erin looked at it, her heart pounding.

"A Christmas present?" she asked. "I didn't get you anything."

"Yes, you did. You gave me your time, a great dinner with friends, and you went to the candlelight service with me, just because you wanted me to have a good Christmas. It doesn't have to be wrapped up with a bow to be a Christmas present." He looked at the little box. "I didn't even wrap this one up with a bow."

Erin shook her head. She took the box from his hand hesitantly, wondering what it was going to be and what she would say to him. She wasn't sure it was time to be getting engaged, or if she ever wanted to get married. Their argument had made her reevaluate their relationship and, even though she fully intended to stay with him, she couldn't say that it would be forever, or that they would ever get married. If his plans were different from hers...

"It's okay," Terry said, stroking the hair beside her face and following one tendril down to her neck. "Trust me."

Erin took a deep breath and opened the box.

It was not an engagement ring, but a locket. Erin examined it, smiling. "It's beautiful, Terry." It had her initials engraved on it. No message from him and not his initials, only hers.

She ran her thumbnail around the crack between the halves of the locket and pried it open. There was no picture inside, just a flat, smooth glassy surface.

"It's electronic," Terry said. "Like one of those picture frames. It loads and charges wirelessly. You can put as many pictures in it as you like."

Erin beamed.

"You tend to collect people, and I couldn't imagine you picking just one or two people to put in it," Terry went on. "This way, you can include everyone you love."

She should have trusted him. He really did know her.

Terry reached over and clicked the top of the locket. It lit up and, as Erin watched, she saw pictures of Terry, Vic, Charley, and even her dead parents, Clementine, and Bertie Braceling. She teared up.

"It's perfect, Terry. Thank you so much."

"Merry Christmas, Erin. And may the next year bring everything you want."

"And nothing that you don't," Erin finished.

He looked at her and shook his head, eyes twinkling.

Neither of them knew what the New Year would bring, but it seemed like things were never quiet for long in Bald Eagle Falls.

Did you enjoy this book? Reviews and recommendations are vital to making a book successful.

Please leave a review at your favorite book store or review site and share it with your friends.

Don't miss the following bonus material:
Sign up for mailing list to get a free ebook
Read a sneak preview chapter
Other books by P.D. Workman
Learn more about the author

PREVIEW OF COLD AS ICE CREAM

AUNTIE CLEM'S BAKERY #13

CHAPTER 1

$\mathcal{A}$s soon as Erin got home from work, Orange Blossom was underfoot, meowing and yowling in greeting, winding around her legs, telling her all about his busy (or not so busy) day at home. Erin put down her purse and took off her jacket and picked him up.

"Hey. Quiet down. Relax. This is the time I get home every day, I'm not late."

He started purring, a loud rumble that filled the room. Erin pressed her face into the short velvety hair at the top of his head and scratched under his chin.

"There. You like that, huh?"

Marshmallow hopped out from behind the couch and waited patiently for Erin to scratch his long ears, nuzzling at her toes.

Terry looked out from the kitchen. His jaw was dark with five o'clock shadow. He'd had an early shift and clearly hadn't shaved afterward.

"Whatever he is telling you about me, it isn't true."

Erin stroked Blossom's back, smoothing down his ruffled fur. "I think he's telling me about K9."

"You'd think he would be used to K9. Most other cats would have resigned themselves to a dog being around here by now."

Erin nodded. She could see K9 lying on the kitchen floor behind Terry, bored or tired after his patrol with Terry. Terry still wasn't back to working full-time at the police department since he had been attacked during an investigation. He was getting gradually better, but was still suffering from headaches, insomnia, and problems with concentration. Not something you wanted to worry about with your police force. K9 had been his partner for a long time and was used to patrolling all day.

"Maybe it's because K9 chased him when he was a kitten," Erin said, "back when we first met. K9 really scared Blossom, so maybe he was traumatized… instead of it being like a normal situation."

Terry raised an eyebrow. "I'd forgotten all about that," he said. "Funny. That seems like a long time ago."

"Maybe she has some kitty PTSD," Erin said, cuddling Orange Blossom up to her face again. "And here we are, just trying to get him to be friends with the person—animal—who traumatized him."

Terry rolled his eyes. "Well, something to think about. Are you hungry?" He segued to food, which Erin assumed was to avoid discussing PTSD any further. Neither of them was particularly good at discussing their feelings or their own symptoms. Terry had been mandated to undergo some counseling through the police department following his attack; he probably wouldn't have chosen to do it himself. Erin had been to enough headshrinkers in the past that she really didn't want to have to deal with another. She would do the best she could to deal with the nightmares and other issues that she had. At least after going through his own ordeal, Terry had stopped suggesting she get therapy. It seemed like a pat, easy answer, but it wasn't as simple as it sounded. It wasn't a matter of going to see a doctor, getting a prescription, and being okay. Even with intense, ongoing therapy, it could last for years, and while pills could help with the depression and some of the symptoms, they didn't fix the underlying problem with the brain.

"Yes. I don't know what you made, but it smells wonderful." Erin put Orange Blossom down and entered the kitchen. Marshmallow hopped along beside her, still waiting for attention. Erin looked at the red sauce bubbling in the pot and the various other pots and bowls on the stove and counter and smiled. "Wow, you went all out. This looks great." She bent down and petted Marshmallow. Terry wasn't an experienced cook, so she wasn't sure how any of the dishes had turned out, but he had obviously been pretty busy since he'd gotten off of his shift.

"I wanted to buckle down and make you a real meal for once. Not just a sandwich or warming up a can of soup. I keep promising to make you something, so…" He gestured along the length of the cluttered counters. "There you go. That's what I did. If you don't like it… well…"

"You must have been talking to Vic and Willie," Erin suggested. She remembered Vic getting after Willie and telling him that opening a can of soup did not constitute making her dinner. Not for a date night, anyway. Maybe other nights of the week it would be acceptable.

"Well, to Willie," Terry admitted. "We're going to do another fishing trip soon. He says it's a good time of year for…" Terry trailed off. "Hmm. I don't remember. But something is good this time of year. I don't think it really matters, as long as we have something to do while we sit around and relax. So no one calls us lazy. If you fish all day, then even if you don't come home with food, people still think that you've spent your day being productive. Not quite the same as if you just sit on the couch all day."

Erin nodded. She went to the cupboard to get out the dishes they would need. She cleared various items off of the table, which he had apparently used as a preparation area when he ran out of counter space, and set out the plates and cups. She cleared various open containers of ingredients as Terry started to fill serving dishes and take them to the table. That way, when they were done, there wouldn't be so much to clean up. Erin always felt more tired after she'd had a chance to sit down and eat. Best to get it done before the lethargy overtook her.

There were some odds and ends of vegetables left over from Terry making a salad, and she fed a few pieces to Marshmallow. Orange Blossom started to yowl and complain about how she was feeding Marshmallow and hadn't yet given him a treat.

"Okay, okay. Your treat is coming." Erin let herself into the pantry, but pushed him back and wouldn't allow him to follow her in there. A few weeks ago, she wouldn't have bothered, but since he had gotten sick, apparently after having eaten something he shouldn't have, she was far more careful about keeping him away from people food, whether it was something she thought would be okay for cats or not. He was only allowed to eat food that came in a package with a picture of a cat on the side.

And the crumbs that K9 left behind. Once Erin had slid a few treats across the floor for Orange Blossom to chase, she got a gluten-free doggie biscuit out of the cookie jar and gave it to K9. He lay with it between his paws, munching on it. Blossom saw that his adversary had also been given a treat and after gobbling down his own, he slunk closer to K9 to see if he could snatch a few crumbs. It was the only time he would get close to the shepherd without hissing and puffing his fur out.

With the food preparation areas mostly cleared, Erin sat down to eat with Terry, looking over the variety of dishes that he had put together.

"This looks great," she told him.

Terry beamed.

CHAPTER 2

She was happy that Terry was feeling well enough after an early shift to cook a meal for her. A few weeks before, that wouldn't have been possible. He had barely been able to get through his half shifts, let alone do anything productive afterward.

They sat on the couch after eating, sharing details about their days.

Nothing exciting had happened, and that was perfectly fine. They didn't need any more crime or mysteries. Just routine, everyday baking and policing work. Muffins and parking tickets.

There was a knock at the back door, then the sound of the door opening and Vic's voice. "Y'all decent?"

Erin straightened slightly and smiled at her young employee. "What would you do if we weren't?"

"Well, I guess I'd go all the way back to the loft and entertain myself there," Vic drawled in her slowest backwoods Tennessee accent. "But it isn't like the two of you are ever doing anything… sensitive… out in the open." She chuckled. "Y'all know you could have drop-in visitors any time."

The blond young woman sat down on one of the easy chairs, smiling at her boss.

"Long time no see," Erin said. Vic had driven her home in Willie's truck after they had closed Auntie Clem's bakery for the day. Erin's car had been wrecked before Christmas and she hadn't yet replaced it. Vic didn't have a car of her own, but frequently borrowed Willie's. And it wasn't like they couldn't walk to and from Auntie Clem's if they needed to. It was only a few minutes away. Though neither of the menfolk liked them walking in the predawn hours when they had to start baking to have fresh bread and muffins in the case by the time they opened up to the early-morning customers. Bakers began the workday very early.

"Where's Willie?"

"He took the truck out to one of his claims." Vic shrugged. "I didn't get any details. Something important in the world of mines and minerals."

While Vic sometimes went spelunking with Willie on days off, she wasn't involved in his mining operations. Willie always had a dozen different jobs on the go and he sometimes kept strange hours, especially if Vic used his truck during the bakery hours.

"How is the mining life?" Erin asked. "Things… going well?"

"I have no idea. He doesn't tell me about it. He keeps his head above water, so I guess it's going well. Or his other ventures are going well. I don't get into any of the business details."

Erin nodded. She rolled her shoulders and rubbed her neck, trying to work out a few knots. Terry pushed her hands away and turned her so that her back was to him, so he could rub her muscles. Erin closed her eyes and rolled her neck, trying to relax into it. His fingers were hard, digging down into the muscles and trying to massage away the tightness.

"How's that?" he murmured close to her ear.

Erin nodded. "That's good." She was sore, but even though it hurt, she knew it would help later. "I'll do some tai chi before bed. And then I'll be nice and relaxed to sleep."

Terry's fingers paused for a moment, but he didn't disagree. Both of them had difficulty getting to sleep, but discussing how difficult it was and the likelihood that either of them would be able to get to sleep when they wanted to would not be productive. And neither of them wanted to talk about it in front of Vic, either. She always noticed when Erin had a difficult night anyway.

"There was some mail for you," Erin told Vic, nodding to the side table. Even though they had a separate mailbox for the loft over the garage where Vic lived, the mailman didn't always get the mail sorted properly between the two boxes. Erin and Vic just passed mail back and forth as necessary and weren't really bothered by it.

Vic stretched out one of her long, slender arms and managed to snag the pile of envelopes. She sorted through it, pulling out the couple of mail pieces that were hers. One of them was just a bill, Erin had noticed, but the other looked like a personal letter. It was rare to get actual personal postal mail, so she couldn't help but notice. Everybody used email and social media.

Although that wasn't entirely true. Erin remembered that Vic had also gotten postal mail from an old girlfriend, crazy Theresa, someone that they all wanted to avoid running into again. Ever. There were warrants out for Theresa's arrest after the murder of Bo Biggles and her attack on Terry and Jack Ward when they had gone over to talk to her about it. But so far, she was in the wind and no one had been able to bring her to justice.

Erin eyes the envelope nervously. She didn't remember enough about Theresa's handwriting to know if it was the same writing or not. Theresa had known about Vic's gender transition but had thought that Vic would still be interested in renewing their relationship. Even though Vic was already in a committed relationship with Willie.

Vic examined the letter in the green envelope. She glanced over it at Erin. "What's wrong?"

"Nothing."

"You look like you're in pain. Terry, I think you're massaging too hard."

Terry stopped. He leaned forward, trying to see Erin's face. "Are you okay? You need to tell me if I'm hurting you."

"No." Erin gently rubbed the sore muscles that he had been working on. "It wasn't that. I was just…" She shook her head. "Nothing. I just wondered who the letter was from. Not that it's any of my business. Just curious."

Vic's brows came down for a moment, and then she understood. "Oh! No, it's nothing to be worried about." She worked her finger into the corner of the envelope and slit it across. "It's not from… her."

"Oh." Erin swallowed and nodded. "That's good. I was just wondering. I know there's nothing to worry about, she's not going to show up here or start anything… she would risk getting caught and sent to prison for a few decades. She wouldn't do that."

"Crazy Theresa," Vic intoned, shaking her head. "You can never be sure what that one is going to do."

Erin's stomach clenched. Vic must have seen a change in her expression because she hurried to change her words.

"She wouldn't come here, though, you're right. She'll stay far away from Bald Eagle Falls and anyone who knows that there are warrants out for her. Maybe she'll go north to Canada."

Erin rolled her eyes and gave a little laugh. "To Canada? She'd freeze."

"Good. Maybe a little chill would be good for her."

Vic herself hadn't been too impressed with the northern weather when they had taken a cruise to Alaska. Born and bred in Tennessee, her blood was too thin to appreciate the cooler weather. She'd been chilled the whole time she'd been north of the forty-ninth parallel.

Vic pulled the paper out of the envelope and unfolded it. Her eyes scanned over the page. "Oh, it's Clayton." She raised her eyes to Erin and Terry. "He was one of the group on the cruise," she said. "One of the people I met onboard."

"Oh." Erin nodded and tried to look happy about this. She *was* happy that it wasn't from Theresa. But she couldn't help feeling a little twinge of disappointment that one of the LGBT group that Vic had made friends with on the cruise was sending Vic letters. Vic was already with Willie and she already had a best friend in Erin. She could have however many friends she liked, but Erin couldn't help feeling like the men and women that Vic had become friends with on the ship were somehow trying to wedge themselves between Vic and Erin.

That was ridiculous, of course. It didn't affect her friendship with Erin at all. But Erin had grown up without many friends and felt possessive. Vic shared experiences with the LGBT group that Erin would never have. Erin knew about the challenges that Vic went through living among the cis men and women in small-town, Bible-belt Tennessee, but she would never understand it with the same depth and nuance of people who had lived through it. Erin could never fully be a part of that side of Vic's life.

She would have to settle for being Vic's friend and working side-by-side with her.

"So, how is Clayton?" Erin asked, trying to inject warmth that she did not feel into the question.

Vic's eyes moved over the page. She didn't look up to answer Erin. "Good…"

Erin leaned back against Terry, resting into his warm body. She waited for more information from Vic. Vic's voice was far away, not really engaged with the conversation as she read Clayton's letter.

Terry resumed rubbing Erin's neck and shoulders, but with gentle hands this time, soothing the sore muscles. Maybe he understood how disconnected Erin felt from Vic at times like that. She felt like the little girl left at home when the others went out to play. Erin scratched at a drop of bread batter that had dried on her slacks. She wasn't sure how it had managed to get past her apron. She always seemed to have a few spatters that made it to her street clothes.

"He's coming to Bald Eagle Falls," Vic said.

"Coming here? Why would he be coming here?" Erin answered too quickly before she thought through her answer.

Erin looked over the letter at her again, eyebrows quirked, shaking her head. "Why not? There's no reason he *couldn't* come here."

"No, I didn't mean that. I just meant I was surprised. It's sort of out of anyone's way. Is he coming just to see you, or is he on his way to something else...?"

"There's some kind of contest. He knows that you and I got the tickets to the cruise as part of a prize package, so he says maybe we can give him some pointers on how to win..."

"We?"

"You and me. We did win it together."

"Did he say me? Or just you?"

Vic's eyes went back to the letter. "Does it matter?"

"No. Of course not. Just curious. I don't think he really wants my input, does he?"

"I don't know. I doubt if he really wants anyone's advice. It's just something to say. Small talk."

Erin nodded. "Yeah, I guess. What contest is it? I hadn't heard anything about a contest. Is it in the city?"

"I don't know. I haven't heard of it before. Not one of the big ones like the Pilsbury bake-off or something. There are little ones running all the time."

"I guess."

"Especially in the rural areas around here. It's entertainment. A good way to get people together. Have some fun, raise some money. Make people remember your name for the next time that they're buying groceries at the store."

The Fall Fair was the first baking contest that Erin had ever entered, but she had noticed since then little contests that popped up here and there.

"I think we just got lucky with our entry. It wasn't like I really knew what I was doing."

"It wasn't just luck," Vic disagreed. "We worked hard on that cake. It was the perfect selection for the Fall Fair."

Erin's cheeks warmed a little. Vic had been instrumental in picking out their entry and teaching Erin about the traditional way to make it, but it had been Erin's recipe and execution. They had both contributed. But she was glad that Vic didn't think it was just luck that had gotten them the prize.

"When is he coming?"

Vic looked at her phone face. "Uh… in just a couple of weeks. I'll have to give him a call and make sure he has everything he needs while he is down for the contest and make sure that he is going to come by for a visit."

Cold as Ice Cream, Book #13 of the *Auntie Clem's Bakery* by P.D. Workman will be available at pdworkman.com

ABOUT THE AUTHOR

Award-winning and USA Today bestselling author P.D. (Pamela) Workman writes riveting mystery/suspense and young adult books dealing with mental illness, addiction, abuse, and other real-life issues. For as long as she can remember, the blank page has held an incredible allure and from a very young age she was trying to write her own books.

Workman wrote her first complete novel at the age of twelve and continued to write as a hobby for many years. She started publishing in 2013. She has won several literary awards from Library Services for Youth in Custody for her young adult fiction. She currently has over 60 published titles and can be found at pdworkman.com.

Born and raised in Alberta, Workman has been married for over 25 years and has one son.

∼

Please visit P.D. Workman at pdworkman.com to see what else she is working on, to join her mailing list, and to link to her social networks.

∼

If you enjoyed this book, please take the time to recommend it to other purchasers with a review or star rating and share it with your friends!

facebook.com/pdworkmanauthor

twitter.com/pdworkmanauthor

instagram.com/pdworkmanauthor

amazon.com/author/pdworkman

bookbub.com/authors/p-d-workman

goodreads.com/pdworkman

linkedin.com/in/pdworkman

pinterest.com/pdworkmanauthor

youtube.com/pdworkman

www.ingramcontent.com/pod-product-compliance
Lightning Source LLC
Chambersburg PA
CBHW070712100726
47907CB00001B/153

* 9 7 8 1 7 7 4 6 8 0 8 5 8 *